CAROLINA

FOUR DISTINCT NOVELS SET IN THE BLUE RIDGE MOUNTAINS

YVONNE LEHMAN

BARBOUR BOOKS

An Imprint of Barbour Publishing, Inc.

Mountain Man © 1996 by Yvonne Lehman.
Smoky Mountain Sunrise © 1996 by Yvonne Lehman.
Call of the Mountain © 1997 by Yvonne Lehman.
Whiter than Snow © 1999 by Yvonne Lehman.

ISBN 1-57748-970-5

Cover design by Robyn Martins.

All scripture quotations, unless otherwise indicated, are taken from the HOLY BIBLE, NEW INTERNATIONAL VERSION®. NIV® Copyright ©1973, 1978, 1984 by International Bible Society. Used by permission of Zondervan Publishing House. All rights reserved.

Published by Barbour Books, an imprint of Barbour Publishing, Inc., P.O. Box 719, Uhrichsville, Ohio 44683, www.barbourbooks.com.

ecpa Member of the
Evangelical Christian
Publishers Association

Printed in the United States of America.
5 4 3

YVONNE LEHMAN

As an award-winning novelist from Black Mountain in the heart of North Carolina's Smoky Mountains, Yvonne has written several novels for Barbour Publishing's **Heartsong Presents** line. Her titles include *Southern Gentleman, Mountain Man,* which won a National Reader's Choice Award sponsored by a chapter of Romance Writers of America, *Catch of a Lifetime,* and *Secret Ballot.* Yvonne has published more than two dozen novels, including books in the Bethany House "White Dove" series for young adults. In addition to being an inspirational romance writer, she is also the founder of the Blue Ridge Christian Writers' Conference. She and her husband are the parents of four grown children and grandparents to several dear children.

MOUNTAIN MAN

Chapter 1

D o I dare?"

The question rolled around like thunder in Meera Briskin's head as she watched the lightning skitter across the midnight sky, shimmering above the forest. Outside her third-floor bedroom window, the clashing of the elements reminded her of the heated exchange earlier.

Family members had gathered at the mountaintop estate—a majestic, brick mansion with great white columns—to honor the memory of Elias Briskin on the one-year anniversary of his death. And rather naturally, the conversation had turned to the selling of a piece of property they had jointly inherited from him.

"You can't be serious about selling to a developer," Meera had protested. "They might build a shopping center or condos across the top of the mountain."

"Humph! That's not our concern," an uncle had declared.

"Of course it is," Meera had countered, glancing at her dad who looked thoughtful but did not come to her defense. "We need to think of the beauty of North Carolina's Blue Ridge Mountains. And we have to consider the environment."

"Oh, really, Meera," her cousin Louisa snorted. "There you go with another of your do-gooder projects! Ever since you took a few environmental courses, you think everybody is out to pollute the atmosphere. You did the same thing when you studied nutrition. Suddenly, we were all condemned for eating junk food and animal fat."

Laughter followed, not unkindly, but as a show of appreciation for Louisa's theatrics. Meera hadn't attempted a defense. She'd grown accustomed to her cousin's tactless jabs. She took a deep breath, and with her pulse beating like the rain against the windowpanes, she'd plunged in before she lost her nerve. "We could at least inform the Maxwells about a possible sale."

Stunned silence fell upon the little group gathered in the drawing room.

"The land adjoins their property, you know," Meera continued. They stared in stark disbelief. "It's only fair. . . ." Her voice trailed off, and she lowered her gaze from the unsympathetic faces of her family.

"Really, Meera," Louisa rebutted, "the Maxwells never cared about the environment. They built Chestnut Lodge smack-dab on top of the mountain.

And they never cared about human life either." Her next words were ominous, throbbing against the background of the rumbling thunder. "Or have you forgotten that old man Maxwell tried to *kill* our grandfather?"

"Stop it!" came Aunt Clara's sharp reprimand. "That name should not be spoken in this house."

"I'm sorry," Meera apologized. It *was* regrettable if anyone thought her disloyal to her beloved grandfather's memory. But she also had her conscience to deal with. "I can't give my consent to sell without further thought."

Later that night, Louisa had come into Meera's bedroom and approached the subject again. "Look, Meera, I don't mean to be unpleasant," she said, sitting in the middle of the bed in her babydoll pajamas. "This might sound selfish, but Gramps did leave a share of the land to me, and frankly, I want the money." She waved her hands dismissively. "Let the big shots decide what to build on the mountain and whether or not it's harmful to the environment. Goodness knows, *I* can't do anything about it."

Meera began to brush her silver-blond hair and watched her vivacious, dark-haired cousin reflected in the mirror as she talked.

"You know, Meera, the decision to sell doesn't need to be unanimous. If the rest of us agree, we don't need *your* consent. And who's to say the Maxwells wouldn't do something worse than the developers anyway?" Louisa added earnestly.

"Like I said, Louisa," Meera put in, eager to ease the tension between them—tension that had originated not with the discussion of the property sale, but with a more personal matter, "I'll think about it."

"Well, think fast," retorted the disgruntled Louisa as she jumped off the bed and strode from the room.

Meera switched off the light and stood at the window, watching the intermittent light flashing like a distress signal in the spring sky. She had "thought fast" when she'd flung the engagement ring at Clark Phillips after she'd caught him responding to Louisa's outrageous flirtations. But when he told her she was making a mountain out of a molehill, she had been persuaded to put the ring back on her finger.

That incident—and the deep-rooted hostility between the Briskins and Maxwells—were not matters she should "think fast" about. She had dared mention the name of Maxwell to her family, and the result had been alienating. She had dared to become engaged to Clark Phillips, and she had to admit she might have been mistaken. If she dared do what she was considering now, the repercussions could be. . .disastrous.

Meera knew the biblical injunction to love your neighbor—but it also said something about not casting "pearls before swine." How was she to know which Scripture to obey? Or was she simply expected to perpetuate the feud that had begun three generations ago and now seemed to be her legacy to pass on to future generations?

A loud crash of thunder jolted her from her reverie.

Or maybe it was her sudden jarring decision. Yes! In all good conscience, she must find out for herself whether or not the Maxwells were decent human beings who deserved to know about the property sale, or if, in fact, they were unmitigated scoundrels who should remain her bitter enemies to the death.

The question was—if she did anything—what would it be? And how would she do it?

Where there's a will, there's a way, she reminded herself, glancing over at her purse, which held a particular writers' conference brochure. Yes, she knew of a way; she just didn't know if she dared pursue it.

⊗

By morning Meera had decided that the only place to really think was in the solitude of her grandfather's hunting lodge. With a stab of loneliness, she realized that it was *her* cabin now. He had left it to her, along with a small section of land adjoining Turkey Creek.

She put on some shorts and a sleeveless shirt, rolled the top down on her convertible, and left the big house. Fluffy, white clouds dotted the gray-blue sky, washed clean by the rain and rose-stained by the early sun just peeking over the mountains.

The wind blew her hair back from her face, and the scent of fresh earth and pine filled her nostrils. The car dipped into the shadowed forest. Her descent along the paved, one-lane road curving down the back side of the mountain led her to the dirt road running alongside the creek, swollen now from the previous night's storm.

Meera could almost see herself and her cousin Louisa as children, wading and splashing on the Briskin side of Turkey Creek, singing at the top of their lungs, "Feudin', a-fussin', and a-fightin'. Sometimes, it gets downright excitin'."

Time and again, their boisterous melody had lifted like the morning mist rising from the forest floor to meet the sun at break of day. The sound had reverberated around the mountainsides and bounced back at them like an approving chorus, echoing, "Citin'. . .citin'. . .citin'."

Those days had been exciting! The Briskin-Maxwell feud had provided the impetus for their greatest fears and sparked their imaginations as to how they might conquer the Maxwell monsters. It had infiltrated their daily life and was incorporated into most of their childhood games.

In a race, the last one home was not a rotten egg—but a Maxwell.

When it rained while the sun was shining, it wasn't the devil beating his wife—it was a Maxwell.

In a fight, the nastiest word one child could call another was—*Maxwell*.

Such memories weren't exciting anymore; rather, disturbing. Meera parked the silver car beside the log cabin, got out, and surveyed the place so close to her heart, acutely conscious of familiar mountain sounds. She'd missed them. The creek singing over the rocks. The birds chirping their greeting to the day. Small animals scurrying about their woodland chores.

She hadn't visited the cabin in over a year, not since her grandfather's death. Now, as she stepped up on the porch, her heart was heavy. Grandfather Elias had purposely built this cabin from blighted chestnut wood, deliberately facing Maxwell property. Maxwells would not listen to anything a Briskin had to say, so this was his mute statement. He had nothing to hide—nothing to be ashamed of. Her grandfather had wanted only peace, but Maxwells were not receptive to that message.

Meera had inherited not only the cabin, but the blighted legacy of discordant families. For the moment, however, determined to face whatever memories awaited her inside, she stooped down and took a key from under the mat. Then she opened the front screen, unlocked the door, and went inside.

She was not quite prepared for the stunning emotions that met her when she crossed the hardwood floor and looked around at the golden chestnut walls and the old stone fireplace. Tears came to her eyes. She and her grandfather had spent some wonderful times here together.

She felt an overwhelming sense of his presence as she walked through the familiar rooms. Seeing his rocking chair, she recalled the times she'd crawled into his lap during a storm and felt his protective arms around her. Walking over to his bed, she trailed her hand across the patchwork quilt he had liked so much. It was a double wedding ring pattern, quilted by the grandmother she'd never known, except for her grandfather's description. On the bedside table was his Bible that had been his guidebook for living.

In the kitchen Meera plugged in the empty refrigerator, and it began to hum. Her eyes roamed over the hardwood table. Then she went to the window over the sink to look out at the slope of the wooded mountainside behind the cabin.

Walking back to the bedroom she always used, she twisted the ring from her finger and held it in the palm of her hand. Clark had said that after she had a little time to think, he wanted her to return to Venezuela and make a more serious, lasting commitment to their relationship. They were meant for each other, he'd said. That's what she'd thought, too. . .at first. Then she'd had some niggling doubts. Now, back in her own territory, she was less sure than ever.

Suddenly, the sound of a chain saw startled her from her thoughts. She put the ring on the bedside table, hurried into the living room, and looked out the window.

Four men in waders were working farther downstream. Her gaze wandered to the shotgun above the mantel and back toward the men. But upon closer inspection, she could see that they were removing part of a huge oak, apparently split by lightning during last night's storm. The fallen portion lay across the swollen creek. The men, working from the Maxwell side of the creek, were having difficulty removing the limbs. She wondered if they dared not trespass on Briskin property.

Several yards away stood a blackened tree trunk, sheared off halfway down. That would have to be felled.

She didn't know if the men working in the creek were Maxwells or their hired hands. She did know that across the creek, on the Maxwell side, her grandfather had been shot, a friendship had ended, and the feud had intensified between the two families.

She'd grown up to despise the name of Maxwell, yet she'd only occasionally glimpsed them on the opposite side of the property line. And only once in her life had she even stuck her big toe in the Maxwell half of Turkey Creek, and that action had caused her to fall smack on her bottom.

Meera turned back into the room and lit a fire to dispel the dampness. The sun wouldn't reach the cabin before midmorning. After the men left, she would open the windows to air out the musty cabin. That was time enough to begin some serious cleaning.

For now, she sat in her grandfather's big, worn recliner and stared into the fire. "I wish you were here to advise me, Grandfather," she said aloud to the cabin, so full of him, yet so empty without him.

She could not feel the comfort of his loving arms around her but knew what he'd say if he were here. He'd taken his philosophy straight from the Scriptures. He would lift his eyes up toward the hills and say, "From there comes my help."

Meera knew he had been referring to God. But whenever she stood on the porch, held onto the banister, gazed beyond the rippling creek, and lifted her eyes to the hills—they were Maxwell hills.

She again thought about the brochure Cathy Steinbord had given her when she'd visited with her in the valley a couple of days ago. Although she and Cathy weren't close friends, they had a common bond. They were both natives of this area, and both had studied journalism together at Chapel Hill.

The famous Trevor Steinbord, Cathy's brother, would be the banquet speaker on the final night of the conference. If Meera acted upon the idea that still rumbled like a spring storm in her head—attending that conference—it wouldn't be entirely a farce. She did have a degree in journalism! She'd even had several travel and food articles published! Besides, she really would like to discover if she had real writing ability—particularly now that she had doubts about becoming Mrs. Clark Phillips.

The conference would be held this coming week at Chestnut Lodge, owned by the Maxwell family, and located, as Louisa had said, "Smack-dab on top of Maxwell Mountain."

A song Meera had sung years ago in Sunday school came to mind: "Dare to be a Daniel." The story was a familiar one. When the prophet Daniel was thrown into the lions' den, God had shut the lions' mouths, and he had escaped unharmed. But Daniel had been forced there, she mused; he hadn't gone in willingly and tempted fate.

Regardless, the gooseflesh rose on Meera's arms, and she felt the tingle of excitement. It was the most adventurous thing she'd ever considered undertaking. Would she? Should she? Could she? Just as the chain saw stopped buzzing, so did the jumble of thoughts in her head. Suddenly she knew the answer.

Yes! She would dare! She would venture into forbidden Maxwell territory. It might be worth the risk.

Chapter 2

A week after she made the decision—one she hoped wouldn't prove to be fatal—Meera felt she was ready for the most daring adventure of her life. To make the whole thing more legitimate, she had called the editor of *Fabulous Places*, for whom she'd written several articles, and had gotten his approval to write a series on noteworthy inns of western North Carolina.

Chestnut Lodge was, as the locals said, only "a hop, a skip, and a jump" from her home. And if she didn't have to do this incognito, she could simply walk across the creek, tramp through the forest, and hike up the mountain.

Needing to conceal her identity, however, Meera drove the long way around via the Blue Ridge Parkway where the mountains met the sky. If the lodge looked anything like the picture on the brochure, it would be an impressive place. In summer, the foliage was much too lush for her to be able to see the complex, but in the winter, when the trees were bare, she had glimpsed lights twinkling high on Maxwell Mountain. With the coldest weather behind, the trees were awakening, trembling with tender, young leaves. Maples, bursting with new life, sported red buds. Willows swayed golden in the sunlight, and dogwood blossoms, fragile as a whisper, looked like white butterflies flitting on the mountainsides.

She felt them in her stomach when she actually turned onto the exit marked with a green sign, bold white letters proclaiming, "Chestnut Lodge." After traveling for awhile along Biltmore Avenue, Meera turned onto Maxwell property and began the ascent up the mountain, feeling much as she had felt that time she'd flown in a small plane all the way to Hawaii. She'd hung onto her seat for dear life—as she was holding onto the steering wheel now. Then and now, she reminded herself, she was at one of those points of no return, so she might as well relax.

The road forked at the entrance to Chestnut Lodge. Now she couldn't turn around—even if she wanted to—without considerable difficulty. Concentrating on every detail of the drive, she tucked away the information she would need if she were to accomplish her purpose.

For more than a mile, the narrow, paved road was bordered by great pines whose branches intertwined like giant fingers to form a green arch overhead.

Younger pines grew between the large ones, and Meera could appreciate the obvious planning for future growth, when the older pines would be replaced.

Before long, she came upon a section that was wild and natural, reminding her of Briskin property. At two different places along the curving road, a tumbling creek was spanned by expertly erected stone bridges.

Then, she was once again winding over the road beneath spreading pine branches that exuded a fresh, fragrant scent. The road turned into a long concrete incline bordered by low stone walls in which were set pink and white flowering dogwoods, thick rhododendron, and yellow blooming forsythia. Myriads of white and yellow daffodils, like welcoming miniature trumpets, swayed on green stems.

Suddenly there it was. Crowning the mountain amid a thicket of lush evergreens and great maples, oaks, and poplars was a three-story, white structure beneath a gray slate shingled roof studded with chimneys.

Meera knew that the hub of the lodge had once been the Maxwell family residence, decorated in a restrained Queen Anne style, with thirty rooms and many fireplaces. Surprisingly, her grandfather had spoken of the place appreciatively, though the Maxwell taste in architecture had differed from his own. The Briskin mansion was an expression of modern elegance—a three-story brick with great white columns and a lower level that boasted a gymnasium and heated swimming pool.

Meera parked at the side of the drive, near the entrance, then walked to the edge of a cliff, where a waist-high stone wall formed a protective railing. From here the view was spectacular. The drive over, made in early-morning shadows, had not prepared her for the effect of the sun bursting upon the lush rolling hills and valleys, transforming them into a green-gold wonderland.

At one time or another, Meera had visited all the lodges, inns, and castles in the area—except this one. Biltmore House and gardens was in a class by itself. Grove Park Inn was a masterpiece carved in stone. The unique architecture of the Assembly Inn at Montreat reminded her of a medieval castle. Then there was Pisgah Inn and Black Forest Lodge. She could have named more. Having been brought up in this area, she was familiar with all of them.

But this one—not as grand as some, larger than others—compared favorably with other inns. She had seen pictures, of course, and had read about it. But Chestnut Lodge itself had been off limits. Now she was here and could see for herself.

Turning back toward the lodge, Meera reminded herself that she had every right to be here. After all, it was open to the public, she was paying her own way, and she meant no harm. With that resolve, and ignoring the gooseflesh that prickled up and down her arms, she opened the massive glass doors, marched across the marble floor of the lobby, and zeroed in on her destination—the registration desk.

She stood waiting for the next available clerk, then signed in as "Meera Brown." It wasn't exactly a lie. She'd used that pen name on the few published articles she'd written.

"Any Maxwells around?" she asked, careful not to trip over the name.

"Always!" The clerk, a curly-headed young man with a friendly face, chuckled.

Not wanting to betray her interest in the Maxwells, Meera began asking about the conference beginning that afternoon.

"There's the man who can answer your questions." Glancing over her shoulder, the clerk lifted his hand to hail someone. "Sir!" he called just as a thud sounded from behind her, and she turned to see what had caused it.

"Be right with you, Tom," came a masculine voice.

The man, dressed in a suit and tie, bent to retrieve a box that had fallen from a cart onto the floor, and with the sudden exertion, Meera couldn't help noticing the straining of taut muscles against the dark fabric of his suit coat. Being a physical fitness enthusiast herself, she could appreciate the discipline required to keep one's body toned and fit. She also noticed the man's air of firm authority in cautioning the young employee who had been unloading the boxes. This man was obviously someone in charge—the conference director, maybe, or a faculty member.

While she waited, Meera lifted her gaze to the the octagonal-shaped ceiling, dominated by a great crystal chandelier hanging from the center. Fans on chestnut crossbeams droned softly. She was acutely conscious of the paneled walls made of now-extinct golden American chestnut paneling and a magnificent, wide staircase that rose three stories high, from which one could look down into the elegant, yet cozy lobby with its furniture groupings, its fine, thick rugs, lush plants, and huge stone fireplace.

Over the fireplace hung a painting that caught her eye. It was a forest scene—no doubt depicting the chestnuts when they were alive and well—*when all was well between the Briskins and the Maxwells,* she added mentally.

What am I doing here? Meera thought and felt an urge to escape, to forget this ridiculous idea of hers. She shifted the straps of her bag from her hand to her shoulder. Instinct told her to return the room key to the desk clerk and make a hasty departure.

However, the man Tom had hailed was now striding her way in the manner of one accustomed to walking up and down mountains so that on level ground it seemed almost too easy. He was tall, with the muscular build and take charge aura she had already noted.

As he approached, he glanced at Tom, who gestured toward Meera. "Miss Brown would like a word with you."

Although the man's eyes held a trace of admiration as his deep blue gaze shifted from the desk clerk to her, Meera was conscious of her casual attire—denim shorts, T-shirt, and wind-blown strands of hair that had worked their way free of the confining knot on top of her head. Unaccountably, she wished she had taken more pains with her appearance.

Smiling, she extended her hand to the attractive man whose dark, wavy hair, neatly trimmed, topped a ruggedly handsome face. Maybe her task here wouldn't be so bad, after all. She could observe the Maxwells from a distance while making new friends and developing her writing skills. "You're here for the conference?"

His voice was pleasantly husky. "For the duration," he replied and reached for her hand. "I'm Elliot Maxwell." The sun glinted in his eyes and the rest of his greeting was lost on her.

Meera tried to withdraw her small hand, but it was engulfed in his large one. She'd never before touched a Maxwell. She had supposed the sensation would be something like holding a frog, that she'd get warts or something. But it was warmth she felt—not warts—traveling from her hand and into her arm before a hot blush flooded her face.

He must have felt her tremble, for he gave her hand a firm shake, then released it.

It wasn't easy, making the transition from finding an attractive man appealing, to realizing that he was supposed to be her mortal enemy. This man was a Maxwell! She had to do something—say something. "Could I have a word with you? I mean. . ."

"Certainly," he said with a devastatingly charming smile and gestured toward a door near the entrance. "We can talk in my office."

She hadn't meant to do it this way. Not dressed like a high-schooler. And not stuttering and stammering like a ninny! She had thought she was prepared to invade Maxwell turf. But meeting one of them in the flesh had unnerved her more than she might have suspected, and she mentally kicked herself for being caught off guard.

Besides, she had thought all the Maxwells were old, and this man couldn't be much more than thirty. She supposed her assumption had been based on childhood impressions. She'd never seen a child on the Maxwell side of Turkey Creek. Only on rare occasions had she even glimpsed one of the adults walking in their part of the woods.

Inside the room—more like a cozy den than an office—Meera stepped into an even greater reminder that she was an intruder. The sun, streaming through the windows, had turned the chestnut walls to gold. How appropriate, she thought ruefully. The chestnut trees had been like gold to the Maxwells once—before the blight that had started the feud between her family and his.

She needed air. Abruptly Meera walked across to the open windows and inhaled deeply of the cool mountain breeze, filled with the fragrance of pine and warm, moist humus. Her gaze fell upon the nearest mountaintop that belonged to her family, and she was reminded of her purpose here. Reminded that a developer wanted to buy that mountain, shave off the top, and build condos—or worse, a shopping center. The appeal of Chestnut Lodge would then be threatened.

Honesty forced her to admit, however, that this was not her primary reason for being here. She could have had an attorney inform the Maxwells about the sale. Wasn't she really trying to be the first Briskin to make peace? After all, she had no quarrel with these people. Or was she merely trying to satisfy her curiosity? *Curiosity killed the cat,* she thought.

Why couldn't she just turn around and say, "I'm Meera Briskin, and I want to give you the opportunity to buy our mountain—to preserve the beauty of these forests and to protect our environment"? Why? *Why, my foot! That kind of offer is what started the blasted feud in the first place.*

Thus justifying her little deceit, she squared her shoulders and turned to face Elliot Maxwell. Her gray eyes couldn't quite meet his blue ones this time. Instead, she glanced around and said the first thing that came to mind. "This is the most beautiful wood I've ever seen."

He smiled his approval at the compliment and motioned her toward an easy chair by the fireplace. She sat and crossed her long, slender legs, concentrating on the green peace lilies with their white blooms, standing in brass pots in front of the fireplace.

"Genuine American chestnut," Elliot said proudly. "There's no wood like this anymore." An expression of sadness crossed his handsome features. "Every American chestnut tree has been destroyed—gone forever. But you may know all about that. Are you from this area?"

She would be as honest as she could. "My parents have a home in Charlotte," she said but did not mention the one on the French Riviera or their joint ownership of the Briskin estate.

Meera had read the historical account of the chestnut blight. She knew the Briskin version of how the blight had sabotaged not only the trees but the Briskin-Maxwell friendship. But she had not heard the Maxwell version. And since there were always two sides to every story, she was willing to listen to what Elliot Maxwell had to say.

She glanced over at him and saw that his eyes followed the movement of her hand as she unconsciously traced a pattern with her room key along the denim of her shorts, a few inches above her knees. Then their eyes met and she put her hands in her lap.

Moistening her lips, she plunged in. "That's one reason I'm here. I'm interested in doing some research and writing an article about Chestnut Lodge."

He broke into a wide smile. "That's what you wanted to talk to me about?"

She nodded, not comprehending his attitude.

"That's a relief. I thought you had a problem with our establishment. You seemed so uncertain. . .reluctant. . ."

"Well. . .I was a little hesitant to ask you about this," Meera admitted, thinking fast. "And I hadn't intended to do it just yet. This is hardly a professional approach." She glanced down at her bare legs and wrinkled her nose.

"Perhaps not," he replied, sobering, and her heart did a quick flip. "Perhaps not professional, Miss Brown. . .but you *have* caught my attention. And I must confess, normally I would have turned down such a request by now."

But he hadn't. And seeing a flicker of genuine interest in his eyes, she heard herself asking, "So, you've heard this line before?"

"Probably," he said matter-of-factly. "Probably as many times as you've heard that you're a strikingly beautiful woman."

Meera's breath caught in her throat. Yes, she'd heard it and had never failed to be pleased. But she had never expected to hear it from a Maxwell. And if she had, she would never have expected to like it. Then why this sudden elation? Why this feeling of having received the ultimate compliment?

This was madness! She should not be sitting here, smiling at a Maxwell, enjoying his company. "Then. . . ," she pressed, realizing she might never have this opportunity again, "does this mean yes?"

He laughed, and again she was stirred by the sound of his pleasure. "It means I will take the matter under consideration, Miss Brown. That is," he paused, uncrossing his legs and placing his hands on the arms of his chair, "if we could proceed on a first name basis."

"Meera," she said as his desk phone rang.

He rose to answer it and quickly turned toward the window, then glanced back at her while he listened. He replied in a few unrevealing words and turned away again, but not before she detected a look of sheer frustration in his eyes. His lips thinned, and his squared chin now seemed to jut forward slightly.

"Yes, I'll be out in a moment," he finished and hung up.

Meera stood. Her emotions ran rampant. She desperately wanted to be honest with Elliot Maxwell. But to confess that she was a Briskin would result in her being thrown out of Chestnut Lodge without having accomplished anything—except to add fuel to the flame of the family feud. "I've taken up enough of your time," she apologized and moved toward the door.

"Just a second." Elliot walked around the desk and leaned back against the edge, arms folded across his chest. "We were interrupted. Did you say your name is Mirror. . .as in looking glass?"

She laughed lightly and spelled it for him. "M-e-e-r-a. It's a family name. My great-great-grandmother. I think it has something to do with the sea."

"Unusual," he murmured. "Is that your car out front? The silver convertible?"

"Yes. Is it blocking traffic or something? Was that what the phone call. . . ?"

"No, no," he said, dismissing her concern with a wave of his hand, though she sensed something different in his mood. "Your car is in the unloading zone," he was saying, "but traffic's not backed up out there. You're okay for awhile. But we will talk again. . .Meera."

❧

Yes, Elliot was thinking as he stared at the door that closed softly behind her, they would talk again! She had stirred something in him. . .curiosity, fascination, perhaps even a gnawing suspicion. Perhaps there was a reason for that feeling of deja vu that had come over him when he'd seen her standing in the lobby.

With a quick movement, Elliot reached for the phone and punched out a couple of intercom numbers. "Tom, pick up, please."

"Yes, Mr. Maxwell?"

"Send someone out to get the license plate numbers on that silver convertible in front. . .discreetly. . .and get back to me as soon as possible."

Elliot hoped, with all his might, that this would prove not to be an act of condemnation, but an act of acquittal.

❧

Elliot crumpled the slip of paper in his fist, wishing he could as easily dismiss the thought of the numbers he had written down.

He shouldn't be standing in the shadows beside the front window, spying on that beautiful, long-legged girl while a bellman helped with her luggage. But his suspicions had been aroused the moment he'd heard the name. The only Meera he'd ever heard of was a. . .Briskin!

When she had introduced herself, the name had triggered a startling memory. Years ago, after spring rains, he'd gone with his dad to check out damage to the mountain. A giant pine had snapped and dammed up the creek that snaked across Briskin and Maxwell land. Briskin men were at work removing the tree.

Elliot had seen a young girl, probably just barely into her teens, wading in the creek. Thick, silver pigtails hung down the front of her shirt, and her face was a delicate oval with enormous eyes that reflected the color of the Carolina gray-blue sky.

He'd been twenty-two then, and not at all interested in the tall, lanky girl who'd stared at him as if he were an alien. The only expectation he had of Briskins was that they stay on their side of the property line.

Then to his surprise, she had raised her hands to her ears, waggled her fingers, and stuck out her tongue. He had reached down to pick up a rock. He'd had no intention of throwing it, but it had served its purpose, for she had turned and tried to run. Then, before he knew it, she had slipped and fallen with a tremendous splash into the rushing water.

An involuntary laugh had escaped Elliot's lips, and he had instinctively reached out to help.

"Don't you dare touch me!" she had screeched just as a man called, "Mirror!" And she had shot Elliot a murderous look before rising awkwardly, sopping wet, and splashed huffily to the bank.

"Don't worry, 'Mirror'! I wouldn't touch you with a ten-foot pole!" he'd called out, laughing at her discomfort.

At the time he had thought it a strange name—"Mirror." And he hadn't seen it again until years later when he read it in the newspaper. The name was not "Mirror," but "Meera." A picture of a pretty face surrounded by a cloud of hair like sunlight, along with an engagement announcement, confirmed that she had grown up.

He'd seen the name Meera one other time—in old man Briskin's obituary, where she was listed as a grandchild.

Now Meera Briskin—or Brown—was a guest at his lodge. She couldn't be the same. Meera Briskin could go to a writers' conference anywhere in the world. She could certainly afford it. The Briskins had made their fortune by cheating the Maxwells out of theirs!

So what was she doing here? And why use a fake name? Or was it? Had she married a Brown? The tumultuous thoughts bathed his forehead in sweat, and he clenched his fists. She'd called herself "Miss." Or had Tom used that term? She wasn't wearing an engagement ring or wedding band. And the challenge he thought he'd seen in her eyes did not send the message, "Don't touch!"

In fact. . .

No! He mustn't fall for this. It was the ploy of a Briskin three generations back. *They pretended to be friendly, then stabbed you in the back.* He didn't want to think about that feud, nor did he want to perpetuate it. All he wanted was for them to stay on their side of the creek, and he'd stay on his.

Still, it appeared that another trouble-making Briskin was up to something. Fortunately for him, she hadn't used a fake *first* name. He had to know. As much as he hated such an underhanded act, he had no choice. He owed it to his family, his establishment, and his own peace of mind.

All afternoon, he had toyed with the idea of running the license number by a friend of his on the police force. He picked up the phone and called Joe Angel and called out the digits on the crumpled piece of paper, smudged from his damp palm, and asked him to check out the registration.

When he turned again toward the window, Meera and the silver convertible had disappeared. He had a hotel to run, a conference director to greet, a million things to do—but it had to wait. One impossible young woman had turned his orderly world upside down.

Impatiently, he paced. Crossing the room in front of the fireplace, his gaze fell on the chair where she had sat. He sank down in the chair opposite, a wry smile on his lips.

He should have known she was too good to be true. Perfect toned figure. Perfect oval face. Perfect features—arched brows over clear gray eyes with just a hint of blue that reminded him of a calm lake on a summer day. Small nose that twitched intriguingly when she talked. . . . He'd even gone so far as to suspect that the heightened color in her softly curved cheeks was a result of her being drawn to him as he was to her.

Her look of fragility accompanied by a confident manner reminded him of the delicate blossom on the hearty rhododendron bush. Or a ripe raspberry hanging on the vine in late summer. Fortunately, he was not a teenager who might be tempted to reach for the fruit without considering the briars!

He stood and paced the floor again. There was no question about it. She had sparked his interest—her looks, her manner, everything about her. He hadn't been genuinely moved by a woman in. . .how long?

He'd lost count of the number of years that had passed since Kate was killed. She'd meant the world to him, though he couldn't be sure he would have married her. Tragically, she'd gotten mixed up in drugs and the wrong crowd and had been murdered. It was the shock of her death that had changed Elliot's life. And that of his friends. They'd all been forced to grow up overnight. Look at life differently. Take things more seriously. Important things like life, death, and spiritual matters were no longer abstract concepts, but facts with eternal implications.

Even the Briskin issue. When and if he married and had children, Elliot didn't relish the idea of telling them that they couldn't even step into certain sections of Turkey Creek because some of it was on Briskin land.

He hadn't thought about the feud in a long time. Now it was staring him in the face. Maybe he was wrong. Perhaps it was just that any reminder of the Briskins was like someone waving a red flag or like stepping barefoot on one of those excruciatingly painful Chinese chestnut burrs. . . .

He jumped when the phone rang. Joe confirmed his suspicions. The car was registered in the name of a Meera Briskin.

"Thanks, Joe," Elliot murmured. "I owe you one." He wadded up the paper and threw it into the trash can, then stomped toward the door. He stopped, however, with his hand on the doorknob. A wave of nausea churned his stomach, and he felt clammy, like he had the flu or something.

It was a disease, that's what it was. The mere mention of the Briskin name was enough to sicken a Maxwell. She'd walked right into his life and infected him with the plague!

Walked right in! Well, no slip of a girl was going to get away with that—particularly not a Briskin. Nausea or no nausea, he'd march out there and order her off his property!

Chapter 3

In a huff, Elliot wrenched open his office door and stormed into the lobby. "Where'd she go?" he mouthed to Tom, from behind a line of guests the young man was registering.

A light of curiosity glinted in Tom's eyes as he rolled his eyes toward the staircase and grinned.

It was no laughing matter, Elliot thought, but he knew the first thing that would pop into Tom's mind. Well, a romantic relationship with that disturbing young woman was the *last* thing he wanted!

Elliot arrived at the bottom of the stairs just as she reached the third landing. She had a room on the third floor? With his luck, her room would be next to his. Had she planned that, too? His blood began to boil.

At that moment she looked down, spotted him, and lifted her hand in greeting. Elliot drew a deep breath. The manager of the lodge couldn't very well shout from the lobby, now could he? He grasped the railing, and the adrenaline rushed through his veins as it had in his football days when he was preparing to make an all-important tackle.

A reprimanding voice stopped him in his tracks. "Mr. Elliot, I told you on the phone I needed you in the kitchen. Where've you been?"

Elliot swiveled around to stare into the worried face of Bertha, the dining-room supervisor, who was wringing her pudgy hands. "What is it?" Elliot asked distantly.

"The dishwasher quit."

Trying to focus on the problem at hand, Elliot faced her. "The dishwasher? Which one?"

"We only have one," Bertha informed him with a sniff.

Elliot lifted his eyebrows. "You should have three. Scheduling is your responsibility. This is a conference check-in day. If you scheduled only one, then I guess you'll have to wash the dishes yourself."

"You got a bug in your breeches, Mr. Elliot?" she snorted. "I'm not talking about no human dishwasher. I'm talking about that mechanical contraption in there. Now, if you want to handle this job. . ."

Elliot knew what he had to do. It wasn't often he scolded Bertha. She was a tough cookie, and that's what he needed to keep the dining room running smoothly, especially during summer season when they hired so many young people. But when it came right down to it, the woman had a tender heart.

He put his arm around her plump shoulders and led her toward the dining room, consoling and apologizing. "I'm sorry, Bertha. I'll get maintenance on it right away. In the meantime, I know you can handle things. You're the only one who can at a time like this. . ." He glanced at his watch, "with over three hundred people to feed in less than an hour."

He could trust good old Bertha to get the job done in the kitchen. But it was up to him to handle the likes of Meera Briskin!

By the time he'd gotten maintenance to work on the dishwasher, Elliot's wrath had settled down to a mild case of indignation. The way for a Maxwell to fight a Briskin was not to become infuriated and grab a shotgun, as his own grandfather had, but to keep his cool. At least she probably wouldn't burn the place down while she was staying here.

A Briskin. . .in his lodge! He still couldn't get over it. How and where had she found the nerve to trespass? But then, she obviously hadn't expected to be caught!

Leaving the kitchen area, he made his way toward the dining room. Many guests enjoyed formal dining from a menu in the Golden Room, but most groups, like this one, found it more convenient and less time-consuming to eat together in the main dining room, where they had a choice of two entrees and several vegetable dishes, along with salad, fruit, and dessert bars.

While the conferees filled their plates from the buffet and seated themselves at the long tables or on the veranda overlooking the mountains, Elliot picked up the microphone and welcomed them. He informed them of the available facilities: a small chapel, an exercise room, swimming pool, and tennis courts. The trails were off-limits to hikers except when accompanied by a guide provided by the lodge. The library shelves were stocked with articles, books, and videos on local history, including the demise of the American chestnut tree and the beginnings of Chestnut Lodge. Amid polite applause, Elliot handed the microphone to Harold Wright, the conference director.

Elliot saw her then, one of the last in line. She looked more like the newspaper picture he had seen, with her flaxen hair framing her face in soft curls. Angel or vixen? He couldn't tell. Only that she looked stunning in a yellow sundress that enhanced her feminine charms. He was acutely conscious that her appeal could easily light a flame in any red-blooded male. That is—if the male didn't know who she was.

Meera Briskin, he said to himself, *I was already a man while you were still playing with dolls, so I just might have a few tricks of my own up my sleeve. What game do you want to play this time?*

She looked his way and his full lips spread into a genuine smile, a smile induced by a fascinating mental picture. It was a picture of Meera the day she fell into Turkey Creek and came up spitting and sputtering, while he stood laughing on the bank, his feet firmly planted on Maxwell property.

Meera rushed up the stairs to her room as soon as the "get-acquainted" session ended. She couldn't remember ever having felt so elated. It was as if a whole new world had opened to her, and it had started with her meeting Elliot Maxwell. She was grateful that her first impression had not been colored by her knowing he was a Maxwell, or she might have felt differently.

Part of this euphoria, too, was the motivating keynote speech of Harold Wright, who had inspired her to attempt more than she had ever intended. Then when published writers were asked to stand and tell about their publications, the unpublished had made her feel that she had already accomplished something marvelous.

More importantly, however, was the feeling that she, without the name of Briskin to pave the way, was part of a group who aspired to the same goal: to produce something of value that could be shared with a reading audience.

Even the air seemed charged with electricity. The sheer adventure of all this—being incognito in Maxwell territory—gave her a sense of challenge akin to the reckless danger in which she and Louisa had placed themselves when they'd ridden around the mountain curves on motorcycles as teenagers.

Oh, Clark had presented a sense of intrigue when he'd taken her out into the wilds of Venezuela to his oil fields. But nothing had so elated her as this foray into enemy territory.

Just being near Elliot Maxwell buoyed her spirits. And, of course, she knew why. All of her life she'd been led to believe that a Maxwell was an ogre, ready to murder a Briskin on sight. But tonight at supper, Elliot had told about the lodge's chapel. He'd even mentioned it first in his list of facilities. A family who included a place of worship in their place of business couldn't be all bad.

It was time for all that feuding foolishness to end, and the challenge of being the one to end it had created a spark in her that threatened to break out into flame. It was as if a light had been turned on inside herself.

At her door, she flicked on the light in her room. Again she was struck by the room's appearance, as she had been that afternoon. Earlier, the paneled wall, big double bed, and carpeted floor had been awash with golden sunlight flooding into the room from the skylight in the ceiling that sloped down toward her own private balcony. From here, she had a view of the grounds and

Olympic-sized pool at the back of the lodge.

Now, with the darkening sky, the light from well-placed lamps lent a warmth to the room, as welcoming as Elliot Maxwell's initial greeting. Suddenly, she wished for a roommate to discuss far into the night this first thrilling session of the conference. Or better yet, she longed for the once close relationship with Louisa, with whom she had shared everything.

That thought brought a slight sinking feeling. Meera wouldn't dare tell anyone, especially Louisa, about this venture of hers. She did need to call home, however.

Laying her notebook on the bedside table, Meera sat on the edge of the the bed, picked up the phone and punched "9," then the number at the Briskin estate. Louisa answered after the second ring.

"Meera! Where are you? Down at Gramps's cab. . .I mean, *your* cabin?"

"Not exactly." Meera couldn't very well tell Louisa, of all people, that she was at Chestnut Lodge on Maxwell property, unless she wanted to be pruned permanently from the family tree.

"What does that mean?" Louisa asked petulantly.

"It means, Cousin, that I wanted to get away for a few days. I have to think."

"The family's starting to worry, Meera. I've called the cabin several times and gotten no answer."

"That's why I phoned, Louisa, so the family won't worry. Please tell them for me that I won't be home tonight."

"Then I'm coming down there. We have to talk."

"No, Louisa!" Meera said quickly. "I told you I'm not at the cabin."

Louisa's exasperation was evident in her loud sigh. "Well, where are you?"

Meera looked down from her third-floor window. A few guests were frolicking in the swimming pool, lighted by the moon and the soft glow of electric lanterns placed high on poles. To the far right of the pool, she spotted Elliot talking with a couple of men she'd seen go into the kitchen earlier.

The men were wearing coveralls and tool-laden leather belts around their waists, so she suspected they were maintenance men. Elliot grasped the arm of one in a friendly gesture, then turned and walked back into the lodge. It was difficult getting used to a Maxwell behaving like an ordinary human being—and a most appealing one at that. But she couldn't admit that to her cousin. "I'd rather not say where I am, Louisa."

Meera heard Louisa's sharp intake of breath, followed by an unmistakable lilt in her voice when she spoke. "Meera! You're with. . .another man."

"I'm not with anyone!" Meera shot back, bristling. "I'm engaged, remember? To Clark!"

At least she had been. Until she'd walked in on Louisa and Clark in each other's arms. No, it wasn't Meera who had forgotten. "I'm. . .spending the night with a friend, Louisa."

"Look, I've got to see you, Meera. We have to talk. I'll be at the cabin first thing in the morning."

"No," Meera said quickly. "I mean, I can't leave in the morning." She had signed up for a class on "Effective Interviews" that she mustn't miss. Not if she was going to do a good job on the Maxwell article—that is, if Elliot allowed her to do it. "Tomorrow afternoon, okay? Say. . .about four o'clock."

"Okay. Tomorrow at four," Louisa conceded. "Be on time, Meera."

"I'll do my best. Now I've really got to run." When Meera hung up, she stared at the phone for a long moment. Talking with Louisa had returned a spark of reality to the situation. A tremulous thought reminded her that she was Meera Briskin, trespassing on Maxwell property, and a shudder traveled down her spine.

"But I'm also Meera Brown," she reminded herself aloud, going into the bathroom and standing by the clawfoot bathtub as she looked into the mirror and freshened her lipstick. "I'm Meera Brown, freelance writer, on a noble mission, and I will not let Louisa, Clark, or anyone else send me spiraling back into a lifetime sentence of animosity with people I don't even know."

But I want to know them—him! she admitted unashamedly. And with that determination, she switched off the light and headed back downstairs to mingle with other writers in the lovely, new world she intended to explore.

❧

It was after nine o'clock before Elliot rolled his sleeves down, put on his suit coat, and left the kitchen. Fortunately, the maintenance men had managed to get the dishwasher going again, and Elliot had made peace with Bertha for the time being. He breathed a sigh of relief when he entered the lobby and heard the murmur and chatter of happy conferees who had finished with their opening session and were now enjoying a reception. Harold Wright, the energetic conference director, strode toward him with a clipboard in his hand and a determined look on his face.

Harold had been bringing the conference to Chestnut Lodge for five years now, liked to work directly with the management, and expected near-perfection. Elliot braced himself for whatever had not measured up to Harold's expectations.

"I'm always a little apprehensive, Elliot," the director began, "as to whether the rooms will be set up properly, the reception ready on time, and everything will be just the way I asked." He shook his head. "Especially this year, since I couldn't work with your dad."

Elliot prepared to offer an apology for some as yet undefined problem. He didn't intend to make any excuses. His dad had had a heart attack three months ago and was now recuperating well, but the doctor had strictly forbade the older man's working for awhile. In fact, he was not to put in an appearance at the lodge for quite some time to come. So Elliot had hired a couple of workers to replace himself, but he hadn't seen a need to hire extra management staff. No, this was a challenge that he expected to handle personally—an opportunity to prove something to himself and his dad, he supposed.

Surprised, Elliot listened to Harold's glowing report. "You're doing a great job, Elliot. Everything's running like clockwork: registration, dinner, and as you know, we can't predict what time our 'get-acquainted' session will end." He gestured toward the long tables set with refreshments. "But here it is—a fabulous reception waiting for us."

Elliot smiled, not bothering to explain that he had stationed a staff member near the doorway, to let him know when Harold's session seemed to be winding down. In this business, one couldn't leave anything to chance. "Thanks," he said, breathing a sigh of relief. "Just let me know if there's anything else you need."

Harold reached inside his suitcoat, withdrew a pen from his shirt pocket, and moved the pen along a list on the clipboard. "I do have a few changes."

Elliot grinned. This was more like Harold.

"We'll need an overhead projector in the Laurel Room. Sorry, but the faculty member didn't tell me ahead of time."

"We can handle that."

"And we had more conferees sign up for the 'Inspiration Workshop' than anticipated, so we'll need about five more chairs in Dogwood."

"No problem," Elliot assured him. "Looks like you've picked up in attendance."

Harold nodded. "Trevor Steinbord's coming in as banquet speaker is a real drawing card. I have you to thank for that, too."

"How's that?" Elliot asked, registering surprise.

"He said he's a friend of yours and wouldn't want to pass up a chance to come to Chestnut Lodge." Harold's chagrin was obvious. "If I had known that, I'd have asked him a long time ago."

Elliot laughed with him. "I'm looking forward to seeing him again."

Harold glanced around at the happy conferees, buzzing with enthusiasm. "It's such an inspiring place, Elliot. The former students keep coming back, and we've picked up quite a few new ones this year. It's going to be the best conference yet. Enthusiasm's high. Great potential here." His roving gaze fell on one particular student. "Take *that* young woman, for instance. I understand she's going to write an article on Chestnut Lodge."

"You understand. . .what?" Elliot echoed.

Observing the unexpected reaction, Harold added uncomfortably, "During our get-acquainted session she mentioned that you might allow it." He laughed uneasily. "However, beginning writers sometimes confuse aspiration with reality."

Elliot clenched his fists. *The nerve of that woman. First, she trespasses, then she lies, and now she has eliminated any genuine aspiring writer from the competition.* "She did speak to me about it," he conceded, making an effort to recover from that temporary jolt.

"Excuse me," Harold said, gesturing toward a passing faculty member, and away he went.

Elliot hardly noticed. But without really looking, he'd noticed Meera in the crowd. Trying not to appear obvious, he saw how she moved with equal ease among faculty and conferees, relating, fitting in, but in no way blending. Meera Briskin was not one to blend. She was like the angel on top of the Christmas tree—all eyes were drawn to her.

Now she'd gained the conference director's attention. Harold made no bones about this conference being his mission in life. And if Elliot did anything to discourage Harold's "favorite" student, he could wave good-bye to the conference. Now, that would really impress his dad!

No doubt about it, Elliot thought, she was worming her way into his life. . . and into his business, just like the blight that had eaten away at the chestnuts until they were all destroyed. And she was doing it with such ease and grace. But then she'd been reared by experts who had written the book on conniving!

With a mental snort, Elliot grasped a discarded paper cup and threw it into a trash can. More irritating than the label "Briskin" was the packaging. He was a man now, and he knew you couldn't judge a Christmas present by the wrapping anymore than you could judge a book by its cover. This conference provided the apt analogy for that.

If he were honest, however, the scary thing was that if he hadn't found out who she was, he could have been taken in. Totally smitten. Not an easy thing for him. Not with his track record with women.

With determined steps, Elliot strode toward the registration desk. There was one more thing he had to do before the night was over, and that was, without provoking her conference director, to put Meera Briskin in her place.

"Break time already?" Tom asked, looking at a make-believe watch on his wrist when Elliot reached the desk.

Only for a second did Elliot ponder that remark. Tom had no specific break time. His job required his presence for whatever the desk duties demanded, whether registering guests for six hours straight or sitting and doing nothing for the same period of time. Then Elliot remembered that Tom had asked to browse through the display materials at this conference, said he might write a book someday. Seemed everybody said that. He'd even considered it himself. . .briefly. Trevor held the monopoly on celebritydom around here.

"Sure, go on. I'll relieve you for awhile," Elliot said to Tom, who quickly left the desk area and began to mingle with conferees at the display tables.

Normally, after being on his feet most of the day, dealing with the innumerable problems of a hotel in keeping his guests pleased, Elliot would be ready to slump into an easy chair or even go to his suite and unwind. Tonight, however, the adrenalin was still flowing. He sat on the high stool that allowed him a bird's-eye view of the lobby, pretending not to be watching for anyone in particular.

He'd tried not to let her get under his skin. Had even tried to convince himself, while standing in a puddle of water in the kitchen, that she was just a conferee who would be here for a few days, then leave. Would that be so terrible?

Perhaps not. But she'd sought him out to ask for an interview. Why? And why not approach him honestly, with a forthright explanation of her intentions? Ha! A Briskin! Honest?

She did have a lot of nerve. The Briskins knew better than to trespass. That was an unwritten law since his grandfather had shot Elias Briskin in the leg, leaving him with a permanent limp. And when his dad had tried to intervene, it had ended up in a fist fight.

Suddenly, unexplainably, Elliot missed Kate. *Kate?* Now what had brought that on? Why was he suddenly aware that he was thirty-two and single?

In that respect, he, Josh, and Trevor were all in the same boat. But Trevor had gone on to achieve fame and fortune as a novelist. And Josh had filled his life with activity—teaching psychology, calling square dances, and working with troubled young people. Elliot, on the other hand, spent most of his time outside office hours simply trying to come to grips with his loneliness. But now it weighed heavily upon his mind. What if? What if Kate hadn't gotten mixed up with drugs? What if they'd married and had kids?

And what if Meera Brown were not a Briskin? Wouldn't that be a most enviable challenge?

Tom returned with an armload of magazines. "Mr. Wright said I could have these," he said with wonder and delight as he placed the reading material under the long bar. He straightened and, keeping his voice low so as not to be overheard, he asked, "Did she have a record?"

"What?" Elliot asked, unable to grasp his meaning.

"You know. . .the license plate." Tom's gaze darted toward the lobby and back to Elliot.

Elliot didn't have long to puzzle over the mischief twinkling in the young man's eyes. For Meera was walking toward him, looking like an angel of light instead of a Briskin with a dark and devious heart. And yes—she definitely had a record. The Briskins represented a long line of pretenders!

She stepped up to the desk, holding two long-stemmed glasses of the lodge's own special nonalcoholic, red, sparkling punch. She smiled, her soft, shiny lips matching the pink of her fingertips. Her perfume—a fine, delicate scent like yellow jasmine on a balmy spring night—wafted to him from the little pulsepoint on her creamy neck.

"I thought you could use this," she said, offering him a glass.

He accepted it and took a sip, staring into the lying eyes—as clear as a morning sky, as soft as a whisper of mist hovering over a mountain peak. A line from Mary Poppins crossed his mind: "A spoonful of sugar makes the medicine go down," and he swallowed hard over his resolve not to give that sugar-coated beauty the medicine she deserved and kick her out on her ear.

He felt his cheeks flush and was grateful for the cooling liquid. "Thanks," he said and took another swallow. "How's the conference going?"

Meera's face came alive. "Great! For years I've been accused of being a rebel. And tonight in the keynote speech, Mr. Wright used that very word." She set her glass next to his and lifted her fist above her head. "We're not rebels," she said, imitating Harold's enthusiastic manner of speech, "we're pioneers! Communicators! The power of our pens can change the world!"

She laughed, and Elliot couldn't help responding to her friendly, congenial manner. "It's my first conference," she confessed.

"What prompted you to attend?" Elliot asked abruptly, wondering if she'd come clean.

Meera decided she would be as honest as possible. "My friend Cathy told me about it. Her brother is the banquet speaker for the conference."

"Trevor Steinbord is a friend of yours?" Was that why Meera had come to the conference? Because of Trevor?

"I doubt that he would call me a friend exactly," Meera admitted, and Elliot was inclined to believe her. Trevor was rather a loner like himself and would not use the term lightly. "I suppose *acquaintance* would be more accurate."

Elliot nodded and Meera continued, a little apprehensive now, noting that his manner had changed since their initial meeting. He was such a handsome man, with eyes that could be gorgeous when alight with warmth as they had been earlier. Now he appeared reserved, distant, and his gaze was guarded. What had changed?

"Anyway," she rambled on, "I heard him speak at Chapel Hill. Cathy and I were students there at the same time, and she introduced me to Trevor."

She looked into Elliot's eyes then, and something flickered in their blue depths. She felt heat rise to her cheeks. He must think her an idiot to give the impression that an introduction to Trevor Steinbord was the highlight of her life. Good grief, she'd been among the guests at a dinner in Venezuela thrown by the American ambassador!

"I know Trevor," Elliot acknowledged with a cool nod. "His entire family, as a matter of fact. His younger brother was the local football hero before his accident, and his dad designed this lodge."

"I didn't know that." Meera glanced around her, grabbing at this new topic of conversation to ease the awkward moment.

Elliot shrugged. "How could you have known?"

At the edge in his voice, Meera dropped her eyes. He'd already made it quite clear that he usually refused requests for interviews. She was close to tears. It all seemed so hopeless. If she didn't interview him. . .if he didn't get to know her and like her, then her mission would have ended in failure.

No, that wasn't it, she reminded herself. Her mission was not to win the Maxwells' approval, but to discover whether or not she approved of *them*. But somehow, it had become very important that at least one Maxwell—Elliot Maxwell—approve of her.

She lifted her head to look him straight in the eye. "I'm sorry. I've gone about this all wrong."

"You *are* an experienced writer, aren't you?" he asked casually.

"To be honest," she began and Elliot resisted the urge to laugh in her face, "I'm not a creative writer like Trevor, nor do I have any such aspirations. I've only done an occasional factual kind of article, usually a travelogue. The editors liked my writing and gave me an assignment to report on the best inns in western North Carolina."

Once again Elliot clamped his lips shut rather than tell her that all he'd have to do was to pick up the phone and almost any major magazine in the country would send a reporter to cover the story—an experienced one at that. It was almost more than he could do not to reveal that he knew her true identity. But he'd resolved to wait—to see what she was up to. He lifted the glass to his lips and gulped down the contents.

Coolly, with perfect composure, she sipped from her glass, studying him over the rim. Why was she really here, he wondered? If just to attend a conference, then why was she continuing to pursue him—not once, but twice today? He glanced at his glass. It was empty. He'd drained it like a man stranded in the desert. Probably looked like one. Maybe even smelled like one.

"Look," he said, feeling suddenly grungy. "Give me five minutes to shower. Then we'll talk. Okay?"

She nodded. "Don't you ever go home? I mean, don't you have a wife or. . . anything?"

"No wife," he answered abruptly, "or anything." Now why would his marital status concern Meera Briskin if all she wanted was to write an article on Chestnut Lodge? "And I am home," he said, pointing upward, and noticed her surprise. "Third-floor suite."

"You do put in long hours. Are you always so busy?"

Busy? The word struck him as odd. "I suppose," he began, as much to himself as to her, "leisure to me is a walk in the woods, planting a tree. . ."

He paused when he saw her eyes light up with understanding. Then he reminded himself that she was a Briskin. She would know that the Maxwells had been involved in research with the Forestry Service ever since the deadly *cryphonectria parasitica* had destroyed the chestnut. She would know the hard work—cutting, planting, erosion control, ecological studies—these forest lands demanded. The hard work the Maxwells had done through the years just to survive.

But she might not know the damage her presence here could do to his father. "My dad had a heart attack several months ago."

The blue-gray eyes deepened with concern. "How is he now?"

"Doing well. He should be back here before the tourist season begins in mid-June."

Tom looked his way and Elliot motioned to him. "One other thing," he said to Meera as he turned to go. "Before making a decision about your writing the article, I'll need to see your credentials."

He gloated inwardly when he saw the look of chagrin on her face. It felt great to best a Briskin! But what had she expected? Had she actually thought he'd take her at face value, lovely though it was? Now what would she do? 'Fess up. . .or pack her bags and leave?

Chapter 4

Meera was waiting near the registration desk when Elliot returned wearing a knit shirt and jeans, his still-damp hair curling on his neck. A quick glance told him that she'd exchanged her high heels for flats.

She held out a manila envelope, and he felt a tremor vibrating inside. *Get hold of yourself, man!* he scolded himself. He took the package containing her credentials and eyed it as if it were a brown recluse spider. But he wasn't ready to be bitten just yet.

"Put this in my office, will you?" he asked, handing it to Tom.

Seeing the expression of pleasure on Meera's face, Elliot had the distinct impression that the article was not uppermost in her mind, and he determined to find out why. He returned her dazzling smile, but tried to ignore the spark that leapt into her smoky eyes, warning himself that any flame ignited by a Briskin could be as destructive as fire rampaging through the forests during a dry spell.

Feeling warm, he tugged at the collar of his shirt. "Let's walk outside," he said and led her to the back deck that spanned the entire width of the lodge. Guests sat in rocking chairs in casual groupings, admiring the deep purple mountains silhouetted against a violet sky.

"Oh, Elliot," she breathed, "this is. . .beautiful."

He felt certain she'd never seen the distant Briskin mountains from this vantage point. Not only that, she'd probably never spoken to a Maxwell before either.

Deliberately he let his hand touch hers where it lay on the chestnut railing. Her words caught in her throat midsentence. But she didn't move away.

Pulling her with him, he led her along the stone pathways and down rustic steps, where they descended the terraced mountainside with its gardens and trees held at bay by stone walls. In the ornamental gardens, Meera found manicured shrubs and fountains playing beneath a grove of giant oaks, maples, and mimosa. Rhododendron sprang up in wild profusion, its showy blossoms almost eclipsing the beauty of the more delicate mountain laurel and fragrant calacanthus.

Elliot's fingers pressed lightly at her waist as he guided her expertly past other guests strolling along the lighted garden paths or sitting on stone benches beneath the tall trees.

When they came to the end of one path, where lush native ferns ran riot, Meera stopped and looked back at the three-story lodge atop the mountain. "I couldn't have imagined all this," she said in a near whisper. "It's. . .magnificent." She turned her glowing face toward his.

Elliot felt his heart lurch. This woman was sincerely moved by the natural beauty surrounding them. *But who wouldn't be?* he decided.

Following a dirt path that led deep into the thick forest, Meera felt a flash of childhood fear—not of bears, rattlesnakes, or mountain lions, but of a dreaded Maxwell lurking behind every tree!

As she walked along beside Elliot, Meera thought how like her own life was this path, dappled with light and shadows. Childhood fears remained, but she was an adult now, coming into the light of her own knowledge. . . about life. . .about the Maxwells.

She liked Elliot Maxwell. She'd liked him on first sight. He had complimented her, had been encouraging, yet had remained polite and respectful. She'd watched him in action, had noted his competence, his concern for his guests, his love for his dad. He was proud of Chestnut Lodge, related well to his staff, was a hard worker. These were attributes she could admire in a man.

As they stepped into the shadows, a nagging doubt surfaced. Where was he taking her. . .and why? He hadn't yet given his permission to write the article, hadn't even looked over her credentials, as far as she knew. This couldn't be part of the coveted interview. So why was he giving her his time?

Still, he was a Maxwell, and she'd always been told that Maxwells were not to be trusted. She wasn't afraid, though, she told herself. One little yell of "Fire!" would echo around the mountainsides, and the sirens would be shrieking to the scene within minutes. Besides, he didn't even know who she was. Could it be that he was as intrigued with her as she was with him?

Meera lifted her hand to her ear. "Do I hear water?"

"Turkey Creek," he explained and gloated at the mental image of her landing kersplat in the middle of it. "On the other side of these boulders."

He reached for her hand and led her along the dirt path, around the rocks, and to the banks of the creek. Directly across from them was the Briskin hunting lodge. "Know what that is?" he asked, watching her closely.

"Well, I—I. . . ," she stammered. "It's a cabin. But. . ."

Still hand in hand, Elliot felt the tremor run through her body. He understood why. He'd known it all his life—dread, fear, anger toward the Briskins. She must feel the same about the Maxwells. He pretended not to notice when she attempted to move away, but continued to hold her firmly.

She had started this. . .she could stay and face the music.

"It's a symbol," he went on relentlessly, ignoring her discomfort. "A mockery. The Briskins built it out of chestnut wood, as a reminder to the Maxwells of their victory in selling us worthless land. It stands there in the clearing like a perennial slap in our faces."

Oh, that's not the reason! she wanted to cry out. What twisted and terrible tales had he been told? But she'd heard the edge in his voice, had seen the hardness in the planes of his face, the bitterness that shimmered in his eyes. She could not dare say what she was thinking: *You're wrong, Elliot! I'm one of them. And my grandfather was one of the kindest, dearest men in the whole world!*

"My dad and granddad brought me here when I was just a kid," Elliot continued, his lips thinned to an angry line. "They took me up and down this creek, pointing out how it ran across Maxwell land in some places and Briskin land in others. But here," he gestured toward the water tumbling noisily over the rocks, "the creek crosses the line in two places. I was warned never to step over that line."

He tossed a look over his shoulder at the boulders and confessed, "I used to hide behind those rocks and spy on the Briskins."

She looked up at him warily. "What did they do to you?" she whispered, as if she didn't know.

"The old man who died last year," he began and saw the flicker of sadness that crossed her face, "sold my granddad thousands of acres of worthless timberland. The trees were primarily American chestnut. . .infested with blight. All of them died. I can show you little shoots that still come up, struggle, then wither away. . .just like the Maxwell fortune," he added bitterly. "The Briskins took it all. For decades my granddad, then my dad fought that blight, but nothing made any difference. It choked off the nutrients while the trees starved to death. It was like watching a loved one suffer, while you stand by, helpless to do anything but watch her die a slow, agonizing death."

Meera felt his pain and sensed that this was not the time to reveal her true identity, or to tell him that he had it all wrong, that her grandfather had not known the trees were blighted. Looking across at the darkened cabin, she felt again her loss. She could almost see her grandfather rocking on the front porch, while she sat on the step looking up at him while he told the Briskin-Maxwell story.

Elias Briskin had discovered ruby in his mountains and had needed money to develop the mines. Jonas Maxwell was eager to buy the land, abounding in chestnut, for his lumber business. The nuts alone would bring a fortune.

In those days, Elias and Jonas were the closest of friends, both competing

36

for the hand of Carrie Spearman, the prettiest girl in the county. But when the blight was discovered, Jonas wouldn't believe that his friend hadn't known in advance. And Carrie, having the highest of standards, refused to speak to him from that day forward and soon announced her engagement to Jonas.

"I would have stepped aside had Jonas won fair and square," Elias often said. "But he poisoned Carrie's mind against me."

It was a dozen years before Elias fell in love again.

"Your grandmother was as sweet and gentle a woman as ever drew breath, yet she didn't mind facin' the devil himself if it came down to it. Pretty as a picture, too," he'd told Meera many times. "You put me in mind of her. . . ." Then he'd stare off into the sunset, remembering the young wife who had died when their last child was born.

"I didn't know about the blight," her grandfather always insisted. "Jonas felt I robbed him. But 'twas the other way around. Jonas robbed *me*. . .of my good name, my reputation, my girl, and our friendship."

Then he came to the part that always choked him up. "The day before they married, I tried again. Jonas wouldn't listen to a word I had to say. He chased me down the mountain, and, when I got to the creek, I stopped and turned around." Elias would rock, stare at the Maxwell forest, and shake his head as if he still couldn't believe it, even after all those years. "My best friend tried to kill me."

Meera shuddered. Believing that, would Elliot Maxwell listen to her, she wondered, when the time came? For now, she couldn't defend her grandfather, could only ask, "Didn't the trees die on Briskin land, too?"

Elliot detected controlled defiance in her tone. "That's not the point," he scoffed. "Their livelihood did not come from the chestnut trees as it did with the Maxwells. With the money they got from selling blighted trees, they developed their ruby mines. I wouldn't be surprised if you're wearing a Briskin ruby yourself." He lifted her hands to take a look.

"Diamonds," she countered as he looked at the dinner ring on the finger of her right hand. "It's my birthstone."

He stared at her hand, narrowing his gaze. The brilliant moonlight that had turned her hair to silver and bathed her face in a soft glow also revealed a thin, white line encircling the ring finger on her left hand. She had worn a ring there recently. Why was she not wearing it now? Was she pretending to be unattached for some reason?

He released her hands and looked at the cabin. "It's been drilled into me that if I ever set foot on Briskin property, I'd be shot on sight."

"Have you?" she wanted to know. "Ever been there, I mean?"

"Never!"

"Then why not now?"

What was she trying to do? Get him shot? "Sure," he mocked. "I'll just hop over there, and you know what will happen. . . ." He lifted an imaginary rifle to his shoulder and took aim. "*Bang!*"

Meera started at the sound and involuntarily clutched his bicep. "Oh, Elliot," she pleaded, "let's talk about something more pleasant."

Now was the perfect time to set her in the creek—either physically or verbally, or both. In the distance, a wild animal howled, and nearby insects hummed to their mates.

He gripped her shoulders. How warm and soft her skin felt beneath his fingers. And beneath a velvet sky sprinkled with diamonds, an ingenious plan came to him as naturally as the gentle breeze that stirred her hair. Even the creek seemed to be applauding.

In dealing with the Briskins, his grandfather had used a shotgun, while his dad had used his fists. But then they hadn't been fighting with a beautiful blond. Surely this generation could come up with something more original.

He looked into her upturned face, her moist lips slightly parted, her misty gray eyes filled with emotion.

There was one way to find out.

With one hand against the small of her back, he entwined the other in her hair, feeling the sensation of corn silk brushing against his palm. Her feathery lashes closed, sweeping her cheeks, as the warmth of her breath mingled with his.

Elliot's lips traced a light pattern over hers, so soft and warm and tasting of sparkling punch. He felt a rush of warmth and pulled her closer. Drawing in an unsteady breath, he covered her mouth with his own in a long, searing kiss.

Suddenly, frightened by her response, Meera wrenched herself away, staring at him with startled eyes. Then she turned from him and hugged her arms to her body, shivering in the cool, night air.

Elliot gazed into the distance, watching Maxwell and Briskin water spraying white foam as it churned over rocks in the creek, as if it, too, were in upheaval, like his emotions. He'd wanted to do that from the moment he'd laid eyes on Meera *Brown*, so he wasn't all that surprised at his own spontaneous action, despite his reservations about Meera *Briskin*.

But he was surprised by the intensity of her response. Or had he imagined that she had grown soft and yielding in his arms? And why had she pulled away? Was it a sudden stab of conscience? Or had she planned this, then been unable to bear the touch of a Maxwell, after all?

Still, suppose she had welcomed it. Now wouldn't her little game be in danger of backfiring?

Somehow he found no satisfaction in that thought. He really didn't wish her any harm. All of his life, he'd simply avoided the Briskins and hoped they'd stay out of his way. But she had crossed the line. That kind of action called for a response. First, though, he'd have to try to discover why she was really here.

"We should be getting back," he said quietly.

"Yes, it's getting late." She ran her fingers through her hair, not quite meeting his eyes.

In a shadowed corner before they reached the patio, he took her hand and felt her tremble. Did she think he would try to kiss her again? But he said what he would have said to any woman whose response to him he might have misinterpreted. "I'm sorry if I offended you."

Offended her? She looked at him wonderingly, overwhelmed that any Maxwell could be such a wonderful human being. He was mistaken about the Briskins, but she'd find a way to remedy that. "Oh, I was not at all offended," she assured him. "I just hope you didn't get the wrong impression of me."

At the moment he had the distinct impression that she wanted him to take her again in his arms, Briskin or not. He lifted her hand and would have brought it to his lips but remembered the white circle. "Are you. . .married?"

"No." She swiveled out of his reach.

"Engaged?" If she said no, he would ask her about the thin, white line.

But she looked at him with unmistakeable misery in her eyes. "I don't know," she whispered into the quiet night. "I really don't know."

Elliot stood like a stone as she hurried away and climbed the steps to the upper deck. She wasn't the only one who was confused. There were several things he didn't know. Why he hadn't thrown her in the creek as he'd planned to do, for instance. And why he'd kissed her instead!

Was he all that cunning. . .or just cowardly? Perhaps his method of dealing with the Briskins was more pleasurable than guns and fists, but it could prove to be catastrophic.

❧

Elliot Maxwell's apology echoed in Meera's head all the way to the third floor and even after she had rushed into her darkened bedroom and heard the lock click behind her. For a moment she stood in the shadows, with her back pressed against the door.

She was not offended! She had secretly wanted him to kiss her. Had been fascinated by the idea of finding out if all the Maxwells were of the same stripe. And the feeling had been. . .exhilarating!

Her fingers moved to her lips just as another thought brushed across her mind: Elliot had kissed Meera *Brown*, not Meera *Briskin*. But it had not been

Meera Briskin who had kissed him back. That Meera knew better!

No doubt, "Meera Brown" seemed terribly naive or foolish to him. Even when he'd made it clear that he was more interested in her personally than in her writing credentials, she had walked through the dark woods with him and down to the creek. She hadn't even protested when he'd stolen a kiss, had practically asked for it! How could he think she'd been offended?

Suddenly she was aware of light spilling into the room from the skylight and filtering through the windows. Crossing the floor, she stepped to the window and reached out her hand to push back the drape. Her eyes fell on what Elliot Maxwell must have seen—the white band circling her tanned finger. Like. . .a brand. Clearly it was the mark of a ring—Clark's ring—signifying an engagement that she had not acknowledged. An engagement she had considered breaking when he had betrayed her with Louisa.

Clark had almost convinced her that the kiss hadn't really meant anything. Of course, she knew men and women kissed all the time—friendly kisses, innocent kisses, casual kisses. But Elliot's kiss had been anything but casual! And. . .if he learned to like her, maybe that would make acceptance easier when she confessed later that she was a Briskin.

Meera stood at the window, watching while the pool lights were turned out and guests left the area for the night. She replayed her conversation with Elliot, understood his adverse feelings toward the Briskins, hoped someday that their silly family feud would all be behind them. And tried not to give too much credence to the kiss they had exchanged.

At last, Meera opened the glass doors and slipped out onto her private balcony and felt the cool breeze on her flushed cheeks. She scanned the dark mountain peaks silhouetted against the starlit sky and reminded herself that nothing must be allowed to mar that breathtaking view. How many thousands of people must have stood here on Maxwell property, delighting in the natural beauty of the Briskin mountains!

Hearing a splash, she looked down. A lone figure was making swift, graceful strokes through the water. The moonlight glistened on his powerful arms and shoulders while the water sparkled and rippled, accommodating his strong frame.

Meera stared, transfixed, while he swam several laps. Finally he swam to the side, hoisted himself up effortlessly, took a towel from a nearby chair and began rubbing himself dry.

Then he straightened. The moon, as if a spotlight, revealed his well-formed physique—the narrow hips, the tapered waist. . . .

She'd wanted to know what the Maxwells were like. Well, now she knew. At least, she knew that at least one of them was incredibly attractive.

It remained to be seen whether there was more to the man than good looks and business savvy.

She returned to the bedroom, still wondering why she had responded to Elliot Maxwell so passionately. Apparently she was drawn to men she should be wary of. Her experience with Clark was teaching her that.

But she didn't want to think of Clark just now. And the thought struck her forcefully: Particularly not Clark!

Later, lying in bed, watching the stars blink above the skylight, Meera thought of how strangely wonderful she had felt in Elliot's strong arms. For those few moments she had even forgotten that he was a Maxwell, her dreaded enemy. She refused to think of the possible consequences if he should discover her identity before discovering that there was more to her than outward appearances.

Shivering, she pulled the covers closely around her. Suddenly, the writing of that article took on enormous proportions. It was more than a means to approaching Elliot Maxwell. It was a means of proving herself. And suddenly, she did not feel very confident—only determined.

❧

Elliot had hoped to exercise away in the pool the disturbing memory of his emotional moments with Meera Briskin, to accept the impetuous kiss as a normal reaction to a beautiful, desirable woman, then to leave it behind with the chlorine that was intended to kill germs and prevent disease.

Just then he looked up and saw her stepping from the balcony into the bedroom. And like the bad blood that had existed between the two families for generations, the memory of their brief encounter roiled in his brain. Nothing had been able to eliminate or subdue the blight that had jeopardized his family fortune. Nor had his strenuous swim banished the infestation of Meera Briskin from his mind.

Slipping into his office to change into his clothes rather than meet up with some late-night guest in the hallways or on the elevator, his eyes fell upon the manila envelope on his desk. If he examined it and saw her real name, he'd be obligated to go to her room and demand an explanation. But tonight, feeling his vulnerability, he knew he might be inclined to believe whatever flimsy story she might concoct. Better not risk that.

He dressed quickly and took the elevator to the third floor. His glance swept the hall, stopping on the door of the room where Meera was ensconced. But he entered his own suite, which was in the central part of the building, commanding a view of the Maxwell side of the mountains and the winding road leading to the valley far below.

Showering, Elliot told himself he'd wash all traces of Meera Briskin's elusive fragrance down the drain. Then he dried himself, wrapping a thick towel around his waist. Catching a glimpse of himself in the full-length mirror on the back of the bathroom door, he made a wry face. His emotions had not been in such a turmoil in a long time, but he felt he could explain it. There were two reasons: the Garden of Eden. . .and Kate.

Just like Adam and Eve, he'd been tempted by forbidden fruit. He'd tasted. And in so doing, his paradise was threatened.

And Kate? She was on his mind tonight, he told himself, because her brother Josh would be at the lodge tomorrow night to call a square dance for the writers' conference.

He switched on the hair dryer and began blow-drying his damp curls. The high-pitched hum of the machine accompanied the poignant thoughts that wouldn't let him be. Seeing the telltale evidence on Meera's finger, he had asked about an engagement. Her words, "I don't know," held the ring of truth. Or maybe he just wanted to believe them. Believe that her intentions were somehow honorable.

He was reminded of the many times he'd asked Kate why she didn't just walk away from her so-called friends who encouraged her drug use. She had cried and said, "I don't know, Elliot. I will. Oh, Elliot, I don't want to live this way. I'll get help, I promise I will!"

And she had tried, really tried. But two weeks after coming out of rehab, she was found dead in a wooded area. She had reportedly OD'd on a lethal drug, and since no conclusive evidence was found to the contrary, her death had been ruled either accidental or a suicide.

Those who knew her best—Elliot, Josh, and the rest of her family— knew she wouldn't have taken her life that way. She would have left a note. Josh had vowed he'd find her murderer someday. Maybe then, they could lay her to rest at last.

Elliot switched off the hair dryer and went into his bedroom to stand in front of the open window, breathing in deep draughts of brisk, fresh air. Far down in the valley, he could see the town's lone traffic light as first one, then another blinked on. Green for go, red for stop. Green for go, red for stop. How symbolic of his own inner chaos.

Turning from the window, he tossed aside his towel and reached for his pajama bottoms. Then he climbed into bed and drew the sheet up over himself.

A stab of loneliness caught him unaware. He hadn't found anyone to fill the void in his life since Kate's death. But he'd accepted it. Oh, there had been a few relationships in the years since she'd been gone, but he'd never kidded himself—or the women—that any of them would lead to a lifelong commitment.

He and Kate had taken for granted that there was something special between them, though they had never made any promises to each other. Then why was she pressing on his mind?

Maybe because he'd learned so much from her misfortune. He and Josh had discussed it many times. Now that Josh was a psychologist, the subject had come up often, along with analysis of many other young people who had not found themselves or gotten a grip on life.

Or maybe he was just looking for some kind of excuse for Meera Briskin having trespassed on Maxwell property and pretending to be someone she was not. Kate had come from a basically moral family, with high standards. If someone like that could go astray, then what chance did a Briskin have?

He reached over to the bedside table and switched on the radio, hoping to distract himself from this litany of conflicting thoughts. Much later, somewhere in the oblivion of another world, he heard the sound of a crooner singing a plaintive love song from a bygone era: "I try hard. . .not to give in. But I've got you. . .under my skin."

Perfume filled the air. . . . Corn silk cascaded through his fingers. . . . A longing took possession of him, and he awakened with a thudding heart, murmuring the words the crooner had sung.

His eyes flew open, and he stared into the night. It was not Kate who had invaded his senses. It was *Meera*.

A terrifying realization penetrated his consciousness. Meera Briskin had not disappeared with the night. She was not, after all, something he could scrub off his skin. She was real and warm and alive. . .and she was driving him to distraction.

Chapter 5

Early morning was Meera's favorite time of day, but she couldn't ever remember a dawn as gorgeous as this one. She rubbed her eyes and peered again through her bedroom window at Chestnut Lodge. The low clouds, hugging the mountaintops as if in a last farewell, slowly lifted, revealing the scenery an inch at a time, as if God were completing a mountain landscape on the canvas of the sky.

She could barely keep her mind on the devotional reading for the day. But she had no problem whatsoever in her morning prayer time, keeping her eyes open and praising God for the beauty of the early sun touching the mountainsides that she had explored, roamed, hiked through, but had never before viewed from this angle.

Delicate, white dogwood blossoms, keeping their promise of spring, were bringing to life a forest that had lain dormant all winter. Tender new leaves sprouted from the limbs of trees. And though she couldn't see them from here, she knew that wild flowers, bulbs, ferns, and myriads of other colorful blossoms were springing up all over the forest floor. The air was fragrant with the scent of new life.

Meera knew in her heart that, if her family insisted upon selling the mountain, it must be offered to the Maxwells first. To take this view from Elliot or to mar it in any way would surely be a terrible injustice.

Her gaze wandered down to the pool. Its smooth surface reflected the first light in a shimmering haze. But in her mind she saw Elliot, and she looked for him, half expecting to see him farther down the mountain, toward the creek, near the outcropping of rocks where he'd held her in his arms.

Meera shook off the heady memory. She reminded herself sternly that she was no longer paying attention to her prayers. Or was she? Wasn't it her heart's desire that somehow this ridiculous animosity between the Briskins and the Maxwells would end?

Like spring, this was a new generation, a new era. She liked Elliot Maxwell. And he liked her—even if he did think the woman who had caught his fancy was Meera Brown. This was a time for new beginnings. She must tell him who she was and why she was here. He would understand. And it would be foolish to wait until she'd written an article. That was such a small thing compared to two people healing old hurts and building a better relationship, rather than letting them lie, rotting like fallen logs on the forest floor.

"I'll tell him who I am," she whispered aloud. "The very first chance I get. I'm sure he'll appreciate what I'm trying to do. I just know it."

On that resolve, she quickly showered, shampooed, dried her hair, and twisted it into a topknot, pulling a few, short strands over her brow. There were more important things to do than worry about her appearance, so she applied mascara only and a light lipstick after slipping into a blue sundress and sandals.

She would begin by asking Elliot if he'd looked over her credentials and read her articles. She didn't even want to imagine that he might turn her down. Not after last night. No, she'd keep a positive attitude.

But she didn't see him at breakfast. She sat next to Marlene, another Southerner she'd met at the "get-acquainted" session. The animated conversation at the table kept her spirits buoyed, and Meera felt again the same surge of hope she had felt during the keynote speech the night before, when Harold Wright had so motivated her, making her believe she could accomplish much with her writing if she simply gave it the attention it deserved.

For the next few hours Meera attended several workshops, including Effective Interviews, and found the information to be invaluable if she decided to pursue a writing career.

The session on Inspirational Writing did just that for her. It seemed incredible, but she began to believe that her words might inspire others as she had been inspired during the morning. Why, with all the insights she was sure to glean during her experiment at Chestnut Lodge, she'd have enough material to write a book on resolving family squabbles! Somehow, though, the family squabble no longer loomed as large as it had all her life.

Elliot just had to understand. Her eagerness to talk with him began to wane slightly when she didn't see him during the morning break. Neither he nor Tom were at the registration desk. A different clerk was on duty, and a mature woman appeared to be in charge. Nor was Elliot anywhere to be seen at lunchtime either.

After lunch, Marlene and some others had planned to go into Asheville. But Meera turned down the invitation to join them. Instead, she bought a few books in the conference bookstore and browsed through the display tables in the lobby.

But her mind was not on effective writing techniques or how to conduct a successful interview. *Maybe he read the articles and didn't like them,* she fretted. Maybe her credentials weren't professional enough. Or. . .maybe he was regretting the kiss and was having trouble facing her.

Worse yet, maybe he had learned her true identity—the scenario played itself out in her mind—and his dad had had a relapse. . . . It was a terrifying thought to imagine that she might be the cause—however unintentionally— of even more problems for the Maxwells. If so, there would never be a chance to end the hard feelings between the two families!

By midafternoon Meera was ready to leave the lodge for her appointment with Louisa. She was almost tempted to keep driving and never look back. Maybe this was a harebrained idea in the first place.

As she sped along the Parkway, taking the scenic route, the panoramic views that spread out before her around every turn lifted her spirits. How could she have succumbed to such doubt and worry when the One Who had created all this also had the answer to her problems? Of course! Elliot Maxwell simply had a day off. And there was no reason why he should have reported to her. Smiling at her foolishness, she switched on the radio and listened to inspirational music as she drove through the mountains and onto Briskin property.

Louisa's black sports car, with Louisa still at the wheel, was parked in front of the cabin when Meera drove up. She pulled around back—just in case Elliot Maxwell might be strolling through the woods or down by the creek.

Louisa bounced out of her car and walked around to meet Meera, her dark eyes flashing. "What took you so long? You know I don't like being out here in the boondocks alone!"

Meera stepped up onto the porch and opened the back door. "Sorry. I got away as soon as I could."

"You know, anybody could be hiding in there," Louisa remarked skeptically, standing back until Meera had checked it out.

"Grandfather Elias always said that's partly what the cabin's for. Sometimes people get lost in the forest. They're welcome to find shelter here."

"Humph! Sounds dangerous to me," Louisa sniffed. "Besides, you can't trust anybody these days. They'll take advantage of you."

Meera didn't reply to that. Her own cousin—her lifelong friend—had taken advantage of any opportunity to flirt with Clark. . .until he finally responded.

"There's no coffee," she said, holding up a box of teabags. "But I'll heat some water for tea." While the water heated, she took inventory of the cupboards, mumbling, "Have to buy groceries soon."

Louisa lifted a sable brow. "Then what *have* you been doing all this time, Meera?"

Meera looked over her shoulder. "Let's just say it's something I've wanted to do for a long time."

Louisa's mouth flew open, and her eyes widened. "You've been hang gliding!" she said and plopped down in a kitchen chair.

At that ridiculous observation, Meera laughed and turned to face her cousin, not bothering to correct the impression. "Well. . .it's challenging, dangerous, and quite intriguing," she replied, describing how she felt about the Maxwell venture.

"Why didn't you ask *me*?" Louisa pouted.

"That's something people should decide for themselves, Louisa. Now what's so urgent that you had to see me today?"

Her cousin rose, still eying Meera quizzically. "We need to know if you're going back to Venezuela with us next week. We have to make arrangements, you know."

"I'm not going yet." Meera reached inside a cabinet for two cups and saucers. "I have a lot of thinking to do, and I can't do it in Venezuela."

"You're not wearing Clark's ring," Louisa said with surprise, noticing the bare finger. "What does that mean?"

"What does it mean?" Meera said, and the cups rattled against the saucers as she set them on the cupboard. "Really, Louisa, do you expect me to wear a rock like that while hang gliding?"

"You're not hang gliding now."

"No, and the ring is in a safe place." Meera got up and walked to the window, remembering the day she had walked in on Louisa and Clark in the midst of a passionate embrace. Seeing her, they had quickly sprung apart, looking sheepish. Later, Clark had tried to insist that it had been only a friendly hug. Then he'd put Meera on the defensive, accusing her of keeping him dangling. He didn't want to wait any longer.

But how could Clark, if he were serious about marrying her, have embraced Louisa so passionately? For that matter—and she blushed to think about it—how could she herself, if she was serious about Clark, have responded so ardently to Elliot Maxwell?

Maybe it was because she had been so overwhelmed to find a decent Maxwell that she had felt like celebrating! At least, she wouldn't have to teach her children to hate the Maxwells—to distrust them—to carry bitterness in their hearts all of their lives. No, it wasn't the same as the incident between Clark and Louisa at all, Meera told herself. She had not been responding to a man, but to a miracle.

How different Elliot and Clark were, she thought, staring at the teabags steeping in identical cups. Elliot was more serious than Clark, but he was six or seven years older, a mature man with heavy responsibilities. Having done some ecological studies herself, she had to be impressed with the Maxwells' work in that area, including forestry, and expected that Elliot, too, was personally involved. She admired his ability to run the resort, serving his guests efficiently while keeping the surrounding forests well maintained.

Clark would be entering the last year of his doctoral program in the fall, but he was primarily interested in spending his allowance. She smiled. That was not a complaint. She'd helped him spend it on more than one occasion! They'd had some exciting times together.

But this—this feeling for Elliot Maxwell—was something entirely different. There had been that wonderful moment when she'd lost all sense of who she was and why she was trespassing on Maxwell property.

"Twenty-five thousand dollars for your thoughts," a voice said in one ear while the teakettle whistled in the other. "Meera," Louisa said sharply, "are you listening to me?"

"I'm sorry." Meera reached for the whistling kettle. "I didn't hear you."

"I asked," Louisa said, looking at her strangely, "what will Clark think about your not coming back with us?"

"Why don't you ask him, Louisa?" Meera retorted, quite certain that her cousin needed no encouragement to do just that.

"You're still upset about the day you walked in on me and Clark, aren't you?"

Meera sighed and brought the cups to the table. "Yes and no, Louisa. If you and Clark are interested in each other, then I won't stand in your way."

Louisa snorted. "Meera, you know good and well that any guy who gets a good look at you and your blond hair never gives me a second glance!"

"That's not exactly a compliment, Louisa."

"I didn't mean it as one," her cousin replied saucily. "It's just the truth."

Meera felt a sudden wave of nostalgia. She'd grown up with this girl. Louisa had been an only child, getting everything she'd ever wanted. . .except time with other children and a family life where one learned the art of sparring and sharing. Louisa had never learned to share. She'd always wanted whatever Meera had—including her current love interest.

"Was that all you wanted to talk to me about, Louisa?"

The dark-haired girl poked at her teabag with a spoon. "I wanted to explain, Meera. I was going to when we were in Venezuela—then we got the word about Gramps and. . ."

Grandfather Elias, as Meera had called him, had been her closest friend. Under his tutelage, she had learned to care about the forests, the mountains, and the Creator who had carved them out of the wilderness. She wanted to spend time at the cabin alone, remembering and cherishing the memory of their times together.

"Don't worry about it, Louisa," Meera consoled, her heart going out to the girl who often seemed so lost. Louisa had everything, yet was unsure of herself. "We'll just say it was a mistake, and I forgive you."

Louisa's eyes widened. "Oh, but it wasn't."

"What?"

"I mean," Louisa hastened to explain, "I. . .like Clark. It would be a mistake for you two to marry if he didn't even know I was in the running until it was too late."

"Oh, Louisa, you haven't changed a bit!" Meera sighed. "You've always made a play for any man I was ever interested in."

"I just wanted to see if I could take them away from you," Louisa admitted smugly, then on a serious note, "but this is different. That day with Clark, I just couldn't help myself."

Before last night Meera could easily have replied that there was no excuse for them to have been in each other's arms. It was betrayal of trust, blood relationship, and friendship. At the moment, however, she had no room to talk.

Louisa filled the awkward silence. "Meera, do you really want to marry a man who can't stay away from me?"

Meera's stormy eyes met Louisa's. "So that wasn't the only time!"

"Yes. . .it was," her cousin admitted, and Meera believed her. Judging from her downcast appearance, she was telling the truth. "But once is enough, isn't it? I mean, it sure sent you into a spin."

"I felt betrayed. . .by two people who are supposed to be close to me. But like I said, I'm willing to forgive."

"Well, that's certainly a change of heart."

Meera drew herself up. "I think it's possible for a man to be tempted by a woman, and his response doesn't necessarily mean he's fallen for her. It may not have anything to do with love at all."

Louisa eyed her skeptically. "You don't talk like yourself, Meera."

"Maybe I'm growing up, Louisa. And it's time you did, too."

"I've grown up enough to know I'll fight for what I want, Meera," she threatened.

Meera stared at her. "There's no contest, Louisa. I'm engaged to Clark. He asked me to marry him, and nothing has changed. . .even after that unpleasant little episode you concocted."

"I didn't find it unpleasant," she said spitefully. "And neither did Clark."

"Remember what I said about temptation." Meera toyed with her cup.

"Then you're going to stay here while I return to Venezuela?"

"Well, I don't intend to ride herd on you or Clark or anybody else for the rest of my life."

"You're that sure of yourself, huh?"

Meera didn't feel sure at all. She had grown less sure of her feelings for Clark over the past year—and in so doing, she'd grown less sure of herself. To reject Clark would seem like the ultimate rebellion—in defiance of what appeared to be a perfect match, a union that would greatly please both families. She didn't know the answers. And it seemed that each day she further complicated her own life. "Look, I've got to go, Louisa. I have an appointment."

Louisa nodded and got to her feet. "Let me leave first. I don't want to be stranded down here on the road somewhere. There might be a Maxwell on the prowl."

Meera watched her cousin drive away, thinking how often she had made similar comments about the Maxwell family. But she was tired of perpetuating that silly prejudice—not without evidence. And so far, the evidence she'd seen exhibited by Elliot Maxwell was nothing to fight about.

She pulled away from the cabin after Louisa's car was out of sight. She'd gone too far to back out now, and she found herself actually looking forward to returning to Chestnut Lodge, where she would revert to being Meera Brown, freelance writer.

Engrossed in her thoughts, Meera failed to notice the lowslung, black sports car parked behind a grove of trees. Nor did she see it follow her as she pulled out onto the highway, keeping well back but never losing her.

While the day manager was on duty at the lodge, Elliot visited his dad and mom. He'd jogged down the exit and taken the private road from there, hiking out to the family home a couple of miles beyond.

The house was a contemporary marvel—completely round, built of stone, cedar, and glass, and perched on the side of the mountain with a breathtaking view of the lower mountains and valleys stretching as far as the eye could see.

It's all God's, he thought. *It doesn't belong exclusively to either the Briskins or the Maxwells, and we sure can't take it with us. True,* he argued with himself, *but we've got to get along with each other on this earth. God put us here to live together in harmony and to have dominion over the earth.* Sure, there was such a thing as forgiveness, but there was also such a thing as taking a stand on what's right and wrong. Even though Meera had had nothing to do with the terrible injustice that had triggered the feud, she belonged to the Briskin family. And regardless of his personal feelings, there was a family loyalty to which he must adhere.

A warmth, different from that of the sun beating down upon him, welled up within when he saw his dad on his knees, working in a flower bed.

"Morning, Dad," Elliot greeted his father as the older man looked up, wiping beads of perspiration from his forehead. "How's it going?"

"Great, son." His dad's laughter held a touch of irony. "I, who have cut trees and lifted logs all my life, am now reduced to *this*!" He flourished a handful of crabgrass, then got to his feet and stripped off his gloves.

Seeing the scowl on Elliot's face, he put his arm around his son's shoulders. "Oh, I'm not complaining. In fact, I feel a little guilty because I'm enjoying this so much. It even occurs to me—and Janie likes the idea—that I might just retire from the lodge. Oh, I could do some bookwork or something, but I've been needing to slow down. Now come up here and tell me how things are falling apart over there without me."

Elliot laughed this time. Strange how, as he'd grown older, he'd come to appreciate his dad's sense of humor. It seemed that the heart attack had only reaffirmed the depth of his love and respect for his father. He had to face the fact that he would lose him someday—maybe sooner than he wished—and it was not an easy thought.

His dad sat in the swing, and Elliot dropped down beside him. From the smile on the older man's face, Elliot knew he was pleased with his progress report. It's what his dad had always wanted—a son to follow in his footsteps.

That subject exhausted, his dad began to reminisce, retelling stories of Elliot's childhood, never mentioning the Briskins, as if they had dropped from the face of the earth. Elliot was quiet, recalling how his father had often told Bible stories as well, including the one about the Garden of Eden. "As you grow up, Elliot," he'd said seriously, "you'll be tempted to eat of the fruit of forbidden trees. . .just like Adam and Eve. That fruit comes in many forms. But if you eat of it, you'll have to pay the consequences."

His dad hadn't mentioned that story in years. No doubt he expected Elliot to have learned that lesson by now.

While Elliot had filled his dad in on most of the latest news, he had carefully avoided mentioning the proposed article. No way could an article about the Maxwells be written by a Briskin. It would kill his dad.

"You look worn out, Elliot," his mom said over their lunch of beef stew and hard rolls. "Max, this boy's working too hard."

"Now, Mother, he knows he can hire all the help he needs. Besides, a little hard work never hurt anybody."

Elliot shrugged. "It's not the work. I just didn't get much sleep last night."

Jane Maxwell looked over the rim of her tea glass, then set it down with a little thud. "You've got a girl, Elliot," she said hopefully.

"No," he denied, and hurriedly took a bite of stew as a defense against further conversation.

When he glanced up, he saw the gleam in his mom's eyes. It was no secret that she was eager for her only son to find somebody, settle down, and give her some grandchildren and Maxwell heirs.

He shook his head again, but the light in her eyes remained.

"Well, it's nothing to be ashamed of, is it?" she persisted. "After all, it's about time."

"Don't start that again," Max said to his wife.

Jane insisted that Elliot take a nap, and he lay across the bed in his old room. He had moved into Chestnut Lodge when he'd begun working there while attending college. But occasionally, it felt good to come home and let his mom treat him like a little boy again.

It was late afternoon when he returned to the lodge and learned from the manager that all was well. Bertha had the dining room under control, Tom was manning the desk, and no complaints had been registered with the conference director. Satisfied that all the guests were being well cared for, Elliot stepped into his office to catch up on some paperwork and to make decisions about applications from college students wanting summer jobs.

He had not been at his desk long when a knock sounded on the door. At his invitation, big Joshua Logan came in, looking like a burning bush with his heavy beard and mustache, and an unruly thicket of auburn curls springing up all over his head. Kate's hair had been that color. But she'd been a good foot shorter than her brother, who stood several inches over six feet.

At the moment, Dr. Josh Logan resembled anything but a psychology professor in his square dance costume—Western jeans, cowboy boots, and a white, pleated shirt with a red bandana knotted at the neck.

"Josh!" Elliot hurried around the desk and put out his hand.

"Good to see you, buddy. Where have you been keeping yourself this last month?"

The two settled into the lounge chairs in front of the fireplace and caught up on their activities. It was good having Josh back in town. For the past eight years, he'd been teaching in Charleston. Now he was back to fill an opening at the University of North Carolina at Asheville. Josh had told Elliot that those years away had given him time to cool off after his sister's murder, and he could now go about the business of finding the murderer more objectively. Elliot knew Josh's mind would never be at rest until that case was solved.

"School was out last week, so all that's behind me till fall," Josh said with some relief. "What's new with you?"

Elliot shook his head. "I'm really not sure." He picked up the unopened manila envelope on his desk and handed it to Josh. "Take a look at this."

Josh removed the papers, examined them casually, then glanced over at Elliot. "Nice-looking magazines, El. Am I supposed to be looking for something in particular?"

"The author, Josh. Look at the name on the paper-clipped articles."

"Meera Brown," Josh read. "So?"

"Let me see that!" Elliot reached for the magazines. He'd been so sure she had written under her real name that he hadn't bothered to look. "So, I've been duped again," he said ironically and explained his dilemma. "She's a *Briskin*, Josh."

Josh was puzzled. "But what has she done to you, pal? Or is this a carry-over from three generations back?"

Elliot sighed heavily and leaned his head against the back of the chair. "Oh, I have no personal grudge. But I've always accepted the fact that as a Maxwell, I'd be loyal to the family. As far as I know, they haven't done anything to *me*. . .until now, that is. Now she comes along, pretending to be this Meera Brown."

Josh tapped on the magazine, pointing to the byline.

"A pseudonym," Elliot explained. "She's still a Briskin."

"But she's also Meera Brown, writer, attending a writer's conference."

Elliot understood what Josh was getting at. His sister Kate had been two different people, too. One was the moral, intelligent, attractive young woman from a good, middle-class family. The other was a person addicted to mind-altering drugs. The real Kate had been buried deep inside somewhere, and all her friends and family had tried in vain to reach her.

He and Josh had talked it over many times—how they'd become more tolerant of troubled people, less judgmental, since the experience with Kate. "But this is different, Josh," Elliot insisted. "We knew Kate's behavior was drug-induced—although I'm not excusing that. But Meera's is deliberate."

"Would it be so bad to let her write the article under the name of Brown?"

Elliot let out a sigh of exasperation and rose to pace in front of the fireplace. "Josh, it's not just the article. The woman seems to be going out of her way to get to me."

"And apparently she's succeeded."

Pausing in front of his friend, Elliot stared. "For the first time in many years, I've let my guard down. That is, I could be vulnerable if I didn't know who she really was."

Josh pulled on his beard thoughtfully. "Do you? Know who she really is, I mean?"

The implication was obvious. The drugged Kate was not the real Kate. Not at all.

Elliot shoved his hands in his pockets and continued pacing. "That's the problem. I don't really know. I know she's a Briskin. But then, there's this beautiful, warm, very appealing woman I'd like to know better." He shook his head sorrowfully.

Josh nodded. "I understand where you're coming from, Elliot. But as any good psychologist will tell you. . ."

"I can't tell you what to do," they finished in unison.

Josh laughed and stacked the magazines neatly. "But I will say this: If fueling your family's feud is your objective, then order her to get off your property."

He grinned at the doleful look on Elliot's face. "On the other hand, if you're serious about getting to know her as an individual, then perhaps you might ask not what she might be doing to you, but what you can do for her. There's a tremendous opportunity here, Elliot."

"I know you're talking in spiritual terms, Josh," Elliot said hesitantly.

"Yes, and I know you're thinking physical. I understand. I'm an old single guy myself, remember? And we are physical beings, as well as spiritual."

Elliot smiled wryly. "I guess what it comes down to, Josh, is what I've known all along. Which Meera do I want to deal with? And more importantly, in what manner?"

Chapter 6

Meera arrived at the lodge before suppertime, quickly showered and changed, then stopped by the desk to ask Tom if Elliot had left anything for her.

"Sorry," Tom replied, "nothing."

She walked across the lobby, trying not to feel rejected. After all, she'd learned in the writing classes that it takes longer for an editor to say yes than it does to say no. The same principle could apply to an interviewee, she consoled herself. Or maybe he wanted to give her his reply in person. Her heart skipped a beat, both in fear and in anticipation.

Brushing aside these conflicting emotions, Meera gratefully acknowledged the approach of Marlene, who was decked out in a wide-brimmed straw hat, coveralls, red shirt, and a red and black bandana.

Marlene waved and hurried over. "You look great, Meera, but then you always do."

"I wasn't sure what to wear," Meera admitted. "The brochure said 'Western square dance.'" She glanced down at her full skirt of stonewashed denim paired with a ruffled peasant blouse. Her hair, falling in one long braid over her shoulder, was tied with a ribbon. "I think my costume may be more 'Spanish' than 'Western.'"

"I think mine's more 'hillbilly,'" Marlene said, wrinkling her nose in dismay and thrusting her hands into the pockets of her coveralls.

Meera laughed at her new friend's rueful expression. "Look over there." Several of the women were dressed in skirts styled with tiers of ruffles over stiff crinoline petticoats.

Marlene shrugged. "Well, it looks like anything goes. Let's head into the dining room."

The table decor—red and white checkered cloths and bright red napkins—carried out the Western theme. A tape playing country-western music set the mood of the evening.

Glancing around, Meera saw that Elliot was again nowhere in sight and tried not to be disappointed. She tried telling herself that if she never saw him again, she had already gained much with the week's discoveries and should be counting her blessings.

"Mmm," she said, taking her own advice. "This barbequed chicken is delicious."

"And wait till you taste the baked beans! Heavenly," Marlene sighed, closing her eyes in ecstasy. "Must be an authentic recipe."

After supper the group moved to the tennis courts, located beyond the steps at the back of the lodge, where Meera and Elliot had walked the night before.

There she spotted Elliot who was scurrying around, checking cables hooked up to some sound equipment on a table. He, too, was wearing jeans and a Western-style shirt with a braided, leather tie. In his boots, he appeared even taller and more striking than ever.

Then her attention turned to the big, bearded man who was testing the microphone. "One—two—three. Josh Logan here. Good evening, pardners." Meera and Marlene exchanged dubious glances, having already discussed their ineptness at square dancing.

But soon she was caught up in the exhibition of colorfully costumed professionals who stomped and turned and twirled as their appreciative audience looked on, applauding wildly. At the conclusion of the performance, Joshua told them that the experienced dancers would now mingle with the crowd, dancing with the inexperienced ones, and the costumed group headed for the sidelines. Meera thought one man was staring directly at her, when suddenly he held out his hand and asked Marlene to dance.

Feeling a little embarrassed, she was wondering why she had been passed up when she sensed someone standing behind her. His warm breath tickled her ear as a deep voice asked, "May I have this dance?"

She turned and looked up into Elliot's smiling, blue eyes. There was no guardedness in his expression, only pleasure in seeing her again, it seemed. In fact, his lingering look set her pulses to racing. So she was being completely honest when she replied regretfully, "I'm afraid I don't know how."

He surprised her by saying, "It would spoil the fun if you did. Come on. I'll give you your first lesson."

Meera gave him a scrutinizing look. "Have I shrunk, or are you wearing high heels?"

His lips twitched slightly. "That's a dangerous kind of statement," he warned.

"I live dangerously," she said with a flippant toss of her head, and pushed away the truth of her statement. What would he do if he knew a Briskin was deliberately flirting with a Maxwell?

She placed her hand in his outstretched one, and they walked out onto the tennis court. She was strongly tempted to tell him the truth about her charade. Was this the right time? Would he take her in his arms and assure her that it didn't make any difference?

"The answer is yes," he said abruptly.

Meera inhaled sharply. Had she actually voiced her thoughts? "Did. . .I ask you a question?"

He nodded. "Several times, in fact. I believe you wanted to write an article, didn't you?"

Her eyes lit up with relief and understanding. "Oh, so you're granting me permission?"

At a second nod from Elliot, Meera's heart thudded. Maybe. . .just maybe her mission would be accomplished after all.

"Thank you," she whispered just as Josh called, "Make a big circle. Ladies on the men's right. Now all join hands and circle left."

She followed Elliot's expert lead, circling left, then right, then allemanding with her corner, taking the arm of the person on her right and swinging around, then returning to her partner. *Partners!* A Briskin and a Maxwell! Only in this moment of fantasy would such a thing be possible, she decided.

There was no time to think beyond that, for Josh called out, "Now dosey-do!" and she and Elliot circled each other back to back, then obliged when he added, "Now look your partner in the eye." Her eyes met Elliot's laughing ones.

"I must look ridiculous," she said, breathless, aware of Elliot's easy rhythm and grace.

"Au contraire. . . ." He swung her close before twirling her around and taking both her hands in his. "It gets easier with practice."

With time, she thought. What would time bring? Was there any hope that the animosities between the Maxwells and Briskins could ever end? Or was she just a fool—rushing in where angels feared to tread?

❦

Meera and Elliot stood in line for ice cream, then found seats in folding chairs set up around the tennis courts to watch another exhibition by the professional dancers he had hired for the evening.

"Do you do this often?" Meera wanted to know.

He finished a big bite of strawberry ice cream, then smiled. "Not very often. But I used to dance a lot. . .in my younger days."

"Your younger days?" Meera would have laughed, but his face had taken on a serious expression, and there was a distant look in his eyes.

He glanced at her. "Josh, the caller, is the brother of a girl I was very close to. Since her death, I suppose I haven't considered myself very young anymore."

"You could have fooled me out there," Meera said quietly.

"I even fooled myself." He looked her directly in the eye. "Since Kate's death, my social life has been somewhat curbed."

He said it matter-of-factly, but Meera could see the stiffening of his jaw. His ice cream was melting, and she set her own half-eaten bowl next to his.

"Do you have any more classes tonight?" Elliot asked at last, breaking the long silence.

"No."

"Then let's walk. . .and talk about. . .the article."

"Yes," she agreed in a small voice.

They disposed of their plastic dishes, and Elliot glanced at Josh who was ready to call another dance for the conferees. Josh winked, but his expression was sober, acknowledging his concern for his buddy. No woman who followed his sister Kate in Elliot's affections would have an easy time of it. . . particularly if her name was Briskin.

As they walked, the music faded, and the sun's last rays flamed in the sky, painting the horizon with gold and orange. As if in homage to the dying day, the insects began to make their own music.

"You were in love with Kate?" Meera asked.

"I don't know," he admitted. "I suppose that's why I could identify with you when you said you didn't know whether you were engaged or not. If things had been different, Kate and I might have made a lifetime commitment. In any event, no one else has come along who has meant as much to me as she did." He shrugged. "Maybe it was love. . .or maybe it's just that I hate to see a promising life wasted."

"She. . .died, you said?"

"Several years ago. It was on TV, in the papers. You may have read about it. It happened on a hot day in mid-July."

Meera shook her head. "No. But several years ago I was spending my summers abroad." There was a long pause, then she added softly, "You can't forget her, can you?"

He gazed out at the distant mountains. "I've never found a woman who could make me forget. . ." Hesitating, he turned to face her, grasping her shoulders with both hands, "Until you, Meera, until you."

Meera held her breath, then swallowed hard. "Then I'm. . . therapeutic."

"Hardly," he moaned. "You're more disturbing than any woman I've ever met, Meera. . .Brown!"

So that was it! he explained to himself. When she was in his arms, she was not a Briskin—she was sweet, lovely Meera Brown, freelance writer. Or maybe she was just playing the part to the hilt. If so, just how far would she go with this act? And a more pressing question still—how far would *he* go?

Then he recalled that Briskins were masters at pretense. There had been many years of friendship between their grandparents, so Elias Briskin had apparently faked that, too. And his blood ran in Meera's veins.

Elliot knew she was pretending to be Meera Brown, and in that role he'd sensed a certain innocence in her warm, passionate kisses. But Meera Briskin was a confident, rich socialite from a dubious background, who could buy whatever she wanted, go anywhere, do anything. And that Meera wore the impression of a band on the ring finger of her left hand.

He closed his eyes to clear his head. Josh had made him see, without really saying it, that he had a responsibility not just to react to Meera—but to be the kind of man she needed him to be, the kind of man he should be. But it wasn't easy when his heart was saying one thing and his mind another.

He opened his eyes and reached for her hand. The heightened color in her cheeks betrayed her excitement—or what he interpreted as excitement. She even managed to look disappointed when Elliot stepped away to lead her from the terrace to a more secluded area.

The truth was, Meera had mixed emotions. She had half-hoped he would try to kiss her again, but all her instincts told her it was wrong to continue to mislead him. She must tell him. . .*now*. He would have every right to resent her if she allowed him to care for her while she deliberately concealed her identity from him. "Let's walk down to the creek, Elliot," she said, making the decision at last.

Elliot felt a sudden elation. Perhaps she was ready to open up. Or maybe she was just bored with her life and had decided to play cat and mouse with a Maxwell. Even so. . .even so. . .he still had an obligation as a mature man dealing with a possibly errant young woman.

When Meera heard the babble of the creek, an old melody ran through her head: "Love and marriage, love and marriage, go together like a horse and carriage. . . ." Years ago, she and Louisa had chanted: "Briskin and Maxwell, Briskin and Maxwell, go together like skin and poison ivy."

At least, if her confession caused him to break out in red splotches, she could escape to the other side of the creek. Surely a Maxwell would never follow her there!

When they reached the boulders, they climbed up to sit and look down on the murmuring stream. Stealing sidelong glances at Elliot, Meera was mesmerized by the way his eyes, now flame-colored, reflected the blazing sky. She sensed a need in him, a pain, a kind of familiar longing. She wanted to make him forget this woman who had meant so much to him. Wanted to be rid of this river of problems that separated them like the creek separated their property. She had to tell him who she was—and she had to do it now.

She drew in a deep breath. "Elliot," she began, "there's something. . ." She stiffened as a new sound reached her ears—the slam of a car door. "Get down," she ordered Elliot in a hoarse whisper, and slid off the rock to the hard ground, crouching low.

Elliot turned his head to look for the source of Meera's concern and saw the car stop in front of the cabin. He ducked and slid down beside Meera, where he peeked through an opening between the rocks. "She's rolling down the window," he whispered.

Louisa's voice rang out loud and clear on the once-peaceful evening air, bringing into play all the bitterness of their deep-rooted hostility and fear. Some very unladylike words rolled off Louisa's tongue, before she added, "I know you're hiding behind those rocks! You dare slither out of there, and I'll blow your head off! Worse than that, I'll—I'll. . ."

"That phony," Elliot said under his breath. "She's sitting in the car, making those empty threats. I ought to go over there and. . ." He balled a fist, glancing at Meera to see her reaction.

Her eyes were wide. She grasped his hand. "Don't chance it! She might have a gun!"

"She's driving away," he reported, still peeking through the small opening.

"She's probably as scared of you as you are of the Briskins."

Seeing that the car was gone, Elliot stood up and scoffed, "Where did you get the idea that I'm scared?"

Meera rose from her crouched position and lifted her chin saucily. "You wouldn't cross the creek last night, and now some frightened female has prevented your slithering out from behind the rocks."

"Always challenging me, aren't you?" he said threateningly. "Maybe, Meera Br. . .Brown. . . ," he corrected himself, "maybe I just prefer to choose a more suitable time and place for my demise."

She laughed lightly with him before they both sobered. She could see that he was waiting for her to finish what she had begun before Louisa's arrival had interrupted her. But she chose another tack. "What has a Briskin ever done to you, Elliot? Personally, that is?"

Elliot turned from her questioning eyes, feeling compelled to use caution. Propping his forearms on a boulder, he stared at the cabin, while Meera backed up against the boulders, studying his profile.

Three short days ago, he could have said that the Briskins had remained a thorn in his side only from a distance. Now, however, a Briskin had invaded his private world as surely as the blight had invaded the chestnut trees. Now he was in danger of losing his heart. . .to the enemy!

But aloud he said, "Briskin and Maxwell animosity runs deep, Meera.

There's always the feeling that I have to be on guard against them. You heard that girl. Just the thought of a Maxwell turned her into a raving maniac. Well, the Maxwells have the same kind of anger and mistrust just beneath the surface."

"That shouldn't be," she said sadly.

Elliot regarded her with a puzzled frown. Meera Briskin was either entirely sincere or a consummate actress. Why didn't she just tell him the truth about herself and be done with it? But what was the truth? He still didn't know what she was doing here. And what was this thing that had sprung up between them? He felt it, and he knew she did.

He reached for her, and she came into his arms without hesitation. Resting his chin on top of her silvery head, he sighed. "The enmity is so deep. That's why, in the article, you mustn't mention the feud. I'm afraid it might have a bad effect on my dad."

Feeling her tremble, Elliot moved away slightly and looked down into her troubled face. "Can't you tell me what's bothering you?"

She wanted to. But she didn't want to hear his words of disgust. Didn't want to hear all the negative remarks that struck her heart like an arrow each time he mentioned a Briskin.

Too, she kept wondering why Louisa had returned to the cabin. Louisa had made it very clear that she didn't like to be there at night. Perhaps something was wrong at home. She should call. "Now," he prodded gently, giving her every opportunity, "what was it you were about to tell me before we got a prime example of how a Briskin feels about a Maxwell?"

Meera knew she couldn't blurt out her identity here and now—not with all the conflicting emotions still so near the surface. Not with their standing only a few feet away from the spot where Jonas Maxwell had shot her grandfather. But she had to tell him something.

She took a deep breath. "Last night you asked if I was engaged. I'd like to explain about that," she said, a doubtful look crossing her eyes, "if I can. If you want to hear."

"I do," he said, surprised that he was relieved rather than disappointed. Perhaps he was a coward, not wanting to deal with the reality of hearing it from her own lips.

She sat down on a low rock, and Elliot sat near her.

"It was a whirlwind romance," she began. "Two summers ago. I met Clark in Venezuela. His family is one-half of Phillips/Coleman Oil."

Seeing Elliot's quick glance and a slight twitch of his mouth, she knew he'd heard of Clark. "You can't believe everything you read in the tabloids," she reminded him curtly.

It was not from the tabloids, but from the more reliable news media that he'd heard it: Clark Phillips—international playboy—linked romantically with numerous socialites and screen stars.

"He swept me off my feet," she confessed, almost apologetically. "But I wanted some kind of proof that I was more to him than his 'reported' exploits."

"Wasn't the proposal and ring proof enough?"

She looked down at her naked finger. "He's been engaged more than once. And now, he's. . .wanting proof that I'm willing to make a more serious commitment."

"Marriage?"

"I. . .don't think so," she said in a small voice.

"And that's why you took off the ring?"

"Not just that. . . ."

"Another woman," he said, guessing correctly.

"I see her as an immature, spoiled brat and a conniving flirt who places little value on our friendship," she said adamantly.

"And *that's* when you flew into a jealous rage and threw the ring at him."

"Quite the contrary," she countered. "I was upset, but I waited, thought about it for several days, then calmly removed the ring." She lifted her chin and gave him a sidelong glance. "*Then* I threw it at him."

"But you said you weren't sure. . .about your engagement," Elliot prompted.

She sighed. "He persuaded me to—to put the ring back on my finger."

"Mmm," Elliot said, squinting at her finger. "It's pretty small for a guy who's filthy rich."

She gave a weak laugh, but Elliot saw the discomfort in her eyes. "I. . . took it off again while I sorted out my feelings. But I am not one to mope around, so I decided to get on with something. . .more worthwhile."

Worthwhile, Elliot thought. The picture she had painted of Clark Phillips struck him as reprehensible. How dare the guy put a price tag on her affections and expect her to prove her love by making a "more serious commitment"—as if he didn't know what that meant! Though, if he were honest, he supposed his own behavior might not appear to be any more exemplary than Clark Phillips'.

"And what 'worthwhile' thing did you decide on?" he asked.

She looked him in the eye. "I decided to come here. . .to the writers' conference."

He regarded her steadily for a long moment. Then, "I'm glad you did."

Her eyes searched his, roaming his face. He wanted to take her in his arms and kiss her again. But he resisted the impulse. Her eyes clouded before she lowered her gaze to the tumbling creek. Apparently she had clammed up again. But why shouldn't she? As far as she could tell, he was no different from her erstwhile fiancé! He hoped he'd have a chance to prove that he was interested in more than her sweet kisses.

Elliot jumped down from the rock and held out his hand. "Meera Brown," he said, "let's go back to the lodge. I have some pictures and information that should be helpful in writing your article."

She smiled, and he added, "Bertha might even give you the recipe for our famous chestnut dressing." Then he grimaced. "On second thought," he contradicted, "no one's ever been able to pry it out of her with a crowbar."

"Oh, I don't know. She's already talked to me about the macaroon glacés," Meera said, to his astonishment.

"But she wouldn't tell you where we get them!"

She cocked her head in a delightful gesture. "I believe you import them from Italy, Sir. Now your secret will be out. Everyone will know those aren't American chestnuts."

He laughed, finding it incredible that a Maxwell and a Briskin could be jesting about such a thing. "Everyone in these parts knows there hasn't been an American chestnut since the 1940s at the latest. What you need is a history lesson, young lady, if you're going to write a decent article about this place."

She was instantly contrite. "Oh, I'd never write anything you wouldn't find acceptable."

He grinned. "I know. 'Subject to my approval.' That was our agreement, wasn't it?"

"I want to make you proud, Elliot Maxwell."

"I hope you will," he murmured under his breath and looked off toward the tennis courts where the conferees were singing now as Josh led them in some old cowboy favorites. "Want to join them?" he asked, indicating the group with a nod of his head.

She shook her head. "Not unless you do. I. . .need to make a phone call."

He sensed she needed privacy. "Use the phone in my office. Then come to the library. The desk clerk can direct you, if you don't know where it is."

In Elliot's office, Meera called the Briskin estate to say that she was fine and still visiting with friends. "That's what your parents have been doing every night this week," Aunt Clara retorted. "Don't know why we even need this big house. Oh, Louisa just came in. Do you want to talk to her?"

Meera declined. She had nothing to say to her cousin at the moment. Promising to report in again soon, she hung up.

When Meera wandered into the octagonal-shaped library off the main lobby, her footsteps were muffled by the plush carpet, and Elliot didn't look up from his rummaging through a stack of magazines.

Stepping inside the room, she caught the pungent whiff of furniture polish and old leather. Libraries had always fascinated Meera, but this one was particularly inviting with its tapestried couches and chairs, stone fireplace, and roll-top desk. Her eyes were drawn to a portrait hanging above the fireplace. It was a painting of a man and woman, and on first glance, the man appeared to be Elliot. Walking closer, however, she saw that though this person was just as ruggedly handsome, he was much older than Elliot, his dark hair silvering at the temples. The small plaque beneath the gold frame read: "Jonas Elliot Maxwell and Carrie Margaret Spearman."

So this was the woman her grandfather had loved so long ago! The woman, with dark, curly hair and determined deep blue eyes that reminded her of Elliot's, was the opposite of the pictures Meera had seen of her own grandmother. Her face, though not delicately pretty, was quite attractive with a look of strength. Meera couldn't help thinking that the more gentle woman her grandfather had married was the better choice for him.

She didn't notice Elliot walking up beside her until she felt his fingers at the small of her back.

"My ancestors," he said, wondering how Meera felt, looking at the woman her grandfather had lost through his chicanery.

But as he studied Meera, then his grandmother's portrait, he had a ridiculous thought. If it had turned out differently, he might be the blond with gray eyes, and she the dark-haired beauty with the very stern expression. . .if the two of them existed at all. He was suddenly glad she did and longed to kiss her and tell her so. But seeing her quizzical look, he resisted the temptation.

"Come over here," he said, changing the subject. "I'd like you to see the video."

Meera watched the brief overview of the Asian fungus that was accidentally introduced into the United States at a time when every fourth tree in the Appalachian forests was an American chestnut. The blight had invaded the trees through its bark, which had developed cankers, identifiable by their orange blush. The spores were then transferred by wind, insects, and birds throughout America, Europe, and Asia.

Threadlike filaments had fanned out and girdled the trees, choking off water and nutrients, until the trees died within months. Nothing was able to stop the blight or control it. Generations fought the blight, spraying, razing, then burying their failed efforts. Within forty years, several billion chestnut trees had been obliterated from the Eastern forests.

Meera learned that the mightiest of the trees were almost seventy feet tall and sixteen feet in circumference. The lumber of one sixty-foot tree would have brought in over five hundred dollars. When sound, the trees had been a favorite for cradles, coffins, telegraph and telephone poles, and fence posts because of the wood's weather-and rot-resistance. Its three brown nuts, nestled in sable-soft downy fur and protected by a sticky burr, was food for squirrel, deer, bear, wild turkey, and people.

When a tree was cut, it grew back from the roots—and after the blight struck, so did the cankers. The brave new growth struggled fiercely for survival, but soon withered and died.

"Surely you don't blame the Briskins for that," she said, wiping a tear from her eye at the dismal spectacle.

"Of course not," he replied immediately. "Just for selling the land to my granddad, knowing that the trees were blighted."

"And suppose the Briskins didn't know?"

He stared at her. "Elias Briskin knew." But she looked so downcast that Elliot felt compelled to add, "At least, that's what my granddad believed."

The next footage showed the building of Chestnut Lodge. Wings were added onto the main house, utilizing as much of the good chestnut lumber as possible, and given the name Chestnut Lodge, in memory of a bygone glory.

When the video rolled to an end, Elliot pushed the rewind button. "My ancestors nearly lost their shirt in that deal," Elliot said, striking fear to her heart, "but my grandfather always thought he lost something more valuable. . . and that was a lifelong friendship with Elias Briskin."

Meera knew that any rebuttal she might make would not be believed. Three generations of animosity and misunderstanding couldn't be erased with a few words. But she would keep trying to find a way.

Maybe one of these days, Elliot thought, he'd have an opportunity to remind her that he hadn't even been born when Jonas Maxwell shot Elias Briskin—and that she hadn't been around when Briskin sold the blighted land to the Maxwells. But for now, he focused on her upcoming article, giving her some tips and loading her down with with resource materials. Because it seemed to be so important to her, he'd begun to want her to do a good job on the article. And when the evening wound down, he prided himself on having behaved like a gentleman.

Rising to go, she stood framed in the doorway, her shiny hair swinging softly against her shoulders as her lovely face turned toward his. "I want you to know that I'm not on the rebound, Elliot," she informed him seriously. "When you kiss me, I don't even know Clark Phillips exists."

To his chagrin, while he was still halfway across the room, clinging to the back of a chair to resist the impulse to rush to her side, she smiled sweetly and disappeared into the lobby.

Chapter 7

I 'll make you proud," Meera had promised last night, and she began making good on that promise from the moment she put in an appearance early the next morning at the breakfast buffet.

Elliot knew he was seeing more than Meera Brown, fledgling writer, uncertain of her skills and her relationship with him. He was glimpsing Meera Briskin, the polished young woman—educated, intelligent, confident.

"May I join you?" she asked, coming up to the table where Elliot and Harold Wright sat discussing the conference.

More than once, Elliot had observed Harold advising a student to make an appointment through the registrar, or to wait until a break when he might have a few minutes. But this time the conference director surprised him. Harold brightened and rose to acknowledge the beautiful young woman in her crisp, beige linen business suit, her hair pulled back in a no-nonsense twist.

"Oh, don't let me interrupt if you're discussing business. Mine can wait."

"Not at all," Harold replied. "I think Elliot and I have finished, haven't we?"

Elliot's lips twitched almost imperceptibly. "If you'll excuse me."

"Oh, this involves you both." Meera flashed him a smile brighter than the morning sunshine streaming through the dining room windows.

"Could I get you something to eat?" Elliot asked with concern.

She was opening her notebook. "A bran muffin and a glass of orange juice, please."

He motioned for one of the servers, gave her the order, then deliberately allowed his eyes to linger on Meera's lips. The only indication that she had noticed was the slight flutter of her lashes and the becoming shade of pink that rose to her cheeks.

She turned her attention to Harold. "May I interview you, Mr. Wright, and include information about the conference in my article on Chestnut Lodge?"

"Of course! That is, if Elliot agrees. After all, it's his lodge." Harold glanced over to Elliot for confirmation.

Elliot spread his hands. "It's your conference."

Harold was wise enough to know that the publicity would have the potential to boost his conference, both in enrollment and prestige. Apparently, Elliot thought, whatever Meera B. asked of him, he would deliver. And she began to present her requests, in her gentle, but intelligent manner. Considerate of his time, she asked nothing that she could obtain from brochures, and before the hour had ended, she had managed to secure some excellent quotes from Harold, along with his promise to put his photographer to work for her. Then she made several appointments for ten minutes each—with Elliot and his staff, including his day manager and the chef—working around the Advanced Interviews session and the Inspirational workshop she yet wanted to attend.

When Meera had finished, she thanked them and followed the photographer into the kitchen while other students were making their way to Rhododendron Hall for the large group session. "I'm surprised to hear that she's just a beginner with only three articles published," Harold told Elliot. "She knows her way around an interview." He frowned. "Too bad she didn't enter anything in our competitions."

"I have her articles in my office," Elliot suggested. "Would they do?"

"I'll take a look. Come by during the break." With a nod, Harold was off to introduce the morning speaker.

Later, in Elliot's office, leafing through several issues of *Fabulous Places*, Harold paused to read Meera's articles. Elliot detected a wistful note in the director's voice when he commented, "Not just anybody can get published in this magazine."

He returned the material to the folder. "Faculty members normally recommend names for Most Promising Student. I usually stay out of it."

Harold appeared to be debating with himself. Then he grasped the envelope tightly. "I suppose as director, I *could* recommend someone. We have several entries, so I'll pass this around to the judges."

By noon, Elliot realized he was keenly anticipating the upcoming banquet. For one thing, he was looking forward to seeing Trevor again. And then there was the possibility of seeing Meera win an award. It was an altogether pleasant thought.

Although his staff was perfectly capable, Elliot himself personally inspected Rhododendron Hall, where the banquet would be held. Set beneath the vaulted cathedral ceiling were tall panes of glass so clear it seemed he could reach out and touch the lush foliage dappled by the afternoon sunshine.

Inside, the hardwood floor was polished to a glossy sheen, and three hundred wooden folding chairs with leather seats and backs were arranged in rows on each side of a center aisle. The podium, where Trevor would speak, stood on a platform. Behind it was a small table where awards would await some well-deserving conferees.

"Testing, testing," he said over the microphone and adjusted the sound.

At the back of the room was a chestnut table where the conference bookstore would display Trevor's books. He would be available to autograph them after his speech.

Surveying the room, Elliot smiled with satisfaction. The staff had out-done themselves. Everything was perfect. The main topic of their conversa-tion as they set up chairs and polished silver was Meera's proposed article about the lodge. Their names might be mentioned. Some of them might even appear in the candid shots taken by the photographer to illustrate the piece.

Others had taken note of the special attention Elliot had paid Meera. And since the first day she walked into Chestnut Lodge, Tom had worn a perpetual grin.

The conference would end tonight. She would have to tell him about her deception tonight—if she intended to tell him at all. Or at the latest. . .in the morning.

Suddenly realizing how quickly time was passing, Elliot went into the alcove and turned up the dimmer lights, for it would be dark outside when the group came in for their closing session. The air would cool quickly after the sun went down, but with a crowd of people in the room, they wouldn't need heat. He turned the ceiling fans on low for circulation.

In the formal dining room, staff members were setting up the tables. Overlays of cream-colored lace topped skirts the color of winter rhododen-dron leaves, enhanced by goldware and dark green napkins embossed with the "CL" emblem in one corner. To block out the early evening light when they ate, the drapes would be drawn, the great chandelier dimmed, and on each table the short, cream candles in golden holders would be lighted to lend an air of cozy elegance. No detail had been overlooked.

Everything seemed to be proceeding on schedule, with not a hitch. Even when Elliot was summoned to the desk to take a call, there was no warning of impending trouble.

But the smile left his face and the satisfaction in his eyes turned to dis-tress when he heard his dad's voice. "Son, your mother and I are coming to the lodge tonight to hear Trevor."

"But the doctor said. . ."

"The doctor said no work," Max interrupted, "and I don't intend to work. I'm going to stick to my diet—no fat, no cholesterol—so I'll skip the prime rib and the chocolate mousse and eat my salad. Just wanted to let you know we'd be there."

Elliot felt as if all the air had left his lungs. His folks were coming. With a Briskin on the premises!

But. . .they wouldn't know her. Would they?

Suddenly he felt as if he'd eaten that forbidden fruit. . .and it had turned out to be a little, sour, green apple. He could feel the consequences beginning to churn in his stomach.

☙

It had been a busy morning. Now, during afternoon free time, Meera pointed her silver bullet toward the Briskin estate. She'd need something special to wear for the banquet.

Never had a spring been so beautiful. Never had she felt so alive! So fulfilled. She was accomplishing something on her own. Well, not exactly on her own. But her dependence upon her grandfather—his presence, his advice, his love, his faith—had always been so much a part of her. She had felt so lost without him. But now, she could remember him with joy instead of pain.

And this thing with Elliot Maxwell. Well, it was going to work out. It just had to. He was an intelligent person. He would understand perfectly why she had felt compelled to conceal her identity. It wouldn't matter.

The inspirational classes had helped, too. Not just with her writing, but in defining problems and finding solutions through prayer and seeking the wisdom of God. The instructor was a very strong Christian who had emphasized her own faith and pointed out the place of divine inspiration in writing. Meera felt like the faith of her grandfather was becoming more solidly her own.

Yes, there were a few things to work out, but Meera had every confidence that, if she handled them the right way, these could be accomplished without anyone being hurt. The last sessions had been very revealing, and she was proud of her actions during the morning when she had pushed her insecurities aside and dared act like a writer who knew what she was doing. It had worked! She had felt thoroughly professional. Truly this conference had given her a new direction.

Not only that, but miracle of miracles, Elliot Maxwell liked her! She would have to tell him tonight. She dared not think beyond that.

"Woooo-oooo Woooo-oooo Woooo-ooooo!"

The sound finally registered, and Meera looked in the rearview mirror to see a flashing blue light. She gripped the steering wheel. Then, as if some kind of automaton took over, she obediently pulled over to the side of the road.

Her heart was beating even faster when the officer got out of his squad car and walked up to the window. A pad and pencil were in his hands.

Oh, no! Elliot must have discovered her identity and was having her arrested for trespassing! Was that really possible? Maybe a charge couldn't stick, but obviously an arrest could be made. The officer lowered his head and peered at her over a pair of nonexistent eyeglasses.

It would be plastered all over the papers. Her reputation would be ruined, not to mention her relationship with her family. And Elliot—would he really do such a thing? Yes, came the answer from deep within. He was a Maxwell, wasn't he?

"Ma'am," the officer growled, "did you know you're driving down the Blue Ridge Parkway?"

"Y—yessir," she stuttered.

"Do you know the speed limit on the Parkway?"

Was she going to get a speeding ticket? Not be arrested for trespassing or falsifying information? "F—forty-five?"

"Then why were you doing fifty-five?"

"I'm sorry," she said. "I guess I was preoccupied. I just didn't think about the speed."

"What are you so happy about? Is it your birthday or something?"

Meera laughed lightly. "No, Sir," and even as she answered, realization was dawning. "I understand you have to give me a ticket."

He quirked his brow. "So this isn't your first one?"

"Oh, it is! But I know you're just doing your job."

"Well. . .consider this a warning, little lady. You keep speeding, and you won't have any more birthdays."

"I understand," she said. "And thank you."

He walked back to his car and waited until she pulled out onto the road again.

My birthday! she thought, keeping her eye on the speedometer. *Oh, it's better than that. It was a new-birth day! A new beginning!* Little niggling doubts clawed at her when she reached home, however. Hearing the TV, she realized she hadn't seen one in days, nor had she read a newspaper. She had been in a different world for the past few days, a fantasy world—just Elliot Maxwell's and hers.

She would have to return to reality soon. But she had one more night, and she would make the best of it. Peeking into the study, she saw Louisa lying on the couch watching the soaps.

"Well, so you decided to come home!"

"Nope," Meera countered. "Just came for a party dress."

Louisa began her third-degree again, but Meera hastened on to her bedroom. As she figured, her cousin was too wrapped up in the story to follow.

Meera thought of calling Cathy Steinbord and telling her to ask Trevor not to reveal her identity, if he knew it. But she decided against it. She shouldn't be dragging other people into this.

The dress she chose was a white, shimmery satin that she'd worn to the ambassador's dinner party in Venezuela the last time she was there. A row of small Briskin rubies, alternating with silver sequins, bordered the V-neckline. The skirt flounced daintily from a small waistline and fell to just above her knees. She would wear it with matching shoes—a silver iridescent sling with a white satin high heel. At the last minute, she grabbed her favorite earrings—a delicate cascade of small rubies and silver dangles.

As she recalled, the outfit had made a big impression on the ambassador. She wondered what Elliot would think. Suddenly his approval seemed more important than all the ambassadors in the world!

❧

Meera hoped to see Trevor Steinbord as soon as he arrived for the banquet. He probably wouldn't remember meeting her, but if he did, he might recall that she was a Briskin, and she couldn't chance her name slipping out inadvertently in conversation. Since he was a friend of Elliot's, she'd have to tell him that she was using her pseudonym here at the conference. Like everyone else in the area, he would surely understand that she wouldn't want a Maxwell to know that a Briskin was on his property. She'd simply have to intercept him before Elliot did.

Having met Trevor at Chapel Hill, Meera knew that his blond head could always be seen several inches above that of the tallest person in the room. He was certainly something to look at, but after she and several of her college friends had read his first book, *Undivided*, they had concluded that he was pining away for some mystery woman who could never be his. The air of intrigue made him appealing, but put him slightly out of reach—the kind of man one tended to admire from a distance.

Elliot was nowhere in sight when Meera entered the lobby and moved toward the sweeping windows across the front of the building. Soon, a long, black Lincoln Continental pulled up and parked in front. A tall, classically handsome man got out, closed the door, and fastened the buttons of his suit coat, then ran one hand across his blond hair. Trevor Steinbord!

So engrossed was Meera in her inspection that she almost forgot she had intended to corner him before he could speak to Elliot. Now, however, she realized that the conference director and several faculty members had also been waiting to see him, and, as soon as he entered the door, Trevor was surrounded.

Meera's heart stood still while he spoke to the group, then shrugged aside his professional air and walked over to greet Elliot, who was standing near the registration desk. To her horror, Elliot spotted her, and the two moved in her direction.

"You remember Meera Brown?" Elliot asked, watching Trevor closely for

71

signs of recognition.

A polite smile touched Trevor's lips, but Meera could see the confusion in his eyes. "Oh, he probably doesn't," Meera said quickly, extending her hand. "Your sister Cathy introduced us several years ago when you spoke to our journalism class at Chapel Hill."

"Meera Brown," Trevor said, shaking her hand. "Cathy mentioned that you visited in our home a couple of times."

So he did remember! "Yes, but you were out of the country, I believe," she responded with a smile.

Elliot saw the eye contact between the two—Trevor's, guarded; hers, pleading not to be betrayed.

While this little scenario was being played out, Harold Wright came over and touched Trevor on the arm. "If you'll follow me, I'll show you to the head table."

"Nice meeting you again, Miss. . .Brown," Trevor said, then glanced quickly at his friend. "Hope to see you later, Elliot."

"Sure thing." Elliot knew that Trevor Steinbord could mask his true feelings better than anyone he'd ever known. But he also knew that since Trevor remembered having met Meera in his parents' home, he must also remember that she was a Briskin.

At least, he'd covered for her when Elliot introduced them. And Elliot was grateful to him for that. As grateful as Meera must be. That confession should come from her—and no one else.

Meera glanced at Elliot and gave him a tentative smile.

He winked. "Did I tell you how beautiful you look tonight?"

She shook her head. "Thanks. So do you."

"Well, I'd like to pursue this line of thought," he said with a grin, "but I need to open the dining room doors and greet my other guests." He hurried away with one last, lingering look at Meera.

❧

Elliot mingled with the conferees, noting the aura of celebration that pervaded the atmosphere. It had been a successful conference, and everyone seemed upbeat. After greeting the guests and checking in with the kitchen staff to be sure everything was proceeding on schedule, Elliot filled his plate from the kitchen and joined his parents, who had arrived without fanfare, at a small table nearby.

"Who was that young woman?" his mother wanted to know immediately.

"What young woman?" Elliot asked innocently.

"The pretty blond you and Trevor were talking to in the lobby."

Elliot pretended thoughtfulness. "Oh," he said as if suddenly remembering, "she's someone he met through Cathy. Well, Dad, how am I doing here?"

"I can't say as far as the pretty girls are concerned, Son. . . ."

Max Maxwell laughed at his own joke. "But you seem to have everything else at the lodge under control. Harold's happy, the place looks great, and this is the best London broil I've ever eaten."

His wife smacked him playfully on the hand. "That's because you haven't eaten anything like that in months, Max, and you're not supposed to be eating it now. Put that down!"

"Now, Mother, a bite or two won't hurt. I know what I'm doing."

Elliot couldn't very well reprimand his father. That "pretty blond" he'd allowed to stay on Maxwell property for the past few days was enough to give anyone heart problems. He'd just have to make sure they didn't meet. But if they did, he'd try and pass her off as Trevor's friend.

After the banquet, Elliot sat at the back of Rhododendron Hall where the staff could signal him if he were needed. His parents sat next to him. Normally, they would not sit in on a session, but they were eager to hear Trevor's speech. As expected, it was quite impressive.

He watched his friend—the suave, handsome, renowned novelist—weaving his spell over his audience. Only his family and a few close friends knew that he'd written his first book at a very early age, out of an aching heart over a lost love. The book had made him famous. Only in an occasional private moment did Trevor let his guard down, but the pain and pathos showed through, creating an instant rapport with his listeners. Elliot understood that kind of pain. Maybe that's why he and Trevor had remained friends, though they rarely saw each other anymore.

Typical of Trevor, once he had gained the full support of his audience, he turned their attention to God, Who gifts people with creativity and drive and expects them to develop and use those gifts to the best of their ability.

Elliot's reverie was broken by a wave of deafening applause, and he stood to acknowledge the speaker, along with the students and faculty.

When they sat down for the closing ceremonies, Elliot remained rather than leaving to check on the front desk. Knowing there was more to come, he felt the quickening of his pulse. He smoothed his silk tie, tugged at the lapels of his dark blue suit, and brushed an imaginary speck of lint from his pants.

When Harold Wright rose to announce the awards, Elliot's anticipation mounted. Several awards were presented—Most Improved Writer, Best Juvenile Entry, Best Young Adult Entry, Best Adult Entry. Then it was time for the most coveted award of all—Most Promising Writer.

Elliot's heart was in his throat when Harold called out at last, "Meera Brown."

He glanced over to see her reaction. Meera was obviously shocked, and her name had to be called a second time. A red-headed girl seemed to be assuring her that she had, indeed, won the award. With hands to her flaming cheeks, Meera left her seat and hurried up the aisle toward the front, where Harold stood at the microphone, holding an engraved silver cup.

Elliot was stunned when she took the microphone and began to speak. And his enchantment had little to do with the illusion of angelic beauty she presented in her white dress studded with stones that winked and sparkled as it caught the light. He'd come to believe that Meera Brown—at least a part of her—was a beautiful, capable person. For the next few minutes, she proved him right.

"For one of the few times in my life, I don't know what to say," she began, and the audience laughed kindly.

She spoke quickly, emotionally, swiping at the liquid joy that filled her eyes. "I don't know if you can imagine what this means to me. . . . ," she said and paused. "No, that's not true. I suppose, being writers, you can imagine *any-thing*." Her audience laughed again, appreciatively. "I didn't know I needed an award, or even wanted one," she said to Harold Wright who was beaming his approval of her, "but I did, and I do, and I'll try to live up to it."

Elliot thought about the professionalism she had displayed last night in his office when they'd finally gotten down to the interview, then again this morning. Now, he watched as she shook Harold's hand and hurried straight down the aisle toward the back of the room, amid applause and Harold's announcement that Trevor would be autographing books in the front lobby, where the conference would host a reception for him.

In the excitement, Elliot had completely forgotten his parents. Too late, he realized he should have ducked out the moment Meera left the stage. She was making a beeline for him.

"I know I'm acting like an idiot," she said, when she came up to Elliot and regarded him through cloudy eyes.

He shook his head.

She held out the cup for him to see. "This is like confirmation that I'm becoming my own person, apart from family. Oh, Elliot, I know you must have had something to do with this. . .and I love you for it," she choked out.

He saw the terror that leapt into her eyes at this slip. But he couldn't let her stand there with her success falling down around her ankles like an old sock. "Well, I rate tonight," he said, hating the thinness he heard in his voice. "One of my secretaries told me she loved my tie."

Thankfully someone grasped Meera's arm and dragged her off to receive congratulations from other fellow conferees just as he noticed his parents staring at him as if he were the boogie-man. He left the room before they could accost him.

The word was used much too casually, almost blithely, he mused. Writers, of all people, should know that. *I love your tie. I love that song. Some people even love broccoli.*

"Mr. Elliot. Your daddy never frowned at my reception tables like that," came a disdainful wail, and he turned to see Bertha with sparks in her eyes hotter than the candles she'd just lighted.

"Oh, Bertha, there you are. I was just on my way to look for you. . . . ," he began as he walked with her toward the dining room, knowing he'd spend the next thirty minutes trying to placate her.

Elliot couldn't very well say his daddy would do more than frown if he knew the real truth about the situation here. More than likely, his dad would say that there was only one thing worse than feuding with a Briskin. . .and that would be *not* feuding with one!

Chapter 8

Before Trevor left, he stopped by Elliot's office and tapped on the door. "Just wanted to say that it's good being back at Chestnut Lodge and seeing you again, Elliot," he said, poking his head into the room. "Saw your parents, too. Glad your dad's getting along all right."

"Thanks, pal. Come on in and have a seat." Elliot motioned to the chairs in front of the fireplace, then went over and sat opposite Trevor. "I want an autographed copy of that new book before you leave."

Trevor nodded. They chatted briefly about his travels and his next writing project. Then Elliot broached the subject that was uppermost on his mind. "What do you think of her?"

"Very attractive. . .gifted. . .interesting." Trevor grinned, his blue eyes twinkling. "I got the impression there's something going on between the two of you."

"We—ll, you know she's a Briskin." From Trevor's noncommittal look, Elliot could see that the statement didn't surprise him. Of course, he knew about the feud. "I'm afraid it may be an impossible situation."

The veil that Elliot knew so well fell over his friend's face.

Trevor had his own impossible situation—loving a woman he couldn't have—so he'd poured his heart and soul into his writing. "I suppose it comes down to this," Trevor said pointedly. "What exactly do you want out of this relationship?"

Leave it to Trevor to get right to the point. He knew what and who he wanted and had resigned himself to the fact that it could never happen. So, he often appeared at public functions with beautiful women on his arm who understood that there would be no long-term, serious commitment.

With Elliot, it hadn't been that easy—or that difficult. Kate was dead. But he supposed Trevor had nailed it down. What *did* he want from Meera?

"I'm not sure," Elliot mused aloud, "that there *is* a relationship, Trevor. I think she may be playing some kind of game."

Trevor lifted a brow. "Have you agreed to the ground rules?"

Elliot laughed wryly. "Yes and no. I'm beginning to feel like a compulsive gambler who's losing his shirt and then becomes so desperate to win that he goes deeper and deeper in debt."

"There's a major difference, Elliot," Trevor said after a thoughtful moment.

"With a compulsive gambler, the odds are in favor of the casino, or the fall of the cards. Here, I'd say, the odds are pretty much even."

"In some ways," Elliot admitted. When it came to family, Meera had as much to lose as he. Her family would not approve her being here—unless it was a deliberate set-up of some kind.

Trevor made a suggestion. "Maybe you should look at it as a challenge, not a gamble."

"What you say makes sense," Elliot agreed but met Trevor's steady gaze with one of his own. "But what makes sense when it comes to emotions?"

Trevor jabbed his thumb into his chest. "Look who's giving advice," he said with irony. "Of our friends, Josh is the psychologist."

"And all he did was shrug his shoulders and wink at me," Elliot said, laughing.

The companionable smile faded from Trevor's face. "When it comes to matters of the heart, Elliot, advice doesn't help much. We're pretty much on our own in that department."

Elliot stood. "You going to be around for awhile?"

Trevor nodded. "A few days. Give me a call. Maybe we can get together. Double date?"

Elliot saw the mischief in the blue eyes and knew without a doubt his friend was aware that a Maxwell couldn't be seen in public around here with a Briskin. It would be sure to make the front page of the newspaper and provide fodder for local TV talk shows. Besides, no place was private when in the company of the famous Trevor Steinbord. "Thanks a lot!" Elliot intoned with playful sarcasm.

Trevor laughed. "At least you know what you're up against."

"Fortunately," Elliot said, then added, "I think."

Trevor's parting words were succinct. "When you find something in life you want, Elliot, and if it doesn't hurt anyone else, then go for it."

Elliot knew the other side of that coin. If it was possible that someone would be hurt, then step out of the picture—as Trevor had.

Later, after his parents came by the office to say they were leaving, Elliot walked out back, past a few milling guests, thinking about his conversation with his successful friend. Trevor had pursued his second love—writing. *Suppose Meera is first on my want list,* Elliot thought, *there are certainly those people who would stand to be hurt if I go after her.* But if not, must he revert to fear, mistrust, and animosity toward her and all her family—people he would have continued to write off if she hadn't come here, dispelling forever the myth that all Briskins were cut out of the same cloth?

No! He couldn't go back. The Briskins were no longer mere legend. Now they were personified in the form of a very lovely and desirable blond. Perhaps Meera had devious motives. Even so, she was an innocent victim, the same as he, of the venomous feud that had been bequeathed to them.

He walked down the steps from the deck. Now that the conference was over, would she leave without an explanation? Without revealing her identity? Or had she really only come here to pursue a writing career? Elliot sighed deeply. If so, she had accomplished her purpose.

As the evening wound down, most of the local conferees left the lodge for home. Others gathered to talk in small groups or to stroll the gardens one last time. Meera took her award cup to her room, then went in search of Elliot. When she didn't find him in his office, she walked out back.

The determined click of her heels against the stone patio came to an abrupt halt when she stumbled upon Elliot who glanced at her, said, "Shh," and put his finger to his lips. She cautiously tiptoed to where he stood gazing up into a young dogwood tree.

"Look," he whispered, and her gaze followed his as she peered up into the spreading branches of delicate, white blossoms against a bright moonlit sky.

His arm came around her shoulders. Startled, she looked into his face.

"Do you see it?" he asked.

Yes, she saw it. She saw the determined chin, the strong jawline, the firm full lips that had taken possession of hers, just as he had taken possession of her heart. "Right here," he said, and she looked again.

Just when she began to suspect he was playing a silly game, she saw it. "Ohh, how beautiful," she breathed. "I've never seen anything like that."

Hanging from a low branch of the dogwood tree was a cocoon from which a butterfly was emerging. Involuntarily, her hand came up as if to caress it.

"Don't touch," Elliot warned. "It's still wet. One touch can impair or even destroy its ability to fly."

"You remind me of my grandfather," Meera said wistfully. "He taught me so much about nature. But I've never seen a butterfly leaving its home. I didn't know it was such a tedious chore."

"Like humans in some ways," Elliot pondered. "Breaking family ties is difficult. Family is the strongest bond we have."

Staring at the butterfly, she thought of his words. How wise he was. Even though her family might be wrong in their attitude toward the Maxwells, she still felt a fierce loyalty toward them, that obligatory bond of blood.

She turned her face toward his. "I know. I love my family, Elliot. My dad gave me the silver convertible for my birthday. But. . .that little silver cup tonight meant more. . . ."

He nodded in understanding. "You earned it. No one could buy it for you. That makes all the difference."

"Then you must feel this kind of accomplishment in what you do here at the lodge."

Elliot narrowed his gaze, squinting into the night. "There's nothing out there for me that can compare with these mountains. This is my own little niche."

She drew in a breath of the pure, crystalline air, perfumed with the scent of mountain laurel and calacanthus and pine, so different from the Venezuelan oil fields. "I wanted to tell you," she said, "that I appreciate the way you handled the interview."

Elliot shrugged, puzzled. "It was you who handled it."

"Yes, but you kept things on a strictly businesslike basis."

"That's what you wanted, wasn't it?"

"Exactly," Meera replied, not daring to meet his eyes.

He lifted her chin with his finger until she was forced to look at him. "You thought I'd get personal?"

She smiled and nodded. It occurred to her that she had come here to discover whether or not she could respect a Maxwell. When had the tables turned? When had it become so important that a Maxwell respect a Briskin?

"I saw a professional side of you, Meera. And I was impressed."

"You know something, Elliot Maxwell," she said, cocking her head to one side. "I. . .I like you."

She had thought he might reciprocate, but when he didn't, she was grateful for the cloak of near-darkness that concealed the rush of heat to her face. She forced her attention back to the butterfly. "Will the little creature be okay?"

He stared a moment longer, then he looked up into the tree. "It takes hours for a butterfly to emerge. But eventually it will break free of that inhibiting cocoon and. . ." He lowered his voice, "And fly away."

A long moment passed before he faced her again and asked softly, "Are you going to fly away, Meera Brown?"

She closed her eyes and bit on her lip. She wished she were really Meera Brown. But she had been as slow to leave that pseudonym behind her as the butterfly was to release itself from the cocoon. Her wings had been touched. Elliot Maxwell's fingerprints were on them. She would much rather make love than war.

"There's something I have to tell you, Elliot. Something that will make you despise me."

His pulse quickened. She was going to confess at last. They could get her little deception out of the way and honestly explore their feelings for each other. If they wanted to put an end to the Maxwell-Briskin feud, they could do it. . .together.

He wanted her to be honest with him. And in that moment of being honest with himself, a shocking realization dawned: He wanted more of Meera Brown—Meera Briskin—than a few stolen kisses.

"First," she said, and he heard the reluctance in her voice, saw the fear in her eyes, "promise me you'll hear me out . . . ," she swallowed hard but did not look away, "before you condemn me."

"I promise." It was all he could do to suppress the flood of joy that coursed through his veins. *Darling*, he was thinking, *if you don't like your last name, we'll change it!* By George, there were more important things to consider than that stupid feud.

He found himself enjoying this little charade of his. There was enough Maxwell in him to feel a sense of satisfaction over her discomfort. Someday they could perhaps laugh about it. But for now, he deliberately pasted a frown on his face and tried to furrow his brow as he snorted, "You're married! Is that it? Is that the reason for this white circle around your finger?"

"No, no," she said quickly.

"Divorced?"

She shook her head, and the little sparks in her gray eyes reflected the twinkling stars in the velvet sky.

"So you're engaged after all!" he said and placed his hand on his forehead.

She laughed at his antics, loving his playfulness, knowing he was trying to make it easier for her to come forth with a confession.

"I do have to think about that part," she said, "the engagement, I mean."

"I can deal with that." She could not possibly think Clark Phillips was right for her.

Meera glanced around, realizing that the place was suddenly deserted and that she and Elliot were alone. She breathed deeply of the cool, fragrant night air and lifted her eyes again to the butterfly whose wings had emerged a little farther. How long before it would fly away?

She looked at Elliot again. Not knowing any subtle way to do this, she plunged in. "What is the worst thing you could think about me?"

A few days ago, he would have responded instantly, "Being a Briskin." Instead, he said, "You're an ax murderer!"

She giggled in spite of the gravity of the moment. "Oh, Elliot, be serious!" Then she sobered. "I wish it were that simple."

"Wait," he said, lifting his hand in a gesture of protest. "Before you say anything else, I want you to know. . ." With his fingers he touched the moonlight on her face, traced a pattern across her mouth, gently drew her closer. Then he bent his head and let his lips say it for him.

Meera knew this could be the last time he ever held her, and she put her arms around his neck and ran her fingers through the hair that curled at the back of his head, returning his kisses with a warmth that surprised her.

At last Elliot moved away, managing to say huskily, "I've never wanted anyone in my arms as much as I want you."

"I've never felt quite this way before either," Meera said earnestly, "but I have to tell you. . .now. . .or I'll never be able to."

Suddenly, Elliot wanted no more games, no more delays. *Say it and be done with it,* he was thinking, and grabbed her hand, bringing her fingers to his lips. Then he pulled her close once more, cradling her head on his chest. "You can tell me anything, don't you know that?"

"Elliot," she said in a whisper, trembling, both from the impact of his thorough kisses and the confession she must now give, a confession that could change everything between them. "I'm. . ."

But the next words he heard came from a different source.

"Well, well! This is quite an exhibition. Looks like you're not the only one who walks in at unexpected times, huh, Meera?"

Meera whirled to face her cousin, who looked as smug and satisfied as the cat who swallowed the canary. "Louisa!" she gasped, grateful at least that the young woman had not divulged her last name. It would never do for Elliot to hear it from someone else. "Wh—What what are you doing here?"

Louisa laughed, lifting her lovely face toward the sky. "That's really not important. What *is* important is that *I* know what *you're* doing here," she said in a silky voice. "Apparently, you're hang gliding from the Maxwell mountains."

Meera glanced at Elliot's troubled face. Oh, no! He would recognize Louisa from last night! He had seen her at the Briskin cabin. The old fear rose up, suffocating her. He might just shoot them both!

Louisa was backing away, as if the full implication of what she was doing had just occurred to her.

"I'll explain later," Meera said over her shoulder to Elliot and reached for Louisa, grasping her arm. "Let's get out of here."

"Hold it!" Elliot shouted.

They stopped dead in their tracks, and Elliot read the alarm in their faces. Served them right. Maxwells could play games as well as Briskins. Two of them now! Okay, he'd play along. "Haven't I seen you somewhere before?" he asked, walking closer, scrutinizing the girl.

Louisa shook her head, her eyes wild with fear.

"Aren't you the nightmare on Briskin property who threatened to shoot me last night? Who are you? What do you want?"

Louisa looked from Elliot to Meera and pointed a shaking finger at Meera. "Well, she's. . ."

Before she could finish, Elliot directed his remarks to Meera.

"I'm calling the police! Or better yet, I'll deal with this in my own way. Never let it be said that a Maxwell doesn't know how to handle a Briskin!"

He rushed past them and hurried into the lodge.

"This is awful, Louisa," Meera said fearfully. "He doesn't know who I am."

"Ohh, he's going after a shotgun. I know it!" Louisa wailed, rocking back and forth on her high heels.

"Then get out of here. I'll meet you at the cabin."

Louisa took off up the steep drive and ran around the lodge.

It served her right, Meera thought, then added to herself, *Serves me right, too.*

Elliot stood beside the window in his darkened office and watched the frightened woman jump into the black sportscar parked in front of the lodge. She fumbled nervously with the key, then started the engine, and roared out of the drive.

With this incident, a new insight was surfacing, Elliot mused. It seemed the Briskin clan felt more fear than hatred for the Maxwells. At least, this was true of two of them.

Gloating inwardly, he relished a small sense of triumph. At last he had the upper hand. Now, Meera Briskin would be at his mercy. He waited for a few minutes, then called her room.

He heard her intake of breath before she answered in a faint voice, "Hello?"

"I think we should talk," he said seriously, hoping she would not detect the enjoyment he was experiencing or the relief he felt that this charade would finally be over and they could get on to more pleasurable things.

"In the morning?" she asked weakly.

"Now," he said with mock severity. "Privately, of course. Would you come to my suite, please?"

His suite? She blinked back the moisture in her eyes. Before now, she might have insisted upon a more appropriate meeting place for their confrontation. But now it didn't matter. He wouldn't try anything. It was too late for that. Louisa had ruined any hope of a reconciliation between the Briskins and the Maxwells.

Louisa? No! Meera had no one to blame but herself. "Give me a few minutes," she begged.

Yes! He could wait. . .for a few minutes.

He hung up and smiled at the telephone. In a "few minutes," it would all be over. They could declare a truce.

When she didn't show up in twenty minutes, he knew.

He went through the motions anyway. First, he called her room. The phone just kept ringing. He was tired of the game that was no longer a game.

He went to her door and knocked. He would make it easy for her. He'd tell her the truth: that he had known from the beginning. Then he'd take her in his arms and console her, convince her that everything would be all right.

But she didn't answer. He used his pass key, half expecting to find her slumped on the bed, crying with remorse—sorry that she had deceived him, asking his forgiveness. His pulse quickened at the thought.

He opened the door, calling her name. There was no answer. No sobbing. No tearful, "Go away."

He switched on the light. There was no Meera. He went into the bedroom. No sign of anything. The bed was made just as room service would have left it that morning. In the closet, there were no suitcases. Only an extra blanket on the top shelf.

The bathroom door was open. She wouldn't be in there. He looked anyway.

The last futile effort was to go out onto the balcony. Nothing—but a dark Briskin mountain looming ominously ahead like a barrier flung against the sky. A cold breeze struck him in the face and went straight to his heart.

She hadn't even said good-bye.

He dragged himself through the lonely rooms once more. Then his gaze fell on the phone. He lifted the receiver and called the front desk. The night clerk answered.

"Did Miss Meera Brown check out?"

"Yes, Sir."

"How long ago?"

"Ten. . .fifteen minutes. Anything wrong?"

"No," Elliot lied. "Everything's fine."

A few minutes later he walked out toward the parking lot where she'd parked the silver convertible. The spot was empty. There would be no more Meera Brown/Briskin. She'd apparently accomplished what she'd come for—whatever that was.

Maybe it really was to hone her writing skills. Maybe it was to hear the famous Trevor Steinbord. Maybe it was to avenge her family honor by breaking a Maxwell's heart.

She had accomplished one positive thing. He would no longer brood over Kate. That was done—over—finished, although he would always cherish her memory.

Coming back toward the lodge, Elliot neared the dogwood tree and stopped to see the progress of the butterfly. It was gone. It had flown away.

Head bent, hands shoved into his pants pockets, Elliot stared at the ground in front of him as he returned to the lodge.

He didn't hate Meera Briskin. But she had closed the door to his loving her. He would simply forget her.

Chapter 9

"It didn't mean anything. It was a mistake," Meera said defensively when Louisa hurled the expected accusations in her face.

"You see," Louisa crowed triumphantly, holding the screen door open while Meera passed through with her suitcases, "a person *can* end up in somebody's arms without it meaning anything." Louisa followed her into the bedroom. "It meant nothing when you barged in on me and Clark. . .just like it meant nothing when you kissed that man."

Meera knew Louisa was being facetious, making her point by saying the opposite of what she really meant. At least, Louisa didn't know who "that man" was. She only knew she'd seen him on Maxwell property.

"Who was he?" Louisa asked then.

"That's irrelevant!" Meera snapped. "John Doe—Sam Smith—a rose is a rose is a rose!" She threw a suitcase on the bed, opened it, and began taking out her clothes.

"Not if it smells like a *Maxwell!*" Louisa retorted.

Meera slammed the suitcase and shoved it into the closet. "I don't have to answer to you, Louisa."

"True." Louisa perched on the bed and crossed her long legs, looking very pleased with herself. "I'm sure Clark will understand."

Meera drew in a deep breath before she closed the closet door and turned to face her cousin. "I'm not so sure, Louisa. I don't think Clark will understand at all. He seems to have a double standard when it comes to men and women."

Louisa shrugged. "He just knows what he wants in a relationship, and frankly, Meera, I think you're too independent to fit the bill."

"But *he* proposed to *me*, Louisa," Meera shot back.

Louisa picked at the chenille bedspread. "I think you'd both be making a big mistake."

Meera resented the turmoil in her life, for which she'd blamed Clark and Louisa, ignoring the fact that she'd felt a burden drop from her shoulders when she took off the engagement ring. Nevertheless, her heart went out to her cousin whose downcast face and trembly lips said much more than her words. Louisa was in love with Clark—and Meera could understand her frustration.

"Look, Louisa," she said softly, "I don't want to fight with you or Clark or anyone anymore, including the Maxwells."

Louisa's head came up, her eyes wide. "You told him about the property?"

"Not yet. But I intend to."

Louisa shook her head, disbelieving.

"I might as well tell you. The family will have to know." Meera slumped down into an easy chair. "I went to Chestnut Lodge under the name Meera Brown so I could study the Maxwells and decide for myself if they were worthy to be informed about the property sale."

"And were they?" Louisa prompted.

"I only met. . .one," Meera confessed, her voice trailing off. "He's. . .just like us, Louisa. A human being who's been raised to hate the name of Briskin, like we hate the name of Maxwell. But he's fair, and decent, and. . ."

"You let a Maxwell kiss you!?" Louisa screeched, jumping from the bed and placing her hands on her hips.

"Oh, cut the threatrics, Louisa."

But Louisa stood her ground, nodding accusingly.

"He thought I was Meera Brown. He—he liked me, and I couldn't be too resistant or I couldn't get to know him, and my purpose there would be defeated."

"And now that you've accomplished your purpose, does it mean that you're going back to Venezuela with us?"

"I have some thinking to do first. Anyway," Meera continued gravely, "the family might disown me after they find out what I've done and. . .what I intend to do."

"Who's going to tell them?"

Meera drew in an exasperated breath. "Well, believe me, Louisa, I'm going to try to beat you to it."

Seeing her cousin's crestfallen expression, Meera was immediately contrite. She'd tried not to strike out at Louisa, who had been reared as a spoiled, only child, accustomed to getting whatever she wanted. What could she expect? "I'm sorry."

"I guess I deserved that," Louisa said humbly, much to Meera's surprise. "I've already done a lot of thinking." She turned a mischievous grin. "Didn't know I could, did you, Cuz?"

"I didn't know you *would!*"

"Well, I've made a decision," Louisa announced, and, seeing that Meera wasn't going to ask, she added, "I'm not going to Venezuela until you do."

Meera gave her a skeptical glance, then began to unpack the cosmetic case and place the items on the dresser top.

"I mean it. I'm going to back you in this Maxwell thing. I really don't care who buys my slice of that mountain. I just want the money. Also," she paused, waiting until she knew she had Meera's full attention, "I'm not going to try to take Clark away from you."

Meera looked at her cousin's reflection in the mirror. "You already tried that."

"Not very hard," Louisa contradicted her.

Meera grimaced. In that case, Clark had succumbed to Louisa's charms with only the slightest provocation. "That's sweet of you, Louisa. But I want to be alone for a few days."

"Oh, I wouldn't stay here. I'll stay at the estate."

Meera shrugged. "That's your decision, but don't do it on my account. If you and Clark have something going between you, then I want to know it before I make a lifetime commitment to him."

"I'm staying," Louisa insisted. "I don't like this bickering between us. We're behaving like. . .like Briskins and Maxwells."

Meera gave her a sharp look, walked through the cabin, and banged the front screen behind her. She heard the gurgling creek, but refused to look on the other side. Instead, she dragged her clothes from the silver convertible and returned to the bedroom where she laid them across the bed.

"If you stay, Louisa," Meera began skeptically, "what's your real reason?"

Louisa gave her a searching look, then tossed her dark hair behind one shoulder. With much more candor than Meera would have given her credit for, she affirmed, "I want to find out how you intend to deal with that rose of yours. . .without getting stuck with the thorns."

⟡

Thorns? No, not anymore, Meera decided. Elliot Maxwell had done her no harm, nor had any other member of his family. As far as she was concerned, the feud was over.

With that determination, she put the silver cup on the mantel, set herself a deadline, compiled all the notes she had taken while at Chestnut Lodge, laid out the information and photographs Elliot had given her, and proceeded to make an outline. Meera was delighted to discover that the article came together more quickly than articles she had written previously and attributed it to the conference instruction and handouts.

It was past 2:00 A.M. when the excitement and motivation fueled by adrenaline were replaced by sheer exhaustion. Meera opened a window far enough to allow a stream of cool evening air to invade the bedroom.

Turning down the bedspread, blanket, and top sheet, she put out the light, removed her robe, and crawled into bed. Safe from prying eyes, Meera allowed herself the luxury of a good cry, telling herself that it was the memories of her beloved grandfather triggered by her first night in the cabin, nothing more.

With the pungent odor of the forest floor permeating the room and the babble of the brook in her ear, Meera gave herself to the wave of nostalgia that swept over her. She'd never talk to her grandfather again, or see his face, or listen to his sage advice. But before she fell asleep, she heard herself say, "Grandfather, am I doing the right thing? Would you approve? You'd never disown me, would you? After all, the Bible does tell us to 'love our enemies.'"

Her face still damp with tears, Meera finally fell into a deep sleep and did not awaken until the bright morning sun crept through the window. She blinked her eyes open to greet the day. Outside, the sound of squirrels and other woodland creatures scampering about industriously stirred her to action.

Hearing a car drive up outside, she jumped out of bed and, throwing on a robe, hurried to the front window to peek out. It was Louisa! She was unloading several heavy grocery sacks from the back seat. Meera ran out to help her.

"Did you tell the family?" Meera asked dubiously, wondering whether to welcome her cousin or send her packing.

"You know I've always been loyal to you, Cuz," Louisa pouted. "We've kept each other's secrets all our lives, haven't we? It's just that little one with Clark, and you're letting it ruin our friendship."

Meera sighed. It wouldn't do any good to say "that little one with Clark" was quite different from all the other secrets they had shared as children. "What is all this?" she wanted to know, tightening the sash of her robe and stepping carefully in her bare feet on the gravel drive.

"Didn't want you to starve to death, dear cousin."

Meera was touched. It was just like Louisa. Despite their past differences, they'd always made up. First, a quarrel. Then a peace offering. This time Meera was truly grateful. It would save her a trip to town for supplies.

"Thanks. Guess I was just shocked to see you up and around so early."

"Early?" Louisa scoffed and handed Meera a sack. "It's almost eleven o'clock."

"Oh, no," Meera moaned. "I've wasted half a day already."

Louisa cocked an inquisitive brow. "What do you have to do?"

"Oh, come on in," Meera said with a sigh of resignation. "I'll tell you over coffee."

"Oh," Louisa said, peering intently at the surrounding area, "someone was sneaking around over there across the creek the other night."

Meera refused to follow the direction of her cousin's gaze. Instead, she headed for the porch with the bag of groceries.

Louisa followed her in pursuit. "I saw a man. And you know what, Meera? I would swear he was the same one you made that 'mistake' with last night."

So that's why Louisa was here? To rub it in! Devious little cousin! "You're incorrigible, Louisa! You know that?"

Meera opened the screen door, balancing the sack. Louisa stuck out her foot to hold the door open. "I'd say we're cut out of the same cloth, cousin," finished Louisa on a triumphant note.

"We'll see," Meera mused. Maybe her cousin was right. "We'll just see."

While the coffee perked, Meera showed her the layout for the article—pictures, recipes, outline, notes.

Over coffee and sweet rolls, Meera confided to Louisa that she'd decided to inform Elliot Maxwell of the impending sale of the property. "I don't like being part of some feud that I didn't start. I want it stopped. Do you, Louisa? Do you want to help me put a stop to this? I mean, if two of us approach the family. . ." She paused, noting the fear that leapt into Louisa's eyes. "Then again, maybe you and I aren't cut from the same cloth, after all."

Louisa picked at her sweet roll and poked a crumb into her mouth. Then she looked over at Meera. "Well, we do tend to go after what we want. . .in spite of what the family might think."

Meera stared at her cousin. Was Louisa saying that she had deliberately gone after Clark, regardless of the pain it might cause anyone else? If the shoe had been on the other foot—if Louisa and Clark had been engaged—Meera would never have made a play for him. At least, she didn't think she would. But then, only last week, she would have sworn she'd never in her wildest dreams have found herself in the arms of a Maxwell. And *liking* it! She looked over at Louisa. "Then you'll help me?"

"As they say on the soaps," Louisa said, anticipation sparking her dark eyes, "try me."

If Meera couldn't trust her cousin with Clark, maybe she could trust her with this. It was worth a shot. Besides, it was inevitable that her family would find out anyhow, and she might as well start with Louisa.

Meera laid out the plan: Louisa would go to the Arboretum in Asheville to pick up some information on the chestnut blight. She would also bring a good typewriter from the big house. Meera herself would call the family and tell them that she would be at the cabin for awhile, writing, but she'd get in touch with them next week, before returning to Venezuela.

Louisa's mouth dropped open. "You're going back. . .next week?"

"Of course. Does that surprise you?"

"Well, I thought you were so mad at Clark and me that you might never go back."

"I'm not mad anymore, Louisa. But something as important as a marriage proposal requires a face-to-face confrontation, don't you think?"

Louisa glanced over at Meera's hand, resting on the table. "But you're still not wearing his ring."

Self-consciously, Meera put her hand in her lap. "It's what's in my heart that counts, Louisa, not what's on my finger. But if it makes you happy. . ."

She retrieved the ring from an inner zippered compartment of her purse and put it on. It felt heavy. . .like a rock. But now maybe Louisa would hush.

Unpredictably, her cousin was silent, though her face clouded over.

Meera began clearing the table. "I have more room on this big table. I think I'll put the typewriter in here."

Louisa accurately took that as a dismissal. "Anything else I can do?"

"You could get our airline tickets."

There was a glint of rebellion in Louisa's dark eyes. "What day did you have in mind?"

"End of next week. Um, Friday, I think. I should wrap up my business here by then."

"You're not going to tell him who you are?"

Meera walked over to the sink and set the coffee cups down. "I can't," she said sorrowfully, looking out the window at the towering mountainpeaks beyond.

"You can't?" Louisa repeated.

"Not yet. Not until after he approves the article. Sees that I mean no harm."

This scenario was beginning to unfold like one of Louisa's favorite soaps. "Then. . .when will you tell him?"

"I'm not sure I will," Meera replied. "I might just have the attorney inform him of the sale and stay out of it myself."

It was a long moment before Louisa spoke again. "I'd better go, but I dread it. Mom and Dad are not going to understand why I'm waiting till next week to return to Venezuela. I'll just tell them you need me here. So. . .you know where you can find me. I'll be at the big house."

Meera turned to face her cousin. "After all I gave you to do in town?"

"Oh, I mean I'll be at the house when I'm not running around playing secretary," Louisa said with a toss of her dark hair. "I guess you know this is going to cost you."

Meera smiled. She didn't doubt that for a minute. Louisa's favors were few and far between, and she apparently hoped there might be something in this for her.

Forgetting Meera was as difficult as Elliot had imagined it would be. She had made him remember Kate. . .then she had made him forget Kate and put her in her proper place with bittersweet memories. But the beautiful blond with soft gray eyes was an image forever engraved on his mind. Her warmth, her caring, her sweet, passionate kisses had created a turmoil inside that he couldn't shake.

The matter wasn't really ended—he knew that—and he was eager to know what the outcome would be. Would she finish the article, then tell him who she really was? Or did she intend to have it published, thinking he'd never know the author was really Meera Briskin? Was it some kind of joke that she and the dark-haired woman were playing on him?

No. There would be a confrontation of some kind—at some time. However, he didn't feel it was his place to contact her. She had started this, and she should be the one to pursue it toward whatever end she had in mind.

Putting the troubling thoughts aside, Elliot busied himself with the never-ending work at the lodge. Although the peak season began in mid-June, spring was more demanding in many ways for the full-time staff. It was a favorite time for many tourists. And when there were no guests to deal with directly, there was always paperwork, inventory, ordering, and maintenance. He tackled the applications for summer staffers and made his decisions within two days. Also, there was correspondence from former guests who had known his dad for years and wanted the latest update on his condition.

But despite the busyness, Elliot could not stave off the memories of Meera for long. Even before Josh had mentioned it, Elliot had realized he was falling for her, but didn't want to face the complications of loving a Briskin. But he could no longer dismiss the reality. It was a problem they must resolve. . . together.

Maybe she was frightened of him. Maybe she was wise to wait until emotions had cooled. But she would contact him again. He was sure of it. . . well, almost sure.

He lunched with Trevor at a small restaurant in the valley. They talked of mutual friends, books they had read and enjoyed, world events, and future goals, which served as a welcome diversion from his roiling thoughts. The subject of Meera didn't come up, and Elliot was relieved, though he knew Trevor rarely discussed his own private life.

Late at night, when the sky had turned to a velvet showcase of starry diamonds, Elliot found himself lonelier than he had ever been. Since there was nothing pressing at the lodge, he tried reading a book Trevor had suggested. But he couldn't concentrate. Instead, he swam in the pool, his eyes wandering frequently to the third-floor balcony.

Perhaps he should go to the cabin to be sure she was all right. But he knew a Briskin would be as adept at survival in the forest as a Maxwell. She would have grown up with guns and rifles. Besides, the hunting lodge would be equipped with modern means of reaching help if needed. In any event, the same security officers who patrolled Maxwell property also patrolled Briskin property, to protect against trespassers and poachers, but more importantly, to report the first ominous sign of a forest fire.

Due to his grim mood, even the staff had stopped asking about the article and if he were still talking to the attractive writer about it or knew when it would be published.

"These things take time," he would snap, so they now took pains to stay out of his way.

Elliot's mom called to remind him that he hadn't been by the house in days and asked solicitously if he were working too hard.

"I have been," he said with sudden clarity, realizing he wasn't handling this whole thing very well. "But I'm taking the rest of the afternoon and evening off, so I'll drop by."

"Then come for supper, dear," she encouraged. "I'm having your favorite stew."

Over dinner, his mother, who could read him like a book, grilled him. "What's bothering you, Elliot?"

Rather than shrug aside her question, he answered honestly. "Just something I have to work out by myself, Mom."

His dad observed him over his bifocals. "I've found, son, that when we're troubled, it's usually not because we don't know what to do, but because we don't want to do it."

"Dad, it's not that simple," Elliot protested.

"Didn't say it was." Max Maxwell picked up his fork and dug into his apple cobbler.

For the rest of the meal, there was little conversation. Elliot thought back to his younger years and the "problem" that had existed for as long as he could remember. His parents and grandparents had instilled in him a respect for the forest and its wildlife, as well as survival techniques for coping with its dangers. When he was thirteen, his dad and granddad had deemed it time for him to accompany them and a few of their hired hands to the forest. They taught him how to spot trees that were to be cut—which should be cleared and which should be left—and when new saplings should be planted.

He had worked alongside the adults all that summer and fall, feeling the tug of growing muscle and flesh and the still, small voice within as he communicated with the God who had created the wilderness.

Then in the winter of his fourteenth year, his grandfather had died. Being the only grandchild, Elliot had been showered with love and attention, and the pain of losing his grandfather had been severe. Growing up was tough.

In the spring of his fifteenth year, his dad had taken him for a walk through the woods to show him where they intended to clear away some of the forest near the creek so that it might serve as a natural fire break. Elliot had welcomed that time of hard work to keep his mind off the loss of his grandfather, and his closeness with his dad deepened. As the work progressed and they moved farther up the property line, they saw that workers on the Briskin side of the creek had similar ideas and were building a road.

It was a hot day, and the Briskin help was burning a big pile of rubble near the creek that curved sharply into Maxwell property. Here, because of the topography of the land, the line was indistinct, though it was soon apparent that Max Maxwell was sure his sworn enemies were too close for comfort.

Elliot saw a muscle flex in his dad's jaw. "It might be a good idea to burn that stuff a little closer to the creek," he called to the workers.

A silver head lifted, and Elliot knew from the anger that washed over his face that he was not just an employee but one of the Briskins themselves. "I think we're capable of handling this. . .without any help from a Maxwell," he said stiffly.

"Apparently not," Max snorted, "or you wouldn't be burning so close to our thickest stand of trees! One little spark can send these mountains up in smoke in a matter of minutes."

"Look here," Briskin ordered, "keep your nose out of our business, and we'll all be just fine!"

Elliot's dad bristled. "If you destroy one leaf on my property, you'll wish you'd never seen a forest!"

Briskin laughed derisively as his boots splashed into the creek on his way over to the Maxwell side. "And just what are you planning to do about it? Shoot me like your ol' man shot my dad? I won't be the one to run away limping, I can tell you that!"

Elliot had reached out to take his dad's arm, but his father had shrugged him away. Workers on both sides glared at each other, ready to defend their respective employers.

The two men fired a volley of accusations and denials that turned the air blue, taking the quarrel back to their own fathers and the chestnut blight. Their tempers flamed hotter than the burning rubble, and Elliot's dad stepped over into the creek himself, onto Briskin property. They began shoving each other, while their language grew ugly and vicious.

The shoving turned into a flurry of punches, fists striking at whatever portion of the anatomy presented itself—knuckle on cheekbone, chest, gut. At last they both tumbled into the creek, wallowing like pigs in a hog trough.

Before he knew it, Elliot was in the creek, pulling on the Briskin man and crying like a baby. "Stop it! Leave my dad alone!"

At this point the workers got into the fray, pulled the men apart and led them, dripping, from the creek.

"What kind of man are you anyway, fighting in front of your own kid like that?" Briskin growled.

"The kind who will protect his heritage from the likes of you!" Max shot back. "We lost enough because of Briskin, and it won't happen again! Like I said, if a single leaf on one of my trees is destroyed, you'll answer to me personally, and I won't be as kind as my dad. . .I won't shoot for the knees!"

"Don't threaten me, Maxwell. You think I'm not ready for you?" Briskin snorted and glanced around at his own men. "You can't reason with a lowdown so and so like that. Put the fire out. He's not worth wasting our time on. You can see he doesn't even care about what he's doing to his own kid."

"My dad's not. . . ," Elliot yelled, but Max stopped him with a look.

"No, Son, not a word." Shrugging out of the grasp of his men, Max came over and put his arm around Elliot's shoulder. "Let's go home."

And when Elliot glanced back, he saw the Briskin workers getting a pump from the back of a pickup truck, apparently either planning to douse the fire or to be ready in case of an errant spark.

Elliot didn't feel like a man that day, but a helpless child. He'd been warned all his life about the Briskins, but this was the first time he'd seen the animosity in action, and it was a fearful thing that had possessed his dad like a fever. It had also shown Elliot how unreasonable the Briskins could be, how dangerous, and how easily a good man could lose his cool when provoked.

His dad had talked to him for a long time that day, reinforcing what Elliot had been taught all his life—that Briskins were conniving cheats and not to be trusted. Elliot knew his dad was not a violent sort, so he blamed the Briskins. And thereafter, rather than risk facing one of them, he deliberately took the long way around the creek.

Now Elliot thought of something his dad had said recently: "It isn't that we don't know what to do, it's that we don't want to do it." Looking back, he wondered if his father might have been referring to that incident. Could it be that he knew he had been in the wrong, but wasn't willing to make amends? Wouldn't he like to make it right now?

Maybe I need to do something, Elliot debated with himself. Meera had taken the first step. At least, she had crossed the boundary. Had dared to set foot on Maxwell property. And after the fiasco with the dark-haired woman who had been spotted on Briskin property, Meera knew that he knew she was somehow connected to the Briskins.

Is it time to take some initiative of my own? Elliot mused. Were Meera a man, it might be a different matter. But he wasn't at all concerned that he would be tempted to fight with Meera Briskin.

By Thursday night and still no word from Meera, he decided to go to the cabin and confront her. He'd be reasonable. Simply ask a few questions. Let her know she had no reason to fear him. On a couple of occasions, he felt sure she had been about to tell him who she was. He could stop behaving like a kid playing games and make it easier for her.

With that resolve, he became more and more fidgety as the day wore on. And right after supper, he knew he needed to get it over with.

When he reached the creek, he was shocked to find that her car was gone. Darkness had come early, but no lights appeared in the windows. The cabin was apparently empty.

He stood near the rocks, feeling foolish and as helpless as the day he'd seen their dads fighting. Then it dawned on him. Why should Meera be living in that little cabin when she had access to the Briskin estate and her parents' home in Charlotte? Well, this little escapade had backfired on him. With his hands in his pockets and his eyes on the ground, he followed the path beside the creek, seeing white dogwood petals—like so many butterflies—floating on the light breeze.

Ignoring the distant rumblings of the heavens and thick, gray clouds rolling in, he shuffled on. Too late he realized that the spring storm was more severe and closer than he had imagined, and the cold pellets of rain that struck his face sharply came as a surprise.

He turned around and hurried back up the creek. When he glanced toward the cabin once more, he saw the front of the silver convertible and a light glowing against a window. His heartbeat quickened. She was home! Had she hidden the car out back in case he returned to the scene of their little rendezvous? Maybe she was afraid to let him know she was there, afraid of his reaction. After all, he had said some pretty nasty things about her family.

With that thought, he moved toward the lodge. But the jarring rumble raised the hair on the back of his neck, and he knew that lightning was about to strike. Making a beeline for the rocks, he crouched low against them as streaks sizzled through the sky.

It didn't take a mountain man to know that the worst place to be during a storm was under a tree, and there was nothing but trees all the way back up Maxwell Mountain. He could stay here, huddled close to the rocks and hope for nothing more than a light case of pneumonia. Or. . .he could do something *really* dangerous. He could see if Meera would take him in.

He had never set foot on Briskin land before, but he decided that he'd rather risk the wrath of a Briskin than stay here and be struck by lightning. After all, she had been the first to trespass, he reminded himself as the lightning flashed a warning, making the cabin dance in the forbidding darkness.

He took a deep breath, stood to his feet, and made a run for it straight through Turkey Creek. With a sudden downpour soaking his clothes clear to the skin, he hopped from rock to rock, losing his footing and getting a shoeful of icy water. Running across the lawn, he bounded up onto the porch, under the shelter of the overhanging roof. Then while the jagged streaks split the night sky, he jerked open the screen door and pounded furiously.

Chapter 10

Meera pecked away at the typewriter while the rain poured, tapping on the tin roof in time to the rhythm of her keys. Outside, the wind howled, lightning flashed in brilliant bursts, and thunder rattled the windowpanes. Although familiar with sudden spring thunderstorms, she was slightly annoyed with the distraction.

When she was little, her grandfather had told her that the rumble of a storm was no more threatening than a growling bobcat. It simply wanted to assert its authority and establish its territory.

Resolved to assert her own authority over the storm's intrusion, Meera smiled at the typewritten pages, pleased that this new project was developing so well. Last night, the final draft of the Chestnut Lodge article had been finished. Today, she'd researched the new one until midafternoon, then she'd napped.

After that, Meera had hiked up the mountainside behind the cabin and looked over at Chestnut Lodge. It was no longer the mystery it had been for twenty-four years. She'd met a Maxwell and had felt his arms around her. Did he wonder why she hadn't gone to his suite that night? Did he even care? Had he guessed that she was a Briskin? Did he hate her now?

After a sudden chilling wind had blown up, she had hiked back down the mountain, tempted to fish the stream for trout. But fearing Elliot might come down that way and see her, she'd hurried back to the cabin. She couldn't face him yet—maybe never. She'd showered, slipped on a pair of coral cotton-knit shorts and matching tank top, then had sat on the back porch with her sandaled feet propped on the only step. Her meager supper had consisted of a piece of cold fried chicken, followed by a yellow mountain apple. Then she'd stretched, reveling in the feeling of isolated freedom and the sense of security the surrounding mountains presented.

It was inevitable that she do some thinking. There were questions that must be answered. Did she want to tackle the ecological issues here on Briskin land or become a bridge-playing, charity-ball-going Venezuelan socialite married to a man who could be tempted by the likes of Louisa? Or was she herself even ready for marriage—having been tempted by a. . . Maxwell?!

As twilight stole through the woods, she returned to the kitchen table with a cup of hot tea sweetened with honey and tackled the second writing project with renewed vigor, working all evening. She had almost finished when the wind began banging the front screen as if trying to rip it off its hinges. She'd better secure it.

Meera reached for the door just as lightning lit the sky, revealing a hulking figure holding the screen door open while she tried to close it. Startled, she jumped back and grabbed the rifle standing in the corner behind the door that was there for such an emergency. She had just swung it around to aim at the intruder when a loud voice boomed, "Hey! Hold it! I'm leaving."

"Elliot!" she gasped. "Is that you? I thought it was the wind! Or a black bear or something. What are you doing out there?"

"I'm either going to drown or become a lightning rod if I stand here much longer," he yelled above the storm. "But I suppose getting shot couldn't be much worse. After all, I *am* a trespasser."

As if to punctuate his remarks, another bolt of electricity split the sky, bathing them both in the neon flash. They stood staring at each other for a second longer before Meera lowered the rifle and stepped back. "You'd. . .better come in," she said, while all sorts of tangled emotions tore through her.

She switched on the living room light, and he moved inside, shaking himself like a wet puppy. Meera closed the door and replaced the rifle in the corner. "I didn't think you'd ever set foot on Briskin property. What possessed you to do it?"

"Basic self-preservation. I'm trying to save myself from the storm. The question is. . .what are *you* doing here, Meera Brown?" he asked, as if he didn't know, telling himself that he was giving her one more chance to tell him the truth. "Did you get caught in the storm, too? Or did that wild dark-haired woman kidnap you?" He glanced around as if half expecting her to appear.

She ignored his question. "I'm alone. Would you like to—to sit down?"

"Do you think we could be completely honest with each other now?" he asked, sounding as forlorn as he looked with water puddling at his feet.

Meera's heart lurched crazily. "Oh, I want that, Elliot! I really do!"

He stared at her for a long moment, touched by the uncertainty in her eyes and the contrition in her voice as she added, "And I hope you won't be angry with me."

That reasonable tone of voice sounded a note of alarm. "Should I be?

"No, Elliot. Not if you hear me out." Her thin reply was almost drowned out by the pounding of the rain that whipped the house and slammed against the windows. Outside, the usually benign creek surged outside its banks like a wild thing, and thunder shook the cabin. Suddenly the lights flickered and went out, plunging them into pitch black darkness.

Elliot did not feel any compulsion to make her feel ill at ease or play any games as he'd intended the night before. Instead, by the intermittent light flashes outside the window, he could see her soft tremulous lips, the hesitancy in her eyes, and wanted more than anything to take her in his arms and reassure her.

"There's a flashlight in the desk drawer," she told him, but did not move to find it. Instead, she remained where she was, finding it curious that he was here, willing to talk, willing to listen. She fought a fierce desire to be cradled in his arms when she made her confession, but dared not risk rejection.

A sudden loud sneeze punctuated the silence, and Meera was jolted out of her reverie. "You're going to catch your death of cold, Elliot. You'd better get out of those wet things . . .your shirt, at least."

She gestured toward a low stool near the hearth, and he stumbled toward it, guided by the flashes of light outside the window.

Feeling some of the tension ease, he joked, "Socks too?"

She attempted a feeble laugh. "Sure. I'll look for the flashlight."

Making her way to the desk, Meera fumbled through a drawer until she found it. Then she turned it on and followed the yellow circle of light to the couch where she lifted her grandfather's afghan from the back. Turning, she captured Elliot in the beam. Squinting, he put up his hands, and she quickly lowered the flash to his bare chest.

"Here, wrap up in this." She handed him the afghan and set the flashlight down beside him.

Elliot draped the wrap around his shoulders, grasping it with one hand. She was so close that he could smell the scent of her freshly shampooed hair, could almost feel the warmth of her. "Does the storm frighten you?" he asked softly.

"No," she said in a small voice, noting how the occasional bursts of light outside the window outlined his solid frame. But when a crash of thunder sounded, nearer than before, she instinctively reached for him, taking comfort in the strength of his muscular forearm beneath the soft wool wrap.

Unexpectedly, the lights came on again. Meera blushed, her hand still on his arm, her body nestled close to his. Then, too late, she realized that he was staring down at her hand. . .her *left* hand!

Elliot was stone cold—as cold as the wet breeches clinging to his legs. His gaze was locked on the hard object that glittered like cold fire on her finger. "Well, I see you've made your decision," he said blandly, his unemotional tone belying the ache in his heart.

"No. . .you don't understand," she choked out. "I mean. . ."

99

In the face of his shriveling disapproval, she stepped away. Feeling suddenly hot, the scratchy afghan prickling his skin, Elliot undraped himself. He was reaching over to lay the afghan in the recliner when he noticed an official-looking envelope on the end table.

"International Airlines." The cold steel of his voice sent a chill through Meera. "Somebody going away?"

"Oh, please. . .don't," she pleaded, but he had already picked up the open envelope, its contents protruding.

"Meera Briskin," he read. "Now who might *that* be? Leaving tomorrow. No," he corrected coldly, "leaving *today*." He tossed the envelope and ticket back onto the table.

She thought his eyes were raking her as if she were a—a *Briskin*. She felt dirty. . . untouchable. "Please, Elliot, let me explain."

"Explain?" In two strides he reached the hearth, pausing long enough to hurl an accusation. "What's to explain? Isn't it quite obvious. . .Meera *Briskin?*"

He plunked himself down on the edge of the hearth and forced his feet into wet shoes, then stood and stuffed his socks into his pants pockets. "And just for the record, I've known who you were since the first day you arrived at Chestnut Lodge."

Meera gasped. "You knew? And you've been pretending all this time?" Realizing the irony of her question, she dropped her eyes.

"No! *Waiting*. . .to see if you'd be honest with me. But, of course, that's a lot to ask of a Briskin! Be sure you include that part when you joke about your little deception with your dark-haired friend and your boyfriend—or husband—in Venezuela."

Meera stepped closer and touched his arm. "I'm not married."

Elliot shrugged her away as he reached for his shirt. "What's the difference? We both played our little games. Now it's over. That's all. But I can't see that anybody won." With difficulty, he wriggled into his wet, knit shirt, then strode to the door. "I can't get out of here fast enough."

He held onto the doorknob, pausing long enough to deliver one last barb. "I know the article was some kind of ploy. I don't even want to know what kind. But just in case you have anything else in mind, let me make this clear. There is to be no article. If you try to publish one word, I'll sue!"

"Please, Elliot, you don't understand!" But he jerked the door open, oblivious to her desperation and the raging elements, and with a slam of the screen, he was gone.

The jarring sound was like the rumble through the heavens, as if Someone had tried to warn her. Her grandfather had been right—a Maxwell wouldn't listen to anything a Briskin had to say. And if Elliot had known her identity all along, then his emotional response to her had been. . .an act!

She closed the door and leaned back against it. The lights went out again, leaving the room dark except for a red circle where the flashlight still shone on the hearth. After switching it off, Meera sat on the cold, damp stone, hugging her arms to her body.

Her good intentions had turned out to be nothing but ashes. *So what,* she said to herself, *if some developer builds condos all across the top of the mountain? I won't be here to see it. I'll go to Venezuela and to Clark—where I belong.*

All morning, Elliot worked like a bear getting ready to hibernate. During the long night he had vowed to himself that he would never trust another woman as long as he lived, mentally kicking himself in the seat of the pants for letting himself get caught up in a Briskin scheme.

He couldn't believe he had been in the Briskin cabin, half-dressed. What a laugh the Briskins would have about that! Or they might not consider it a laughing matter. He'd never made such a fool of himself in his entire life. And the rotten thing about it was, he'd walked into it with his eyes wide open.

His intercom buzzed, and the morning clerk broke into his train of thought. "Mr. Maxwell?"

Elliot growled into the phone, "I thought I told you to direct everything to the manager. If she can't handle it, then we don't need her."

"But she says it's a matter of life and death."

"She who?"

"Um. . .the young woman."

"Young woman!" he muttered under his breath. "Tell her I'm. . .out of town!"

"She says she knows you're here, and she's not leaving until you see her, Sir."

Elliot leaned back against the cool leather chair back and closed his eyes. How much more did he have to take? "Is she a blond?"

"Blond?"

"You know. . .hair color!" he yelled. "Does she have blond hair?"

"No, Sir."

Elliot threw down his pencil and stared at the door until it burst open. In charged the dark-haired hellion he'd encountered for the past two nights. He punched the intercom. "Get security in here," he demanded.

The woman marched up to the desk, gave him a scathing look, and threatened, "You call security, and I'll yell 'Fire!' to the top of my lungs!" And with that, she threw a manila envelope on his desk. "Now shall I start screaming?"

"Just say what you have to say, and then get out," he snapped, not doubting for a moment that she'd do it. . .and enjoy the process.

He punched the intercom. "Forget security. Everything's okay in here."

"You're sure, Sir?"

Elliot hesitated. He wasn't at all sure. "It might be a good idea to pass by my door occasionally."

She grinned while Elliot got up and propped the door wide open.

"I'm Louisa Coleman," she said, putting out her hand. "Meera's cousin."

"You people have your nerve," he spat, ignoring her hand and returning to his chair behind the desk, hoping to put as much distance as possible between them.

"I'm also her friend."

"Well, as the saying goes, 'With friends like you, who needs enemies?' " he growled. "You're the one who tried to steal her fiancé, aren't you?"

"She told you that?" Louisa said, disbelievingly. Then after a moment, she shrugged. "Well, Meera doesn't know how to treat a man. She's kept poor Clark dangling all this time. It's no wonder he came on to me." She grinned again. "You can understand that, can't you?"

He wouldn't give her the satisfaction of hearing what he had on his mind at the moment. "Sounds like you and poor Clark are two of a kind," he said simply.

"I quite agree." Louisa lifted her chin defiantly. Then her mood changed and she purred, "And what kind are *you*, Mr. Maxwell?"

He could have laughed. "What difference does it make?"

"A lot." She got out of the chair and sauntered over to the desk, leaned across and rested her chin on her elbow. Then with her red lips pursed prettily, she challenged him. "I think you and I could have a lot of fun. I'm not nearly as stuffy as my older, but more naive, cousin."

"You come any closer," Elliot snapped, "and I'll be the one to yell 'Fire.' "

Her eyes narrowed. "Just testing you, Mr. Maxwell."

He got up and, against his better judgment, turned his back on her to look out the window. "Why do you two feel you have to test me? Why can't you just leave me alone?" he asked dejectedly. He'd had enough. Too much.

"Meera's reasons are in that envelope. Mine are more. . .creative, shall we say. But you needn't worry. We're both leaving for Venezuela tomorrow morning. That is, *if* you read what's in that envelope." Her voice took on a threatening tone again. "I'm not going anywhere until you do."

Leaving tomorrow morning? Good riddance! He whirled around, sat down, and tore open the envelope.

"She sent you with this, huh?" he asked, taking the papers out.

"Oh, no! Meera would kill me if she knew I was here. You can't imagine what I went through just to get her to say I could mail it."

"Sure," he retorted sarcastically. "You look like you've been through the wringer, all right."

She giggled. "Why, Mr. Maxwell, I do believe you almost paid me a compliment."

He smiled wryly. "Some of the most beautiful flowers are among the most deadly."

Louisa cocked her head and studied him. "What did my cousin do to you?"

He couldn't very well say that Meera had deceived him, since he'd known who she was almost from the beginning. And he wasn't about to tell Louisa the real truth—that her cousin had trespassed on his property and stolen his heart. "I don't want to discuss her!" he muttered and began reading the article.

"This comes as no surprise," he said when he had finished. "It compares with other articles she's written. It's well done, but I don't want a Briskin publishing an article on anything about the Maxwells. And that's final!"

"Read the other one," she urged.

Elliot sighed but picked up the other paper-clipped stack of papers. When he was well into it, he swiveled around, his back to Louisa.

He read Meera's well-documented account of the chestnut blight and how it had destroyed the country's most valuable hardwood tree. He already knew that, quite well! But he had not known the Briskin version of the feud.

She outlined it in an objective way, reporting what Elliot had told her. Then she gave a moving rendition of Elias Briskin, not the monster he'd always imagined, but a great man, a fine man, whose heart and life had been broken by a Maxwell.

It was an account of the blight upon two families, infected by the parasite of misunderstanding and unforgiveness. Her version was something to think about. But it didn't change anything.

He turned around and faced Louisa again. "I've finished. You can leave now."

"One more thing," she said and took a white envelope from her bag and held it out to him.

Elliot looked at the letterhead, imprinted with the name of a prestigious law firm. He recognized the name of the attorney. *What now?* Was he being sued for trespassing last night? Or worse—had Meera recorded his late-night foray with a hidden camera so she could blackmail him? He felt sick to his stomach and sweat beaded his forehead. How could he ever explain his way out of that fiasco—wearing an afghan and little else in the middle of the night at the Briskin cabin?

Slowly, he opened the envelope. It stated simply, clearly that the Briskin mountain adjacent to Maxwell property was expected to be placed in the hands of a realtor in the near future and that Meera Briskin wanted the Maxwells to be so informed.

Elliot bristled. "What's this all about? You expect me to believe that a Briskin would sell to a Maxwell? The last time that happened, the Maxwells were ruined and a Briskin got shot."

"It's Meera's idea," Louisa said defensively. "A developer is interested in that land. Meera wanted to be fair. She's that way." She rolled her eyes toward the ceiling. "She convinced me to go along with her, and my mama and daddy will do what I ask. The other relatives don't really care that much, so it's just Uncle George and Aunt Clara and Meera's parents to convince, but you're already informed so I think you may have a legal right even if some of them say no."

"I don't intend to do battle with any more Briskins," he said, tossing the letter aside. This had to be some kind of sinister scheme. These two cousins playing some kind of sick game. He rose. "If that's all, Miss Coleman, I have work to do."

Louisa got to her feet. "Just one more thing," she said and walked over to him, standing so close that he caught a whiff of her heady perfume. "You're really not bad for a Maxwell, you know. And I'm a Coleman, not a Briskin. Couldn't we forget that silly ol' feud and get better acquainted?"

Elliot put up both hands and backed away. "No offense, Ma'am, but I'm not interested."

"I didn't think you would be," she said lightly. "I should be used to it by now. The only time a man spurns me is when Meera gets to him first."

Elliot stiffened. Maybe he'd move to Hawaii. Trevor had had the right idea at one point in his life. "Look," he said between gritted teeth, "I'm not falling for any more Briskin schemes."

"Amazing, isn't it, Mr. Maxwell," she said, eyeing him through narrowed lids, "what we fall for sometimes. . . . I'll leave now."

Louisa moved toward the door but halted in the doorway. "Meera says she's going to. . ." her voice broke, then she added, "to marry Clark. If you want her, you'd better stop her."

❧

Stop her. . .stop her. . .stop her. . .if you want her. The words rang in Elliot's head for the rest of the afternoon. But it was not just a matter of what he wanted. He, Trevor, and Josh had talked many times about what *God* wanted for their lives. He felt a sudden burst of conviction. When was the last time he had consulted God in all this?

Now it was too late, he supposed, even for the Lord to intervene. Besides, he'd seen the ring on her finger. So. . .what was there to say? *Don't marry that rich playboy, Clark Phillips? Forget your family and I'll forget mine, and come away with me and live happily ever after?* Oh, it was no use.

Scuffing through the woods, he continued to hear the refrain. *Stop her. . . stop her. . .stop her.* It whispered through the trees on the wind. It laughed at him from the waters of the creek. Even the small forest animals seemed to be repeating its message, taunting him.

Later, back in his suite at the lodge, unable to rest, he rose from his bed while darkness still blanketed the hills and valleys outside, and wandered down to the chapel. The glow of the wall sconces in the hallway cast a triangle of light along the aisle that separated the shadowy benches. Faintly outlined against the back wall was a six-foot cross made of rugged chestnut beams.

He closed the door behind him, plunging the room into a chilling blackness, then quickly switched on a small lamp at the back. In the subdued light, the cross seemed to be beckoning, and he moved nearer and sank down in one of the pews.

What am I supposed to do now, Lord? he prayed silently. He thought of Meera's grandfather, Elias Briskin, who had been in love with his grandmother, Carrie Spearman. Was Meera trying to get even for old Elias—trying to make a Maxwell fall in love with a Briskin—then break his heart?

He shook off the cloying thoughts. Whatever her motives, he loved her. He loved Meera Brown. . .who was also Meera Briskin. But she was like the elusive Christmas angel—always just out of reach. And now he had lost her forever to a man who didn't deserve her. . .any more than *he* did!

The revelation was startling. Since when was he himself a paragon of virtue? *I'm no saint,* he thought ruefully. And in the darkened chapel, alone with God, Elliot Maxwell repented. "Lord," he prayed, "I'm sorry. I've been a disappointment to You in this situation. I haven't asked You for Your input. You know I want that girl. But if I can't have what I want, help me to want what is best for me, and for her. Give me the integrity to face up to it. Lord, I understand that this is not just a matter of two people—me and Meera— but two families who need to be reconciled. Although I'd like to make a deal, I'll try not to put conditions on my serving You. . .but I don't mind admitting it would be easier if I could have her by my side."

When Elliot rose from his knees, he saw that morning had come, for a soft glow filtered in through the skylight to the center of the room. With his eyes on the shaft of light, Elliot walked through it, then returned to his room to get ready for whatever the day would demand of him.

He did not feel his burden lift. As he showered and dressed, he thought of Josh who had never found a girl intended just for him. Josh had told him that he'd met someone in Charleston whom he'd hoped was the one, but their first conversation had revealed that she was in love with someone else, so Josh contented himself with being her friend.

Trevor had loved a wonderful woman who had ultimately entered a convent, and he had—with integrity and maturity—channeled his emotions into his novels and speaking engagements.

But I, Elliot chided himself, *what have I done? I've behaved like a sophomoric fool.* Love, he remembered, is action—not just feeling. Love wants the best for the object of one's affection, even if the best is. . .someone else.

His mind accepted the truth of that statement, but his rebellious heart was not so receptive.

❧

Three days later, after careful investigation by the Maxwell attorney, Elliot discovered that a developer was indeed interested in Briskin property, although the property was not yet on the market.

Elliot told his parents that he'd learned of it from a Briskin who felt the Maxwells should know in case they got a chance to bid on it. The only drawback was a dogwood fungus, but that was a problem on Maxwell land, too, and was currently being dealt with successfully.

To Elliot's surprise, his dad appreciated the information and delivered the startling statment that, although he'd never expected a Briskin to sell to a Maxwell, perhaps there was a Briskin with a trace of goodness in him.

"It's a 'she,' Dad. Not a 'he,' " Elliot said quietly.

He told them what he knew about Meera Brown, who had come to the conference to pursue a career in writing. They remembered the lovely young woman who had won the award.

"I stand corrected," his dad said slowly after reading her articles. He glanced at his wife who lifted a quizzical brow. "Perhaps there's a Briskin with a trace of goodness in her."

"I never thought I'd hear you say a thing like that, Dad," Elliot replied.

"Well, that heart attack brought me close to death, Son," his dad said seriously. "Before that, I felt I was invincible, immortal. Now I know how fragile life is. . .and how precious. Makes a man consider what's really important. . .like finding the right partner." He reached across the table and grasped his wife's hand. "And getting things squared away with the good Lord."

There wasn't much Elliot could do about finding a wife right now. The one he wanted was on her way to Venezuela to join the man she had promised to marry. But there was plenty he could do about his spiritual life. And he wouldn't waste another moment.

Chapter 11

The summer season passed quickly for Elliot. By mid-June, the lodge was filled with guests and conferences that had been booked for months. Summer staffers were housed in their quarters near the lodge. And Elliot had made some headway in his quest for a closer relationship with God. He'd even spent more time than usual in the chapel where his breakthrough had occurred and in the woods, taking long, solitary prayer walks.

Elliot had resigned himself to the probability that Meera had married Clark by now. He had only himself to blame for letting his emotions take precedence over his good sense. But then, he'd never felt this way about a woman before. His feelings for Kate had eventually been affected by the drugs that ravaged her personality. Still, he had seen the potential there and had begun to love the kind of woman Kate should have been. . .could have been. . . if!

Meera's obvious beauty, her warmth, her inner worth had been qualities he had admired from the beginning, far outweighing any fault he found in her. He had even begun to feel a kinship with Elias Briskin, who had lost the woman he loved to a Maxwell.

Remembering the fight between his father and Meera's, Elliot now realized that the two men had not been angry with each other—they had simply been victims of the feud that fed upon misunderstanding, always ready to break out. It was a spirit of discord that permeated both families. But because of Meera, he would never feel that way again, and he loved her for releasing him from that bondage.

He would tell her someday. . .maybe. . .if they ever met again. But during the summer, he stayed as far away as possible from the creek and any view of the cabin.

Then, one hot day in August, she called. "This is Meera. . . ," she said hesitantly.

"Hold on. . . ." He raced to another phone, hoping she wouldn't hang up on him. "Sorry, I wanted to take the call in my office."

"You're not going to believe this. . . ."

"Shoot!" he said, then laughed lightly. "Uh. . .please don't take me literally."

"I don't know how this happened," Meera continued apologetically, "but *Fabulous Places* magazine has a copy of my Chestnut Lodge article. They sent me a check. I swear I didn't submit it. . . ."

"*I* did."

"What?"

"It's a very good article. My dad gave his approval."

"Does he know who I am?"

"Yes," Elliot said. "Or at least he did. And who are you now, Meera? Brown, Briskin, or Phillips?" He caught his breath. "I'm sorry. I shouldn't have put you on the spot like that." His words came quickly then. "I wish you well."

"Thank you," she said, hating herself for feeling like she had static on the brain—static that seemed to be transferring to the telephone line. "The connection's going bad," she said, and closed her eyes against the pain that washed over her. As Meera Brown, she had connected so well with Elliot. But that was over now.

How long they listened to the crackle on the line, he didn't know. And when he spoke again, he wasn't sure how much she had caught of his message. "If they don't use a picture of Bertha, I'm liable to lose a very good employee."

"I'll insist," she called over the crackle. "I'll bring. . .extra copies."

Bring, she had said, not *send.* "You're in the States?"

"Venezuela."

The line went dead, and Elliot stared at the phone for a long time. A sense of abandonment like he hadn't felt since the last night he'd seen her, washed over him, shaking him and leaving him bent double like a sapling in a strong wind.

Apparently she had been in Venezuela all summer. She had intimated that Clark wanted a stronger commitment. Maybe the international playboy had actually married her. A person like Meera would not settle for less, he knew. He'd heard that love has the power to change people. Maybe it had changed Clark Phillips.

"Maybe someday I'll discover that my feelings for Meera were based on the game she and I were playing," Elliot told Josh when they talked later, "and the euphoria over the fact that a Maxwell and a Briskin were communicating."

"Do you really believe that, Elliot?"

Elliot shook his head. "No. . .I don't."

"It's easier for me to give advice than for you to take it, old pal, because I've never been in love. Oh, I've met women that I would like to have fallen in love with, even wished our relationship might grow into it. But it never happened. So, in my limited experience, I can only say: Trust the Lord to know what's best and to work things out according to His will."

Elliot grinned. "Yep, it's easier said than done. But I know you're right." He grew suddenly serious. "But I'm afraid the Lord has already decided there is to be no relationship between Meera and me. That is, Meera and Clark Phillips have decided."

"You can't reverse what's happened, Elliot," Josh reminded him.

Elliot nodded. "And I can't force her to love me. All my attempts at relating have resulted in failure."

"Then wait on the Lord," Josh advised, "but stay busy."

❧

Elliot tried, but he was still in limbo. Maybe news would come that Meera had definitely married Clark, and he could begin to put her out of his mind. Or somehow his longing for her would subside. But nothing he did eased the ache deep within.

Then autumn came. The lush green of the mountains blazed in a rich tapestry of brilliant color, and the air turned crisp. The tourist season would end soon after the turning of the leaves.

When the cold, rainy season set in, the leaves lost their color and fell to the ground, leaving the limbs barren except for the evergreens that darkened to yet a deeper green. Then in mid-November, Indian summer came to the dun-colored hills and valleys. Autumn, punctuated by the blood red leaves of the flame bush and fiery oranges and yellows of the marigolds in the flowerbeds around the lodge, seemed determined to go out in a blaze of glory.

Elliot took some comfort in this, his favorite season, and spent more time outside, involved in ecological activities in the forest. And for the second day in a row, he and his workers saw surveyors on Briskin property.

❧

During the second week in November, Meera returned to her parents' home in Charlotte. The family was planning to gather at the Briskin estate for the holidays and those who could would arrive by Thanksgiving. Meera had research to do and interviews to conduct. *Fabulous Places* had scheduled an April date for the publication of her Chestnut Lodge article and assured her that they would use the picture of Bertha holding a dish of macaroon glacés. In addition, the editor wanted to see other articles in her proposed series on western North Carolina inns.

"I've called a surveyor, Meera," her father told her one morning just before Thanksgiving. "Your mother and I will be driving up to the estate tomorrow afternoon."

It couldn't be put off any longer. That night, Meera told her mom about the writers' conference, the article she had written on Chestnut Lodge, and her strategy to make peace with the Maxwell clan.

"I married into this family, Meera," she said dolefully. "And regardless of my private opinion about the feud, my place is to stick by my husband. You know that."

While telling her mother had been a breeze, telling her father was another matter. Meera weighed her words carefully. "I'm going to close the cabin for the winter," she told him early the next morning. "Will you go down with me?"

He was more than willing. "The surveyors are coming at nine in the morning I'll come by the cabin after I've shown them which piece of property we intend to sell."

Around noon, she served sandwiches and lemonade to the surveyors on the back porch and left the pitcher and glasses for seconds when they completed the job Mr. Briskin had outlined—to guarantee Meera access to the cabin from the main road as well as the back way down the mountain from the estate.

After lunch, while she cleaned out the refrigerator, her dad checked the pipes to make sure they were securely insulated for the winter. Seeing him straighten from his cramped position under the sink, Meera suggested, "Time for a break, Dad."

And with a quick prayer for guidance, she stepped into the living room, took her silver cup from the mantel, and brought it into the kitchen.

"What's that?" he wanted to know.

Meera sighed. "You'd better sit down."

Over coffee, Meera told him about her escapade at Chestnut Lodge, the article that would appear in April, and how she had inadvertently perpetuated the feud, causing at least one Maxwell—Elliot—to consider her devious and conniving.

Her dad was silent for a long time, pondering the gravity of what she had told him. Finally, he shook his head. "You say the fellow knew who you were, but pretended not to?"

Meera nodded.

He ran his hands through his silver hair. "It's just like I've always said, there's no reasoning with a Maxwell. Don't suppose you could expect any more than that from the son of Jonas Maxwell."

Meera stared at him. "Elliot is his *grand*son, Dad."

Now it was her father's turn to stare. "The boy?"

"Well, he's not exactly a boy."

"He was the last time I saw him," he said slowly, reminiscently. "I think Maxwell had only one. And the boy? He's not. . .married?"

She shook her head. "He loved someone who was murdered. Kate. . . Logan, I believe."

There was a moment while her dad pondered this latest information. Then, "Yes, I remember. It was several years ago. Made all the papers. Terrible tragedy for one so young and for those. . .left behind."

Meera closed her eyes, feeling the moisture trickle down her cheeks while he sat watching her. Then he took a handkerchief, leaned over, and blotted the tears. "You've been through a lot this past year, Honey. We lost your granddad, then this noble venture of yours turned sour, then this thing with Clark. Do you think that's really over, Baby?"

"Clark is not right for me, Dad. At least, not as a husband. He and Louisa are much better suited to each other."

"Well, all I know is that my beautiful girl should be happy," he said softly. "You seemed so happy with Clark. What happened, Honey?"

Meera took the handkerchief from his hand and finished mopping up. "I *was* happy. . .for awhile. But I guess I learned that happiness isn't all there is to life."

"Doesn't the Constitution say we're entitled to the pursuit of happiness?" he joked, hoping to make her laugh.

She obliged him with a watery smile. "Well, the Bible doesn't say anything about that. I think it talks about an *abundant* life, and that means more than just having a good time." She sobered and looked down at the damp handkerchief knotted in her hands. "I want my life to count for something."

Her father covered her hand with his large one. "Oh, Honey, it does, and it will. You have a terribly wonderful conscience and a warm heart. You just continue to pursue that abundant life, and it will be yours." He stood and looked down at her. "But I know this is a trying time for you. So, let's get that property on the market, forget the Maxwells, and get on with our lives. Now, how can I help you?"

For the next half hour they packed her grandfather's personal papers and pictures and put them in the car. Meera hoped to write a novel about the chestnut blight and the misunderstanding that had made bitter enemies of friends and destroyed what might have been a beautiful relationship between herself and Elliot. Someday. . .she'd write it.

It was midafternoon when they left the cabin and returned to the estate. Meera unpacked the box of memories and set the silver cup on her dresser. She would keep it always, just as her grandfather had kept letters and a diary of his early, happier days with the Maxwells and his memories of Carrie Spearman.

Yet, in spite of everything, her grandfather had lived an active, productive life. She would strive for that, too.

It was almost dark when it sounded—like a jet breaking the sound barrier—yet somehow different. Suddenly a screaming wail sent a chill through her veins.

Meera bolted from the bedroom and ran down the two flights of stairs to the drawing room where her mother stood listening as her dad talked on the phone. It was the fire department.

Fire! It had to be the cabin.

Elliot came in at sunset and went directly to his office. It was there he heard the loud boom. . .varoom. . .that seemed to shake the very foundation of the mountains, followed by a moment of silent panic.

Then came the shouting. "Fire!" "There's a fire in the forest!" "Down by the creek. . ." "Fire!"

The dreaded word ricocheted off the mountainsides and came over Elliot's voice pager. He pushed the intercom button to all offices. "Fire!" he shouted. "Sound the alarm!"

But Tom had already flipped the switch. Upon hearing the ear-splitting alert, guests began pouring into the lobby and spilled out onto the patio, peering into the forest to determine the source of the billowing smoke.

Elliot stood by the desk phone until the location of the fire was reported.

"It's the Briskin cabin, sir," said an employee. "Should we just keep the Maxwell side watered down?"

"Is anyone there?" he yelled.

"We don't know. Can't see a vehicle. Smoke's too thick."

"Sometimes they park at the back. Check it out."

"Sir, there was an explosion. It's. . .pretty far gone."

"Do what you can!" Elliot slammed down the receiver. "Call the fire department and report the fire at the Briskin cabin," he instructed his secretary on his way out. "Then tell Tom to break out the shovels and rakes and line up some people to help. I'm going down there."

He raced down the mountain at the back of the lodge, the tinder-dry leaves crunching beneath his feet. He could see the ominous glow—not the sunset painting the sky orange, but the glare of fire against the late evening sky. Clouds of gray smoke billowed above the trees. The pungent odor of burning pine needles and dry leaves mingled sharply with the cooler, crisp air, taking from it some of the oxygen and leaving behind a strong scent of woodsmoke.

When Elliot reached the creek, he saw that his men had driven Chestnut Lodge trucks across the creek onto Briskin property and were raking leaves into the clearing surrounding the cabin, while others were pumping water from the creek and hosing down the perimeter. They were helpless, however, to prevent the fire from racing up the mountain at the back of the cabin, for their hoses wouldn't reach that far.

Crossing over, Elliot felt his heart plummet to the pit of his stomach, seeing that the back of the cabin was in flames and part of the roof had already caved in. American chestnut wood was virtually fireproof and relatively smokeless, but the cabin had been standing for decades, and there had been an explosion. The cabin was burning steadily.

"We couldn't get inside, Mr. Maxwell!" someone called. "I don't think anyone was in it, but if they were, it's too late now!"

Too late! screamed through his head like the sirens coming on the scene, immediately followed by the fire engines, now lining up along the creek and the back road from the Briskin estate right behind a long, black car that pulled to the side of the road to let them pass.

At this point, it was far more important to sacrifice the cabin, if necessary, than chance letting the fire spread, endangering thousands of acres of timberland. Since the firefighters were hard at work, however, Elliot directed his efforts to dousing the cabin. He had to save it for Meera, if possible. It meant so much to her.

Within minutes, the fire marshal had assessed the situation and praised Elliot and his staff for their prompt and professional action. He then directed the firefighters to move on up the mountain to build a firebreak above the fire. A staging area was set up on the Maxwell side of the creek with trucks, equipment, and an ambulance.

Several hours later, they had done all they could and now could only try to contain the fire. The terrain was too steep for bulldozers, and they could only hope the wind did not pick up and that the flames would not jump the firebreak. Additional workers arrived and went up the mountain with five-gallon tanks on their backs to put out any scattered fires. Others carried tools and equipment. Helicopters wouldn't be able to drop their barrels of water before morning.

Many of them, like Elliot, could now only stand by and watch as one tree after another ignited, like giant candles on a birthday cake.

After the eleven o'clock news, a fresh crew arrived, along with volunteers who had heard about the fire on television. Wearily, Elliot handed his hose over to someone else. As he turned, wiping his face with a handkerchief, he spotted Meera and her father relinquishing their rakes.

Startled, his eyes met hers. "You're safe!" he breathed, relief washing over him like the water over the now smoldering cabin.

113

With one hand, Meera reached up to brush away a strand of hair. She couldn't believe what she was seeing. He had tried to save her cabin. . .after all she'd done. . . .

Then he looked from her soot-streaked face to the astonished gaze of Bruce Briskin. "Maxwell?"

Abruptly, Elliot turned away, pretending not to hear. He was too exhausted to deal with a Briskin at a time like this.

Walking toward his own property line, he saw his mom and dad standing near the boulders, talking to the fire marshal. Soon afterward, the marshal announced over the speaker that any firefighters going off duty were welcome to shower and change at Chestnut Lodge. And there was plenty of food for everyone!

Soon tired, smoke-blackened workers were crossing the creek and heading for the lodge.

She and her father would not be among that number, of course, Meera thought as she watched them go. But she was startled when her father interrupted her musings. "I owe that boy an apology," Bruce Briskin said, staring after Elliot. "Years ago, I got into a fight with his dad in front of him. The guilt over that has never left me. No wonder he despises me."

"It's not you, Daddy. It's me! I made a mess of everything! He. . .hates me!" Meera blurted, unable to meet her father's inquiring's gaze.

"If that's so, he has a strange way of showing it," he remarked solemnly. "The boy risks his life by trespassing on Briskin property, puts his men to work saving land that, according to you, he knows will not be offered to him but might be sold to a developer, and spends hours protecting Briskin property when his own is in no imminent danger."

He put his arm around his daughter, and she nestled her head against his shoulder. "Suppose I should thank the Maxwells personally," he mused. "Maybe even offer to sell the mountain to them."

"Oh, Daddy!" she wailed, and he held her closer.

"That should make you happy," he said. "Isn't that what you wanted all along?" He tilted her chin upward with his finger and looked into her face.

Meera nodded gratefully.

"Maybe you should thank him too, Honey. It's your property—your cabin he tried to save."

❧

It was a small fire by forest standards, not much more than a brushfire, they said later when the assessment had been made and only four hundred acres were found to have been burned. By now all the firefighters were gone, except for the few who would linger until the rains came.

After it was all over, Max Maxwell consented to see Bruce Briskin. And promptly at nine the next morning, Briskin walked through the doors of Chestnut Lodge. He wore a dark suit and tie, and every hair on his silvery head was in place.

"Good morning," he said politely.

Elliot nodded. "Come this way, please," he said, leading the way to his father's office.

Although Max offered the man a seat, he remained standing, as did Elliot, who waited with his arms folded across his chest.

Despite the fact that Briskin had praised the Maxwells publicly for preventing what might have been a disastrous forest fire, Elliot was not convinced of the man's sincerity. Privately he might say something to upset his father, and Elliot was determined to be present in case he had to escort Briskin out of the office.

But to their utter amazement, Briskin thanked them once again, explaining that the investigation had shown the explosion had been caused by a gasoline container. Elias Briskin had kept it under the back porch for his chain saw, and apparently over time, the plastic lid had melted, allowing noxious fumes to escape. There was also evidence that someone had smoked a cigarette while sitting on the back steps. When questioned, one of the surveyors admitted that he had smoked but was fairly certain he'd dropped the stub in a glass of lemonade. But everyone knew it took only the flick of an ash to kindle a fire among the dry leaves.

"The mountain adjacent to your property is for sale," he went on. "It's yours if you wish to purchase it—a prime parcel."

"We'll check it out, of course," Max said guardedly.

Briskin colored. "I understand. Guess I can't blame you for not taking my word for it."

"I'll leave the final decision to my son." Max nodded toward Elliot, whose stance had not changed. "You'll have to deal with him now."

"Then you're the man I need to see," Briskin said, pausing. "I have a score to settle with you."

Elliot waited for what he suspected had been coming all along. But he was bowled over when, instead of condemning him for his conduct with Meera, the man apologized instead for the fight staged in Elliot's presence on that long ago afternoon. "Now. . .my daughter would like to speak to you, too. She would have come with me, but she feels she would not be welcome here."

Elliot's startled expression told Bruce all he needed to know, so he added, "She's down at the cabin, assessing the damage."

Chapter 12

E lliot paused at the boulders that bordered Turkey Creek, seeing the devastation on the other side. Where the Briskin cabin had once stood proudly was now only a blackened stone chimney and a few twisted, charred objects, scarcely identifiable.

Scanning the mountainside, he saw burned stumps and scorched tree trunks, shorn of their limbs. He and the others might have managed to save a forest, but the vale was a black hole, lifeless and dark. The firefighters had gone. There was nothing left to fight. No fire smoldered in the gray ashes.

But Elliot felt keenly the unseasonably warm day when he spotted the hood of a silver convertible winking in the sun far up the road. Then she emerged from the trees. Despite his knowledge that she might be married, his blood sang at the sight of her. She was wearing a simple T-shirt and blue jeans, but she had never looked lovelier to him. A cloud of silver-blond hair fell around her shoulders, catching the glint of the sunlight that filtered through the trees.

With her head down, she appeared wistful, moving forlornly along the path, scuffing the scorched earth with the toe of her tennis shoe. He could only imagine what she must be feeling.

❧

Meera had been watching for what seemed like hours, wondering if her dad had lost his courage and decided not to show up at Chestnut Lodge after all. Or maybe Elliot and his father had turned him away. Still, she wished she could see Elliot once more, if only to thank him again for trying to save the cabin. Who would have thought a Maxwell would have done that for a Briskin!

When she saw a jeaned figure approaching, she stopped her aimless pacing and watched as he hopped effortlessly across the rocks and strode resolutely along the creek bank toward her. The breeze, smelling of burned wood, lifted his curls and tossed them across his forehead. His tan had deepened during the summer, she noticed. And when he stood in front of her, she saw that his knit shirt was the exact color of his deep blue eyes.

He read the profound loss in her glance, then turned to follow her gaze toward the chimney.

"I'm so sorry," Elliot said, seeing the sad spectacle. "We did all we could to save it."

"You and your men saved the forest, Elliot. Perhaps even the Briskin home. Thank you. . .so much."

"I only wish we could have done more. But you could build another cabin someday. . .in your grandfather's memory."

Meera stared at the charred landscape and sighed. "It wouldn't be the same."

Respecting her grief, he waited. "This may be little consolation, Meera, but losing this piece of land to a fire has brought our families closer than they have been in generations."

Even you and me, Elliot? she yearned to ask. Her hair swung about her shoulders as she turned her imploring, smoky eyes to his, and her voice trembled uncertainly. "Maybe. . .this could be made into a little haven in memory of *both* our grandfathers, who were the best of friends. . .once."

Elliot lifted his gaze toward the distant mountain peak. He had thought the clearing might be left to grow wild, erasing any memory of Meera, thus easing his pain. Now, with a glance toward heaven, his excitement began to build. Some good could come from this, after all, and she would not be completely lost to him. "I like that. We could turn this spot into a place of. . .love and friendship."

Meera ran a few steps ahead and turned, stirring puffs of ash along the path. The sun, rising higher, sparked her gray eyes with blue. "Guests could come here from Chestnut Lodge. Families could bring their children." She brightened. "You don't have a children's park at the lodge, do you?"

"No," he said, delighted with the idea. "And our own children could play here."

Our children? She stared at him. Saw him grimace as if he'd said the wrong thing. He scuffed his shoe in the ash which settled as gray dust on the toe of his white tennis shoe.

Meera caught her breath and dared to test it. "I couldn't very well have children without getting married first," she quipped. "Unless I wanted to start another family feud."

"Let's don't do that," he countered. "We've just begun to work this one out."

She moved to face him. "I'm sorry for all the trouble I caused you, Elliot. But I didn't know how else to approach you."

He reached over and took her hand. "Your approach was quite unforgettable," he replied and finally looked from her shining eyes to her hand. There was no ring on her finger. No white circle. "Do you know why I was so upset with you the night of the storm?"

She ducked her head, feeling the heat stain her cheeks a becoming shade of pink. He gently lifted her chin with his finger. "Because I was afraid I could never have you. That you were going to marry that guy, and I'd never see you again. Never hold you. Never kiss you."

"Oh, Elliot, I feel the same way. It started the moment we met. Then you turned out to be one of those unscrupulous Maxwells." She giggled.

He searched her face, her eyes, and could hardly believe what he saw there. "You're. . .no longer engaged?"

"I returned Clark's ring as soon as I reached Venezuela."

Afraid to believe the joy that began to engulf him, he stomped about in mock disgust, raising the dust. "So you let me sweat it out all summer!"

Her voice was soft with wonder. "I thought you. . .despised me."

Ignoring any apprehension, he said sincerely, "Without you, there's a constant ache in my heart."

"Oh, Elliot, I thought you didn't want me. You said it was a game."

"How could you believe that?"

She shrugged. "How could our grandfathers have believed such terrible things about each other?"

"I think," he said, moving nearer, "it's time we put this animosity behind us."

"You mean. . .start over?"

"I mean. . .take up where we left off."

"Oh," she said in a small voice. She brushed her hair back from her face and looked toward the creek. "We could build a bridge across the creek so people won't have to rock-hop or wade through."

"Good idea, Meera." His enthusiasm grew. "There's an old shed on our property made of American chestnut wood. We've talked about tearing it down, but it has symbolized our heritage and how we've built on the loss of the forest. We can use those boards across the bridge and make a wooden railing above the stone. That will be *my* grandfather's contribution."

"Oh, Elliot," she breathed, "don't you think our grandfathers are hearing us. . .and approve?"

"Without a doubt," he said staunchly, "Jonas Maxwell is the one who put the bug in the ear of the Lord to bring us together."

"Oh, you!" she teased, hitting him playfully on the arm. "If anybody, it's Elias Briskin. He's the one who wanted to make peace all along."

"My foot!" Elliot exclaimed. "He came to the house on my grandfather's wedding day so he could try to get his girl back!" He looked down into her upturned face, so close to his, and grew serious. "But when a Maxwell marries a woman, he's not going to let her get away."

"I don't want to get away, Elliot."

He smiled down at her. "Our home will be built on the Word of God, Meera, and faith in the One who created this fantastic beauty. Let's always obey that greatest commandment of Jesus. . .to love one another."

She nodded. Then an impish look crossed her face, and she could not contain the sparkle in her eyes. "There's something I've been wanting to do. I've always wanted to stand on the Briskin side of the creek and put my big toe in the Maxwell side. . .without falling down, that is."

A wide grin spread over his face. "And there's something I've wanted to do for the past ten years. Let's go!"

He grabbed her hand and ran with her to the creek, sitting down on the bank to take off their shoes and socks. Meera waded in until the water was up to her knees. Balancing herself, the water flowing around her, she lifted one leg and planted her foot on the other side. Then, lifting her arms in victory, she threw back her head and shouted as the warm sun caressed her face.

Elliot waded in to stand beside her. "How does it feel?"

"Brrr! It's cold!" She shivered. "But exhilarating!" A frown wrinkled her smooth brow. "But. . ."

"But what?" Elliot asked.

"It's not quite the same as when I was a little girl, challenging the Maxwells with a song Louisa and I made up while trembling uncontrollably, pretending it was only because of the cold creek water."

"Well," he said, rubbing his jaw, a strange glitter appearing in his eyes, "*your* childhood dream has at least been realized. You did stick your toe on the Maxwell side of the creek. Now, it's my turn. There's something I need to get off my chest."

"Then do it," she encouraged him.

"All right, I will!" he said and with that he reached out, scooped up the startled Meera in his arms, and deposited her smack dab on the Briskin side of the creek.

Mouth agape, she sat up, the icy water creeping up to her chest, and stared at him.

He moved back and shouted, "I wouldn't dare touch you, Meera Briskin! Not even with a ten-foot pole!"

"Po—le. . .po—le. . .po-le" echoed in the still forest.

Then Meera remembered. "That was. . .*you?*" she shrieked.

"Yoooooo! . . .ooooo. . .ooooo!" bounced back to them from the Maxwell-Briskin Mountains. Their laughter rang through the hills and surrounded them with joy.

She began to scoop up the water and fling it at him, but he didn't back away. Instead, he came closer and dropped down beside her, sitting in the Maxwell side of the creek. Then he pulled her to him, and they sat shivering on the Maxwell-Briskin property line. "Elliot," she said on a quivery breath, "I was wrong in what I said years ago." His look of love encouraged her to continue. "Life doesn't have to consist of feudin,' fussing,' and fightin'. . .to be excitin'."

In acknowledgment, he lowered his dark head to her silvery one and their lips began silently, but profoundly, proving that point, while the laughing waters of the creek flowed around them.

SMOKY
MOUNTAIN
SUNRISE

MOUNTAIN MAN

Mountain man, a rugged man
    Whose frame is lean and leathern
As one who lives with giant hills
    His home is nigh to heaven.

Mountain man, a loyal man
    He loves with depth and feelin'
In pain and sorrow stands like steel
    His faith is strong, revealin'.

Mountain man, a lonely man
    Whose gaze is far, revealin'
His words are few, and smile is slow
    His wisdom is inspirin'.

Mountain man, a learned man
    In nature's realm of schoolin'
His refuge is the One above
    The God of Spirit rulin'.

            —LOUISE BARKER BARNHILL

copyright February, 1960. Used by permission

ACKNOWLEDGMENTS

The setting is Camp Rockmont for Boys,
located in the Blue Ridge Mountains
of Western North Carolina. The camp is awe-inspiring with
its incomparable beauty and panoramic views
and is situated on the site of the former Black Mountain College.

Chapter 1

A ndré's in trouble!"
Rae glanced up startled by Mimi's explosive announcement as the girl rushed into her office and flung herself into the nearest chair.

With another school year behind, Rae had been cleaning out her desk drawers. Now she paused to study the beautiful brunette who gazed at her with soulful, blue eyes. One could never be sure when Mimi Doudet was serious or merely exaggerating.

"Why do you say that, Mimi?" she asked, now stacking papers into a cardboard box.

"I don't really know. . . ." She hesitated, confirming Rae's suspicion that Mimi didn't mean her brother was in *real* trouble.

"Why don't you tell me about it while you help take those books off the shelves. We're not teacher and student now, you know. Just friends."

"Fine friend you are, making me work on a hot day like this!" Despite the protest, Mimi smiled in her winning way and walked over to the bookshelf, lifting her shoulder-length hair from her neck.

"Hottest May day ever recorded by the weather bureau in Atlanta, Georgia!" Rae reported, mimicking the noonday weathercaster. "Now, tell me about your brother."

"He's in Florida."

Rae glanced at her. "That's bad?"

"It's *strange*." Mimi forgot the books and leaned back against the shelf. "Both Uncle Lucas and André had planned to stay in Switzerland for another week. When I told Uncle Lucas that you had invited me to spend this week with you, he was delighted. Now," she spread her hands in frustration, "André has called me from Florida and started asking about you."

"Me?" Rae straightened immediately, surprised. She'd never met André, but she knew Mimi was from a wealthy and close knit family. "Does he make it a habit to check on all your friends?"

Mimi laughed. "André wouldn't check on my friends. But it seems he *does* want to check *you* out!" She shrugged, then the typically mischievous look sparkled in her eyes. "Maybe he's between girls!"

"That's ridiculous, Mimi."

"Not for André," she countered.

"Let's get these things packed." Rae's tone was no-nonsense now. "The sooner it's done, the sooner we can enjoy the air conditioning in the apartment."

With that inviting idea, Mimi returned to her chore with renewed enthusiasm, but she couldn't resist talking about her brother. "At first he asked about you casually; then he got really interested when I told him how terrific you look."

"He wouldn't think so if he saw me today," Rae contradicted, touching her hair that curled into tight ringlets when damp. She could feel the tiny beads of perspiration on her face.

"Anyway, he's coming here," Mimi continued.

"Here? To the university?"

"No, he's going to pick me up at the end of the week at your place. Then we'll drive home to North Carolina together."

"Really, Mimi," Rae said with a sense of exasperation, yet affection for this girl who always twisted things out of proportion. The famous André Doudet was linked with beautiful women from all over the world. He certainly wouldn't be interested in someone he'd never seen. "That explains it. There's no trouble. It's just brotherly love. You don't spend much time together, so this is just a good chance to catch up with you."

Mimi was shaking her head. "He was more interested in you than in me. And André doesn't like to drive. He always flies if possible. Oh, are these the exams we took today?"

"Don't you dare touch those!" Rae warned. "I haven't graded them yet, and when it comes to exams, I'm all teacher, and you're still the student. But you don't have to worry about your grades."

"On the written part I do," Mimi moaned. "Come to think of it, I don't think I could *ever* be as good as you in the gymnastics routines, either."

"The teacher is supposed to excel," Rae chided gently, accepting the compliment.

"I'll bet when you were my age, you were better than I am *now*," Mimi said with admiration.

"I had the best possible teacher," Rae reminded her and caught her breath. They grew quiet, and the only sound was that of books and papers being piled into boxes.

Both women were remembering Rae's teacher, her father, who had died a few months earlier. A famous coach in years past, he had sent several young hopefuls to the Olympics before coming to teach at the university in Atlanta where Rae had been on the faculty for the past three years.

"School's out at last!" Mimi piped suddenly, lifting her arms into the air and dispelling the reflective mood that had momentarily settled upon them.

Rae smiled, remembering the years she had uttered those words as a student, then as a teacher. But it was different this year. An entire summer without her father was not appealing. It would be lonely. Her spirits lifted as she remembered that Mimi would be with her for a week. And that week would be climaxed by a visit from André. It wasn't often one had a chance to meet an accomplished athlete like André Doudet.

"Looks like everything's packed," Rae said after taking a quick look around the office.

As they lugged boxes through the gym, Rae's mind replayed the physical education classes she taught there. Her favorite this year had been *gymnastics moderne*, in which she had had an opportunity to exhibit her extraordinary skills along with her instruction.

After driving the few blocks to the apartment house and unloading the boxes, they collapsed into chairs, enjoying the refreshing effect of the air conditioning.

"As soon as we cool off," Mimi said, wiggling the toes of one foot propped on a box of books, "you and I are going to have a great week—seeing everything in Atlanta and doing all there is to do!"

Rae laughed. She didn't doubt that. With her own fair hair and green eyes, she knew that she and Mimi differed in more than physical appearance. In lifestyles and temperament, too, they were exact opposites. Mimi was a fun-loving extrovert with the tendency to laugh at life rather than take it seriously. Yet, Rae knew Mimi had depth that rarely surfaced. Rae's faith in God had given her strength to face life with courage after her father's death. But it had been Mimi, herself an orphan, who came offering friendship during a difficult time.

As promised, the week was filled with fun and laughter, then ended all too quickly. Rae had become increasingly excited about André's arrival, for Mimi had proudly pointed him out in numerous sports magazines. "That's André at Uncle Lucas's ski resort in Switzerland." Another pictured the smiling athlete poised on the slopes of a similar resort in North Carolina. He was on the cover of still another, having won the national tennis competition that year.

The only thing that marred Rae's excitement at the prospect of meeting André was the fact that he would take Mimi back to North Carolina, and she would be left to face the reality of her loneliness and to make a difficult decision about her future.

Rae kept telling herself that Mimi was mistaken about her brother's desire to meet her for any particular reason. After all, they were strangers.

Nevertheless, on the day of his arrival, she decided to wear one of her prettier summer dresses. She had tamed her naturally curly hair with hot rollers, brushing it away from her face on one side and allowing it to fall in a soft wave on the other. The long-on-top, short-in-back style was ideal for one so active and complemented the color her father had often referred to as "spun gold."

Expectantly Rae watched from the porch of the modest, white frame apartment house. Mimi ran down the front walk to embrace her brother who was exiting from a low-slung, bright yellow sports car. Towering over his sister, his brown hair gleamed in the sunlight. He was wearing casual slacks and a short-sleeved shirt, but Rae could visualize him in tennis and ski wear, stepping from the pages of sports magazines she and Mimi had devoured.

Now this perfect specimen of masculinity was walking toward Rae, flashing the dazzling smile that had the power to charm, even from the glossy pages of sports magazines.

Her green eyes met his twinkling brown ones as Mimi introduced them.

"Call me Andy. Most of my American friends do," he invited, extending his hand. "And tell me why a gorgeous girl like you is named Ray?"

Rae laughed, having heard that question hundreds of times before. "It's Rae with an *e*," she explained.

"I suspected something like that," Andy teased. "You should have told me about her sooner, Mimi. You know blonds with green eyes are my weakness, especially those with freckles sprinkled across an adorable nose."

"How would I know where to find you?" Mimi quipped, her long hair falling below her shoulders as she turned her face toward his. "Last month it was Paris and Switzerland. Then last week it was Florida. Now, you're here!" Mischief played in her eyes. "What attracted you to Atlanta, André? Was it the red clay or the Georgia peaches?"

Rae felt that Andy's laughter was a polite recognition of his sister's double entendre, for his glance slid away from her. Sensing his uneasiness, she recalled Mimi's premonition that he was in trouble.

"Shall we go inside?" Rae invited, holding open the screen door.

"I made your favorite drink," Mimi said as she and Andy followed Rae into the kitchen.

"Sounds like lemonade," he said, smiling down at Mimi before pulling out a chair and taking a seat at the small, round table. "It's nice of you to ask Mimi to stay with you this week, Rae."

"It was my pleasure," Rae assured him. "Mimi and I have become close friends since my father died."

"Your father was Raymond Martin," Andy said, his eyes lighting with sudden realization. "I didn't make the connection when we were introduced."

Anyone seriously involved in sports knew the name. In addition to his coaching, Raymond Martin had helped to make the gymnastics program at the Atlanta university one of the finest in the nation.

"I'm sorry to hear about it," Andy continued softly. "The sports world has lost a great man. Mimi and I know about that kind of loss. Our parents died when we were quite young. But there was always Uncle Lucas and Gran. Do you have relatives?"

"No, and I think that makes losses easier to bear. But I try to think not so much of what I've lost, but of what my father has gained. My mother died ten years ago. At least now I have the consolation that they're together again —in heaven."

Rae spurned the grief that threatened to overwhelm her. Feeling Andy's intense gaze, she was grateful when Mimi brought the glasses filled with lemonade.

"Is Uncle Lucas back home?" she asked

Andy shook his head. "He won't be for a couple of days yet. We'll get home before he does, even by car." He tasted the frosty beverage and nodded appreciatively. "Good lemonade."

"Nothing's too good for my big brother who loves me so much he wants to drive me all the way from Georgia to North Carolina." Mimi replied with exaggerated playfulness, cutting her eyes toward Andy.

"Well, there is another reason, Mimi—something I must discuss with you." He seemed uncertain whether to continue as he poked absently at a lemon slice. "As you know I had to make a trip to Florida. That's where I picked up that little gem out there."

Rae assumed he meant the car.

"Okay, what's her name?" Mimi asked, amusement coloring the inflection of her voice.

Andy's look of chagrin confirmed his sister's assumption that a female was involved. "We have a long drive ahead of us, Mimi. We'll talk about it later." He turned his handsome face and charming smile in Rae's direction. "Right now, I'd much rather talk about your friend here."

Mimi tugged at his shirt sleeve. "You know I have no patience, André! Besides, Rae doesn't mind. We've shared many personal things."

"I couldn't burden her with this one," Andy said, but Rae had the distinct feeling he wanted to talk about it, and her curiosity was aroused.

"It wouldn't be a burden, Andy," she assured him. "If you want to talk about it, I'm a good listener."

With a sigh Andy leaned forward, propping his elbows on the table.

"There *is* a girl," he admitted. "Celeste imagines herself in love with me. Her parents wrote to Uncle Lucas, mentioning wedding plans. I was shocked when he confronted me with that news, so I had to go to Florida to see Celeste. I think I've convinced her to make a clean break, but I don't know. . . ."

Mimi shrugged, "Oh, André, you've been in worse situations. What about. . ."

Interrupting, Andy shook his head. "This is different. Uncle Lucas feels I haven't been honest with Celeste. That I haven't made my intentions clear from the beginning. He doesn't like her parents' getting into it, and he even mentioned the possibility of a breach of promise suit."

"Can't you explain to your uncle that you made a mistake, Andy?" Rae asked. "Tell him Celeste misunderstood your intentions?"

"He doesn't take such things lightly, I'm afraid," Andy assured her.

"Sounds like a happily married man who enjoys matchmaking," concluded Rae.

"No, he's a bachelor and vows to stay that way. It's just that he strongly believes in being responsible for one's commitments."

"He doesn't like women?"

The quick note of ironic laughter shared by Mimi and Andy dispelled that notion from Rae's mind.

"He likes women just fine. The problem is," Andy paused, looking sheepish, "that this is not the first time something like this has happened."

"You *have* left a string of broken hearts around the world," Mimi scolded affectionately.

"It hasn't been all one-sided, Mimi," he protested. "But that's the way Uncle Lucas is beginning to see it. He says there have been too many indications that I'm not being honest in my relationships."

"Why doesn't your uncle let the two of you work out your own problems?"

Andy shook his head. "Celeste's parents involved him when they wrote to him, and he feels responsible since he's my guardian. Besides, it hasn't been easy working things out with Celeste. You know how it is when a woman believes she's in love and wants to get married."

Rae lowered her eyes to her glass. No, she didn't know. She had had a few casual dates, a few kisses, but nothing that threatened to disturb her placid existence. In her twenty-five years she had been content to bask in her father's love and to devote herself to making her parents' last days as joyous and meaningful as possible. Now that they were gone, her world revolved around her work. She now felt happiest, most fulfilled, on the balance beam, the floor mat, and the parallel bars. Here she could be herself—expressing her innermost feelings within the rigid constraints of the sport.

"Celeste wanted to bring her parents to our home to meet Lucas," Andy was saying. "That would be disastrous for a girl like that. She would take one look at the place and believe herself even more deeply in love. You can't imagine what that girl has cost me in clothes and jewelry." He took a deep breath. "Now we have matching cars."

Noting the shocked expressions on the girls' faces, Andy looked from one to the other. "It was *her* idea," he said helplessly.

"André, didn't you tell her you were through with her?" Mimi almost shrieked. Rae, though silent, found the idea equally incredible.

"Yes, but Celeste is not the kind of girl one drops suddenly. You've heard the proverb about a woman's wrath? No, this will have to be done carefully and discreetly."

"Well, if Uncle Lucas plans to invite them to the house, what hope is there?" Mimi's voice sounded despairing. "He'll insist you marry her."

Andy traced a pattern on the tabletop. "I lied to Uncle Lucas."

"Oh, André," Mimi moaned. She reached over to take his hand and his fingers tightened around hers. His expression was more that of a remorseful little boy than a grown man of twenty-six. "What did you tell him, André?"

"The only thing that would make any difference. I told him I had been wrong about Celeste and was going to Florida to make her understand. Then I said I couldn't marry Celeste because," Andy paused, cleared his throat, then continued in a desolate tone, "because I had fallen in love with the perfect girl, the kind he always wanted for me. A nice, Christian girl!"

Mimi looked delighted. "Oh, André, have you?"

"No," he admitted, shaking his head. "I haven't exactly been looking for that kind of girl, I'm afraid."

The three sat in silence, staring at cold lemon slices resting on ice. Rae knew only that Mimi's older brother had graduated from a university in Switzerland and helped to manage his uncle's ski resort there when he wasn't playing in tennis tournaments all over the world. He had probably earned his playboy reputation, she thought.

She could well understand how females would be attracted to André. Physically and materially, he had much to offer. But from this brief encounter, she suspected he lacked the spiritual qualities that would make a long-term relationship possible. He needed guidance but seemed instead to be manipulated by what she supposed was a domineering uncle.

Mimi's concerned voice broke through the wall of silence. "Did Uncle Lucas believe you when you told him you had fallen in love with a Christian girl, André?"

Had it not been such a serious matter, Rae would have laughed at the scowl on Andy's face as he imitated his uncle in a booming voice, " 'Fantastic Andy! She must really be some girl if you're thinking of settling down. Go to Florida. Clear up this misunderstanding with that young woman and her parents. Then bring your perfect girl home. I want to meet her. Within the week! Otherwise, I'll have to take drastic measures which includes cutting your allowance'."

"You see," Andy explained to Rae, "I don't come into my inheritance until I'm twenty-eight." He looked helplessly at the two women. "Then he told me if I didn't bring my fiancée to North Carolina, he was going to do what he should have done in the first place and invite Celeste and her parents to our home." Andy grimaced. "If he finds out I lied on top of everything else, I'm doomed! My only chance is to come up with a girl Uncle Lucas would approve—a nice, Christian girl."

"Oh, André," Mimi sighed in exasperation, but love for her brother glowed in her eyes. "How do you manage to get mixed up in such scrapes?"

Their laughter was tinged with irony. Mimi had already confided to Rae some of the childish pranks she and Andy had instigated while growing up, which included extravagant shopping sprees. Remembering her years at the university, Rae suspected, too, that the lively girl had left her share of broken hearts behind.

The laughter subsided as they sat trying to think of a solution. Rae traced a design through the moisture collecting on her glass, while the silence grew increasingly uncomfortable. When she looked up, Andy and Mimi were staring at her with a peculiar gleam in their eyes. Almost simultaneously, they broke into triumphant grins.

Rae swallowed hard. A strange sensation crept over her. *Heavens, what must they be thinking?*

"More lemonade?" she asked in a strained voice. They shook their heads. Rae rose from the table, gathered the glasses, and took them to the sink. Looking out the window at the backyard, she noticed the brilliance of the sunshine bathing the new growth of the leafy trees. Twin maples. After his first heart attack, her father had spent much time under the shade of those trees.

Rae returned to the table, aware that Mimi and Andy were watching her every move. Under their scrutiny, her fair complexion was fast becoming a scarlet flush. Finally she sank into the chair, shaking her head.

"Rae." The confidence in Andy's voice indicated he had found the answer to his dilemma. In spite of the physical differences between brother and sister, there was definitely a family resemblance. Now it was one of sinister determination.

"Oh, no!" she cried in dismay, their incredible scheme suddenly transparent.

"Oh, come on, Rae! You could do it. You could pretend to be André's fiancée. And we wouldn't have to pretend about your being a Christian." She turned to address Andy, "Rae and her father headed up the Christian Athletes Club on campus."

"I'm impressed," he said. "As Uncle Lucas would be." He leaned across the table and took Rae's hand in his. His voice was low and persuasive. "Would it be so unthinkable to be engaged to me for a short while, Rae?"

"Andy, it wouldn't work." She was adamant. "Just tell your uncle how you feel."

"You don't know my uncle!" he replied, as if such an admission were out of the question.

Rae could agree with that statement. She *didn't* know Lucas. Mimi had made frequent references to him in their late-night talks. She knew that he acted as guardian and provider to his wards, but he had remained a distant parent figure in Rae's mind. One she found rather foreboding, now that she thought of it.

"I'm sorry, Andy," she said. "I wish I could help. I really do. But it just isn't possible."

"Well," André sighed. "At least I *thought* I had found the solution. *Do* you have plans for the summer, Rae?" he asked, apparently dismissing his scheme.

Rae withdrew her hands from Andy's. Studying one pale pink-tipped nail, she thought about his question. She had not signed the contract to return to her position at the university in the fall. The administration and faculty had been more than understanding and sympathetic throughout her father's illness and death, assuring her that the position would remain open indefinitely. Now, she felt, a complete change was in order. But she hadn't yet decided what that would be.

Rae looked around the kitchen of the cozy apartment. She and her father had moved here over two years ago when they sold the house. They had been fortunate to find a rental so near the campus. Now that she was entirely on her own she had wondered if she should renew her lease at the end of the month or go away for an extended vacation to think about her future.

"I'm not sure, Andy," she admitted finally. "I've considered a vacation. I may even try to find a summer job. A change of scenery might be good for me."

"A job?" Andy's eyes lit up. "I have the perfect job. And for a teacher of gymnastics, who is also the daughter of Raymond Martin, it would probably *seem* like a vacation. Our summer camp for young athletes opens up in June."

"André, how ideal!" Mimi said, her eyes bright. "You should see Rae when she's teaching. She's *magnifique!* Everyone loves her, but she commands respect, too. And she makes us believe in ourselves—that we can do anything we set out to do. She could head up the gymnastics program. She's equally good in swimming and. . ."

"Wait a minute," Rae protested. "You don't know if your uncle would approve of me as an employee, even for the summer. The job sounds challenging, but I just don't know. . ."

"I understand," Andy said finally, a look of resignation settling on his face. "There's a special guy here. There would be for girl as attractive as you."

Rae recognized his ploy, tried to keep the blush from her face, but knew she was unsuccessful. "No, there's no one special."

A strange silence followed. Then, without taking his eyes from Rae's face, Andy addressed Mimi. "You know, Mimi, I believe Rae is the kind of girl Lucas has in mind for me. He thinks my friends are too flashy, too worldly, too caught up in materialism. Rae is sensible, sweet, and probably the most honest person I've ever met—not to mention the most beautiful."

"Flattery will get you nowhere," Rae said quietly, quite afraid she was in error. She wished she had thought of something more original than an old cliché.

"I'm not trying to flatter you. Rae; I'm even beginning to understand your viewpoint. We aren't exactly infidels, Mimi and I, although we probably appear that way to you. I can see that it would be against your principles to pretend an engagement." He leaned forward. "Tell you what—I won't ask you to do that. Just come with us to North Carolina and consider taking that summer job. Be my special girl for the next few weeks. Perhaps you don't find that idea too unpleasant."

"It's not unpleasant at all, Andy," she assured him. "I'd love the job, but. . ."

"But you can't accept the offer?"

"Oh, Andy, not under the circumstances."

"Don't you like me a little, Rae?"

"I barely know you."

"Don't be difficult, Rae," Mimi pled.

Rae knew there was no way these two impetuous siblings could understand her reluctance. But sensible people just don't do things like that.

"All right," Andy said with resignation. "I won't ask you to pretend anything. Just let me tell Uncle Lucas that you're my girl, from my point of view. Is it so unthinkable that I could take you seriously? And is it so impossible that you might consider really being my girl?"

"Well, no," Rae admitted, "as long as I don't have to pretend a relationship that isn't there." She gasped to realize how close she was to agreeing to Andy's scheme. Being André Doudet's special girl did have its appeal, even to a sensible girl like her. She quickly reminded herself that Andy wasn't really taking her seriously but needed a girl in a hurry to get him out of a jam. If she remembered that, she could guard against ending the summer with a broken heart.

A change of scenery would be good for her, and could provide the opportunity for the serious thinking she had to do. She was well aware that her funds were not unlimited, and she must soon decide what direction her life should take.

Yes, there seemed to be so many reasons why she shouldn't accept his offer. *Mimi will be in Paris during the summer,* Rae remembered.

"I would be a stranger there."

Andy shrugged. "There will be plenty of people around. Our summers are very busy. And I promise you won't be lonely."

"Your uncle must be"—she stifled the urge to say, "an old tyrant," and substituted—"very strict."

"As I mentioned, without Uncle Lucas, there's no allowance." Andy explained. "He holds the purse strings."

"And the purse," Mimi added, laughing.

Andy grinned. "True. Until we're married or twenty-eight—whichever comes first. And for me, twenty-eight is a few years away yet."

"But, Andy," Rae persisted, "I might not meet your uncle's requirements. I'm really a very ordinary, uninteresting person."

Andy looked amused. "And you are well-trained in gymnastics—an excellent reason why he would hire you!" Then he leaned closer. "But if he doesn't give us his blessing, I'll marry you anyway!"

"Oh, Andy," she laughed helplessly. At least the summer promised to be anything but dull.

Chapter 2

The low, sleek sports car sped around the mountainsides like a small yellow bird, flitting from treetop to treetop before eventually nestling in the heart of the Blue Ridge Mountains.

Around every bend of the Parkway was another scenic delight—deep, emerald valleys; rocky ravines slashed with crystal waterfalls; tangled thickets of flowering shrubs carpeting the forest floor on either side of the highway. The retreating sun flung visual blockades as subdued peaks of blue and green were thrust against a graying sky. Wide-open landscapes, endless highways, and skyscrapers had given way to a world of almost primeval splendor, and Rae wished the sun would linger so she could drink in the beauty of this paradise.

"It's incredibly beautiful," she whispered reverently.

Andy reached across the front seat of the car and squeezed her hand. "This part of the country compares favorably with any spot in the world," he said. "At times I take it for granted, but you have a way of making me appreciate things, Rae. As if seeing them for the first time." Giving Rae's hand a final squeeze, Andy turned his attention to the serpentine curve ahead.

Rae had not felt comfortable with his one-handed driving, yet felt sure her apprehension was due to her own lack of familiarity with the mountains, for he maneuvered the car expertly, even in the fast-approaching darkness of night.

Turning her face toward the window, Rae concentrated on the fascinating world opening up before her. The closer they came to their destination, the more intrigued she became. There was a sweet fragrance she could not identify, and the pungent odor of pine.

Soon Andy turned off the main road onto a paved, private one. The car began its curving ascent as it wound higher through trees that joined limbs in a conspiracy against the moonlight.

"It's like a jungle," Rae said in wonder.

"The only place in the world where there is a greater variety of trees is in China," Andy informed her. "Around this next curve you will find our haven from this crazy, chaotic world."

After the turn, both sides of the road were flanked by rustic, split-rail fences. Orange trumpets on long, green throats swayed and bent, heralding their coming. Suddenly, like a mirage, the great stone structure appeared.

Mellow light gleamed from windows, and floodlights illuminated the landscape. Rather than dominating, the two-story structure blended majestically with its surroundings. Circular wings did not distract, but conformed to the natural undulations of the land. Behind the mansion rose an even higher peak, darkened by the night, as if it were some strange sleeping beauty.

Rae could not begin to comprehend what the scenery must look like in bright sunlight, for, even now, shadowed by darkness and lightly bathed with artificial light, the colorful array of springtime was much in evidence. Even her brief glimpse provided the spectacular picture of the fragile among the stately, the delicate in the midst of strength. There were dark evergreens; leafy maples; yellow-green poplars; pink and white dogwood blossoms; and bushes laden with purple, red, pink, yellow, and white flowers.

At the beginning of a long, sweeping drive was a rustic wooden sign with the words *Mountain Haven* carved into it.

"That's Lucas's name for the house," Andy explained.

It was a place like none Rae had ever seen. The stone mansion with its great expanse of glass windows seemed to draw nature into itself, and at the same time the shingled roof appeared to touch the sky.

Andy didn't turn into the drive bordered by natural rock and lush greenery, which circled in front of the house, but drove onto a secondary gravel drive, around a stone wing, then came to a stop beneath a redwood roof.

As soon as they stepped from the car, Rae was bombarded with a sweet fragrance. "Strawberries!" she exclaimed, inhaling deeply.

Mimi laughed and pointed to a row of bushes along the stone wall. "That's calycanthus," she explained, "more commonly called 'Carolina allspice'."

Rae walked over to them. The blossoms looked like rust-colored wooden flowers. When she touched them, they felt like wood, but when she sniffed, they smelled nothing like wood.

Each taking bags, they climbed the redwood steps alongside the stone wall leading to a high deck at the back of the house.

"It must be something in the air," Rae said incredulously. "Tell me flowers don't look like wood, and rocks don't shine."

"Wrong, wrong," Mimi corrected. "There is mica in the rock, and when the light strikes just right, it *does* shine. These stones were hewn out of our own area mountains."

Rae stood on the deck for a moment, marveling at the sounds of nature, almost deafening in the absence of car horns, train whistles, and airplane engines.

Andy took their luggage upstairs while Rae and Mimi whipped up a quick snack, which they ate at the kitchen table. After the snack, Mimi checked the lounge for mail, leaving Rae and Andy to tidy up.

As they worked, Rae thought of the past two days and Andy's helpfulness with arrangements she had had to make before leaving Atlanta. Their close proximity during the drive had provided an insight into his personality. His interesting conversation had been flavored with humor and intelligence as he related experiences associated with his many travels. She was growing to *like* this roguish charmer.

Her parents' illnesses had occupied her time and thoughts during recent years, so Rae had not seriously considered a life's mate. But in the back of her mind was the assumption that the man of her dreams would be both a Christian and an athlete. Andy certainly fulfilled one of those requirements. And the other was partly her responsibility in this world: to set an example for unbelievers. Yes, with a faith in God to put his priorities in the right order, Andy could become the kind of man a Christian girl could consider seriously.

Their fingers touched as they reached for the same dish. Andy grabbed her hand and lifted it to his lips just as Mimi came in from the lounge, carrying a bundle of letters.

She held an envelope toward the light. "Wonder what Isobel has to say." she mused.

"Better not snoop in Uncle Lucas's mail, Mimi." Andy reprimanded her, and Rae wondered if his irritation was caused by Mimi's interruption or by the letter.

"Who is Isobel?" she asked curiously.

"Very likely the future mistress of this house—if she has her way," Andy explained. "She's a widow with a young son who very much needs a father. So she has set her cap for my uncle."

"You really think they'll marry?" Mimi asked. She didn't appear happy about that.

Andy sighed, as if resigned to the situation. "They've been seeing each other for quite awhile now. Wouldn't be surprised."

Mimi nodded in acquiescence, shuffled through the letters, gave Andy his mail, then returned to the lounge with the other letters.

"We should say good night, Rae. Tomorrow's a big day."

She knew he was referring to the fact that tomorrow she was to meet his Uncle Lucas.

His face grew pensive. "It's not going to be so bad, is it Rae?"

Although she hadn't yet absorbed her new surroundings, Rae was looking forward to working in a mountain setting. And she believed Andy needed her as a buffer against his uncle. But there was something else to consider.

"Much depends on what your uncle thinks of me, Andy," she reminded him.

His hand touched her shoulder, and he spoke reassuringly. "He'll like you, Rae. Any man would. But the important thing is that he believes I want to marry you."

Rae sighed. "The burden's on you then, Andy. I'm only supposed to be thinking over our relationship."

His smile was warm. "I don't think it's going to be at all difficult." He leaned close to whisper. "I suspect we've already convinced my sister."

Rae turned her head in time to see Mimi step quickly back inside the lounge doorway. She looked up curiously at Andy, but he only grinned and said, "Good night, Rae. And thanks for everything."

Mimi rejoined Rae only after Andy had gone upstairs and closed the door to his bedroom. Approaching Rae, she shook her head. "André surprised me tonight," she said. "He's treating you like someone very special."

Rae laughed it away. "Mimi, you're imagining things. Your brother's just being polite and charming. It seems to be part of his nature."

"It is. But I know André. He doesn't seem to be acting." She stopped on the stairs, her lovely eyes aglow. "You and André! Rae, that would please me so much."

"Don't be silly, Mimi. Andy isn't looking for a girl like me."

"And why not?" Mimi asked.

"Different backgrounds. He's rich, I'm poor. He's internationally known, I'm relatively unknown. He's. . ."

Interrupting, Mimi stopped on the stairs, her hands on her hips. "That sounds like you think we're terrible snobs. And I sincerely hope you aren't calling me a snob, because if you are, I'll challenge you to a duel of—of racquetball."

"You know you always beat me at racquetball."

"That's why I chose it!" Mimi laughed, and they walked up the stairs arm in arm.

❧

In spite of her exhaustion, Rae couldn't sleep.

The cool mountain air, moist and misty, drifted in through the open bedroom window, stirring the curtains. Outside, the shadowy hulk of the mountains spoke of permanence and endurance. She was glad she had come. But there was something mysterious and compelling out there in the night that beckoned to her on air heavily scented with the perfume of a thousand unknown blossoms.

Tossing the coverlet aside, she rose and put on her robe, tying the sash around her tiny waist. The flimsy garment was designed for comfort on hot, city nights, she realized too late. Glimpsing her reflection in the mirror, she shrugged. *No one will see me,* she reassured herself.

Quietly she closed the bedroom door. Her slippers made no sound on the carpet in the upstairs hallway. Following the light from the lamp that had been left on, Rae made her way down the stairs, looking up momentarily at the exposed beams of the cathedral ceilings

This is no mountain cabin, she thought. She reveled in the aesthetic blend of log and hardwood and beam that carried the hallmark of a sensitive designer, just as the out-of-doors bore its Creator's mark.

Leaving the back door ajar, Rae stepped out into the night. She crossed the redwood deck, walked down the steps to the second deck and on out to a third that was completely surrounded by a veritable jungle.

Inhaling deeply, she savored the wonderful, musty fragrance of earth and trees and wild, growing things. Somewhere a gurgling stream made its noisy way down the mountainside. Insects sounded a symphony, and night birds called to their mates. Everything here was so wild, so untamed, so free, and she responded with a sense of exhilaration she had never felt before.

Lifting her face to the cooling breeze, her eyes were met by the sight of lush foliage—the intertwining branches of the trees so dense that only slivers of moonlight penetrated to splash on her face and hair, turning it to gold.

She wasn't sure how long she stood there, listening to the night music, absorbing the peace, before she heard footsteps. They were heavy, swift, hesitating only momentarily to locate her. She did not turn to look. It would be Andy. He wouldn't be able to sleep, either.

Her eyes were closed when his arms slid around her waist, and she did not open them when he turned her toward him, but lifted her face willingly. His lips met hers with a thoroughness that surprised her.

She had expected, would have welcomed, a sweet, gentle kiss. But the intensity of this encounter shook her. Feeling his strong hands gripping her arms, Rae gasped and pushed herself away.

"You're not. . .Andy!" she whispered.

"No," he said in a bemused voice, still holding her in a tight embrace, his eyes slowly sweeping her face, the wide, frightened eyes, the soft, parted lips. "And you're not Isobel."

Rae shook her head, unable to look away.

"You a friend of Andy's?" he asked, his eyes lingering on her face.

Rae nodded. There was no mistaking who *he* was. And he was nothing like she had imagined. There was no way she could call this man "uncle."

"You must think me impulsive—kissing you like that," he murmured, a smile tilting the corners of his mouth.

The man reminded Rae of the unknown that had so intrigued her about the night—fascinating, wild, and untamed. His shirt sleeves were rolled up and the neck of his dress shirt was open, as if he had recently discarded a tie.

"Yes," she said finally, "I–I thought you were Andy." It occurred to her that not only was she surrounded by beauty in this place, but there were things out there in the night to be wary of—like bears and snakes and who knew what else?

"Forgive me," he breathed. "I didn't mean to frighten you." And he released her, somewhat reluctantly it seemed.

Still, his very nearness was disturbing. Something about him was like the unknown wilderness beyond the safety of the railing—compelling, deep and mysterious, captivating. And something deep within her stirred, reaching upward toward the light and warmth, like some fragile forest flower.

She was aware that she was part of something greater—and that things could never be quite the same again.

Sensing her discomfort, he moved away, putting a respectable distance between them.

"What is your name?" he asked.

"Ramona," she whispered, looking up into his eyes, amazed to discover that the sensation was the same as when she had first glimpsed the mountains. There was majesty here, power, and unspoken challenge. "I–I mean Rae." she corrected herself, using the familiar nickname with which she had been tagged ever since the day she had begun toddling after her father, imitating everything he did.

The man's voice was soft, melodious, flowing over her wounded spirit like a spring rain. "Ramona," he echoed her given name.

The sound of it restored her to reality. No one ever used that name—except her father.

The man reached out to wipe away the tear that trickled down her cheek. "And now I've made you cry? Why?"

Rae didn't know how to tell him that she didn't understand her own behavior, didn't know why her emotions were suddenly as unpredictable and precarious as the mountain roads. Perhaps it was his gesture that had moved her so. It was such a gentle touching—like the soft, sweet caress of the night mist.

Turning from him, Rae stepped into the shadows. "It's just that no one ever called me Ramona but my father. . .and he died recently."

"Do you mind if *I* call you Ramona?" he asked kindly.

"No," she shook her head, and found that she didn't. Rather than feeling a stab of loss, it brought a flood of warm memory, and she turned her face toward him again with a faint smile. He did not smile back but gazed at her in a strange way that she could not fathom.

"Have—have we met before?" she asked, some vague impression forming in the back of her mind.

"That's not a very original line," he said in an abrupt change of mood, taking a step nearer. "Now," he said, reaching out his finger to trace a pattern down her nose and around her soft, parted lips that trembled beneath his touch. "Wherever did Andy find you? Tell me what acting school you're from, or how much Andy paid you for this little job, and I'll repay him. Then you and I can get on with more pleasurable things."

The insinuation in Lucas's tone began to penetrate Rae's consciousness. Was he intimating she was like some of the women in Andy's past? But what else could he think? She had even admitted she thought he was Andy—as if she were there on the deck waiting for him.

Suddenly aware of her attire, she grasped her robe closed in front, then turned and fled across the decks as if some wild beast were in pursuit.

Breathless, she slammed the door of her bedroom harder than she intended, and, without turning on the light, went to the window that overlooked the area she had just left. The dark figure stepped into the light and looked up, as if knowing where she would be. She moved out of sight and sank on the edge of the bed, taking in great gulps of air. How could she ever face the man again and behave normally? Or more to the point, would she ever *be* normal again?

After taking off her robe in the darkness, Rae climbed beneath the covers that Mimi had insisted would be needed. "The nights are quite cool here," she had said.

Rae shivered in spite of the down coverlet. She could not dismiss the tangled emotions she had felt with that mountain of a man. No one had ever evoked such a response in her. In those brief moments he had touched something deep within her that she hadn't known existed. Then he had casually dismissed the moment with his accusations. But what could he think of a girl who not only allowed him to kiss her, but responded to it like that? After all, they were strangers. He was the loathsome Uncle Lucas, who in an instant could cut off Andy's allowance, force his marriage to Celeste, and send her packing!

She tried to rationalize. Perhaps it was because of the loss of her father that she had responded to a man's arms around her. Maybe it was the need to feel cherished and safe. *No*, she whispered into the darkness. It was not her father's touch she needed.

She faced the window, looking out past the billowing curtains, breathing in the misty, cool air. The stars were huge, almost as if she could reach out and touch them. Everything here seemed larger than life.

Tossing restlessly, she knew sleep would not come. Hers had been troubled nights since her father had become ill many months ago. She had simply accustomed herself to dreamlike snatches of sleep. There would be none at all tonight, it seemed, but perhaps she could will her body to relax. *Inhale. Hold for a count of ten. Slowly release the breath, allowing tension to drain away. Inhale. . .* It was a technique she had used before gymnastic competition. It always worked. Tonight it wasn't working at all.

She thought of Andy. He resembled his Uncle Lucas. Maybe that's why Lucas had seemed so familiar. Even Andy's voice held a quality that might someday mellow into the same resonant tones as his uncle's voice. But Andy's eyes were not as dark, nor was his hair, nor was his skin. Andy wasn't as tall, nor his shoulders as broad, nor his body as muscular, nor his grip as firm.

"Oh, no," Rae breathed, as if in prayer. "I know what it is now. Andy is like a shadow compared to his uncle." She liked Andy. In fact, she more than liked Andy. His masculinity, his charm, his good looks, his youthful vulnerability appealed to her, and she had even looked forward to getting better acquainted.

Now she knew that Andy, in comparison with Lucas, was but a reasonable facsimile. Andy was a hill that could be conquered; but this man was a mountain too steep to scale. He was rocks and cliffs and sheer drop-offs and ledges.

Exhausted, Rae lay with her eyes closed, and, though she did not sleep, she did not open them again until the early morning hours.

⮾

Rae was instantly aware of a difference in the atmosphere. Getting up, she pushed the curtains aside. She had expected to see a spectacular view of mountains and trees and valleys beyond. But she could see nothing through the dense fog.

Opening a suitcase, she pulled out a pair of shorts and a long-sleeved shirt and dressed hurriedly. Brushing through her hair, she left the room, retracing her steps of the early morning.

The patter of her tennis shoes stopped abruptly when she neared the back door. He was there, with his back turned to her. The mist seemed to be swirling about him, threatening to invade the house. He had changed into jeans and a plaid shirt.

"Don't you ever sleep?" he asked, without turning around. She wondered how he knew it was she. But Andy would have spoken. And Mimi would have called a cheery greeting and rushed forward to embrace him.

Rae took a deep breath before answering. "I have slept very little since my father died several months ago."

"You'll find this place to be very conducive to rest." He paused, as if wondering how long she planned to be a house guest. "Are there relatives?"

"No. No one. Oh, friends, of course. . ."

"Like Andy."

"And Mimi," she added.

He turned toward her, and in the early light of day his face astonished her. It was as handsome, rugged, commanding, frightening as she had remembered, and she caught her breath.

His eyes swept over her trim, perfect figure. She was accustomed to admiring glances. but this appraisal seemed different, as if evaluating, perhaps deciding if she were a suitable friend for his niece and nephew. And after their first meeting, how could he think so?

He took a step forward, and Rae abruptly moved back.

"You're afraid of me," he said incredulously. "Aren't you? Did I cause that? Or have you been told that I'm some kind of ogre? Or, is this some kind of act?"

"I'm not an actress," she answered truthfully.

"If you belong to Andy, I shall give you no reason whatsoever to be fearful of me. If Andy is serious about you, then I will not attempt to interfere with that. That's how it is."

His words held the ring of truth, and Rae felt a terrible longing that nothing could be done about. This morning she had experienced the first real kiss of her life, and he seemed to be saying, "Forget it, it won't happen again."

Before she could speak, he was asking if she would like coffee.

"I was going to run," she said.

"Again?" he teased, and a grin played about his lips.

She knew that he was making a joke about her having run from him on the deck during the early morning. But she could not help but respond with a smile, seeing a strange, warm glow in his eyes. It crossed her mind that it might be wise to run from him now. He reached for her hand, and she did not move away.

"You'll need a guide," he said, leading her out onto the deck where they became enveloped by a velvet fog. Soon they fell into step on a pathway. "The fog is a precarious thing. It may have obscured the entire mountain range for miles, yet we can walk through it for ten feet and find the sun shining through."

Rae's eyes brightened at the prospect. "I've never experienced anything like the feeling the mountains give me." she said. "And I've seen so little of them. I can hardly wait to see more."

Just at that moment Rae stepped on a twig and tripped. Instantly Lucas's strong arm was encircling her waist, preventing her from stumbling and falling. With his arm around her, she felt completely safe, and she proceeded with confidence.

Maybe it was her lack of sleep, Rae surmised, or maybe it was the mist that rendered the world so dreamlike, so lovely, so different from anything she had ever seen before. The scene was like a lady dressed in all her finery, with the fragrance of perfume to complete the effect.

Just as Lucas had promised, there were spots on the climb where the fog had dissipated, and rays of golden sun peeked through leafy branches. A light breeze stirred tender, young leaves. Moisture lay heavy on the pink blossoms of rhododendron, azaleas, and mountain laurel.

Stopping at a stream, they scooped up handfuls of cold, clear liquid and drank laughingly, wiping the drops from their mouths. Then Rae followed him to higher ground until, finally, he stopped on a rocky ledge. The fog lay below them, obscuring whatever lay in the valley that stretched on forever before rising to another peak, and yet another.

"Does it never end?" she asked in wonder.

Lucas laughed lightly, enjoying her discovery. "It's different each time you see it. Here," he said, reaching for her hand, "front-row seats."

She climbed down onto the ledge which provided not only a seat but a back on which to lean.

The sun was turning her hair to gold, making a halo of dampness that had transformed the soft wave to little tendrils of natural curl.

"I'm accustomed to vigorous exercise and running every morning," Rae defended her heavy breathing, "but I haven't been in top shape since. . .for several months. And this is different." She gestured toward the valley. "The air here seems thinner, cleaner. It takes my breath away."

As if knowing instinctively what she was thinking, he said quietly. "You've had no one to comfort you since your mother died."

Rae bit her lip and frowned thoughtfully. "My father and I were a great comfort to each other. My mother was so brave during her illness. Even then she reached out to others, and her Christian faith inspired me to reach out in my health. It's true that some good comes from even the worst situations, if we keep believing in God."

Rae looked up then, to find Lucas staring at her in a different way—sort of a studied, interested way—and she felt he would understand if she continued.

"I know Mother is in a better world," Rae said distantly, looking out into the distance as if seeing that other world. "But," she admitted, "it's still hard to go on without those you love. My father was never the same without her. I think his missing her eventually led to his stroke. I was not enough for him."

"We need God in our lives," Lucas agreed. "But we also need people with whom we can share the hard times." He lifted her chin with his forefinger and forced her to look at him.

"I thought he was enough." she replied in a thin voice. "He's the only man I ever really cared about."

Rae did not immediately understand the expression in his eyes as they searched her face. "The only man?" he finally asked with skepticism. "What about Andy?"

What about Andy? Her mind was clouded, and she had to look away from his questioning gaze. Turning her head, she saw the fog hovering over the unseen valley. Though she couldn't see it, she knew the valley was there, just as she knew that somewhere beneath this strange upheaval, this indefinable convolution of Lucas, was Andy. The vague impression began to register that her reason for being here was Andy.

How much could she say without betraying Andy's confidence? Without endangering their tentative friendship? Her relationship with Mimi? Summer job possibilities? She would try to be as honest as she could possibly be.

"I haven't known Andy very long," she said truthfully. "But I hope to know him better before the summer is over. He offered me a summer job, so I'll be working with him—" she quickly added, "that is, if you agree."

Lucas's silence and thoughtful expression puzzled her. Perhaps he would question her job qualifications. Instead, his words were tinged with incredulity.

"Andy told me he had met a Christian girl who was special to him. . . I didn't believe him."

Rae didn't know what to say. To be completely honest with Lucas would mean she must damage her budding friendship with Andy. She suddenly felt caught in the middle of something, and she had the strange feeling her relationship with Andy was not going to be quite so simple as remaining silent while he pretended she was his special girl. But that was something she would have to work out with Andy.

Sighing shakily, Rae leaned her head back against the rock. She was aware of extreme fatigue accompanied by a quivery feeling, something akin to the sensation of having practiced for too many hours on the athletic equipment.

"What will happen to the fog?" she asked.

His dark eyes now seemed to hold a strange resignation as he looked away from her toward the valley below. Rae closed her eyes, listening as he talked in the deep, resonant tones that both excited and soothed her. He was as much a part of the mountain as the rock on which they sat.

"Sometimes it drifts away," he was explaining. "At other times, it clings to the mountainsides. This morning it is rising. Soon it will envelop us. Then it will become thinner, and the sun will shine brightly as if the fog had never existed."

Turning her face toward him, Rae breathed in the odor of his clean, fresh, vital masculinity and knew a man like that would never wear a sweet-smelling fragrance. The out-of-doors was fragrance enough.

"What are you thinking, Ramona?"

The sound of her name, as her father had spoken it, touched her deeply. And she found herself pouring out her heartache over the loss of her parents, her indecision, her loneliness. Her voice droned on and on while Lucas sat beside her, silent, immovable. At the moment he did not seem to be a stranger at all, but someone in whom she could confide, someone for whom she had been waiting, unaware, all her life.

She spoke of her mother and father who had both coached gymnastics at the famous school, of the young athletes they had championed to Olympic wins. Ramona had been born when her mother was in her early forties—the child they thought they could never have. Then her mother had become ill and died when Rae was fifteen—the year she was to have won at the Olympic Games. After that, Rae had lost her will to try for the gold. She had gone on to win some national awards, was part of the college team, and had stayed on to teach at the university.

Then, several months ago, her father's stroke had left him physically unable to return to his duties on campus. The doctor's bills from her mother's illness, combined with the new expenses, had piled up. The money was gone, and her own future, uncertain.

Rae sensed, rather than saw, the fog when it lifted to surround them. Her eyes were closed, but she felt the dampness as in enveloped them, then moved away to be replaced by gentle fingers of sunlight.

It happened inside her, too, as the emotion of her losses overwhelmed her, spilled over, then moved away with the mist.

"I doubt that I'll return to the university," Rae said, her voice catching in her throat. "Without my father. . ." She couldn't tell if her face was damp from her tears or from the phantom fog.

"I understand," Lucas said at last, breaking his long silence. "Andy, Mimi, and I faced such a crisis when our parents—all four of them—died in a plane crash in the Swiss Alps. It was such a freak thing. They were young—too young. Acceptance didn't come easily. It had not seemed a real possibility when we talked about my becoming Mimi's and Andy's legal guardian in the event of a disaster. In fact, we joked about it, since I'm only ten years older than Andy. Then suddenly, it was only too real. Mimi and Andy came to me so lost and forlorn, their world in pieces. Their father—a spirited, dashing Frenchman—was gone. Their mother, my sister—a lovely, exciting woman— taken from them."

Rae watched his face, thinking he was so young to have borne such a responsibility.

Lucas smiled at her and sighed deeply. "I may have overindulged Mimi and Andy at times," he admitted, "but I've done my best. And I'm fortunate to have my grandmother nearby with her wisdom and faith. It was through her I learned that dependence on God you speak of." His next words were spoken almost reverently, as though he were afraid he might shatter the spell between them. "I didn't really believe Andy when he told me about you, Ramona. He was right. You're exactly the kind of woman I've always wanted. . ." he paused, adding, "for Andy. Strange as it may seem, he's like a son to me."

His words were no real comfort to her, she realized miserably. She should be glad that Lucas approved of her. . .for Andy.

Following Lucas's lead, Rae braced her feet against the huge boulder in front of them. In spite of herself, she felt herself drifting off into an exhausted sleep.

When she awoke, they were resting in the shadow of the rock, and the sun was blazing high in the sky. Rae raised her head to find Lucas's head thrown back against the rock, leaning to one side, his lips parted in easy breathing. Her shoulder was pressed against his.

As Rae shifted her position, Lucas opened his eyes. Only a second of incomprehension dulled them before he smiled a lazy smile. The stubble of beard was more pronounced.

"Feel better?"

She could only nod. She did not only feel better—she felt newborn, alive!

Lucas stood and stretched languidly. Rae's pulse beat faster at the sight of his supple grace.

"Want to run back?"

"Lead the way!" she answered, eager.

He started slowly, then increased the speed until his long legs were beating the downhill path at a steady, rhythmic tempo. Rae's movements were perfectly synchronized with his. She was so close behind him that when he swept an occasional branch out of the way she was already past it before it could sweep back. Though the temperature had risen with the sun, the trees shaded them as they jogged down the twisting path.

When Lucas's pace slowed, Rae knew they must be nearing the house.

They ran up the steps of the lower deck with Lucas still in the lead. He stopped suddenly, causing Rae to collide with him. Reaching out to break her fall, he encircled her waist, lifted her off her feet for a second or two, then set her down again.

"How was that?" he asked, breathing hard from the strenuous workout.

"Invigorating!" Rae inhaled deeply, then automatically swung her arm around his waist, seeing nothing but his smiling face turned toward her.

They were almost upon the lounging figures on the second deck before they realized there was anyone else in the world.

Chapter 3

I see you've met Uncle Lucas," said Mimi, mischief dancing in her dark eyes. Then she rushed into her uncle's waiting arms, delighting in his hug. Lucas kissed Mimi's cheek and turned to greet Andy.

"I *thought* you might be out running, Rae," Andy said uncertainly. Looking at Lucas, he added, "I didn't know you were back."

Rae thought she must have imagined the tense moment between the two, for Andy stepped forward and Lucas's arm went around his shoulders in an affectionate gesture.

"Let's go in," Lucas said. "We're famished. Mind eating in the kitchen?" he asked, but didn't wait for an answer. Going inside, he shouted, "Selma, where are you?"

When the plump, mature woman appeared, Lucas gave her a big hug. "Now there's a woman for you. Best cook in the world!"

"You know that sweet-talking means nothing to me," Selma said, but the look on her face denied the words.

Lucas laughed and took a seat at the wooden table. He and Andy sat opposite each other with Rae beside Andy.

"Eggs and ham, Selma," Lucas said.

"I'll get the juice," Mimi offered and went to the refrigerator.

Lucas filled the water glasses from the pitcher on the table. Rae, looking over the rim of her glass, thought of the gurgling stream on the mountainside.

"You look awful, Rae," observed Mimi as she served the orange juice.

Rae laughed. "I don't care," she replied, and she didn't. "I haven't felt so free. . . ," she searched for words and shrugged, "*ever.*"

"When did you two meet?" Mimi cast an inquisitive eye in her friend's direction.

Rae hesitated, but Lucas replied immediately, grinning. "I would say about two o'clock this morning."

Mimi gasped, and Andy was noticeably paler. "You've been on the mountain all night!"

"Oh, no," her uncle answered. "We took an early morning hike."

"Coffee, anyone?" Andy's voice was distinctly cool. He poured a cup for Rae. "Sorry," he apologized as some of the coffee spilled over in her saucer.

"It's okay." Rae hoped her expression would convince him he had no cause for concern. But Andy had walked back to the breakfast bar to refill the coffeepot.

"When are you leaving for Paris, Mimi?" Lucas asked.

"Next week," she said, her eyes lighting up when she looked at her uncle. Their mutual affection was obvious. "Rae and I are going to have one great week before I go and before she settles down to work."

When Selma appeared, bearing steaming platters of ham and eggs, hot biscuits, and grits, Lucas asked God's blessing on the food.

"You haven't told me your last name," Lucas said, looking at Rae. When she opened her mouth to reply, he continued, "But I know. Your father would be the famous Raymond Martin. He is one reason I sent Mimi to the university in Atlanta. Not only did I want her to have the finest academic training available, but the finest physical training."

The flush of pleasure staining Rae's cheeks betrayed her delight. For a moment it seemed they were the only two people in the room. But she soon became aware of Mimi's wide-eyed stare, and she felt her face grow hotter still under Andy's questioning glance.

Looking at Lucas, Rae saw that a strange grin quirked his lips. "Ramona Martin," he boomed, "we haven't been properly introduced. Welcome to the world of Lucas Grant."

Rae's laughter halted in midair, and her fork dropped to her plate in a clatter.

"*Lucas Grant?*" she gasped. She had only heard him referred to as "Uncle Lucas" and assumed he was a Doudet, too. "I knew you looked familiar, but I thought it was because Andy looks so much like you. . . . You're the Lucas Grant who won the gold medal in skiing and was expected to win again the year I was fifteen. But you broke your leg on the slopes in Switzerland."

She did not add that, because of the rash of articles and pictures reporting the event, she had also experienced a painful, teen-age crush.

Lucas was grinning now. He picked up his fork. "One and the same," he said.

"Why didn't you tell me.?"

"It didn't occur to me."

"I cried for you," she said. "That was the year I didn't get to go. Thinking you must feel as disappointed as I, I identified with you."

"Well, thanks for that." The grin was still on his face. "I must have sensed your concern, because the disappointment was not the heartbreak for me that it was for you. I had already proved what I could do on the slopes. And—I had my 'children'." He looked fondly from Mimi to Andy. Mimi beamed, but

Andy did not raise his eyes from his plate. "Besides, I was all of twenty-five and you were only fifteen—much too young for me then," he quipped.

"Then, Uncle Lucas?" Andy's voice chilled the atmosphere, and the group grew strangely silent. Putting her fork down, Rae leaned back. Had she not known better, she could have easily believed Andy's look of hurt and frustration.

"A figure of speech, Andy." Lucas spoke without malice.

Andy's next words were uttered quietly, but with perfect clarity. "Are you trying to steal my girl, Uncle Lucas?"

Rae gasped and stared from one to the other. "Please!" she whispered but was completely ignored.

Mimi shrugged, apparently not understanding the tension arcing between her uncle and her brother.

Andy lowered his eyes while Lucas studied him thoughtfully. "You know better than that, Andy."

"Stop, this instant!" Rae demanded. "You can't talk about me as if I were not here!"

Lucas glared at her. "Please be quiet, Ramona. This is probably one of the most important issues Andy and I have ever discussed."

It was shock that silenced her.

"I don't think you could accurately accuse me of ever stealing a girl from you, Andy," Lucas said, returning his attention to his nephew.

"Not exactly," Andy admitted, "but several of them have seemed to prefer you."

"Oh, this one girl fell so hard for Uncle Lucas," Mimi began, trying to ease the tension of the moment, "that she climbed the high diving board down at the lake in her evening clothes and threatened to jump in and drown if Lucas didn't come 'save' her!"

Apparently unconcerned, Lucas drank the last of his coffee, then held out the cup for Selma to refill. He and Andy did not seem to be hearing Mimi, but were lost in their own private battle.

"Uncle Lucas told her to jump and be done with it!" Mimi continued. "Of course, she didn't, and her audience left, so she climbed down, and someone drove her home."

Neither Lucas nor Andy responded, and Rae and Mimi grinned at each other. For a moment it was like the days at school when Mimi had regaled her with wild accounts of childhood pranks.

"This one's special to you, Andy?" Lucas continued to probe.

"You ordered me to bring her here within the week, Uncle Lucas. I know you wanted to get to know her, but. . ." Andy shrugged uncomfortably.

For the first time Andy seemed to have struck a sensitive note with his uncle. Lucas appeared discomfited, running his hand through his unruly, dark curls and stroking the stubble of beard.

"Andy," he began, his tone slightly defensive, "how am I to know which ones you're serious about and which ones you're trying to set me up with? Now, you have to admit you and Mimi have been guilty of that kind of thing before."

"You can tell she's different, Uncle." Andy said matter-of-factly.

"Surely you didn't expect me to take your word for that, Andy. As your provider and guardian, don't I have an obligation to make sure you're making the right choices?"

"I think you forget that I'm no longer a child, Uncle Lucas. There are some things I must decide for myself."

"André." Lucas spoke his name with the kind of authority that forced eye contact. "I want the truth. Is this girl special to you?"

Rae held her breath, fearing what was to come. It was apparent that Andy loved and respected his Uncle. She was sure he would have to tell the truth. Rae was only grateful that the question was not directed to her.

Andy did not take his eyes from her when he spoke quietly. "Uncle Lucas, Rae is different from any girl I've ever known. And, yes, she is very special."

Rae swallowed hard. She could scarcely believe the ease with which Andy had lied to his uncle.

Lucas cleared his throat. "Well, Andy," he said uncomfortably. "I'm sorry if I was out of line. Perhaps I should have tried to get to know Ramona in your presence instead of alone. . . ," he faltered, then turned to Rae. "Did I offend you?"

"No," she answered truthfully, shaking her head. "Oh, no, not at all!" For a moment she couldn't look away. It was as if her favorite song had been recording: This is a test, only a test. In case of an actual emergency, you would have been instructed to. . . .

So Lucas had been testing her, trying to discover if she was really Andy's girl. The conversation, the comfort and protection of his strong arms had meant nothing. It was only a test.

Lucas turned from her confusion with a mocking smile and lifted his eyebrows. "What I can't understand, Andy, is how you could have allowed her to be missing all morning without tracking her down. I don't understand you. She has beauty, passion, intelligence, sensitivity. . . . How could you let her get away?"

Rae knew Lucas was trying to laugh it all away. He wanted truth from

Andy, yet Lucas himself had deliberately played with her emotions, deceiving her into thinking that he cared how she felt about things. That was despicable! She could not, would not, sit docilely and be discussed as if she were an inanimate object.

"Stop it!" she protested, rising to her feet. "Andy knows how to treat me, Lucas. Like a. . .like a. . .lady." Her green eyes sparkled defiantly as she lifted her chin.

Lucas threw back his head and laughed heartily. "That's exactly my point. I couldn't have stated it better."

Rae's audible gasp was an automatic recoil from the stinging slur. Was Lucas inferring she was not a lady?

"Oh, how could you?" her voice quivered. "How could you?"

Uncontrollable fury gripped her, and, before she knew what was happening, her hands had closed around the water glass, and she had dumped it over Lucas's head.

He jumped from the chair so quickly that it crashed to the floor. Rae turned to run from the room, but his hand shot out and grasped her wrist. His expression was fierce.

"I'm so sorry," she breathed, her voice choked. "I don't know what possessed me. . . ."

Water dripped from his curls and ran in rivulets down his face.

"I was not insulting you," he said, "I was referring to the fact that, if Andy wants to keep you, he should start treating you more like the woman you are. He should have been the one to hear about your family, your fears, your dreams." He paused in an effort to control his emotions. "But maybe you need some time to cool off a little, too. After you've rested, you'll feel better."

It sounded like a dismissal, and Rae ran from the kitchen, Mimi right behind her.

In the bedroom, she fell across the bed, thoroughly humiliated. She did not understand Lucas Grant. Nor herself, for that matter.

"Oh, Mimi," she wailed, her voice muffled in the bedspread, "how awful! What have I done?"

"Awful?" Mimi asked, flopping down on the bed beside her. "I don't think it's awful at all. I think it's wonderfully romantic. Don't you see? Uncle Lucas and André are fighting over you."

Rae sat up, staring incredulously. "Are you out of your mind, Mimi? It's horrible. And. . .embarrassing. I talked to Lucas about such personal things. Now I've behaved like a—a child. I can't face either of them again. I'm leaving!"

Mimi slung her dark hair behind her shoulders.

"You can't leave now, Rae. André needs you at the camp, and you did agree to help him out." Then Mimi's eyes sparkled. "Where did you find the nerve to pour water on Uncle Lucas, Rae? Nobody's ever done such a thing before."

"Oh, Mimi! I don't know! I didn't mean to. He'll never forgive me. Now I've ruined everything—for everyone."

"Oh, no, you haven't. You've just made it more interesting. Really, Rae, it does seem that André was truly concerned—about you, I mean. After all, he did ask you to come here. And it's no secret how attractive Uncle Lucas is to women. . ."

"Oh, hush, Mimi!" Rae burst out. Suddenly a hot bath and bed sounded very appealing. "I have better sense than to consider becoming involved in anything like that. If I hadn't, that little scene downstairs just now would have convinced me."

"Well, there's one thing for certain, Rae."

"What's that?" Rae stepped out of her shorts.

"Uncle Lucas obviously likes you. And he has one weakness. . ."

"Lucas—with a weakness?" Rae jested, her hands on her hips. "What could that possibly be?"

"André and me!" she gloated. "He loves us very much. He's a strict disciplinarian and has done a marvelous job with us, as you know."

They laughed together, relieving the tension of the past few moments.

"But he has spoiled us, too." Mimi continued. "Since André is obviously interested in you, Uncle Lucas will do everything in his power to nurture that interest."

A sudden, inexplicable surge of anger flared again. "And I'm to have absolutely nothing to say about any of this?"

Shaking her head, Mimi replied. "Not a word. Around here, darling, Lucas has the last word. And if André wants you—and I believe he does— Uncle Lucas will get you for him. One way or the other." She walked to the door, put her hand on the knob, and paused as if debating whether to say what was on her mind. "I can't think of anyone I'd like more for a sister-in-law!" she mused and slipped out the door before Rae could think of a suitable retort.

Delighting in the warm shower, she noted how much softer the water was here than the city. *Fewer chemicals*, she surmised, remembering a crystal-clear stream she had seen that morning on the mountain.

The light spray cleansed her hair and tear-stained face. She determined to put aside any ideas about Lucas Grant, just as surely as she was now washing away the feel of his lips on hers, the strength of his muscular arms around her.

Determined to shut out the disturbing thoughts, Rae shut off the shower, dried herself, slipped into a nightie and slid between the sheets, admiring the feminine room. The decor was antique white and sky blue, with plush blue carpeting matching the patterned wallpaper. Obviously no expense had been spared in furnishing the room, with its solid cherry canopy bed and ornately carved highboy. To one side was an inviting chaise lounge, deep in pillows, and an assortment of interesting reading material on a round, skirted table nearby.

She turned toward the windows where the white curtains seemed always to be stirring from some invisible breeze. Rae must remember her original intent in coming here, before the romance and intrigue of this exotic setting overpowered her. She had come to escape heartache, not to invite more. With a sigh she burrowed her head in the soft pillow.

※

The next thing Rae knew Mimi was shaking her shoulders and calling her name.

"Rae! Wake up! Come on now. You're sure making up for all those months you couldn't sleep. You've slept all day!"

It took awhile for the words to register. When Rae sat up in bed and looked out the window, she saw the dwindling light of late afternoon.

"It's five-thirty," Mimi informed her. "Dinner is at seven. Hurry! You've only one hour to make yourself beautiful."

Pushing the sheet aside, Rae stretched and yawned. "I've slept like a log. Must be the mountain air. But. . . ," her grin was mischievous as she looked in the mirror at the wilted figure and head full of drab ringlets, "it will take more than an hour, I'm afraid."

"I've plugged in your hot rollers. I'm wearing my red. Wear your green. We'll wow 'em!" Mimi teased, then left Rae to her privacy.

Less than an hour later, with the hot rollers to relax the tight curls, and a vigorous brushing to bring out the highlights, her golden hair was anything but the tangled mess of the earlier morning.

She never completely concealed the sprinkling of freckles across her small, straight nose for she had been told they were quite alluring. The green dress brought out the color of her eyes, and they were shaded by long, dark lashes. She reached for her glossy lipstick to apply to her full, soft lips. A faint blush heightened the color of her cheeks.

Standing and viewing herself critically in the mirror, she wondered what Lucas would think of her now that she looked more like a mature woman who was a teacher at a university rather than an early-morning jogger who cried on his shoulder, or a moonlight temptress who invited his kiss.

She sat down again, losing her nerve. That speculation and pep talk did no good. Her dumping water on Lucas Grant reigned uppermost in her mind, and she was sure he wasn't about to forget that! Facing him again would not be easy.

"What's keeping you, Rae?" Mimi asked, knocking on the door and interrupting her friend's reverie. "Don't you know that you don't keep Uncle Lucas waiting?"

Chapter 4

Mimi's eyes widened when Rae opened the door. "You'll dazzle 'em tonight!"

Surveying the dark-haired girl in scarlet, she shook her head. "Not a chance with you around, Mimi."

Mimi had been one of the most popular girls on campus, not only because of her startling good looks, but because of her effervescent personality. It was in Rae alone, however, that she had confided the deeper longings of her heart.

"Well," Mimi was saying, "I will admit I may have a job keeping Brent at a distance."

"Brent?"

"Oh, I've never mentioned him before, but he would make the 'perfect husband,' or so Uncle Lucas insists." She wrinkled her nose. "I can't think about anyone except Pierre anymore—you know that, even if Uncle Lucas doesn't!"

Rae nodded, understanding.

"Pierre!" Mimi exclaimed, hugging her arms to herself. "I'll see him next week, Rae! Not a word to anyone, though. If Uncle Lucas knew, he wouldn't let me go to Paris. But I feel about Pierre. . .oh, how can I describe it? I know," she said, with sudden insight, "I feel like you looked this morning. You were a mess—no make-up, hair in all those funny little ringlets—yet when you and Uncle Lucas came out of the woods, you were—radiant."

Rae shrugged it off. "Well, we had run down the mountain and. . .oh, come on! We're late."

"I'm glad you're here, Rae," Mimi said sincerely.

Rae wondered how wise it was, her being here. But what else could she do. . .now?

Rae descended the staircase, determined to make the best of the evening. At the landing Mimi went to greet Brent, who was talking with Andy. Rae knew immediately what Mimi had meant about the tall, young man with the handsome face, good clothes, nice smile, and charming manners. When he looked at Mimi, a spark ignited in his eyes. He couldn't conceal his enchantment with the girl in red.

"Now for the blond bombshell," said Mimi under her breath after she had introduced Rae to Brent.

Standing behind one of the two plush couches facing each other in front of a massive fireplace were Lucas and Isobel.

Before the introduction could be made, the woman stepped forward. "You would be one of Mimi's little friends." Rae cringed inwardly.

Upon closer scrutiny Rae realized the blond with pale blue eyes was not as large or imposing as she had thought at first glance. It was just that so much of her was showing in the shimmering white sheath. No doubt those were real diamonds around her neck and at her ear lobes. Her light tan set off a flawless complexion, as did her dazzling white teeth when she spread her lips into a smile. There was no denying she was sophisticated and beautiful—at least Lucas's age, if not older. So this voluptuous woman was an example of Lucas's preference in women.

Rae suddenly felt angry—angry with herself for caring what Lucas liked or thought, angry with the woman before her whose eyes did not reflect the warmth of her smile. She seemed to thaw a little, however, when Lucas stepped forward and said, "Ramona is André's friend, too. Ramona—Isobel Patrick."

"Well, Ramona. I'm very glad to meet you." Even the voice was well-modulated.

"Rae," she corrected. "Everyone calls me Rae, Mrs. Patrick."

"Oh, you make me feel ancient, calling me Mrs. Patrick. Please call me Isobel."

Rae suddenly realized that Lucas couldn't have possibly mistaken her for Isobel in the early morning. Her gaze swung sharply toward Lucas and found his eyes on her, an amused expression there. Her glance raked his face, taking in the smooth-shaven skin, deeply tanned, the eyes that had seemed so tender earlier. His broad frame was now attired in an obviously expensive, formal, brown suit with velvet lapels and a beige silk shirt and tie—so different from the mountain man in jeans and plaid shirt of the early morning. This man was cool, self-possessed, so in control of his surroundings, the king of the mountain—a perfect escort for the perfect Isobel.

Suddenly Andy was at her side, offering a glass of ginger ale.

Gratefully, Rae turned to him, surprised at the affectionate look in his eyes. "You're especially beautiful this evening, Rae," he said softly.

Her smile was one of genuine pleasure. "After this morning, I suppose anything would be an improvement."

"Come on," Andy said, "I want to show you something."

They walked around the great stone fireplace that separated the lounge area from the library in which they now stood.

Andy gestured toward the three walls, lined from floor to ceiling with books. "I'm not sure I ever want to read again," he grumbled. "I haven't yet recovered from my college days."

She laughed with him. "I know exactly what you mean. Such torture is not easily forgotten."

He steered her over to a trophy case displaying Lucas's gold medal. Flanking it were other lesser awards, conferred for his superb skiing skills. Some of the trophies were tributes to Andy's expertise in skiing, tennis, and swimming. Listening to Andy now and watching him describe the various meets, Rae realized why women were so attracted to him. He was irresistible when he was talking animatedly about the sports he loved, his eyes alight with his intense passion for the game.

"I've got to talk to you, Rae," Andy said fervently.

"Fine," she agreed.

"I mean—alone. Perhaps we'll have a chance after dinner."

He placed his arm lightly around her shoulders, and they walked back into the lounge to find Mimi and Brent.

When dinner was announced, Rae was pleased to see that she had been right in her earlier supposition that the dining room overlooked the decks. Small-paned windows covered almost all the wall facing the back of the house. There were no curtains. None were needed. The effect was that of a rustic setting, as if the jungle outside were an integral part of the room.

"I must see this," Rae said to Andy, then walked over to the windows.

Shadows were stealing across the wooden deck as the sun swiftly made its descent behind the mountains. How different the scene appeared each time she looked at it—once in the moonlight; another time in the mist; again in the sunlight; now in the shadows that gave the deep green leaves the appearance of ebony.

"Perhaps she's just one of those spoiled brats who refuse to eat anything as ordinary as paella Valenciana!"

Mimi's banter finally reached her ears, as did the good-natured laughter of the others.

"Oh, I'm so sorry," Rae apologized, quickly taking the seat that Andy was gallantly holding for her. "It's just that it's all so fascinating—so very different from Atlanta. I'm afraid I got carried away."

"The only thing that disturbs me," Andy was saying as he settled himself beside her, "is that Selma might get tired of waiting, take it all away, and serve us grits instead."

To Rae's extreme discomfort, she realized that she had been seated to Lucas's right and that Isobel was on his left, directly across the table from her.

She suffered a momentary pang before remembering that she was the new-comer, the honoree at this affair. Brent and Isobel had obviously dined here many times before.

While the salad was being served, Rae took the opportunity to look about her and was once again reminded of the unique blending of elegance and luxury on the interior with the lush, untamed vegetation beyond. The walls themselves were of dark paneling, like the kitchen. The rectangular room was designed with a brick fireplace at the far end, and Rae could see that two overstuffed armchairs could be drawn up to the fire for conversation or quiet contemplation on a winter evening. She would be gone before winter.

They were seated at a long dining table in gold velvet, padded chairs with very high, straight backs, enhancing the aura of formality and precision in this room. Suspended over the table were two magnificent crystal chandeliers and, beneath them, the *piece de resistance*, bringing life to the otherwise austere surroundings—two huge silver bowls displaying miniature clusters of pink blossoms set against the background of thick, waxy, dark green leaves. They had been gathered, no doubt, from the grounds.

Rae realized she was smiling when Lucas asked, "I'm sure you recall our brief lesson in mountain flora and fauna from this morning?"

He *had* pointed out several plants and identified them during the early morning hours.

"Mountain laurel," she replied confidently.

"Rhododendron," he corrected playfully.

"Oh, yes. Rho. . .do. . .den. . .whatever," she finished feebly.

"Don't worry," Andy consoled her. "It takes time to become a mountaineer."

"Oh, darling—" Isobel touched Lucas's forearm, apparently bored with the conversation—"before I forget, Kevin made me promise to thank you for the card and lovely game you sent him."

Lucas smiled warmly. "I'm glad he's feeling better."

"Oh, he is. Much. He wouldn't miss opening day at camp for anything!"

André leaned toward Rae. "You are about to discover that Selma is a real cuisinier."

"I'm already convinced," she replied, discovering the hidden delights of Selma's Paella—chicken, vegetables, rice tinted a dull yellow by the addition of saffron. And were those clams? And shrimp? This was more than a meal. It was an adventure.

During dinner conversation, Rae learned that Isobel's home was in Raleigh, the state capitol, and that she and her son Kevin, despite a virus that had hung on for several weeks, were visiting Isobel's parents who lived in nearby Asheville.

The conversation turned to Andy's activities of the past year, then to

Mimi's present interests, which led quite naturally to discussion of Rae's summer employment. This bit of information surprised Isobel.

"Will you be staying here at the house, then, after Mimi leaves for Paris?" Isobel asked her.

Lucas spoke before Rae could answer. "She will stay in one of the cottages at the camp—with the other staffers."

"Oh, I see," Isobel said and smiled sweetly. Rae looked past Brent to Mimi, who was making a valiant effort not to laugh. She would have to remember not to glance at Mimi too often. No doubt Isobel would be wondering how Andy had become acquainted with an ordinary working girl. The woman's next question proved her correct.

"I'm always interested in romances," Isobel said brightly. "How and when and wherever did you two meet?"

Andy answered immediately, "On one of my stops to see Mimi in Atlanta."

"Oh? Love at first sight?"

Rae felt a stab of resentment at Isobel's assumption and her patronizing tone.

"Something like that," Andy replied and returned to his eating, as if the discussion were closed. But where Isobel left off her questioning, Lucas took it up.

"I would have thought a sensible, intelligent girl like Ramona would not believe in love at first sight. Perhaps you are speaking for yourself only." His tone sounded accusatory, and Rae suspected he had not totally accepted Andy's apparent sincerity.

"I don't think love is necessarily sensible," Rae said defensively, looking directly at Lucas, "or reasonable. It can be quite disconcerting, unpredictable, and unexpected." She had at least *read* about that kind of love. "I think the important thing is whether it is treated lightly, as some passing fancy, or treasured for a lifetime."

Lifting her chin, she determined to meet Lucas's sarcasm head-on, but discovered something surprising in his eyes. He looked as if he could not agree more.

Blessedly, Mimi started up a conversation about Brent. Now twenty-two, he would receive a master's degree in business in another year, then would go to work in his father's firm.

"Where he will eventually work his way up to the presidency," Mimi informed Rae. "It will probably take all of five years."

"Well, I think Dad plans to hold that position for awhile yet," Brent countered. "But it is a real possibility for the future." The way he looked at

Mimi indicated he would be happy to have the beautiful girl as a part of that future.

Rae knew it was not Brent who interested Mimi. Her heart belonged to Pierre. Mimi's thoughts were with him, too, for she began to speak of Paris, fashions, and trips abroad. Isobel, quite a traveler herself, joined the discussion enthusiastically.

Invariably the conversation drifted back to sports—a subject Rae never tired of.

"Ramona's father was a famous coach," Lucas informed Isobel and Brent.

"Rae," Isobel corrected, and smiled condescendingly.

"I'm allowed to call her Ramona," Lucas replied.

Rae picked up her spoon. She didn't dare look at Lucas but busied herself with the dessert.

"Her father called her Ramona," Lucas continued in his explanation. "I represent an uncle figure, I suppose."

"That's certainly refreshing," Isobel said, laughing lightly. "How many more of those diving board episodes could one stand?"

Disliking the implication, Rae could not resist a retort. "You needn't worry. I could tumble off a diving board, do tricks in the air, or dive in with my mouth wide open, and still not drown."

Lucas laughed heartily while Isobel's smile still did not reach her eyes.

"A fish, huh?" asked Lucas, still laughing.

"At least half," she replied, glancing at Mimi who winked.

"And I know what the other half is," Lucas said, as all eyes turned to regard him curiously.

Rae drew in her breath and held it for a long moment.

"A gymnast!"

Mimi immediately began telling of Rae's athletic abilities, including her medals and honors.

"I suppose I would be classified as just a homebody," Isobel said.

"If telling your maid and housekeeper what to do classifies you as a homebody, I suppose you're right," Lucas said, chuckling.

"Now, Lucas," Isobel reprimanded, placing a well-manicured hand on his sleeve, "I'm turning into a regular gourmet cook. And I can prove it. I insist on cooking for you one evening soon."

"I suppose I'll have to take you up on that," he responded.

After dinner Isobel regretfully announced that she had to return to her young son. Taking her arm, Lucas led her from the lounge to show her the gifts he had brought back from Switzerland.

Unsuccessfully stifling a yawn, Mimi stretched luxuriously. "Guess I'm still tired from the long drive from Atlanta."

Taking the hint, Brent stood to leave. "Some of the gang are coming to my place for a luau on Friday. Would the three of you care to drop in—especially since it will be Mimi's last night in the States for awhile?"

"We'd love to!" Mimi replied, then rose. "I'll walk you to the car."

As soon as the couple had left, Andy moved closer to Rae. Emotionally drained, she had leaned her head back against the couch and closed her eyes. At the touch of his hand on hers, she opened her eyes.

"Rae, it's time for that serious talk," he said.

And then Mimi and Lucas were back, lounging on the sofa opposite them, and Andy released her hand and reluctantly moved away.

Lucas removed his tie, then unbuttoned his shirt at the neck as if, now, for the first time since dinner, he could truly relax.

"You managed to get rid of Brent in a hurry," he scolded Mimi fondly.

"Like you managed to get rid of Isobel?" she asked with a saucy toss of her head.

"It's not the same, and you know it."

"To tell the truth, Uncle Lucas," she pouted, "I could hardly tear myself away from him."

Lucas snorted. "You could barely tolerate him, you mean!"

"You know me pretty well, huh?"

"For several years now," he said, nodding.

"But you've ruined me for all men, Uncle Lucas. Not one of them can measure up to you."

"None?" he asked quizzically.

"Almost none," she replied, stealing a glance at Rae. They exchanged knowing smiles.

"Anyway," Mimi said, looking back at Lucas, "I promised Brent he could come by and take me to church in the morning."

"Be back in time for lunch, Mimi," Lucas said. "Gran is coming to meet Rae. Would you like to worship with Gran in the morning, Andy?" he asked his nephew.

"Sure," he replied, "if Rae wants to. It really doesn't matter much to me."

Rae's voice was quiet, but firm. "It matters to me, Andy."

The soft music from the stereo did not fill the uncomfortable silence that followed.

Ever diplomatic, Mimi hurriedly changed the subject. "Is extra help coming in next week, Uncle Lucas?" she asked.

"Marie will be here on Monday morning." His voice held a note of wry humor. "Don't worry. You won't have to do your own laundry."

"I did plenty of it at school. But that reminds me," she said, jumping up, "I'd better see what I have to wear in the morning."

As soon as Mimi left, Andy excused himself, too. "I'll be right back," he said to Rae. As he walked through the doorway, he was removing his tie.

"How long have you been here?" Lucas asked when they were alone.

"Almost twenty-four hours," she said and looked down at her hands folded stiffly on her green dress.

His next words echoed her thoughts. "Incredible!" he said under his breath. "It seems much longer. I feel I know all there is to know about you."

Chapter 5

Y ou haven't even seen all the house, have you?" Lucas asked, standing. When Rae admitted she hadn't, he exclaimed, "Ah, let me show you the best part of the living room."

Despite the fact that was the one room she saw each time she ascended or descended the stairs, she walked with him from the lounge. He mentioned that his study, bath, and bedroom were behind the closed doors next to the lounge.

The foyer and staircase were separated only by space from the living room with its cathedral ceiling. A dim light burned on the wall near the foot of the stairs.

"Over here," Lucas said, without turning on another light. They stood looking out beyond the wide picture window where the mountainsides were dotted with tiny lights. The dark outline of mountain ranges seemed to stretch on forever, eventually fading into the sky. Expecting Lucas to comment on the view, Rae was surprised at his question.

"Is it so important to you, Rae?"

"Is what so important?" she asked, studying Lucas's profile as he looked out toward the mountains.

"Attending church tomorrow—and Andy's lack of interest."

"I believe the most important thing in a person's life is commitment to Jesus Christ as personal Savior," she replied thoughtfully. "Church attendance is just one expression of that commitment. But I do think families should worship together. For example, I can't imagine being married to a man who doesn't share and understand my beliefs."

"Perhaps it's not an insurmountable problem," Lucas replied, and she felt his eyes search her face in the near darkness.

The subject shifted to the magnificent view before them.

"Asheville lies in that direction," Lucas said, pointing. "Not to be compared with Atlanta in size, of course, but it supplies our needs. In front of you is the Swannanoa Valley and, off to your left, is a little town called Black Mountain. . .You're not looking," he said with surprise.

No, she had not looked at anything but his face since he had come to stand beside her. She could think of nothing but how she had felt in the early morning with his arms around her. Did he remember?

"I—I see only mountain peaks dotted with light. A whole blue ridge of them."

"I've looked at this view so many times," he laughed, "that I can see it with my eyes closed."

Suddenly brilliant light flooded the room.

"Wondered where you had gone," Andy was saying, striding across the floor toward them. His eyes held a strange gleam of triumph. "I just talked to Gran," he said, reaching for Rae's hands and holding them out in front of her. "She's delighted that we'll be going to church with her in the morning. She's eager to meet you, Rae."

'That's wonderful, Andy," Rae said sincerely.

"Now," Andy continued, "let's ride down to the camp. The lake is very romantic in the moonlight. But you'd better get a sweater. It'll be cool by the lake."

"Andy," she said when they neared the staircase, "Would you mind very much if we waited until tomorrow? I think I really did eat too much, and I feel I might be getting a headache."

At his look of disappointment, she almost changed her mind, but instinct told her she shouldn't. "I haven't unpacked," she explained. "After all, I don't have closets full of clothes like Mimi!" Her banter did little to lighten Andy's dark mood.

Reaching out, he placed a hand on her shoulder and the warmth she had detected earlier returned to his eyes. "I understand. There's plenty of time for us to see the lake—tomorrow, or even next week." He shrugged. "I really should spend this evening with Uncle Lucas, anyway. We have a lot of catching up to do."

Leaning forward, he touched his lips to hers. She was uncomfortably aware that Lucas was probably watching. But it was a very nice kiss, and Andy was really a very nice person.

After a moment, she moved back and smiled up at him. "Sleep well, Andy."

"See you in the morning," he said softly, then turned to rejoin his uncle.

Rae was pleasantly surprised on Sunday morning when Lucas appeared at the breakfast table and announced that he would drive them to church. Gran had planned to meet them there.

She was waiting for them in the foyer of the church. Rae was not surprised to find a tall, elegant, handsome woman who appeared twenty years younger than her seventy-plus years. Her silvery-white hair was beautifully coifed, and her alert brown eyes held the speculativeness of Lucas's and the warmth of Andy's. Upon being introduced, Gran had immediately insisted that Rae call her Gran.

There was no time for conversation, but Rae felt comfortable sitting between Andy and Gran during the worship service.

After church, Gran got into the Lincoln with them to accompany them to lunch, and on the way back to Lucas's house, she told Rae about the historic sites in the area: The Biltmore House and Gardens, Vance's Birthplace, Thomas Wolfe's home, Carl Sandburg's home, Mt. Mitchell, the Parkway.

"Stop!" cried Rae. "I'm overwhelmed just looking at the mountains. And now you tell me there's more!"

"Not to mention the boys' camp and the ski resorts," Andy teased.

Then Gran told her about the religious conference centers in the area, as well as several colleges. It all sounded fascinating, and Rae feared she would never be able to visit all those places in a single summer. It would be over all too soon. . . . But she mustn't think of that now.

During lunch, and afterward in the lounge, Rae learned that Gran was active in church work, served on several civic committees, and was athletic like her children and grandchildren. She had her own exercise room and remained a member of a tennis club. A live-in staff took care of things during her frequent travels.

"A woman friend travels with her," Lucas explained. "Gran has turned up at many of Andy's competitions and at mine when I was more actively involved with sports."

"Well, Lucas. We Grants have to stay busy. We have a capacity for activity," Gran said. "Too many evenings spent alone can make one old before one's time."

"But that's enough about us. Let's hear about this fascinating girl." And she turned her full attention to Rae, who already felt a bond of kinship. "I'm so pleased to meet the young lady whom Mimi mentioned every time she wrote. It was a comfort knowing she had a friend she could speak of so highly, and one who wasn't afraid to lecture her when she needed it!"

Mimi pursed her mouth in a pout, but smiled at Rae.

"When my granddaughter wrote to me about you, I thought to myself: *Now there's a girl Mimi should bring home for all of us to meet,*" Gran continued with a sparkle in her eye. "I just hope you have the good sense to take this adorable girl seriously, Andy," she said.

Andy perched on the arm of the couch, near Rae. "I told you last night, Gran. Rae means more to me every day, but she insists on time to think it over."

Only for a second could Rae meet the warmth and acceptance in Gran's eyes.

"I thought I detected a more serious note in your voice when you told me about her on the phone last night," Gran nodded. "I also sense that Rae is a fine young lady. Now, you win her over!"

Rae tried to smile with the others. Gran would not think well of her when she knew the truth. Such lying seemed to come so naturally with Andy. But Andy was a desperate young man. Now she felt herself being drawn deeper and deeper into his predicament. What had begun as a seemingly innocent suggestion was fast becoming a full-blown deception. What was worse, these people accepted her, liked her, wanted her to be part of their family.

"What is it, Rae?" Gran asked quietly.

"Oh—" Rae said, shaking her head, "my mind was somewhere else. I'm sorry."

Then Lucas was explaining for her. "Rae isn't as ready as we are to express her feelings, Gran. I think we embarrass her by speaking of personal matters."

"We *can* be rather blunt," Gran agreed.

But there had been a time when Rae was open about her feelings. That morning with Lucas. When he had conducted his cross-examination.

❧

Monday morning began with Rae and Mimi running along the horse trails that wound around the camp area and down beside the lake that Mimi said covered six hundred acres. When the sun began to peek over the mountains that surrounded the camp area, Rae was reminded anew that God's handiwork could not be imitated by mere man. Gentle rays filtered through the cool morning air, moist with mist. The fragrance of honeysuckle, sweet and clean, delighted the senses as they ran past rustic cabins, soccer fields, tennis courts, and even a miniature golf course. But it was the modern gymnasium that intrigued Rae.

"The outside of the gym is used in teaching the fundamentals of beginning rock-climbing," Mimi explained.

There was a spot high above the camp where they could look down upon a pastoral scene with cattle grazing in the valley beneath, surrounded by sloping hills and mountain peaks, green, purple, and gray with haze at various levels.

The evergreens were alive with golden yellow-green fingers at the tips of each limb, stretching toward heaven to catch the sunlight.

❧

Andy and Lucas were usually finishing their morning workout when Rae and Mimi were ready for theirs. The fully equipped exercise room was immense, encompassing the entire area beneath the first floor of the house.

The next few days passed quickly. While the two men spent much of their time on the campgrounds, Mimi and Rae were busy with exercise, swimming, tennis, shopping and visiting some of the quaint little shops on Cherry Street in Black Mountain.

Suddenly it was Friday and time for Brent's party.

"Since the theme is Hawaiian, we have to dress the part," Mimi said, rummaging through her closets.

She brought out a brightly patterned silk dress for Rae and one of blue, green, and orange for herself. They donned low-heeled sandals before walking downstairs, where Andy waited in khaki pants and an exotic short-sleeved shirt. All thoughts of how handsome he was vanished the moment Lucas walked in from his bedroom and joined them in the foyer.

"Well, you look festive," Lucas said, smiling at them.

"Join us," Mimi invited. "It will be fun."

Lucas laughed. "I'm afraid I have other plans."

"A gourmet dinner?" Mimi teased. "In a romantic A-frame?"

Lucas gave her a noncommittal glance before saying, "Don't be out too late and—behave yourselves."

"If you will, Uncle Lucas," Mimi said mischievously.

He looked at his watch, said a hurried good-bye and strode from the foyer.

Rae stared after him. "What was that about the A-frame?" she asked.

"Isobel's mountain hideaway," Mimi replied.

Rae suddenly realized how the three of them, dressed in their Hawaiian costumes, must have looked to Lucas—like children playing dress-up.

Upon arriving at Brent's, Rae discovered it was anything but a children's party. After winding their way up the mountain, Andy pulled the car to a stop in front of a magnificent, two-story, brick home with huge, white columns.

Walking around to the back patio was like stepping into an Hawaiian travel poster. The three of them were immediately presented with fresh flower leis. A live musical group strummed musical instruments in accompaniment to native Hawaiian songs. Long tables were laden with festive decorations and elaborate foods, with centerpieces of pineapple and every conceivable kind of fruit.

"Brent does have a knack for giving a party," Mimi said brightly.

"It's fabulous!" Rae agreed. "I've never seen anything like this."

"We'll have one of our own when I get back from Paris," Mimi promised. "Oh, but I mustn't think of Paris. Tomorrow, Rae. Tomorrow I leave."

"Then stop thinking about it, Mimi," Rae said. "Here, have a. . . .whatever this thing is."

They laughed and sampled the food. Rae determined to forget everything but the party and for the next few hours did just that, wondering briefly at only one point if Lucas were enjoying his evening with Isobel.

When Andy came up to her and led her away to a secluded part of the patio, she welcomed the retreat from the noisy guests—until he pulled her close. "After we take Mimi home, let's go somewhere, Rae. We haven't had any time alone." A rather desolate look appeared in his usually twinkling brown eyes.

Rae searched his face, and her heart went out to him. "Why don't you take me back to the house, Andy?" she asked kindly. "Then you can come back to the party and find another girl. I'm afraid I'm not very good company tonight."

"Rae," he whispered miserably. "I don't think you understand me. I don't want to be with just any girl. I want to be alone with you."

Rae lowered her eyes from his searching gaze.

"Look at me, Rae," he said, and she lifted her eyes to his. "It's not what you think, Rae. I want to talk to you. I want to tell you my dreams and my plans. And I want to hear yours."

Rae was surprised at his earnestness as he continued, almost hesitantly. "I've never wanted that before, Rae. There's never been a girl who made me think seriously about my future, and my personal actions, like you do. I'd like to think that if you knew me better, you'd see more than a–a playboy."

"Oh, Andy, who am I to judge?" Rae protested. "You haven't always made good decisions, but we all make mistakes."

"Not you," Andy replied with conviction. "You're sensible. . .and wise."

He didn't know that at this very moment she was struggling with a ridiculous girlhood fantasy that had come to life in the person of a man who had listened while she poured out her heart to him on a mountaintop. That was not at all sensible, or practical or wise.

But it would pass. Apparently, this was a common reaction of women to Lucas. As she became more accustomed to that mountain of a man, she would be better able to deal with her own emotions. And then. . .there was Andy. He had great potential. His skills were admirable. He was personally very attractive. Once she settled down to face reality again, she would accept these things about Andy with her heart as well as her head. It would just take a little time.

"I would like to know you better, Andy," Rae said truthfully. "But for now, I have a job to do. That's really why I'm here. I need to take things slowly this summer."

Andy looked up toward the starlit expanse of sky and sighed deeply. When he returned his gaze to Rae, the troubled look had disappeared. "Okay," he said, smiling. "Slow and easy it is."

It took another thirty minutes to say their good-byes, with Mimi promising to write from Paris. Rae could honestly tell Brent and his friends how much she enjoyed the delightful party.

It was when they returned to the house and entered the lounge that Mimi expressed her surprise to find Lucas sitting in the dimly lit room, watching TV.

"Uncle Lucas, you're home early," she said, hurrying over to stand by his chair where his lean frame was stretched out, his feet propped up on a stool. "Is everything all right?"

"Of course. Why shouldn't it be?"

"Did you and Isobel have a fight?"

"Isobel and I plan to spend the day together before she returns to Raleigh tomorrow evening. Now, does that sound like we've had a fight?"

"No," she admitted. "But you looked worried. You don't usually sit in the dark, watching TV."

"And you aren't usually home at this hour," he countered, looking from Mimi to Andy.

"I'm too excited about Paris to keep my mind on anything else for long," Mimi said, adding, "which reminds me—I have to finish packing." After a quick kiss on Lucas's cheek, she left the room.

"Did you enjoy the party?" Lucas asked Rae.

"Very much," she replied and looked at Andy. She wanted to give him an opening to return to the party. "But it *is* early."

"Maybe I'll watch TV with Uncle Lucas," he said.

"Fine," Lucas said. "Care to join us, Rae?"

"No, thanks," Rae replied. "I promised to help Mimi pack."

She started to turn but Andy reached for her arm and gently drew her to him, then placed a light kiss on her lips.

Rae stepped back immediately, expecting Lucas to be watching, but he seemed absorbed in finding a channel on TV. As Andy said good night, there was the sound of a lively commercial in the background. But it was Lucas's low, deep-throated, "Good night, Ramona," that lodged in her consciousness.

Chapter 6

Rae greeted Sunday morning with both anticipation and apprehension. She was excited about beginning her job at the camp, but wondered if she were equal to the challenge.

Mimi had insisted on arising before daybreak. Gran had arrived early. She and Mimi were already on their way to the airport. Lucas left for the campgrounds.

"Our lives won't be the same for the rest of the summer," Andy assured Rae, when it was time to head down the mountain toward the camp to begin a week of staff training and indoctrination before the campers' arrival.

"Short cut," Andy explained while he drove down the steep, winding incline which led to the side of the gym and onto the gravel road in the center of camp. A short distance farther, he parked the car and took her bag. They hiked up a winding path leading to a log cottage posted with a crudely carved sign reading: "Off Limits."

"It means what it says, too," Andy said emphatically. "None of the males are allowed up here." Rae suspected its authority had been challenged more than once.

A pleasant-looking woman in her mid-forties came out onto the deck as Andy and Rae set the luggage down. Andy introduced her as Marge, the director's wife.

"I've heard a lot about you from Lucas and Andy," she said. Marge's rather plain face, surrounded by very short, brown curls, came alive when she smiled, and her blue eyes expressed warmth. Rae liked her immediately.

"I'd better get myself down to the dining hall and meet the incoming staff before Lucas or Carl call for me over the PA system," Andy said, as if reluctant to leave, but he lifted his hand in parting and hurried down the steep path. She watched as he got into the yellow car, turned it around and drove down to the dining hall. Her eyes swept the lake as she thought of the infamous diving board incident.

Marge stood beside her and pointed out her house, several yards from "Off Limits." A rustic mountain home with a shingled roof, it was situated in the center of camp. The house was almost obscured by lush, green foliage and thick clumps of rhododendron, growing down the banks of a fast-flowing stream that ran in front of it. A bridge arched high above the stream, leading to the deck across the front of the house.

"That long, modern building at the far end of the lake houses office space on the top floor and the infirmary on the lower floor. The nurses have quarters there during the summer. But we'll see it all later," Marge promised.

She opened the screen door, and they stepped into the living room, furnished with utilitarian but comfortable furniture. "The fireplace is the only source of heat. Some evenings are quite cool, but you won't notice it most of the time. You'll be so tired, you'll simply fall into bed," she laughed.

"That's encouraging," Rae said and wrinkled her nose in mock dismay.

A doorway to the left led to Rae's bedroom. The furnishings were spartan in their simplicity—two cots, a dresser, and a chest of drawers. From the front window, she looked out upon the deck, then out toward the view of the lake and mountains beyond.

"You'll share your bedroom with the rifle instructor," Marge told her. At Rae's quick glance, Marge laughed. "*She's* an expert. Has won marksmanship awards for years. And she's only twenty-two. She was with us last year."

Two crafts instructors would room together in one of the other bedrooms; the crafts director, in the third.

"I'll take all of you on a complete tour this afternoon. Go ahead and get settled. I'll see you in the dining hall at noon."

The crafts director, who insisted upon being called by her first name, arrived first. Rae learned that Adele was a librarian at a private girls' college, had never married, and looked forward all year to leaving the heat of northern Illinois for the coolness of the western North Carolina mountains. "I've always been interested in crafts," she explained, "and these campers keep me young."

So that's her secret, Rae thought, for in spite of her gray hair, her sparkling blue eyes reflected a lively spirit and love of life. "I would almost pay them to let me come here," she added, then jested, "but don't tell Lucas."

Rae was equally delighted when the crafts girls, Peggy and Linda, arrived. Peggy, an art major just finishing her junior year, was a tiny, cute brunette whose dimples accompanied a ready smile. Linda was a lovely girl from the Cherokee reservation. She would be teaching Indian crafts.

Leslie, the rifle instructor, was the last of Rae's cabinmates to arrive. Her red hair was her outstanding physical characteristic, followed closely by at least a million freckles. A tall, trim girl whose forceful personality was contrasted by warm brown eyes, Leslie was a college graduate who would begin officers' training school in the fall, to continue in the family military tradition.

Shortly before noon they walked down to the dining hall where the kitchen staff had set out, on long tables in the main part of the building, hamburgers with all the trimmings; crisp, raw vegetables; and platters piled high with fresh locally grown fruit.

Carl stood at the head of the line, restraining the hungry staff. When everyone was in line, Lucas went to the microphone and asked that they bow their heads. His prayer was a short, simple one, thanking God for the food, for the staff, and asking His guidance as they prepared to share their lives with young men.

After the "Amen," Rae regarded him long and seriously.

Lucas's acknowledgment of God was not just a ritual, but seemed to be as much a part of him as breathing. Though much about Lucas was a mystery to Rae, she sensed a deep religious conviction within him. She had felt it when they were on the mountain that first morning together, when he said he wanted a Christian girl for Andy, and when he admitted his own dependence on God.

Considering all the things that appealed to her about Lucas, she realized he had never appealed to her as much as he did at this moment. Regardless of how much money a person had, or how physically attractive, a man was never taller, nor stronger, nor more intriguing, than when he admitted his need for God.

Rae turned and moved with the line to fill her plate. Her sudden elation was replaced by a sinking feeling. Her own faith in God would mean nothing to Lucas without a life to back it up. No matter how able she might prove herself to be on the job, she was sure that, when he learned the whole truth, he would not approve of her. . .not even for Andy.

Rae forced her mind from these unhappy thoughts and followed Marge and the others to the screened-in deck overlooking the lake. From this vantage point, they could see a huge, colorful float near the diving station.

Marge explained that it was called the "blob." A boy could crawl out to the edge and sit on it. A counselor or several small campers would then jump off the diving board, land on the air-inflated blob, and the camper would fly up into the air, then come screaming down into the water, arms and legs waving wildly. "They all love it," she said.

After lunch, Lucas welcomed the staff and introduced Carl and Marge, praising their efforts in directing the camp operation all year in preparation for these few weeks during the summer.

When Lucas introduced Andy, he stressed his experience and training—leaving no doubt that Andy held his position as junior camp director, not because he was the nephew of the owner, but because of his own unique qualifications.

"This is a time for self-analysis and recommitment to the young men who are sent here from all over the world to receive the best training and finest influence available. We're here to give them just that!"

How will I ever learn all these names? Rae wondered, as Carl asked the entire staff to stand and introduce themselves. Being able to state her own qualifications for being a part of such a select group gave her a good feeling. She was grateful she had the opportunity to speak of her father and saw some knowing nods, indicating that many of the staff knew of him.

After lunch, Marge took Rae and her cabinmates on a tour. She parked the Jeep in front of the long, two-story office building. In the infirmary they met two of the nurses, Mable and Suzie, who assured them that at times those rooms would be filled to capacity. Sometimes a virus ran through the camp. There would be the inevitable scrapes, sprains, and bruises. And, occasionally, young campers would be stricken with homesickness.

"One little patient woke me up in the middle of the night," Suzie told them. "He looked so pitiful, and, when I asked what was wrong, he said he couldn't sleep. Luckily, I had just the medicine," she said, laughing. "We keep ice cream in the refrigerator for just such emergencies."

Marge took them upstairs to the offices and introduced Ann, the executive secretary and receptionist. Before Ann could finish her greeting, the urgency of the phone demanded her attention.

Crossing the hallway, they entered another long room, where a bright smile from a very pretty face welcomed Marge and her entourage. Nina was introduced as the registrar, who processed the applications and kept all the information on each camper. "Her skills on the word processor are invaluable," Marge told them.

"And I'm Cindy," an attractive blond said when they turned her way. She began asking about each of them, and Rae knew she was one of those rare, enviable persons whose warmth and vibrant personalities shone through immediately.

"Now let's get your summer uniforms," Marge said, and they walked down the hallway to the clothing room where they met Laura, a young woman whose blue-gray eyes held a clear, direct expression, and her sweet smile gave the impression of early morning sunshine, fresh and pure.

Each of the girls was issued several sets of forest green shorts and khaki shirts. The shirts displayed a tennis player emblem on the left pocket, and the word *staff* embroidered above it. White socks also bore the emblem.

After leaving the office building, Marge drove them along the main road, which led to a front and back entrance. She pointed toward mountainsides dotted with cabins, each of which would accommodate eight to ten campers, a counselor, a junior counselor and a counselor-in-training. Nearer the lake were cottages for male staff and tribal directors.

Again it was the gym that fascinated Rae. Running the entire length of the huge building was storage space for all kinds of athletic equipment. One large room was devoted solely to gymnastic equipment.

"The gym is also used for church services on Sunday morning," Marge explained. "It's the only building large enough to accommodate all the campers at one time, except for the dining hall. Some of the campers are sons of noted Christian athletes, so Lucas often asks the fathers to speak. Even Bill Graham, who lives about fifteen minutes away, in Montreat, has spoken to our campers."

Soon Marge headed back toward "Off Limits." "You should get to bed early tonight," she suggested, handing each of them a packet. Later, when Rae looked over the papers, outlining the schedule during the next week of training and orientation, she had the feeling Marge had given good advice. The would be needing all the rest they could get.

After they turned out their lamps, Rae lay on the bunk nearest the front window, where she breathed deeply of the cool, moist night air and snuggled under warm blankets. All was quiet except for the sound of crickets and insects claiming their right to the night. She could feel herself drifting off to sleep before she had finished her prayers.

Chapter 7

Wsinging, "Nothing could be finer than to be in Carolina in the morning!" accompanied by a loud trumpet.

With a groan, Leslie turned over. "I'm afraid that's our alarm clock for the entire summer!" she explained. "It's a tape they play over the PA system. And we will be warned that if anything happens to it, they have plenty of spares!"

Chuckling, Leslie flung aside her covers and sat on the edge of her bunk.

Soon figures clad in green shorts and khaki shirts were jogging down the mountainsides toward the dining hall.

Lucas, attired in camp uniform like the others, welcomed everyone. After breakfast, the staff sat around the tables on the dining hall deck for Lucas's indoctrination, much of which included an explanation of the material in the packet Marge had given her.

"Our most obvious purpose," Lucas said, "is to provide the campers with a fun-filled, enjoyable three weeks. The campers will be divided by age: Junior camp, ages seven to eleven; Senior camp, ages twelve to sixteen. After that, into tribes—Apaches, Seminoles, Cherokees and Comanches. The younger, unskilled camper will strive—by improving some skills and learning others— to attain the rank of Brave and Pathfinder, the ultimate goal being Little Chief."

Normally a camper of thirteen, fourteen, or fifteen who had attended the camp for several years was ready to be tested for physical endurance and mental aptitude. Attitude was a major test, for a "Little Chief" must be gentle and helpful, as well as brave and strong.

"We will expose each camper to a variety of activities and encourage him to excel in at least one area," Lucas continued. "Staff members must make written reports on each camper under their care. This will demand careful, meticulous evaluation."

Rae grew increasingly apprehensive as she listened to the stringent goals that demanded professionalism and organization. Every other staff member had submitted an application, with references that had been thoroughly checked. She had not. Each of them had been accepted with the clear under-standing that he or she would be tested in a particular skill before acceptance was final. She hadn't had to pass a single test.

After this briefing, the staffers were told to get into their swimsuits and meet at the lake in fifteen minutes. Because of the many water sports—swim-ming, diving, canoeing, sailing, and life-saving—water safety was a must. Rae was perfectly at ease in this area, for she had always felt comfortable with water sports and was especially skilled in diving. Even Lucas and Carl joined the others in the life-saving course.

Rae marveled at the way Lucas's great body glided through the water with such grace and ease. His muscular frame was surpassed only by that of David, a body builder and one of the tribal directors.

Testing in all the other disciplines continued through Monday and Tuesday.

The staff gathered around the tennis courts to watch as the applicants for tennis instructor were carefully scrutinized during play. Though Andy was unexcelled, of course, the games provided excellent opportunity for the young men to demonstrate their skill, style, knowledge of the game, and attitude.

Rae's turn to demonstrate her expertise in gymnastics came on Tuesday morning. She would compete with two young men who had applied for a position in gymnastics.

"Could the guys go first?" Rae asked Andy.

"Sure," he said, after a moment's hesitation. His smile was warm, but she saw the questioning look in his eyes. She knew she had paled, for she felt that crazy case of jitters that often struck before competition. She must prove—to herself, as well as to Lucas, who insisted on the best in what he offered young campers—that she was a qualified instructor.

Rae watched from the sidelines as the two young men took their turns. They were good. Excellent, in fact. Her heart hammered, her palms grew moist, and she felt nauseous, in spite of the fact she had known better than to eat any breakfast.

Rae had spent some time in the gym the night before, practicing a few routines and testing the surface of the tumbling mat. She had decided to per-form barefoot. The exact routine was familiar, one that she had used hundreds of times in competition, exhibitions, and classes.

Now her tape recorder, as much a part of her equipment as her warm-up suit and leotards, was ready on the sidelines. She joined in the enthusiastic applause for the young men, for it was well deserved. But she had been trained by Raymond Martin, and she was ready to demonstrate what he had taught her.

Were this a match of physical prowess alone, she knew she would fail, for the young men had displayed superior strength on the pommel horse and parallel bars. But her *gymnastics moderne* classes and their stringent routines had given her an undeniable edge.

She knew what she must do. She would not give less than her best. She would not simply display the correct movements, the results of many years of discipline and training, but she would give an exhibition. It would be a tribute to her father and his years of tireless effort. She would draw upon the inner strength he always stressed.

And then Andy was calling her name—"Rae Martin."

Her father had always said, "When you see nothing but that vault, it's time to go." She stood, forcing the spectators from her mind, telling herself it was not Lucas she must please ultimately, but herself. She welcomed the intense surge of concentration.

Unconsciously she tugged at her leotards, brushed at the hair that was already turning into ringlets, positioned her body, lifted her chin, felt the silence of an audience holding its breath, then stared at the horse until nothing else occupied her mind.

Her flight began. In an instant her body somersaulted in a tuck position, reaching the horse in a handstand. The next instant she completed the vault by a somersault identical to the first, then landed with a flourish, her back to the horse. The effort, concentration, and years of practice that had gone into the vaulting, was culminated almost as soon as it began.

Rae wiped her hands and her forehead, allowing herself time to catch her breath and decrease the rapid beating of her heart before she moved to the balance beam. In competition, one slip on the balance beam could cost a medal or a career. While teaching the young campers, she would not have to follow all the rules or perform the more difficult maneuvers. She would be expected only to demonstrate a knowledge of the basic tenets. However, for herself and her father, she intended to perform as if the gold medal were the prize.

She mounted by jumping from the springboard and landing on one foot at the end of the beam, keeping the other foot free at the end of the beam, and extending her arms. Her graceful movements incorporated the *moderne* technique. Strength, balance, agility, and personal innovation were evident as she performed her cat leap and turn, arabesque holding position, forward springs, aerial walkover, and, unrelentingly, a standing back somersault. She worked the entire beam, first supporting herself on her hands with one foot touching the beam, then kicked up to a handstand, turned 180 degrees to face the opposite direction, then executed a forward walkover and dismounted to land with her back to the beam.

With this part of the routine successfully completed, Rae couldn't allow the tension and pressure to leave her yet, but she could breathe a little easier. The uneven parallel bars gave her opportunity to exercise creativity in a way the vault and balance beam could not—these required much more rigid, meticulous movements. The asymmetric bars demanded a continuous movement, calling upon strength, agility, flexibility, and stamina developed through a regular program of exercise.

From a running position, Rae jumped from the springboard into the air, executed a 360 degree spin, grasped the low bar, circled over it forward, down and up again, supported herself above the bar, and dropped down. Then, hanging from the low bar with arms straight, she moved her legs forward in a piked position and propelled herself through a 180 degree turn upwards to grasp the high bar. With fluid grace she performed the swinging movements, suspension, and passage of her body between the bars. Finally, after circling up through a headstand on the high bar, she swung down, did a backward somersault, and dismounted, facing the bars.

Rae's father always had told her to smile before she began her floorwork. She knew she had not failed her father this day, nor herself. Her broad smile reflected her appreciation of the audience's applause. Her next routine would be for them.

She could not relax completely yet. The floorwork, however, was her forte and called for the kind of movements she had taught almost daily at the university for the past three years.

Standing at the edge of the floor mat, she lifted her arm. The music began. For the next minute and a half her routine displayed the beauty and elegance of the female form as she combined artistic and gymnastic movements in her handsprings, somersaults, handstands, pirouette spins, and jumps.

Rae loved this, for it was the most aesthetically beautiful of the gymnastic events, providing graceful interludes between the tumbling movements. She perfectly performed a roundoff and a double back somersault, landed in a gymnast's graceful stance, then finalized the movements with a body wave by bringing her feet together, and standing on tiptoes with her head and shoulders back, knees and hips forward. After a quick bow, and a lift of her arms, she ran from the floor.

Her radiant face, framed by damp curls, turned toward the audience that had risen to its feet spontaneously, applauding enthusiastically. That tribute was especially appreciated, for many of them were just as capable as she in their own particular skill.

She looked toward Lucas for approval, but he was talking to Carl and Andy, studying the clipboard in Andy's hand.

One by one, or in clusters, the staff began to leave the gym. Rae slipped into her warm-ups, then sat on a bench to put on her socks. When she saw the great hairy legs in front of her, she looked up.

"Raymond Martin would have been very proud of you today," Lucas said in a voice meant only for her ears.

Chapter 8

By Wednesday, the testing was complete, and final assignments were given. Rae would instruct gymnastics for both junior and senior camps, with the two young gymnasts assisting her, and would also take her turn on the waterfront.

The next several days were spent studying and absorbing camper applications. Rae felt she knew all the campers well, even before their arrival, for complete files were provided, along with photos.

Schedules and lists were made, revised, and approved. Plans were finalized concerning the skills that would be taught in beginner, intermediate, and advanced classes for both junior and senior campers.

By Saturday evening, after the intensive week of training, everyone was ready for a change of pace. Rae had been told that it was traditional for a girls' camp staff from another part of North Carolina to travel to Lucas's camp for a square dance the night before opening day.

Rae had become so accustomed to seeing the green shorts and khaki shirts that it seemed strange now to be confronted with hillbillies dressed in jeans and western shirts. She had asked Andy to bring her a pair of jeans and a checkered shirt from the big house.

Lucas was standing near the door of the gym, greeting many of his guests for the evening, when Rae walked up.

"You'll be a converted hillbilly before the night's over," Lucas predicted. His friendly manner and mountain-man attire reminded her of the first morning they had spent together on the mountaintop.

"There's definitely a twang in the air," Rae laughed as she started to walk past him.

Lucas reached out and grabbed her arm, then steered her through the doorway. "The Mountain Creek Boys," he said, gesturing toward the small bluegrass band.

"Oh, look!" Rae pointed. "I didn't know Andy could do that!" She was intrigued to see Andy clogging with an attractive brunette from the girls' camp. There was toe-heel-toe tapping to the hip-slapping music of guitars, and those on the sidelines clapped to the beat, patting their feet and calling out a few "Ah-haws."

After the clogging exhibition, a square dance was announced. Andy and the brunette paired off, while others formed a circle.

"Now it's your turn," Lucas said, but Rae shook her head.

"I don't know how," she said regretfully.

"You don't need to know how. Just follow me." There was a challenge in his eyes.

Taking a deep breath, Rae squared her shoulders and walked to the circle with Lucas.

"All join hands," the call was given.

Lucas grabbed her left hand and, simultaneously, she felt the right one being grasped. She looked around into the smiling face of Hank, one of the tribal directors. Before she could object, the caller was singing out, "Circle left," and for the next twenty minutes, she wasn't able to utter a word.

The circling was easy, but the calls confused her: "Texas star. Circle four. Swing that opposite girl. Now your own."

The only thing Rae understood was that when the caller said, "Now your own purty little gal," she was in Lucas's arms, then just as quickly was whisked away. It didn't take long for her to realize that no matter how confused she became, or how lost, Lucas always found her.

At one point, only briefly, Andy was her partner. "Having fun?" he asked.

She could only nod, fearful that by the time she answered, she would be handed off to another.

"Promenade around the ring, promenade that purty little thing." Two by two they circled, Lucas's arm around her shoulder, his hand holding her lifted one.

After the dance, Lucas was introducing Rae to the director of the girls' camp when Andy came up to claim her. When the next round began, he asked, "Want to try it?"

"I've had enough for awhile," Rae said, laughing. "Go find yourself a good dancer and have some *real* fun."

Andy squeezed her hand and looked down into her eyes. A special gleam was there, and his smile was sweet. "You're one girl in a million," he said, winked affectionately, then walked away. Andy found his clogging partner, and they joined the square dance circle.

Slipping through the doorway of the gym, Rae inhaled deeply of the brisk air. The coolness felt refreshing on her warm skin.

"You're apparently not the jealous type," Lucas said, joining her.

"It wouldn't change anything if I were," she replied noncommittally.

"No, I suppose not." Lucas's face wore a forbidding frown.

"I encouraged Andy to find a good partner," Rae explained. "After all, *you* danced with me."

"I'm part of the family," he countered.

Rae looked away. "Beautiful, isn't it? The stars are so bright."

"You should see them reflected on the lake," he said. "And tomorrow, we'll have about that many young men *in* the lake."

Rae laughed. "Noisier, I expect."

"Ah, quite!" He took her elbow. "Even noisier than that." He gestured toward the gym where the bluegrass music could be heard. They walked down the path, toward the lake.

"Is Isobel's son still ill?" Rae asked.

"No," Lucas replied, glancing toward her. "He's fine now."

"I'm surprised she isn't here tonight for the festivities."

Lucas grinned. "This kind of primitive exertion doesn't appeal to Isobel."

"Doesn't she like camp life? I mean, if you marry her, wouldn't she help you run the camp?"

Lucas's inquisitive glance made Rae wonder if she had become too personal. He gazed out into the distance before answering.

"Isobel appreciates what the camp does for her son. During the winter Kevin attends a private school. At summer camp we give him discipline, attention, and a sense of belonging. He needs that, and Isobel knows it." Rae felt her face flush under his sudden scrutiny. "Do you think I would marry a woman because she might be an asset in my chosen field?"

Rae had to answer honestly. "No. I don't think you would."

"If you must insist upon knowing my deepest secrets, fair maiden," he said, taking her arm and leading her to a canoe tied up in a stall along the lakeshore, "then I shall whisk you away to yon faraway deserted island."

Laughing, Rae settled into the shaky craft. Lucas was a man of many moods. This was a side of him she had not seen before. "Yon island" was all of about fifty feet from the edge of the lake and not more than that in length, with two solitary trees on it.

"Now," he said, paddling on alternate sides of the canoe, "what were we talking about?"

"Why you never married," Rae reminded him. She felt strange being out on the lake alone with Lucas, beneath the stars. The music was so faint now that the sounds of night life were becoming more predominant. Her voice sounded strange to her own ears. "Why haven't you?"

Lucas looked surprised, then laughed low. "Ramona Martin, I have the sneaky feeling you're prying."

"Well, it works both ways," Rae said, lifting her chin. "You have asked me all sorts of questions. Do I not have the same privilege?"

"Yes," Lucas replied quickly, more serious than she thought he would be. "You're interested in Andy. His lifestyle and relatives are a part of him."

Rae stared down at her tennis shoes, then glanced up through lowered lashes. Lucas was still quite serious. "I think you're a girl who follows her heart instead of her head."

"You're wrong," she argued. "I'm like my father. I think things through before I make a decision. . .that is, generally." The absurdity of her claim struck her forcefully.

"Probably," he conceded. "It's just that the things that seem important to you are not the things most women in your position would consider priorities—financial security, social status, the right clothes. No," he spoke with conviction, "I believe you would be wondering if you could live with a man for a lifetime, bear his children, love him when he's at his worst." He paused, not expecting an answer.

Rae's voice was softly thoughtful. "During my mother's illness, my father and I were extremely close. There is something about the bond of suffering that draws people together. Because of her hospital expenses, we had financial difficulties, but no amount of money could have bought the love we shared. And our faith in God gave us strength to face her death. Then, when my father became ill, I learned all over again the sufficiency of God's grace. I suppose that's why, although I enjoy material things, I know there are more important things in life."

Lucas was silent, only occasionally stroking the water with the paddle. He took the oar and laid it across the canoe in front of him. "I'm going to tell you something I've never told anyone," he said.

Part of Rae wanted to hear how he felt, what he thought, what was going on inside of him. Another part feared what he might say. Everything was still as she waited. There was no sound of music now, and even the night noises were being driven into the background by the sound of her own heart's beating in her temples. There seemed to exist only the two of them.

The thought flashed through Rae's mind that the lake looked different tonight. This morning it had been blue, clear, without a ripple on the surface, giving the appearance of polished glass, the reflection of trees and the island and the dock perfectly reproduced. In the afternoon the lake had been a summer-leaf green. A light wind had stirred the surface much like one dips a spoon in frosting and lifts it, leaving slight indentations and peaks. Tonight it was a deep gray-blue, reflecting a myriad of brilliant stars. This would be the impression she would carry with her always.

When Lucas spoke, the sound of his voice, resonant and deep, lay gently on the still, starlit night. He mentioned having been acquainted with many women of many types, from many countries. "But there is a mountain in Switzerland that intrigues me," he added.

Rae looked at him quizzically.

"We're not compatible—that mountain and I," he continued. "She's treacherous, has thrown me many times, but I get up laughing, determined to accept her challenge. When I am skiing down that slope, I feel that I make an important conquest if I reach bottom upright. Frankly, I rather like it when she wins." He looked at her then.

"And that's the kind of woman you want?" Rae choked.

His laugh was light. "I used to think so. I often wondered if there was a woman out there for me who expected, even demanded, more of me than gliding smoothly along the slopes of life. But there always seemed to be a missing ingredient."

"Do you know what was missing?" Rae asked in a small voice.

"Of course," he replied immediately, that mocking expression on his face. "I thought I would fall in love. I had visions of such delight. As you seem to have done."

Rae found his sarcastic tone irritating. "I wouldn't marry a man I *didn't* love," she assured him.

"Ah, love," Lucas said with amusement. "Is love some tangible thing, or some illusory fantasy? Is it not some figment of imagination one finds in a novel? Is it not wiser to be practical, sensible? Chasing love might be like chasing rainbows. Looking for that pot of gold that can never be found."

"You mean you think I should consider how much I might gain financially when I marry?" Rae asked, resenting his cynicism.

"I didn't say that," Lucas replied in a low voice. "I was merely suggesting that you consider your options."

In that instant Rae realized that what often seemed like tender moments with Lucas turned out to be another of his attempts to explore her motives regarding Andy. And she had fallen for it every time. That angered her. "So you no longer believe in love!" she fired.

Looking at her levelly, he lifted his eyebrows. "I know the mountain exists. Perhaps the woman does."

Rae shook her head in confusion. She did not understand him. Glancing over at him, she saw he was amused. It was difficult, if not impossible, to know when he was serious and when he was not.

He sighed. "As one grows older, however, the tendency is to be more of a realist, and less a romantic. I think I have come to the conclusion that such a woman does not exist. . .at least, for me. Perhaps I should settle for compatibility."

Rae watched as his jawline tensed. She almost regretted having been engaged in such a conversation, for now he seemed remote and sad.

"But there have been times, Ramona," he said softly, almost as if talking to himself, "when I have longed for a woman, not just to fill my arms, but to fill my heart. I think the most irresistible woman in the world would be one—" he spoke the words hesitantly, almost fearfully—"one who truly loved me."

His rugged profile seemed to be carved from the mountain itself. There was something touching about this man beneath whose steel and fire ran deep reservoirs of tenderness and longing, springing up like some subterranean stream from the heart of the mountain. He was a man who had everything, yet longed for something more.

"You have Isobel," Rae said quietly, and his gaze returned to her.

"Of course. And Isobel would fit perfectly with my lifestyle."

"But you said she wouldn't care for camp life."

Now he looked at her as though she were a foolish child. The intimate sharing was over.

"This is only a small part of my life, Ramona," he explained. "The camp is very important to me, but I also have a winter resort in North Carolina and one in Switzerland. And perhaps you aren't aware of my line of sports equipment. Isobel would be greatly admired in those circles."

"You seem to so enjoy preparing for camp, the boys, the square dance," Rae said weakly, remembering his vitality and verve, his hearty laughter. He was a part of these mountains, this culture.

"I can live without it," he replied tersely. "All this will be Andy's someday. You would be an ideal partner to work alongside him. You're good for him, Ramona."

To cover her sudden discomfort, she sought a subject that would take his mind off her relationship with Andy. "It has occurred to me that it seems a shame that only young men will be here to take advantage of the expert skills of your staff. Have you ever considered making the camp coed?"

"You must be a mindreader," Lucas replied immediately. "I've even thought of discussing the possibility with you. It would take a very special kind of woman to direct it. With your background, skills, and Christian commitment, Rae, parents would admire and respect you. They would feel comfortable sending their girls to such a camp."

"I wasn't speaking of myself, Lucas," Rae protested quickly.

His smile was warm and beautiful. "But I believe you are that very special person who could make it successful." He reached for the oar and began to maneuver the small craft toward the island.

Rae felt the rising panic within. Her thoughts were in turmoil. She wanted to blurt out hers and Andy's deception, free herself of the weight of guilt before things went any farther.

Strange, when she had agreed to accompany Andy to North Carolina, it hadn't seemed so complicated. She had justified his silly scheme in her own mind by telling herself she was helping a young man who had made a foolish mistake. She had even thought she might be a good influence on him. But now it had grown all out of proportion. Confession would ease her conscience. She could then obtain Lucas's forgiveness and try to set a genuine Christian example for the camp.

But the timing was all wrong. Beginning tomorrow, each of them faced tremendous responsibilities. Lucas had emphasized that the campers were their top priority for the summer. Her confession would cause division among Lucas, Andy, and herself. Rae would just have to suffer silently—for the sake of all of them.

Feeling trapped in a web of deceit, Rae lifted her hand to her head, then looked for any sign of distraction from her thoughts.

"Oh, look!" she exclaimed as a fish broke the surface of the water farther out. She leaned over just as Lucas swung the oar.

"Watch it!" he cautioned abruptly, but too late. The canoe was tipping, and, before she could regain her balance, she was plunging headlong into the water.

Lucas released the oar and followed her. For an embarrassing moment, both of them flailed about, reaching for the paddle.

"Oh, Lucas!" Rae sputtered away the lake water. "What an awkward thing for me to do!"

"I quite agree," he said, attempting to right the canoe.

Rae swam around to the other side. "We'll never get back into this thing," she wailed.

"We'll just have to drag it back to shore. And to think," Lucas said with amusement, "we were almost stranded on a deserted island."

"Almost," Rae repeated, trying to imitate his joking manner, then added incredulously, "Am I doing all the work?"

"It would appear so," he replied. "Why don't you relax and try walking?"

"Walking?" Rae stammered, then realized they had reached shallow water.

They both laughed. After Lucas secured the canoe, he came over to where Rae stood shivering. "Your clothes are at the Haven, aren't they?" he asked.

"Everything except my camp uniforms."

"Let's jog up there," he suggested. "We can change, then I'd like to discuss some plans with you."

When they neared the gym, Lucas spied a counselor. "Tim," he called, "would you please find Andy and tell him that Rae and I have gone up to the Haven?"

"Sure," Tim replied, a grin spreading across his face at the sight of the soggy couple. "He was inside just a minute ago."

"Let's go," Lucas said to Rae, and they began to jog up the road by the gym, their tennis shoes squishing with every step.

After reaching the house, Lucas and Rae sat on the top step of the first deck to remove their shoes and socks. "Sorry I ruined your evening." Rae said apologetically.

"Ruined my evening?" Lucas asked, as if the idea were preposterous.

"You probably weren't ready to come home yet."

"If I hadn't been," he replied, pulling off his socks, "I would have stayed there and drip-dried."

"I'm glad you're not angry," she said sincerely, grateful for his lenient attitude.

"I will admit I hadn't planned to swim in my jeans," he said, taking her shoes and his own. He set them side by side at the edge of the deck, with the wet socks on top. Then he came back and drew her up by her hands. "But the evening was not a total loss," he assured. His voice grew soft. "I enjoy teaching you things."

Rae looked up at him, his dark eyes shadowed as he bent his head toward hers. "I like teaching a city girl how to adapt to our mountain ways. How to square dance. How not to rock a boat."

Rae told herself Lucas was being very kind, trying to make light of their misadventure. Perhaps that intense look on his face was her imagination. But the feel of his warm breath against her cheek was all too real. "Fortunate is the man who will have the privilege of teaching you," he added, "everything."

Rae longed to tell him she wished that he might be that man, but his next words seemed to contradict any such possibility. "I believe he's here now," he said as tires screeched against the gravel on the driveway.

A concerned Andy was bounding up the steps. He stopped suddenly, taking in their wet clothing and bare feet at a glance.

"This time it was not a glass of water, but an entire lake," Lucas laughed. "She dunked me—right out of the canoe!"

Chapter 9

U ncle Lucas tells me you have some terrific ideas about including girls in the camp program," said Andy after Rae entered the lounge, clad in a warm sweater and slacks. In her haste to shower and change, she had not bothered to dry her hair, and it curled in tight ringlets about her head.

"I don't know anything about camping except what I've learned this week. And that knowledge hasn't been proven yet," she shrugged. "So I'm not about to tell you how to run a girls' camp," she said adamantly.

"You look terrific, Rae," Andy said admiringly, "even without your hair fixed, and with your nose all shiny."

"Thanks, Andy," she smiled and sat down beside him on the couch. "But I really don't know how I can help you, so flattery will get you nowhere."

"We don't expect that much, Rae," Lucas assured her, handing her a cup of steaming hot chocolate which she accepted gratefully. "We just want your opinion on a few things. There were times when I had hopes of Mimi's taking an interest in this venture, but I've abandoned that hope. I've been waiting until I felt the time was right. Perhaps, now, it is."

Lucas walked over to a file cabinet near his desk and removed a folder, then returned to the easy chair he had pulled up to the coffee table, across from Rae and Andy. He moved the tray aside and laid the folder on the table.

"This is the area at the back of the camp, beyond Marge's and Carl's house, where cabins could be built. And this mountain here," he said, pointing to a plat of his property, "could be leveled and a new gym built there. Do you think the girls' gym should be separate from the boys'?" he asked Rae.

"I think so," she asserted. "It would be good to have some interaction between the boys and girls—even competition—but their training should be separate. They would want to impress each other with their skills, but I don't think they would be comfortable together while in the learning process."

To prove her point, Rae related some experiences she had had as a child at church camp. "They should be together for meals, though," she smiled, remembering.

"Then I would need to extend the dining hall," Lucas mused, looking at Andy for his opinion.

"There's plenty of room to expand," Andy said. "And even for extending the deck out over the lake. How many girls should be enrolled?"

"What do you think, Rae?" Lucas asked

Rae felt he knew exactly what he would do, but wanted to hear her answer. "If," she began, emphasizing the conditional stipulation, "if it were my decision, I would limit the number of girls. I would employ staff with exceptional skills, like you have for the boys' camp, and accept only girls who are interested in athletics. It's so important to train them properly when they're young. Some of the girls in my classes at the university had learned habits that were almost impossible to overcome and hampered their technique."

"A small group of girls, seriously interested in athletics," Lucas nodded in approval. "That would diminish some of the supervision problems that have concerned me."

"It would be a great service to young girls," Rae suggested. "A real ministry—if handled properly."

"Yes," Lucas agreed readily. "If we get the right person to direct it." He handed them blueprints of the cabins and an area marked off for a swimming pool. "We could make the swimming pool Olympic size," he said.

"Oh, to be young again!" Rae exclaimed. "I'd like to be one of those campers myself."

"I'm sure Uncle Lucas will let you sign up, Rae." Andy laughed, reaching for her hand.

"I've kept you two long enough," Lucas said, gathering up his blueprints. "You probably want to get back to the square dance."

"Shall we?" Andy asked Rae, and she felt he was eager to return to the campgrounds.

"It's fine with me," she said agreeably.

"Thanks for your opinions and suggestions," Lucas said, closing the folder and standing. "And Andy," he continued seriously, "although you have done a good job with the camp in the past, I detect a new sense of direction and a more positive attitude about you this season. I'm confident this will be our finest summer yet."

"Rae has a lot to do with that, Uncle Lucas." Andy smiled down at her. "I'm beginning to understand what you meant when you talked to me about taking life and relationships more seriously. Maybe it just takes that special person to make a guy realize it."

Lucas nodded. "I want you to know something else, Andy. Whenever you're ready to settle down and take over the running of the camp, I'm ready to begin releasing more responsibilities to you. And Rae," he continued, looking deep into her eyes, "I consider it a privilege having you on our staff. I can well picture you heading up the girls' camp. Think it over."

Lucas's acceptance and approval of her was not only reflected in his words, but in his eyes. Rae felt lost in his poignant gaze for a moment. How pleased he seemed to be in believing she and Andy might marry.

"Lucas," she began helplessly, and his questioning gaze invited her to continue. But she felt Andy's hand grip her shoulder, and she recognized his signals that a confession at this moment would destroy the confidence his uncle had just expressed in them. "Good night, Lucas," she said.

Andy steered her out the door before she could reconsider.

"How could you possibly put on such a blatant display of hypocrisy, Andy?" she blurted out angrily when they were in the car. "It's bad enough to know we're playing this deceitful game, but you're behaving as if everything is settled between us. That's going too far!"

Andy was undaunted by her anger, and tenderly touched her lips with a finger. "I'll tell you all about that in about three weeks. A date?"

"Definitely!" Rae assured. She knew she must try to come to terms with her emotional conflict. But she couldn't think about that now—not with three weeks of camping just ahead.

❧

Sunday morning dawned bright and clear. Although registration was scheduled from one to five o'clock, campers were piling from cars, and buses full of noisy boys were arriving from the airport even before the eleven o'clock church service scheduled in the gym.

It was a memorable moment when nearly one hundred staff members, campers, and guests joined in the singing of several favorite hymns before Chuck, one of the tribal directors who would return to the seminary in the fall, sang a solo in his beautiful baritone voice.

The famed area evangelist spoke on the wonder of the body, the temple of God. He praised Lucas for his ministry to the physical growth of young men and emphasized the even more important need for spiritual growth, which could be accomplished by an acceptance of Jesus Christ as one's personal Saviour, then a daily exercise of the Lord's teachings.

After the service, everyone was invited to share in the picnic lunch to be eaten outdoors, since part of the dining hall was being used for registration lines.

Rae was to assist on the waterfront. Each camper had to be tested in order to determine if he belonged in a beginner, intermediate, or advanced swim class.

She knew they'd have to give time for lunch to settle before allowing the boys into the water, but by one-thirty she was clad in her swimsuit and a floppy hat that Tim had found to keep her nose from turning into a beet in the hot sun. On her clipboard was an alphabetical list on which to rate the swimmers.

Time passed quickly and by four o'clock over half the expected three hundred campers from all over the United States and abroad had completed the test. Standing, Rae stretched, feeling the tightness of her muscles from having sat so long observing and evaluating the style, speed, stamina, and confidence of young men as they swam.

"Take a break, Rae," Tim urged. "You deserve it."

"I do need to stretch my muscles," Rae replied and turned.

It was the woman's platinum hair that caught her attention first. Holding tightly to Lucas's hand was a little boy with hair the same startling shade.

So intent was she on the newcomers that Rae scarcely noticed the camper who walked up to her on the dock. Vaguely she saw what appeared to be a rope around his neck and was about to tell him he couldn't go into the water with it.

"Will you hold my snake while I swim?" he asked innocently, extending his arm, the slithery creature coiled tightly around it.

Rae shrieked and was forced to exhibit some of her fanciest diving technique.

Realization of what had happened was instantaneous. Everyone was laughing, and Johnny reached for her hand to help her back up on the dock.

Tim was telling the stricken camper that he couldn't keep the snake. He must either put it back where he found it or take it to the nature center.

Rae's heart went out to the little fellow. Careful not to get too close, she apologized for screaming. "I just didn't expect to meet him," she explained. "It's really a very. . .nice. . .snake. I hope I didn't scare him."

"Oh," the camper said with a grin, "he'll be all right. I'll just put him back. You think he'd like that better than the nature center?"

"I think so," Rae replied, and he smiled with relief.

There was no longer any way to avoid the trio waiting at the edge of the dock. She was dripping wet, had lost her hat, her hair was in tight ringlets, and she could feel the heat in her face.

"I. . .he had a. . . ," she began, but found herself stammering under Lucas's amused expression and the cool, tolerant look on Isobel's placid face.

"We saw," Lucas assured. "Congratulations. You've been fully indoctrinated into camp life. I want you to meet Kevin."

Feeling uncomfortable in the presence of the immaculately groomed Isobel, Rae knelt in front of Kevin, who was still clinging to Lucas's hand.

"I've heard a lot about you, Kevin. Are you feeling better?"

"I've heard about you, too," he said. Unexpectedly he leaned forward. "I know how you feel," he whispered.

"You don't like snakes either?" she asked.

Frowning, he shook his head. "But if you let anybody know, they'll try to scare you all the time—on purpose!"

"Then I'd better act bravely," she said with wide eyes. "You want to be brave with me?"

He straightened his frail shoulders and nodded.

"Bobby," Rae called, "may I go with you to put the snake back? Kevin's going along to protect me."

"Sure," Bobby replied and walked over to them. "Girls are scared of snakes," he confided in Kevin.

Isobel's thin smile was Rae's only clue that the woman was pleased with the attention Rae was giving her son, but Lucas winked his approval. She and the two little boys and the snake headed off down the path.

After Kevin and Bobby were tested, Kevin was breathless.

"Can I be in intermediate?" he asked, his eyes large and pleading, his new friend beside him. "Bobby and me can be buddies if we both make it."

There was no doubt that Bobby qualified for the more advanced rank, but Kevin was another matter. Yet Rae felt it was important to Kevin. He was a very lovable child, but she doubted that he made friends readily.

"You got very tired, Kevin," she reminded him kindly.

"That's because I've been sick. But I'm okay now. Honest! Ask Tim. I was in beginners last year, and he said I might could move up this year."

Knowing determination could play a major part in one's accomplishments, she relented. "I'll talk to Tim about it, and we'll see."

"All right!" Kevin shouted and grinned over at Bobby.

By Tuesday, the camp was settling into the routine it would follow for three weeks: Breakfast, at eight o'clock; classes, beginning at nine.

Kevin was in Rae's beginner gymnastics class, and just as she had feared, he was not well coordinated and hadn't the strength for many of the routines. Due to his agility, she suspected he might be good at tumbling, so she encouraged him to try. It was soon apparent that what Kevin needed most was a personal touch and, since there were only ten boys in this class, she was grateful that she and her assistants could give him the individual attention he craved.

Lucas put in an appearance during her first beginner class.

"You're doing wonders with Kevin. Thanks. There's more to camp life than athletic training. I appreciate your sensitivity." He looked at his watch with a grimace. "Hey! I've got to go. See you around." And he was on his way.

Rae turned her attention to the boy with the mop of pale hair. He was an adorable child, eagerly reaching out for affection. Yes, Kevin needed a father—a father like Lucas, she admitted ruefully.

Almost before she knew it, the beginner class was over, and the intermediate had taken its place, demanding more than training in balancing, tumbling, handstands, and cartwheels. Coaching the advanced class required all her discipline skill, for the young men had already learned techniques that needed to be refined. Here, however, they did not utilize music which she had found so valuable in her teaching at the university, for it provided rhythm, an aid in timing.

During the remainder of the week Rae felt that her head never quite touched the pillow before the now familiar strains of "Nothing could be. . ." were calling her to a new day.

Like a spring, she bolted from under the covers, so welcomed during the cool nights, and leaned over onto the windowsill to read the Bible and meditate. Each day the view was different—sometimes clear, sometimes with a smoky haze encircling or resting upon the lush, green mountain peaks. Inhaling deeply of the fresh morning air, she thanked God for the beauty He had created and for the joy of sharing it with others.

It was not until Sunday that Rae had a day off. After attending church services in the gym and eating in the dining hall, she went with Andy and Carl to see what was being done to the mountain behind the boys' camp.

"That's where the new gym will be," Carl said, pointing to a portion of mountain that had been leveled and cleared, readying it for the foundation.

"Lucas mentioned naming the gym after your father, Rae," Andy told her. "It will be known as the Raymond Martin Gym."

Rae was speechless. Finally she managed to ask, "Lucas would do that? For me? For my father?"

Emotion welled up in her eyes. She was hardly aware of Andy's arm circling her waist. They walked over the mountainside, discussing the cabins, the spot for the pool, the plans for the dining hall. What had been only marks on paper that night in Lucas's study were becoming a reality before their eyes.

She longed to ask Lucas about it, to express her appreciation for his tribute to her father, but there was not the opportunity during the next week, nor the next. Rae was aware, reluctantly, that the first session was rapidly coming to a close.

In the evening as she sat on the deck of "Off Limits" or in her room by the window, working on evaluations or contemplating three hundred "little Indians" who were scattered about the mountainsides, she was amazed at how much learning and fun could be packed into three weeks.

Suddenly it was Sunday afternoon again, and the first session was over.

Rae stood in front of the dining hall saying good-bye to the many campers who promised to write to her.

When Kevin came by, his handshake was surprisingly firm. Rae felt her eyes misting and there was a catch in her throat when she told him good-bye. In case she wanted to write, he gave her his address in Raleigh, then added that he would be staying with his grandparents in Asheville during the following week.

Isobel, too, seemed strangely moved when she came to collect Kevin and his belongings. "Thank you for what you've done for my son," she said, before the icy veil of reserve dropped over her eyes once more. Only once did they brighten as she looked past Rae. "I'll see you tonight, darling," she called in her soft, Southern drawl.

Rae didn't bother to turn. There was only one person to whom Isobel could be speaking.

"Mimi called early this morning," Lucas said to Rae when Isobel and Kevin had left. "It appears there's to be a wedding. I suspected that would happen when she left for Paris."

"Oh, she loves Pierre so much!" Rae turned then to face Lucas. "I'm happy for her. But I didn't know you knew."

"I make it my business to know everything about my wards," he retorted. "Mimi's grandparents in Paris are well aware of her actions and keep me informed."

Rae detected a certain reticence. "You don't approve?"

"From all I hear, Pierre is a fine man. And you're right. Mimi does love him very much. Incidentally," he said, changing the subject. "You will stay at the Haven this coming week. Most of the staff will be gone until the weekend. Then we begin again."

"Is it all right if I come to the Haven tomorrow?" she asked. "Andy is taking me out tonight, then later I have to finish my reports for Carl. So, I would like to stay at 'Off Limits' tonight."

"Fine," he said and added, "Gran will also be coming to the Haven tomorrow to spend the week with us."

Only Selma was at the Haven when Rae and Andy arrived there to dress for the evening. After taking a leisurely bath, Rae put on a chocolate-colored dress that fell in soft folds to just below her knees. She fastened gold earrings at her ear lobes and a thin gold chain around her neck, then stepped into high heels. Her skin had acquired a bronze sheen during the past three weeks, and her cheeks glowed with natural color. Only a little green eyeshadow was needed to enhance the color of her eyes. Her hair had taken on the effect of spun gold which her father had loved, and her soft, full lips shimmered faintly with a touch of gloss.

Feeling ready for a night out, she hurried to the lounge, expecting Andy to be waiting. She stopped short. Lucas stood inside the doorway, dressed in evening clothes.

"You look lovely," he said and then, as if to explain his comment, added quickly, "Our costumes are quite different from that of the past few weeks."

But Rae knew that did not explain why she didn't seem able to take her eyes from him. His physical attraction was undeniable, but even more than that were the wonderful inner qualities he had displayed during the past month. She had seen it in all he did—in his expressed purpose for the camp, his involvement with the staff, his concern for a fatherless boy, his kindness to a. . .fatherless woman.

"Lucas," she said, remembering, "the new gym. Have you really considered naming it after my father?"

"I intend to," he replied. "Your father made a significant contribution to the sports world. Through his daughter, that contribution has been extended to my camp. His name will not be forgotten. I'll make certain of that."

"Why?" she whispered. Rae did not mind that his dark eyes were probing hers, as if seeking out her innermost thoughts. Her gratitude was something she wanted him to see.

"Why?" he repeated, then she felt some kind of withdrawal in him as his eyes left her face. "I would do anything within reason for my family. And you're likely soon to be a part of it. . . . Enjoy your evening," he said, looking away from her to speak to Andy, who just entered the room.

Andy had reserved a table by a window on the twelfth floor of Grosvenors. Here they could look out above the traffic of Asheville, beyond the city lights, to the dark peaks forming a protective background against the graying sky.

The silence was not uncomfortable as they smiled across the intimate table for two. Rae sensed that this would be a significant evening. The very ambiance of the elegant restaurant suggested intimacy and sharing.

After their order was given, Rae looked out where the land touched the sky. "The stars are shining," she said softly. "I sincerely doubt there is a more beautiful place in the world than the Smoky Mountains."

Andy made no comment and Rae turned to look at him. He was twisting his glass thoughtfully.

"There's a little village in Switzerland, near Uncle Lucas's ski resort. It's quaint and charming. There's a certain chalet on the side of a mountain where you can look out and see for miles. When the area is covered with snow, there's nothing else like it anywhere."

Rae was surprised at Andy's declaration of love for Switzerland. He seemed to be trying to convince her, pausing only long enough for their food to be set before them, tasting it, and making complimentary remarks.

"There is a sports shop on a main street in that small town. It's for sale. A friend and I have talked about buying it and seeing if we can make a go of it."

"I love hearing about your dreams, Andy," she assured him, sharing his excitement. "Have you told Lucas?"

"That's the only problem," he confessed. "You've seen how Uncle Lucas is so eager to turn the camp over to me. He has trained me, set his hopes on me. I've tried, but I don't seem able to tell him that I would turn down a probable lifetime security with the camp for a shop in Switzerland that might fold at any minute. It really doesn't sound very responsible, does it?"

"You've proved you can be responsible, Andy. I've seen it this summer. So has Lucas. And I think your plans are commendable. Lucas would understand you wanting to do something on your own. I don't think he wants to force you to run the camp. He's just offering it to you."

"When I go, Rae," he said with determination, "I want to take you with me. As my wife. Surely you know I've fallen in love with you."

Did she know? There had been indications, but it hadn't really registered. They had been so busy during the past weeks. Her gaze slowly turned from Andy's waiting eyes toward the sky, twinkling in its blanket of stars.

It occurred to her that her acceptance would be the perfect solution to almost all her difficulties. Lucas would not have to wait any longer to marry Isobel. Kevin could have his much-needed father. She and Mimi could be life-time friends. She and Andy could be—compatible.

But slowly creeping into those thoughts was something more akin to the dark peaks beyond—so unmovable, mysterious, foreboding.

"I'm not asking for an answer right now," Andy said across the silence. Just think about it. Hey, this is delicious steak. How's yours?"

"Perfect. Just perfect."

"And the pianist?"

She looked toward the dark corner. "Excellent." Then it dawned upon her that Andy was trying to put her at ease, telling her to relax. "It's really a wonderful evening, Andy," she smiled then, with genuine pleasure.

"There can be many more like them, Rae."

Yes, she knew. An exciting, romantic life could exist for the two of them. Here, or in Switzerland. A lifetime of being loved by Andy should be all, and more, that a woman could ask for.

When Andy parked below "Off Limits" later that night, Rae did not protest when he pulled her gently toward him and pressed his lips against hers in a lingering kiss. Wishing with all her heart that she was in love with him, Rae allowed herself to be wanted, to be desired, to be loved, until his mouth became more demanding.

When she gently pushed him away, Andy sighed heavily. "Rae," he said seriously, "there have been many things I've wanted to hang onto rather than settle down. But now, I would give them all up. . .for you. You will think about what I've said, won't you?"

"Yes, Andy. I will," she promised. She would try, with all her might, to think about what Andy had said.

Too tired to stay awake, Rae postponed her thinking and her work. The following morning was spent in finalizing evaluations and making reports. It was late afternoon before Marge drove her and her few belongings up to the Haven.

Seeing no one about, Rae went upstairs to the room she had occupied a month before. After a leisurely bubble bath she slipped into shorts, a thin summer blouse, and sandals. Rae put away her few personal items, then felt the sudden change in the air. She walked over to the window where the wind was restlessly stirring the curtains.

The late afternoon sky, heavy with clouds, looked as if it had deliberately waited until after the campers left before spilling its contents. The blue sky became gray, then almost black, as the rain began to pelt the house and deck with heavy drops. The heavens rolled and rumbled. Bright flashes of light revealed the downpour upon the foliage. Gutters could not hold it all, and water splashed upon the deck. Sheets of lightning lit up the world, while streaks sizzled down the mountainsides.

Rae was unaware that the bedroom door had opened wider, admitting a shadowy figure, until Lucas spoke nearby, "Rae, are you frightened?"

"Frightened?" she asked, turning around.

"The electricity is out," he explained. "Andy is bringing lamps."

Rae shrugged. "I didn't know. I hadn't tried to turn them on."

He came to stand beside her. "That doesn't sound like a city girl talking."

One moment the lightning bathed his tall, athletic frame in light, its strange reflection in his eyes; the next moment, he was clothed in semi-darkness. The air was so still in the room that she parted her lips for breath and gazed up at the darkened figure, the face turned toward her, the man not touching her, yet seeming to. She was not sure if the vibration she was feeling was from the thunder or from somewhere deep inside.

"I don't think my training as an athlete prepared me for city life," she said in a strained voice. "I simply tolerated it. I seem to be awakening here in this primitive country, and I don't quite understand it."

Rae was allowed only intermittent glimpses of his inscrutable face, with the lightening gleaming in his eyes, his face shimmering with silver streaks, then fading into the darkness again.

"But you aren't afraid."

"Maybe I *am* afraid," she said, her voice in a whisper.

The world was so strange with the turmoil outside contrasting with the breathless calm inside the room.

"The fear of a storm is a healthy respect," Lucas said. "Even those trees, which have weathered many storms and have grown strong and tall and seem indestructible, can be reduced to shreds in a storm like this. No matter how mature, they are quite defenseless against the forces of nature."

"Defenseless," Rae breathed as his face came nearer, suddenly illuminated, and a tremendous rumble of thunder set the hills to quivering. The crash was that of a cymbal.

In response Rae clung to him, trembling, as vulnerable as the time-worn trees. All sorts of things could happen—in a storm like this. All sorts of things, and they were happening—in her mind, in her soul, in her heart.

Chapter 10

Rae opened her eyes to a yellow glow in the doorway. It was Andy, carrying a lighted oil lamp.

She stood frozen, immobile, conscious only that she and Lucas had been silhouetted against the window. She could not be sure that Lucas had stepped back before Andy appeared.

"Storms can be frightening," he was saying as if in explanation. "Go with Andy, Ramona. I'll close the window."

Andy left the lamp on a hall table for Lucas. In silence, with Rae's hand on his arm, they walked down the stairs and into the kitchen. Another oil lamp burned in the center of the table, and others, casting crazy shadows on the walls, flickered around the room.

Lucas entered the kitchen, saying, "Gran called before the phones went out. She felt it best not to venture out in the storm."

Andy nodded, but Rae had the distinct feeling his mind was not on what Lucas was saying. Even Selma's cold supper of ham, green salad, applesauce, and spice cake was eaten without enthusiasm.

Rae tried to keep her mind on the few comments made about previous storms and the damage they had done. Even Selma, apparently concerned, kept looking out the kitchen window.

After they had finished eating, she came over to clear the table.

Finally, Andy broke the silence. "I'm not sure how to say this," he began and Rae's heart seemed to stop beating.

"If you have something to say, Andy," Lucas said quietly, his voice carefully detached, "then out with it. I can't read your mind."

Rae braced herself.

Nervously Andy ran his hand through his thick, brown hair. "I had a letter from Celeste today." He raised troubled eyes to his uncle after looking apologetically at Rae. "She knows the camp schedule and that I have this week off. She's coming here."

"I thought that was over and done," Lucas said bitingly, his eyes sparking in disapproval.

"It is as far as I'm concerned," Andy assured him, glancing again at Rae, then adding helplessly. "But she didn't ask. She just announced that she was coming. And," he cleared his throat, "her flight arrives in the morning. She might be expecting to stay here."

Lucas leaned away from the table. Dark shadows clouded his face. "So what do you do now, Andy?"

"I don't know," Andy admitted helplessly.

Lucas leaned forward again, clenching his fists beneath his chin. His dark eyes flashed in the lamplight. "Perhaps we could allow Celeste to stay awhile, Andy. Rae could go to Gran's, or to the cabin, or even stay with Marge and. . ."

Andy's sudden intake of breath and look of incredulity halted Lucas's words. "Uncle Lucas," he said, "Don't you understand?" His voice rose to a higher pitch. "You can't do that. Rae is the woman I'm going to marry."

Rae felt certain Andy would shrink beneath his uncle's stare. Finally, Lucas rose from the chair. "I'm just trying to determine what you're made of. I thought you might be forgetting what you have in this girl here."

He nodded toward Rae who quickly rose from her chair and walked over to the window above the sink. She could hear Andy's reply. "I have no intention of forgetting, Uncle Lucas."

"How many times do I have to tell you?" Rae blurted. "You can't discuss me as if—as if—I'm a tossup. Heads, somebody wins. Tails, somebody loses." Hot tears sprang to her eyes. "And *I've* made up my mind about *everything!* Andy, I will not. . ."

Before she could finish her declaration, Andy was on his feet. Striding over to her, he put his hands on her shoulders soothingly. "I know you're upset, Rae. But let's not discuss it further tonight. You'll see once Celeste gets here that she means nothing to me. There's no one else for me now but you. Don't forget that for a minute."

His grip relaxed, but his eyes in the dimly lit room were pleading for her not to say anything more.

With a sense of resignation, Rae nodded.

"Please, Rae, please be patient with me," he whispered. "This will soon be over."

Lucas interrupted. "I'm going to check on Gran," he said, "and stop by the camp."

"Would you like me to do it, Lucas?" Andy offered.

"No. That won't be necessary."

"May I go, too?" Rae asked. She wasn't sure why she said it. It just suddenly seemed necessary to get away from Andy. And to escape the unbearable tension in this room.

"In this storm?" was Andy's immediate response.

"It's the best one I've ever seen," she retorted and looked toward Lucas for his reaction.

"It seems to have subsided a little," he commented, looking out the window.

"Do you mind if I go?" she asked again in a small voice.

"There's a raincoat of Mimi's hanging on the pantry door, I believe," Lucas said in reply and walked across the room, returning with the coat and putting it around her shoulders. Rae drew it closely to her and the two walked toward the doorway.

"We'll be back in a little while," Lucas said. "Gran might return with us."

The evening was unreal. Rae felt a strange calm, a lull inside, steeled against the storm raging around them. It had eased some, the rumbling distant, the flashes of lightning more infrequent and farther away. The wind wasn't as strong.

After Lucas headed the Jeep down the drive, Rae said, "Perhaps we should have asked Andy to come along."

"He had a lot of thinking to do," Lucas snorted in derision.

Nothing else was said as the Jeep bounced down the gravel road, flanked by swiftly flowing streams, swollen from the downpour. Lucas stopped outside the dining hall, where a faint glow shone from the windows. Staff members were gathered around, playing games, eating, and talking.

Catching sight of the newcomers, Marge called, "Great night for ducks! Why don't you stay? It isn't often we can *really* rough it!" Her gesture included the oil lanterns and the cozy fire.

Carl told Lucas that the electric company had found the reason for the power outage and assured him the lines should be back in service within a few hours.

After climbing back into the Jeep, Rae drew her knees up on the seat and stared at Lucas, who was watching the road, apparently unaware of her fixed gaze.

When he looked in her direction, she shifted her eyes to the wet streets. Although visibility was greatly diminished on the interstate, Rae did not feel frightened; rather invigorated. She was content to entrust herself to the big man with the sure knowledge of the road ahead.

When they pulled up in front of Gran's house, she met them at the door.

"I thought you'd come by," she said. "But I've told you it isn't necessary to keep such an eagle eye on me. I won't break—or melt."

Lucas laughed. "It's such a beautiful night that we couldn't resist the urge to go joy-riding."

"Well, come in before you drown," she invited, opening the door wider.

"We're not staying, Gran. Would you like to go back with us?"

"Not on a night like this!" Gran protested. "But maybe Rae would like to stay here for the night. Would you, dear?"

She shook her head quickly but looked away from Gran and out toward the rain. "Thank you, but no," she said quietly. "I like the rain."

Perhaps it was her imagination but there seemed to be only the sound of rain splashing against the hood of the plastic raincoat. Reaching up, she pulled it off her head, allowing the rain to drench her hair.

"Is Andy in the Jeep?" Gran asked, craning her neck to peer into the vehicle.

"No. And you should know that we're having a guest tomorrow. One of Andy's former girlfriends is dropping in. So be prepared for anything."

"That doesn't sound sensible to me, Lucas."

"Nor to me," he replied and changed the subject. "I suppose we'll see you in the morning."

"I'll be there early. Now you two take care."

"We will, Gran. Good night."

The violence of the storm was past, a steady downpour continuing. Lucas concentrated on the roads, particularly the one up the mountain to his house. "These roads can be tricky," he said.

"If we get stuck, we'll just get out and walk."

"I think you'd like that," he said, glancing over at her, then had to do some fancy maneuvering when looking back at the road.

"Keep your eyes on the road," Rae bantered.

"I'll try," he said, and managed until he pulled the Jeep to a stop and switched off the lights.

When Rae stepped down from the Jeep, her raincoat slipped from her shoulders. Since her shorts and blouse were soaked, she folded the coat over her arm as they walked up the steps onto the deck

"You're all wet," Lucas said, not taking his eyes from her. "There are towels in the pantry."

The oil-burning lamp cast a lonely circle of light on the kitchen table and ceiling. With the brightening of the sky, a faint, natural light shone in through the kitchen window. They squished across the tile floor to the pantry door.

"There's a hook inside the door," Lucas said, opening it. Rae could not see it, but reached.

"Here, let me." Rae felt his hand touching hers and, then his body pressing lightly against hers. His bulk blocked out the light through the pantry door, thrusting her world into total darkness. Or maybe her eyes were closed, and she had ceased to breathe. There was a suffocation, a wonderful, terrible inability to comprehend any other world outside this vacuum created by Lucas's nearness.

One or both of them moved. His hard lips groaned, then found hers. Emotion coursed through her body as his hand slid up and caressed her neck. There was a storm going on inside her, a flood about to break loose. "Ramona, Ramona," he whispered huskily against her ear, her lips. Then his warm breath was labored against her cheek.

"Oh, Lucas. I've never felt like this before," Rae whispered against his lips, standing on tiptoes, never wanting to leave the magic circle of his arms. Looking up into his face, barely outlined by the dim light, she whispered the truth she had long refused to acknowledge. "I care for you so much, Lucas." She wanted him to know her heart belonged to him.

But before she could say she loved him, he was speaking. "And we all care for you. Andy loves you. Mimi and Gran care. And," his voice was shaky as he added, "and I."

Then he moved her away from him. Rae could not even lift her head. She was wrong when she had assumed she could take such a dive and survive. She felt as if she had drowned. "I'm wet," she whispered. "And cold. Let me. . .go." She did not think she could ever face him again.

"Ramona," he said. The way he spoke her name sounded so helpless, then he began plummeting her self-esteem. "Please forgive me. I can't explain it. Perhaps I'm just a man who has not led a disciplined enough life. And tonight you were especially vulnerable, knowing that Andy's former girlfriend is on her way here. Can you? Will you forgive me?"

She was nodding. "Yes," was all she could whisper. Then she reminded herself not to panic. It was like losing a major competition. On second thought, she had not even been in the running. She had not stood a chance with Lucas from the very beginning.

Surely he could not see her tears in the darkness. Please, not that, too. Then his arm lay gently across her shoulders. There was nothing to do but fall into step beside him.

At the kitchen table he stopped, took the lamp and handed it to her. Whatever words he attempted to speak were not forthcoming. He sank into a kitchen chair, leaned forward with his elbows on the table, his face in his hands. Rae quickly left the room.

Chapter 11

After removing her wet clothing, Rae dried herself and slipped into a gown, then lay in the darkness, listening to the distant mumblings of the abated storm. She would like to drift with those clouds, sail off into the night, disappear somewhere.

The wonder of Lucas's arms around her, the hope that he was beginning to care for her as she did for him was shattered when he drew away. He regretted his actions and had asked for her forgiveness.

Trying to force the humiliating scene far from her mind, her thoughts turned to how far they had all come since that afternoon in her kitchen in Atlanta when it seemed her part in this charade was simply to allow Andy to say he wanted to marry her. It had seemed to be Andy's dilemma ultimately. Not anyone else's.

But it wasn't that way at all. This family was so closely knit. What affected one, affected all. The Scripture verse came back to haunt her that what one sows, one surely reaps. Now, the pretense would be extended further. Even to Celeste.

Lucas must have a very low opinion of her, she surmised, throwing herself at him that way in the pantry. And it was not the first time! There was that morning on the deck. He must wonder what kind of girl invited his kisses while she was supposed to be Andy's girl. When he knew she and Andy had played such a game with him, his scorn would be unbearable. She was torn between wanting Lucas to know the total truth while another part of her wished he never had to find out.

❧

Her muddled mind was invaded by sporadic snatches of sleep, but when nature's limbs stretched toward the gentle rays of morning sun, her own lay listless. While feathery, white clouds skipped gaily along the blue ridges outside her window, her own inner longings were suppressed by a smoky, gray haze.

Tossing the covers aside, she willed her body to move. The back of her neck ached with tension. Perhaps later she would go to the exercise room and work the kinks out of her body. She wished there were such a room for the mind and the soul.

After brushing her teeth and washing her face, she slipped into shorts and a shirt. Last night's wet clothing still lay in a heap in the bathtub. There wasn't much she could do with her hair without washing it, so she gave up and let it curl in wayward ringlets. Circles beneath her eyes indicated her inner turmoil.

Hearing voices, she walked to the window, then stepped back and sat on the edge of the bed. On the deck, Lucas and Andy were conversing with Gran. A few minutes later, Rae peeked out to see the two men retreating down the steps. Gran was lounging in a chair.

When she thought it safe, Rae went downstairs. "Good morning," she greeted Gran, who was apparently enjoying the fresh coolness of the morning.

"It's always so clean and clear after a heavy rain," Gran said. Rae returned her smile. She walked over to the edge of the deck. The scent of earth and pine perfumed the air.

She turned when asked where she would like her breakfast served. "Eat out here if you like," Gran suggested. "Bring some coffee for me, Nancy, please."

Rae was grateful for Gran's suggestion. It would be impossible to choke down a single bite in the kitchen. She sat in a chair by a table, near Gran.

"I hope you aren't coming down with a cold, Rae, after being out in that downpour."

Rae shook her head. "I don't think so." Her hand went to her hair. "I haven't done anything to myself yet."

"It's charming, dear. No, I just meant that you seem a little tired, that's all." Gran smiled. "This week should be for relaxing. There are still three hectic ones coming up at camp."

Rae thanked Nancy when she brought her breakfast. It looked good, but she wasn't very hungry. Feeling the need for black coffee, she reached for the cup.

Gran pulled her chair closer to the table. "There was quite a discussion going on when I arrived this morning." The older woman sipped her coffee. Rae stirred the scrambled eggs with a fork. Selma had prepared them with mushrooms—a gourmet treat. Still, her appetite was not tempted.

"I hope you aren't letting this disturb you too much, Rae."

She looked away from Gran's worried eyes, wishing she could tell her that it was not Celeste's arrival that was upsetting her. Instead, she forced a bite of food into her mouth.

"But of course you're upset," Gran added with a sigh. "Everyone in this household is. That's why Lucas has ordered Andy to bring Celeste here."

"Ordered?" Rae gasped, almost choking on the bite of food.

Gran nodded. "He's greatly perturbed with Andy. I don't think Lucas slept last night, either."

Rae reached for her orange juice. "Can't he just let Andy handle this?" she asked weakly.

"That's what Andy asked him. He said he was going to tell Celeste that he loves you, and put her on the next plane to Florida." At Rae's quick glance, Gran continued. "But Lucas said he had tried that before. That Andy was supposed to have settled the matter with Celeste over a month ago, but hadn't. Since Andy doesn't seem able to handle his life maturely, Lucas is taking matters into his own hands."

Rae was almost afraid to ask. "What is he going to do?"

"Lucas said that Andy is not going to play his philandering games with you." Gran said, looking out where the gentle breeze stirred the leaves of a tree. Then she glanced back at Rae, with a strange light in her eyes. "He's going to demand that Andy make his intentions clear concerning you and Celeste, right in front of everyone."

"Everyone?" Rae questioned, afraid of the answer. Gran's concern was apparent as she replied slowly. "Yes. He had planned to discuss Mimi's engagement with the family tonight at dinner. And, Isobel mentioned that she wanted to discuss Kevin with you since you had spent so much time with him at camp. So. . ."

Rae pushed the plate away and stood. "I can't," she said, shaking her head. "I can't sit at a dinner table across from," she choked back the sobs before adding, "everyone. It's just impossible."

"My dear," Gran said in a whisper. "We're all on your side."

Yes, she knew. Lucas had told her how they all cared for her. A sob escaped her throat. "I'm sorry," was all she could say before turning from Gran's sympathetic eyes and running across the deck to the safety of her room.

❧

The tears had dried on her face when, over an hour later, a knock sounded on her bedroom door. Andy called her name and pleaded for her to let him in.

"Just a minute," she said, went to the bathroom to douse her face with cold water, then returned to sit on the edge of the bed. "Come in," she called.

"Gran told me how this is upsetting you." Andy said, pulling up a chair. Misery was written on his face. "Believe me, Rae. I never intended to hurt you in any way."

"I know that, Andy. No more than I intended to hurt your family. But they will be when they know what we've done."

He took her hands in his. "Rae, I know I was wrong. But we don't have to confess our mistakes to my family. You and I can deal with it ourselves, can't we?"

A ray of hope sounded in his voice. "You see," he continued, "what started out as a lie has become the truth. I have asked you to marry me. You did say you would think about it. So why do they have to know?"

"Andy," she said quietly, "I hope I will never be able to deceive people and feel good about it, or explain it away. Even if they never knew, *I* would know. I can never have peace of mind, or seek God's forgiveness, without telling your family and asking their forgiveness."

"I knew you'd say something like that," Andy sighed. "Can you be here tonight when I tell the truth in front of Lucas and Celeste?"

"Truth, Andy?"

"That I love you and want to marry you."

Her heart went out to him, for she knew how it felt to have love rejected. She opened her mouth to protest, but he stood to leave, with a look of determination in the set of his jaw.

"I don't want Celeste here at the house today. I'm going to drive her around the area and convince her that she and I have no future together. And tonight," he promised, "everyone will know for certain where I stand with you."

"Please don't, Andy," she said, but he ignored her plea, leaving her to stare at a closed door.

∞

Rae awakened with a new determination. She had slipped from a balance beam upon occasion, failed in an attempt to grasp an asymmetric bar, even during competition. But she had forced herself to continue while knowing her final score would be lowered.

She reminded herself that a team member in gymnastics pushes herself, even after an embarrassing fumble, to keep on for the ultimate good of the entire group. That's what she must do tonight. There was the ultimate good of the camp to consider, as well as Andy's feelings.

But there was one thing she could not do. And that was to sit at the dinner table and pretend that she was not in love with Lucas Grant.

When Nancy came to her room to say the family was ready to dine, Rae truthfully replied that she was not feeling well and would not join them for dinner. A short while later, Nancy returned with a tray, exemplary of Selma's culinary expertise.

Rae forced herself to eat a little, then pushed it aside. She decided not to sit in her bedroom and wait to be summoned.

She stood at the window in the shadowed living room, watching the sun go down behind distant peaks, when the sound of voices traveled toward her from the hallway. Turning, she saw a young woman between Isobel and Andy.

Andy must have lost the courage to tell Celeste he didn't love her, Rae surmised. Otherwise the young woman could not be holding onto his arm like that, while engaging Isobel in such lively conversation. Celeste was not the picture of a girl whose heart had recently been broken.

They walked into the lounge, followed by Lucas and Gran, talking quietly. Gran entered, but Lucas stopped at the doorway.

He glanced toward the staircase, then, as if sensing her presence, turned and looked in her direction. He was silhouetted against the light, and Rae stood in near darkness, yet she felt his eyes on her. *How*, she wondered, beginning to move, *can it be easier to walk a balance beam than to cross that expanse of floor?*

Neither spoke as she passed him, and the other voices soon died away.

Andy, looking uncomfortable, walked forward with Celeste, who was still holding onto his arm possessively. After a quick appraisal, Rae realized the brunette's dark eyes held the expression of a confident woman prepared to do battle with her rival.

If sheer outer beauty of dress, face, and figure enticed a man to fall in love, then Isobel and Celeste were unsurpassed. They had dressed elegantly for dinner in a mountain mansion, and their beauty complemented the attractive men in that room.

In contrast, Rae had chosen a simple cotton dress, enhanced only by a single strand of pearls and pearl drops at her ears.

She was not inhibited by the girl's vivacious beauty, nor by the trace of hostility in her voice after they were introduced.

"Rae?" Celeste questioned skeptically. "A boy's name?"

Rae's smile was genuine. Celeste couldn't be more than twenty-one and reminded Rae of some college students she had known who were still young enough to believe that verbal combat was the only method of dealing with a rival.

"I was named Ramona, for my father, whose name was Raymond," Rae explained. "I like it, but it doesn't compare with yours. Celeste is a beautiful name, and you're a very beautiful girl."

Celeste's mumbled thank you quickly covered her momentary confusion.

Not wanting any undue attention, Rae looked around and found a place to sit between Gran and Isobel. Celeste began to remind Andy about the good times they had together, as they sat on a couch opposite Rae. Seeing a shadowy figure move behind them, Rae was grateful when Isobel mentioned Kevin.

"He was like a different child," Isobel said with genuine pleasure, "when he showed me the certificate he received for tumbling."

"A little encouragement can go a long way in building a child's confidence," Rae replied and suggested some exercises that would increase Kevin's physical strength.

A glance across the way told Rae that Andy was well aware of his uncle's presence behind him, and he was talking in low tones to Celeste. Just when there seemed to be nothing else for Rae and Isobel to say, Celeste's voice was heard asking, "Don't you still love me a little, Andy?"

One word penetrated the hushed silence that fell upon the group. It was the first time Lucas had spoken. "Andy!" he said, and the sound carried all the force of a speeding arrow, heading straight for the bull's-eye.

Andy drew a ragged breath, and Rae knew what courage it must take to stand and surrender to his grim-faced uncle's staunch demands.

"I told her, Uncle Lucas," Andy said and looked down at Celeste. "I told Celeste that our relationship is over, and," he looked at Rae then. "I love Rae and have asked her to be my wife."

Rae quickly looked down, embarrassed for the girl. Gran reached over to pat her hand.

"Celeste," Isobel said, rising from the couch and smiling at the girl, "why don't you come home with me tonight? Tomorrow we can shop in some of those quaint little places I mentioned during dinner."

Celeste stood, threw a defiant glance in Lucas's direction as if he were some kind of villain, then said, "I'll call you tomorrow, Andy."

She walked swiftly toward the door, followed by Isobel, who had just proved what an asset she could be to Lucas, in helping to ease a difficult situation. She looked around. "We can find our way out," she said, smiling sweetly at Lucas.

After they left, Rae felt she must make her escape. "I think I'll go to my room," she said, but Andy detained her.

"Not yet, Rae," he said with determination, striding over and sitting on the edge of the couch opposite her. "I don't want you carrying this burden any longer." His voice softened. "I only want to make you happy." He looked around at his uncle. "It's time you knew the truth."

"The truth?" Lucas asked, as if that were something all the philosophers in the world had sought, but to no avail.

Andy told the entire story. From beginning to end. He took full blame, explaining that Rae was only the victim of his persuasion. He told of her reluctance to go along with the scheme initially, and her need of a job.

"I'm sorry, Uncle Lucas. It seemed the easiest way to get myself out of this situation with Celeste."

Lucas had leaned forward with his elbow on his knee and his hand on his forehead, moving his head from side to side as if he could not believe what he was hearing.

Rae couldn't look at Gran, sitting so still beside her. She could not bear to see the hurt and disappointment on that dear face.

"Andy," Rae said after a long pause, "stop blaming yourself. Your family knows that I make my own decisions. And I made a wrong one. I'm sorry, too." She shook her head in remorse. Tears stung her eyes. "I'm sorry I allowed you to accept me for something I'm not. I'm so sorry."

Lucas's words cut like a spear. "You two think that's all there is to it? Confess? Receive instant forgiveness?"

It was difficult to face his expression of fury, but she looked at him resolutely. "No, I don't. I know I have failed each of you. I know you thought I was that fine Christian girl you wanted for Andy. You certainly can't think that of me any longer. It didn't seem so wrong in the beginning. But now, I'm so ashamed."

Andy halted her words of apology. "Rae, it's over," he said. "We aren't going to be spanked like naughty children. We've said we're sorry. There's no longer any pretense."

"That's right, Andy," she replied miserably. "And I can't pretend that I'm going to marry you. I'm not, Andy. You have to understand that. I can't marry you." She hated what she was doing. How could she tell Andy she didn't love him? Humiliate him further? Break his spirit? She could only repeat, "I can't."

"You don't mean that Rae," Andy soothed. "You're understandably upset. You'll see. Tomorrow, everything will be different. Let's just drop the subject for now."

"I agree," Lucas said and stood as if the matter were ended. "We will get through the next three weeks of camping. Then Mimi will be here, and we will all sit down and discuss this in a reasonable manner."

Rae jumped up. She couldn't bear his treating her like a wayward child. "No, Lucas," she said. "I'm not your ward to be told what to say and when to say it. And whether or not you believe it, I'm not going to discuss this further."

"Believe you?" Lucas asked. "How can I know when to believe you, or what to believe? I asked both of you about your relationship. And each time I came away convinced of the probability of your engagement."

He inhaled deeply, but wasn't finished. "And now I'm supposed to believe Andy is in love, but you won't marry him? And you don't want to discuss it reasonably. Is there more? Are there other deceptions you are covering up?"

"Uncle Lucas," Andy said and stood. "Don't talk to her like that."

Rae felt she couldn't stand any more. "Both of you stop this. You don't have to argue over me! I'm leaving!"

"Please, Rae. Please don't." Andy pleaded.

Defiantly she turned to Lucas. "I'm leaving!"

"You signed a contract to work at the camp for the full season," he reminded her, strangely calm. "It's only half over. The going gets tough, and you want to quit. Is this really Raymond Martin's daughter I'm hearing?"

The fight went out of her. She could only stare down at the floor. "He would be as ashamed of me as I am of myself," she replied, her voice in a whisper. "I'll stay. But I can't stay here. I don't belong at the Haven. I'm going to pack my bags now and go down to the campgrounds with the rest of the staff."

"Wait until morning, Rae," Andy suggested.

"No." She shook her head. "I have to go tonight."

Lucas did not protest, and she knew he felt that was best. She was just an employee now, not a prospective member of the family.

Rae turned to Gran. "I'm sorry," she said, choking back her tears, then hurried from the room.

She had packed everything she had brought from Atlanta and set the bags in the hallway. Lucas appeared to drive her to the campgrounds.

On the short Jeep trip to "Off Limits," Lucas's tone was that of an employer talking with his employee. He simply informed her what to expect and what would be expected of her during the week between the camp sessions.

He parked in front of "Off Limits" and took her bags up. Adele appeared long enough to speak and see Lucas setting the bags inside the screen door.

"Ramona, can I trust you to stay until the end of the camping season?" he asked, and the quietness of his voice surprised her.

She looked up at him, and his seemed to be the only face in the world, the only eyes, as she stared at him and nodded.

"And to think," he said so low she almost didn't hear. "That slope in Switzerland broke only my leg."

He turned and left the deck. Rae looked after him for a long time, wondering why he made that remark. Had he meant she had done worse? He probably meant she had broken his trust in her. Perhaps his faith in human nature. Those things were more important to him than human limbs and bones.

Chapter 12

How simple things might have been had Rae fallen in love with Andy rather than Lucas, she thought. But she hadn't. And in spite of the ache in her heart, and the belief that neither Gran nor Lucas could ever again respect her, she felt a great burden had been lifted now that the truth was known.

Rae was grateful for the stringent demands of the second session's youngsters, who needed and wanted her undivided attention, and left her exhausted at the end of each day.

She saw Andy and Lucas only briefly. Andy dropped by during some of the morning junior classes; Lucas, in the afternoon, each of them seeming determined to concentrate only on camp business.

One evening when most of the campers had gone with their counselors to Cherokee to see the play, "Unto These Hills," she and Andy walked by the lake. The sky was star spangled; the evening, mild and clear.

"Would you reconsider our relationship, Rae?" he asked seriously.

"I'm sorry, Andy. But I can't."

He sighed deeply. "I've been thinking some more about Switzerland."

"Tell Lucas," she prompted.

"I can't just yet. I've pulled too many surprises on him recently. But, Rae," he said, taking her hands in his, "I do love you."

"Thank you, Andy," she said softly. She knew it was true, but he probably loved Switzerland better, and she was glad.

Lucas did not approach her, unless it was a matter of business. Through Carl she learned that Lucas was aware of her interest in the plans for the girls' camp and heartily approved.

Time moved so swiftly. It seemed she had just watched the sun go down, only to rise to the sound of "Nothing. . . ."

Nothing! The word echoed in her mind. *Nothing* from Lucas ever. Not his respect. Nor his admiration. Nor his love.

She went for one last swim the morning the young men left the camp. After leaving the lake, she tied the terry cloth wrap around her, then spotted Lucas sitting in a wrought-iron chair near the dock. She had to pass him in order to get to the cabin. What could she say?

He stood when she came near. "Beautiful morning," he said. She stopped, nodded, and looked around as if seeing it for the first time.

"It's over," he said, but she was already aware of that. This was her last day. She could leave anytime. Her paycheck would be ready.

"There's something special about working with young men who have such potential for accomplishment," he said.

Rae nodded. Next year someone would be working with the girls in the same capacity. She had offered some valuable suggestions. It would be a good program.

"I've loved the work," she could say honestly. "It isn't just work, but a sharing of one's self."

"You have a feeling for it," Lucas said, then looked out over the lake and mountainsides. "I really expected you and Andy to be working together this time next year."

"I'm sorry I disappointed you," she said, but avoided his gaze, staring down at her bare feet on the wooden boards.

"It seems the other way around," he countered. "I believe we disappointed *you*. We couldn't offer you the things you find important. And you aren't swayed by money or outward appearances."

Not swayed by outward appearances? Not swayed by the personal magnetism of a man whose appearance was superb—breathtaking as a tall pine, glorious as a vivid sunset, calming as a gentle breeze on a misty morning, sweet as a ripple on a lake, fragile as a blossom on a shrub, strong as a mighty oak, all-encompassing as a leafy maple? Not swayed? Of course not. Her rapid heartbeat was a figment of her imagination; the sudden quickening of her pulse when he came near was a fantasy; the deep longing for his arms about her and his lips on hers was not real at all. It was all a mistake—another mistake.

She could only lower her head, hoping he would not see what was in her eyes: the truth, the longing, the desperation, the misery. The silence seemed interminable.

"Do you have plans?" he was asking.

She shook her head.

"Would you do me a favor?"

"I'll try."

"Go with Gran to pick up Mimi at the airport."

She looked at him. "When?"

"This afternoon."

Rae's eyes brightened and her smile was genuine. "Of course. I'd love to." The smile he gave her in return was beautiful and the sunlight gleamed in his dark brown eyes. "At least there's one member of our family who hasn't disappointed you," and added, "yet. She would never understand if you didn't have dinner with us to share her excitement over the engagement. Then we'll talk."

Rae stiffened. What was there to talk about? She had already expressed her caring for him, but either he didn't believe it or disregarded it.

"I have nothing more to say, Lucas, and I really don't feel like socializing."

"Only the family will be there—Andy, Mimi, Gran, you, and me. As I've explained before, Ramona. All of us. . ."

She couldn't bear to hear him say *that* again. "All right. I'll be there." She turned quickly and began walking toward the cabin.

He is relentless, she thought. He would not rest until everyone was completely debilitated with their sense of guilt for having deceived him. She would attempt to bear one more night of humiliation.

On the way to the airport Gran commented on the oppressive heat. "We can expect a few days like this toward the end of July." Gran explained as if apologizing because it was not another of many perfect days. Rae wore a cool sundress and had slipped her feet into high-heeled sandals, grateful that her tanned, smooth legs did not require hose.

It was a wonderful reunion. Mimi's face shone almost as brightly as the huge diamond on her finger. Love certainly agreed with her.

Rae felt that Andy and Lucas were as glad as she that dinner consisted of a full-course meal of Pierre. Tonight she was here just as Mimi's friend. It was good not to have to pretend anything with Andy, who was quieter than usual, but obviously pleased for Mimi.

After dinner they settled in the lounge with coffee while Mimi discussed her plans. She wanted to return to Paris, marry Pierre right away, and complete her last year of college at the university where he taught. She might even decide to teach there until she and Pierre were ready to have children.

"You would be satisfied settling down like that, Mimi?" Lucas asked seriously. "You've never really worked. I probably failed you there."

"I've settled down for three years with my studies, Uncle Lucas, and I didn't do too badly. Study is very confining. Oh, Uncle Lucas! I could live in a tent with Pierre and be utterly content! I would slave for him!"

Lucas was nodding. "Of course you could. For a month or so."

"Oh, it's going to be fun, Uncle Lucas. He has a nice home near campus. We would be at the same school every day. But," she teased, "if you feel we would be too confined, you could, for a wedding present, give us a little place on the Riviera where we could escape on weekends."

"A little place on the Riviera," he repeated. "Just like that."

"Oh, Uncle Lucas," Mimi said, running to him and putting both arms around his waist. "I love him so much. He'll take care of me. He loves me. You know how impulsive I can be. Well, Pierre is the sensible one and has made me see that we have to work at a growing relationship. He was afraid I would have my fun with him, then leave and break his heart. He wouldn't let me do that. Don't you know, Uncle Lucas, how hard it is being away from the one you love?"

"Yes, Mimi. And I'm beginning to approve of this Pierre, but I'll reserve judgment until I see for myself." He unwrapped her arms and ignored her deflated look. "First, we have another matter that must be settled. It seems we have done this young lady a terrible injustice."

Rae put her hand to her throat. What on earth did he mean? She looked at Andy, who had leaned forward, elbows on his knees, and was staring at the floor.

"You mean *me*?" Rae gasped.

"Yes, I mean you." Lucas replied. "This entire summer has been a fiasco of lies, conniving, false pretenses, and taking advantage of you."

"Nobody took advantage of me," she protested. "You've all been wonderful to me. I had nowhere else to go. Nothing to do."

"Right," he said, his eyes bright.

Mimi meekly took a seat near Gran, who took her hand and patted it in a consoling gesture.

Lucas looked from one to the other. "You were supposed to be her friend, Mimi. Yet, knowing she had no one and had just lost her father, you did not offer her a home in the name of friendship, but as an accomplice to your brother's scheme."

He looked at Andy. "And Andy, you didn't offer this girl the job she needed as a gesture of kindness. You planned to use her for your own benefit."

Andy and Mimi paled under Lucas's stern gaze.

"What kind of friendship is that?" Lucas asked, staring at Mimi, who would not look at him.

"You wanted a real engagement, Andy. But how could she ever trust you to tell the truth? You think a girl wants to marry a man who has lied since the first moment she met him?"

"Please, Lucas," Rae began, but he silenced her with a look. "You'll have your turn. I'm talking to Mimi and Andy now."

Rae leaned back against the couch helplessly. Gran gave her a sympathetic look.

Mimi's lips trembled. "I'm sorry. It didn't seem so serious. It was just a little game to help Andy out of a spot. Rae needed a job, and I thought it would be terrific if she and Andy got together. I was thinking of what might result from a summer spent together."

She lifted moist eyes to him. "It did occur to me to ask her here. But I was only going to be here a week before leaving for Paris. I guess my mind was on my trip. . ."

"Even in the midst of her trouble, she didn't hesitate to invite you into her home, did she?"

"You make it sound so reprehensible," Rae protested, unable to keep quiet.

"It is," Lucas replied.

"And Andy, did you think of the possibility of Rae's falling in love with you? She had nothing and no one. You were offering her a world of plenty. Suppose she had fallen in love with you, but you couldn't return her love? Would you give her a car or jewelry, then tell her to run along?"

Andy was twisting his fingers uncomfortably as Lucas continued. "She wouldn't have accepted those things, Andy. She would have had nothing."

"You're right, Uncle Lucas," Andy agreed meekly. "I can't blame her for not loving me."

Rae fought the impulse to say she loved Andy, would marry him. Anything to stop this torture.

"All right," Lucas said. "So you two are sorry. And what do we do now? Mimi will go to Paris and marry her beloved Pierre. Andy will gallivant off to Switzerland and find someone else to console him while his heart is mending. . . But what about Ramona?"

Mimi rose and started toward Lucas. "You're not going to let me marry Pierre, are you? I know you won't! Oh, Uncle Lucas, I love him so. Don't you understand?" She was shaking her head, a fearful look in her eyes. Her voice became accusatory. "You don't know what it's like to love someone!"

"Oh, don't I, little girl?"

Mimi was properly chastened as he continued. "When love—what some people know as love—becomes the only important factor in a relationship, then it is a destructive element. Love can be a selfish thing, when all else is excluded. Real love is something that two must share, must build upon, must cherish. You might be able to survive it, to meet its challenge, if you give it the deference it deserves. But love can be as devastating as it is beautiful. And how do I know these things?" His tone was curt. "I've been around just a few years longer than you—and your uncle isn't immune to Cupid's fiery darts."

Mimi muttered a faint, "I'm sorry, Uncle Lucas."

Andy rose from the couch without looking at Lucas and walked over to the fireplace. He stood with his back to them. Rae saw Gran's eyes were fastened on Lucas. When his eyes met hers, a smile settled about her lips. Lucas shifted uncomfortably and looked away from her.

When his gaze swept her way, Rae could not meet it. With bowed head she stared at the floor. Lucas had been, or was, in love. Perhaps he had discovered that Isobel was like that challenging mountain after all. Maybe that was part of the redeeming and devastating qualities about love; it wasn't particular about whom it attacked.

"Now sit down, Mimi," Lucas said sternly. She obeyed him, looking lost and forlorn. Rae's heart went out to her.

"What do you think I should do, Rae?" Lucas asked. "Is there any way we can make it up to you?"

Rae swallowed hard, not sure what to say. "Lucas, I know you feel you have to reprimand them because you're their guardian. But they didn't intend any harm. Intentions mean a lot. Mimi is my friend, and I've come to appreciate Andy. The job opportunity was a lifesaver. Being here this summer has been—" she looked down at her hands clasped together "—the most wonderful time of my life in many ways. I don't blame Mimi and Andy. I'm grateful."

"Your opinion doesn't ease their guilt," he protested.

Mimi's sob was audible. She turned to Gran with pleading in her voice. "He's not going to let me marry Pierre."

"You're wrong, Mimi," Lucas said coldly. "If you want to go to Pierre right now, I'll write the check for your plane fare. You can have a new wardrobe. I'll finance the wedding. I'll hand over to you many times more than Rae has worked for all summer."

"And, Andy, I'm not going to disinherit you. You have money coming to you from your parents' estate. If you want to travel all over the world, I'll finance it, and deduct it from your inheritance. I'm not going to tell either of you what to do, so don't look so downcast. You're going to make your own decisions this time. Mimi, send your good friend a post card from Paris sometime. And, Andy, call her from Switzerland. Show her how much you care."

Andy turned and faced his uncle then. He looked crushed. "I would marry her if she'd have me, Uncle Lucas. That's how much I care. I'm not the insensitive cad you make me out to be. Okay, I was wrong. I admit that. But it's not the end of the world!"

"Isn't it?" Lucas asked abruptly. "I haven't finished."

Chapter 13

Lucas leaned forward, his feet wide apart, his hands clasped between his knees. He stared at the floor for a moment, as if uncertain whether to speak. A weariness seemed to settle upon him. "You're right, Andy," he said slowly. "It's not the end of the world. Rather, it's the end of something that never really had a chance to begin."

He got up and walked around to the back of the couch, his fingers absently moving along the printed fabric. "I've given this a lot of thought. At first, I decided to remain silent, or perhaps talk to each of you separately. However," he drew in a deep breath, "since your offenses have been brought out and confessions made openly, I feel I should do the same."

"*You*, Uncle Lucas?" Mimi asked suddenly, disbelieving.

"I am the worst offender, Mimi," he assured. "I need to apologize and ask forgiveness, too. Just as the two of you have done." He looked from Rae, sitting by Gran, over to Andy by the fireplace.

He paced slowly as he talked, glancing occasionally at his audience. "You see, from the first moment I saw Ramona, I wanted her for myself. My tactics were not exactly those befitting a gentleman. But I could not believe Andy had found a girl he really wanted to marry, and certainly not the kind I had always wanted for him. It seemed too sudden—too pat. I'll admit I was suspicious."

Lucas looked at Rae. She wondered what condemnation might follow now, but she was not prepared for the gentleness in his voice. "And Rae," he began, "when you and I sat on that mountain, with all of nature around us responding to the rising sun, something was happening inside myself. You needed me that morning. Like no woman ever has. It was like a revelation. You know, Andy," he said, turning his attention toward his nephew, "the kind of girl I always said I wanted for you, was in reality the kind of woman I wanted for myself. It was wrong of me, I confess, but I sincerely hoped you were playing one of your games with me. And the only thing that prevented my telling Ramona was my belief that she might belong to *you*."

Andy paled and could no longer look at his uncle.

"That morning, as the sun rose to warm our bodies, your inner beauty warmed my heart, Ramona," he said. "And if I hadn't been unsure of the relationship between you and Andy, I could have begun to love you then."

The sudden elation that had begun to soar in Rae plummeted to the depths. *Lucas could have loved me. But that was in the past. He said it was over, before it had a chance to begin.*

She wanted to protest that it was not Andy who occupied her thoughts, who had stolen her heart, but she could not say such a thing in his presence. It was too late anyway.

Lucas asked that they bear with him just a little longer. Now that he had begun, he must say it all.

"Rae, when you asked me what kind of woman I wanted to marry, I couldn't be honest. But I want to be honest now. My fulfillment does not come in seeing the Grant label on sports equipment and clothing. Nor does it come from socializing at ski resorts. It comes from sharing myself with growing young men, who demand more of me than I normally would give. It comes from being a part of their spiritual and physical growth. It is my ministry in this life. I've always wanted a woman to share that ministry with me. But I could not say it, for I would have been telling Andy's woman that it was she who had captured my heart."

"You see, Andy," he said turning to speak to his nephew who could not meet his eyes, "I would never betray you—even for the most marvelous woman I've ever met. So, I did the next best thing. I tried to arrange it so you two could have the life I wanted, working together in the two camps. And Rae," he said, his voice husky with emotion, "I'm so sorry that I was in a position that allowed you to witness my weakness, rather than my strength."

Rae felt the hot liquid scald her cheeks. She could hardly fathom his words. They were so beautiful, yet so terrible. So loving, yet so impossible. Each hope that rose in her was being dashed to pieces. There were so many things she wanted to ask him, but this was not the place, not the time.

Then an uncontrollable sob escaped Mimi's throat. "Please, Uncle Lucas. We didn't mean to hurt you."

"I know that, Mimi. I'm not condemning you. I don't expect any of you to be perfect. We all know I'm not. But when we do wrong, we should be big enough to admit it, learn from it, and make it right if we can."

They each looked at him as if expecting answers. "I can't tell you what to do," he said. "You're adults now. You will have to find your own solutions."

Rae sat frozen in her seat, unable to lift a hand to wipe the tears from her face.

"Rae, I can understand if you have lost respect for this family. However, I know how much this summer meant to you. You are the kind of person who needs to give of herself, and those young people needed what you had to give. So, entirely separate from any family involvement, I'm offering you a job with the camp. You would work with Carl in the planning of the girls' camp, and if you would, direct it next summer. Otherwise I will have to abandon the project until a later date. But if you leave, as you have threatened to do, I wouldn't blame you. This family will never harbor any ill will toward you—whatever your decision."

Rae looked at him then, but before she could speak he said, "Now if you will all excuse me, I will be at Isobel's. There are some things I should have said to her a long time ago."

With that, he strode from the room, leaving them all in a state of shock. Gran dabbed her eyes. Mimi sobbed aloud. Andy's face was pale.

Her heart sinking, Rae ran from the room. Just as she reached the deck, she heard his car retreating down the drive. She slumped, defeated, against the door frame.

Then Andy was standing beside her. "You love him, Rae?" She couldn't answer. "You do," he said incredulously. "You have all along. I can see it now."

"Oh, Andy. I'm sorry. I never intended to hurt you, or anyone else."

"I know," he said, "nor did I. But I've done all sorts of damage with that impetuous scheme of mine. I can't blame you for loving Lucas, Rae. I'm not half the man he is. Maybe someday I'll deserve a girl like you."

"Andy, go after him. Tell him you don't love me."

"Rae," he said with determination. "I don't ever intend to lie to Uncle Lucas again. I'm sorry. I can't tell him that."

Andy turned and walked back through the house, leaving Rae staring out across the deck where she had first met Lucas. There had been a chance that he could love her. Now it was gone. And Lucas had turned to Isobel. If he made a commitment to her, he would never back away from it. He was that kind of man.

Rae didn't know where she would go, but she knew she could not be there when Lucas returned to announce his engagement to Isobel. He might even bring her back with him. . . . She was throwing things into her suitcases when Mimi came in.

"Oh, Rae," she wailed. "Do you hate me?"

"You know I don't, Mimi. Neither of you meant any real harm."

"Then why are you packing? Where are you going?"

Rae shrugged helplessly. "I don't know, but I can't stay here."

She tried to finish packing, but the blur before her eyes prevented her even seeing what she was doing. Collapsing on the bed, she let the tears come. Mimi was right beside her. "You love Lucas, Rae?"

"Doesn't everybody?" she asked miserably. "The girl on the diving board. Isobel. What difference does it make? He's gone, to Isobel."

"Let me help you pack," Mimi said, then added firmly, "We're going to Gran's."

"To Gran's?"

"Yes, we have a lot of thinking to do."

❧

The following day Andy appeared on their doorstep, more exuberant than she had seen him in weeks. "I told Uncle Lucas! Rae," he said, taking her hands in his as they walked out back on the patio at Gran's house. "I told him about Switzerland. He liked the idea. I didn't think he would."

"That's wonderful, Andy. I know you'll make a success of that little shop."

"Go with me, Rae. We could have a good life together."

Rae was shaking her head. "You're a fine man, Andy. You'll find. . ."

"Don't say that," he interrupted. "It doesn't help. Maybe I've grown up a little. If I can't have you, then I hope you and Lucas get together, Rae. I really mean that."

She lowered her eyes. "It's much too late for that."

After a long moment, Andy leaned over and kissed her on the cheek. "If you change your mind, let me know."

❧

A week passed before Gran, Mimi, and Rae felt it was time to relate their plans to Lucas. The four of them sat in the padded redwood furniture on Gran's patio.

Tall, frosted glasses of lemonade were a welcome respite from the warmth of August. After raising the back of the chaise, Mimi slipped out of her sandals, stretched her legs out and wiggled her red-painted toenails; Gran, nearby. Rae's and Lucas's glasses sat on a table between their chairs. Rae was grateful she didn't have to face Lucas, but could look out upon the dark green canopy of trees that obscured the view of nearby houses.

"I want to tell you what I've decided, Uncle Lucas," Mimi began hesitantly.

Lucas said nothing, waiting.

"I've decided to finish my senior year at the University of Asheville before marrying Pierre. I'm going to move in with Gran while going to school. It will be easier since Rae refuses to move to the Haven, and I need her to help me with my wedding plans."

Rae suddenly realized Lucas might want Isobel to help with the wedding. That would be logical if he were planning his own marriage. "You may have other plans, Lucas. This is a big event, and I'm sure there's more expert advice available than mine."

"We'll hire all the experts we need," Lucas assured her. "But I'm not making Mimi's decisions any longer. And I can readily understand her wanting a friend to talk things over with."

"I want you to be proud of me, Uncle Lucas," Mimi said, as if being released from his dominion was not as appealing as it might once have seemed.

"Your decision to finish school before getting married could not have been an easy one. There are many plans to be made in Paris. To show you how proud I am of you, I'm sending the three of you to Paris during Christmas holidays."

Before Rae could protest, Mimi shrieked, jumped up, ran over to her uncle, and hugged him fiercely.

"Oh, I love you, Uncle Lucas!" and in the next breath added, "I've got to go call Pierre and tell him."

"Then you're not going to Paris, Lucas?" Gran asked.

"No, at least not now," he replied. "I plan to fly to Switzerland and spend Christmas with Andy."

Gran looked at Mimi's sandals, left behind in her haste to call Pierre. "I'd better go remind that girl whose telephone she's using for that Paris call." She went inside the house.

Rae reached for her glass, thinking she might join the women, but Lucas spoke. "Carl tells me you're on the permanent payroll as of Monday."

Rae leaned back, looking out where the sun was retreating. "I have no real ties in Atlanta," she said, beginning to relate her decisions, a result of much thinking and praying during the past week. "The job you offered me is a place where I can share with others the faith and values my father stood for, and have become a part of my own sense of purpose and commitment. If you agree, I'll work with Carl, then help direct the girls' camp next summer. You have a wonderful ministry, and I'm honored that you want me to be a part of it."

He stood and stepped over in front of her, looking down. "Without you, those dreams of mine could not materialize for next summer." She must have been mistaken in thinking his hands moved forward as if to reach for her, and that his eyes held a kind of excitement, for he straightened, silhouetted against slopes darkened by a dying sun.

"Any ideas you have will be welcomed, Rae. After you have worked with Carl for awhile, we'll discuss the plans and decide exactly what direction to take. And believe me when I say we are fortunate to have you join our staff."

☙

They didn't see Lucas for awhile. Gran said he was committed to several meetings and speaking engagements. A former gold-medal winner was always in demand.

Rae shared her letters from Andy with Mimi and Gran. He was now co-owner of the little shop and apparently loved every minute of it. He said he might go big time and expand, possibly handling Lucas's sports equipment and clothing and opening a branch office.

"There isn't much time for girls, Rae," he wrote. "But I manage to see them occasionally. I hope you get all the good things you deserve. Give my love to Uncle Lucas."

I wish I could give him mine, she thought, putting down the letter.

Since Lucas was away on business most of the time, he made the house and lake available to Gran, Mimi and Rae during fall break.

Even when Lucas was in the house, Rae never found herself alone with him. It was as if he were deliberately avoiding her. He seemed to want her to understand that the awakening love he had thought possible had fled. It would never surface again.

The day before he was to leave for the North Carolina resort, then Switzerland, dawned bright and clear. He drove the Lincoln up the Parkway with Gran in front; Mimi and Rae, in back.

"Of all the seasons in the mountains, I do believe fall is the most beautiful," Rae exclaimed when they stopped at Craggy Gardens. "I've never seen such spectacular colors." The mountainsides were splashed with brilliant reds, golds, oranges, greens, yellows—deep, rich colors that gleamed in the sunlight.

Lucas moved closer, pointing out the garden before them. "Magnificent," he said, then their eyes met. "You'll never want to leave the mountains, will you?"

"No," she said. She would like to come to this spot again, remembering the man who might have loved her. What might have been. What was no more.

They walked back to the car, and Lucas drove higher and higher, where the balsams were scarce, their limbs growing on only one side of the trunks. Many trees were bent, all in the same direction. Others were lying on rocky ground.

"The winds," Lucas explained, "are terrific up here in the wintertime. These roads are closed and there's snow on Mt. Mitchell most of the season."

Fog, mist and clouds obscured much of the view from the lookout. *Does Lucas remember holding me in the early morning mist?* Rae wondered.

Lucas was to leave right after breakfast the next morning. Rae didn't sleep well, thinking about it.

When breakfast was served, she ran down the stairs, calling over her shoulder, "I'll eat later." She didn't want Mimi to have a chance to ask where she was going or offer to go with her.

Running down the mountain to the lakeshore, she shed her shorts, shirt, tennis shoes, and the towel she had around her neck. Clad in a bathing suit, she ran around to the deeper part of the lake, jumped in, swam back to the shallow side, then climbed out and lay on her back on the towel, allowing the early morning sunshine to dry her.

It was quite cool at first, but soon the constant rays of the October sun warmed her skin, causing her to doze off. She must have slept about thirty minutes before she was awakened by the sound of a car coming down the gravel road. She didn't want to say good-bye. She didn't move, not even when she heard the footsteps on the wooden planks.

Chapter 14

Sitting up, she reached for her shirt and slipped her arm through the sleeves.

"I'm a mess," she said.

"You're always saying that," Lucas replied, reaching out to touch her tangled curls. "Crazy, the way your hair curls like that."

Her heart skipped a beat, and when he spoke again, it was about trivialities.

"You haven't seen the place in wintertime," he said, and she shook her head. "You'll love it when it snows. Light a fire in the fireplace in the lounge."

She looked up at him and he was staring at the mountainsides on the other side of the lake. "All right, Lucas. Thank you."

"Any message for Andy?"

"Tell him I hope he's well." Lucas looked at her sharply. "I didn't mean to hurt him, Lucas."

"I know that, Rae. It's just hard for me to grasp sometimes that you really aren't Andy's girl. And never were." His voice was distant and saddened. "Do you think he will ever stop loving you?"

"Of course," she replied quickly.

Lucas sighed. "It can be pretty miserable, pining away for a girl who can't be yours. But I suppose the way to know for sure is to ask him. I'll be back," he assured with a smile, then walked toward his car, got in, and waved as he drove away.

Rae lifted her hand but did not smile as the black Lincoln moved away from her, down the gravel road.

❧

The leaves lost their brilliance and fell to the ground, reflecting the bleakness of Rae's world without Lucas. But the prospect of Paris was exciting, and Mimi's exuberance proved contagious.

The trip was far from a sightseeing tour, however. Christmas Day was spent with many guests, including Pierre's family, at the Doudets' fashionable Parisian home. Most of the conversation centered around the wedding. It seemed all of Paris held or attended a party for Mimi.

The highlight of the season was a card from Lucas which read: "How do you like Paris? The snow here is great. See you in a few weeks. Lucas."

Back in North Carolina ice and sleet marked January and February. Mimi's classes were canceled several times, and Rae didn't even attempt to drive to the campgrounds.

Then the rains came, accompanied by swollen streams and flood watches. Mimi laughingly called it "liquid sunshine" and marked the days off on the calendar.

Finally the warm rays of sunshine began to dry the saturated earth, and tiny green shoots made their appearance. Lucas appeared, too, in early spring, during Mimi's break from school. He and Carl finalized camp plans to allow Rae time to help plan Mimi's farewell party at The Haven. She wouldn't be seeing her friends for awhile after leaving for Paris.

The April showers ceased long enough for the sun to shine on the day of the party. A fabulous dinner was followed by a surprise "This Is Your Life" game in which some of Mimi's childhood escapades were revealed.

"Tell us about the wedding," was all Mimi needed to fill the next hour with details. "All of you are invited," she said at last. "It's a huge wedding. Since Pierre teaches at the university, all the faculty and administration are invited, along with students. *Grandmere* and *Grandpere* know everyone in Paris, as do Pierre's family. Uncle Lucas has friends and business acquaintances there, not to mention my own friends."

Lucas held up a restraining hand. "Why don't you just invite the whole world?" he boomed.

Mimi looked surprised. "I thought we had!" She laughed and went over to hug him.

"At least it's only once," he said affectionately. "How long until you graduate?"

"Seven weeks," she replied. "Then I'll have my degree. I'm on a rain break right now."

"Why don't you all stay here tonight?" Lucas suggested after Mimi's friends had gone.

"I don't have to be asked twice," Gran replied, walking out of the lounge toward the stairway. "Good night."

"What does one do with five toasters?" Mimi asked, then turned her eyes around at Lucas. "I'll bet you think I don't know what to do with one."

"Do you?"

"No," she admitted, and grinned. "But I do know I have to write some thank-you notes." With that, she began to rummage around in boxes scattered all over the lounge floor until she found the note papers. Then, with a cheery wave of her hand, she hurried up the stairs.

"Let's have a cup of coffee," Lucas suggested to Rae when the excitement had died down.

Selma was leaving the kitchen when they walked in. "There's fresh coffee in the pot," she said and shook her head, a knowing smile on her lips. Someone *would* start dirtying dishes after she had just cleaned the kitchen.

Lucas took two cups from the cupboard and poured while Rae sat at the table. "I'm bushed," she admitted, rubbing the back of her neck.

"I can imagine," Lucas sympathized, bringing the coffee over. "My main role is bill payer, and I'm ready to call it quits for at least another twenty years or so."

Yes, Rae thought, *if he marries Isobel, and has children of his own, he probably will be ready to give away a daughter at the altar at just about that time.*

Refusing to entertain such a dismal thought, Rae mentioned the project that was uppermost in both their minds. "It's amazing how much progress has been made on the new camp," she said. "The gym is ready, the cabins built, and Carl says the pool will be finished within a month after the rains stop and the crews can resume work."

"And in two short months, your young girls will be here," he added.

Rae glanced over at him and smiled. "I remember your telling me that about the boys' camp. I couldn't have dreamed of the excitement and wonder of being involved in their lives. Oh, Lucas, it's so exciting to see the applications coming in, reading about those fresh-faced young girls with their goals and ambitions. It's such a tremendous challenge that I sometimes wonder if I can possibly live up to the responsibility."

"I have confidence in you, Rae. I brought some folders up that I want to look over with you. That is, if you're not too tired."

"Oh, not at all." Rae drained her cup, wondering if she had reacted too enthusiastically. "Talking about something other than the wedding is refreshing."

Lucas pushed his chair away from the table. "I'll meet you in the study in a little while."

Rae went to the room she had occupied when she had first come to the Haven. She turned in front of the mirror as if expecting something to be out of place. It wasn't. Not even her hair, for it still fell softly along one side of her face and was brushed back on the other, exposing a small, gold earring, matching her choker.

The soft green, knit dress was the color of early spring leaves and suitable for this in-between weather. She applied a bronzed gloss to her lips and noticed the unnatural brightness of her eyes, and the flush on her cheeks. *How ridiculous,* she told herself, *to have a rapid heartbeat over a business meeting with an employer.*

Lucas was already in the study when Rae arrived. He had removed his suit coat and tie, and his sleeves were rolled up as if he were ready to work. "I thought we'd be more comfortable on the couch than sitting at the desk," he said.

Rae sat on the couch near him. Folders were spread out on the coffee table. He began to discuss the staff and soon Rae was recommending counselors, activity directors, skills leaders, and even talked about interviewing secretaries to work only for the girls' camp.

"Much of the decision making is up to you, Rae," Lucas reminded her.

"I appreciate your confidence in me," she said gratefully. "But I'm not as experienced as you are."

"Your sensitivity to the inner needs of the girls is important," he assured. "It would be easy to overlook that and focus on what we offer in the way of physical facilities and equipment. Your suggestions of having Marge serve as sort of a mother figure is an excellent one. Each of us needs someone to share our feelings with, don't we?"

Rae nodded, not daring to look at him.

"You can't imagine what this means to me, Rae, the two of us working together like this. I've always dreamed of. . ."

His words were interrupted by a light tapping on the door. Mimi walked in. "I'm going to bed. Night has long passed, so I'll say good morning." She handed them each a piece of paper, then walked away, yawning.

"Oh, Lucas, look. Thank-you notes."

He smiled down at the loving words Mimi had written. "I've trained her well."

"You've met Pierre now, haven't you? Do you approve?"

"I think so. He's a very dashing fellow. Not the stereotyped teacher at all. He's tall, good-looking, a sports enthusiast. And Mimi is impressed with his mind—and his heart. He counsels many of his students, I understand." He turned a little to face Rae. "And he's several years older than Mimi. She needs someone like that, I believe. All those years I felt they needed me," Lucas smiled reflectively, "I needed them just as much."

"We all need people," she said and realized she mustn't stare into his wonderful face so intently. Suddenly she had to know. "Are you going to marry Isobel?"

Surprise flooded his face. "Never!" he responded immediately. "What gave you that idea?"

"Well, you said you had to get things settled. I assumed. . ."

"I meant I had to be honest with her and let her know there's no chance of that. I never said there was."

Mimi's thank-you note was becoming wrinkled from the pressure of her fingers, so she reached over and laid it on the coffee table. His sudden question surprised her.

"Do you not love Andy a little?"

"Yes," she answered honestly. "I love Andy a lot. Like I do Mimi. I want to see them happy."

"Was there some glaring reason why you couldn't marry him?"

"Yes, Lucas. I'm not in love with Andy." Her finger nervously traced a pattern on the knit dress.

"I think his broken heart is healing," Lucas assured. "Otherwise I don't think he would even look at another girl."

"I'm glad," she said sincerely.

His hand reached out and covered hers. "I've waited a long time for that, Rae. I could not approach you as long as I felt Andy was in love with you, or there was a chance for the two of you. Even though you can't love me, Rae, perhaps you and I. . ."

"What. . .what do you mean. . .I can't love you?" she asked haltingly, her green eyes full of wonder.

"Well," Lucas said hesitantly. "It was pretty clear. When I admitted my love for you, you said nothing."

"When was that?" she asked, amazed.

"The night I admitted to the family how I felt about you from the moment I saw you," he said with incredulity.

"But Lucas, you talked as if that was something in the past. That you *might* have loved me, but that it never had a chance."

He was shaking his head. "Rae, I thought you would know what I meant. I couldn't be so blunt in front of Andy. He was still hurting. I tried to make myself clear, so that you would understand."

"Lucas," she said, glad recognition dawning in her eyes. "A person doesn't assume a thing like that. It has to be said. And the night I tried to tell you how I felt, you stopped me."

"You mean, when you said you cared?"

She nodded.

"I thought you were going to tell me that you belonged to Andy. I stopped you because I couldn't stand to hear it. Ramona," he said suddenly, "could we start over?"

"No, Lucas," she said. "I can only continue. I began to love you long ago. I love you still—now and always."

"Just so there is no further misunderstanding, let me say, I love you, too. And I want to marry you right away."

"Oh, Lucas!" she cried, her heart overflowing with love for him. "But when will I ever find time now? The camp—the girls—"

"You'll *make* time." His laughter exploded from deep within. "Even if I have to fire you! And I'm not waiting twenty years. But I suppose you want a big wedding like Mimi."

Rae shook her head.

"A small one. Maybe in Gran's church. I do want to walk down the aisle in white, toward my husband-to-be. Maybe Marge as matron of honor and Mimi as bridesmaid. Nothing elaborate, just simple and beautiful. Then a small reception with a few of your friends and those I've come to know from camp."

"That sounds perfect," Lucas said in amazement. "How long have you had this planned?"

"Well," she said, a lovely glow on her face, "I've never thought of the wedding before, but I have dreamed of spending my life with you. That's the important part."

"We should be married before we go to Paris for Mimi's wedding," Lucas said. "We can have a short honeymoon there before coming back for the camping season. We won't have much time together for awhile."

"We'll have a lifetime."

"Yes," he sighed, "a lifetime."

"Lucas," she said quietly. "Why don't you stop looking at me, and take me in your arms. That's where I belong. Where I want to be."

"I've spent almost a year trying not to do that. I'm afraid I will take you in my arms only to awaken and find this is all a dream. Just like that first morning. It was a nightmare, Ramona, thinking you could never be mine."

"I know, Lucas. I felt that way, too."

Still holding her hand, he stood and gently pulled her to her feet. "Come on," he said, and led her through the house and out onto the deck and down to the third one, where they had met that first morning.

They stood looking out upon the dark green foliage and upward toward the smoky gray haze lingering along the peaks, visible evidence that the moisture had risen from the forest floor.

"This setting will always be a reminder to me, Lucas," Rae said regretfully, "of all the misunderstandings and heartaches of the past year."

"Yes, Ramona, but beyond that darkness is the beginning of a new day."

One arm went around her shoulder, and he held her closely as he pointed with the other hand. "Look. You can see it. There in the gap between those highest peaks."

Rae could see the faint fingers of dawn just beginning to reach into the shadowed coves and hollows.

"It's like us, Lucas," Rae whispered. "Like all human beings. The sun doesn't move—it's the earth that turns away, causing the night. God doesn't move—we look away from Him, bringing darkness into our own lives."

Lucas was nodding his agreement. "And like our love. It didn't disappear. It was there, waiting for us until we could recognize it and express it in the right way and at the right time."

As they watched, the glow spread along the ridges, dispelling the last shadows, touching the smoky haze and turning it to gold.

Lucas drew Rae closer into his arms. His dark eyes mirrored the majesty of the awakening mountains. "Ramona, I love you."

She lifted her face for the touch of his lips on hers. Neither of them turned to watch the sun rise higher into the vaulted sky, feeling only the warmth of its gentle caress.

CALL OF THE
MOUNTAIN

Chapter 1

He replied, "Because you have so little faith. I tell you the truth,
if you have faith as small as a mustard seed, you can say to this mountain,
'Move from here to there' and it will move. Nothing will be impossible for you."
MATTHEW 17:20

Beth Bennett had read somewhere that if you save a life, then you're responsible for that life. She'd wanted to save the life of that unborn baby but never dreamed she would become involved to this extent. A few hours ago, twenty-four-year-old Beth was footloose and fancy-free, as her Aunt Tess would say. She was single, had never been intimate with a man, but in six and a half short months she was going to be a mother!

Beth's thoughts spiraled back to the heated conversation with her sister, Carol, who threatened to have an abortion. Beth had given every reason she could think of why Carol should not take such drastic measures. But Carol offered every reason why she should.

"I'm twenty-one, single, and the father doesn't want marriage or a baby. And how could I give it away? I'd be worried forever about whether the child was being cared for properly. I'd rather it never be born. Anyway, it's not a baby yet."

"Oh, Carol," Beth protested. "It's like a seed. It has everything necessary to make it a baby at the time of conception."

"No way, Beth! It's just a fetus." Then, pressing her hands against her still-flat stomach, Carol challenged, "But if you're so intent upon this baby being born, then you take it and raise it."

"Me?" Beth squeaked. "How in the world could I raise a baby?"

"That's exactly how I feel," her sister exclaimed triumphantly. "You do-gooders spout your religious ideals, but you're not willing to get involved. You, who want babies to live, should provide homes for them."

"I'm sure there are hundreds of people just waiting for a baby," Beth said. "I'll help you find a good home."

Carol shook her head again. "Nope. This is the deal. You take the baby and raise it. Otherwise, I'm having an abortion."

There was only one thing Beth could say. "Yes, I'll take the baby and raise it."

Skepticism filled Carol's eyes. "Beth, I've had over two months to mull this over. When you've had time to think about it, you'll realize it's not so easy to take care of a baby."

"I won't change my mind," Beth retorted emphatically.

Carol smiled wryly. "You're my older, sensible sister, but you're not thinking clearly. I understand where you're coming from, but you don't understand where I'm coming from. I'll give you two weeks to come up with a great excuse for why you can't do it. Now, promise me you won't tell Mom and Dad."

Beth promised, adding, "Under the condition you don't do anything foolish like having an abortion."

⁓

Don't you *do anything foolish, Beth,* her conscience rang out as she stood in the airport phone booth, listening to the phone ringing at the Crenshaw home in New York. She and Randy had planned that she'd call from the airport so he would know when to meet her. But, no way could she drop a bombshell on her boyfriend like this. *Hey, Randy. Guess what? In a few months I'm going to be a mother!*

"Hello?" Randy's voice answering the phone interrupted her thoughts.

"Hi, it's me," she said. "I'm at the airport."

"Great! What time does your flight get here?"

"Randy. I can't get a flight out of here to anywhere. Everything's booked."

"We've got big plans, hon." Disappointment sounded in his voice. "Tomorrow's New Year's Eve, you know? Times Square. Mom and Dad are looking forward to meeting you."

Would his mom and dad be eager to meet her when they discovered she would have a baby in about six months? Could she go to New York and act like nothing had changed? At least she didn't have to make that decision right now. The weather had done it for her. "I'll take the first flight I can get, Randy, to New York or Baltimore."

"Be sure and call, Beth. You can leave a message if no one's here. You know how this gang is."

"Yeah," she said as he chuckled. She did know. They were a fun-loving bunch. A few months ago, ten of the airline's employees took off on the spur of the moment and flew to Cancun. That was an advantage of working for the airlines—free flights. "I'll call," she said, a wave of disappointment washing over her. This had been the first time Randy had said he wanted her to meet his parents. That was significant, wasn't it? Did it mean their relationship was taking a more serious turn? It was too bad Carol's boyfriend hadn't been that serious. That must hurt Carol—deeply.

Well, Beth thought as she hung up, *Carol had been right in saying there was*

236

more to this than meets the eye. Her life was changing already. Randy could think about flying to anywhere in the continental United States, or Hawaii, or even abroad. That would have appealed to her greatly a few days ago—before her promise to Carol threatened to turn her life upside down. What she needed was to get back to Baltimore where she lived with her Aunt Tess. But she couldn't seem to get to Baltimore.

⁂

"Any cancellations yet for Baltimore?" Beth asked the Eagle Airlines ticket agent for the third time in the past hour.

"Sorry," the young man replied. "Booked solid, and with all the storms approaching this part of the country, it's not likely anybody's going to take a chance on being stranded."

Beth closed her eyes against the feeling of desperation that had mounted to the point of a dull throb behind her eyes. The prospect of staying overnight at the airport wasn't very appealing, and she didn't relish the idea of going to some strange hotel and spending her hard-earned money. As usual, after Christmas, it would take several paychecks before she'd have bills paid off and be even again. *How will I ever be able to support a baby?*

"Can't you smuggle me in somewhere?" she asked. "After all, I am an Eagle Airlines employee." Beth had worked as a ticket agent in Baltimore for the past two years.

"Which means," the young man replied with a note of chagrin, "we take what's leftover, if anything. And frankly, there's not a single seat available, and there're only two more flights out tonight for Baltimore. You know how booked we are over the holidays." His sympathetic smile and shrug indicated his helplessness in the situation. "Maybe someone will cancel at the last minute."

"Not with my luck," Beth retorted, remembering the fiasco that had occurred at her family home and the promises she'd made to Carol. "Look," she reasoned, "it doesn't matter if I have to go in a roundabout way. I'd rather be in the air and changing planes, than stuck in an airport all night."

A furrow appeared between his brows, and his eyes traveled from her face to her dark brown, layered haircut that she had thought looked wonderful this morning. Now, it must appear as bedraggled as she felt. And by now, she'd probably harassed this ticket agent to the breaking point. She felt like slinking into a corner somewhere instead of insisting he perform the impossible.

His eyes lit up, and he lifted an index finger. "Just a minute." He picked up the phone. "You may just be in luck."

Luck, she thought. That, and fate, and her own common sense were all against her. She only wanted to reach New York before Randy flew off into the wild blue yonder, or go to Tess's house and have a heart-to-heart talk with Aunt Tess and Randy, both of whom were as opposed to abortion as she. But now, she was in Charlotte, North Carolina, with little prospect of getting out.

"Ah, ha!" the young man said suddenly, causing Beth's deep blue eyes to look at him speculatively. "There's a commuter flight leaving in about thirty minutes for Asheville. It should get there just in time for you to connect with a departure and take their one empty seat to. . .ta daaaa. . ." He spread his hands. "To Baltimore!"

"You're not kidding?" Beth's eyes were wide and her mouth open. He had performed a miracle. Finally she closed her mouth.

"Sort of wish I were," he said, with frank admiration in his eyes and a lowered voice. "I've been entertaining the idea of taking you home with me. We've spent a lot of time together in the past hour or so."

Beth laughed. "Thanks, but I really need that commuter flight." She really needed the compliment, too, however vague or insincere. She needed anything to take her mind off the predicament she'd gotten herself into by promising to become a mom in six and a half months. She looked around. "Where do I go?" She'd never been in the Charlotte Airport and knew nothing about their commuter flights.

He pointed toward a flight of stairs. "Downstairs. You'll see the desk on your left when you get down there."

"Thanks." She smiled.

"Glad to be of service, Ma'am," he said with a mock salute.

His dimpled smile reminded Beth of how cute he was. His slow drawl was southern. The evaluating look he gave her, however, was universal. She didn't resent it, having felt she'd come to know the difference between ogling and appreciation. In exchange for free flying time, Eagle expected their employees to be a complementary representation, in looks and deportment, even when off duty.

Beth had dressed in a black, wool suit with a midcalf-length skirt. It was the suit she'd raved about when it came to Aunt Tess's dress shop and had ended up, as she expected, as an early Christmas present. The royal blue, silk blouse deepened the color of her eyes. She'd begun to long for a pair of sneakers instead of her stylish, new, black, chunky heels as she quickened her pace toward the stairs.

After a short delay, the few passengers boarded the commuter flight. No seats were assigned, and Beth chose a window seat near the rear of the plane. She leaned her head back, then fastened her eyes upon the flight attendant. The girl looked so young, as if she hadn't a care. Her cornsilk hair hung straight to her shoulders, and she wore bangs. Beth thought the sprinkling of freckles across her nose gave her a storybook wholesomeness.

Beth concentrated on the girl's smiling oval face while she gave emergency instructions. When Beth took advantage of free flights, she didn't really consider that the craft might crash. However, this noisy crate being kept in the air by spinning propellers conjured up images of all sorts of crashes. There were only two rows of seats along one side of the plane and a single row on the other.

The plane flew into an air pocket, and for awhile it was rocky sailing over pointed mountains almost obscured by clouds. She felt an uneasy churning in her stomach as if her lunch might come up. It suddenly occurred to her that she hadn't eaten lunch. Her stomach felt strangely like she'd heard morning sickness described.

There were only a few passengers, and no one next to anyone except one middle-aged couple. There were two elderly women and nine men in suits and ties, looking like stereotypical bored businessmen eager to get home. The windows misted over, and Beth could no longer view the sight she'd decided to label "the twilight zone." This definitely was not her day.

The flight attendant caught her attention again. Beth could sympathize with the girl trying to keep her balance by leaning her hip against a seat while bringing soft drinks and coffee. The tray could at any moment topple, and drinks might go flying all over the passengers. Beth accepted a Sprite with a smile for the girl who worked in the same profession as she and wore one of the required maroon, gray, and white uniforms.

A short while later, Beth was staring out the misty window when a voice registered in her ear. Her head turned to see the flight attendant sitting beside her.

"Do you mind if I sit here for a minute?" the girl asked rather timidly.

"No, that's fine," Beth encouraged. She welcomed any distraction that would get her mind off her personal situation.

"I'm Faye," the girl said.

"Beth."

"Are you visiting people in Asheville?"

Beth shook her head. She didn't want to explain.

"I didn't think I'd ever seen you on this plane, and I've come to know just about everybody who commutes to Asheville. There're not all that many."

Beth smiled, finding Faye's southern drawl an interesting point to focus upon. She sighed. "I'm trying to get to Baltimore."

"Kind of a roundabout way," Faye said curiously.

Beth nodded. "I work for Eagle, too. Ticket agent in Baltimore."

Skeptical brown eyes held Beth's. "Are you planning to stay in Asheville till morning?"

"Well, no," Beth stammered, feeling something strange in her stomach again and knowing it wasn't hunger or because the small craft took another bumpy dive into an air pocket. She had to wave her cup of Sprite to go with the flow of the plane's movement. "I was told," she said, performing her balancing act, "that a flight was leaving there tonight and there was an empty seat."

Faye grimaced. "That flight leaves at 5:30."

Beth looked at her watch—5:20. "How long does it take to get to Asheville?"

"Twenty more minutes. Maybe you didn't know we were delayed at Charlotte."

Beth had known. But she'd been so grateful about getting any flight, she hadn't thought of the connection being that close. And she'd been delayed all day long. She squeaked, "I'm going to miss it?"

Faye nodded, and Beth turned her face toward the cold, misty window. Finally, she turned back to Faye. "I guess I can fly somewhere else."

Faye shook her head. "That's the last flight out from the Asheville airport tonight."

"I see," Beth said, as if the words were ripped from inside her. "I'll bet the airport doesn't even stay open all night."

She'd made that statement as a point of irony, but Faye nodded. "You're right," she said sympathetically. "It doesn't."

Beth closed her eyes and bit on her lip, knowing she was up a creek without a paddle. What should have been a day of triumph was turning out to be the worst day of her life. *Where do I go from here?* she wondered.

"I'm so sorry," Faye said.

Embarrassment welled up in Beth for several reasons: one, allowing herself to come unglued about what had saved an unborn baby's life; two, being so unprofessional as to go flying all over the sky without a destination; and three, causing this nice, friendly girl to lose her pleasant smile and feel sorry for her.

"Don't mind me, Faye," Beth said quickly. "I'm wearing my feelings on my sleeve. It's only a temporary setback. I'm the kind of girl who rolls her sleeves up and gets busy with a new project." With that sense of determination, Beth handed Faye her cup, half filled with Sprite.

"That's the spirit," Faye agreed, then said seriously, "Beth, do you know that things work for good to those who love God and serve the Lord?"

Beth nodded. "I do. But sometimes it's hard when we don't see the outcome immediately."

Faye nodded. "I know exactly what you mean."

Beth believed the girl and was impressed that Faye had been open about faith in God. Aunt Tess had led Beth to the Lord years ago, and when Beth was eighteen, she'd moved in with her aunt rather than stay with her own parents and sister, who considered Aunt Tess some kind of religious fanatic and warned Beth about following in her footsteps. Beth had become stronger in her faith but couldn't at all see how God would work in this situation. Maybe she'd been wrong to say she'd take Carol's baby. But if she hadn't, the baby would be aborted. Sometimes it seemed there wasn't really a right answer to life's problems. She looked at Faye.

Faye smiled, then got up and moved along the narrow aisle, speaking to the other passengers. Soon the pilot's voice came over the intercom with instructions concerning their landing. Beth breathed a sigh of relief when the landing wasn't any more bumpy than when they'd flown into the air pocket.

"Wait for me inside, and I'll see what I can do to help," Faye said as Beth walked past her at the doorway.

"Thanks," Beth responded and descended the steps, feeling homeless and helpless. How could such a person raise a child? She lowered her head to ward off the cold, moist wind that struck her face, then hurried across the runway and into the airport that had only one waiting room. No one was heading toward it. She went straight to the ticket counter and confirmed that she was, indeed, stranded.

What else could she do but wait for Faye and whatever advice the girl might offer? Suddenly her eyes grew wide as she looked toward the glass front doors. "Oh, no," she wailed aloud. That couldn't be snow. It would be the perfect final touch of irony added to her day filled with unexpected events.

Faye finally appeared, wearing a heavy tweed coat and carrying a large canvas bag. Her face was grim. "They're ready to get out of here," she said. "A snowstorm is expected. Did you need to get to Baltimore because of some emergency, Beth? Or are you scheduled to work?"

"Baltimore's my home. There's. . .no place else to go."

"Sorry," Faye quipped with a mischievous grin. "Asheville is the home of Thomas Wolfe who is famous for saying, 'You can't go home again.' "

At Beth's snort, Faye quickly apologized. "Well, at least not tonight."

Beth inhaled deeply and shook her head. Oh well, what harm could a little more honesty do? "Actually, I've gotten myself into a pickle—with my sister." She shrugged helplessly. "I'm not sure how to handle the future or even if I'm capable of facing what I've gotten myself into."

Freckles across Faye's nose became more noticeable as her face paled. "Oh, Beth, there's always a way."

"Oh, don't mind me. I'm being melodramatic."

Faye nodded and smiled uncertainly. The two young women headed toward the baggage claim area.

A baby started crying. A young woman was trying to reach for bags while keeping an eye on the baby on the floor in one of the regulation seats required by the airlines for infants. She had a shoulder bag and a diaper bag over her shoulder, a suitcase on the floor, and she reached for another but missed, so she was waiting for its return on the conveyer belt.

"I think somebody could use some help," Faye said, grabbing the bag. "This yours?" she asked, walking over to the woman whose baby was now screaming.

"Oh, thanks," the woman said. "Now if I can just find his binky." She rummaged through her purse. Then she sighed in relief as an older woman came toward her. "Oh, thank goodness you're here, Mom. The baby won't stop crying. I'm—"

Beth felt suspended for a moment, watching, while holding her single bag. She could travel anywhere she wanted with one bag. That would change after the baby came. She'd have to lug around a regulation seat, a diaper bag, a binky—whatever that was. Oh, boy!

"Here, let me take something," Faye said, returning to Beth. "Look at the size of those flakes! Let's go," she ordered, "before we're unable to."

Yes, Beth was thinking. *Before I call my sister and say the deal is off!*

Chapter 2

B eth didn't ask questions as she followed Faye out a side door and into a private parking lot. Snow fell on her hair and melted into the shoulders of her suit coat while she waited for Faye to unlock the doors of her little, red economy car.

"Front-wheel drive," Faye said, upon starting the engine. "So the snow shouldn't give us any problem. However," she added, glancing over at Beth. "I still feel safer in the air than on the road."

"I know what you mean," Beth agreed. "Baltimore traffic is the pits." She fastened her seat belt in preparation for heavy traffic on a snow-slick road. Faye drove from the parking lot, took several turns on two-lane roads, then pulled out onto Interstate 40, a four-lane highway separated by barren trees lining the median strip. Patches of blowing snow obscured visibility, and huge flakes splattered the windshield as fast as the wipers could remove them. A few cars moved slowly along both sides of the Interstate.

"Where's the traffic?" Beth asked after several minutes. "Are the storm warnings so bad that people aren't driving?"

Faye laughed lightly. "Oh, it's never that bad here." She leaned forward for better visibility. "And there's not a lot of traffic during the winter. Quite the opposite during the other seasons, however. The Blue Ridge Mountains of western North Carolina are a tourist attraction, you know."

Beth supposed she had known, but it wasn't something she'd kept in her mind for any reason. "What kind of attractions are here?"

"The mountains," Faye said with a quick glance toward Beth, then back at the highway, where the snow was beginning to stick.

Beth looked down at her hands, folded together on her lap. Early this morning she'd been at sea level. The Pacific Ocean, in fact. What was she doing in the Blue Ridge Mountains, where the attraction was. . .mountains? "By the way," she asked suddenly, "where are we going?"

"You're going home with me," Faye said. Before Beth could question that, Faye turned off the interstate onto an exit marked "West Asheville." At the end of that, she drove onto an almost-deserted road where an approaching car slithered toward them before the driver regained control. Faye's little, red car kept puttering along, the front-wheel drive behaving efficiently.

Faye glanced over at Beth's hands, grasping the seat on each side of her. "There's a lot more snow than this in Baltimore, isn't there?"

"Yes, but it lies on relatively flat streets. And you can see buildings all around." Beth peered out the window for a description. "Here, what I can glimpse through the blowing snow is forests or rock barriers, right on the edge of the road."

Faye laughed. "I don't suppose I can convince you that this area is called 'Land of the Sky'?"

Beth leaned forward to glance up through the windshield. Huge white flakes were falling from a black background. "No way," she said.

"Well, you really need to see everything from Josh's place."

"Josh?" Beth questioned.

"My brother. He has a cabin way up. . .oops! Shouldn't have stepped on the brakes. That's the hardest thing not to do when you start to slide." She let out a breath and smiled broadly. "We missed it."

"It?"

"The ditch on the side of the road. But we're okay now."

Beth mumbled, "Mmm," but felt like her physical life was in as precarious condition as her emotional life. Whoever said that when you're down, there's no place to go but up was wrong. She'd gone down in San Francisco, come up to Faye's Land of the Sky, only to be in danger of rolling down the side of a mountain in a little, red bug.

"Oh, Faye," she exclaimed suddenly. "Look at that. It's gorgeous."

A wide road stretched out before them like a white carpet. Evergreens, mingled with blackened branches of deciduous trees, lifted their arms to catch the falling snow. The greenish hue of vapor lamps accentuated the soft flakes.

Christmas Day had come and gone, but signs of it remained. A huge cedar glowed with loops of colored lights. Smaller trees winked and blinked from yards and behind picture windows.

Houses, each with their own individual designs, sat charmingly against, below, and upon the rolling hillsides. Curling, white smoke rose from chimneys. Snow fell upon angels guarding the baby Jesus in the manger, safe and warm inside the stable. Had young Mary been afraid of rearing the Christ-child? Carol didn't feel competent to rear her baby. *And I am getting more nervous by the moment,* Beth conceded.

"Now," Faye said, breaking Beth's reverie, "all we have to do is slide down this hill, turn into our driveway, and we've got it made."

She did just that. The driveway was long and curved around and up toward a brick house that appeared to be one level on top of a hill.

Faye gestured toward the house. "We're home." A truck was parked in the carport behind a huge van. Faye drove past the carport and house, where colored lights beckoned from a tree in the picture window, then turned into the driveway below the house and parked beneath a wooden deck. An outside light glowed on the brick walkway, leading to the entrance, untouched by snow. Beth realized there was a lower level to the house.

"This was built to be a garage," Faye said, unlocking a door beside a wide window. "We never used it for that. Dad had it converted into an apartment for me." She walked in and switched on an overhead light.

Beth stepped inside. "It's darling," she exclaimed, looking around the cozy living room. Having an eye for style, Beth appreciated the pastel colors accented with bright splashes in a painting and a vase of artificial flowers, serving to lighten and brighten the rectangular room that had windows only along one wall.

Beth followed Faye across the light blue carpet into a compact kitchen. "I rarely cook," Faye said. "My parents live upstairs, and it's much simpler just to pop up there." She wrinkled her nose. "Pleases Mom and Dad, too."

Faye opened a door on her right and invited Beth into her bedroom. The overhead light showered down upon twin beds, one made and the other with covers tossed aside. Faye spread her hands and grimaced. "So, I'm not the world's greatest housekeeper."

"Looks great to me," Beth replied, unmoved even by the pieces of clothing on the floor and the bathrobe draped across a straight chair. "I like this." She looked around at the paneled walls, the nightstand and lamp between the beds, the corner closet built out into the room, a small dressing table and mirror between two, wide windows with drawn drapes, and a chest of drawers. There was no particular style that she could pick up on, but she could honestly say, "It's cozy and inviting."

Faye looked pleased, dropped her bag onto the unmade bed, and began to peel off her coat. "Mom and Dad keep telling me I'd have more room if I got rid of one of the beds. But I like having two, in case of company."

Beth unfastened her suit coat. "Why do I get the feeling you're one of those persons who bring home stray cats, lost dogs, and stranded humans?"

The way Faye shrugged before going to hang up her coat and the sheepish look on her face convinced Beth she'd correctly diagnosed the girl. "I'm nothing compared to Josh," she said, and held out a hanger. "Hang up your coat, and we'll go meet my parents."

Josh? Beth started to question, then recalled Faye had said Josh was her brother who lived on the mountaintop. "Faye, do you have a bathroom?"

"Couple of outhouses down the hill," Faye began, and Beth's mouth dropped open. "I'm kidding, Beth. It's under the stairs. Just step back into the living room and turn to your right. It's small, with a shower. When I want a marvelous bubble bath, I go upstairs."

When Beth returned, Faye said it was time to meet her parents. The staircase to upstairs was beyond the open doorway Beth had observed earlier. Her first impression upon stepping from the upstairs hallway and into the living room was one of warmth and comfort. Not only because of the matched furniture and glowing fire in a brick fireplace, but the attitude of Faye's parents.

The trim, blond woman in jeans and plaid shirt stood to one side of the lighted Christmas tree, looking out. An auburn-haired, broad-shouldered man, also in jeans and flannel shirt, set down a box of wood and wiped his hands on his jeans.

Wearing welcoming smiles, they both came toward the girls. Jean and Sam, as they later insisted upon being called, hugged both girls before the introductions were made. Then they all discovered last names. Beth Bennett. Jean, Sam, and Faye Logan.

"It's one of those soft, light snows that just lays on everything," Jean said, looking toward the window and back at Beth. Then she smiled up at her big, rugged-looking husband, at least a head taller than she.

Sam's face lit up with a smile, and his dark brown eyes looked down upon his wife in a way that made Beth feel they had a very special relationship. It was rare that she'd ever seen her parents be so casual and open about their feelings for each other.

"We've got a warm fire and plenty to eat," Sam said. "What more could we ask for? You girls come on over here and get yourselves warmed up."

He hurried over to the fireplace, threw on another log, and poked it with a poker. "Little lady," he said to Beth. "Prop your feet up and sit right here by the fire." He gestured toward the big, overstuffed couch, several feet away, but adjacent to the fireplace.

"Thanks," Beth said with a smile, and didn't have to be asked twice. Faye took a seat at the other end of the couch. Sam sat in a well-used recliner at the other side of the fire. Jean walked up beside Sam and perched on the chair arm.

Beth braced herself for inevitable questions she didn't feel like answering. To her surprise, they never came. Jean simply asked when they'd last eaten, told Beth to make herself at home while she raided the refrigerator, then exited through the dining area and into the kitchen. She peeked in at them occasionally, confirming, contradicting, or adding to what Sam had to say.

Sam described a world Beth had been unaware of. Her adult role model had been her dad, an executive with a big office in a corporate conglomerate. Now she listened to a man talk about his years of being a ranger on the Blue Ridge Parkway. Clearing trails. Cutting logs. Digging ditches. Fighting fires. Using hands and muscles in a way she hadn't even imagined. She'd thought muscles came from weights in a health club. But Sam, even in middle age, obviously had well-developed forearms, chest, and biceps, although they were covered by a long-sleeved shirt and an undershirt exposed at the neck.

How fortunate Faye is to have a father like that, Beth thought. One who tracked a wounded animal for miles so he could help. One who cared about preserving the forests and keeping virgin land safe. He talked about how he had taken his family into the forest and taught them survival.

"All this is probably boring you, Beth," he said. "I get to talking and don't know when to stop."

"I love to hear it, Sam," Beth said honestly. "I've always lived in a city. San Francisco, now Baltimore. So, hearing about your work and family life is fascinating to me. My maternal grandparents lived on a farm, but they were killed in an automobile accident when I was thirteen."

A sympathetic expression passed over Sam's face. Suddenly he looked quite tired, and Beth was aware of the deep lines that furrowed his brow, the crow's-feet at his eyes, and the creases at the corners of his mouth, now turned downward. She became conscious of how much gray sprinkled his auburn curls.

"I'm sorry to hear that," he said finally and reached over to take Beth's hand in his. "We lost our Kate several years ago. She was about your age. Well," he patted her hand, "I don't need to get into all that. Just know you're welcome as a summer shower after a drought."

"That's the nicest thing anybody could say to me, Sam." Beth glanced at Faye, whose eyes were filled with warmth and acceptance. Then Faye looked toward the kitchen. "I smell something good. Let's see if Mom has that food ready." She rose from the couch. Beth followed her lead, leaving a silent Sam staring into the fire that had burned low.

Jean set spaghetti, homemade sauce, and salad makings before them.

"The sauce is leftover," Jean said, "but we all think it tastes better that way."

They all watched while Beth sampled it. "Mmm, this is the best sauce I have ever tasted, and I'm not just being polite. Honest."

"I believe you," Jean said, laughing. "After all, you did say you haven't eaten a decent meal since last night."

"Well, I admit I could eat a horse right now, but I'd still know if it tasted good or not."

The need for food overwhelmed Beth, and she indulged along with Faye, much to the pleasure of Jean, who sat down with a cup of coffee and talked about the weather for awhile, then mentioned her country-western apparel store at the mall.

Beth could identify with the apparel store and related her own experiences of having worked in her aunt Tess's dress shop on weekends and holidays before going with Eagle and starting classes at design school. She could not identify with the square dance apparel Jean talked about. The closest she'd ever come to anything like that was during one college semester of folk dance, which consisted of a skimpy introduction to numerous international dances. Her favorite had been the polka, when she and her partner jumped and leaped all over the gym floor. It had been such fun.

Beth heard a phone ringing in another room and Sam called, "I'll get it." A short while later he appeared in the doorway. "Josh called. He wanted to make sure Faye got home all right. I told him she did and that she brought a friend with her." He smiled at Beth.

"Is he stopping by?" Jean asked expectantly.

"No, he's getting ready to go out on the mountain." Sam explained to Beth, "When the weather's like this, he goes out to search for anyone or anything that might be wet, cold, or disabled."

Beth would like to have asked more about Josh, but Sam pointed at the kitchen window. "Look at that!" Huge, white flakes fell fast and thick.

When Beth and Faye could eat no more, Jean insisted they leave the cleaning up to her. The girls said good night and went downstairs.

"Would you like to talk about your pickle?" Faye asked.

Beth stared for a moment, then remembered she had described her dilemma that way. But she couldn't help laughing a little at the way Faye made it sound. "Thanks for the offer, but it wouldn't help. I need to talk to my aunt about it. Oh, I should call her."

Faye said to use the phone between the beds.

Aunt Tess was surprised to hear from her. "I thought you'd be in New York by now," her aunt said.

Beth knew she shouldn't relate the baby situation over the phone. She could honestly say, "There were no empty seats on a flight to New York. I'm coming back to Baltimore as soon as I get a flight. Don't worry. I met a flight attendant who brought me home with her. She and her parents are wonderful, so I'm fine. How's the weather there?"

After completing the brief conversation with her aunt, Beth told Faye, "Aunt Tess said storms are forecast for Baltimore tomorrow. Maybe I can get out early in the morning before they hit."

"Then you'd better get some rest," Faye said. "Sounds like you've had a rough day spent in and out of airports." Without coercion, Beth snuggled beneath the comforter and felt blessed sleep coming over her as soon as her head sunk into the soft pillow and she began to pray. But she wasn't sure how to pray about the situation. Should she ask that God change Carol's mind so that she'd keep her baby? Or should she pray for the wisdom to raise the child herself?

Beth realized she was beginning to feel like an unwed mother. In fact, wasn't that exactly what she was becoming?

⌘

The next thing Beth knew, someone was calling her name. "Beth. Beth. You're okay. Wake up."

Beth sat up in bed, clutching the covers, ready to cower in the corner. She looked around, then focused on the clock. It was morning. Then the identity of the girl struck her. "Faye," she said with relief, and pushed her dark hair away from her face.

"It sounded like you were moaning and yelling about a baby," Faye said with a question in her eyes.

Beth shrugged. "It's a problem I have to work out."

"Sure you don't want to talk about it?"

Beth shook her head. "Thanks, but I'm not even sure what I think about it yet."

"You should talk to my brother Josh."

Beth doubted that. "The one your dad says roams the mountains trying to find people?"

"Yep. That's Josh's way. Oops! There's my teakettle," Faye said as a shrill whistle pierced the air. "Dad bought it for me. Says I can't boil water. He thinks I might burn the house down." Her eyes turned toward the ceiling then back again. "Want some instant coffee? We can get the real stuff upstairs later."

"I'd love it," Beth said. "First, I need to call the airport."

"Number's right there on the front of the phone book," Faye said, waving her hand toward the bedside table, where the book sat beneath the phone.

Beth watched thoughtfully as Faye left the bedroom. The scare of her dream hadn't quite left her. It had something to do with a baby swaying precariously in a treetop while the wind blew. She knew the dream was based on unanswered questions in her mind. Agreeing to rear a child responsibly could change her entire lifestyle! Well, she couldn't worry about it yet. And she was sure this Josh couldn't help. Only Aunt Tess and Randy would have advice and answers about this problem, if anyone could.

For the first time in her life, Beth felt she could really empathize with a single, pregnant girl. If Carol didn't change her mind and decide to keep the baby herself, then in two weeks Beth must seriously consider herself an unwed mother-to-be.

Chapter 3

A few minutes later, Beth wandered into the compact kitchen in her bare feet, wearing the pajamas Faye had lent her. She'd rolled up the legs. "All flights canceled indefinitely," she moaned. "Also, I called Aunt Tess—collect. She said an ice storm is supposed to hit Baltimore at any moment."

"Which means," Faye correctly surmised, "even if you could get out of here, you might not be able to land in Baltimore." She set a steaming cup of coffee in front of Beth, who had pulled out the kitchen chair and sat in it, her feet propped on the rungs instead of on the cold tile.

Beth accepted cream that Faye took from the refrigerator.

"Guess you're stuck with us," Faye said with a pleased grin. Her glance turned toward the open doorway. "I think that's the smell of Mom's bacon in the air. Her voice will soon follow."

They laughed together when a few seconds later they heard, "Faye. Beth. You all up?"

"Yes, Mom," Faye answered. "Be right there."

Beth dressed in jeans and a tee shirt. The same friendly accepting attitude reigned throughout breakfast. Then Sam left in the van to go to the post office and supermarket and run some errands for Jean. Beth helped Jean wash the dishes that Faye brought to the countertop. They could look out the kitchen window at the whitened landscape. Jean began to tell about other snows and when the three children were little.

Beth enjoyed the stories. Then a wistful look came onto Jean's face. "It's just the two of them now. Faye and Joshua."

"My sister took her life a few years ago," Faye said, setting down a stack of plates.

"I'm so sorry," Beth said. "My problems seem small compared with yours."

"No problem is too small, Beth," Jean said. "That's why I mention this. We thought Kate's problems were just those of growing up. But they went much deeper. We assumed too much, but we can never do that again, with anyone."

Beth felt she understood the Logans better. That would explain Sam's sadness when Beth said she'd lost her grandparents and their reaching out to her as if she were part of their family.

"Well," Jean said quickly. "Since you can't get to Baltimore, you'll just have to join us in our New Year's Eve celebration."

Beth hoped her smile looked genuine, but her mind was on the irony of how her entire life had changed in an instant and how uncertain her future looked. Should she celebrate—or lament—the coming of the new year?

By midafternoon Beth accepted the fact that there would be no flights out of the Asheville airport that day, and more snow was predicted for later in the night.

She was surprised to discover that the New Year's Eve celebration would not be a family dinner and conversation around a cozy fire, then turning on TV and watching the ball fall in Times Square in New York while everyone counted down to midnight and the new year. Randy would be in Times Square, but Beth wouldn't. Nor would she be here to try and pick him out of the crowd on TV. She was to join the Logans at a square dance at The Barn, between Asheville and Hendersonville.

Beth expressed her delight when Jean and Sam appeared, dressed in country-western costumes. Sam wore denim jeans that matched Jean's full denim skirt that she wore over a crinoline. Their western shirts were a softer denim with sequins sewn along the shoulder and pocket seams. Jean wore chunky-heeled shoes, and Sam wore boots.

Really stylish, however, was Faye in a beautiful suede outfit. She wore a full skirt that fell to midcalf and a vest with a cream-colored shirt. Her boots were a darker suede. "You'd make any cowgirl envious," Beth remarked.

"You're not too bad yourself," Faye replied.

Beth was pleased with her recent haircut. She only had to shampoo her hair and blow-dry it just right, and she didn't even need to use a curling iron. The feather cut kept its shape without too much effort on her part. She'd brushed it out well, fluffed it around her head with her fingers, pulled a few strands over her forehead, shaped it back from her ears, and smoothed it down to her shoulders. "Looking at you guys," she said, "I do feel under-dressed, although Faye loaned me this beautiful, white western shirt."

"Your jeans are fine," Jean assured her. "The important thing is to have fun, not how you're dressed. There will be other women there in jeans. Anyway, this New Year's Eve celebration brings together many country-western groups. There will be western square dancing that's structured and requires lessons. There will also be line dancing, some that requires some lessons, but others that you can do with or without a partner."

A disturbing thought crossed Beth's mind. *Will I have to do a lot of things without a partner—like raising a baby?*

Sam and Jean rode in the van. Beth rode with Faye in the red car. The snow lent a brightness to the evening, almost like day. Everything looked like an unreal picture postcard. She could appreciate the scenery and anticipated the festive evening ahead.

This wonderful family had kept her mind off the few short months before she would become a mother. She bit on her lip and inadvertently shook her head. Had she done the right thing? But what else could she have done? How would Randy accept this? Were his feelings strong enough to include marriage? Were hers? But how could she raise a child. . .alone?

"Want to talk about it, Beth?" Faye asked, breaking the silence and settling back in a more relaxed attitude after reaching Interstate 40.

"Not all of it," Beth said. "But I was wondering how my boyfriend is going to react to the situation I've gotten myself into. I've got two weeks to make a decision that is irreversible." She sighed.

"I've learned that the best thing to do is pray, seek God's will, and let Him work things out. Nothing is too difficult for Him, Beth."

Beth smiled at Faye's response. Aunt Tess was like that—always with something encouraging to say. And Beth did appreciate Faye's trying. "I wouldn't mind confiding in you, Faye, but it's all so new to me. I have a lot of thinking to do."

Beth knew Faye's silence was to give her a chance to say more if she wanted to. But Beth was determined not to put a damper on these people's New Year's Eve celebration. "I never dreamed I'd be spending New Year's Eve at a square dance in North Carolina," Beth said, thinking of the irony of it.

"Did I tell you Josh is the caller?" Faye asked, slowing as she turned off I-40 and onto I-26.

"Caller?"

"You know, the one who tells you to promenade, seesaw, or California twirl."

"I just did that one," Beth retorted. "The California twirl, that is."

Faye laughed lightly. "At least you can joke about it. That's a good sign."

Beth looked out the side window. It wasn't a joke. It was true. Her head was still spinning from the turn. How was she ever going to do what she promised?

"Joshua's a great guy, thirty-three and unattached," Faye said. "Officially, I mean. He's not married. But all he has to do is snap his fingers, and they come running."

"I'm sure Joshua must be as nice as the rest of your family, Faye." In her mind, Beth could picture a tall, blond, male replica of Faye.

"He's the most wonderful brother a girl could have," Faye said affectionately.

"I always wished I had a brother."

"I'll share mine," Faye said, with a sly gleam in her eyes as she looked over at Beth.

"I have a boyfriend," Beth politely reminded her.

Faye turned right, drove around a horseshoe, and slid onto an icy side road. She turned into a parking lot with at least one hundred cars in it, surrounding a huge, red barn with golden beams of light slanting out onto the snow. Faye pulled around to the side, next to her parents' van.

"We'll bring the clothes in, and you girls set them up," Sam instructed when Beth and Faye went over to help them unload. After he went in with the first load, a couple men went out to help.

Upon entering The Barn, Beth looked helplessly toward Faye. The loud, twangy sounds of guitars and the words, "Baby likes to square dance," reached her above the mumble and roar of conversation, people moving around, greeting each other, removing coats, shaking hands, hugging, bringing food, putting on name tags, and being introduced.

Faye introduced Beth to a few people as she steered her across to a side of the barn where tables were set up for the country-western apparel. She met Billy, dressed in western clothes. He was a tall, trim, handsome, dark-haired guy with a nice smile, polite manner, and friendly handshake. He appeared to be in his mid-twenties, and Beth realized that if someone put him in a suit and tie, he would remind her of a slightly younger version of Randy.

Beth became interested in the costumes being brought in and glanced at a few price tags. Wow! They were expensive! There were even coats made especially to wear over the full skirts. And the jewelry. . .everything from earrings, to broaches, tie tacs, cuff links, neckerchief holders. . .gold, silver, precious stones. . .some smooth, some cut in the figures of square dancers, boots, hats, stars. This was a world of fashion completely new to her.

"Okay, now. Let's have some cloggers up here while everybody's finding their partners for our first square dance set of the evening," encouraged a voice from the stage.

Faye grabbed Billy's hand. "Watch us, Beth." Away they went.

Beth looked at the singer on the stage, assuming him to be Joshua. He looked older than thirty-three, but she supposed a head that was bald on top and dark over the ears would make a man look older. He looked nice enough and had a good, strong voice.

What fascinated Beth was what the cloggers began to do with their feet. They resembled disjointed wooden puppets she'd seen once upon a time.

Strings had pulled their legs and feet in wild directions. Toe-tapping, heel-clicking, knee-knocking dancers were doing the seemingly impossible while the onlookers clapped and cheered.

As the accolades abated, the singer admonished the trained dancers to find their partners and square up. He welcomed guests from several classes who had come together for the occasion of celebrating the new year. "And now," he announced, "our guest caller for this special occasion—our one and only." He swung his arm and hand in a circle, drawing out the name, "Josh-uuuu-aaaa Lo-gaaaan."

Thunderous applause like one might give a noted popular celebrity sounded as a tall, muscular guy, wearing tight-fitting western jeans, cowboy boots, and white shirt, jumped up onto the stage and took the mike from the other man, at least a foot shorter than he. The overhead lights lent an auburn sheen to his thick, dark brown curls. Joshua also had a short, neatly trimmed beard, reminding Beth of a contemporary Christian singer she'd thought particularly handsome.

"Circle to the left," he called and the eight persons in each square joined hands and shuffled left in a circle to the beat of recorded music. Then Joshua's deep voice reverberated around the room as he began to sing and call:

> *Pretty lady, walking down the street*
> > *Pretty lady, the kind I'd like to meet*
> *Left allemande your corner, do-si-do your own*
> > *Promenade your lady, all the way home.*

Beth didn't know what she had expected, but stereotypical TV portrayals of mountain and southern people had nothing whatsoever to do with that fine specimen of a man on stage. His looks and strong resonant singing voice reminded Beth of Kenny Rogers. She had a quick impression from a limited vantage point—being half a barn-length away—that Joshua was a younger version of Sam.

Her eyes did not linger upon him, however, for she became fascinated with the many squares of dancers on the floor. They reacted in unison to Joshua's calls of "Eight-chain thru, load the boat, bucket of worms, circle left, and ladies-center men-sashay." When he called that inevitable, "California Twirl," the women whirled beneath their partner's arm.

Wishing to put the "California Twirl" out of her mind for the moment, Beth turned to speak to a woman looking at the country-western apparel, then looked to the other side of the room. Men and women were spreading food on tables, making coffee, and setting out punch bowls.

It wasn't until the second set ended that Beth realized she'd been tapping her foot against the floor in tempo with the music and even chuckled at times when some of the dancers failed to execute the call correctly and the square of eight would crack up with laughter. Very few, she noticed, ever missed a step.

From the announcements Joshua made, Beth surmised this was a party for several dance classes in the area. The beginners and guests were admonished to fill their plates first, while the angels took a whirl on the floor. Beth decided the "angels" must be experienced dancers.

"Pete's callin', and I'm gonna dance," Joshua announced.

"On one condition," Pete replied good-naturedly, after taking the mike. "I'll call if Josh here will show us some of that fancy stepping I've seen him do."

The crowd began to applaud. Pete played the music and called while Joshua and Faye, Sam and Jean, and two other couples smoothly executed the seemingly impossible calls. When it ended, most of the crowd lined up for food. Many, however, to the beat of Pete's calling, began to gather for line dancing.

"Don't be glum, chum," Faye's elated voice sounded. Beth glanced up at her and Billy. Faye reached out her hand. "Let's get something to eat."

Beth smiled. It wasn't easy to wear a frown when two hundred people were so happy. On the way to the line at the tables, in between more introductions and greetings, Faye managed to say, "I told Josh about you."

"What do you mean?" Beth questioned.

"Oh, just that you're stranded and staying with us." Her cheeks were plumped with a healthy glow, but Beth suspected the color deepened when she added softly, "I did feel obligated to say that you have a problem and a boyfriend. That way he'll understand if you don't think he's the greatest thing since sliced bread."

"Thanks lots," Beth said, uncertain how she felt about that. But maybe it was best. She couldn't go around like a single girl, anticipating meeting eligible men, now that she was going to be a mother. And what guy would take a second look at her, if he knew it?

However, during the dancing and singing, she'd developed a curiosity about Joshua. There was something intriguing about a grown man so obviously excited about kicking his heels up and singing to the tune of country-western music.

Faye handed Beth a plate. She took it and looked out toward the floor. Josh was surrounded by a group of dancers. He certainly was popular. But, she supposed, as a square dance caller, he probably was considered by the dancers, as he'd sung earlier, "king of the road."

She filled her plate with finger food while being urged to take twice as much as she did. It certainly looked appetizing—raw vegetables and dip, wheat and rye quarters of sandwiches filled with chicken salad and alfalfa sprouts, cheese balls and crackers, miniature ears of corn, baby beets, ham and biscuits, hot sausage balls, assortments of sandwiches and cheeses. There was also a generous supply of fudge, light and dark, cookies galore, and fruit.

After selecting two pieces of fudge, Beth limited herself to some potato chips and dip and, at Faye's insistence, a small sandwich and a few vegetables. She and Faye found places to sit on the edge of the stage. Beth struck up a conversation with the woman next to her whose costume reminded her of Holland. Beth said so, and the woman replied that she'd bought it in Germany, when she'd square danced there. Beth learned that square dancing was international folk dancing and not limited to any particular section of America. The woman explained that she had square danced in several foreign countries.

Beth felt an arm press against hers and figured Faye had moved closer to allow someone else to sit. At a pause in the conversation with the woman, who said she'd been dancing for nineteen years, Beth turned her head to tell Faye there was a lot about square dancing she'd never even suspected. Frankly she'd never given the dance a second thought. When she turned, she had to balance her punch cup much like she'd done with her Sprite on the commuter plane when it hit an air pocket. With mouth agape, she stared into the dancing eyes of Joshua Logan.

Chapter 4

Howdy, Ma'am," he drawled. His speaking voice had that slight reso-nant raspy quality of his singing. "Joshua Logan here." A golden glint touched the brown flecks in his hazel eyes as they traveled to her open mouth. She closed it at the same time she lowered her punch cup to her plate.

"Beth." She extended her hand. She certainly didn't want him to think it was he who unnerved her with a firm, muscular arm fitted up against her. These people thought nothing of touching. It appeared to be as natural as breathing to them—and all done in such a casual, friendly way. "I expected to see Faye," she said, hoping that would explain her momentary flustered behavior.

"I'm her brother, and she's right on the other side of me," Joshua said, as if reassuring her. "She says you're a city girl and don't square dance."

Beth glanced away from his face that looked a lot like his dad's. A younger version of a very handsome man. Joshua had that healthy glow in his cheeks, despite the rugged appearance of a mature man. She'd never before encountered such a mountaineer, so tall, muscular, yet somehow. . .comfort-able—except for his bicep, which had become rather disconcerting. "I can't begin to even understand the language of square dancing."

"Then we'll have to do the bingo for you," Joshua returned, and scooped a piece of broccoli through his dip and popped it into his mouth.

"Bingo?" Beth looked at him in surprise. This conversation reminded her there was more to a man than a ruggedly handsome exterior, muscles, and a raspy voice that sort of tingled up one's spine. What kind of man celebrated the new year drinking punch and playing bingo? Maybe she wasn't as citified as Randy, but. . .bingo on New Year's Eve?

"I'd like to get a cup of coffee," she said, looking away from his eyes that seemed to probe into her mind.

He immediately stood, towering over her by head and shoulders. His eyes held hers for a moment, then he nodded politely, turned, and started a conver-sation with Faye.

Beth threw her paper plate into the trash, set the punch cup on a table, got her coffee, and returned to the tables where Jean was selling her apparel.

Then she sat and watched the activity on the floor, although her mind kept wandering to Carol, wondering how she was celebrating the new year. The prospect of having a baby sure changed one's thinking—in a hurry!

"As you know," Joshua announced from the stage, causing Beth to realize that the dance had ended, "we celebrate the New Year at eleven o'clock so we can get home before the drinkers hit the road." He thanked all the participants and made a few announcements about upcoming events. Then he said a song had been written for square dancers that would be sung by every group, throughout the world, at eleven o'clock. He had them all join hands in a big circle while he sang the words that spoke of friendship, fellowship, and peace on earth.

They all applauded, Joshua bowed, saluted them, smiled, then with exuberance, shouted, "We can't leave without bingo! And nobody's better at calling bingo, than our own. . .Pete!"

Pete hopped up on stage and took the mike to the crowd's thunderous applause. Beth glanced toward Joshua when he headed her way but refused to look directly at him. She was not going to play bingo! She could tell him that some people considered it a form of gambling. However, feeling four hundred eyes staring at her, she had little choice but to stand and place her hand in Joshua's large, extended one.

"Circle up," Pete called, and they all joined hands. "Now just a little instruction, in case some of you don't know how to bingo." He had them go through the movements. They held hands while sidestepping three times to the left, then they all kicked their right legs out toward the middle of the circle, then turned and faced their partners. They pulled by each other, first with a right hand, then a left, spelling b-i-n-g-o as they passed each person. After spelling "bingo," they had to "yellowrock" the next person. Yellowrock turned out to be a big, friendly hug. Then they started the same procedure over again, going around the entire circle until they returned to their partners.

The music started. Trying to be a good sport, Beth felt good about doing the steps correctly, even if Joshua was whispering, "right leg out, right-step-step, left-step-step, b—" and pulled her by him. The "yellowrockers" turned out to be all kinds. Some did the A-frame hug, not allowing the body to touch, while others did it exuberantly, but all were friendly. It was fun and allowed no time for thinking of anything but the next step. Everyone had twinkling eyes, smiles, and some word of greeting or a good night as she passed them.

Then it was time to yellowrock Joshua. Beth couldn't resist, wondering how it would feel to have such a man envelop her. However, he turned out to be an A-framer with her, although she'd noticed he'd given bear hugs to some of the older, married women. The hug was friendly but quick, and his eyes turned toward the stage as Pete began the countdown from ten. When he passed one and shouted "Happy New Year," Beth noticed that most of the couples paired up, ready for their traditional kiss. Beth glanced up at Joshua as she faced him. She held her breath, but didn't move away as his hands moved to her shoulders.

I should be doing this with Randy, she thought, ready to turn her face away. However, Joshua Logan's words warmed her heart as he said sincerely, "I wish you a year filled with excitement and happiness, Beth."

"Thank you. Happy New Year, Joshua." She smiled as others cheered the year in. *I don't know about the happiness,* she was thinking, *but I can pretty much count on excitement.*

⬡

Joshua drove his Jeep along the interstate until he turned onto the exit leading to the road to his home on top of Black Mountain, east of Asheville. The highway patrol and police would cover the main roads. He drove the most treacherous back ones that had not been salted, rarely felt the sun, and would still be frozen solid. He found a car in a ditch, the engine still running, with two young people huddled closely together, and used his cell phone to call for assistance.

They had known enough to keep a window rolled down a few inches to prevent asphyxiation from carbon monoxide, but he felt compelled to caution them about icy back roads, although he felt they'd already learned their lesson. He couldn't help but think of what might have happened if he hadn't come along. Would they have stayed there all night and run out of gas? Would they have frozen in the car? Would they have attempted to walk to a house and have gone in the direction where there were no nearby houses?

He needed the four-wheel-drive Jeep in order to get up and down his own mountain in bad weather, and he also needed it for his peace of mind in attempting to find persons who might be stranded out there. A part of him knew the young couple probably didn't mind being stranded for awhile, and they most likely would have found safety or even walked a long distance without freezing. Another part of him felt an exhilaration at having found them, for the possibility existed that the worst could have befallen them.

The Jeep crept along the mountain curves as it made its way higher, toward his log house. Joshua pulled into the carport under his deck, next to the enclosed garage where his black Mazda RS7 was parked. He held the box of leftover finger food that the women had insisted he take, opened the door, and reached inside to switch on the light that illuminated the small foyer outside the game room and gym. After closing the door, he shucked out of his heavy denim jacket, hung it on a coatrack, then ascended the narrow stairs. At the top he opened a door onto the upstairs landing, switched that light on, and the lower one off.

He went to the kitchen to refrigerate the food, then retraced his steps to the hallway, through his bedroom, and straight to the bathroom to shower. Afterward he donned his faded blue terrycloth robe. He blow-dried his dark hair, knowing that otherwise he'd wake up in the morning with unmanageable curls.

Normally, he'd have a bite to eat, then jump into bed and immediately fall asleep following such an evening of exercise, excitement, and a long drive enjoying the beauty of his mountains, topped off by the sense of well-being by having done his good deed for the day. He would not fall asleep quickly tonight, however, and reading wouldn't help.

He returned to the kitchen, drank a glass of milk, and ate a few small sandwiches. He rinsed out the glass, turned off the light, and walked over to the glass door. There was no need for artificial light. The moon's silver glow that illuminated the magical landscape and reflected the snow filtered through the glass wall, brightening the dining area and living room almost like day.

Beth was very much on his mind. He'd noticed her when she arrived with his family, which aroused his curiosity. Who was she, and why was she so sad? Faye had told him that Beth had gotten herself in some kind of pickle, had two weeks to make an important decision, and was reluctant to tell her boyfriend. Josh was familiar enough with the workings of the Lord that he believed God had led the young woman to the Logans for a reason—and that reason wasn't likely to be for his own personal pleasure.

He had no idea what was bothering Beth, but he determined to find out. He whispered a prayer for God to show his family what to do. They mustn't ever fail anyone again—as they had failed Kate.

Chapter 5

The alarm rang at seven. Beth bolted up in bed, like someone had touched a button causing her to spring to life. The covers fell away from her, and she reached over to shut off the shrill sound. Faye was turned away, toward the wall.

Beth called the airport. A recording said they expected to have runways cleared and operable by 10:00 A.M.

"Faye, Faye," she called, jumping out of bed.

Faye turned, but didn't open her eyes.

"The airport will open at ten. It took us about thirty minutes to get here the other night, didn't it?"

"Um-hmm," Faye replied, her eyes still closed. "But the roads should be clear now. Anyway, Dad will probably want to take you in the truck. He can make it in twenty, twenty-five minutes." She sat up and blinked her eyes open. "When does your flight leave?"

"I don't know. I got a recording. But I should get there as soon as possible. That way, I'll be ready whenever a flight goes in the direction of Baltimore. After all, you guys have plans and don't need a fifth wheel around."

"You're not that at all, Beth. We're your new friends, and we're loyal."

Beth was smiling. She didn't doubt that. She'd already discovered they were not fair-weather friends. She took a quick shower in Faye's bathroom, then dressed in her black skirt and blue silk blouse. She draped the coat over her arm, got her purse and suitcase, then went upstairs.

The TV was on in the living room and various work and road closings were being announced. She set her overnight bag and purse near the TV and draped her coat over a chair.

Faye was setting the dining room table, and Jean stood at the stove, scrambling eggs. Both wore robes and house slippers. Looking into the kitchen, Beth saw that Sam had his back turned and was gazing out the window over the sink. He was dressed in a red plaid shirt, tight-fitting jeans, and hiking boots. He certainly looked young from behind. That was probably a result of exercise from clogging and square dancing.

"Can I help?" Beth asked.

"You just sit down. We've got it under control," Faye told her, with a strange little smile. Sort of impish, but Beth had noticed that trait of Faye's before.

Jean dished up the eggs and brought them to the table. "Sam had his breakfast an hour ago, but the ham and biscuits are still warm in the oven. Faye, get the orange juice, honey."

Beth reached for the pitcher that Faye took from the refrigerator and began to pour the juice. Four glasses. Faye had set the table for four, but Jean said Sam had already eaten. Well, she wouldn't say anything to make her feel badly.

Beth started pouring her own juice when Sam turned. Only it wasn't Sam's voice when he said, "I believe that's the weather forecast. Whoa, Beth!"

Beth looked to where, not Sam, but Joshua, pointed. Orange juice had run over the top of a glass and was flowing across the table. She apologized, knew she turned red, and wanted to crawl under the table.

"No big deal," Joshua assured her as he grabbed a roll of paper towels, tore off a few for her, then crawled under the table to sop up the juice running from the table to the floor. Beth tried to listen to the weatherman while cleaning up and watching Joshua on all fours. The forecast didn't really make sense.

It sounded something like the clouds were coming in from the direction of Tennessee. Very slowly. About six miles per hour. They held all sorts of treachery. Snow, ice, sleet. Depending upon the wind, the storm would hit the Blue Ridge Mountains anytime between midmorning and noon. It was vague. Perhaps that's because at the same time, Beth felt like kicking herself for making a mess simply because she hadn't expected to see Joshua Logan. What must he think of her?

During breakfast, Beth attempted to keep the egg off her face and was grateful the Logans were a talkative bunch. They had it all planned. Sam had been called in for some kind of emergency on the parkway, but they expected him back in time to take Jean and Faye down to Old Fort to spend New Year's Day with Billy's parents. Beth learned that Old Fort Mountain was the most dangerous road in the Blue Ridge, with a downward grade of four miles, going east. Joshua would drive Beth to the airport.

"I feel like I've known you all my life," Beth said sincerely. "Thanks so much. And tell Sam, too."

Jean nodded. "Consider yourself a part of us, Beth. We won't let you forget us. We'll be in touch."

That made Beth want to cry. Especially when Jean added, "You can call us or come here, anytime. Now don't you forget it."

Beth knew the invitation was sincere.

A short while later she climbed into the Jeep, then waved at Jean and Faye, shivering in the cold carport. The long driveway had been scraped, and snow was piled high along the sides. Sam must have done that.

Joshua said nothing, and Beth could hardly blame him. He was obviously fun-loving, vital, happy, content. What could he say to a girl who couldn't even handle her own affairs maturely, behaved miserably, and poured juice all over a table? Well, she should make an effort. Would it sound foolish to ask if he went to school to learn to be a caller? Of course, it would!

She could say he was fortunate to have such a nice family. But that was obvious. He might think she'd say anything, just to get to talk to him. She sighed deeply, leaned her head back, and closed her eyes.

He began to hum. Then he turned on the radio and started to sing with it.

> What would you think
> > I would do at this moment
> When you told me
> > You don't love me anymore?

He sang several verses with that raspy sound that she had to admit was intriguing the way it seemed to tingle along her spine. Strange. . .she knew there were sounds that grated on one's nerves, like fingernails across a blackboard, but she'd never before thought of the reverse. He certainly wasn't inhibited.

Beth moved her head to the side only far enough to unobtrusively observe him through half-closed lids that could shut quickly if he looked. Soon, however, her blue eyes were mesmerized by the movement of his lips. She'd never thought of a man's lips being lovely. But his were. Instinct had told her that last night. They seemed large, but in proportion to the rest of his face and body. He was a big man. The lips were full, and a ruddy pink, and seemed to dance across strong white teeth.

When he finished the song, he switched off the radio. "You sing?"

Beth looked out the windshield, rather than at him. "No," she said. "At least, not often, and not like that." She looked toward him. "You have a beautiful voice."

"Thanks," he said, with a smile. "And you don't dance."

"I've learned a few steps in P. E. classes in high school and college, but no, I really don't dance. I've never learned to square dance."

They were on Interstate 40 before he spoke again. "You have family in Baltimore?"

"Aunt Tess."

"What's she like?"

"Wonderful," Beth said, glad he wasn't asking questions about herself. She was glad for the opportunity to praise her aunt. They were as close as a mother and daughter could be. "She would take Faye in if she were stranded, just as your family did for me."

"Would she take me in, too?"

"What kind of question is that?" Beth asked curiously.

Joshua shrugged. "I'm just wondering what kind of family you come from. That's all right, though. You don't have to tell me."

"Well, I will tell you," she said, her voice rising slightly, as if a member of her family might have been insulted. "She probably wouldn't take you in."

"Why not?" he asked, pretending to pout and stuck out his bottom lip.

Beth laughed. "She's not naive. She'd never believe you were stranded. And she wouldn't approve of you and me living in the same house."

"Me?" he quizzed. "I'm harmless as a dove." He shot her a quick glance, and a grin played about the corners of his mouth.

Harmless, my foot! Beth thought. Just being near Josh had an effect on her. Even his own sister had warned her of that. She turned slightly in the seat toward Josh. "Well, Aunt Tess is a little old-fashioned. And besides," she added, with a tilt of her chin and a coy look in her eyes, "all the doves I've ever seen always have a mate, and they coo a lot."

"Nothing wrong with that, is there?" he asked in a slow drawl.

"Nothing at all," she replied softly.

Joshua's glance traveled over her face as naturally as he expertly maneuvered the Jeep around the curves of the interstate. At any other time or in another situation, he wouldn't mind pursuing that line of reasoning. However, in about fifteen minutes, this lovely girl would be flying out of his life and no doubt into the arms of the man who would solve her problems.

"I went to live with Aunt Tess after I finished high school. She's in her sixties. Owns her own dress shop. She's kept herself in good shape. But she does complain lately about arthritis in her bones."

"Have the doctors confirmed that?" he asked.

"No, but she says she knows the symptoms."

"Several of the people you met last night find that square dancing helps such afflictions. The exercise is not too strenuous, and it helps keep the muscles and joints flexible."

Beth thought about that for a moment. "Keeps away old age, too, doesn't it? Most of those old ladies have great legs."

Joshua laughed at that. "It does seem so. Maybe you could interest your aunt in dancing."

"I don't think it's her style," Beth replied, and wondered if he would be offended.

"Like it's not yours," he returned.

"Well, I've never given it any thought. But last night—it just isn't how I expected to spend New Year's Eve." That thought brought with it the realization that this was New Year's Day. What a way to begin the year. She looked out the window and longed for her home in Baltimore, where she could confide in Aunt Tess about how her youth had seemed to vanish overnight and now her every thought and action must be for that little, unborn baby.

Joshua hummed the rest of the way until he turned right at the airport sign. The parking lot was almost deserted, and only one car sat in front. Joshua parked in the unloading zone and went inside with her.

"Sorry, Ma'am. Baltimore's socked in completely," the ticket agent informed her. "We have a few flights out to Florida, but no way is anything going north." He smiled wryly. "Expecting another storm, too."

Beth turned her back to the ticket counter. Joshua had to do the talking, asking when the Baltimore Airport would reopen. He was told not today and that if the overcast conditions remained, which they were expected to do, it might be tomorrow, or the day after. Who knew? Certainly not the weatherman.

Chapter 6

They decided to go back to Josh's place for the day until his family returned.

"How incredible," Beth exclaimed, pointing ahead, after she and Josh reached the interstate. Whitecapped mountain ranges spread out as far as the eye could see. Trees, gray against the white sky, fringed each rise. "The trees look like some fuzzy decoration on top of the mountains. Like whipped cream on top of vanilla ice cream. Sort of."

"Or maybe," Joshua queried, "like an elephantine chin with a beard on it?"

"Exactly. Of course he's lying down, and his chin is sticking up in the air."

Joshua laughed. "I wonder if that's where they got the name, 'Gray Beard?' There's a mountain near my place called that."

"I'll bet it is. And look, you can see all the little towns and villages. Oh, my. We're on top of the world, aren't we?"

"Not quite," Joshua contradicted, then added triumphantly, "but we soon will be."

At his place, Beth surmised, turning her head to look out the window beside her. She could certainly understand why people came here just to see the mountains. She could feel the exhilaration from being in these panoramic surroundings.

The feeling remained, even intensified when Josh pulled over to the side of the interstate, parked, and pointed toward a distant range until finally her eyes could see the outline of an A-frame against a mountainside.

"Looks like a doll house from here," she said when she finally saw it.

"Doll house!" Joshua snorted. "Never describe a man's castle as a doll house, girl!" He started the engine and pulled back out onto the road.

He began to talk about the mountain having belonged to his grandfather, who left a piece of it to his only son and grandchildren. "The top is mine," he said proudly, then frowned at the ice that had begun to hit the windshield. "We'd better stop by the supermarket."

He left her in the Jeep to stay warm and returned a short while later, pushing a cart laden with several bags of groceries.

Soon, they left the main roads and began their ascent up the mountain ridges. Beth had complete faith that Josh and the Jeep could conquer any icy road. "I've never seen frozen trees like this," she said, feeling like a child at Christmastime. "And look how the snow is lying on the icy branches." She gazed at the wonder of the scenery when a glimpse of mountains and villages below them appeared through a break in the forest of trees.

Josh didn't take his eyes from the road, but she saw his smile. Soon the smile was replaced by total concentration. The higher they got, the more fierce the wind, and snow became almost blinding. The Jeep appeared to be lost in a maze of white, going right for a short distance, turning left, then right again. At one point, they came to the edge of the world where they could plunge hundreds of feet below. Beth grasped the seat and pushed her foot into the floorboard. A sound like pain emitted from her throat.

"Don't worry," Josh said, making a turn she didn't even know was there. "I always said I could go around these curves blindfolded. This is my chance to prove it."

"Don't talk," she cautioned. "Just. . .do it." She closed her eyes and held onto the seat.

"Here we are," he said a moment later, stopping the vehicle. She opened her eyes to see they were safe and sound inside an enclosed, log structure. A doorway was on her right.

He switched off the engine and got out. "If you'll take one of these," he said, handing her a bag of groceries, "I can get the rest."

She took it, then stood by the door.

He came around with her suitcase and another bag of groceries. "Go on in."

"Oh, it's not locked?"

He laughed. "No need. The bears could break through a window if need be."

"Bears?" She looked toward the entry furtively. "They do hibernate during the winter, don't they?"

"Most of them," he said. "Light switch is inside on your left. The stairs are straight ahead."

Beth led the way and stood shivering in the upstairs hallway while Josh walked past with the groceries, informing her needlessly, "It's about twenty degrees colder up here than down the mountain."

"No kidding," she replied through chattering teeth, hugging her arms to herself.

Josh laughed. "Thermostat's right down the hall on your left. Turn it up. I'll set your suitcase in the bedroom here." He walked into a room on her left.

Beth turned the thermostat to seventy degrees, then followed him into the spacious kitchen, where they put the bags on the center island. "Be back in a sec," he said, switching on the light. A warm glow revealed knotty pine cabinets and white countertops and appliances. The floor was a beautiful white tile with a subdued golden pattern, resembling marble. Across one entire wall was a row of windows above lower cabinets, except for one corner where there was a small, wooden table with a basket of lush, green ivy in the center and two chairs. Josh was apparently a good housekeeper. Everything looked immaculate.

A countertop with cabinets underneath separated the kitchen from the dining area. Being interested in design, Beth would have liked to have gone into the dining room but decided to make herself useful. She began taking groceries from the bags.

"Thanks," Josh said when he returned with the other bags. "I'll put these away."

"Do you mind if I use your phone?" she asked.

"There's a phone on the wall over there, or if you'd like privacy, there's one in the bedroom where I set your suitcase."

"Thanks," she said, getting her calling card from her purse. She opted for privacy and went into the bedroom, where the subdued light of fog and mist pressed against the windowpanes. She smiled at the rustic appeal of the room—paneled walls, patchwork quilt thrown over the bed, oversized pillows propped against the headboard. Hanging from the beamed ceiling was a fan with wooden panels. A captain's chest sat at the foot of the bed, and a hooked rug lay beside the bed on the hardwood floor.

Beth liked the cozy, inviting appeal of this guest room and saw that it even had a private bathroom. She sat on the bed and picked up the phone receiver from the end table. First, she called Randy. A mature-sounding woman answered the phone.

Beth replied, "This is Beth Bennett."

"Oh, yes. Randy said you might call. Just a moment, please."

Beth wondered if that were Mrs. Crenshaw. She sounded very polite. What were Randy's parents like? Would they be as warm and friendly as the Logans?

Randy came on the line. "Hey, Beth. Any luck?"

"Nothing is leaving this airport going north," she said. "The only place I could go is Florida."

"Been there, done that," he said, and laughed. Yes, she and several others had gone there together more than once. "I'm sorry this had to happen," he said. "Dad surprised us with tickets for all of us to go to a Broadway play tonight." He raved on about their plans. "The weather here is nothing to brag about today," he said. "We're considering going where it's warm and sunny."

Did he even miss her? She swallowed hard. "I'll just plan to see you when we both get back to Baltimore."

"We'll plan something special when we get there," he said. "Okay?"

"Okay. Have fun."

"How can I not with this bunch?" he said, and laughed.

Beth took a deep breath before calling Aunt Tess. "I'm still in North Carolina." She gave her a rundown on the situation and the Logan family. "The Logans are wonderful people, Aunt Tess. They insist I stay with them until I can fly out. Now, how are you?"

Beth discovered that Aunt Tess was iced in, too. After being assured that Aunt Tess had everything she needed, Beth said, "Take care, now. I love you, too."

Beth returned to the kitchen where Josh was putting the stack of folded paper bags in a cabinet under the sink. He straightened and smiled, gesturing toward the windows. "You might want to look at the view, Beth."

Beth walked over to the windows. "It's the same view we had during our drive up here, except the wind's not blowing the snow as much."

"What?" he said, and they laughed. "Visibility obscured, huh?" he said. "Okay, what about food? You hungry?"

"I could eat something."

With Beth following his instructions on where to find what and his taking leftovers from the refrigerator, they had lunch set out on the small table in no time and sat down to eat.

"This is terrific, Joshua," Beth said. "You make dainty sandwiches just like the ladies at the square dance."

Josh gave her a wicked look, then smiled. "It might surprise you, Beth, but I can make the dainty sandwiches myself. However, I prefer more substantial meals. And," he added, shaking a piece of raw broccoli at her, "I'd put my pot roast up against any woman's."

Beth didn't doubt it could compete admirably and probably win. He struck her as being quite self-sufficient. However, she lifted her chin and challenged, "You haven't eaten until you've tasted my shrimp scampi, not to mention lobsters and crabs and. . ."

"Stop!" Josh interrupted, closing his eyes and licking his lips. When he opened his eyes she noticed faint crinkles at the corners of them when he smiled. "You have that wonderful East Coast seafood in Baltimore. Tell you what, I'll trade you a steak dinner for some of that shrimp scampi and lobsters and crab and whatever else you want to throw into the pot."

"It's a deal," Beth said, then felt her words were suspended in space. Her eyes locked with his momentarily, then she looked away from him and toward the window, with gray daylight hovering against it. It was not a deal. Once

270

the airports opened, there would be no reason for her and Joshua to ever see each other again.

"Don't worry, Beth," came his deep, strong voice. "I won't hold you to it. I know the difference between serious conversation and idle chatter. Believe me, you're under no obligation whatsoever to reciprocate for a steak dinner or those finger sandwiches. Besides, I ate most of them myself."

Beth glanced back at him, feeling quite foolish. Joshua was like Faye, he'd take in a lost kitten. But it did give her a sense of satisfaction to be having lunch on top of the world with a ruggedly handsome mountain man.

Shaking away her thoughts, Beth knew she could not afford even a mild flirtation with Joshua Logan. Too many serious matters had to be decided. And she needed to get back to Baltimore so she could plan for this change that was taking place in her life. She kept the conversation light, talking about her work and her design classes. She quickly finished her lunch.

"I'd like to change into my jeans," she said. "Then I'll help clean up."

"Go right ahead," he said. "If you're not going to be on the phone, I need to make a few calls."

Beth changed into jeans and tee shirt, then made her way back through the hallway, toward the kitchen. Josh was hanging up the phone. "We need to go up the mountain," he said.

"Up?" she questioned. "I thought this was the top."

"Well, it is the top of this one. We'll go down, around, and then up another."

"What for?"

"To check on an elderly couple. I couldn't get through on the phone. I'd love for you to go with me, but if you want to stay here, that's fine."

Beth couldn't imagine staying alone instead of accompanying this intriguing man down, around, and up a mountain. This was akin to anticipating a ride on the world's highest roller coaster—frightful, yet exhilarating. "I'll go," she said. "But I'd better exchange these flats for sneakers."

"Good idea," he agreed. "You might find a jacket you can wear in the closet. Faye keeps a supply of clothes here."

As she left the room she heard him softly singing:

> I'll go where You want me to go, dear Lord,
>   I'll be what You want me to be,
> I'll do what You want me to do.

Why not make the best of this? she told herself. All the worrying in the world over her situation wouldn't change a thing. And there were worse things in the world than being stranded in this winter wonderland with an intriguing man like Joshua Logan. While tying her shoestring, she found herself humming the tune Joshua was singing.

Three hours later, Josh pulled into the carport again. He couldn't help but grin as he watched Beth get out of the Jeep while holding the peach pie Mrs. Henson had given them and trying to keep his pile-lined jacket from slipping off her shoulders. She hadn't found one of Faye's but had found a heavy sweater that he insisted she wear in case something happened and they had to walk.

On the way over to the Hensons, she'd worried about how she looked with the sweater sleeves folded in thick layers at her wrists and a jacket that fell to below her hips. It hadn't taken long before she forgot herself and warmed to the Hensons as they did to her.

"Go on up," he said. "I'll bring up some wood and build us a fire."

She set the pie on the hood and looked out at the entrance. "Wait a minute," she said. "What is that?"

He walked with her to the opening. She pointed to a nearby tree. "It went behind that tree."

Josh looked. He didn't see anything but started to walk toward it.

"Be careful," she whispered.

He glanced back, shrugged, and carefully plodded on. Just as he reached the tree he was jolted to a stop by a thud on the back of his head. Momentarily stunned, he didn't move. Then he realized she had thrown a big snowball at him. He'd fix her! With a groan, he fell to his knees and bent his head, balancing with one hand in the snow and the other at the back of his neck.

"Oh, Josh, I'm sorry," she called, running up to him.

Just as she got there, he grabbed a handful of snow and splattered her right in the face with it.

"You faker!" she screamed, and started scooping snow at him as if they were in a pool and she was splashing water.

He grabbed handfuls of snow and started rolling it into a ball while standing to his feet. She screamed and hid behind the tree. He simply went up to it, reached around each side, caught her arm with one hand, held her, and came around to rub the snow in her hair. What he didn't know was she had a snowball in her hand, and she reached up and managed to dump it down the front of his shirt where his jacket wasn't zipped up all the way to his neck.

He roared at that one. "Cold," he said, rubbing it in to melt instead of freezing a hole in his chest.

"Serves you right," she said, "for calling me a dog," and she headed for the carport entrance.

"When did I do that?" he asked, following, still rubbing his chest.

"When Mr. Henson asked where you found me and you said you couldn't very well leave me stranded out in the cold."

"Right," Josh said, as he picked up the jacket that must have fallen from her shoulders when she'd run out to him, believing he was hurt. "And I distinctly remember he is the one who said I'm always picking up stray dogs and taking care of them till I can find their owners or a home for them."

She stopped, looking up at him with accusing, blue eyes, her dark hair standing in arresting contrast against the snowy background. "You agreed," she said. "And I distinctly heard you say that some of those little dogs are hard to resist. I saw the glance and grin you two shared. Shame on you," she said, quickly picking up another handful of snow and trying to get it down his shirt.

He caught her wrist and held it fast, away from him. "You don't suppose you misinterpreted?" He released her wrist, and she let the snow fall, as well as her eyes. She quickly turned and trudged toward the carport. Her clothes were covered with snow.

He laughed as they reached the entrance. "Oh, I wish I had the camera out here. You're a sight, you know that?"

She gave him a threatening look as she brushed off the snow. "And I wish I had another snowball—with a rock in it."

He jumped inside the carport, pretending to be scared.

She laughed then, and went over for the pie. "If you don't behave yourself, you're getting no pie for supper."

She enjoyed this afternoon as much as I, he thought, following her inside the house and hanging up the jacket she'd worn. A beautiful girl, who had momentarily forgotten her problems, who enjoyed spending time with an elderly couple, who loved the views from his mountain, who felt comfortable enough with him to joke and play. And what should he do about that? Drive her back down the mountain?

I'm making too much of it, he told himself. *She's still a young woman with a pressing problem and a boyfriend. What I need to do is just remember who I am. . . and what I am.*

When they got upstairs, Josh checked his messages. He had one. "Josh, this is your dad. We can't get up Old Fort Mountain tonight. There's a couple tractor trailers jack-knifed, so we're spending the night with Billy's parents. Thought I'd let you know in case you tried to get in touch with us."

Sam's voice carried into the bedroom. Beth had taken off her wet shoes

273

and socks. She walked barefoot into the kitchen. "I heard the message," she said. "So. . .I won't be staying with Faye tonight?"

"I have a key to Mom and Dad's, but the way this weather is acting, I'm not sure we could make it back down the mountain safely, even with my Jeep. If you want, I'll try."

Beth thought of some of the skids they'd gotten into on the way back from the Hensons' home. Even though Josh was obviously an experienced driver in rough weather conditions, he'd needed total concentration to keep the Jeep on the road. Now the roads were even worse, and they weren't going to get any better. If he managed to get her down to his parents' home, would he make it back up here safely? And there was no telling what obstacles might be blocking the roads already because of the storm.

Beth shook her head. "Josh, I appreciate the offer, but we both know it would be foolhardy to try navigating the roads on a night like this."

"I'm glad you feel that way," Josh replied. "I've seen too many bad accidents caused when people didn't respect the power of these storms. At least here we're dry and warm—and we have food," he added, with a teasing smile. "I do have a couple steaks in the freezer."

"Now, how could I resist that?" She shivered. "I'd better get out of these soggy clothes before I catch pneumonia."

Chapter 7

Maybe the Lord knows I need the diversion of extra time with Josh and the rest of his family before I get back to Baltimore and face decisions that will last a lifetime for myself and all my loved ones—particularly Randy, Aunt Tess, Carol, and the baby, Beth thought as she ran bathwater.

All the worry in the world wouldn't change the facts. *I'll simply trust the Lord,* she decided as she lay her head back against the tub, allowing the fragrant bathwater to warm her chilled body. *In any event, I certainly can't change the weather.*

It has been fun, she thought, smiling, remembering how she and Josh had frolicked in the snow. For hours, she'd forgotten about herself and concentrated on the man who'd checked on his neighbors and took them food, who'd intimated she was hard to resist, who'd held her wrists to him to keep her from putting a snowball down his shirt, and who had gazed intently into her eyes and thought her funny enough to want to take a picture.

She felt at ease and comfortable with Josh. Maybe it was because she wasn't trying to impress him or live up to some kind of image. After all, as soon as the airports opened up, she'd never see Josh Logan again. He would fade away like the mist on the mountain.

She decided against wearing the dress she'd planned to wear on New Year's Eve and chose instead a pair of slacks and a short-sleeved sweater. Finally she emerged from the private bathroom with freshly shampooed hair. She examined her reflection in the mirror over the dresser. Her cheeks were naturally colored from the day's activity. All she needed was a little powder for her shiny nose and lip color to moisten her lips to a glossy sheen. After slipping on her flats, she tripped lightly into the kitchen. "Mmm. What smells so wonderful?"

"It's me," Josh replied. "I showered and shampooed, too," he said, his eyes sweeping over her, and he nodded and grinned as if he were quite pleased. With tongs, he lifted a foil-wrapped potato from a baking dish and placed it on a plate.

"You didn't shave," she quipped.

He glanced up as he lifted another potato. "But I did splash on a little cologne."

275

Beth walked closer as he tilted his head to the side and pointed to behind his ear. She laughed and sniffed. "Ah, yes. That's the new Steak-and-Potato brand of cologne. It does smell delicious."

He gave her a pseudo-hurt look, and she laughed again. Actually she had gotten a faint whiff of the musky fragrance of his cologne. This afternoon it had been a fresh, clean, outdoorsy aroma. She liked the way Josh Logan acted, smelled, and looked. She realized the light cast a burnished red-gold sheen to his dark hair. A few gray hairs glistened at his temples. He wore casual slacks and knit shirt. After all the trouble he was going to for her, she could at least reciprocate by being pleasant company. "Can I help with anything?"

"You can take the salad into the living room." He took two dessert dishes from the refrigerator.

"Oh, that looks good," she said, admiring the white-topped red cranberry sauce on dark green lettuce leaves.

"Chock full of orange pulp and walnuts," he said, placing them in her outstretched hands. "You go make yourself comfortable, and I'll be right in with the main course. Does sparkling white grape juice suit you?"

"Sounds perfect," she said.

"Perfect," Beth echoed upon entering the living room that was separated from the dining room by a staircase leading to an upper level. The room was beautiful. Soft light gave the paneled walls a mellow glow. A ficus tree stood tall and lush in a far corner where wood met stone. A chair and end table were placed near it. The brown and cream furniture, large to accommodate a big man like Josh, made her want to curl up in a corner with those big cushions behind her and gaze into the flames licking the logs in the fireplace, emitting a welcoming warmth. Candles burned on the mantle against the rock wall reaching from floor to ceiling. He'd pulled a side table away from the wall and set it near the fireplace. Two white candles in crystal holders glowed in the center of the table covered with a white satin cloth.

Her eyes roamed the welcoming, rustic setting. Looking around at flower arrangements, floor plants, pictures on the wall, the furniture grouping placed perfectly to accommodate the fireplace, the high-beamed ceiling with a fan hanging from a long chain, the thick rug under the coffee table and smaller rugs placed in strategic patterns on the hardwood floor, Beth wondered if he'd had a decorator design this room. It looked perfect—even to the staggered candle holders, with each one taller than the next. She was sure that most men, maybe most women, would have their candle holders the same size. And pieces on the end tables and mantle were correctly placed as one item, or sets of three. It wasn't likely this was done accidently.

She walked over to the glass wall. A deck stretched as far as she could see along the side of the house, across the living room wall, and toward the dining room. The whitened landscape made everything appear almost as light as day. Clouds still covered some mountain ranges in the distance. A crescent of yellow moon and a couple of bright stars decorated the darkened sky.

Hearing Josh's humming before she heard his footsteps, Beth turned and exclaimed, "It's so beautiful out there. And in here, too."

He thanked her and smiled, then placed their plates on the table. He didn't seem to think she was referring to him. And she hadn't been. But upon thinking about it, he was a beautiful man, not just in appearance but in his character. And he was so easy to relate to.

Josh pulled a chair out from the table and gestured for her to sit. She did, then he took his seat and stretched his forearms across the table with his palms up. Beth placed her hands in his and felt his strong fingers envelop hers. They bowed their heads, and he prayed: "Our Father in heaven, thank You for the beginning of a new year, when we reflect upon the past and look toward the future. Thank You for this food and for Beth, who is here to share it with me. Guide us with Your Spirit. In Jesus' holy name we pray. Amen."

"Amen," Beth said softly, after he gently squeezed her fingers, then released them. She took a sip of sparkling grape juice, then unfolded her cloth napkin and placed it on her lap. She looked over at him and smiled. "This is a lovely room," she said. "Did you design it?"

"I chose the furniture I liked and had a few ideas of how I wanted the room arranged. But the accents, tree and plants, etc. were suggested by a friend who was in our singles' group. She has a silk flowers and trees shop downtown."

His girlfriend? Beth wondered as he continued to speak in glowing terms of the woman's expertise in design.

"Her shop is downtown on a main corner," he continued. "You might have noticed."

"I don't recall being downtown."

"You must have blinked your eyes," he chided playfully. "It's small, but we have a wonderful, little town. And a street of antiques and specialty shops that you should see. Particularly the silk flowers and trees shop."

Why is he telling me so much about her? She must be special to him.

He swallowed a bite of steak, took a sip of juice, then pointed his fork at her. "Incidentally, now that she's married again and expecting a baby, she's looking for help. She does trees and arrangements for the Grove Park Inn, one of the finest hotels in the area. She has a helper but would like to have someone with a background in design. Interested?"

Beth saw the twinkle in his eyes and knew, behind the facade of white shirt and tie, the playful Josh was right there. She grinned. "Yes, I am. I love the idea of beautifying rooms that cause a person to feel the kind of appreciation and welcome that I felt when walking into this room earlier. But I still have a lot to learn, and I don't finish design school for another year. I'm taking one or two courses each semester." She smiled. "So, tell your friend to hold the job."

Josh felt reluctant to get into more serious matters, but knew he must. He loved the idea of spending an evening with a lovely woman on a personal basis. But at the same time, he knew God had brought Beth into their lives for a reason. He thought of the attributes she'd shown. She hadn't resisted any of his references to the Lord and to his praying, which he interpreted as indicating such things were part of her life. She'd enjoyed the Hensons and spoke lovingly of her aunt. She and his family had connected. She was fun-loving and natural when she let herself go and forgot her problems. But the fact remained—she was a young woman with a problem and a boyfriend. In his position, he must accept and deal with that—but not until after dinner.

"Do you have a special girlfriend?" Beth asked.

Josh continued cutting a bite of steak, contemplating why she'd asked. Was she interested, curious, making dinner conversation? He quickly reminded himself it didn't matter why. This was one evening out of a lifetime. And how well he knew how one evening, one mistake, could change an entire life. He was neither young, foolish, nor naive and had no excuse but to behave with the utmost responsibility.

He pierced the bite of steak and looked across at Beth. "Not really serious," he answered.

"Are available women scarce around here?"

"Available women, no," he replied immediately. "But a compatible companion, yes."

Beth thought she detected a note of regret in his voice. Something had happened to him, she was sure. "Have you been married, Josh?"

For a moment she thought he wouldn't answer. "No," he said finally. "I've had some meaningful relationships. I suppose I've at least briefly considered, consciously or unconsciously, every unattached woman I've encountered." She smiled with him as he gave a rueful laugh. "But each time something has happened with her or with me to change our minds. I've learned to find fulfillment within myself rather than expect it to come from another person."

"Maybe you're right," Beth said slowly. "I often think in terms of being attached to another to feel complete."

"Now, don't get me wrong," Josh quickly added. "Most of my friends are blissfully married, some with children, and I often envy them. On the other hand, I've encountered many singles who struggle daily because of broken marriages and dysfunctional families."

What will mine be? Beth wondered briefly as she looked down at her plate and forked a bite of baked potato.

Josh had cleaned his plate before she finished. While she ate, he told her about his friends and some of the women he'd seriously contemplated marrying. There'd been Shelly Landon, a bright energetic cheerleader turned aerobics teacher whom he'd really admired. But one of his best friends had been in love with her, and they'd eventually married and now lived in Hawaii. "We visit occasionally and have exchanged homes for a couple of weeks. You might have heard of him. Trevor Steinbord."

"The writer?" Beth asked, and he nodded. "I've read some of his books."

Josh nodded. "Most everyone has. All his books have been best-sellers. And then there was Norah, when I spent some time in Charleston, South Carolina. Beautiful redhead. Oh, you may have heard of her sister." He told about the actress who was killed in a car crash with her actor boyfriend several years ago. Yes, Beth had heard of that. It had been all over the news for days.

"Anyway, Norah married the actor's brother, who owns an island. We don't visit each other," Josh said with a wry smile. "I'd taken Norah out several times, and that doesn't set well with the rich dude." He lifted his hand. "He's a good guy, though. Right for Norah."

Beth was fascinated with Josh's friends. He certainly was a multifaceted guy. He hobnobbed with the rich and famous, and yet he befriended ordinary people who lived on the mountainsides or went to square dances. . .or were stranded in a snowstorm.

He scooted back from the table. "Okay. Ready for peach pie and coffee?"

Beth shook her head. "Maybe later. I couldn't hold another bite. It was great, Josh. Thanks so much."

"My pleasure," he said, and they cleared the table together and stacked the dirty dishes in the dishwasher. Afterward, they returned to the living room. Josh threw a couple logs on the fire, and Beth propped a couple big cushions in the corner and leaned back against them, with barely a thought of Baltimore, New York, or anything but the fascinating man who poked the fire, then turned and walked to the easy chair across from her.

Josh saw Beth turn slightly to face him directly as he sat in his chair. She appeared relaxed, as if no longer stressed over getting back to Baltimore. He'd like to ask what was there and why she'd planned to go. If Kate had not killed herself, he'd be a different person, and he could perhaps ask what kind of music she liked, if she liked seafood better than steak, what she intended to do after design school, and how serious she was about her boyfriend.

But Faye had said she had a problem that she couldn't tell her boyfriend. He could not attempt to ignore that. In his position, he couldn't say anything that would give the impression he wanted to be personally involved with her. He couldn't be overly complimentary about how much he had enjoyed spending the day and evening with her. Tell her how beautiful she looked in the candlelight or with the firelight caressing her face. How he liked her full lips that laughed and smiled so easily. How little lights danced in her eyes like evening stars in a deep blue sky.

Another time, another place, another person, and he could show her a few steps of line dancing, watch her twirl beneath his uplifted arm, draw her near and let her know he found her most attractive and would like to see her again. That is not what he could do. He didn't want to spoil the mood of this easy camaraderie between them. But he must.

"I've enjoyed this day with you, Beth," he said. "And there's a lot I'd like to know about you and share with you. But I have to ask this. If you don't want to get into it, that's your choice. But Faye mentioned that you have a problem. If you'd like to discuss that with me, I'll be glad to listen."

He couldn't read her expression. Perhaps at first, mild surprise, then a thoughtful look before she spoke. "Maybe you can help, Josh. I think you'd honestly tell me if you think I've done a foolish thing or if I should continue in my predicament."

Looking him straight in the eye, she distinctly said, "I'm going to be a mother in about six months."

Okay, Lord. So this is it. You've brought another desirable woman into my life and have given me the task of pointing her away from me. If there's any way, I must help her unite with the father of her unborn child. Let Your Spirit guide me.

As she began her story, Josh could hardly fathom that she really was talking about her sister. Carol was pregnant, but Beth was going to be a mother? Then, as she continued, his skepticism was quickly replaced by fascination. He knew that some unmarried, expectant mothers had periods of denial, but this had the ring of truth on Beth's part. She had honestly agreed to take that child as her own to prevent an abortion.

"I thought I'd heard everything," he said contemplatively, watching Beth carefully. "But I've never heard of this. You are really going through with it?"

She sighed deeply and slipped to the edge of the couch. "Carol gave me two weeks to change my mind or come up with a better solution. She won't consider giving the baby up for adoption. So what choice do I have, Josh? If I refuse to take this baby, Carol will have an abortion, and I'll be responsible."

After a thoughtful moment, Josh slowly shook his head. "No, Beth. My family lived with that idea for a long time after Kate's death. But in the final analysis, reasoning adults are responsible for their own actions, their own decisions. But I certainly understand why you feel you have to do this."

"Do you think I'm right?"

"I think you're one in a billion," he said, nodding. "I know a lot of people who would do anything they could for a girl in that situation. In fact, my parents and Faye have helped several young women. I've assisted in some ways. But," he added pointedly, "I don't know anyone who would go this distance. Many of us are willing to go the first mile. You're willing to go the second mile. I'm impressed," he said with admiration in his voice. "Very impressed."

Beth felt suddenly shy, seeing such admiration in his eyes and hearing it in his voice. She wanted his approval, but this was a time for honesty. "Frankly," she said, her eyes meeting his warm gaze, "I'm scared."

"Sure you are," he said quickly. "That means you know this will be no picnic."

She smiled wryly. "I never imagined all the things an unwed mother must consider until these past few days, and I'm sure I haven't even scratched the surface. I know it's going to change my life and the lives of everyone around me." *Yes*, she decided, *I might as well get some male insight into this*. "Josh? I'm learning you can't really know how you'd react until you're faced with a situation, but. . .consider this. Suppose your fiancée dropped a bomb like this on you? How do you think you'd react?"

So this is what bothers her about confronting her fiancé, Josh realized. *She shouldn't worry. Surely he knows what a fabulous woman he has here. If not, he will know it when he discovers she is willing to sacrifice her life to save the life of an unborn baby. How fortunate that man is. How fortunate that child is. And this incredible woman doesn't even realize the extent of her sacrifice.*

He looked her straight in the eye, and his voice sounded convincing. "I would marry her so fast it would make her head swim. Then I'd do everything in my power never to let go of such a remarkable person."

Beth caught her breath. Yes! Josh Logan would do that. He was one in a bil. . .no, zillion! She got to her feet and walked over to the fireplace that was burning low.

"Are you cold?" he asked.

"No, I just wanted to stretch my legs a little."

"I usually let the fire die down before bedtime."

Beth's eyes rose to the mantle. The candles were burning low, too. Then a picture caught her eye. A picture of Sam and Jean with three young people. The youngest girl resembled Faye, complete with straight, blond hair and bangs. "Is that Faye?"

He got up and walked over to her. "Sure is, about ten years ago. She was sixteen then."

Beth stared at the picture awhile longer and turned her eyes toward Josh again. He began to whistle nonchalantly and looked up at the high-beamed ceiling. *She knew!* "That's you!" she exclaimed. "You looked like Sam."

"That's what everybody said. I have nothing against his looks, but I prefer to look like me."

Beth looked a moment longer at the picture and focused on the young girl with auburn curls down to her shoulders, framing a pretty face. She wore a smile, but somehow Beth felt it was posed. But then, it wasn't always easy to smile on cue and mean it.

"That must be your other sister," she said. "Your mom said there were three children."

Josh nodded. "Kate," he said.

Beth returned to the couch and sat on the edge. Josh stood by the fireplace, holding the picture as he told about a teenager, a freshman in the local college who got caught up with partying. Before the family realized her problems, she was hooked on drugs.

He returned the picture to the mantle, then faced Beth again, leaning against the stone and crossing his arms over his chest. "I was busy having my own brand of fun, a lot of it away from the Christian principles I'd been taught and claimed to believe in. Even then, it was as if the Lord were telling me that it was all temporary, and I wore a guilt trip for years. I couldn't say too much to my eighteen-year-old sister when my own life wasn't exactly exemplary."

He uncrossed his arms, walked over to the chair, and placed his hands over the back of it. "There was one difference between us that we didn't discover until her brain was fried. I never tried drugs, and I thought she knew better. She did know, but she was an addict."

He came around the chair and sat on the edge of it. Beth could see and feel his pain.

"When we realized what was happening, Mom and Dad had her put into a rehab facility. Her recovery was long and painful. Finally, she came home and did all the right things."

Sam had said his daughter killed herself. "It didn't last," Beth said softly in the silence of the room that was broken only by an occasional gust of wind splattering frozen snow against a window.

"Only for six months. One day the police came and said they'd found her dead body in the woods near the college campus. She died from an overdose." He spread his hands. "I couldn't believe it. By that time I'd straightened up, committed my life to the Lord without reservation, and vowed that I'd find her killer. I was in Charleston for several years, and my burning desire was to return and find who did that to my sister."

"And did you?" she asked softly, wanting to console him.

He shook his head. "When I talked of having her body exhumed and an autopsy done, my parents showed me a letter Mom had found in one of Kate's coat pockets when she'd finally been able to clean out my sister's closet." He paused and cleared his throat. "Kate couldn't face the family with her secret. She'd returned to even stronger drugs. She was pregnant and feared the child would be affected by the drugs. She wrote that she wasn't fit to be a daughter—let alone a mother."

"Oh, Josh," Beth said softly.

Josh got up, walked over to the windows, and gazed out toward the ice, snow, and wind.

Beth walked over to him. He faced her, and she saw his moist eyes. "Thank you for sharing such a painful experience. I know that was hard for you. And I know you did it to reinforce my decision about what's going on in my life."

"I believe God intends for me and my family to be involved in this, Beth."

"I think you already have been, Josh," she said softly. "Just to know that kind, caring people like all of you exist helps me. I wouldn't hesitate to call any of you in a time of need."

He gazed into her deep blue eyes. She was a lovely woman. They were natural together. She was a committed Christian, trying to do what she felt God would want her to do, sacrificing her life in the process. That appealed to him. Very much.

"Whoa!" he said suddenly, tearing his eyes away from hers. "What kind of host am I? I haven't even given you a tour of my house."

She laughed. "I think I've seen most of it, haven't I?"

"Not the laundry room in the basement," he said.

"That can wait," she said. "But what's up there?"

"A couple bedrooms and my office."

"Office? Square dance callers need offices?"

He looked surprised, then he laughed, as if she were joking.

They ascended the staircase. "Back there are two bedrooms," he said. "Filled with some of the furniture that my grandparents had. Sometimes Faye or I have sleepovers here, and our friends pile in wherever they can find a bed or a floor."

He opened a door opposite the bedrooms, and the natural light from the whitened landscape and a bright moon lent a silvery sheen to the room.

"Wait," she said. "Don't turn on a light yet."

Walking on a moonbeam making a path across the carpet, she walked to the French doors that led out onto a balcony, a miniature of the deck below. The night was awesome. The storm had abated, and the white mountains were caressed by moonlight. A hush had settled upon this magical setting.

"Oh, Josh," she said, turning to look at him, still by the door. "This must be how God feels when He looks at His creation. This is so beautiful, so perfect."

He'd gazed upon that setting many times, feeling as she did. He hadn't done so with such an appealing young woman silhouetted against it, however, with moonlight caressing her hair, giving it a silvery blue sheen. "It is beautiful," he said softly.

"Okay, you can turn on the lights now."

He did.

The room flooded with light. Along the right side of the wall sat a couch with a long coffee table in front of it. A table and a lamp was at the far end. On the left was a file cabinet, then an easy chair, a computer on a desk, then a straight chair. She walked over to the computer, about to ask if he surfed the net, but her eyes lit upon an envelope. "Joshua Daniel Logan, Ph.D." She realized there were framed certificates on the wall. What were they?

He had picked up a magazine from the coffee table and was reading something. "Do you have to go to school to be a square dance caller?" she asked.

He looked up, then laughed lightly. "No. Although there are conferences and sessions that help. What I had were parents who wanted some kind of activity the entire family could participate in. I liked the singing and calling more than the dancing."

"I didn't mean to pry, but I saw this envelope that has your name followed by Ph.D."

"Yes," he said, simply.

"What kind of doctor?"

When he said, "I have my degree in psychology," Beth decided to sit in the nearest chair, which was the straight-backed one at the desk. Josh sat on the couch and laid the magazine down. "I teach a couple of classes at the university in Asheville, and I have an office at the mental health clinic in Asheville where I work a few hours a day as a Christian counselor."

Counselor! No wonder he was so easy to talk to. He did this professionally. "Why didn't you tell me?"

"Beth, I wasn't trying to keep anything from you. That subject just never came up."

She stood. "I just feel like I've been your patient without knowing it." She turned and walked out of the room. He'd done nothing but try to help her. Why this feeling of disappointment?

Josh switched off the light and followed her down the stairs. "I didn't once think of you as a client, Beth. Would it have made a difference if you had known?"

She stopped at the bottom of the stairs, feeling rather foolish. Then she lifted repentant eyes to his. "I probably wouldn't have thrown snowballs at you if I'd known you were a doctor."

"Then I'm glad you didn't know," he said seriously. "But look, if you want to throw a snowball at me now with a rock in it, I'll understand."

She saw the mischief in his eyes and a boyish grin on that manly face. The tension eased.

"Please believe that I would not try to mislead you for anything in the world. Whatever job a person has is tied up with who that person is. But during this entire day, my relationship with you was on a personal basis, not professional."

Beth nodded. "It was a good day for me, Josh. Very good."

He reached for her hands and held them. "For me too, Beth. Thank you for giving me something to remember from a most remarkable woman. But this is not the end," he said. "I'll be checking on you to see how things work out. Remember, you have a friend here. And I don't use that word lightly."

"Thank you," she said. "Now, I think I'd better turn in."

He smiled, gently squeezing her hands, then let go. "Good night, Beth."

"Good night, Josh."

❦

Beth slept peacefully during the night, with no remembered dreams, and awoke to the aroma of coffee. For a moment, she lay in bed, thinking how grand it would be never to leave this mountaintop house far above the hustle and bustle of civilization. But, she could not afford such a luxury. There were plans to make. There was a little baby whose needs must come first.

In jeans and tee shirt, she trekked into the kitchen to get a cup of hot coffee. "Are we going to get out of here today?"

Josh's response didn't bring the elation she should have felt. "We can always slide down this mountain in the Jeep or on our backside. Since we didn't have any more snow during the night, the main roads should be cleared. So. . .whenever you want to leave, just say the word."

Beth nodded, walking over to the windows to gaze at the incredible view. Yes, she understood Faye's descriptive phrase of this being the Land of the Sky. Beneath an incredible blue sky, dotted with a few fluffy, white clouds, were miles and miles of white mountain peaks, many covered with clouds, others with their tips above the clouds.

She understood, too, the remark Josh made. It wasn't a matter of when she wanted to leave here. It had to be a matter of when a plane could land at the Baltimore airport.

Chapter 8

Later that afternoon, after having gotten a flight out of Asheville around noon, Beth shivered in the cold Maryland air while she stood beneath a gray sky that looked like thick gravy. She unlocked her car that she'd left at the airport before leaving for California. Driving along the Baltimore highway, she thought how different this flat country was from the curving mountain roads of North Carolina. Dirty ice and snow bordered the highways that had been salted and scraped.

Beth felt at home driving along the street with row houses on both sides. The residents were proud of their brick two-story homes, with their marble stoops that were swept daily. Beth couldn't help but contrast the spaciousness of the mountains with these homes, wall-to-wall on either side with long, skinny backyards.

Dark tree trunks and limbs like outstretched arms looked helpless against the frozen ground and winter sky. It was the second day of January, but Aunt Tess's Christmas tree shone from the living room window like a welcome sign. Beth knew it was for her. Aunt Tess understood how much Beth loved the look of Christmas mixed with snow and how she dreaded the end of the holiday season.

Beth unlocked the front door and walked on through to the toasty-warm kitchen. Immediately she was met with the aroma of a roast cooking in the oven and the sweet odor of peanut butter cookies—her favorite. Aunt Tess knew how to welcome a person. Beth pulled out a kitchen chair and sank into it. With her toes against the heel of one shoe, then the other, she freed her aching feet and wiggled her toes.

"I thought I heard you," Aunt Tess said, hurrying into the kitchen with open arms and welcoming smile. "Oh, I'm glad you're back safe and sound."

Beth wasn't sure about how sound, but at least she felt safe here with Aunt Tess, who had been her mentor for several years. Beth stood and embraced her aunt, a couple of inches shorter than she and several pounds heavier. Aunt Tess had a glow about her pretty face.

"And how are Vera and Dean?" Aunt Tess asked, speaking of Beth's parents.

"Like always," Beth returned, with a slight furrow between her brows.

"They're having a wonderful time enjoying the social life. They think they're happy, Aunt Tess. But I wish my mom and dad were spiritual leaders in our family. I honestly believe their lives would be more fulfilled. Maybe Carol would be more responsible, too. Or maybe I failed my younger sister by moving away from home. Perhaps I should have stayed and influenced her."

"You tried that, Honey," Aunt Tess reminded her. "After you accepted Jesus as your Lord and Master, you tried to impart that to your family. But they didn't listen to you any more than they listened to me. Your mom considers me an overbearing older sister, and to your dad I'm a religious fanatic who also is an in-law." She laughed, but a tinge of sadness glazed her eyes. "They are the ones who have missed out, Honey. And I've been so blessed to have you with me."

"I'm the lucky one, Aunt Tess," Beth replied. "But I really need to take a long, hot bubble bath and get into something decent like jeans and a tee shirt. Not that I don't appreciate this designer suit you got me for Christmas, but I've worn it for three days. It's like you say, when you've eaten steak for a week, you kind of want the taste of hamburger."

"Oh?" Aunt Tess said with lifted eyebrows. "Then I'll just eat that roast myself and thaw out a hamburger for you."

"Don't you dare," Beth said. "I'm famished." She didn't say that she'd had the most delightful, unforgettable steak dinner of her life the night before—although it hadn't been the meat that had impressed her. With a flourish she turned. "How long till dinner?"

"Soon as you finish your bath," Aunt Tess said, picking up a pot holder and heading for the oven. "I want to hear all about what put that spark in your eyes. And I have a few things to talk over with you."

Beth didn't think talk of the baby was a subject to simply drop on Aunt Tess, nor did it seem like appropriate dinner conversation. During dinner they talked about the weather and Beth related her experiences with the Logans. Aunt Tess was particularly anxious to find out more about this Josh in whose home Beth had stayed during the storm.

"He's a psychology professor and a Christian counselor," Beth explained. She grinned. "Like you said, my parents and Carol think you and I are religious fanatics—well, they'd think the Logans are religious looney-toons—especially Joshua."

"Ah, this Joshua is the kind you wouldn't mind submitting to, huh?"

Beth gasped. "Aunt Tess!" Her heart thudded at the thought.

"Honey, I'm speaking in the spiritual sense, of course." Aunt Tess took on an innocent expression.

"Oh, um, yes, exactly. He is definitely a spiritual leader and would be that in a home."

"Did you two talk about Randy?"

"Well, I. . .we. . ." Seeing the twinkle in Aunt Tess's eyes, Beth sighed. "Yes, we mentioned Randy. And talked about you."

"Me? And how does he like me?"

"A lot—when I said you're one of the greatest cooks this side of the Chesapeake."

"So is he coming to sample my culinary delights?"

Beth shook her head. "No, I don't think so. I'll probably never hear from the Logans again."

The phone rang. "I'll get it," Beth said. "Probably Randy."

She walked over to the wall phone, picked up the receiver, and said hello. "Who? Oh, Josh. I just didn't expect to hear from you. I thought the call would be Randy—" *Now why did I say that?*

"I won't keep you then if you're expecting a call."

"Oh, I'm not."

"You don't expect him to call?"

"Well, yes, but I'm not sitting here waiting for it."

"Going out, huh?"

"No, I mean. Oh, Josh, stop it!"

He laughed. "I wanted to check to see if you arrived safely."

"I'm here," she said, wondering whatever happened to her good sense. Maybe she never had any. Lately she seemed to be proving she had little or none.

"I'll let the family know you arrived safely. Give Aunt Tess my regards. We'll be in touch, Beth. You know we're here if you need us."

"Thanks. Bye."

She hung up, took a deep breath, and smiled as she faced Aunt Tess. "Josh sends his regards," and added quickly, "now, what was it you wanted to talk to me about?"

Aunt Tess gave her a long, studied look, then said, "Let's take our coffee into the living room. I don't like to sit too long in these kitchen chairs."

The old radiator clanked as they entered the living room. Beth set her mug on the coffee table, shook out of her house slippers, and pulled her jeaned legs up onto the couch. She sipped the creamy liquid and put the mug down when Aunt Tess sat in the recliner opposite her.

Would she raise the baby here? They'd have to keep a screen around the radiator with a baby around. She'd need a playpen. Would Aunt Tess baby-sit while she worked? But Aunt Tess was at the dress shop six days a week. She had two salespersons, and Beth helped out sometimes. Was it right to take on the raising of a baby, then leave her with someone else—even if it was her great-aunt?

How can I say I'm raising her if I'm off working every day? Or leaving her with Aunt Tess? Or with a baby-sitter? But how can I stay home with a baby unless I go on welfare? And wouldn't that be a catch-22 that I couldn't get out of for years?

An inadvertent groan escaped her throat, and she realized she'd been staring into space and that Aunt Tess was staring at her.

"Beth, Honey, what's the matter? Are you in pain? You have a sore throat?"

"Oh, no, Aunt Tess, I just had to clear it. Something was on my mind, but go ahead with what you wanted to tell me. I'll try to be more attentive."

"First," Aunt Tess said, "I want to know how things are going with you and Randy. Are you two really serious? He didn't give you a ring for Christmas, so I'm just wondering how long. . ."

Before now, Beth would have laughed off such questions. Aunt Tess wasn't being a busybody. She'd often worried that Randy didn't really appreciate her. This time Beth didn't say she had a lot of living to do before settling down. She didn't say she had places to go and things to do and see. She'd wanted to do that before settling down. She'd seen some of the world. She'd flown over the oceans, seen the famous old churches in England, the castles of Europe, the museums in France. She'd lolled on the beaches of Hawaii and the blue Pacific, and just yesterday she experienced being on top of the world in the Land of the Sky.

She'd done those things. Now, in a few months she'd be forced to settle down. She longed for Aunt Tess' advice. But Aunt Tess had something on her mind. Let that come first. Beth replied, "That's something I need to find out, Aunt Tess. Just how serious Randy and I are about each other."

Aunt Tess's eyebrows lifted in mild surprise. "Second thoughts?"

"A lot of thoughts," Beth said. "We've been seeing each other for a couple of years."

"And as I've told you, things don't stand still."

As Beth recalled, Aunt Tess had said that emotions don't stand still—they wane or they grow more intense. "Be aware of that, child," Aunt Tess had warned.

She was well aware of that. She had been in Josh's house and was sure the emotions he had stirred would wane—probably already had or would the moment she saw Randy again. "You had something to tell me," Beth prompted.

Aunt Tess seemed uncertain. She massaged her fingers. "You know my arthritis has been acting up more," she said, and Beth nodded. "And during these storms it was worse."

Josh said exercise would help.

"So, I'm considering giving up the dress shop. Selling it. You're not interested in it anyway, and that would be my only reason for keeping it."

Beth's heart leaped. Was this God's way of saying He was making a way for this baby? Aunt Tess would be home every day? Oh, a baby couldn't be more blessed than having Aunt Tess with her. Beth wouldn't have to worry at all.

"Oh, Aunt Tess, you work too hard anyway," Beth said, and a thought occurred to her. She'd heard there was no work harder than raising a child, or more demanding, or more time-consuming. Aunt Tess wouldn't have to be on her feet for long periods of time. But if she married Randy, Beth could stay home and take care of the baby herself. Aunt Tess could be around every day to help out, give advice, tell her what to do. "Would you be content just to stay home?"

"Well, not home exactly. I'm thinking of selling the house."

"Where would you live? I mean. . .oh, Aunt Tess, you know you can always live with me, wherever I live." Was that why she asked about how serious Randy was?

"Oh, no, child. It's time you had a life of your own. And I don't ever want you burdened with me." She lifted her hand when Beth started to protest. "You don't need to say it. I know how you feel. You wouldn't consider me a burden and all that, which I believe. But I would consider myself a burden. I'm getting older and getting older means wearing out."

"Well, how soon do you plan to wear out?" Beth said, looking at the woman still youngish although she complained of stiffness in her joints and occasionally in her hands. Otherwise she was in good health. A fear struck Beth. "Have you been to a doctor? Are you keeping something from me?"

"No." Aunt Tess laughed. "I'm fine. I'm just looking out for my future. I'm thinking of moving to a retirement center. You're going to be moving on with your life and rightfully so. You'll either marry Randy and settle down, or keep gallivanting all over the world, or finish that design course and get a glamorous job somewhere. I want to help make that possible. I'll give you a nice little nest egg and go off to a retirement center and slow down."

"Aunt Tess, you're not ready for a retirement center."

"And why not? It's not a nursing home for old folks. It's a retirement center where you can do what you want and not worry about repairs and grass-cutting and snow-shoveling and getting out on the ice. I've read up on it, and a lot of people really get active at those places. And I'd be in contact with people my own age."

"You have friends here, Aunt Tess."

"Yes, my Sunday school class members and a couple of neighbors. But we don't really pal around. I'm busy with work six days a week and don't feel like doing much but going to church meetings. Most of the people I know are married, and I don't want to be third or fifth wheel, and I don't want to turn into a single fuddy-duddy."

"And just what are you planning to do at a retirement center if you're not going to be a fuddy-duddy?" Beth said accusingly with a mischievous grin.

"Now you're talking to me like I used to talk to you when you wanted to go to some of those college parties—what are you planning to do that you want to stay out beyond midnight?"

Beth remembered. Aunt Tess had warned her explicitly about sex, drugs, alcohol, smoking, and anything else a young person might be prone to do—leaving no room for anything but a strong conscience when she was tempted to do anything wrong. She was grateful. Maybe things would be different for Carol if she'd had stronger warnings. But it hadn't worked for Kate. Like Josh said, each person had to make her own decisions. "I appreciate those days," Beth said.

Aunt Tess nodded. "But now, I'd like to see some of the world during my retirement years."

"Aunt Tess, you know I can get you discounted tickets to anyplace in the world. I've offered—"

"I know, and when we went to Hawaii together that was wonderful. But now I'd kind of like to run around with someone my own age. You need to be with young people, and I need to be with older people."

Beth felt a burden of guilt. Aunt Tess had sacrificed so much for her. How much of Aunt Tess's life was lived the way she wanted, and how much was sacrifice for Beth? She didn't know. But if this was what Aunt Tess wanted now, Beth would not stand in her way. "You should do what you really want to do," Beth said.

"I want to do what's right," Aunt Tess said.

"You always have."

"I hope so, Beth. I truly hope so."

Beth knew she couldn't mention the baby now and cause Aunt Tess to change her plans. Her arthritis must be worse than Beth had suspected. Aunt Tess was not one to complain, so even a mention of it must mean terrific pain. *I need to think, not about how Aunt Tess can help me, but how I can help Aunt Tess.* "If this is really what you want, Aunt Tess, I'll help any way I can."

I'll tell her about the baby after she begins putting her plans into effect. I wouldn't want her to change them because of me. I'm the one responsible for the decision I impulsively made. But she needed to talk to someone. Her eyes inadvertently moved to the phone on the desk near the far wall. When was Randy going to call?

Not only am I unmarried and going to have a baby, Beth thought as she stared at the clanging radiator, *but soon I'm going to be homeless.*

✥

Randy called later that evening, expressing his relief that Beth had returned to Baltimore safely. Not having it fixed in her mind how to approach Randy with the fact she was going to be a mother, Beth was content to talk with him on the phone. He was having a great time with his family and friends, he missed her, wouldn't get in until late Sunday night, weather permitting, and would see her first thing Monday morning at work.

Sunday morning at church, Beth listened more intently to the sermon than she normally did. Everything was taking on a different perspective. She had to consider Randy in a different way than she ever had before. The possibility of marriage—a subject she hadn't been particularly interested in—loomed large in her future.

She got to work early Monday morning, expecting Randy to do the same, although his job wasn't always on the line like hers, since she was in operations and he was a customer service supervisor. Fraternization was frowned upon, but she and Randy had started seeing each other when he, too, was in operations. She was in her Eagle Airlines uniform, the white blouse and maroon skirt, waiting at the ticket counter, talking to other employees when Randy strode in, tall and handsome in his fashionable overcoat.

He nodded and said "good morning" to the employees at the ticket counter. His fingers touched Beth at the waist, and he leaned close to her ear. "I'll see you in my office immediately, Miss Bennett," he said gruffly. The look in his eyes was anything but gruff, however. They were a teasing gray in a pleasant face that was handsome in a classic way, surrounded by black, wavy hair, conservatively cut. He was pleasant to look at. It was not hard to see why he got promotions easily. He was capable and had the kind of personality that attracted others. Beth had been particularly pleased when he had sought her out from among the many women who thought him rather terrific.

They walked together to his office. He unlocked the door, pushed it aside for her to enter, switched on the light, removed the overcoat, kicked the door closed, and held his arms wide. "Come here, you," he teased.

Beth laughingly went into his arms. Her arms went around him, and she lifted her face to his as she'd done many times, without thinking. This time she thought, even as his lips touched hers. She was analyzing, wondering, considering—*Is this what I want for the rest of my life?* Why wouldn't she? He was nice-looking, had a great career, a wonderful personality, and often went to church with her and Aunt Tess.

Could she submit to him for the rest of her life? And why not? She liked being in his arms, being kissed by him, feeling special. Aunt Tess's words popped into her mind, "submit spiritually, I mean." Actually, Randy wouldn't expect that. He wasn't particularly demonstrative about being a Christian and often engaged in what Aunt Tess called "compromise," believing moderation was the key to successful living.

She really wouldn't need to submit to Randy spiritually because he wouldn't be leading spiritually. Was that the kind of man she should spend her life with? And yet, she'd heard the remarks many times that very few men ever led their families spiritually. But what man or woman ever lived up to God's perfect will? What man knew how to lead spiritually? As the question formed, so did an image in her mind—and it sang from beautiful lips.

But wasn't she seeing Josh Logan as some kind of white knight in shining armor? Anyone could be on their best behavior for a couple days. If she were to be around him longer, she would probably discover weaknesses and faults. Everyone had them! And when two people were talking seriously, they always put their best thoughts, their best words, their best behavior at the forefront. Everyday living was a different thing.

Anyway, she wasn't comparing Josh Logan and Randy Crenshaw. There was no need. Josh was a counselor who helped people. Randy was her boyfriend of two years, the one she must decide whether to spend the rest of her life with.

She felt his kiss wasn't as thorough as usual or perhaps she wasn't responding as usual. Her mind had been on other things. He smiled, and she thought he didn't mind letting her go, as sometimes he was reluctant to do. He'd often said that she was too good to be true—the kind of woman a man thought about settling down with, as if other women he befriended were not that kind. He respected her, and she wanted it to stay that way.

She knew he and a group of employees often flew to other states and foreign countries, and she suspected from what many had said that their good times often involved a great deal of partying. She never questioned Randy about his life when he was away from her because they had not made a commitment to each other. They liked being together, talking, going out and sampling different restaurants, going to the theater, finding interesting things to do.

"I'd like for us to go out tonight, Beth," he said. He told her where he'd like to make reservations—The Brass Elephant—and she lifted her eyebrows appreciatively. High-class all the way. "I have something special to talk over with you. I hope you'll be as excited about it as I am."

What? For an instant she thought about how Aunt Tess had wanted to talk over something and how it was going to change Beth's life drastically. But God knew how to work things out. Wouldn't it be just like Him to instill it in Aunt Tess to make her moves just about the time Randy was about to make his move?

This is what I want, isn't it? Or am I just considering marriage because of the baby? Is this the way unwed mothers feel? They have to consider marriage when they hadn't before. But she couldn't honestly say she'd never entertained the idea. It was always in the back of her mind when she dated anyone or related to a single man—*Could this be the one?* Even. . .even during the past few days when she was stranded and became Joshua Logan's. . .client!

"It's so good to be back and see you, Beth. I had a great time, but you're my stability. I need you. You're so good for me." Randy paused, looking down at her. "More tonight. Pick you up at seven?"

"That would be great." She glanced at the clock. "I'd better get to work. See you tonight."

❦

Randy hadn't seen her designer suit, but after having been stranded in it, Beth decided to wear that soft, light-blue wool dress that Aunt Tess said was made for her. She knew by the way Randy's eyes lit up when he came for her at Aunt Tess's that she'd done the right thing.

"You're a class act, Beth," he complimented.

"Aunt Tess gets the credit," Beth said. "She recommended it."

"Some credit," he agreed, "but it would never look like that on a mannequin." His eyes swept over her approvingly.

I hope you can be as approving of what I've done, she thought. On the drive to the restaurant in Randy's sleek Thunderbird, Beth told him about the Logans and about going to the square dance.

Randy laughed. "On New Year's Eve, of all times. You sure got yourself stuck with a bunch of local yokels, Beth. Hillbillies, that's what they're called, isn't it?" He laughed again. "Beverly hillbillies." He glanced at her. "I saw one of those shows on TV one time. Thought I'd die laughing. Did they feed you possum gizzards?"

Beth was shocked. "Randy, these people aren't like some of those stereotypical hillbilly TV programs."

"I wouldn't expect them to be exactly like them, Beth."

"No," she said, irritated, "they didn't discover oil on their land and didn't move into a Beverly Hills mansion. But Faye is blond, like Ellie Mae and Josh is big and handsome like Jethro."

The grin left Randy's face. "The one you spent the night with?"

"The one who was gracious enough to offer me his home when I was stranded," she said with icy control, not liking the insinuation but telling herself that perhaps Randy was jealous. "The Logans are wonderful people."

"What does this Jethro do?"

"It's Josh." Rankled by Randy's attitude, Beth said simply, "He's a square dance caller."

"Oh, baby, wait till the guys hear this."

Beth felt her blood begin to boil, but she didn't answer. Randy was turning her wonderful experience into some kind of comedy.

She told herself that the experience with the Logans was wonderful, but Randy couldn't really understand, being from New York and only having some stereotypical TV programs as examples of mountain people. He wasn't a cruel person, and soon he was entertaining her with talk of having been in Times Square on New Year's Eve. Before long, he drove into the parking lot at the restaurant.

This was the kind of life Randy enjoyed. Eating out in fancy restaurants, dressing up, feeling successful. With classical music in the background, Beth couldn't help but compare it to the square dance music of New Year's Eve. That was fun, but this was romantic—but then, so was that night at Josh's. And she had learned a lot more than she would have seeing a Broadway play.

But it was just something she must forget. Oh, they all said they'd be in touch. Josh had followed through and called to make sure she'd arrived home safely. She might get a call from Faye later on, and that would be it. It was sort of like when she left California. She and her friends had kept in touch for awhile, then it dwindled down to Christmas cards only, and then nothing. She hadn't even called any of them when she was out there. She must concentrate on the present and what was at hand.

Beth turned her attention to Randy, who was talking about his time in New York. She'd missed some of it, having been lost in her own thoughts. Apparently he hadn't lost touch with his old friends, but he did return to New York more often than she returned to California. He'd hardly seen his family, being busy partying with his friends. She knew he liked people and the nightlife.

"Ron was in New York over the holidays," he said. "He talked about another promotion. There's going to be an opening soon. The higher-ups prefer a married man."

Would he marry her to get a promotion? Would she marry him to get a father for this unborn child? Was this the kind of thing an unwed mother would consider? Beth knew she might even resent such an implication if

Randy had brought this up before she'd agreed to raise Carol's baby. Strange, how things changed when a baby entered the picture.

No wonder Carol was scared to think of raising the child herself. Beth never knew there were so many things to consider. How glibly she and her friends had condemned those who would consider abortion. Of course, she still didn't believe it was right, but she could understand the fear and uncertainty that an unwed mother must endure. Even how difficult it was to tell other people. Beth hadn't been able to tell Aunt Tess yet. And she was reluctant to tell Randy.

The waiter came. "Let's order," Randy said. "Then I'll tell you what's on my mind."

And in your heart? she wondered.

They ordered lobster thermidor.

After the waiter left, Randy took a drink of water, then smiled. "Ron is really impressed that you're going to design school."

Beth smiled. So Randy had remembered her during his holiday. He had talked about her to Ron, one of his supervisors. "I hope that won't make him think I'm leaving the airline anytime soon."

"No, I told him you had a year to go, and it's more a hobby than a career. Something you're interested in. He said that just before the holidays the station manager was talking about getting his office redecorated, and I mentioned that you had courses in architecture and design and had a real flair for decorating. Ron's going to talk to the manager about it. We all know he's interested in keeping costs down as much as possible. If he'd allow you to do it, they'd save a bundle."

If I'm good enough to do it, then I should get paid well for my work, Beth immediately thought. Then she quickly reminded herself she was not connected with a design firm nor an interior decorator, that she hadn't completed her schooling, and that she shouldn't be offended but grateful that she might make extra money. It would certainly help, with a baby coming along. And it would be good to have on her resume. Maybe she could get a better-paying job. Why? So she could pay a baby-sitter?

The frustration of it all washed over her—those questions again about how to raise a child and work and baby-sitters and what was right.

"You think you could do it, Beth?" Randy asked.

She was about to say no, but then realized he was talking about decorating an office, not raising a baby.

"I've done Aunt Tess's shop windows for years, even before design school. I do them for all holidays. Everyone in town says she has the best window displays of anyone. I've learned about fabric and colors, so yes, I feel I could come up with something good. I would need to talk to him about color. I expect he'd want to incorporate the Eagle maroon and white into the design. Also, I know something about art and could get some great prints."

"You're really talented, Beth."

"It's not all talent, Randy. I do have a knack for design, but Aunt Tess has taught me so much about clothing and what goes together—the fabric and colors. Then my classes. . ."

Randy was shaking his head. "Not only talent, Beth, but you also have ambition and drive. You want more than you have. I admire that. And even if the station manager doesn't choose you to design his office, this will bring both of us to his attention. It will give you a chance to design and me a chance at that promotion."

Beth nodded, knowing she had to say something about the baby before he went any further. She took a deep breath, but before the right words would come out, he said, "I admire and respect so many things about you, Beth. Your abilities, your morals—although I haven't always known how to appreciate them."

Beth knew what he meant. He used to pressure her into being more modern and not adhering to her Aunt Tess's rules. She'd had to remind him they weren't just Aunt Tess's rules. They were God's. He'd stopped dating her for awhile, then he'd begun to appreciate her. She was the kind of girl he wanted to introduce as his girlfriend. Now he was saying there were things he loved about her. Wasn't that a step before saying something more serious?

She looked into his serious, dark eyes. He was quite handsome, especially in the dimly lit restaurant with hauntingly romantic music in the background. He looked like a young executive. And his face was so serious. They discussed many things, and he was always interested in her schooling, in her advancing and improving herself. "You're one in a billion, Beth," he said.

For an instant a different image passed through her mind. Joshua, with his laughing face, his kind eyes. Josh had said she was one in a billion. He'd been so impressed with her decision. Maybe she'd been stranded with Josh as part of the way God had of confirming she had done the right thing. Josh had thought her wonderful for making such a decision.

Beth had difficulty shaking away that image. That time was gone. Josh would fade from her memory. She must think of him as a confirming angel, perhaps. It was Randy who sat in front of her. Randy she had thought about for two years, cared about, expected she might marry someday. But her life had taken an unexpected turn. And all the girls she knew said Randy was the greatest catch and she was so lucky and how they looked so good together, as if they were meant for each other.

The critical moment had come. She had to make a lifetime decision about Randy. There was no putting it off. Aunt Tess had said she wished he were more committed to the Lord, but Beth knew how difficult it was to have to work weekends sometimes and yet be involved with a church group. You certainly couldn't teach a class. And how could she blame Randy for choosing to go to Europe and see the great churches and castles instead of going on a church retreat? He said he would be more inspired by the great churches, and Beth felt she would, too, but she went on church retreats because it was what Aunt Tess felt was right for her. And Beth knew Aunt Tess and others wouldn't have felt too comfortable about her traipsing all over Europe with Randy.

"You and I make a great team, Beth," Randy was saying, and noticing his lowered voice and the serious look in his eyes, she knew she had to tell her secret. He hadn't said "I love you," ever, but he had drawn her to him, had kissed her and held her like he meant it. And he'd said there were many things he loved about her. Wasn't that the same? Shouldn't she believe he was in love with her?

Was that what Randy considered "special" about this evening? The fact that they made a good team? But of course, it was special since they hadn't seen each other in a couple weeks. Just because her life was changing before her eyes, didn't mean his was. Suddenly the food wasn't setting well in her stomach.

"I don't understand, Beth, why aren't you excited about this?"

"Oh, it's not that. The idea makes me nervous, but something like that would look great on my resume."

"It sure would," he agreed. "Then is something wrong with your food?"

"No. It's fine." How long had she been pushing it around on her plate instead of eating it? She took a deep breath and looked at the confused expression on his face. "So much has happened over the holidays, Randy. My life is turning upside down. I thought I'd tell you about it over dinner, but now, I don't feel like this is the right place."

"You look pale, Beth."

She nodded. "I'm feeling a little queasy. I just can't eat anymore. If you want dessert, go ahead."

"No, I've had plenty," he said, looking around for a waiter to signal.

❧

Randy sped along the highway. He already knew about her being stranded and staying with the Logans. Beth told him first that Aunt Tess was putting her shop up for sale and was considering selling her house and moving to a retirement center.

Randy was surprised. "Where does that leave you?"

"Oh, she's keeping the house until I finish my design courses. But, as you know, many of our friends we work with manage to support themselves on a salary like mine."

Randy shared a townhouse with another supervisor at the airlines. They made it just fine. She shouldn't have too much difficulty sharing a small apartment with someone if it came to that.

"But that's not a big concern for me, Randy," Beth continued. "Aunt Tess would never leave me stranded, and surely at my age, I'm capable of being on my own. I haven't moved sooner because I like living with Aunt Tess and vice versa."

He concentrated on the traffic as he neared the exit leading to residential areas. "Then, what's disturbing you, Beth?"

He already knew there had been tension with her family for several years because of what they considered her extreme religious convictions, so she told him about Carol being pregnant. "She said she was going to have an abortion."

Knowing how he felt about abortion, Beth was not surprised when he blurted out, "I hope you were able to talk her out of it."

"I think so, but she's adamant about not wanting to keep the baby."

"There are a lot of childless couples who'd love to have a newborn baby," Randy said.

"I told her that, but she doesn't want that either."

He glanced over, puzzled. "So, she's going to have the abortion?"

"There's only one way to prevent that," Beth said. "She challenged me, Randy. So, to keep the baby from being aborted. . .I promised to take it and raise it."

Randy swerved and almost ran up onto the sidewalk as he stared at her. "You what?"

"You heard me."

"Would you mind repeating it?" he asked, turning onto Aunt Tess's street.

Beth didn't like this disbelieving attitude of his. On the other hand, wouldn't he be as shocked as Brad was when Carol told him she was pregnant? Considering that, Beth decided Randy's attitude wasn't all that surprising.

"Carol is giving me two weeks. . ." Then Beth realized a week had already gone by. "One week," she amended, "to change my mind about taking the baby. If I change my mind or she doesn't change hers about the abortion, then in order to save that baby's life, I will take it and raise it."

Randy parked in front of Aunt Tess's house but didn't turn off the ignition. Maybe that was to keep her warm. Tonight, his arms apparently weren't going to do that.

"Beth, this should be Carol's decision. You shouldn't make it your problem."

"Well, it is my problem." She didn't know what she was feeling. Anger? Frustration? Disappointment? "But it's not your problem, Randy."

"That's not entirely true, Beth. What affects you, affects me. It's just hard to swallow something like this. But you said in a week you'll know for certain?"

Beth nodded.

Neither spoke for a long moment. Finally he shook his head as if trying to clear his thoughts. "There's a lot here to think about, Beth," he mused, then came closer and kissed her lightly on the lips. "See you at work tomorrow."

Beth lay in bed for a long time, staring into the darkness toward the ceiling, trying to reconcile her emotions with reality. She shouldn't be disappointed because Randy didn't think her decision was noble. Josh had thought so, but then Josh wasn't personally involved. Randy said what affected her, affected him. But she really couldn't expect Randy to suddenly call his lifestyle to a halt and want to become a devoted dad to someone else's baby. Of course he'd have to think about it.

Beth had stated more than once that she wanted to finish design school before getting serious about anyone. Randy had said he expected to settle down someday, but for now, he wasn't ready. That was another reason they had hit it off so well.

What must poor Carol have gone through after telling Brad he was going to be a father? She must have felt like he'd stepped on her heart and ground it into the dust. Carol must be spending many sleepless nights staring into the darkness and seeing no light.

Beth had Randy, who was going to think about the situation; the Logans, who understood her situation so well; and Aunt Tess, who would see her through anything. Even with all that, this situation was difficult to face.

Carol has no one, Beth reminded herself, *except me.*

Chapter 9

The next evening late, when it would be about dinnertime in California, Beth called Carol.

"You can't do it, right?" Carol said as if she'd expected Beth to make excuses.

"Carol. . . ."

"I'm sorry I made you promise," Carol interrupted. "You laid a guilt trip on me, and I struck back. But this is my problem, and I'll handle it. So just forget I said anything."

"Now, don't you hang up on me, or I'll just fly out there," Beth said. "You listen to me. I'm calling to say I don't need to think about this for another week. If you decide on anything other than abortion, I'll do everything in my power to help you. But if that's still in your mind, I really mean that I will take the baby and raise it as my own."

"Beth, I know you mean well. But I'm almost three months now. I can tell my clothes are tighter. You're the only person I would let raise my child—the only person I would trust. You and Aunt Tess will find a way to give this baby a chance. Now, if you can't or if you have any reservations, I'll go ahead with the abortion. That's what Brad advised me to do."

Oh, my poor little baby sister, Beth thought, hearing the sob in Carol's voice.

"But I can't wait. I've heard those stories about abortion, and I cringe to think about it. You might think so, but I'm not a complete heathen, and I'm not heartless."

"Oh, I don't think that, Carol. I'm realizing just how serious all this is."

"I won't blame you if you've decided it's too much for you. I know it's a big decision. I know I can't do it."

There was no way in the world that Beth could say that Carol should take the life of that baby. That would be consenting to murder in her mind. And if she were Carol's only answer, then there was only one reply.

"I've decided, Carol," Beth said. "I'll take the baby and raise it the best I can."

"How are you going to do it, Beth?" Carol asked skeptically. "I know Aunt

Tess will always be there for you. Um, have you mentioned it to Randy?"

Beth tried to keep her voice steady. "We talked about it. He realizes there's a lot to think about here."

"Oh, Beth. This won't break you up, will it? I mean, don't mess up your life because of me." Carol had met Randy last summer when she'd visited for a few days. She'd thought him terrific.

But what could mess up a person's life more than living a lifetime knowing you could have saved a baby's life—and didn't? "No, Carol. My decision isn't messing up anything."

∽

Maybe Randy really is thinking about this seriously, Beth told herself during the following days. He made a point of stopping by to speak to her, talk about some trivial matter, or to relate a tidbit of gossip. But he didn't order her into his office for a quick embrace or kiss. That would have been too trite, wouldn't it, when there were such major decisions to make? About midweek, the tension between them had eased, and he was almost like his old self when he said that Ron told him the station manager was going to talk to her about his office suite.

Beth knew Randy interacted well with people of all ages, and he'd described his antics with his nieces and nephews as if he enjoyed them thoroughly when visiting New York. She took particular notice of how Randy related to children in the airport. She saw him kneel down in front of a little boy, crying because his daddy flew away. Randy gave him a toy plane and explained that his daddy would fly back after his business trip. The boy had finally smiled and walked away, hand in hand with his mother, happily holding the toy.

Yes, Randy would make a good dad. The little boy knew that Randy's gesture had been sincere and from the heart. Randy had looked over at Beth and gave a "thumbs up" sign, indicating victory. Is that all it meant? Or did it mean he was thinking seriously about settling down?

∽

I'm right, Beth realized, when on Friday Randy asked if she would meet him in the snack bar for lunch. *He's ready to talk about it.* Or maybe he wanted to find out how things went that morning in the station manager's office. Everyone knew about that, since she couldn't leave the desk for a considerable period of time without a good excuse.

As soon as they were settled at a table and Beth had asked the blessing on the food, Randy asked her about the meeting and then attempted to explain his reticence to talk with her during the week. "I know our relationship has taken a different turn, Beth," he began. "And I understand that. A baby in the picture gives cause for serious reflection."

303

Beth nodded. What anxiety poor Carol must have felt, having to tell Brad and wondering what his reaction would be. She apparently had been devastated by his rejection of the baby and ultimately her. Beth herself felt rather numb waiting for Randy's reaction. She tasted her vegetable-beef soup, then broke off a bite of roll.

"Beth," Randy said, leaning slightly forward, "I have to be honest with you. I've tried to picture myself as settled down and being a dad to someone else's child. I'm not ready to even think about a child of my own. Just the thought of it freezes me over."

Beth felt like shivering herself. "I know," she said, nodding. What else could she say? She didn't feel quite ready either, but time didn't stand still, and a baby would be born in a few months. She sat staring into her bowl, unmindfully stirring the soup.

Randy reached over and took her hand. "I know how good-hearted you are. But you don't owe your life to your sister or to that baby. I can understand your helping Carol all you can. But you shouldn't take on her problem like this."

"I've promised, Randy. Carol trusts me. I can't break that trust."

"Have you talked this over with your aunt Tess?"

"Not yet."

He took a deep breath. "Maybe you and Carol should talk to a counselor."

Beth couldn't control her short laugh of irony. "You could be exactly right about that," she said, thinking of Josh and how supportive he had been. At the same time, she couldn't at all blame Randy for his reaction.

Randy let go of her hands and smiled, as if she were rethinking her decision about Carol's baby. "I don't want to lose you, Beth," he said sincerely.

She pushed away from the table. "I'm not feeling well, Randy. I need to go."

So it's come down to this, Beth mused as she left the snack bar. *I must choose between Carol's baby and Randy.*

❧

Beth got through the day somehow and felt a headache coming on by the time she got off work. After the pampering of Aunt Tess and a good dinner, she was feeling better, but she knew the time had come when she must talk to her aunt about Carol and the baby.

After dinner, they carried their coffee into the den. Beth sat on the couch, and Aunt Tess took her usual place in the recliner. Beth told her everything—all that Carol had said, all about the Logans, the evening with Josh, and then Randy's reaction.

"Oh, Honey," Aunt Tess whispered through quivering lips. "You've been carrying this burden around since Christmas? Why didn't you tell me right away?"

"I didn't want to put the burden on you, Aunt Tess. You deserve to live the kind of life you want."

Tears formed in Aunt Tess's eyes. "The kind of life I want to live is helping you succeed in life, Beth. And you know I'm not talking about worldly things. And honey, I want to ask you a personal question. If this unborn baby were not in the picture and Randy proposed, would you marry him?"

The perfect question, Beth was thinking. Aunt Tess had a way of getting to the heart of things. In all honesty, she had to say, "No. Neither of us are ready for that. We've enjoyed the single life, especially the freedom of flying all over the world if we want to. I've kind of taken for granted that I would think seriously about it after I finish design school."

"And the reason you're thinking differently now is because of Carol's baby?"

Beth nodded. "That has changed everything for me. I have to think seriously."

"Well, I would say if you and Randy love each other and want to marry, this baby could be a wonderful blessing to you both. But if either of you is not ready, you're asking for trouble. You and I and God can handle this, Beth."

Beth realized anew how fortunate she was to be in the company of this loving woman. She swiped at the tears forming in her eyes as Aunt Tess continued. "I have never been more proud of you than I am right now for offering to save that baby's life. I couldn't be more proud than if you'd just become the president of the United States."

Beth rushed over and curled up on the plush carpet at her aunt's feet. She laid her head on her dear aunt's lap.

The older woman's fingers caressed her face and hair while Beth let the tears wash away her doubts and fears. Finally, Aunt Tess said a prayer, thanking God that Beth had saved a life and that the two of them had the privilege of caring for that life.

When her aunt finished praying, Beth looked up. "I took this on myself, Aunt Tess. I can't let you. . ."

Aunt Tess sniffed and got that determined look on her face. "You can't stop me, young lady. When God sent you to me, I took on your joys, your hurts, your responsibilities as if you were my own child. You mustn't even try to keep me from doing what I feel is God's will. You know I've told you that I prayed for children for so many years. We never had them. Then you came to me. You're like my own child. Like it or not, you and I are in this together."

Beth's head slumped down upon Aunt Tess's lap again. This time, her heart didn't feel heavy at all. *Thank You, God, for this wonderful woman. I should have known Aunt Tess would be the answer to my prayer and my predicament.*

Chapter 10

Midmorning on the following day, Beth answered the phone and heard the upbeat voice of Faye Logan. "Here I am at the Baltimore airport, and you're not even here," she said in an accusingly playful way.

"It's my day off," Beth said. "But I'll be right there to get you."

"We have a three-hour layover waiting for another crew to come in. I can't leave the airport. Regulations, you know."

"I'll be right there. Maybe Aunt Tess will come with me."

Less than five minutes later, Beth and Aunt Tess were headed for the airport. "I don't know why I thought you might not come with me," Beth said.

Aunt Tess laughed. "Well, I'm anxious to meet a Logan after the way you've praised them."

Aunt Tess and Faye had immediate comradery. Before long, the three women sat in the snack bar, talking like old friends. Beth even told Faye that Randy hadn't eagerly accepted the news about prospective motherhood.

Faye nodded. "Josh says this happens all the time, Beth. He counsels a lot of young people, and so many times the guy who has proclaimed undying love decides he's not ready for marriage or a baby."

"But it's different with Randy," Beth protested. "He's not the father of this baby. I'm not the mother. It's a shock to him."

"Okay, Beth," Faye said, flicking a strand of blond hair behind an ear and leaning her elbows on the table. "What are your plans?"

"I don't know. I only told Aunt Tess about it last night. We haven't talked it over yet. Aunt Tess needed time to think and pray."

"Well," Faye said, bringing her arms up on the table and leaning on her forearms. "My family has talked it over, and I've come with the results."

Beth and Aunt Tess exchanged curious glances, then stared at Faye.

"First, let me tell you about my sister."

Beth and Aunt Tess listened intently, although Beth had already heard the story from Josh.

When Faye finished telling of the suicide, she added, "We feel God wants us to help others who are in a temporary situation and need help of any kind—material or spiritual. We've had unmarried, pregnant girls live with us for awhile. Through Josh's counseling we know of many in that situation. Now, we believe you were stranded at our home for a reason. The reason is, we're supposed to be involved in your life. My message is: Whatever your need, we'll do what we can to help. You want a home, you've got it. You need money, we can offer a little. You just need a friend, we're that. You need a baby-sitter, we're available."

Beth's face softened, and she looked over at Aunt Tess with moist eyes. Her aunt seemed to be looking at her more than she looked at Faye. What was on Aunt Tess's mind? The older woman's next words surprised Beth. She'd expected her aunt to say she could handle the situation, that she and Beth could make it just fine although she appreciated the offer. Instead, Aunt Tess began to ask questions about their home, her family, their jobs, as if she wanted Beth to take Faye up on the offer.

For an instant, Beth felt abandoned, then she realized Aunt Tess was trying to prepare for her old age. She couldn't go on forever taking care of someone else. She was getting to the age where someone else should take care of her—especially now that she had arthritis. Maybe it was worse than she'd let on.

Faye was excited as she told how flexible their hours usually were. Faye didn't always work the same days of the week. Her dad could plan most of his days around work situations. The baby would be born in June, according to what Beth had told her, and Josh didn't teach during the summer.

"And, Aunt Tess," Faye added, as if she were her own aunt, "you should come to our area. It's the most beautiful place. And if you're looking for a retirement home, we have the best. We know some people who live there, and it's not an old folk's home. It's a place where you can do anything you want, go anywhere you want, and not have to worry about a house, a car, or even cooking your own meals."

"Oh, my, that sounds a little like heaven," Aunt Tess exclaimed.

Beth could see that Faye had won Aunt Tess's heart. That girl was a delight. So natural, and Beth knew Faye wouldn't know how to make offers that were not sincere.

"It sounds tempting, Faye," Beth said. "But Aunt Tess has lived here. . . how long?"

"Maybe too long," Aunt Tess mused, nodding thoughtfully. "I'm ready to move on. It's never been the same since Jack died. But it was a place to be with you, Beth. I think it's time you and I cut the apron strings."

"I don't ever want to be without you," Beth exclaimed.

"Then come to the mountains and live with us, and Aunt Tess can go to the retirement center if she likes it. Tell you what—take a vacation." Faye looked at Aunt Tess. "You are thinking of selling your shop, right?"

After Aunt Tess nodded, Faye looked at Beth. "And I know you can take off from the airline if you want to. And you need a job? You could probably get a job working with me. And, you know, Josh is as convinced as we are that God dropped you in on us for a reason. He's looking forward to this baby and anything we can do to help you. He keeps saying how impressed he is with you, Beth. That you would take this on when so many women your age would take Carol's way out."

Beth sighed. "Maybe I'm just not too smart. There's a lot more involved than simply having a baby. There's the rearing of that child. That's a lifetime commitment, Faye. I'm willing, but am I able?"

"Doesn't the Lord promise He'll provide us with the strength we need?

❧

That evening, Jean Logan called and talked to Aunt Tess after speaking with Beth. But it wasn't until after Josh called and said to Aunt Tess, "We're all in this together; you mustn't shut us out," that her mind was made up.

Aunt Tess beamed after she hung up the phone. "That Josh Logan, with the velvet voice, called me Aunt Tess. Why, Beth, these people think we're related."

Beth laughed. "They're like that, Aunt Tess. They're serious about this. I think they'd truly be offended if we didn't let them be a part of this in some way."

"You know," Aunt Tess said with a tilt of her head, "I think you and I need a vacation. We could talk with the Logans and pray with them and maybe have a clearer picture of how the Lord is leading. Didn't you say that Josh is a counselor?"

"Yes, Aunt Tess, but I don't want him to counsel me. I've made my decision. And I don't want him to think I'm chasing him."

"Why, Honey, why would he think such a thing?"

Beth shrugged a shoulder. "Faye says all he has to do is snap his fingers and the women come running."

"Did he snap, Darling?"

"No, Ma'am," Beth said, and turned away from her aunt's speculative gaze.

❧

"Beth?" sounded the reluctant voice over the phone.

"Carol? Is that you?"

"Yeah."

"What's wrong?"

"It's Mom and Dad. Oh, Beth. They're. . .livid."

"You told them?"

"Well, yes and no. This just proves my point, Beth. I thought I could tell them. I said that I would be going to Baltimore to stay with you and Aunt Tess for awhile. They couldn't understand that until I said there's the fact of an unborn baby coming into the world in about six months."

Beth was thinking that Carol's reluctance had changed. Now she was talking a mile a minute. Her words tumbled over each other. "Their eyes swept over me, Beth, and since I'm not showing yet even though I know my clothes are tighter, Mom said, 'You can't mean Beth?'"

Beth closed her eyes, nodding. She knew what Carol would have said.

"I'm sorry, Beth, but what could I do? When I didn't answer immediately they jumped to the conclusion that you're pregnant. I couldn't say you weren't. That's one of the reasons I was going to get an abortion. I don't want them to know. And if you're going to be the mother, I guess that was the right thing to do. I had to warn you. I think they're planning to call you."

Soon after Beth finished her conversation with Carol, the phone rang again. "Is it true, Beth, what Carol said?"

"What did she say, Mom?"

"That. . .you're. . .I'll just come right out and say it. Are you pregnant, Beth?"

Beth inhaled deeply, feeling the weight of every young, unwed mother who had to face her parents. *I'm not even that close to my parents anymore. We don't believe in the same lifestyle. I've already been ostracized and criticized and called a fanatic. But how can I tell a bold-faced lie?*

"Answer me, Beth," her mother demanded.

Lies! Lies! She hated them. But what could she do? *God, forgive me,* she breathed before saying, "The baby is due in June, Mom."

Beth heard a click and wondered if her mom had hung up on her. But when her mother spoke again, she knew it must have been her dad, hanging up one of the phones.

"Is the father going to marry you?" her mother demanded.

"That. . .doesn't seem likely."

"I see. Well, maybe it is best you moved to Baltimore and saved us the disgrace of this. I'm shocked, Beth. You come here and spout those religious convictions of yours and Tess's, like your father and I are some kind of heathens. And now, this. It reeks of hypocrisy, Beth. It's not that I'm so self-righteous. I know these things happen. We've had our talks on sex, and I would have thought you'd have sense enough to use protection. But what hurts is that you talk and act so moral—like your values are higher than ours—and now, this!"

Her intake of breath was audible. "We're not judging you, Beth. And of course we aren't disowning you. And we're very proud of Carol, who insists upon coming to be with you during this time. If you need anything, let us know."

"Yes, Mom. Thanks."

Aunt Tess came into the room. In a small shaky voice, Beth said, "I really could use a vacation."

"I think Randy was right about one thing," Aunt Tess said adamantly. "What you need is a good talking to from a Christian counselor."

Aunt Tess hadn't meant that Beth should talk to Josh over the telephone. The following evening Beth stood in Jean and Sam Logan's living room, looking out over the landscape and down into the valleys where lights were coming on like fireflies flitting around at a lower level in the darkening night. Patches of ice and snow were still visible along the sides of the higher mountain peaks.

It hardly seemed possible that only yesterday she had been sobbing in her aunt's arms. Now, she felt as if she were surrounded by family and friends. Jean had picked them up at the airport. She and Aunt Tess had found instant camaraderie, but Beth was hardly surprised. How could anyone resist Jean's warmth and sincerity? It was the same with Sam when he came in from work. Before she knew it, Jean and Aunt Tess had gone to the store and returned to spend the afternoon in the kitchen. Faye had left early to go to a wedding rehearsal dinner that she couldn't get out of. Beth and Sam played checkers in the living room. He won two games, and she won the other.

Then Josh had come in, looking vibrant and alive and excited, as if long-lost friends had returned. He looked so professional in his suit and tie and carrying a briefcase. Golden flecks sparked his eyes, and he smiled broadly. Hearing his warm words of welcome as he hugged Beth, Aunt Tess and Jean came into the room.

"Aunt Tess!" he shouted. "Am I glad to see you!" Amid laughter from the others, he opened his arms and enfolded her in a warm embrace.

"Is that one of those 'yellowrocks' I've heard so much about?"

"That's it, and there's a lot of 'em in these parts, Ma'am," he drawled.

"I'm not complaining," she said, and Beth marveled at how this family welcomed her and Aunt Tess into their lives. It was so like what they had done for her when she was stranded in the snowstorm. And yet, although she was no psychologist, she knew they needed this. It seemed people who had tragedy in their lives often started or joined organizations against whatever caused that tragedy. In the same way the Logans needed to have a part in Carol's unborn baby's life. Would it be cruel of her not to let them?

Dinner conversation was light, touching on jobs, dress shops, and square dancing. It was settled that Aunt Tess would sleep in the guest room and Beth in Faye's bedroom. After dinner, Sam went to the hardware store for something, and Jean and Aunt Tess said they'd clean up the dining room and kitchen.

Beth stood at the picture window in the living room. Hearing Josh bringing up a box of wood, Beth turned. He apparently kept clothes here, as Faye did at his house. He had changed from his suit and tie into jeans and a rust-colored knit turtleneck. Watching him build the fire and light it, Beth smiled to herself. He had already lit up her life and could well light a fire in her heart. . .if he were just a square dance caller and not a counselor.

But facts were facts, and she had to face them. Still, as he rose and said he needed to wash his hands, she felt the warmth and the welcome of again being in the Logan home. He'd said he wanted to be her friend. And she knew that she needed both a good counselor and a good friend. Joshua Logan was both.

Josh returned and came over to stand beside her. "The mountains look different each time you see them," he said.

Beth stared ahead of her. "Maybe that's because some people have faith enough to move them," she mused and glanced at him. "My faith is small, Josh," she admitted, as they walked over to the chair and couch, close to where the burning kindling was licking at the logs and lending a warm glow to the room. Beth, wearing jeans and a sweater, drew her legs up on the couch. She told Josh about the conversations with Carol and her parents.

"I didn't contradict what Carol told them. They think I'm pregnant and a hypocrite."

Expecting sympathy, Beth was surprised when he shook his head. "That's compromise, Beth. It's lying."

"I didn't lie, Josh," she protested. "And normally, no, I wouldn't out-and-out lie. But I promised Carol that I wouldn't tell Mom and Dad." She gestured helplessly. "What else could I do?"

"Maybe you shouldn't have promised that in the first place."

"But I did. And I can't go back on my word. If I tell Carol I can't live this lie, then she will decide to have an abortion."

"Beth, a Christian should not lie. It's as simple as that."

Beth couldn't believe Josh was taking that attitude. "I thought you understood this problem, Josh." She didn't feel relaxed any longer. She turned and put her feet on the floor, scooted nearer the edge of the couch, and spoke in a forced-calm voice. "This is not a simple matter of telling the truth or not. This involves the life of an unborn baby. I tell the truth and a baby dies. I lie and a baby lives. That's what it comes down to."

He was shaking his head. "God cannot approve of lying. You know that, Beth."

"Can God approve of that baby dying?"

"I don't know the answer to that, Beth. I know you've done a wonderful thing by agreeing to take the baby. But lying is a different matter."

"They're connected," she rebutted staunchly.

"Look, we know God is working in this situation. Now, don't you think He's big enough to handle this problem without complicating it with lies and deception?"

She sighed. "Of course. He can turn the world upside down if He wants. But Josh, He gave us free will. Carol has free will, and God will let her abort that baby if she wants to."

"Then, that's her decision," he said.

"No, it's not. I would have to live with that decision for the rest of my life—knowing I could have prevented a baby's death but didn't because I wouldn't lie." She shook her head. "No way, Josh. No way could I live with that. I'm not faced with a right-or-wrong situation. I'm faced with two wrongs—abortion or lying. I say lie and let a baby live."

"No, you're not," he said calmly. "You're faced with lying or not. And you know that's wrong."

"I know you're an experienced counselor, Josh. But I can't agree with you on this. To tell my parents the truth would be like gambling with a baby's life."

Josh looked troubled, but he didn't bend. "You have to have faith that God will work this out, Beth. He's with us. He's not going to abandon us now."

Beth still couldn't agree. "I guess my faith is too small, Josh. But I can't gamble with that baby's life."

"God is with you in this, Beth. Don't limit Him by being afraid to let Him work this out."

"It's not just between me and God. Carol is involved. And she's a young, single, college girl who believes in God but is not strongly committed to Him. I never imagined what an unwed mother might go through. My life and thinking has changed completely. The pressure on Carol is magnified greatly."

He nodded. "You've taught me a lot, Beth. Just by opening up your heart and thoughts to me. I've counseled young women in this situation, but I haven't really understood until now. Oh, I'm sure I can't understand completely, but I have a much better idea. There is so much to deal with. But I've never known anyone to do what you're doing, and I find it incredible."

"Maybe I'm just foolish, Josh. I got myself into this without knowing what the consequences would be. I've committed myself to being responsible for another human being's life. Do I have a right? Can I do it? Am I capable?

This is more than just what is right and wrong. How can I support a child? I've brought this on Aunt Tess, too. She'll work or baby-sit—but it's not her responsibility."

"Don't forget my family," he said, but her quick look at him revealed a softness in his eyes and a smile on his lips.

"Oh, I couldn't," she said, staring a moment longer at this beautiful man, larger than life in so many ways: gentle, kind, strong, caring. Firelight and lamplight lent a golden sheen to his auburn curls. There was a glow in his hazel eyes, too.

"What I mean is," Josh continued, "my family feels God brought you here. We will not abandon you. God has made a way. There are numerous possibilities here, Beth. It will be up to you to decide whether to accept or reject, and how much you will allow us to be involved."

Beth looked down and picked at an invisible speck on her jeans. *Oh, Josh, why couldn't Randy have said those things? But Randy is an entirely different person. And too, Randy would have to be involved daily as a father if he accepted this. Josh wouldn't!*

After a long pause, Josh asked, "What are you thinking?"

"About Randy. He thinks I'm wrong to say I'll take the baby."

Josh took a deep breath. "This can't be easy for him, Beth. I've counseled a lot of unwed fathers, too. Most of them find it hard to accept. It would be even more difficult for a man who is not the biological father. But this, too, needs to be given to the Lord. God can be trusted."

Beth looked away from him. "I've considered myself a strong Christian, Josh. I've been faced with difficult decisions, but right and wrong were pretty much clear-cut. I've never been tested like this before. I and the people around me are being faced with a life-and-death decision. A wrong one affects so many lives. I've. . .never felt so weak."

After a long, silent moment, she stole a glance at him. He was looking at her, smiling, as if he were greatly pleased. She stared, questioningly. He moved to the edge of the chair and held out his hands toward her. "Beth, we're all weak. It's when we realize it and know how dependent we are on God and give it all over to Him that He can show us how strong He is. That's when He can really work."

Beth couldn't take her eyes from that beautiful man who spoke such wonderful words, who believed so strongly in God. She couldn't imagine anything being more appealing than a man completely committed to the Lord. She placed her hands in his, and the feel of them brought warmth throughout her being. They were strong, comforting, reassuring. Holding Josh's hands, she could face anything. But he was not asking her to look to him for strength. "Let's pray about this, Beth," he said, and they bowed their heads.

Beth squeezed her eyes shut. His prayer was brief and to the point. He asked God to lead her to make right decisions concerning Carol and her parents. He thanked God for the spiritual growth that each of them could experience if they continued to trust in Him and let Him lead in their lives. He also prayed for Randy, that an understanding might come to him and that God would lead Randy to do the right thing.

"Thank you, Josh," Beth said quietly after he finished praying.

He squeezed her hands, and they smiled at each other.

Josh then got up to tend the fire. Beth could still feel the strength and warmth of his hands as they held hers, the warmth of his prayer, the security of having such a man care, give advice, pray for her.

She whispered a silent prayer of her own. *Lord, let me keep my priorities straight and remember that it is Your Spirit working in Josh, so I may look beyond the man to You.*

Chapter 11

The following morning at breakfast, when Aunt Tess talked about going to a motel or hotel, the Logans said that was no way to treat new friends. If Aunt Tess and Beth could put up with them, they'd be delighted to have them stay the entire week.

"You've been so kind already, we don't want to impose," Aunt Tess said.

"Oh, you wouldn't impose," they all assured her. "We'll be so busy we won't even have time to think about such a thing."

The week literally flew. Faye worked three days, which gave Beth the chance to make her bed, straighten her rooms of only a little clutter, and dust her living room. The two of them hardly entered Faye's apartment except to sleep.

A couple mornings, Aunt Tess helped Jean at her shop, and in the afternoons the two women visited the retirement center in Black Mountain after dropping Beth off at Josh's to use his computer for graphic design and making sketches and designs for the station manager's office. Beth learned that Josh kept hours at the Blue Ridge Mental Health Facility as a Christian counselor two days a week and sometimes made other appointments after teaching psychology three days a week at the university in Asheville. He left there around 2:00 P.M.

On one of those days after she showed him her sketches and ideas for the station manager's office, he suggested she show them to Heather Smith, who owned the Silk Flowers and Trees Shop in Black Mountain.

At first, Beth felt reluctant, not wanting to impose, but after seeing the gorgeous arrangements and the reasonable prices compared to ones she'd seen in Baltimore, Beth knew that, even with shipping charges, she'd save money by purchasing arrangements right here. She told Heather, who was delighted, and before long they were into discussing Beth's ideas. Heather offered some valuable ideas of her own.

Josh decided to run some errands and visit some shop owners he knew while the two women talked. Heather was pregnant, and she'd just begun to show. Beth told her Carol's baby was due in less than six months and that she would raise the baby. Heather shared that she had a little, five-year-old girl with her first husband, who had been abusive and was killed in an automobile accident. Her current husband, Tom, was a wonderful father to Molly. He was a creator of children's videos and had a special way with children.

There had been adjustment problems. But with people like the Logans, Beth could get encouragement and support. After they talked about Heather's business, Heather said she'd love to have someone like Beth to help in the shop. Beth knew this would be hands-on experience that could be more beneficial than taking courses and a way to make a little money at the same time.

Beth would have loved to visit the shops on the main street of Black Mountain, the town where Josh lived, but there wasn't time. They needed to get back to the Logans' for dinner. Tonight, Sam said he was making what he called his "famous spaghetti."

On the twenty-minute drive back to Asheville, Josh and Beth discussed the shop and the job possibilities. "Only a month ago," Beth mused, "I had my life all planned out. I'd work with Eagle, finish my schooling, get a great job with a design firm, marry, have children, and live happily ever after."

Josh smiled over at her as she gave a rueful laugh. "Life has a way of changing our plans," he commented.

"It sure does. I would never have imagined that I'd be planning to become a mother. Or that I'd even consider moving from Baltimore to North Carolina. I'd never been in North Carolina in my life."

"Sometimes, Beth, it's best to stay where you are and face the problems. Other times, it's best to make a clean break and start over. But decisions like this should ultimately be between you and God. My family and I offer our help in whatever way it's needed or wanted, but you mustn't let that sway your decision. It needs to be within the will of God."

That evening, they all gathered in the Logan living room and prayed for God's guidance and presence. Then they seriously discussed the future, the possibilities for Aunt Tess and Beth, the advantages of remaining in Baltimore or moving to North Carolina. It was decided that they needed to consult Carol.

"Carol needs to be included," Jean said. "We mustn't assume she's handling this well just because she's giving away her baby."

Sam was nodding. "Our own daughter appeared to have her life under control."

Jean added quietly, "Yet she took her life."

❧

The night before they were to leave, Josh asked if he could have a word with Beth after the others had said it was time to turn in.

"How are you doing, Beth?" Josh asked seriously, and she knew this was no idle question.

She shook her head and smiled. "I've done wonderfully well this week,

Josh. I really needed this break. And I've learned how important it is to pray and put everything in God's hands. I try to do that, but I see your family really doing it. You guys put feet to your prayers."

"We didn't always, Beth. It was our failure with Kate that brought us out of complacency and into realizing we are to serve others, not get wrapped up in our own desires and feelings. It's difficult. It's easier to be carefree, look for pleasure, and call that living."

"I can't imagine you being that way."

"Believe it," he said. "I'm not proud of it. But it's easy to take it for granted that you have salvation, and that God is loving and good, then go about your life doing things for yourself. Not necessarily sinful things, but selfish things. Life is so much better when it's lived daily for the Lord, and we see each event as some kind of blessing from Him. You have inspired us, Beth, and we're so grateful you and Aunt Tess came here and allowed us to be involved. I know you're leaving in the morning. Don't let this be the end for us, Beth. Let it be a beginning."

"I can't say what will happen. Any major decisions will probably be made by Aunt Tess and Carol. But I could never forget. . .I could never forget the Logans. I think Faye and I are close friends, even in this short time."

"As I've said before, I can't believe your coming here in that storm was a coincidence, Beth. There's a reason."

Oh, Josh. What could it be? Would he intimate anything personal? Was he even aware of her in any way except as a. . . project? A needy person? His next words seemed to leave no doubt. "Randy will realize what he has in you, Beth. I can't imagine he'd let you get away."

What more was there to say? She nodded and looked into the dying fire, feeling that his eyes were on her. Finally, he strummed the guitar, and softly sang, "I'll meet you in the morning, with a how do you do."

She figured that meant it was time to say good night. So she did. When she looked over her shoulder before descending the stairs, Josh was staring into the darkened fireplace.

Going back to work at Eagle after that week in North Carolina held a certain amount of tension. Never before had Beth realized such need for Christian friends around her to give her strength to face a day. She even dreaded facing Randy and kept her eyes on customers at the ticket agent counter. But her smile was genuine. She knew God was working a good thing through her life, and He gave her help. She had it already through Aunt Tess. Now she could have all the support anyone could ask for through the Logan family.

She was learning to give everything to the Lord. A sense of joy passed through her. She looked up at just that moment into the eyes of Randy Crenshaw, who was at the head of the line of customers.

"Have lunch with me, Beth. Please."

When she hesitated, he quickly added, "I'll be in the snack shop at 12:30."

She briefly nodded, looked around him at the next customer, and smiled. "Good morning. May I help you?" Randy stepped aside and walked away.

During her break, one of the workers said she'd heard what Beth was doing for her sister. *So, Randy had talked about it.* Well, she wasn't trying to keep it a secret. Others stopped talking and listened while Beth expressed her beliefs. They were surprised, some skeptical, but all were impressed with her strong convictions and the action she was taking.

As soon as she got back from her break, her supervisor said the station manager wanted to see her in his office. By the time she'd finished that meeting, it was after 12:30 and past time to meet Randy at the snack shop. Randy stood to make sure Beth saw him. As soon as she got her veggie burger and skim milk, she walked over to his table. He stood again as she took her seat. Randy was the kind of man who liked to open doors for women and stand when an older woman or supervisor came into the room. He was very respectful, which everyone liked.

"I'm sorry, Beth," he said, as soon as she got to the table. "I acted like a cad. I know that, and I hope you can forgive me. I didn't think you'd mind if I shared your decision with a few people." He smiled warmly. "Many of them think you're absolutely incredible, taking on the responsibility of your sister's child."

"What about the others?" she asked. How many had he told?

"Well, the general consensus is that your sister is taking advantage of you, Beth, making you do this. She's using you."

"I think you're right," Beth said, agreeing. "I think Carol was trying to make me see that deciding to raise a baby when you're single is not a piece of cake. She was trying to get me to agree to what she felt was her only way out of an impossible predicament. Yes, Randy, she's using me. But more importantly, God is using me. My life has already changed dramatically. It's in turmoil. Sometimes I'm not sure exactly what to do or where to turn. I only know I have some good Christian friends willing to help me."

"I'll help you out, Beth. You know that, don't you? I mean. . ." He grinned. "I'd make a great uncle, don't you think? Uncle Randy."

Beth stared at him. What was he saying? She wasn't sure exactly what to ask.

"Ron and some of the other guys think you're really something special. It's put you on a different level, Beth. You're not just another beautiful, talented girl," he said, and smiled his winning smile over perfect white teeth. "Ron said that specifically. He mentioned your situation to the station manager, who said he, too, was impressed."

Beth couldn't believe she could feel such calm and hoped it wasn't one of those that appeared before a storm. It wasn't Randy saying she was beautiful and talented, but Ron who had said it. Randy was just repeating it. Randy wasn't impressed, the station manager was. And yet, she shouldn't be so quick to jump to conclusions. She had talked to others about Randy, and hadn't they said this would be a shock to him? It certainly was a serious matter that would change a person's life completely.

Then another thought entered her mind. *Is Randy trying to further his career through me? Use me?* But hadn't she been tempted to use Randy—hoping he might decide he was ready for marriage and a baby carriage and the three of them might live happily ever after like in a fairy tale?

"You're right about the station manager. I took some sketches and ideas to him this morning. He told me he's against abortion but has never gone beyond strongly expressing his opinion. Now he's thinking of starting a program in his church where members can help each other. I told him about the Logan family. He was impressed and said he knew there were families who could take young girls in until they got on their feet, could do something on their own. So, Randy, the Lord has used you, by your telling others about this, and something good is coming from it. And the station manager even gave me a generous personal check to help out with the baby."

Randy seemed to take a considerable amount of time absorbing her words. Finally, he took a drink of water and cleared his throat. "Well, just call me," he spread his hands and smiled, "Uncle Randy."

"Exactly what does that mean, Randy?" Did he want to marry her, or what?

Randy never blushed, so she knew what the color in his face meant, even before he said it. "I mean, Beth, I'll be around to help out. I like kids. I could even baby-sit when you go to your classes—give your aunt Tess a break. This doesn't have to change the relationship between you and me." He reached for her hands but she slipped them off the table and onto her lap.

He took a deep breath. "Beth, you and I have something special. You know you're special to me. And someday. . ."

She shook her head as she pushed away from the table and stood. "Someday, Randy," she said sincerely, "I hope you find the girl who is meant for you."

He drew back slightly as if to retreat from her words.

"Thank you, Randy," she said, with a softness in her voice. "It's been a good two years, and I will remember it, and you, fondly."

She turned and walked away. Tears smarted in her eyes. Saying good-bye to old friends was never easy. She hadn't eaten her lunch, but she didn't feel empty. She felt filled and alive with God's presence and the challenge of what tomorrow would hold.

She could almost hear Joshua Logan singing, as she hummed,

Nothing could be finer
    than to be in Carolina
In the mor-or-or-ning.

"We have renters," Aunt Tess said that evening when Beth came home from work.

"So quickly?" Beth exclaimed.

"Well, that comes from offering it temporarily, a month at a time, for a reasonable amount. I'm not trying to make a killing. This house is paid for, and now we'll have a nice sum to use for renting one of those places we saw in North Carolina until we're sure where we want to live. So now we can get down to the business of planning for my great-niece or nephew."

"We?" Beth questioned. "Aunt Tess, please do exactly what you want. God has already shown He can handle this situation."

"You're absolutely right," she agreed. "And He said, 'Aunt Tess, sell your shop and take up your niece and walk—I mean fly—to North Carolina.' "

Beth squinted. "God calls you Aunt Tess?"

"We're on a first-name basis," she said smugly.

The two laughed and fell into each other arms for a hug.

Chapter 12

Beth had been off duty for thirty minutes and kept looking at the clock. In one sense the time seemed to crawl until Carol's flight into Baltimore was due. In another, it seemed to speed by all too quickly. Seeing Carol again would just be more confirmation that this situation was real. Could she keep her concerns from Carol and make her believe everything was okay? How could she make Carol believe everything was fine, that there were no concerns about rearing a child, when she wasn't all that sure herself?

Beth saw Carol swinging up the hallway toward her. Carol looked like a breath of fresh air, her jeans fitted into boots, a sloppy sweater down to her hips. She looked like a young, carefree college student with her soft, dark, short hair framing a flawless face and bright shining eyes. Beth knew she was heavier than at Christmastime, but no one would suspect she carried a baby—a baby that would become Beth's.

Carol breezed right up to her with a genuine smile and shining, deep blue eyes. "Cold out there, Sis," Carol said.

"Aunt Tess's house is warm and cozy. She's making a fried chicken dinner with all the trimmings and apple pie to welcome you. Come on, let's get your bags."

"Is she. . . ," Carol rolled her eyes toward the ceiling as they walked toward the baggage compartment, "you know, in a snit about this?"

"She's looking forward to it. Making all kinds of plans."

"What did she say about me?"

"Nothing. Not one word, good or bad."

Carol's eyebrows rose and fell.

When they reached the baggage department, Beth knew she had to make one thing clear. "Carol," she began, "if Mom and Dad question me about this, I can't lie about it. I can keep my promise to you about the baby, but lying is against God's will and my Christian witness to my parents."

Carol didn't say anything as she bent to retrieve her single bag except to comment that most of her clothes were too tight, and she'd have to get looser ones. They were both silent as they walked out into the cold February dusk.

At least Carol didn't do an about-face and return to California, Beth thought.

"I told Mom and Dad the truth," Carol said, after they got into the car and Beth had headed for the main road. "The way they jumped on you and accused you of being a hypocrite bothered me more than. . ." She paused and took a deep breath. "More than giving up the baby."

"How did they react?" Beth asked.

She sighed. "Well, the whole thing made better sense to them then. They'd already taken out their frustration on you. I guess they weren't too surprised to learn I'm the one who's pregnant."

"Oh, I don't believe that, Carol," Beth replied.

"I don't know. They're glad I decided to come here. This has to be a terrible embarrassment to them. They did ask me to apologize to you. Mom said she'd call and talk to you. Oh, and they sent money," Carol added. "They want me to try and get into school. And another reason I'm glad I told them is they said their insurance will cover my hospital bills."

Hospital bills! That was something Beth hadn't thought about. Yes, that was another hurdle an unmarried mother must face.

"All that doesn't sound like Mom and Dad are too upset with you, Carol."

"Not upset enough to cancel their plans. They're taking a three-month trip to Europe. Dad's opening up a new branch in Germany for his corporation. They debated whether or not to tour Europe, and I think I talked them into it, telling them there was no need to come until after the baby is born."

Beth felt that surge of elation again. She had struggled so about the lying issue. But Josh had prayed, and he had faith. Even before Beth had made her decision to tell Carol she couldn't lie, the Lord had been working, resolving that problem. And her parents had not disowned Carol. It was one more important step in learning to trust her Lord.

⟐

Two weeks later, Beth, Carol, and Aunt Tess drove to North Carolina in two cars loaded with clothes and miscellaneous items. After the all-day trip, they spent the night with the Logans. The following morning, Jean drove the three of them to Black Mountain to see a furnished house, immediately available at a reasonable monthly rent and right on the main street, two blocks from where Josh attended church and four blocks from the Silk Flowers and Trees Shop.

"Josh was so excited about this when he told us," Jean said. "I'm not sure which one it is. We'll need to look for house numbers. Oh, there's Josh."

Josh, wearing a tan topcoat, was standing on the deck at the side of a white frame house surrounded by bushes. Beth tried to concentrate on the landscape.

A couple deciduous trees stood in the yard. A sidewalk ran between the street and the yard. The driveway was to the side, where one could drive into the backyard or park underneath the side deck that she could tell would have a lovely view of the surrounding mountains. A high, wooden fence on the left side offered privacy between the deck and the house next door.

Jean parked in the driveway, behind Josh's Jeep. Beth watched as Carol's eyes evaluated the tall, ruggedly handsome man now bounding down the deck steps and striding toward them, ready to hug his mother, then Aunt Tess. Beth knew what was to follow. She and Carol would be next.

Beth had already warned Carol about the hugs. Carol glanced at Beth and grinned, then hopped out of the car as if anticipating her hug. Beth watched, feeling the hug between Josh and Carol seemed much more natural than she had felt anytime Josh had hugged her. *But then, Carol has a more outgoing personality than I,* Beth reminded herself. *Josh would sense that.*

Beth felt more reticent than ever when Josh hugged her. She would have to work on these growing feelings for Josh Logan. She needed to keep things in perspective. Josh was one of the Lord's lifesavers! And who, but Carol, needed someone like that at the moment?

As Josh unlocked the front door, Beth noticed steeper steps opposite the front ones, leading into what appeared to be a spacious backyard. To the left of the small foyer they stepped into the kitchen. To the right was the living room.

"Go into the living room," Josh encouraged as he held the door open for them to pass by.

It was a lovely room with beige carpet and a picture window at the front and one at the side facing the deck and driveway. A dining room table sat beneath the window. The couch was in the center of the large room, facing a brick fireplace and mantle. Adjacent to the fireplace wall was a doorway leading to a hallway.

Beyond the living room was a large master bedroom with a half bath. At the back of the house were two smaller bedrooms, a bathroom, and the compact kitchen with a booth that would comfortably seat four persons in the corner near the side door where they had entered.

Across from the side entry was a door that Josh opened. "Leads to the full basement," he said, gesturing for the women to precede him.

"We'll be right along," Carol said. "You go on." She took hold of Beth's arm.

As soon as the others had reached the basement, Carol closed the door and faced Beth. "No wonder you wanted to come to North Carolina. If I'd known they grew mountain men like that, I'd have moved here years ago."

Beth laughed with her but turned to walk over to the kitchen window. She'd heard what sounded like a garage door opening below. She looked out and down to see Aunt Tess, Jean, and Josh exploring the backyard surrounded by a wire fence bordered by deciduous bushes and trees. A few stately evergreens stood in the corners of the fence, almost obscuring the view of the neighbor's house and giving the yard privacy.

"No, I didn't come here for him, Carol," Beth said, as her sister walked over to gaze out the window. Beth wondered if she were becoming accustomed to skirting the whole truth concerning this situation. But, of course, she wouldn't quit her job and move away from the place she'd lived for six years just to be near Josh Logan, would she?

"Well," she corrected, "he is a part of it, Carol. He and his family. Had I not been stranded or had I stayed in a motel or with people who weren't this warm and friendly, we'd still be in Baltimore. But this isn't personal. The baby is my first priority, and I realize I'm going to need a lot of support in a lot of ways. Josh is first and foremost a psychologist and a Christian counselor. He made that clear the night I stayed at his house."

"Uh-huh," Carol said knowingly. "So there is more here than meets the eye."

Beth turned to face her. "Yes, there is. He needs to help in this kind of situation because of a family tragedy. It's a healing process like women getting involved in MADD after they've had a loved one killed by a drunk driver or speaking out publicly against drugs after having a child involved with drugs. The Logans need to help, Carol, as much as we need help."

"You don't think you could do it without them?"

"Oh, yes," Beth replied quickly. "Even you could do it without anyone. And it would be a terrific struggle. But when you turn things over to God, He provides ways in which you don't have to struggle as much. Oh, you may still be poor, but there will always be someone to help. I believe God led me to the Logans for a reason. And they believe it, too." She smiled at her doubtful-looking sister. "He led you here, too, Carol, for a reason."

Carol lifted her eyebrows, then glanced outside and back again with a grin. "If I weren't going to look like I'm carrying a watermelon under my clothes, I might hope that reason was a man like Josh Logan."

I doubt there are more like him, Beth thought.

"Oh, don't look so worried, Beth. Even the father of my child doesn't want anything to do with us. I'm not totally unrealistic, and I'm not some unprincipled wayward floozy just looking to throw myself at some man. Frankly, I'm through with men. I've learned my lesson the hard way. Believe me."

Beth smiled and grasped her sister's arm, looking at her affectionately.

"You and I both have learned a lot. And we've got a lot of talking to do. But for now, let's go see what's so interesting in the backyard."

On the way down the stairs to the full garage and basement, Beth thought about Carol's remarks. She felt no man would want her now. Beth understood that. If Randy had ever had serious marriage intentions, they were gone forever. A baby made a difference. But Josh was different. This kind of situation would appeal to him. And the only thing that would keep him from falling for Carol would be her lack of a strong faith. But Beth knew that Carol could not be around Joshua Logan for very long without becoming aware of his faith and her own need to be totally committed to the Lord.

Carol rushed outside in the crisp, late-February air, went right over to Josh, and entwined her arm through his. She looked up at him and said something. He looked down at her and laughed. Then, as if no one else existed, the two of them, arm in arm, walked toward a far corner of the yard, talking and laughing, with their backs turned to everyone else.

Yes, if Josh Logan were to fall for one of the Bennett sisters, Beth had no doubt it would be her baby sister. And wouldn't that be the greatest blessing that could befall Carol? Of course it would!

Then why couldn't her heart rejoice? Such thoughts had eternal implications. And here she was, feeling like her world was falling apart.

"Honey," Aunt Tess said, tugging on Beth's jacket. Beth turned toward her. Surely she hadn't been staring wistfully after Josh Logan! Aunt Tess had a way of reading her, so she tried to cover her emotions with a smile.

"You should hear this, Beth," Aunt Tess was saying. "Jean was telling me about how this house became available."

Jean explained that one of the young couples at Josh's church had recently built a house. This one had belonged to the young man's grandparents, who left the house to him, but he didn't want to live in it, didn't want to sell it, and because of nostalgic reasons, didn't want just anyone living in it. He'd come to Josh, knowing of his contact with needy persons and new people moving into Black Mountain and Asheville.

"Josh told him that a fine Christian woman and her two nieces, one who would become a single parent in a few months, were looking for a place to rent. He was delighted that no lease would be involved."

"So," Aunt Tess jumped in, "we can pay one month's rent. If we decide we don't want to stay longer or even that long, we've only lost a month's rent. And if the landlord decides he doesn't want us here, he will give us until the end of that month to leave. It's ideal, don't you think?"

"It sounds like it," Beth agreed. "Everything seems perfect."

"I think it is," Jean said. "This is not coincidence. God made this house available."

Yes, Beth agreed, with a nod. As if to confirm everything, Carol and Josh walked up to them. Beth hadn't seen Carol look so positive about anything since before December.

"If anyone wants my vote," she said, "this is exactly where I'd like to hang out for a few months. Oh, and I'm going to the university with Josh. He thinks he can get me enrolled in a few classes and has even offered to tutor me until I catch up."

Carol looked up at Josh, and he looked down at her. They exchanged happy, smiling faces as if all was well with the world. Beth remembered when Josh had made her feel warm and welcome and that he and God would make everything turn out all right.

Carol needs Josh, she kept telling herself, *more than I do.*

Beth couldn't be more pleased with the progress that Carol was making in her personal life. From the beginning, she'd said she would cooperate with Beth and Aunt Tess in where they chose to live and in their lifestyle. She seemed intent upon proving she was not a person of low morals, despite her condition which was daily becoming more visible. Carol always wore loose sweaters and talked about being out of shape, although Beth knew no one would suspect she was pregnant.

Josh had arranged for Carol to take several classes at the university, and three evenings a week he tutored her in a classroom at church. Beth tried not to wonder if Carol ever cried and if Josh ever took her in his arms. Then Beth would pray that God would take away her feelings for Josh. If God heard her prayers, He was being slow in answering. Or perhaps He had given her this as a test of some kind. She must learn to be grateful to have a friend like Josh, although his attention and time had transferred from her to Carol. Beth reprimanded herself for wanting him for herself when her sister's future and spiritual well-being were at stake.

Beth knew Carol hadn't been too keen on going to weekly singles' meetings, but she consented when Josh said she might gain valuable insight on what to expect in the final months of her pregnancy. Whenever Josh suggested something, Carol was quick to comply. She made no secret of thinking he was Mr. Wonderful. And Beth could not disagree.

It was at the third meeting when Russ, a quiet man whom Beth had noticed only once, gave his testimony. The group met at the church or at homes. On this particular night, since the roads weren't icy, they met at church and carpooled up to Josh's house. Josh introduced Russ as a clinical psychologist in the mental health clinic where Josh had his office. He occasionally came to a meeting and always gave his personal testimony whenever there were several new singles in the group. He did the same in other area churches.

There wasn't a dry eye in the group, and Beth could tell that Carol was visibly shaken. Russ had lost his young wife and two-year-old son in an apartment fire. Russ dropped out of church, out of graduate school, out of life, and turned to alcohol. A couple years later, a young man approached him in an alley. The young man said he couldn't keep walking past that alley. It was as if something were drawing him into it. Upon seeing Russ, he knew the reason.

"God led me here," the young man said. "He led me to you for a reason."

Russ told the young man he didn't know anything about life and had no idea what had happened to him. The young man said that didn't matter. He proceeded to tell Russ the plan of salvation. Russ had heard it all before. Then the young man said God would let Russ make a choice. He could spend the rest of his life as a drunk in an alley, hating God or he could pick himself up, clean himself up, and be the kind of man God intended.

Russ spent the night in the alley, crying, cursing God, and cursing the young man until his liquor ran out. Then he called on God. The next morning Russ walked out into the sunshine, feeling he was like Jacob and had wrestled with an angel all night. Smelly, unkempt, he walked and hitchhiked from Pennsylvania to North Carolina where an uncle lived. The uncle's wife had died of cancer when she was in her forties. Russ thought he'd understand. He did.

Russ returned to school, got his degree in clinical psychology, and got a job at the mental health clinic. "I give my testimony to anyone who will listen," he said. "It's part of the healing process for me. I would give anything if I hadn't lost my wife and son." The tears were running down his face now, unchecked. "But if I hadn't gone through that heart-wrenching experience, I'd likely have gone through life merely existing. My goals were position and money. It is from the struggles that we learn. It's how we come to know how fragile life is and how important eternity is."

There wasn't a dry eye in the room then, and some people were sobbing openly. "I want the world to know," he said, "how to appreciate their loved ones and not take them for granted."

On the way home, Carol talked about Russ's story and cried again. "When I hear things like that, Beth," she said, "I feel badly that I ever considered having an abortion. I thought only of myself."

"You didn't do it, Carol. That's the important thing."

Carol smiled through her tears, and Beth reached over to give her hand an affectionate pat.

Chapter 13

The month of March blew in, roaring like a mountain lion, accompanied by low temperatures, drenching rains, and flood warnings. However, the Logans' friendship warmed their hearts. Jean and Sam acted like expectant grandparents as well as dear friends. They'd gotten Aunt Tess involved in beginner classes of square dancing, and she discovered that the exercise eased her arthritic pain and loosened her stiff joints.

It had become a standard practice that they ate dinner with the Logans at least once a week. Joshua joined them when he could, as did Faye, when she wasn't out with Billy. The day Carol went for her ultrasound, Aunt Tess invited the Logans over for dinner.

Beth and Carol both were amazed at what the ultrasound revealed. The nurse was almost positive the baby was a girl. They could see perfectly shaped fingers and a spine with every tiny little bone perfectly aligned. "Anyone who doubts God, should see this," Beth whispered emotionally.

"I didn't realize babies were so perfectly formed so early," Carol said, amazed.

Sam and Jean were already at Aunt Tess's when Beth and Carol returned from shopping for the baby girl after the doctor's appointment.

"Okay, what is it?" Sam said as soon as they walked into the house.

Carol went over, poked him in the chest, and lifted her face to him saucily. "I'm not saying a word until Josh, Faye, and Billy get here. But I'll say this: The baby is perfect."

"That's the important thing," Jean said.

"One of you girls set the table," Aunt Tess said.

"I'm going to beat Sam in a game of Chinese checkers," Carol warned, giving him a smug look. They'd bought a game after discovering how much Sam liked to play.

"You've got one lazy sister here, you know that, Beth?" he joked and flinched when Carol poked him in the arm.

"I'm the dumb sister," Carol quipped. "I'd never get the silverware in the right spot, and I'd break the dishes."

"As I remember it," Beth retorted, "you broke dishes after we ate so you wouldn't have to wash them."

"Only once," Carol said. "And you promised not to tell."

"I only promised not to tell Mom and Dad," she said.

By that time Josh had come in, asking what all the commotion was about. Carol and Sam began to playfully tell him and argue about who was going to win in checkers. Josh grasped Beth's arm in greeting, winked at her, then walked over to join the light bantering and the game. Beth set the table. She looked out the window to wave at Faye and Billy as they got out of Billy's car.

"Oh, good. Everybody's here," Jean called, coming from the kitchen to the living room. "Now, what are we having? A boy or a girl?"

"I'd say a monkey, knowing this girl," Sam said.

"Oh, Sam," Jean moaned.

"I feel like a grandfather, so I can call her a monkey if I want to," Sam retorted. "But don't let me hear anybody else do it."

"My dad!" Faye exclaimed, rolling her eyes as if exasperated.

"You tell them, Beth," Carol said. Beth detected her slight embarrassment. Carol often got caught up in the joy of the baby and then would back off, as if she shouldn't.

"I'll give you a clue," Beth said. "Think pink."

"A girl?" Faye squealed. Beth and Carol nodded. The others applauded and cheered.

Which one of us should say thank you? Beth wondered. However, both she and Carol just smiled.

Suddenly Carol gasped and grabbed her stomach.

"What's wrong?" "Is something the matter?" they all said at once.

Carol's mouth was open, and her eyes widened. "It. . .it's moving."

"You mean it kicked you?" Jean asked, beginning to smile.

Carol nodded. "I guess so. It doesn't hurt. It just seemed to be moving around and pow, it started poking at my tummy."

All the Logans touched Carol's tummy and felt the baby move and kick. At times like that, Beth couldn't help but wish it were her tummy, that she was the natural mother. Carol seemed so special. She was carrying a miracle of God, regardless of how it was conceived. Even Carol had come to accept this baby as something priceless to all those around her.

The baby will be mine, Beth thought as she touched Carol's tummy and felt a spot harden as if the baby wanted to feel the palm of her hand. Already she felt a special bond, and this only made it stronger. She loved that baby. She could understand how the Logans could love that baby before it was born. How a father could be all excited. How adoptive parents could love a baby like it was their own. And the expression on Josh's face said he, too, was in love with that little, unborn baby. Was he in love with Carol, too?

"Have you thought about a name?" Jean asked, as they all moved back from where they had surrounded Carol.

Before she could answer, Aunt Tess said, "I thought Beth would want to name it. Don't you all think so?"

Carol shrugged and said, "Sure." Then her lips began to quiver and tears ran down her cheeks.

"No, I think Carol should name her," Beth said quickly. "She is the mother."

"But I won't be," Carol said. "Oh, don't mind me. Everybody says expectant mothers are moody and emotional."

They all smiled at her as she tried to laugh, and Jean handed her a tissue to wipe her eyes and nose. "But I have thought about it," Carol said. "If I were to name it, and if it had been a boy, I would have named him Joshua because he's been so much help to me." She looked at Sam. "And his middle name would be Samuel. Joshua Samuel Bennett. How does that sound?"

"Biblical," Josh said, and they all laughed, which eased the tension.

Carol sniffed. "Since it's a girl, I guess I'll have to name her Bethany Tess Jean Faye."

They laughed lightly with her.

"But I always said when I was a young girl dreaming about the ideal life, I thought I would name my first girl after Grandma Deborah. I could just see a little girl with bouncing, brown curls called Debbie."

"You were like that," Beth said. "And Grandma used to say you couldn't be still. And that your name was like music and you filled her heart with joy." They smiled, remembering.

"Deborah," Beth said. "That's a strong name. Grandma was a strong woman. I think it's a perfect name for. . ." Beth hesitated for a moment. Should she say it's a perfect name for "your" baby or a perfect name for "my little girl"? Quickly, she added the words, "the baby."

Carol nodded, reminiscent. "Those were happy days." She looked around to share her memories with the Logans. "Beth and I spent more time with our grandparents than with Mom and Dad. They were busy working and seemed kind of uptight to me."

Beth saw the smile on Aunt Tess's lips and the moisture in her eyes and knew she was thinking about her parents—or maybe she was thinking about never having any children of her own. And yet, Aunt Tess was such a loving mother to her, and now to Carol. She would be a wonderful grandmother. Beth could only hope she, herself, would be half as good a mother.

It was Jean who tried to explain why mothers seemed uptight. "I guess we new mothers are always uptight to a certain degree," she said. "When that little bundle is laid in your arms, you feel so inadequate, so aware that the child's life is in your hands to such a great extent. And you feel you aren't quite grown-up yourself and yet you're supposed to know how to responsibly rear that child."

"I don't know how you could have done any better, Mom," Faye quipped, then wrinkled her nose at Josh. "With me, I mean."

They laughed, and Beth saw the brief sadness touch their eyes. They were probably thinking of Kate. "I don't know if any textbook is adequate. So much of the time you have to trust yourself and the Lord. Each child is different."

A buzzer sounded in the kitchen. "That's the signal dinner is ready to be put on the table," Aunt Tess said. She and Jean rushed into the kitchen while others began to wash their hands or find a place at the table that Josh and Sam pulled away from the window.

During dinner, the major portion of the conversation stemmed around the baby. After dessert, Beth got around to mentioning what she and Heather had discussed and felt more strongly about daily.

"We'd like to start a young mothers' group at church. Maybe meet one evening a week. We can discuss how we feel, what we expect, what we've read, and share our fears and doubts. Heather says she was so scared with her first one and still doesn't know everything."

"I wouldn't have suspected that," Carol said. "She seems to have it all together. I mean, having that shop, a successful husband, a little girl, and expecting another. She just doesn't seem like she'd have a problem. She could even have a nanny if she wanted one."

"Those are surface things, Carol," Jean said. "Oh, it helps to have enough money. Sam and I started out without anything materially. But we had love and supportive parents. Fortunately, we knew to raise them in the church and according to the teachings of the Bible."

"And I thought you knew everything," Sam said.

Jean hit him on the arm, and they all laughed. Then Beth looked over at Josh. Their eyes met, and she couldn't seem to look away. She tried but felt a flush in her cheeks as she saw the contemplative look on his face.

Finally, he spoke. "Do you intend to have fathers in the group?"

Beth shrugged. "That hasn't been mentioned by either of us. I guess it's something to think about."

"It is. In my counseling I've found so many problems stem from men not knowing how to relate to their wives or their children. Many times, they don't know how to appreciate their wives and don't know how an entire day can be taken up with the care of one small infant. Now, take me. I've had experience." He turned mischievous eyes toward Faye. "Being several years older than Faye, there were times I even changed that little brat's dirty diapers."

"Oh, you!" Faye went over and banged on his arm, just like Jean had a habit of doing when Sam teased her.

Josh grinned at Faye, then grew serious again. "Our pastor's wife is a nurse and works in the obstetrics unit. She would be helpful along the birthing lines. And if you could use me, I would be more than glad to talk about the changing relationship between the husband and wife after a baby arrives."

"This really sounds great," Carol said. "You could even extend it to unwed mothers. Advertise that it's a group who welcomes all expectant mothers, not just married ones or first-time ones."

"Carol, that's a wonderful idea," Aunt Tess put in. "You would have a lot to offer along those lines."

"Oh, yeah," she said, rolling her eyes. "I've been through the gamut of emotions about this baby. And I've learned so much from every one of you." Her glance extended to everyone in the room and then rested on Josh. "Especially Josh. He's taught me so much and just has a way of calming all my fears."

"That's the Lord, Carol," he said.

"I know, but the Lord does it through you. Stop being so modest."

They smiled at each other, and Beth saw how special that look was. It even grew deeper when Carol said, "You can't believe how my thinking has changed. I've heard people say a baby changes everything, but I would never have believed how my life has changed. I thought I could have an abortion, or give away my baby and go back to being like I was before. But that can't happen. I'm seriously thinking about changing my major from business and going into some kind of social work. I think some unwed mothers would open up to me when they might not do that with a man. I could say I've walked in their shoes."

They all were shocked speechless. Finally, Jean whispered, "That's wonderful."

"So you see," Carol said, "I don't want to always be the receiver. I want to give of myself to other people. And if I don't have anything to offer this new group you're starting, I'm sure I could learn something. When Brad didn't want to marry me, I kind of felt like my life was over. If he didn't want me, what other man would?" She paused. "I want to be the kind of person a man would want to marry. I want to have children. But I want to do it in the right order."

All of a sudden, Carol burst into tears and ran from the room. Josh immediately followed. Soon, Josh returned. "Carol and I are going out for awhile," he said.

✧

Jean, Sam, and Faye had left before Carol returned. Aunt Tess was watching the eleven o'clock news, and Beth was making notes about the young mothers' group on the computer at the desk in the living room. Carol burst through the door, her face animated and her eyes glowing. A laughing Josh was right beside her.

"Oh, you guys, stop what you're doing. You've got to hear this. Josh, you stay. He has changed my entire life."

Beth turned from the computer and braced herself for the news. Aunt Tess turned off the TV.

Carol stood behind the couch, holding onto the back of it. "Josh has opened my eyes to what it means to give your life to Jesus. I mean, I've never had any problem believing. He has explained clearly that the devil himself believes, but that's not enough. Oh, I know you guys know that. I've heard it. But it never really got through to my heart and soul. It was only in my mind. But tonight, I opened my heart to Josh, and then we prayed."

Beth felt the tears sting her eyes. She remembered well opening her heart to Josh and his holding her hands while he prayed. Such a beautiful moment was unforgettable. Now, her troubled little sister had had the same experience—and more.

"I've given my life to the Lord. The girl I was seems so. . ." Carol searched for a word and decided on "trite" to complete her thought. "I don't want to be a surface person anymore. I feel clean. And you know what I want to do? I want to be baptized. I want to make that public gesture. And. . ." Her voice lowered, and she looked uncertain. "I'd like to be baptized while I'm pregnant. Am I being silly for wanting to give that gift to my little Debbie? It's something she could be told later."

Beth could not hold back a sob. She rushed to her sister and embraced her. "I can't imagine a better gesture, Carol." Her eyes met Josh's as she held her sister. She mouthed, "Thank you," and he nodded. He even let his own tears trickle down his cheeks.

"Carol, I'm so happy for you," Aunt Tess said, coming over to add her congratulations. Beth couldn't describe the happiness she felt for her sister. Already, she could see so much good coming from what had appeared to be a tragedy when Carol had first said she was pregnant.

Then Beth felt Josh's hands on her shoulders. His beautiful hazel eyes looked down at her. "It's you who made all this possible, Beth. It's you who made the decision to come here, to open your heart to your sister and little

Debbie. You are the one to be thanked."

With that, he drew her to him and embraced her, then let her go after saying a quick, "Good night, Beth." He opened the side door and left.

I needed that, she thought as the cold night air swept over the warmth of her body just from being so near to Josh. Being in his arms was something she desperately wanted. But she had to remind herself that the embrace was just an appreciative "yellowrock." Day by day, moment by moment, Carol was becoming the kind of woman that Josh could welcome into his life.

"Oh, Aunt Tess," Beth sobbed upon returning to the living room and seeing Carol wasn't there. She didn't know how to express her mixed emotions. As if she knew how Beth felt, Aunt Tess led her to the couch and held her head against her shoulder, rocking gently.

"I know how you feel," Aunt Tess said. "We could not be happier for Carol. It is what we want for her and we rejoice. But, my dear, we are human, and we still have our own emotions to deal with."

Yes, Beth could believe her aunt knew or suspected what was in her heart—that she loved Josh Logan. And how could she not? How could Carol not love him? How could anyone not love that remarkable man?

Chapter 14

The landscape looked like it was being baptized for another week. Finally, the rains ceased. A touch of spring filled the air, warmed by the sun's rays that touched the forsythia bushes which began to bud in small, green clusters. Before they could bloom, however, April came, and with it came a soft snow that fell in two-inch layers on everything. The sight was beautiful, even more so than the ice-covered world in December had been.

Just like the rhyme that Beth had learned when she was a child, the March winds and April showers brought forth flowers—hyacinths, daffodils, and jonquils. White dogwood blossoms dotted the mountainsides.

Soft breezes and fragrant, warm air lent a softness to the early days of May. Business at the flower shop picked up. It seemed everyone had flowers and lush, green trees on their minds. Beth's days were filled with activity, working with Heather at the flower shop, visiting with the Logans, shopping with Faye, helping Josh with the singles, going with Carol to her doctor appointments, helping with the church baby shower and the shower Faye and Jean had planned for the baby.

Even on the days when Carol felt uncomfortable and the baby pressed against her ribs or caused her hipbones to feel as if they were stressed to the breaking point, she never missed a class at the university. She passed her finals with A's and B's. She missed only one singles' meeting and smiled appreciatively during all the other activities, although Beth knew how tired and uncomfortable she had become.

"How can I complain," she said to Beth, "when so many people are loving and helping me?"

Then in early June, Beth didn't attend the singles' meeting but sat at the dining room table, making a flower arrangement. The meeting must have lasted longer than usual, she surmised. At 10:15, the phone rang.

Beth answered. It was Josh. "The hospital? We'll be right there."

"It's Carol. The baby's coming," Beth said to Aunt Tess. "Josh will call his parents." Less than five minutes later, the two of them were on the interstate, heading for the hospital.

As previously arranged, Beth was allowed to be in the delivery room for the birthing of the baby. Beth wondered if this were worse for her than for Carol. Beth felt every contraction, every groan, every bead of sweat.

"I'll never do this again," Carol vowed, then with a final push, a dark head of hair appeared in the doctor's hands, followed by the first breath of life, causing the baby to cry with healthy-sounding lungs.

The pink-skinned, dark-haired baby was laid on Carol's chest. "Oh," was all Carol could say, but that one exclamation was not of pain, but akin to what Beth was feeling. Pain, struggle, and prior anxieties had been replaced with tender love.

A nurse placed the baby in a scale, where she registered in at six pounds, four ounces. Then the nurse wrapped her in a blanket and handed her to Beth.

"Little Debbie," Beth whispered. *My baby. The baby I'm going to call my own. Yes, I can love her as if I were the one who gave her life. In a sense, I am. Thank You, God, for this little miracle.* Then Beth was struck by another thought. Having experienced the birth process, seen little Debbie, felt her, heard her cry, how could Carol possibly give up her baby?

❧

"Oh, Beth, I don't think I can do it," Carol wailed later that day, after she had asked to see Beth alone in her hospital room. "You know, we decided the baby would be bottle-fed, and I'd go back to California as soon as I could. Well, when they brought the baby, I decided to feed her myself." The tears flowed down her face. "She's mine. And I love her. I just can't give her up."

Feeling a sudden lurch in her heart, Beth grasped her sister's hand, bowed her head, and cried with Carol. She could not find the words to speak.

"You must hate me," Carol said.

Beth shook her head.

"Then. . .why are you crying?"

"I'm not sure," Beth said and tried to smile, but her lips only trembled. "Maybe because you are. But I know a baby should be with a mother who loves it."

"Oh, Beth," Carol said, reaching out her arms to her, "I owe you so much."

"Whatever you owe," Beth managed to whisper, "give it to the baby. Now, the others are waiting to see you. You can tell them. . ."

Beth walked into the waiting room, still unable to check her tears. Josh came over and asked if he could help. She could only shake her head. Only one thought was dominant in her mind. *A baby should be with a mother who loves it, yes. But one doesn't have to be the birthing mother in order to feel a mother's love.*

❧

Two days later, Carol was released from the hospital, and at the end of the week, her parents arrived in the afternoon, so Aunt Tess picked them up at the airport. Beth had asked Aunt Tess not to bring them by the flower shop but to let them see Carol first. When Beth walked in after work, her parents stared at her as if she were a stranger, then they both began to interrupt each other, apologizing again for what they had thought and said against Beth.

"It's okay," she said. "You didn't know the whole story."

Her mom's embrace was warmer than Beth had felt from her in a long time.

"You don't have to say anything, Mom. You didn't know the whole story."

Her dad hugged her, too, but he was stiff and uncomfortable. He smiled, but questions remained in his eyes, and Beth saw him look from her to Carol several times as if he were trying to make sense of everything.

They both sat on the couch. "And moving to North Carolina, Tess," Beth's mother said. "I'm surprised at you. I've always been the impulsive one, and you so sensible. I can't imagine that you'd just up and move."

"I did what I thought was best for this girl who has been like a daughter to me, Vera. Oh, I'm not trying to take anything away from you, but you've had so much, and I've had little for many years until Beth came to stay with me. I would do anything I could for either one of these girls."

Beth's mom nodded. "You're a good woman, Tess. I wish I had been the kind of mother that these girls could have come to me with this problem." She took a deep breath, and her voice was shaky. "But, in all honesty, I'm glad they didn't."

The silence was incredible. They all stared at her. Then she began to explain. "Beth, Carol told me she had planned to have an abortion. If she had come to me in those early weeks with Brad not intending to marry her, I might have advised her to go ahead. And, at first, after she said you were pregnant, I didn't think I was ready to be a grandmother. I have this social life, you know, and I'm eternally thirty-nine years old."

She tried to laugh, and they all smiled at her, but the tears spilled from her eyes. She didn't even blot them with her hanky. Beth realized she had never seen her mother cry about anything before.

"And now," she said, "I've held my granddaughter. And I can't find words to thank you enough for saving her life. I am so glad I did not influence Carol to. . .harm my own granddaughter."

Carol began crying. Beth suspected her dad might be moved as well, for he quickly rose and walked over to the window, his back turned to them. Aunt Tess looked at Beth with a pleased expression in her eyes.

The rest of the evening and into the night they talked about everything that had occurred during the past months. Long past midnight, Beth's mother declared, "I want to meet this incredible Logan family—particularly this Josh who has changed you so completely, Carol."

"Oh, he is incredible," Carol said. "There is no finer man. I mean. . .oh, Dad, I don't mean you're not the finest man a girl could have for a dad."

"It's all right, Carol," he said in that subdued manner that had colored his actions since Beth had walked into the house. It was as if he were still in shock about everything. "Judging from all you've said, I know what you mean. And you have no reason to apologize."

☙

It was the Bennett parents who apologized after the Logans arrived at Aunt Tess's. "Our hearts are so full of gratitude to Tess, Beth, and all of you Logans," Vera said, and Dean briefly added his words of appreciation.

Dinner conversation centered around everyone's jobs—Dean's, Josh's, Sam's, Beth's, Jean's shop and the fact that Aunt Tess had begun to work there a couple mornings a week, Faye's job and plans with Billy. Beth noticed that her dad was uncommonly quiet and did not dominate the conversation about his business affairs. When had he become such a thoughtful listener?

After dessert, they sat on the couch, easy chairs, and dining room chairs. Vera Bennett again expressed her concern that she had failed her daughters. The Logans told the story about their daughter and how they'd felt they had failed. It had taken a long time before they allowed God's healing in their hearts.

The mood took on an entirely different feeling when Carol said she had some special announcements. She told of her gratitude to Beth and Josh. She gave her testimony of how she had come to know the Lord as her personal Savior and how her earlier lifestyle seemed so trite and meaningless compared with what she saw in Beth, Aunt Tess, the Logans, and others like them—like Russ, who had lost his wife and child.

"I want the kind of faith in my life that shines through the actions of Beth, Josh, and the Logans," Carol asserted. "I want the kind of faith that made Beth care about an unborn child when I myself considered it a major inconvenience." Her lip trembled, but she smiled.

Beth had never seen her little sister look so beautiful nor speak so maturely. She knew the change in Carol was a miracle of God—and of Josh. Only a few short months ago, Carol was interested in partying, her boyfriend, and her own desires.

"Deep inside, I now know I hoped someone would come to my rescue. Beth did that. Through Josh's urging, I became involved with people who are struggling in many ways. Before, I thought this baby would mean the end of my life. Now, I know it's only a beginning. Things began to change in me when I first felt this baby kick. Those feelings have grown, and when I saw little Debbie, I knew I couldn't give her up. Josh, come stand by me while I tell them."

Beth's eyes suddenly locked with Aunt Tess's, and Beth quickly looked down. She gripped the side of the chair, bracing herself for this announcement.

"Josh said you all would approve of this. Because of what the Logans, and particularly Josh, have meant to me, I gave Debbie the middle name of Kate." She looked at Jean, Sam, and Faye. "After your daughter, and sister."

They all seemed to start talking at the same time, saying that was perfect and the Logans felt she was so thoughtful, thinking of that. Then Vera and Dean Bennett said they wanted Carol to return to California with them.

"That's something else I needed to tell you all," Carol said. She went on to explain that she couldn't possibly go away from Aunt Tess, Beth, the Logans, and the singles' group. She needed them.

Then, surprisingly, her parents agreed it was time that they began to rethink the priorities in their lives. They would share in the responsibility for Carol and their granddaughter, Debbie.

Beth felt numb. Why couldn't she rejoice? *A baby will be with her own mother—her mother who wants her. A baby will grow up with loving grandparents. A baby might even gain a father—Josh!* It was all so wonderful. Tears sprang to Beth's eyes, but looking around, she saw tears in the eyes of others.

Then Josh got up and went over to Carol. They embraced for a long time. Beth had heard that things happened in threes. She didn't want to wait around for the third announcement. She left the room, muttering that she needed to get a tissue. No one seemed to hear.

Beth opened the side door and walked out on the deck. The days of mid-June had turned warm, but the nights were always chilly. She needed that cool breeze to blow away her errant thoughts. They persisted, however. Beth felt like she had lost her baby. She'd lost the man she loved but never really had. She loved Josh, but she must not let anyone know. Her parents and Carol were trying to get their priorities straight. Beth felt she must do the same.

Thank You, God, she began to pray silently, *that Carol will keep her baby and rear it. Thank You, God, that my parents want to be grandparents. Thank You, God, that Carol is one of Your born-again children. Thank You, God, that my parents have admitted they might need more in their lives.*

There were so many things. The list could go on and on, but the one thing Beth had to say, even if she couldn't mean it just yet. *Thank you, God, that Carol has the most wonderful man in the world—that the baby will have the most wonderful parents, the most wonderful grandparents. Thank You that Carol and Josh have found each other.*

Someone touched her arm. Beth turned and found Josh's eyes staring into hers. "You need counseling," he said.

"No, I don't. I have everything in perspective."

"Come on," he ordered. "Let's go to my house and talk."

"No," she said. "I need to go back inside."

"I told them you and I needed to have a talk."

She began shaking her head, but he literally swooped her up and took her down the steps to his Jeep and soon was on the interstate, then turned in the direction of his mountaintop home. Did he know she loved him? But then, who didn't love him? The important thing was who he loved. And that was Carol. Her lucky, lucky sister.

"You lost your baby," he said. "An expectant mother suddenly became an aunt after giving up everything for that baby. That must be devastating."

"Yes," she admitted. "But I know it's for the best. For the baby and for my entire family. Nothing I gave up can even compare with what has been gained."

"I agree," he said, "but that doesn't take away the feeling of loss you must be having."

"My mind knows. It will sink into my heart," she said.

He turned off the interstate onto the winding incline toward his home. "Carol even said you might want to go back to Baltimore and renew your relationship with Randy."

Beth didn't answer, instead looking out the window at the trees that obscured the landscape, symbolic of her own inability to see her future.

Neither spoke on the rest of the way up the mountain. After they arrived at the house, Beth walked out on Josh's deck and held onto the railing. He came up and placed his light jacket around her shoulders, then stood beside her.

"You're an incredible woman, Beth. There aren't many people who would do what you were willing to do for your sister. Do you realize how many lives you have touched and changed?"

She was surprised. "You are the one who brought about the major changes in Carol."

"I couldn't have if you hadn't brought her to me. If you hadn't sacrificed your own life. You should be elated, not sad."

"I am elated about that."

"Then why are you sad?"

"Well, like you said, I lost a baby. I. . .it's only natural I should. . .grieve."

She walked to the other end of the deck. The sun streaked the sky with gold and pink, and then the scene began to fade and the cool mountain breeze caused her to hug her arms.

Then he was behind her with his arms around her. "You're shivering," he said.

"Well, the breeze."

"I'm shivering, too," he said, "but it's not the breeze. It's from standing so close to the most wonderful woman I've ever met. The most giving, the most sacrificial. It reminds me of Jesus saying, 'Greater love has no one than this, that one lay down his life for his friends.' Of course, we can only do it on a smaller scale. I talk to people, Beth. And it often makes a difference. But you acted on it. You were willing to give up your man, your career."

"I was lucky," she said, "to find out that man and that career were not so important after all."

Beth told herself she should not be reveling in feeling Josh's arms around her shoulders. He was a counselor, a kind man, a hugging man.

"After Carol said you might return to Randy, Aunt Tess said a strange thing. She reminded Carol that you told her, before even moving to North Carolina, that you realized you were not in love with Randy. I wonder, Beth," he said softly, "what made you realize it?"

Beth lifted her chin and opened her mouth to try and be rather flip about the answer. Then she knew she couldn't. She needed to be honest with Joshua. No more lies and deception. He would understand why she couldn't stick around this area. After all, hadn't he admitted he'd been interested in women who had not been meant for him?

She cleared her throat, took a deep breath, almost choked on it, then told the truth. "At that time, Joshua, I had never met a man like you—so completely devoted to the Lord, and yet so appealing in every other way. I suppose I could be falling for you. I wasn't entirely thinking along spiritual lines." She gave a short laugh, but it sounded more like a groan to her own ears.

It didn't even seem to phase him. After all, he was accustomed to women falling for him.

"You know what, Beth? I'm going to be the best uncle any baby could ever have."

"Uncle?" Beth questioned. It had an entirely different sound than when Randy had used the same word. Now there was definitely room for an uncle in this situation. "Aren't you? I mean, aren't you in love with Carol?"

"No. I'm in love with Carol's sister."

"What?"

"I love you, Beth. I didn't feel it right to tell you while you were heartbroken over Randy and while you were so intent upon making a life for that unborn baby and taking care of Aunt Tess and your sister. I couldn't burden you with my feelings at a time like this. Carol and the baby had to take precedence."

"What kind of psychologist are you? Didn't you know I loved you?"

"No. Psychologists only see other people's dilemmas. We're notoriously incapable of seeing our own, and I was afraid."

"Josh?" She couldn't believe her ears. She never considered herself much of a singer, but the words came: "*Snap your fingers, and I'll come running.*"

Josh grinned and snapped. Beth fell into his arms, and he lifted her off her feet and swung her around.

"Oh, I was so afraid that here was another one who would get away. You can't imagine how hard it was for me to keep my priorities straight, Beth. I had to try and be as sacrificial toward Carol and her needs as you were."

He set her on her feet again but wouldn't let her go. She lifted her face to his. "Josh, I love you. I will always love you."

"Then make my life complete. I'll court you, and woo you, and we'll marry. We'll have our own babies. How about that?"

Beth glanced out at the changing landscape. It was true that the mountains looked different each time she saw them. And now, it looked as if a mountain had moved. A tremendous joy flooded her soul as she thanked God, then lifted her face to Josh.

WHITER
THAN SNOW

Chapter 1

Wake up, Jennifer," Irene Collins implored. "Come on, Honey. You can do it. You've got to, Baby. Please, please, wake up."

Jennifer Collins heard her mother's voice. She heard the plea when she called her "baby," something she did only when something drastic had happened. What happened? Why was her mother distressed? And why did she want Jennifer to emerge from that peaceful blackness?

Jennifer remembered others had tried to awaken her. Or had she dreamed that? It seemed she had been resting in that blessed blackness. A man had ordered her to talk to him. A woman demanded she wake up and tell them what happened. Questions had been fired at her, not giving her time to consider them, much less reply. Fingers had lifted one eyelid, then another, and tried to blind her with a bright light.

No! She had not wanted to answer, nor look at whomever or whatever kept poking and probing her body, bringing pain.

Someone in a tunnel, far away, said, "She's not responding," and Jennifer had smiled inwardly, returning to the security and safety of darkness.

But now her mother was pleading with her to wake up. She'd heard such distress in her mother's voice only once before. That was the morning Jennifer was in her room getting ready to leave for her college classes, her greatest concern being a test on Shakespeare's *King Lear*. She'd just finished trying to tame her naturally curly, long, brown hair, which she disliked almost as much as she disliked the sprinkling of freckles across her nose.

"Useless," she muttered, her green eyes flashing as she laid her brush on the dresser. "You'll just have to look like a bush." She sighed, threw the strap of her purse over her shoulder, and picked up her stack of books. She was midway down the hallway when her mother walked past.

"Breakfast is ready, Hon. Your dad must have fallen back asleep." She continued down the hallway and opened the bedroom door. The way her mother said, "Jim?" as if asking a question, made goosebumps form on Jennifer's arms. Her dad had a weak heart. Already, he'd lived longer than the doctors had anticipated.

Irene shouted his name louder. "Jim! Jim, wake up! Jennifer, call 9-1-1!"

Jennifer dropped her books and ran for the telephone in the kitchen, mechanically obeying her mother's orders, but as a defense against reality, her mind remained blank. She refused to believe what might have happened. She scarcely breathed until she heard the sirens down in the valley, then rising higher and higher, bouncing from one mountain to another, echoing louder and louder. Jennifer rushed out the French doors and onto the back deck, gesturing for the medics as if that would make them faster. She kept telling herself, *This can't be happening. I don't want to be here. Let me awaken from this dream.*

She had awakened into the nightmare of reality when her dad was taken out on a stretcher.

In the days that followed, Jennifer had learned just how much she and her mother needed each other. Now, Jennifer heard her mother pleading, "Wake up," once again. And once again, Jennifer's mind was blank, except for the urgent comprehension that her mother needed her.

"Oh, she's waking up!" her mother cried out.

Then the voices started again, the hubbub, the activity, lights in her eyes, pain in her head. She was so sleepy. But she needed to find out who these persons were so she could tell them to leave her alone.

Finally they did, and Jennifer dared peek through her leaden eyelids only to discover a world of pain and confusion accompanied by her mother's continued encouraging pleas for her to awaken.

Was this a dream? Or a nightmare? Vaguely, in her groggy state of mind, there seemed to be ghostly white figures at the bottom of the bed. *Bed?* Her eyes opened wider. Jennifer realized she was lying in a bed, and her mother was sitting in a chair covering Jennifer's right hand with her own and looking concerned.

She must wake up for whatever her mother had to say. Jennifer took in a breath to ask, and the effort sent sharp pains all along her left side. All she could manage was a torturous moan.

"Ohhh," came her agonizing sound, and her gaze fell in the direction of the pain, only to discover an arm with a cast on it, lying across her chest. Slowly, as her eyes adjusted to the light, a realization dawned. She was lying in a bed in a hospital room. Those ghostly figures were medical personnel. Her mother's concern was for. . . Jennifer herself!

"What. . .happened?" Jennifer whispered on a shallow breath.

"Don't you remember, Honey?" her mother asked.

Remember?

What did she remember?

It had something to do with Don. She'd had it on her mind for days. What she had to do had pressed down upon her like a heavy weight, and she knew she wasn't giving her best to her kindergarten children that day—just going through the motions.

Those adorable munchkins, so full of excitement and energy, seemed to drain her while at the same time energizing her. Particularly young Tina, her most promising student, whose delight with life was an inspiration.

"Are you sad, Miss Collins?" Tina had asked at lunchtime when Jennifer hadn't said "Amen" after Tina finished her usual practice of praying aloud. Some of the other children had begun to bow their heads, too, after prompting by Tina, so open about her faith.

Jennifer knew Tina's concern was genuine and that the little girl would detect any fudging on Jennifer's part. "No, I'm not sad," she said. "I just have my mind on something I have to do."

Tina shook her finger at Jennifer, saying staunchly, "You better pray before you eat your lunch or God will take away your smiley face." While other little kindergartners giggled behind their hands, Tina clamped her lips together, trying not to laugh, but her big, blue eyes were dancing in her pretty face surrounded by her dark brown, pageboy hairstyle.

Jennifer couldn't help but laugh. She gave smiley face stickers when children obeyed and did their work well. "I'll pray," she said, then bowed her head and said, "Amen," after a brief pause.

Jennifer admired that sense of humor in Tina. She could jest about the smiley faces, but when Jennifer threatened to take away Tina's sticker if she didn't stop talking, Tina took the reproof seriously. She was never disrespectful.

On the way home from school, Jennifer had thought about God taking away a person's smiley face if they didn't obey. But it wasn't God who took away the smiles. It was human beings, in their troubles or disobedience, who lost their own smiley faces. Jennifer knew what had caused her to be distracted at school. She couldn't put off talking with Don any longer.

Jennifer remembered leaving school shortly after three o'clock. She had called her mom to say she was stopping by Don's office at church before coming home.

She'd stood in the hallway for a long moment before going into the offices. Don's door was open. With a sense of deep respect and heartfelt caring, she watched him intent upon entering something in his computer. Then as she walked near, apprehensive about what she felt compelled to say, his head turned, and his face registered mild surprise.

He saved the material immediately, then greeted her with warmth in his brown eyes that went so well with his blond, flattop hairstyle. He was tall, lean, and extremely fit. How many singles, and her mother, had said, "Any woman would be blessed to get him!"

Jennifer had "gotten" him, so to speak. They'd started dating over a year ago, soon after he came to the church as youth pastor. But a nagging caution had increasingly invaded her heart and mind to the point that she had to say something.

"Didn't expect to see you 'til later," he said. "Have a seat."

Jennifer sat, wondering how to say it. "Don," she blurted out, "I'm not going on the hiking trip with you and the youth tomorrow. I'm just not into it."

Don propped his arms on the desk. His expression turned serious. "You're not obligated, Jen."

"I know. But it seems we've sort of taken for granted that I go on most of these trips. Oh, don't get me wrong. I've enjoyed every one. That's not it."

"I understand," he said. "This is my calling, not yours."

She nodded. *But shouldn't it be? If Don and I are meant for each other?* "And, I really don't feel like going out tonight. I know we always do on Fridays." That, too, had been taken for granted. Every Friday evening, with rare exceptions, they had dinner together, then decided if they'd see a movie, a video, meet friends, or just talk.

"Are you coming down with something, Jen?" he asked, concerned.

"No," she said, "although the sniffles are running rampant in my class. It's not that." *Boredom* was the word that popped into her mind. How was that possible? Don was the life of any party, able to relate to young and old alike. He had a winning smile and a wonderful personality. Maybe she *was* coming down with something—like insanity!

She smiled faintly when Don said, "We've taken a lot for granted, haven't we, Jen?" When she didn't answer, he added, "Or at least I have." He took a deep breath and glanced toward the ceiling as if asking for divine help. "I was going to say something tonight, but I'll go ahead. Maybe we should, as the kids say, 'cool it' for awhile. Step back and take a long look at where we're going."

Jennifer felt her mouth fall open and promptly shut it. She was shocked! She'd come to tell Don she thought they should do that very thing, but it was Don who was telling her. She was a little upset he'd beaten her to the punch. But now she wouldn't have to hurt his feelings, after all. She didn't have to try and explain something she didn't quite understand herself.

Lest he see her relief and mistake it for joy, she quickly stood and turned toward the doorway, rubbing her still-gloved hands together. "I think you're right, Don. I really do."

"Jen," he said, standing. "Let's talk about this. I mean, I'm not saying we shouldn't see each other at all. I don't mean we shouldn't go out. I. . ."

Jennifer turned to face him. "We don't have to discuss it, Don. You said it, and I agree." She spread her hands. "That's it. I mean, if you want to see me, call. I'll do the same. Okay?"

This was one of the few times she'd ever seen a worried wrinkle cross his brow. He bit on his lip. "I'm probably being a fool," he said.

"No, Don," she said softly, "you're a wonderful man." She quickly left and hurried out into the February chill, alive with winter's bite.

Driving along the main road, she felt like a great burden had lifted from her shoulders. She hoped that she and Don could remain friends, without any regrets. Just as she neared her turn, leading up the mountain to her home. . . yes, she'd been going home and. . . Why couldn't she remember going home?

Life after that was a blank—except for waking up in a hospital room.

"Was there an accident?" she asked.

"Yes, dear," her mother said. "Another vehicle collided with your car."

Comprehension began to penetrate. "Mom," Jennifer whispered, feeling a greater concern than her physical pain. Despite her parched throat, she managed to swallow before asking, "Was anyone else. . .hurt?"

Chapter 2

*I*t's my fault! The thought stabbed at Don's conscience after he answered the phone in his apartment. Irene Collins said Jennifer was all right, but her car was hit by a truck on her way home. "She's in the hospital."

"What—who—?" he stammered. "But she's all right, you said?"

"She's awake now. She has a knot on her head, a broken arm, and several cracked ribs. But yes, she's going to be fine."

Don's free hand swept over his flattop as if trying to sweep away his feelings of guilt and concern. "I'll be right there," he said when Irene confirmed that Jennifer was at Mission Hospital.

"Wait, Don!" Irene added. "I've not called anybody but the pastor and you. Would you call Ashley for me?"

Ashley? Don's eyes squeezed shut. Ashley was Jennifer's best friend. "Sure, Irene. I'll call her."

Waiting for Ashley to answer, Don breathed a prayer. *God, forgive me for what I've done. You sent my way the finest woman a man could want. I turned her away. But not because of her, Lord. You know it was because of my own errant thoughts.*

"Ashley," Don said when she answered on the third ring. "Don here."

"Don?" He heard the surprise in her voice. She knew—everyone knew—that Friday night was reserved for him and Jennifer unless they planned a group outing. "There's been an accident," he said. "Jennifer's in the hospital." He told her what little he knew.

Thank you, Don breathed inwardly when Ashley said she would drop her daughter, Tina, off at a friend's house and go straight to the hospital. He couldn't bear picking her up, then bringing her home later. The farther away from Ashley he stayed, the better off he would be. He mustn't be so fickle as to break up with one woman, then turn right around and keep another woman on his mind.

Ashley was Jennifer's best friend. But he couldn't honestly have made a commitment to Jennifer when he had become increasingly aware of Ashley. Ever since the youth Christmas pageant, when Ashley had been so dedicated and enthusiastic, he'd begun to picture her in his mind, her smile, her joy at growing in the faith, her devotion to her daughter, her brave front although her boyfriend, Leo, had been transferred to another state and said his good-byes.

He remembered thinking, even saying, "How could a man in his right mind, who had a chance with Ashley, abandon her so easily?"

On the twenty-minute drive to the hospital, a similar thought struck hard at his heart. How could any man, in his right mind, pull away from a remarkable woman like Jennifer?

He'd sprung that "cool it" line on her about as casually as Leo had picked up and left for California. *But I wasn't breaking up. Was I? What was I doing? What was I thinking?*

What was Jennifer thinking when she had the accident? Was she crying and unable to concentrate on traffic? Had she been speeding and lost control? Or. . .had someone else caused the accident?

It just occurred to him then. Had the accident injured anyone else besides Jennifer? *Just how much is going to be on my conscience?* Don Ramsey wondered.

❧

Rick Jenkins built a fire in the fireplace, plugged in a pot of coffee to perk, then took a long, hot shower and pulled on a pair of sweats. It wasn't until he poured the coffee that he realized his hands were shaking so badly the coffee sloshed over the edges of the mug. He knew the tremors had nothing to do with having been out in the low-thirties temperature most of the day. Being a volunteer fireman with search-and-rescue certification as well as a tree surgeon who cut dead limbs, trimmed branches beneath power lines, felled entire trees, or cut up already fallen trees around homes or in entire forests, he was accustomed to working outside in sleet, snow, ice, and cold rain.

He went into the living room. Ignoring the blazing fire, he walked to the French doors and looked past his deck, out at the tops of leafless trees and beyond the forest of pines. Creeping dusk began to turn the doors into mirrors, but he didn't see the reflection of a muscular man with still-damp, dark curls, holding a cup with both hands as if it might escape. He didn't see troubled, deep blue eyes. Instead, he saw shadowy images of the past. Quickly, he attributed that to treetops being shaken by the wind.

Turning from the scene, he walked over to a chair and slumped into it. His coffee had turned cold, and he set it aside. Staring at the fire that was burning low, he reminded himself that as a volunteer with search and rescue, he was conditioned to accidents.

He'd seen the same thing hundreds of times: Somebody runs a stop sign. An accident happens. The injured are taken to a hospital. The police question witnesses and make out an accident report. The perpetrator, if not drinking or drunk, is charged with a misdemeanor, is given a traffic ticket, and is free to leave and may go about his business as if nothing happened. Later, he'd be summoned to court, where he'd plead guilty and pay the cost of the ticket.

Rick had never thought that was punishment enough. It wasn't fair.

But his obligation was to attend to the injured parties, not worry about the fairness of life. He'd learned the hard way that the word "fair" might as well be taken out of the dictionary. He'd never learned to be hardened against seeing a twisted, pain-ridden body or a suffering child or a person struggling to hold onto a thin thread of life. But he'd become conditioned to it, like a doctor who has to ignore the horror and concentrate on providing the best and quickest care possible.

Rick tried telling himself that tonight's accident was minor compared to some he'd seen. But this one kept nagging. Instead of getting a call to an accident, he'd been the first one there. He'd seen the accident happen. He could see it now—the heavy, white, four-wheel-drive truck sunk into the driver's side of the small, blue car.

He'd been the one to call 9-1-1, then jump out of his vehicle and run around to the passenger side of the car and open the door. The girl's head had been slumped forward against the steering wheel and her hair had been soaking up a trickle of blood. Her neck hadn't been broken and her seat belt had kept her from being thrown around too much. Her pulse rate appeared normal under the circumstances. She was alive, breathing, but he felt that he hadn't breathed until he heard the sirens.

He knew the routine, but instead of being a participant, he yielded to being an observer. He watched as the medics checked the girl, laid her on a stretcher, put her in an ambulance, and drove away with the siren blaring. The police questioned, made out a report, wrote a ticket, and moved the truck out of the middle of the street. There was only a minor dent in the bumper and a few scratches imbedded with dark blue paint.

The wrecker towed away the little, blue car with its crushed door. Rick stood staring for a long time at the scene that had vanished before his eyes. If he hadn't been there, he wouldn't suspect an accident had just occurred. He got into his vehicle and drove up the mountain.

Now, Rick stared at the ashes in the fireplace, then the darkness shrouding his glass doors and windows. His stomach grumbled that he hadn't had any food since around noon—not even a cup of coffee.

He took his cup to the kitchen sink, poured out the now cold liquid, and unplugged the coffeepot. He had no appetite. He'd try to get some sleep.

Several hours later, without having slept, Rick got up and walked across the hardwood floors and onto the cold kitchen tile in his bare feet and switched on the light. He called the hospital and asked about the condition of the girl whose name he'd heard when the police officer checked her identification.

"This is Rick Jenkins with the fire department. I wonder if you could tell me the condition of Jennifer Collins, brought in earlier."

"Oh, hi, Rick," said Becky, who apparently recognized his name. "Just a sec." A moment later she came back on the line. "She's listed in fair condition. That's all I can tell you."

"That's fine. Thanks. Thanks a lot."

He held the receiver for a long moment. What good would it do to go or call and say he was sorry? None! It would just give the girl a name and a face to resent, even hate. He didn't need that. He returned the receiver to its cradle.

Maybe he should eat something—at least have a glass of milk. But first he walked over to the table and picked up the traffic ticket he'd laid on the table earlier. He stared at it long and hard with one thought ringing in his mind: *The one who caused the accident may go about his business as if nothing ever happened.*

Chapter 3

"I t was three weeks ago today that my arm was broken, Mom," Jennifer reminded her mother during breakfast on Friday morning. "It's healing, and I can use my fingers if I need to."

"Not very well, Jennifer. And I just don't feel good about leaving you," her mother protested.

"I think you're just afraid of leading that seminar on literacy," Jennifer accused, with a knowing grin on her face.

"Well, I am a little anxious about speaking to hundreds of people coming from all over the Southeast," Irene confessed. "But it's such a wonderful opportunity to help others understand the need for this. I'm just going to have to remember to be Christ-conscious and not self-conscious."

"That's the spirit, Mom. And you'll do a great job." Jennifer was proud of her mother, a social worker who'd started a literacy program in her church. She helped other churches do the same and now had an invitation to speak to a women's conference about the program and how others could be involved. "Just go, and don't worry about me."

"There's a winter storm coming," Irene reminded her. The morning newscast included a forecast of an imminent winter storm set to hit the mountains of western North Carolina.

"We've had winter storms before," Jennifer said, appreciating her mother's concern, but tiring of this overprotectiveness. "Anyway, I'm a grown woman. How many other twenty-six year olds even live with their mothers?"

"All of them who have only one good arm with a storm coming, I would hope," Irene replied defensively. "I'm just thinking of your welfare."

"I know that, Mom. But how many people have been to see me since my accident?"

Irene patted the side of her short, permed, dark hair that was sprinkled with a little gray, a habit Jennifer recognized as a defensive measure. "A few," she replied.

They both laughed while Jennifer named them. "Pastor Robbins, Mary Robbins, Don, Ashley, Tina, a half-dozen singles, your friend Jan. . ."

"Okay. So I'm a worrywart," her mother said. "It's just that you've had a rough time, and you're just not able to do ordinary things with only one hand

and cracked ribs. I mean, you've even complained about something as simple as brushing your teeth and. . ."

"Mom," Jennifer interrupted. "I wasn't complaining. I was just stating facts. Actually, I was being grateful that I had two good hands and will again. It just made me realize how much I take for granted."

Her mother sighed and looked out beyond the back deck. "If it wasn't for the storm, I wouldn't worry."

"We've had storms before," Jennifer reminded her mother. "Anyway, it's not like this is January or February. This is the middle of March. We've already had some warm weather. The jonquils are out in all their yellow splendor. So are the forsythia. Look at that line of bushes out there just bursting with yellow blossoms."

Her mother looked and nodded. "It's snowed on the forsythia before."

Jennifer shrugged. "So, it's no big deal. Anyway, Mom, the conference is how far from here? Eight. . .ten miles? You could crawl home to me if you had to."

Irene's eyebrows lifted. "I haven't crawled in several decades. I'd better take my knee pads with me."

Jennifer shook her head at her mom. "Thanks for caring, Mom. But everybody at church knows you're going away for the weekend. Somebody from the singles' group will visit me every day. You've let our neighbors know I'll be alone, and they've promised to keep an eye out for things around here. The church people said to call if I need them. I can always call the pastor or dial 9-1-1. After all," she added, "I still have the use of my legs, my right arm, and my mental faculties."

Irene spread her hands. "Superwoman! My baby doesn't need me anymore."

Jennifer turned her head to look out the window at the wintry landscape beneath a leaden sky and hummed a little ditty absently, as if her mother were right. Then she grinned at her. "I'll always need you, Mom."

"Hmmph," Irene scoffed. "If you listen to me, then get on that phone and make up with Don."

"Mom," Jennifer scolded. They'd been over the situation repeatedly since Jennifer came home from the hospital and told her mother she and Don weren't going steady anymore. She'd tell her once again. "Don and I have the same relationship we've had all along. There's just something. . .missing."

Irene touched her temple with her index finger, indicating she knew what was missing—perhaps a few marbles upstairs. "Well," she finally conceded, "I do believe he's spent more time with you and called more often since you broke up. Maybe you're smarter than I think. Before long he'll be coming around with a ring for that finger."

"Thanks for the compliment, Mom," Jennifer said. Suddenly Irene realized she'd implied that her daughter was a little bit on the dense side. They grinned at each other.

That afternoon, after hugging her mom, wishing her well during the weekend conference, and saying she'd see her Sunday night, Jennifer looked forward to spending the weekend alone, where she could lie around, read, and prepare for returning to class on Monday. Three weeks away from those kindergartners was way too much. The substitute had even brought the class to see her last week as a field trip, and they'd all written their names on a huge card that they'd drawn and colored.

When the phone rang shortly after five, Jennifer looked at it skeptically, expecting the call to be from her mother. However, it was Ashley, who was ready to leave the insurance company where she worked as secretary. She offered to pick up supper for the two of them.

❧

Twenty minutes later, Ashley ground her little, red car to a halt beneath the deck and ascended the back steps. Jennifer had the door open.

"Whoa! It's getting colder. The wind's picked up," Ashley said, putting the fast-food bag on the table. She took off her red scarf and shook out the thick, dark hair that surrounded her pretty, round face. Her cheeks were stained with color from the cold wind. But she was so pretty. Her eyes had an excited, expectant glow to them.

"You didn't bring Tina?" Jennifer asked, looking toward the deck before closing the back door.

"Mama took her to her piano lesson so I could come and see you. But I know you'd rather see her than me," Ashley accused playfully.

"Not so," Jennifer denied. "But that little girl has stolen my heart."

"It's mutual," Ashley said. She put the fast-food bag and some papers on the countertop, then shucked out of her heavy coat and laid it across the countertop that separated the kitchen from the family room. She took off her gloves and walked over to the woodstove, holding out her hands to warm them. "Tina wanted you to see her week's worth of papers. And she made you a card."

"Another one?" Jennifer laughed as she looked at the papers. "All A's."

"She had a B but didn't want to send that one. Don't tell her I said that."

"Never," Jennifer replied, her heart softening as she thought of the little girl who had folded a piece of paper and drew a big smiley face with curly hair, a halo, and wings behind it. She had printed the words "To my favorite teacher" above and below the picture. On the inside she'd printed "Come back to school soon. I love you. Tina."

Jennifer bit on her lip. "Oh, this is so sweet."

"Humph!" Ashley said, going over to the food bag. "You didn't say that about the card I sent you."

"You sent me a card?" Jennifer asked, as if she didn't remember.

"If your arm wasn't broken," Ashley threatened, "I'd break it."

Jennifer got the paper plates out of the cupboard and put the sandwiches and fries on them while Ashley poured two glasses of orange juice. Ashley took the plates in to the coffee table in front of the couch near the stove, then went back for the drinks.

After the blessing, Jennifer laughed at Ashley's grimace while watching her try, with one hand, to get a sandwich to her mouth without the insides falling to the plate.

"You still haven't found out who ran into you, Jen?" Ashley asked.

"I haven't tried. And I didn't see anything in the paper about it. That week there was so much news about the national situation and the awful school shooting. That took precedence over my broken arm and cracked ribs."

"And the person didn't even apologize or anything, right?"

"That's right," Jennifer said.

"Don't you want to know who it was?" Ashley asked, astonished.

Jennifer shrugged. "What's in a name, Ashley? Somebody said a man in a truck ran into me. His insurance is paying for everything. My car's still in the repair shop, but I can't drive yet anyway. Maybe the driver thinks that's enough."

"He could at least say he's sorry," Ashley said.

"Now you sound like my mother," Jennifer accused.

Ashley still sounded like her mother when she added, "Don's been running around like a chicken with its head cut off since the accident. I've never seen him so worried about anything."

"He and Mom both have made too much of this, Ashley." Jennifer knew he was blaming himself for her accident. He'd been to see her several times, saying how sorry he was, and it didn't register with him that she was not heartbroken. But she hadn't sent him away. She did not want to lose such a fine man as a friend, and she wasn't even sure but that "everyone" was right when they said she and Don were made for each other.

"Jen!" Ashley said loudly. "You haven't heard a word I said."

"I'm sorry. What did you say?"

"I asked where Don is tonight. The youth didn't have a trip or anything, did they?"

Jennifer and Ashley had been friends since grade school. They'd grown up together. They'd remained close even during the years when Ashley left college after her second year and married Ted. After a year of marriage, she'd given birth to beautiful Tina. Then tragedy struck. Ted was one of five employees killed in the chemical plant explosion where he worked.

The following years had been difficult for Ashley, but her friends and church members had remained faithful. She'd had her parents and in-laws nearby, who gave constant support. Ultimately, Ashley had ceased to grieve for Ted and had become a radiant Christian who was an example to others, particularly singles who'd gone through great difficulties.

Last year, a widower came to the church and joined in the activities. He and Ashley hit it off immediately until suddenly he announced he was being transferred to another state. Ashley seemed disappointed, but she'd said, and meant, "Apparently God didn't intend for him to be a part of my life and Tina's."

Ashley had always been open with Jennifer and vice versa. Jennifer had hedged, however, about her relationship with Don because she had needed to get it straight in her own mind. She wondered if she had just gotten cold feet about possible marriage because she'd seen so many fail at it. She knew relationships couldn't stand still. They had to move forward or deteriorate.

"Hel-lo-o," Ashley was saying. "Anybody home?"

Jennifer laughed. "I'm sorry. My mind drifted. What were you saying?"

"I asked about Don. You know, your fiancé."

"We're not engaged, Ashley."

"Don't you think it's about time?" Ashley asked.

"If we're headed in that direction, yes," Jennifer admitted. "You know I've had doubts about me and Don. Maybe I'm just not ready for marriage."

"What are you waiting for, Girl?" Ashley blasted, seeming more concerned about it than Jennifer. "You'll never find anyone better than Don."

Jennifer could agree with that. "I know," she said.

"Where is Don tonight?"

"He and the youth are stocking the food closet at church in case the storm does hit. There are always stranded people when that happens." She glanced at the clock. "It's after six. Let's listen to the weather report."

Jennifer punched the remote buttons while Ashley cleaned up from their supper. The weather report was the same. A winter storm was on the way. Possibly several inches of snow. It was expected to be the worst one of the entire winter. High winds were expected, too.

"I'd better get home," Ashley said. "I need to stop by the store in case I get snowed in for a couple of days." She slipped into her coat.

"Tell Tina 'thank you' and that I love her."

"Sure will," Ashley said and hugged Jennifer. "You take care now. Call me if you need anything. And of course I'll call you." She opened the door and jumped back when the wind rushed in, almost knocking her off balance. "Whoa! That wind's getting colder and stronger. And look at that sky. Looks like a sea of lumpy gravy."

Jennifer looked at the sky with a smile. Leave it to Ashley to come up with an expression like that. "Right," Jennifer said. "It looks like any gravy I'd ever make."

Jennifer was still smiling when she closed the door, then glanced around at the cozy room, anticipating spending the weekend alone. She pushed aside a twinge of guilt because one of the reasons she was so looking forward to this weekend was that it wouldn't be spent with Don.

Chapter 4

S udden shrieking bleeps penetrated Jennifer's deep sleep, and her eyes popped open as the odor of smoke awakened her. Howling winds outside seemed to be rocking the house. A quick glance at the windows revealed wind-whipped snow and ice battering the windows.

The storm! A fire! What a combination, especially for a one-armed woman.

Jumping out of bed as best she could, Jennifer switched on a lamp, dispelling the dim shadows made by a nightlight in her bathroom. Her next instinct was to call 9-1-1. However, she saw no smoke, and the alarm was sounding from the kitchen rather than in the hallway near her bedroom. From past experiences of having burned food and needing only to fan the alarm with a newspaper to stop its beeping, her mind rejected the probability that the house was on fire. Maybe she'd left the woodstove door open and sparks had blown out. As she neared the family room, the odor of smoke was more concentrated.

When she switched on the light in the family room, she saw puffs of smoke coming out from around the stove door. The fierce wind was apparently blowing down the chimney. The backdraft stirred the embers, causing them to smoke. She'd put several logs in the stove and closed the damper to keep the family room warm during the night and so she wouldn't have to build a fire in the morning.

Jennifer didn't know what to do about the puffs of smoke. They were only intermittent. She opened the draft, hoping that would help. At least the wood would burn faster. The flames leapt around the logs immediately and the puffs stopped. She was afraid to open the stove door lest a puff of wind would come down and spray flames out into the room.

Grabbing a newspaper, she hurried to the alarm and began fanning. She looked at the kitchen window over the sink, but the wind and snow blew so fiercely against it, she feared she wouldn't be able to close it once it was opened. She might not even be able to open it with only one hand and could even strain her already cracked ribs.

The alarm was driving her crazy, so she finally pulled a dining room chair into the kitchen beneath the alarm. With the newspaper beneath her cast, she carefully pulled herself up and switched the alarm off, then fanned as vigorously as she could. She got down and turned on the hood fan over the cooking stove, then returned to the family room and turned that fan on. Maybe she should turn up the register on the furnace. That would be a good idea anyway, since the strong wind might whip the electric lines down. However, she'd better check out the basement first, just to make sure there wasn't a fire anywhere.

If the lights were going to go out, Jennifer knew they'd do it while she was in the basement. She got the flashlight, just in case, and checked out the basement where the furnace stood along a back wall. All was fine in the downstairs guest bedroom, bathroom, and laundry room, but it sounded like the wind might break through the windows and doors at any minute.

Jennifer returned to the upstairs hallway and turned up the thermostat on the furnace. She repeated the ritual of climbing up on the chair and turned the fire alarm back on. It didn't begin blasting. Apparently all was well, except she wouldn't be able to bask by a cozy woodstove until the wind died down, but she'd better stay awake and watch it until the logs burned. She lay on the couch, watching the wind whip the flames several times, causing a vigorous, bright orange glow. However, only a couple of intermittent puffs of smoke escaped from around the door. Finally, the fire burned down to a layer of ashes, brightly glowing when the wind blew down the chimney.

Checking the clock, she discovered the time was 4:00 A.M. Wearily, she trudged back to bed, hoping to fall asleep again despite the feeling the house might be picked up by the wind and sail out over the mountaintops any minute. She fell asleep praying and was awakened suddenly by another mind-boggling sound. *Not again! Please.*

Then she realized it was the phone. The digital clock was blinking at 12:00, so she had no idea what time it might be but had a good idea who the caller was. Sure enough, it was her mother.

"Jennifer, have you been listening to the TV?"

"No, Mom. I've been sleeping."

"Well, that's good. How is it up on the mountain?" Before Jennifer could answer, her mother gave the weather report. "They're saying that anywhere from eighteen to twenty-four inches of snow has fallen and more is on the way. Do you still have power?"

Jennifer decided against telling her mom about the fire alarm fiasco. "I haven't blown away, and I still have power. I'm lying here in bed, snug as a bug in a rug."

"Oh, good." Her mother's voice was full of relief. "The conference center has power. And of course they have generators here, so they can still operate and cook meals even if the power goes off."

"So can I, Mom. I have my woodstove, you know." She wouldn't dare mention that it would be impossible to use it if the high winds remained. The conference center was tucked away against a mountainside, surrounded by other mountains on all sides. It was made of stone and wouldn't feel the effects of high wind like a wooden house on the side of a mountain.

"People are being told to stay where they are, Jennifer. Only emergency vehicles are to be out."

"Good, Mom. Then you stay right there and enjoy the conference. Don't worry about me."

"Right!" her mother answered, and they both laughed. Jennifer had asked the impossible.

❧

"Oh, my goodness!" exclaimed the trim, well-dressed, middle-aged woman behind the conference center's registration desk. She'd finished a conversation with the night clerk at about the same time Irene finished her conversation with Jennifer.

"Is something wrong?" Irene ventured to ask.

"Well," the woman said with her brown eyes wide and a grin on her perfectly made-up face surrounded by curly copper-colored hair. "It looks like I'm going to have to run this place for awhile."

"Oh, are you the manager?" Irene asked.

"Not officially. My name's JoBetty. This man's my husband, Willy. He works the night shift. He just told me that the manager called and can't even get out of her house. She lives way up on the mountain, so that's no surprise. Then the assistant manager called and said she can't find her car."

JoBetty laughed. "That might be an exaggeration. But from what Willy's been telling me, that's a doozy out there. Oops, 'scuse me."

She answered the ringing phone. "Oh, that's a shame," she said. "Have you thought about putting an aspirin on it?" She hung up and shook her head. "Can you believe that? The bellboy said he can't come in because he has a toothache. I told him to put an aspirin on it, and he said he thinks it's his root canal. I mean, the storm would be a better excuse than that."

Irene smiled at this colorful woman, dressed in a kelly green skirt and matching sweater with long, gold beads tied in a knot and matching balls of gold on her earlobes.

"You must live near here," Irene said, "to be able to get to work."

"Oh, I spent the night. I knew if a storm hit overnight, Willy would have to drive home this morning, pick me up, and bring me back, so I just came last night and spent the night. The cooks do that when snow is predicted.

364

Most of them live down the mountain in Old Fort and Marion. They'd never be able to get up that mountain in a storm like this. Well, Willy, I'd better go see how breakfast is going."

"I'll be right here," he said, running his hand through his gray hair and looking like he could fall asleep any minute."

"Can I do anything to help?" Irene asked.

JoBetty shrugged. "I won't refuse an offer of help. And you guys will be out of luck if you depend on me to cook. I can't boil water without burning it."

"That's the truth," Willy said, perking up. "She burned the bottom out of a pot of water she put on to boil one time."

JoBetty and Willy grinned at each other. "Just a minute," he said when the phone rang again. She waited until Willy hung up. He chuckled. "That was a dining room worker. Said she has a flat tire and can't get to work."

JoBetty looked at the ceiling. "All she'd have to do is look outside or turn the TV on, and she wouldn't have to make up that excuse."

Irene liked JoBetty on sight. She was certainly an interesting person. As they walked across the lobby toward the dining room, Irene noticed her green heels, at least three or four inches high. "You look nice," Irene said, "but are you going to work in the kitchen with those high heels on?"

"Oh, I couldn't begin to wear flats when conferees are here. I know some of them do, but it's just not me. That is, unless I'm doing my aerobics or have been standing behind the desk a long time checking people in. Then I might put on a pair of almost-flats."

After JoBetty and Irene walked into the kitchen, it didn't take more than a few minutes for them to get the impression that the cooks didn't want a desk clerk interfering with their expertise. Silverware, plates, and cups at the drink stations had been put out last night. "We'll cook the meals," said the head cook to JoBetty. "You can organize cleanup after they eat."

"Well, I guess we know who's boss," JoBetty said after they left the kitchen. "Guess I'll just do my aerobics while they're cooking. I'll eat and organize clean-up, then Willy can go get some sleep while I sit at the desk."

Irene walked over to a group of conferees whose name tags helped with identification. When she told them about workers not being able to get in, they all immediately offered to help.

"I'm sure JoBetty would appreciate that," Irene said. "That's her."

They all looked as JoBetty, now in tennis shoes and her lovely green outfit, jogged around the registration section and trotted up the stone steps.

Phyllis, one of the literacy conferees, looked longingly toward those steps. "So that's how she keeps her trim figure. Maybe I should try it."

"Me, too," agreed several others as they turned toward the TV, listening to the continuous weather report and waiting for breakfast.

Irene and the others knew by now that Phyllis had a greater reason than most for being concerned about the storm. Home alone, in a wheelchair, with spina bifida, able to do little for herself, was her invalid daughter, Sue.

Knowing other calls would be forthcoming, Jennifer didn't even try to go back to sleep. She might as well get dressed.

Dressed? She glanced ruefully at her cast. Each day she'd asked for her mom's help with hooks, buttons, and other fasteners. Well, her mom wasn't here. She'd just have to be innovative.

After twenty minutes of tugging, pulling, squirming, and turning her good arm and wrist in odd positions, she finally had managed to get some clothes on. An oversized shirt with wide sleeves slipped over her cast with minimal difficulty, and Jennifer discovered she was much better at single-handed buttoning than she would have guessed. She zipped up her jeans, but putting the button through the hole at the waist was almost impossible. After several determined attempts, she finally succeeded. Getting into socks and tennis shoes wasn't too difficult, but tying the laces was out! She pulled them taut and shoved them under the tongues. Not exactly comfortable, but better than tripping over them.

Count your blessings, her mind chided. *Oh yes!* she thought. *I can dress and do my aerobics exercise at the same time. Lucky me!*

After three weeks without the use of her left arm, she'd gotten the hang of one-handed tooth brushing, face washing, and even brushing out her curly hair that hung almost to her shoulders.

Walking into the family room, she became aware that the furnace was running constantly. She stopped suddenly when a howling rush of wind tried to tear the roof off the house and caused the walls to tremble. She walked past the kitchen countertop and across the family room to the drapes and drew them apart.

Wow! This is incredible. Jennifer stood with her mouth open. For a long while the wind whipped and swirled ice and snow against the French doors, and she could see them give as if the force might even break them. Between gusts, she saw that the deck was piled up with snow, and near the steps against the wall was a drift higher than her head. On some sections of the bannister lay at least two feet of snow. And the snow was not falling—it was pouring like white rain!

A whirlwind of snow swirled like a tornado she'd seen on TV. But this was a white one. Not only small limbs blew into a frenzy; huge trunks were swaying. Suddenly the top of a stately pine snapped, flew through the air, caught for a moment in the arms of an oak, then sploshed to the ground, making a huge impression in the snow, quickly being covered by more falling snow and blowing drifts.

Jennifer laid her right arm over her cast, in a hugging gesture, realizing the danger. Giant trees bordered their house. She'd just witnessed the fact that a wind like that could send a tree right through her roof. Or take the roof off. Or perhaps even push the house down the mountainside. It certainly seemed to be trying to—with all its strength.

Maybe the TV would give some insight on when all this was going to end. Leaving the drapes open in order to view the unbelievable sight, she picked up the remote from the coffee table in front of the couch and clicked on the TV to the local channel.

"A horrible situation," the reporter was saying. "This blizzard is being called the storm of the century. Front after front is piled on top of each other, and we have no idea how long it's going to last."

❧

Jennifer wasn't surprised to hear Don's voice when she answered the portable phone beside the couch. He'd been extremely attentive since the accident, as if he himself were responsible for it. She'd begun to wonder if he regretted saying they should cool it for awhile. When she had her strength back, she'd have a long talk with him.

"Yes, I'm fine, Don. Electricity's on. Furnace is going. Mom made sure I have everything I need to last me for a couple of months with minimal effort on my part. How are things in the valley?"

"It's like a whiteout, Jen. Several of the teens and I, along with the volunteer cooks, spent the night here when the forecast of a blizzard became imminent. Several regulars have called and said they can't get out. The Red Cross and National Guard have started bringing in additional cots and blankets."

Jennifer knew the church was set up as a shelter for emergency needs. She'd been there alongside Don many times, serving Thanksgiving meals to the homeless and travelers on their way to other areas. She'd loved helping at Christmastime. That seemed like the best way to celebrate the birth of Jesus.

"I'll keep checking on you, Jen," Don said with the kind of concern she'd heard in her mother's voice.

"Thanks, but I'm fine."

"It's not over, Jen," he said, and Jennifer caught her breath. The way he said it made her think he wasn't just talking about the storm. His distress over her accident drew her thoughts back to the status of their relationship. Should she pretend the relationship was on hold? Should they make a clean break, or had they just needed to take a step back and assess the relationship? She hadn't had a chance to think it over. Don was smothering her. Ashley was questioning. Her mom was reprimanding, and Jennifer had been dealing with pain and with concern about her kindergarten class and preschool choir at church. She needed peace and solitude for awhile. But now, it appeared that perhaps even God and nature were upset with her.

"Take care," she said.

"You do that," Don commanded gently. "You know how important you are to all of us, Jen."

When she didn't reply immediately, he added, "Just a minute. Somebody else wants to talk to you."

It was Ashley, who said, "You haven't blown away yet?"

Jennifer laughed. "I might any minute. But what's your problem? You sound nervous."

"Nervous, nothing. I'm freezing to death. Tina and I spent the night at Mom and Dad's so we could walk down here this morning. It took us twenty minutes and half a dozen falls before I got here, and once I was nearly blown away. Honest, I had to hug a tree with Tina sandwiched between us when one big gust came, and I was afraid we'd be buried alive in a snowdrift."

Exaggeration was an asset of Ashley's, but considering the news reports and howling outside, Jennifer thought she might be giving an accurate depiction of the storm.

"How's Tina?"

"Oh, she thinks it's a trip! Don's getting her out of her snow clothes and going to fill her up with hot chocolate. Uh oh. Another load of people have been brought in. I'd better go. I know you always do this, so I thought I'd take your place this time."

"So you're saying I'm responsible for your nearly freezing to death," Jennifer said.

"Right, so hurry up and get well enough to take your rightful place beside Don."

Ah, so that's it, Jennifer was thinking. Ashley was one of Don's greatest admirers and often said he and Jennifer were made for each other. She didn't seem to accept that they had broken up. No doubt she wanted to pump Don for information concerning any problem between them.

After talking with Ashley, Jennifer called a couple of neighbors and discovered they, too, still had their power and were fine. She turned up the TV again.

"The interstate is impassable," the reporter was saying. "People are waking up to a monstrous winter storm." Pictures flashed on of trucks and tractor-trailers blocking the interstate. "Stay off the roads," he instructed. "It's treacherous. Stranded motorists are leaving cars in the middle of the road. State and local crews are pushing the snow off major roads as much as possible, but it just keeps snowing. They can't get to secondary roads. Trees are down all over."

The reports gave Jennifer an urge for something other than cold milk on cereal. While she fixed herself a scrambled egg, hash brown potatoes, and coffee, the reports continued. More than twenty thousand people were without power in four counties, including her own. A substation transformer was down and would take four to five hours to repair. "Trees are down all over. Please, please stay off the streets," he pled. "Even with four-wheel-drive, it's virtually impossible to get around."

When it happened, Jennifer was sitting at the countertop eating breakfast, keeping an eye on both the TV and the French doors, wondering what she'd do if the roof blew off. Suddenly, the TV gulped and the screen turned black. The rumble of the furnace stopped. The hum of the refrigerator ceased. The room fell into eerie shadows. Jennifer became aware of the absence of household sounds. She sat stunned for a moment, listening to the ominous wind trying to destroy the house. What would she do if the roof blew off? If she and the house swirled off somewhere over the rainbow, would she be as fortunate as Dorothy in *The Wizard of Oz* and be returned? A glance at the doors, however, revealed there was no rainbow in sight.

Bother! So much for spending a relaxing, quiet Saturday alone.

Chapter 5

C hildren are taught that they can be whatever they imagine they can be," Irene said near the end of her last literacy large-group session before lunch. "But imagination and reading go hand in hand," she concluded, adding with emphasis, "and it all begins with reading."

One hundred thirty-two conferees, almost a hundred of them women, applauded enthusiastically. Irene smiled as she closed her notebook and said they were dismissed for lunch. She felt good about the conference. But she knew she couldn't be credited with all its apparent success.

These conferees had a heart for helping children. And the storm, stranding them together in this lovely conference center, brought them all closer. They were separated from loved ones, so they turned their attention to each other and the needs at hand, pitching in to do anything—clearing dining-room tables, washing dishes, sweeping floors, or answering the telephone when JoBetty had to act like a bellperson and deliver a message to a room, unlock a closet for extra toilet tissue since the housekeepers couldn't get in, or check on things in the kitchen.

"Volunteers! Volunteers!" JoBetty shouted as the literacy group came up the stairs and gathered in the vast carpeted lobby to sit facing the TV or take their turn at the telephone, checking on family members.

Several reached the desk immediately. "I have to check out some rooms to make sure they're clean before I put anybody in there," JoBetty said. "I just got word that a house burned down up on the mountain. The fire trucks couldn't get close enough to put the fire out. Can you imagine, a house burning in all this snow and ice?"

Irene couldn't.

"But, the people got out and managed to get down to the fire trucks. We're the closest facility to them, so the man, woman, and two teenagers will stay here." She grinned. "Far be it from me to say 'There's no room at the inn!' So, I need to make sure the rooms are clean."

"I'll help you," said one woman, and another said, "Count me in."

"We're not following rules anymore," JoBetty said. "Normally you'd be asked to use the phones in your rooms. But," she struck a pose, "since I'm in charge, I say everybody for themselves. Take your turns using the phone

370

ght here at the desk."

Irene waited her turn. She could read the expressions as one after another
sed the phone. A smile and a cheerful voice indicated all was well. They all
new the lines could go dead at any second.

"Oh, I'm so glad you answered, Jennifer," Irene gushed when her daugh-
er answered the phone. "I'll have to be brief. There's a long line waiting to
se the phone."

She turned and smiled at the line behind her as she listened to Jennifer's
aying the electricity was off, but she'd be fine. Irene closed her eyes for a
noment while Jennifer talked optimistically. That was typical of her. But the
irl apparently didn't realize the danger. While standing in line, Irene had heard
he reporter on TV saying they hadn't seen the worst of the storm. There was
aore to come. Winds were going to pick up. Temperatures were steadily falling.

"Call somebody, Jennifer," Irene advised. "You need to get to the church
helter."

Irene felt herself frown and shook her head when Jennifer protested, say-
ag she'd be fine. If she got cold, she'd snuggle under a pile of blankets.

"Okay, you take care, honey," Irene said. "I love you."

She hung up after hearing Jennifer say she loved her, too. Her lips
lamped together, and she nodded as she walked away from the desk toward
group of women concentrating on the TV.

After the others had their turn at the phone, she'd make another call. If
ennifer wasn't wise enough to get help for herself, then it was up to her
nother to do it!

❦

)on was amazed at the ingeniousness of the stranded people at church. Not
nly did they pitch in and help whenever and wherever needed, but when
hovels just weren't enough to handle the snow and ice, they took metal trash
an lids and took turns out in the storm, shoveling out a pathway for emer-
ency vehicles to get in.

Other people had been arriving all day. They were a thankful bunch,
nowing they couldn't survive long out in that storm. One couple, without
eat or power, covered their shoes and pants with plastic bags and fastened
hem with duct tape to keep from getting wet and having their legs freeze
vhile coming a couple of blocks to the church shelter.

He'd hardly had time to think. Meals were being served all day long and
ewcomers given instruction. The TV was going all day, and he knew that the
oof of a mall had caved in from the heavy snow. Houses were in danger of
he same. Tree limbs, laden with heavy snow, were breaking like fragile glass.

He was just getting ready to start dishing out lunch when he got the

message that Irene had called. She said Jennifer was without power, and h
needed to get her down off the mountain. His conscience began to gnaw
him. If he hadn't broken up with her, she wouldn't have had the accident. Sh
wouldn't have a broken arm and cracked ribs. She wouldn't be stranded u
there on the mountain in the midst of one of the worst storms anyone coul
remember. She'd be here with him, serving alongside him.

Yes, he'd have to get her off the mountain.

But how was he supposed to do that?

"Tom, would you take over for me while I make a phone call?"

"Sure," Tom said and came over as soon as he finished putting ladles i
the bins filled with food.

He felt some relief when Jennifer answered the phone. "Your mom sai
your power is off, Jen."

"Yeah, it has been for a few hours. The house was real warm, though. It
getting a little chilly, but we never run the furnace at night anyway. By tomor
row, the wind will probably have died down, and I can build a fire in th
stove."

"Jen, they don't know when this is going to be over. It's supposed to ge
even worse overnight. Even now there's a windchill of minus sixteen degree
below zero."

"Well, I don't intend to go out," she assured him. "How are you guy
doing?"

"It's been a constant flow of traffic. We don't have any relief, either, bu
the stranded people help as much as they can."

"I'm sure Ashley's a big help," she said.

"Oh yes. And Tina's entertaining all the children. She's taken over as on
of the leaders."

Jennifer laughed lightly at the thought of the little girl. "She's a special one

"Yeah," he said, then his voice filled with concern. "I'd feel a lot better
you were down here, Jen."

Jennifer refused to say she'd had that very thought after the difficult
she'd had striking a match to light a candle with one hand. She'd wanted t
dispel the eerie dim shadows that reminded her of scenes from a movie i
which flickering shadows enhance the mystery and foreshadow the heroine
danger. She'd finally sat on the couch, put the matchbox on the floor, stead
ied it with her foot, bent over, and struck the match. The flame went ou
before she could lift it to the candle. Ingenuity told her to set the candle o
the floor so the match wouldn't have far to travel. Ah, success!

But she wasn't about to share such minor problems with her mother or Do

"Don, I'm a big girl," she reminded him. "My power's off, but I hav everything I need right here. Just take care of those stranded people and don't worry about me."

"I do, Jen. You know that."

Jennifer knew she should appreciate that. But sometimes not only her mother, but Don, too, smothered her. She knew they cared. But she needed to feel like she was in control of her life, not be dependent on others all the time. She didn't want them worrying about her. It put a burden on her for them to be so concerned, as if she couldn't take care of herself. This was beginning to give her a tension headache. She needed to end this conversation.

He shouldn't worry about her. After all, even if she were heartbroken, as he seemed to suspect she was, she would manage. Even if she hadn't wanted to break up with him, she'd survive. It wouldn't be a greater loss than having lost her dad, and she had gotten through that.

She felt right about the breakup. Don said he did, too, but he continued to hang on to her. Well, she supposed she was like a bad habit—hard to break! She closed her eyes against the pain of her headache. She needed to end this conversation.

"Thanks, Don, for calling. I don't have heat, but as soon as the wind dies down, I can build a fire. The house is still warm from the furnace heat. I have blankets all around me, and I'm quite comfortable. I have candles, food, and everything I need."

"Okay. You be sure to call if—"

If what?

"Don? You there?"

Apparently not.

❦

"Jennifer. Jennifer? Hello. Hello. Jennifer?"

No answer.

Her phone was dead. Don punched the hang-up button, got a dial tone, and called her number again. Nothing! Her line was dead. She was up there on the mountain with no heat, no phone, no lights, and the storm worsening. She wouldn't even have a weather report to know how bad it was, and the worst was yet to come.

He slowly replaced the receiver in its cradle. Passing a TV on his way back to the kitchen, he paused for a moment, hearing a reporter whose voice was full of amazement.

"This is absolutely incredible," the reporter was saying. "There are sustained winds of forty-seven miles per hour, gusting to fifty-six miles per hour, and a windchill of minus sixteen. Visibility is so low during the whiteout, you can't see other vehicles. Pine trees have dropped limbs all over the road. Road crews can't get ahead of this vicious storm. Even emergency crews are having difficulties. Four-wheel-drive vehicles are running into each other or ending up in a snowbank."

How will Jennifer ever survive this? Don wondered.

Chapter 6

Rick Jenkins had been out in his four-wheel-drive truck since early morning, after having been awakened by the storm battering his log house on the side of the mountain. He didn't need a call from search and rescue to know he was needed. This was worse than any storm he'd ever seen.

He called his uncle, higher up on the mountain, and discovered he was fine, except for his constant problem of arthritis, which kept him from doing much heavy work. But keeping his uncle supplied with firewood and helping him with a few chores was the least Rick could do after all his uncle had done for him.

Getting up a mountain would probably be impossible, but at least his four-wheel-drive could get a grip on the snow as he wound down around the curves. He dressed in his polypropylene long johns, fleece pants and shirt, and Gore-Tex jacket and pants. These would allow him to survive working in the cold all day. His waterproof boots, fleece hat, and Gore-Tex gloves made him ready to battle the elements.

At one point, he had to saw a limb into movable pieces and use the winch to get it off the road before he could even get down his mountain to the valley. He used his truck phone to contact the fire station to find out where he was most needed with his chain saw and winch. All morning Rick worked with the crew cutting trees off downed power lines. Like the other workers, he'd have to stop occasionally and warm up in his vehicle.

Around eleven o'clock, Rick responded to his beeper. "We've got a tree down on a house. People are trapped inside." The dispatcher gave the address. "Anyone near with a chain saw, please respond."

Rick responded. "I'm a few blocks away, but I think I can make it as soon as I finish clearing this path of tree limbs out of my way."

After arriving at the house, he saw a huge maple imbedded in the roof of the house.

"There's a woman with a heavy limb on her leg, and her husband won't leave her side," a crew member explained.

Rick knew the danger of the couple being exposed for too long to the freezing temperatures and the snow falling through the roof, as well as the possibility of the tree limb cutting off the circulation in the woman's leg.

After more than an hour, the bedroom looked like a woodpile, but the EMTs were able to load the woman onto a stretcher. An ambulance took the couple away. Then came the job of getting the rest of the tree off the roof and covering the gaping hole.

It was midafternoon before Rick had a chance to breathe a sigh of relief. "You had lunch?" the operations chief asked.

"Haven't even thought about it," Rick answered.

"Lot of us are taking turns at the church set up as a shelter," the director said. "There's a stranded couple and child in that car over there. Take them down to the shelter, and you can eat a hot meal."

Rick was quick to take him up on that. The family piled into the cab of his truck. The mother held her little boy on her lap.

After taking about thirty minutes to travel only a few blocks, Rick safely delivered the grateful family to the church fellowship hall. Even as a matter of survival, Rick wasn't sure he could go inside. He hadn't been in church in over seven years. However, a middle-aged man reached out and touched his arm as if to drag him inside. The man's brown eyes were friendly. "Come on in," he welcomed with a genuine smile. "I'm Tom. Some people right over here will give you some dry clothes if you need them," he said to the family, then smiled at Rick. "Plenty of food back there."

Rick removed his fleece hat. "A cup of something hot to drink would be. . ." His words stopped. He mustn't say "heaven." But that might be the closest he'd get to heaven, and he was about to the point of risking anything for survival. "Would be fine," he continued.

"Cocoa or coffee?" the man asked, while another man came to take care of the family.

"Coffee, please," Rick answered.

Tom nodded. "Have a seat. We'll get you fixed up in no time."

Rick surveyed the shelter, telling himself that's what it was—not a church. But he knew what it was. He was no stranger to such scenes, even if it had been a long time ago. Long tables were set up around the room. A TV in a corner. People eating, playing games, children running around.

It's a shelter, he consciously reminded himself and pulled out the nearest chair at the end of a long table and sat. The man brought his coffee. It would be foolish to starve himself when the odor of hot food almost made him dizzy. And as if his feet had a mind of their own, he soon stood behind the family, having food dished up for him on a big plate.

He devoured the hot meal of beef stew with potatoes and carrots, a big dinner roll, and two cups of hot coffee before having to battle the elements again.

"I'm Don Ramsey, youth pastor here," said a voice at his ear, and Rick looked up at the tall man with the blond flattop. He'd noticed Don scurrying around helping people and talking with them, encouraging them.

"Thanks for the meal. It hit the spot."

"I'm glad," Don said with a friendly smile. "We appreciate all you guys are doing."

"Just doing our job," Rick replied a little more shortly than he intended, but Don didn't seem to take offense. After all, he, too, was doing what he considered his job, or was it what he'd call "serving people for the Lord"?

"I have a list here of some people we know are up on the mountains and need help. We can't get through up there anymore by telephone. A pharmacist made it to the drugstore, and the medications are just waiting until someone can pick them up."

Rick nodded as he looked over the list of locations, names, ages, and special needs. Marilyn Hill was a diabetic whose insulin supply was low. John Schneider had a heart condition, and his bottle of lanoxin had run out. Sam and Sue Mott, an elderly couple, both had the flu and needed a prescription taken to them.

Jennifer Collins—Rick blinked at her name on the list. That was the girl he'd crashed into! He drew in a deep breath as Don explained her situation. "She's only twenty-seven but was in an accident a few weeks ago. She has only one good arm, and she's alone way up on a mountain. Her power and phone are out. Please, you've got to check on her. Bring her down here if you can."

Rick saw the dark-haired woman who'd been serving victims of the storm pause when Don was talking about the girl. She stepped over.

"Jennifer only has one good hand," the woman said. "Her mother's at a conference and really worried about Jen."

One good hand kept running through Rick's mind. Just how badly was that girl hurt? Regardless, he was as wary about seeing her as he was about stepping foot into a church. He cleared his throat. "I'll see what the crews can do."

Don nodded. "I know you guys are doing all you can, but. . .could you call and let us know if anybody can go up there?"

Rick looked from him to the dark-haired woman who gave him a faint smile, then poured more coffee into his cup before moving on.

"I'll see that my ops chief gets the list."

"Thanks. Thanks a lot," Don said, looking relieved, as if Rick could perform some kind of miracle. Rick didn't say so, but it was getting harder and harder to move around in the valley. Getting up any mountain was a near impossibility.

He downed his coffee and stood, then found the dark-haired woman in front of him again. "It may seem that Jennifer isn't highest priority, but she was in an auto accident and hurt pretty badly. She's my best friend."

A man he'd heard addressed as Tom had overheard the conversation. "Yes, please. Jennifer is Don's fiancée. He's plenty worried. Please see what you can do."

So that's why Don was so concerned. His fiancée! That girl must be in bad shape. When he'd checked with the hospital, they'd said she was in fair condition. Had other complications set in? But that wasn't his problem. There was nothing he could do.

When he showed the list to his ops chief, the chief questioned Jennifer's being on the list. "The older ones are top priority," he said.

Rick told him about the concern of the youth pastor and the fact that she'd been in an accident. When he added that Don Ramsey was her fiancé, the director shook his head. "I understand his concern, but if the young woman were in bad shape, surely she wouldn't have been left alone up on a mountain with a storm coming. We'll have to put her at the bottom of the list. I don't know if we can get to her at all. New calls are coming in. Real emergencies are taking place. I'll give this to some of the other guys. We need you to get a tree out of the middle of the road up there in front of the elementary school."

After a couple more hours of work, Rick and a couple others had the tree off the road. The ops chief radioed that Rick should call it a day. They could barely see what they were doing. Maybe, in spite of reports to the contrary, tomorrow would be better.

Rick welcomed that message. He was exhausted. He didn't care if his cabin had no power; he just wanted to get out of this frenzied mess of ice and snow.

"By the way," the director said. "It was tough going, but everybody on your list was taken care of except that last girl. She's up higher on the mountain than the others. We just can't chance it. It's on your way home, so if you want to try it, okay. If not, I understand. If you try it, radio us when you get stuck, and we'll come dig you out."

"Thanks a lot," Rick said and gave a short laugh, then realized it was no laughing matter. Accompanying the whiteouts, darkness was setting in. He wondered if he could even find his way home.

∞

Rick didn't think he was going to make it. If he could just get up the mountain, he wouldn't worry about getting back down. A couple of times he had to stop when the wind caused a whiteout. He waited, then used his snowplow so he could travel a few feet farther. Often, the wind dumped a drift right where he'd plowed. Finally, he reached the house and parked in front of a garage door that was located underneath a back deck. He radioed his supervisor. There was a lot of crackling and static. He couldn't make out half the words his supervisor said and figured it was the same on the other end.

"In case I can't get through on the radio or a phone, you might let the church shelter know that I'm at the Collins house. I'll check out the situation and let you know. That is," he added, "if I can get through on the radio or a phone."

Chapter 7

Rick carefully made his way up the steps, holding onto the wooden railing, stepping into two feet of snow on each step in addition to some drifts. Bracing himself against the wind, he slid along the wall until he reached the glass storm doors.

He brushed away ice and flakes from the doors so he could peer in, but the blowing snow kept slapping against it as fast as he could wipe it clean. He cupped his hands around his face to peer inside. He detected a faint glimmer of light, but his breath kept fogging up the door.

He wiped again. Yes, someone was there. But. . .what in the world was going on?

He could see the girl with a cast on her left arm. Then she began a strange movement. What was she doing? Throwing something down and dancing? That reminded him of something he'd seen in old movies of a war dance. Stomp, stomp, throw the head back. Stomp. Stomp. Or was she having some kind of seizure?

Rick kept wiping and peering. He saw her pick up a piece of firewood. She hit something with it. Then suddenly she whacked it across the room. Was she practicing her golf stroke? With one hand? Whatever it was, she wasn't pleased, for she tossed the piece of wood into a box near the stove and stomped over to the couch.

The girl's crazy! Had the wreck done that to her?

The back of the couch was facing the doors, but he got the impression her shoulders were slumped and her head moved from side to side. Then she raised her hand to her forehead. Weird.

He didn't knock for awhile, trying to assess the situation. What would he do with a woman having seizures? He'd had training in some areas, but this seemed to call for a paramedic. Maybe he should radio back to the ops chief.

She was still now, though. Maybe the fit was over. Or maybe she was frightened out of her wits by the storm. Some people panicked in times like this. If he didn't get in out of the cold, he was going to panic himself—or rather freeze to death.

Anyway, he could knock her out if he had to. Take her down in his truck. Get her down to her boyfriend at the church or maybe to a hospital.

He had to chance it. If he stood out there much longer, he'd be the one in need of an ambulance—or worse. He began to pound on the door.

Finally her head turned toward the doors. She jumped up and shrieked.

"Let me in!" he yelled.

She put her hand to her chest for a moment as if she had a heart problem, then rushed to the door, released the latch, and tugged. Nothing happened.

Rick shoved. The door creaked and scraped, and he brushed away ice and snow from the bottom groove and finally managed to open it wide enough to enter.

Swoosh! The wind almost shoved him through the door. The girl jumped back. He knew he must look like the abominable snowman, and the frigid air wouldn't do any favors for a house already without heat.

"Oh, my candle," the girl exclaimed, as the faint light disappeared, leaving behind an almost completely darkened room.

"I'm sorry," he said, shoving the door closed. A blanket of snow fell from his shoulders onto the tile floor. He looked down at the wet mess he'd brought in. He'd have to clean it up before they left. He removed his hat and tucked it into a pocket. "I assume you have matches."

"Oh, yes," she said and laughed lightly as if embarrassed. "I didn't mean to make a fuss. I was just remembering what I had to go through to light it."

"Are your matches nearby? I'll light the candle. After all, I am with SAR. That's the least I can do."

"SAR?" she questioned.

"I'm sorry. That's short for search and rescue. I'm a volunteer fireman with SAR, as well as being a tree surgeon."

"I'm honored," she said. Her laugh was pleasant. Not at all that of an out-of-control girl. He took off his gloves and stuffed them in his pocket and followed her across the shadowed room, over to the end table.

He rubbed his hands together. "I'll have to get some feeling in my fingers first."

"Oh, I can do it. I'm experienced now."

Another ritual? he thought as he watched her brace the box under her cast, manage to open it, take out a match, close it, and set it on the floor. Then she set a candle on the floor. She sat on the couch, put one foot on the box, bent over, struck the match, and lit the candle.

"There," she said, picking up the candle and setting it on the table, as if she'd performed a major feat. Well, he supposed, with one good hand, it *was* a major accomplishment. Still sitting on the couch, she smiled up at him.

He stared for a moment. How pretty she looked in the soft glow of a candle. He resented the line of a song that unbidden ran through his mind. Something about if everyone lit just one little candle, what a bright world this would be.

Bright world? His had been dark for many years. And he had no business, no business whatsoever, even looking upon this pretty lady. He quickly turned his attention to the candle and held his hands over it.

From the corner of his eye he watched her as she retrieved other candles, one at a time, from the coffee table, and as he moved his hands away, she tipped each candle to light it and then set it down to give him more heat for his hands.

"That's all I had out," she said.

"This is plenty," he replied. "I'd better thaw out slowly."

"You're shaking," she said. "How long were you out there?"

"Since before daylight," he said.

"Oh, not so," she retorted. "I would have seen you."

He gave a quick laugh. The sound was startling to his own ears. He didn't laugh often. When he did, what he laughed about usually wasn't all that funny. "You mean how long was I outside your door?"

She nodded.

"A few minutes is too long to be standing out in that," he said.

"Well, at first I thought you were a bear."

His eyebrows lifted. "What changed your mind?"

"It talked," she said simply. "And it's been awhile since I've had any company."

His glance held hers for an instant. Was that cabin fever or a sense of humor? Then an impish glint appeared in her eyes. Maybe she did have cabin fever—or something. Hadn't she ever been told not to be too friendly with strangers? "I should introduce myself," he said. "My name is Rick Jenkins."

In the dim light, he watched for any trace of recognition when he said his name. She showed none. Just extended her hand and said her name.

No, you don't know me, he thought, looking into her trusting eyes with an expression as warm as her small, soft hand in his cold, callused one. *But I know you, Jennifer Collins. You are my victim.*

"You, um, seemed to be having a problem there for awhile," he ventured to say.

She grimaced. "You were watching?"

"Well, yes. I was trying to figure out if you were playing golf, trying to make it rain, or doing some kind of war dance before going into battle."

Jennifer laughed, forgetting her headache. "Oh nothing like that. I was just trying to open my bottle of pain medicine."

"I see," he said. "Well, I have a chain saw in the back of my truck, if that would help."

"I may have to resort to that. But I was so aggravated, I was trying to open it with a stick of wood."

He looked around. "Where is it?"

She shrugged. "In the rough, I think. I should have thrown it out into the storm and let it freeze."

Rick grinned. This was such a funny, yet serious matter. But she needed pain medicine. "I can try and find it," he offered, taking off his gloves and dropping them on the floor in front of the door.

"My hero," she said, putting her good hand against her chest. "That would absolutely save my life."

"Where do I look?"

"Back there in the dark kitchen maybe."

Rick took the candle and walked back toward the kitchen. It wasn't in front of the countertop separating the rooms. He bent and lowered the candle. It was darker behind the counter. There the bottle was, in the middle of the floor. A little, white, innocent-looking thing.

He brought it back to her. "Shall I open it?"

"If possible," she said. "It's childproof."

He pushed the top, twisted, and voila! Open!

"You saved my life," she said, taking note of his yellow outfit. "My knight in shining armor."

"Well, I was just making my usual rounds," he said. "How many?"

"Two," she said. "I'm not even sure I need them now, but since the bottle's open, I'll take them. Just leave the top off in case I need them later. You could bring the candle," she said.

He tried to light the way as they walked toward the kitchen. He held it, watching while she put the tablets on the countertop, turned the faucet on, reached for a glass, filled it, set it down, turned the water off, picked up one tablet, then the water. She set the glass down, picked up the other tablet, and picked up the glass again.

It wasn't a difficult task, but it was interesting to watch what a person had to do to take a pill with only one hand. It took much longer than if she'd had two working hands.

Jennifer sighed and smiled broadly. "There, that's done." Then she sobered. "Do you need some pain medication?"

He did have some aches from all the physical work he'd done that day. But it wasn't enough for him to take her medicine. "I'm fine, thanks," he said.

She laughed. "Well, you looked like you were in pain."

"I was just thinking about the effort it took for you to take the tablets."

She shrugged. "Haven't you heard? Going through struggles builds character."

Not always, came his immediate thought. He frowned, picked up the candle, and headed back toward the family room. "Well, let's see what we have to do to get you down the mountain."

Jennifer stopped short. "What?"

Rick looked around at her. He stared at the look of surprise on her face. Her voice was full of incredulity when she declared, "But I'm not going down the mountain!"

"Sure you are. This is no ordinary storm, Ma'am. You have no power, no phone, and you can't even open your medicine bottle."

"It's open now. I don't need heat and phone. I have food, clothing, and shelter." She laughed wryly. "Are you one of those Boy Scouts who takes the little ol' ladies across the street even when they don't want to go?"

"If it's for their own good. And I don't think I'd have too much trouble picking you up and tossing you in the truck," he said, hoping to get another smile out of her.

"I think you would," she said, but the idea rather appealed to her. He was tall, apparently strong, quite handsome now that his face was thawing out. "Do you really think you can just yank me up and take me down the mountain?"

"I would have," he said, "if I hadn't seen you attack that medicine bottle with a stick of wood. You might get the poker after me."

"I might," she said, but some strange scene played in her head. Her hero would swoop her up in his arms and take her screaming and yelling out the door, down the deck steps, and into his vehicle. Rhett Butler did that sort of thing to Scarlett O'Hara in *Gone With the Wind*. But that was on the Romance Channel. This was reality!

"Let's sit down and talk this over sensibly," she said, in spite of her intriguing thoughts.

"I really don't want to sit in this garb," he said. "You sit, I'll stand."

"Well, you can see I'm fine," she said.

"You don't understand," he began. "This storm is dangerous. You have huge trees all around you. They can come down on your house. It's going to get really cold tonight, and there's no telling when power will be restored. You have no business being up here alone in a cold house."

Jennifer knew he was just doing his job. Was it really that bad? She knew it was. There was just a certain amount of security in being in her own home, even if she was rather incapacitated with only one good hand and ribs that still ached with too much exertion and occasional headaches.

"Maybe you're—"

Her words stopped. She and Rick looked toward the doors at the same time. Something cracked and moved in slow motion toward the deck. "Get down," Rick demanded, and Jennifer fell to the floor as gracefully as she could without breaking more bones. She lay as close as she could get to the front of the couch. Rick got next to her as if to shield her in case the tree came through the roof. During the crunching, cracking, and thudding sounds, Jennifer held her breath, wondering if the tree would come through the roof.

After a moment the movement stopped. He was sure it was a tree limb, snapped from its trunk by the weight of the ice and snow.

Still close to her in his Gore-Tex jacket and pants, he said, "We had a tree fall through the roof of a house this morning. I had to be lowered in a cherry picker so I could cut branches away from a trapped, elderly woman."

"Just what I needed to hear," she said.

"I can really cheer a person up," he said. He laughed uncomfortably, got to his feet, and reached down to help her up. "You all right?"

"I think so," she said, standing. Her cardigan sweater slipped off her left shoulder. She struggled to push the sweater behind her back over to the left side, then slung her right arm across her body, trying to reach it to pull it around her left shoulder.

Rick stepped behind her and placed the sweater over her shoulder. "There," he said. "You did need me after all."

"Oh, I would have gotten it," she said. "But I wouldn't want you to see what shenanigans I'd have to go through to get it. I use a fork."

"A fork!" Spontaneous laughter escaped Rick's throat. The image was funny. She was funny. And cute. Good-natured about her incapacitation. But she wouldn't be if she knew he was the one who had caused her predicament.

She struggled to button the top button so it wouldn't slip off again. Rick watched for a long moment. "Could I. . .help you?" he asked, reluctantly.

He detected a slight hesitation before she shrugged, as if she knew she was pretty much helpless. "Sure. You don't want to have wasted your time coming up here."

He walked over and realized it wasn't as easy as it looked, pushing that little button through a tiny hole with his large, still-cold fingers. But the worst part was that awareness again of standing close to an attractive woman who smelled of fresh fragrance. He couldn't help but compare her with other women he'd known in the past few years. There hadn't been many, and they weren't the kind he wanted to get attached to. And the odor had been too much perfume, too much makeup, too much trying to get and keep a man's attention. This girl was different. He sensed it. He knew it. Yes, her fiancé was a pastor. This was the kind of girl that Rick Jenkins didn't want to be around.

He was determined to get that button in, even if he had to cut the buttonhole. "There," he said, "I think that'll do it."

"Thanks," she said and stepped back.

He should leave now. She'd be fine. She would know enough to put a stack of blankets on her bed. His glance moved to the stove. Wood, kindling, paper, and matches were nearby. "Obviously, you know better than to build a fire in this wind."

Jennifer nodded. She told him about the early-morning scare from the smoke.

"Are you sure you won't go down the mountain with me?"

"Honest," she replied. "I feel much more apprehensive about going out in that storm than I do staying here."

Frankly, Rick felt the same. He relented. "I think you're resilient enough to survive a night of freezing temperatures, even if you have to climb into a closet and bury yourself in blankets," he said.

"Oh, yes," she said confidently. "Or I could bundle up in a corner or under the kitchen table and surround myself with candles."

"And you know better than to fall asleep with candles surrounding you."

Nodding, Jennifer replied, "I think the shivers will keep me from falling asleep."

No doubt! Rick was thinking. Unless she got so cold she began to feel numb and warm. But she was young. One couldn't expect to weather a storm like this without a bit of inconvenience.

"Why don't you put one of those candles on the floor in front of the couch so the wind won't blow it out when I open the door," he advised. While she did so, he decided against his wet facemask but pulled on his gloves and pulled the hood over his head.

Jennifer came near him. "Have you been checking on everybody on the mountain?"

"Nope. This was kind of special. I delivered some people to the church shelter, and your fiancé asked me to check on you."

"Ex-fiancé," she mumbled, then sighed. "Oh, Rick. I'm sorry you had to ome way up here for nothing. But thanks anyway."

"You're entirely welcome," he said and stood for a moment, thinking that as the least he could do, after having incapacitated her. But there was no oint in saying so. Instead, he put his hand on the door handle. "I'll get word the shelter that you're fine."

Jennifer moved back as he squeezed through the doorway, opening it as ttle as possible. The wind roared around him, but this time, although the andle flickered, it remained lighted.

Rick felt the frenzied icy wind on his face the moment he stepped out nto the deck. Part of the deck railing was missing where the tree limb had pparently knocked it off as it fell.

He knew that going down the mountain would be much easier than oming up. It wasn't likely he could slide off the road. There were enough ees and banks of snow on the sides of the road where he'd scraped to get p the mountain.

He turned sideways, walking along the wall for support and guessing here to put his feet on the steps, careful to hold tightly to the railing on the ght side of them. He couldn't see more than two feet in front of him due to 1e falling snow and the wind whipping up what had already fallen. At least e knew his truck was only a few feet away from the steps. He bent his head 1to the blowing snow, trying to shield his face as best he could. He reached here his truck was supposed to be but instead ran smack into a nightmare.

It wasn't a limb that had fallen earlier, but a tree! The tree missed the ouse except for the deck railing. However, the front of his truck was sus-ended in air, snow underneath it and the wheels high in the air, as if it were ome kind of giant monster about to pounce. Rick couldn't believe it. ̌autiously, he moved forward several feet. Then he saw the culprit. The top f a giant pine had snapped and fallen smack onto the bed of his truck, mashing it into the ground and raising the front end. It looked like he had everal hours' work cut out for him.

Try as he might, Rick could not get to the bed of his truck. He climbed mong the branches, knowing he could easily fall and not be able to get him-elf out of the tangle of limbs. With the huge, heavy pine on the truck that ʌay, there was no way the truck could come out of it unscathed. He couldn't et to his chain saw. His face was freezing. His limbs became so cold he could eel himself growing numb. He tried climbing onto the tree but kept sliding ff because of wind and ice. If he had a ladder he might be able to climb up nd open the door long enough to call the rescue squad for himself. But a lad-er couldn't stand in this wind. *And neither can I,* he admitted to himself when he was suddenly blown back against the carport door. He wasn't nearly as stu-dy as a pine tree, and look what the wind had done to that.

He had only one alternative to freezing to death.

He'd have to spend the night here at the home of Jennifer Collins.

Chapter 8

With effort, Rick made his way back to the glass doors, hoping Jennifer hadn't locked the door and settled herself in a back closet somewhere. He'd be sunk if she had!

When he pulled on the door, however, he found she hadn't locked it behind him. He shoved it open and stumbled in, bringing ice, snow, and wind with him. Her candles went out again. He closed the door.

He'd been almost blinded by the glare of white; now he was blinded by darkness. "I have a pine tree on the bed of my truck, and there's not a thing I can do about it tonight," he said, nearly exhausted. "I can't even call emergency crews." While he went through the same hat, gloves, and pocket routine as before, she went through her ritual of relighting the candles.

He walked over to help. "I'm sorry," he said, hearing the weariness in his voice.

"It's okay," she said pleasantly. "I've decided to switch to hurricane lamps anyway."

He was too tired to laugh. "I mean, I'm going to have to stay here overnight." Would she be distressed about that? He held his painfully cold fingers over the candles and glanced at her.

A grin was on her face, and she looked very much like she might laugh. How could this girl be so cheerful when he was becoming more aggravated by the moment?

While warming his hands, he reprimanded himself. Why hadn't he minded his own business and gone home after work instead of coming up the mountain? He should have done what he'd done the day of the accident—stayed out of her life!

Now, he had no option. "Well," he said, "looks like we're stuck here. Mind if I borrow a corner?"

Jennifer looked up at him and smiled. "It's the least I can do after my tree fell on your truck. By the way, have you had supper?"

"Nothing since this afternoon," he replied.

Jennifer rose from the couch. "I'll see what I can scrounge up for us to eat."

"I came up here to rescue you," Rick said with a trace of irony. "Now, you're taking care of me. What a twist of fate."

Jennifer stood still, the candlelight reflecting from her face. "I don't believe in luck or fate," she said.

Rick nodded. He knew exactly what that meant. She was or had been the fiancée of a pastor. Rick knew about people like that. He knew how they believed. That God was in control—that He had the whole world in His hands, that all was well.

Not so!

Or at least, if it was so, then God could be very, very cruel.

Her voice interrupted his thoughts. "I've heard suffering produces perseverance."

Without thinking, he finished the verse of Scripture, hearing the weariness in his voice as he concluded, "And perseverance produces character."

His own words startled him. He hadn't opened a Bible in more than seven years. Now he was quoting it—giving the impression he was something he wasn't? But he'd already done that by not telling her he was responsible for her accident. What was another deception?

Upon further thought, however, he decided that maybe it was best if she thought he knew Scripture. After all, they were going to be stranded up here in this house together, all night long.

⁂

Jennifer surprised herself with the surge of happiness that swept over her when Rick indicated he couldn't leave. But of course, she would want company when all the world was blocked out. He was her hero. Strangely, she felt like this was better than spending the weekend with a cozy fire and a good romance novel. Instead, she was spending a weekend with a real, live hero. And to top it off—he knew Scripture. And that verse was not one that everybody went around quoting.

She believed everything happened for a reason to the redeemed who walked closely with the Lord. Or at least, some good came from everything. She couldn't imagine that this rescue worker was stranded here with her by coincidence. Perhaps God had brought him, knowing she would freeze to death otherwise. She knew that people who lived high on the mountain were accustomed to being snowed in for days at a time and were prepared for it. However, with a storm like this, with entire counties and even states covered with ice and snow, it could be weeks before they thawed out. If the wind died down enough that she could build a fire, she'd be fine. But suppose it didn't.

Thank You, Lord, for sending Rick Jenkins to rescue me.

⁂

If you must be stranded alone on a desert island, Jennifer was thinking, *or on top of a mountain, then it doesn't hurt if your companion is good-looking.* And Rick was. She already knew he was helpful. While she took food from the refrigerator, he cleaned up the icy mess in front of the French doors, drew the drapes to further block the icy wind, and then went to the bathroom to clean off his outer suit that had pine needles and resin stuck to it.

When he returned to the family room, his irritation about his truck seemed to have disappeared. She knew people looked better in candlelight and wondered how she looked to him. He looked terrific to her. If she'd imagined a real, live hero, she couldn't have done any better. The shadowed contours of his face revealed a very handsome man. Actually, he was tall and handsome with dark hair falling over his forehead and dark, brooding eyes like the hero in the romance novel she'd been trying to read. She'd rather have the real thing any day than just read about him in a book. Of course he was in great shape from his line of work, doing physical activity every day.

As if knowing she was giving him the once-over, he cleared his throat and walked into the kitchen with his candle. He set it down. His hand brushed hers as he took the knife from her and began slicing the roast beef.

She laid pieces of bread on paper plates, sneaking glances at Rick helping in the kitchen by candlelight. *I always thought I was a realist,* Jennifer told herself. But there was definitely something romantic about a man taking care of her like this. No, she didn't think she'd freeze to death without him. She might get mighty cold, but that was a far cry from freezing. After all, didn't Eskimos survive in igloos made of ice?

But there was something comforting in having a man ask how old the roast beef was, telling her about survival, saying they should eat the meat first and save peanut butter in case the power wasn't restored for days.

She remembered how she'd felt a slight exasperation with her mother for unnecessary instructions, reminding her where the candles were in case of a power outage. Her mom had even printed out the phone number at the conference center in large script and left it by the phone in case she was needed. All those instructions from her mother had been excessive.

But Jennifer didn't find Rick's explanations and plans for survival at all excessive. Maybe the difference was that her mother tended to hold onto her a little too closely since her dad had died. They both needed each other. Her mom needed to "mother" her. Had even talked about how nice it would be when Jennifer and Don married and gave her some grandchildren.

But the last thing Don Ramsey needed in his life was a woman with a thought running through her head like, *If you were stranded on a desert island, what or who would you take with you?* She could think of only one answer: Rick Jenkins! She almost giggled out loud. This handsome, muscular man with secrets in his eyes would know how to cut trees, make them a little hut, and make her skirt from palm leaves or tall grasses. Maybe her mother was right! That wreck had addled her brain.

Neither said anything for awhile. She just stood there watching him make sandwiches in a room growing dimmer by the moment except right by the candle. She did not want to disturb the silence. She could hear her heartbeat, his breathing, any inflection in the voice. Awareness was magnified.

"I've never realized before how noisy this world is," she said softly.

She could hear the storm, could feel the strength of the wind pressing against the windows, pushing on the house, whistling across the roof, invading the chimney. But she felt safe. Without Rick here, she would have worried. Even with her mother, they would both have tried to be brave for each other. But this seemed special, here with Rick. It was as if she knew him. Maybe it was just that she wanted to know him.

Rick was helpful, gentle, kind, but distant at the same time. Of course, as a rescue worker, he'd need to be objective no matter what the plight of those he rescued. There seemed to be apprehension in his eyes. That, too, was natural. Hadn't he mentioned the irony of his being a rescue worker, and yet he was stranded and, in a way, she was rescuing him. The tree could have fallen while he was still in the truck, and he'd have been in a storm without a shelter.

Should she ask anything personal? He had been strictly impersonal, even though doing personal things for her. Of course she should ask. Why did she hesitate? It would be colder than the storm of her not to ask. And she needed to know if she should not be concentrating on his physical appeal, being tall, dark, and handsome. He even had the dark brooding eyes of a romance hero. And he wasn't too much older than she, if at all. Yes, she wanted to know if he was off limits.

For the first time in over a year, she could entertain the idea of another man without feeling as if she were betraying Don. That was a good feeling—like freedom—and she enjoyed it. Particularly since Don had been the one to question their relationship.

"I'm sorry if this takes you away from your family," she said, as he put a slice of bread on top of the roast beef, lettuce, and tomato sandwich.

Jennifer wondered about his hesitancy. She saw his uncomfortable glance before he focused on the sandwich he began to cut into quarters for her. She grinned inwardly that he cut them in squares instead of triangles like she or her mother would do. But he apparently wasn't accustomed to cutting his sandwiches. He left his own intact.

"We'd better drink the milk and save the juice," he said. "The juice will last for awhile, but the milk won't if the power isn't restored soon. If we put it outside, it'll freeze." With the aid of a candle and her instructions, he took two glasses from the cupboard and poured them full of milk. "You'll be warmer over there in the easy chair," he said. "Sit down, and I'll bring your food."

"Now this is what I call service!" Jennifer quipped, but avoided saying, "Service with a smile." He apparently wasn't a smiler. And obviously, he wasn't going to answer her question about a family. She hopped down from the stool and got her glass of milk. She'd let him handle the paper plate with a sandwich on it.

"Just a minute," he said when she reached the chair. He took her milk and set it next to a candle on a table beside the chair. "Let me put this around you," he said, taking the afghan from the couch where she'd sat earlier.

Jennifer stood still. From behind her, he draped the afghan around her shoulders.

"Okay, sit in the easy chair," he instructed, so Jennifer did. He moved another end table in front of her, then got her paper plate and set it on the table. He then placed several candles around her and her food.

He got his own food and sat on the couch. As he started to pick up his sandwich, Jennifer said, "Let's pray."

She bowed her head and closed her eyes. "Dear Lord," she prayed. "Thank You that we have all we need. That we have food, clothing, and shelter. Watch over those stranded out in the storm and give a special blessing to the workers out trying to help people and restore power. Thank You for Rick's risking his life for me. Bless him, Lord, and keep us safe in Your care. Amen."

Rick didn't close his eyes. He sat in the dim shadows, watching Jennifer surrounded by softly glowing candles as she prayed. It didn't really matter what she said. He knew it made her feel good to go through the ritual. He'd been there. . .done that! But those days seemed light years away. And he knew she wouldn't be so quick to ask blessings and thank the Lord for him if she knew he was the one responsible for her being stranded up here during a storm instead of down in the valley, helping others alongside the man who apparently considered her his fiancée. Yes, he knew her type. And it saddened him. He wouldn't mind existing in that oblivious state of unreality when he'd thought God was on His throne and all was right with the world.

Never again. Those innocent, trusting days were gone forever.

He realized he was scowling at his sandwich when Jennifer said, "We have more candles."

"I'm okay," he said. "We may need them later."

A piece of tomato fell from her small piece of sandwich onto the plate. He held his sandwich with both hands, aware of how easily one could take for granted their own arms, hands, and fingers.

There was no sound but the howling of the wind and the creaking of a house being pushed first one way, then another, as if the wind were looking for a weakness or a crack to invade. Somehow that's how he felt. But just as the house was keeping the wind at bay, he could keep at bay any invasion of his privacy. She could ask, she could look soft and warm and lovely, but he'd keep emotion at bay. He'd done it for years. He was a master at it. So he could say as little or as much as he wished. He could at least be courteous enough to answer the question she'd asked earlier about family. He could tell as much truth as he wanted, without laying out his personal misgivings like so much garbage to trip over.

It would be morning before anyone could come and rescue him and his truck. He'd have to make the best of it. He might as well be cordial—or had he forgotten how to be that, too? Would they sit around, shivering, all night long, with nothing but the wind to accompany them?

Rick felt the swallowing of that bite of sandwich was loud enough for her to hear. His glance revealed she didn't notice, but she retrieved the piece of tomato that had fallen from her sandwich onto her plate.

She laughed. "Hmmm. Kinda messy, I am," she said. "And I tell my kindergartners not to lick their fingers but wipe them on a napkin."

"Oh, I'm sorry, I should have gotten napkins for us."

"Don't bother," she said. "The kindergartners aren't here to see." She launched into tales about the little children, their adorable antics, and how they could try one's patience. He laughed with her. In the back of his mind, however, he couldn't help but think about the flip side of such precious children. He'd seen many who had been in car wrecks or for no apparent reason had stopped breathing. EMTs weren't always able to help.

After awhile they grew quiet, and he wondered if she'd picked up on his unpleasant thoughts. He didn't want her to feel anxiety by tuning in on his personality quirks. He took a swallow of milk, realizing he hadn't talked about his family other than his uncle in several years. Now that he thought about it, he hadn't had a decent conversation with a woman in several years except to comment on the trees she wanted cut or to try and reassure someone on the way to the hospital.

"I live near Highway 9," Rick began. "My uncle has a couple hundred acres out there that he got real cheap because it's remote. He lives in an old house he had built when he came back from Vietnam with a leg missing below the knee."

Rick inhaled deeply. He didn't need to tell gory details, even if she did seem interested. But what else was there to be interested in, besides the howling wind? He wasn't very entertaining. "Anyway," he said. "He sold several acres to me some years back, and I built myself a little, two-bedroom log cabin back in the woods near a trout stream. I can look off my deck and see mountaintops spread out for miles and miles."

"Oh, you must enjoy that," Jennifer said.

Rick responded with a grunt of sorts, since he'd just filled his mouth again with a bite of sandwich. Enjoy? Not really. He'd cleared his land where he wanted a house, near a trout stream where he could find a little peace while fishing, and he'd lived in a trailer up there for awhile, then had his own log house built. He'd hoped to find some peace in his solitude. All he'd found was solitude. He didn't enjoy much of anything, frankly.

He saw that Jennifer, having finished her sandwich and milk, pulled the afghan closer around her. He didn't want to tell her that this was only the beginning. It was going to get much, much colder before the night ended. "You want a piece of that chocolate cake I saw in the refrigerator before I start putting the food out on the deck?"

"Yep. And some more milk, please."

He carried a couple candles into the darkened kitchen section, returned for their paper products and threw them into the trash can, and then cut them both a piece of cake.

He stood for a moment, looking at the back of the chair where she sat. *How is a cold-hearted man like me going to keep Miss Jennifer warm during this treacherous night? How can I warm her, when there is no warmth in me? It is she who glows in the candlelight. It is her hair that shines with a halo of light. It is her eyes that express warmth. It is her smile and her laughter that exude a ray of sunshine in a dim world. She has light in her soul. Her heart is alive, while mine simply beats.*

Her vitality only reminded him of his lack. He did not want to be near a woman like her. Lest she feel his stare and feel uncomfortable, he returned to the couch, aware of how the cold temperature was fast invading the house.

After eating a piece of cake, he felt it was time to get the food out of the freezer and onto the deck. When he returned to the couch, he tried to make casual small talk. "Did you say that was, or was not, your fiancé I met down at the church?" He was surprised when she didn't answer immediately but sighed deeply, then looked past him toward the closed drapes over the French doors that continuously rattled in the wind. She pulled the afghan closer, holding it to her chest with her right hand.

"Ex-boyfriend," she said with a sense of finality.

Did she think he was being too personal? Or was there a reason she was as reluctant to talk about him as he was to talk about his family?

Chapter 9

Around 6:45 P.M. everything went pitch black!

Don and Ashley were momentarily frozen in the church food closet.

Ashley told herself she and Don were not holding hands. She was grasping the box of spaghetti noodles he'd handed down while standing on a ladder. Their hands touched. *That did not blow the fuses!* She blushed as the errant thought flitted through her mind.

She had an uncanny sense of humor. But it wasn't funny. Not at all. Those thoughts that she tried desperately not to have seemed to linger on her brain. Like a disease that she didn't know how to cure.

It couldn't have lasted more than a second. Their hands did not linger. Both were startled by the sudden blackout, that's all. Or maybe it was only she. Of course Don wouldn't let go of the box in the dark. Until recently, Don had belonged to her best friend. She'd thought he and Jennifer were meant for each other. Why, oh why, didn't Jennifer marry him and get it over with? Then Ashley could be a maid of honor, Don would belong to Jennifer under God's law as well as man's law, and that would put an end to her foolishness.

After that split second of darkness, the generator clicked in and the lights came on, only slightly dimmer.

Ashley left the closet with the box and took it to the cook. "Mom," she heard, as Tina came near, followed by her new friends, five-year-old tow-headed twin girls who'd become stranded with their parents on the way to spend time with their grandparents in Georgia. "We're finished. Can we watch movies now?"

"Did you throw your plates and cups away?" Ashley asked.

"Yes, ma'am," Tina said.

"We did, too," the twins said in unison.

Ashley looked at her watch. "It's almost seven o'clock. Don will announce the movie in a little while. We want to give all the children time to finish supper before starting the movie. Then Cassie will take you up there."

"Okay," Tina said in her usual bright, excited way. She turned to her friends. "Come on. Let's go see Cassie."

Ashley knew it was useless to try and sit down. There'd just be something or someone demanding her attention, and she'd have to get up. She stood to one side of the kitchen, trying to finish her supper and trying to settle her mind.

She thought of her husband, his death, and Leo. She understood her fascination with Don. He was wonderful. Ashley had been married, had a child, had learned in the singles' group not to look for a man to make her happy, to satisfy her needs, to support her. She had to learn to be independent and think of a mate only as a companion that God would choose for her if he had someone in mind for her. She had to learn to live without a man.

Then why did she have this obsession about Don? It wasn't until Leo left without making a commitment that she began to see Don in a different light. He was a single man whom she came to admire more and more until it seemed to get out of hand. She would find herself thinking of him, wanting to be near him.

She'd reminded herself that Don was not for her. He belonged to her best friend. She'd prayed about it, but the feelings hadn't left. She'd begged God to take her back to the place where she could think of Don as just a friend.

She'd thought Jennifer was perfect for him. Jen was the decent, dedicated Christian that Don needed in his life. More importantly, the Lord had brought them together. And now that Jennifer was having second thoughts, Ashley's own thoughts were even stronger. But Jennifer would probably change her mind and realize just how perfect Don was for her.

Maybe this was the kind of "thorn in the flesh" that the apostle Paul had written about in the Scriptures. And he had also written that there was no temptation that was not common to man. He also said no one would be tempted beyond what they could bear.

Tempted? No, the temptation was not a physical thing, although Don was certainly attractive. Tempted to want the kind of physical closeness she and her husband had, yes. But she'd known many men who were attractive. There was something else that drew her to Don. His dedication to the Lord. His commitment. His selflessness. His giving spirit. But that was not all. The senior pastor had all those qualities, and so did just about every male church member. But she did not love them.

Love? No! No, no! She must not have those thoughts. Oh, God, please, take this from me.

❧

Don couldn't see a way out of his situation. Even if he and Jennifer didn't get back together, how would it look to link up with Ashley? Assuming she'd be interested! It would look as if he'd dumped Jennifer for Ashley, and that would appear as cold and callous as when Leo had dumped Ashley.

I've gone out of my way to avoid Ashley without being conspicuous was in the back of Don's mind while he continued to dish out food and welcome and instruct newcomers that the crews brought in. But with her standing near him, the awareness was there. In fact, it had begun to be there even when she wasn't near.

How could this have happened? Don wondered. His relationship with Jennifer had grown to the point that he'd considered giving her a ring for Christmas. But something had held him back. Almost from the moment that Ashley's boyfriend had left, Don's feelings toward her had changed, or maybe they just came to the surface. Why?

Had he gotten cold feet about the possibility of marriage? His parents had divorced when he was fourteen, and suddenly he'd had a weekend dad for a few years. Fortunately, his mom grew close to the Lord after that, and he'd wanted to make up for the difficult time she'd had making ends meet. He'd come through the difficulties. His mom and dad had been Christians but not strong in that area. Don had gone to church enough and heard his grandparents talk enough that he knew he needed God in his life. At age seventeen at a church summer camp, he quit running from his situation, quit resenting his dad, quit rebelling against God, and made an adult decision to accept Jesus into his heart and life as his Lord and Savior.

He knew immediately where the Lord could use him—with young people. He knew what it was like to be from a broken home. He knew the insecurity and self-consciousness of not having a dad in the household. He knew the Lord could see them through it and make their life meaningful.

Was that the cause of this unwanted affinity with Ashley? Was he drawn to her because she reminded him of his mother's situation of raising a child without a man in the house? Did he simply admire her because Tina was such a well-adjusted, special little girl? Or did he feel the way he did about that little girl because she was Ashley's child?

There were other singles in the church in almost the identical situation as Ashley. And he'd talked with them, helped them, listened to their troubles, cared about them and their children. But there was never anything personal about it except a deep caring and friendship. The feeling for Ashley was different. It gnawed at him. He tried to ignore it, deny it, dismiss it. But there in the closet when their hands had touched, his heart had leaped.

He'd held Jennifer's hand in his many times. He had enfolded her in his arms, and he had kissed her. His admiration and respect for her had grown. Jennifer had become his closest, dearest friend. And shouldn't married couples be friends? But what about this attraction that drew him to Ashley?

Ashley wasn't prettier or smarter or more dedicated to the Lord than Jennifer. She'd been married, and she had a child. That could be a point of contention to some congregations.

What was he thinking? A point of contention? The only way it would even come up would be if he married her. Was he like his dad? Just couldn't stay with the woman he'd made a commitment to and went off to what he thought were greener pastures? *Oh, God,* he prayed. *Straighten out my confused mind.*

Even as he considered his feeling coming from the wrong motives, Don knew that was not the case. Sure, he was aware of an attractive woman when he saw one. He was aware of his own human emotions that he had to deal with. But he didn't want to do anything to be out of God's will or cause Ashley any difficulty. He wanted to. . .what?

"Hey, no sleeping on the job," said a male voice behind Don.

Don became aware that he was holding the spaghetti sauce ladle but that no one was coming through the line. Everyone had eaten supper except himself and a few workers. He looked around to find Tom Taylor grinning. The older man put his hand on Don's shoulder. "You'd better make your announcements, then eat and get some sleep. With the electricity apparently off in this area now, we'll probably have people coming in all night, or at least in the morning, looking for a warm spot."

"Thanks," Don said, grateful that Tom thought his absentmindedness was due to fatigue. He was tired, but his job as a youth pastor required the ability to act like the Eveready Energizer Bunny—go, go, go! There was no such thing as a youth pastor having an eight-hour, five-day-a-week job.

Seeing that it was almost seven, Don stepped to the mike, thankful that the generator could keep most electrical equipment and appliances in the church going. "Could I have your attention, please?"

He welcomed everybody who turned their attention from the round-the-clock weather news on the TV. He told them where the trash cans were located for their paper materials and asked for help in taking down the tables so cots could be set out. He asked that families with children remain in the fellowship hall for sleeping and that singles and couples without children sleep in the sanctuary on the padded pews or on the carpeted floor.

Those who wished could watch the weather report in the fellowship hall. A Billy Graham film would be shown in the sanctuary. Young people could play games or watch TV in the youth department. He introduced the young people and adults who would be available to supervise children who would like to watch some biblical videos. In a side room off the fellowship hall a TV would show some young children's videos. Parents were welcome at all activities, of course. The library was open for those who would like to get books for themselves or their children.

Around eight-thirty, popcorn, cookies, and soft drinks would be available.

After his announcements, one of the stranded guests came to the mike and made a beautiful speech of appreciation for all Don and the church workers were doing. The people applauded. Don nodded, feeling awkward about the praise.

"I'm sure each of you would do the same if this occurred in your hometown," he said into the mike. The group began to clean off their tables and fold the legs beneath them.

Don looked around, and his eyes focused on Ashley. She glanced up from the dishwater where she was washing one of the big serving bins. He had to have some reason for staring at her. He walked over. "Have you heard any more about Jennifer?"

"Don, if a message came, I'm sure somebody would get it to you." He thought there were tears in her eyes when she asked helplessly, "What do you expect me to do?"

She turned from him and set the bin on the counter, but not before he saw the hurt in her eyes, the fatigue on her face. She'd been busy since early this morning. She'd had people to look after besides her very active little daughter. He wanted to console her but could only stand there, miserable.

He saw the trembling of her lips before she brushed by him, saying, "I have to check on Tina."

Don watched her hurry away. He wanted to say it was his fault. He kept pushing the Jennifer issue, as if he had to hammer into both their minds that he and Jennifer had been dating steadily for a year and four months. The natural progression of things was to get engaged, then marry.

Lord, I'm not handling my personal situations well. I'm not sure what's going on with me. Do I have a roving eye? My callousness in telling Jennifer we should cool it had to affect her. It's my fault she wasn't attentive enough to avoid that accident. I hurt her, Lord. And now my words and attitude are hurting Ashley. Should I. . .leave this church and this position?

❦

Irene felt guilty because she hadn't even thought of Jennifer during supper. The meals were fabulous, the noble spirit of everyone being up a creek without a paddle bonded them like family, and JoBetty was an ever ready source of entertainment.

"You may have noticed I'm wearing my beads around my waist," JoBetty announced to Irene's table when she delivered a message to one of the women. "I know you get sick of seeing me all day long looking like a cucumber, so I made this little change. See, I fastened it with a rubber band and let this little part hang down."

She began to twirl the hanging part and swung her hips from side to side like she was doing the hula. She put one hand to the side of her head and droned, "I guess I could pull an Elizabeth Taylor and take down a curtain and wrap it around me."

JoBetty stopped swinging, and her big brown eyes widened. "She did that once, you know. Her luggage was lost or something, and she took down a drape from the hotel room."

They all laughed. "You could get away with it," one of the women said and grinned.

"Well," she said. "Let me run and compliment the cooks so they know I remember they're really in charge here." She lifted her eyes to the ceiling, shook her head, then traipsed across the floor in her high-heeled shoes.

By now, they had the cleaning up routine down to an art. The tables were cleared and washed, dish carts loaded and taken to the kitchen, floor swept, salt, pepper, and sugar containers filled, drink stations set up, plates and silverware set out for morning.

By 8:00 P.M., JoBetty was behind the desk, manning the phone and taking care of any needs that arose. Several of the women began to gather in front of the fireplace that they were afraid to light because of the high winds. Some gathered around the TV to watch more of the same report that had gone on all day, only to hear that conditions were worsening. Over two hundred thousand people were without power in the four nearby counties. Snow and wind increased, and temperatures continued to fall.

Irene was concerned that no one from the church had called. She knew they were busy and expected Jennifer to be fine; nevertheless, she wanted to hear. Her heart went out to Phyllis Johnson, however, who had tried all day to get in touch with her eighteen-year-old daughter who had spina bifida and was home alone.

Phyllis walked over to the group after trying to make a call. She shook her head, worried. "Still no answer," she said, taking a seat. "All circuits are busy. Reports are that lines are down all over Atlanta."

Phyllis had already told them that her daughter, Sue, was in a wheelchair. Irene reminded herself that Jennifer only had a cast on her arm and her ribs were bound. But Jennifer was self-reliant and had everything she needed within reaching distance. "Let's have a prayer for all the stranded victims," Irene said, "and a special prayer for Sue."

After the prayer that Sue would be safe and that someone would get to her and help her, Phyllis seemed to relax. She had planned to stay overnight ad leave the conference after the last workshop this afternoon. The drive to Atlanta was only a little over four hours. She'd left food and everything where Sue could get to it.

That reminded Irene of what she'd done with Jennifer. And Irene was only about ten minutes from home. Yet she might as well be four hours away, or even a continent away.

Phyllis addressed Irene in particular. "I really wanted to attend this workshop," she explained. "I wanted to find out if this is something Sue might do at home. She could teach people to read. It would give her a goal and a purpose. Maybe both of us could do it together since I am home with her all the time anyway."

"Oh, I'm sure she could," Irene encouraged. "That's a wonderful idea."

Phyllis's smile faded almost as soon as it appeared. "I thought I needed to get away," she said, shaking her head. "Now look what happens. If I could reach my daughter's side, I'd never leave again without her."

Irene knew the feeling. How many times after her husband died had she thought that if he were alive, she'd never have another cross word with him. She'd never disagree with anything he did or said if he could just be with her. At the same time, she knew that wasn't true. It's just that she missed him so. She knew she had a blessed life, especially since Jennifer had agreed to live with her.

She didn't like the idea of living alone, but at the same time, she wanted to see Jennifer married and happy. Sure, she had a selfish motive, wanting Jennifer married to Don. He was a fine man and had a good position at church. He and Jennifer could live nearby and rear children. Irene could have grandchildren come and visit, spend the night.

Those were dreams, but they were certainly within the range of reality. Or she had thought so until recently. What held Jennifer back from making wedding plans? Maybe Jennifer was reluctant to leave the nest, to cut off from her mother's apron strings, so to speak. Irene would have to encourage Jennifer to become more independent.

Her eyes focused on Phyllis. Would Sue ever marry? Or have children? With a pang of concern, Irene realized that she needed to focus on what this woman wanted for her own daughter and not be too wrapped up in what Irene wanted—for herself, for Jennifer, for Don.

Chapter 10

Jennifer's heart warmed as she thought about Don and talked about him to Rick, not so much as her steady companion of more than a year, but of how he looked to others.

From the moment she'd met him at a church dinner given in his honor for all the members to meet, she'd found him physically appealing. His blond hair was closely cropped, a style that suited his clean-cut, rather chiseled look. His lean frame caused her to wonder if he had the stamina for an active bunch of young people.

After the pastor introduced him, Don stood to say a few words. The warmth in his eyes and the determination in his voice appealed to Jennifer. Within a few weeks she realized his lean look was not from lack of strength but due to energy bordering on hyperactivity. He could keep up with the most active teenager and at the same time lead them into a deeper faith in the Lord.

"Soon after that," Jennifer said, "my good friend Ashley—the mother of Tina I told you about—pointed out Don's outstanding characteristics. Then he began to come to singles' activities as much as possible. Everyone liked him. Don asked me out, and I discovered his wonderful personality. And too," she said, "I was greatly impressed with his dedication to the Lord and plans to reach young people in the name of Christ."

Perhaps she had romantic notions about her "hero" who'd come through a storm to rescue her and these made her feel like she could talk to this stranger about Don. Or maybe it was because she had an attentive listener. "Anyway," she continued, "Mom thinks he's the greatest thing since sliced bread, and in a way he is. She thinks we're perfect for each other."

She told Rick how Ashley felt about it. More than once, she'd said to Ashley, "You really think Don and I are suited for each other?" and Ashley always replied immediately, "Absolutely, Jennifer. You couldn't find a more suitable mate anywhere." Ashley's steady at the time was Leo, and that was another reason it seemed so perfect for her and Don. He, Jennifer, Ashley and Leo had made a great foursome.

"I haven't told anyone but Mom and Ashley that Don and I have broken up," she said and sighed. "Neither of them want to believe it."

ick thought how right Don seemed for Jennifer. Her mother was right. Her
iend, Ashley, was right. Jennifer and Don were the type of people who
elonged together. They were fine, dedicated Christians who hadn't had their
ves trampled on. . .yet! They had common beliefs, goals, and purposes. They
ad gone steady for over a year. There must be an emotional bond.

"Have you met someone else who interests you?" Rick asked, when she
aid she and Don had decided to stop seeing each other exclusively.

"No," Jennifer said, and he heard the concern in her voice. "There could
ot be a finer man than Don. In addition to his outstanding spiritual qualities,
e's good-looking, has all the physical appeal a woman might be attracted to.
And they are," she added, with a small laugh. "Everybody tells me how lucky
am. So, do you think I'm foolish or what?"

Rick stared through the graylike fog that shrouded him and watched her
ace in the soft, warm candlelight. He focused on her for a long time. He
ouldn't possibly say or even allude to what went through his mind. There was
time when he felt God had a special calling for him. He'd had high ideals
nd an unrealistic view about life until that was suddenly, irrevocably changed.
Had the blinders remained over his eyes and his mind, then he might have
urned out to be the kind of man that Don was. He might have been the one
o come to the church and interest a girl like Jennifer. But those innocent, ide-
listic days were gone. He couldn't go back. He couldn't change things. If life
vere different. . . But it wasn't. And he wasn't.

"I don't think you're being foolish," Rick said finally. "I think it's wise to
oe absolutely sure before you commit to a lifetime with another person. But
rom my limited view, it looks to me like you and Don are suited for each
other. Why do you think you aren't?"

Jennifer laughed lightly. "Maybe I read too many romance novels."

Rick snorted. "I haven't read any, so I wouldn't know."

"Well, that's not it," she corrected herself. "It has nothing to do with a
novel. It's just. . .how I feel inside."

Although she had felt an almost-instant camaraderie with Rick, she didn't
eel it proper to go into detail about her emotions with a man. That would be
getting too personal, and it didn't seem to be a subject two strangers who were
tranded together should be discussing. But actually, it was an absence of
motion. Getting to know Don and realizing he was her ideal man had been
vonderful. Becoming his steady with everyone envious, yet complimentary,
uited her. She'd waited a long time for a man like Don, having believed he
vould come along someday. He had. That had been fun and exciting.

But as the months passed, the excitement was replaced with acceptance,

taking each other for granted, even complacency. "I love Don," Jennifer sa
quietly. "But I don't think my love for him is any greater than the love oth
have for him. He's an exceptional man in so many ways. But. . .I feel li
we've taken each other for granted. I don't think that's how it should be."

Her voice trailed off, and Rick could almost see her shrug. "Maybe t
spark of love just needs to be rekindled," Rick said. "Perhaps a separation w
make you both realize just how much you mean to each other."

"Have you ever been in love, Rick?" she asked softly.

"In high school and college, I fell in love with every pretty girl. Now
call that being in love with love—or perhaps with myself."

"What about since college?"

"No," he said more shortly than he intended. He supposed he'd stopp
believing in love, too. For the first time in seven years he'd let himself g
close to the kind of girl where such foolish notions might be entertained.
don't even consider love or marriage or all those ideal notions of early year

Jennifer gasped. "You don't believe in love?"

"Oh, I believe it exists. It's just not a part of my personality. My life
filled with other things."

"Such as?"

"Work."

"Hmmm," she said.

He didn't bother to ask what that meant. But he figured she thought hi
some kind of weirdo. Perhaps he was. He didn't discuss things like love ar
goodness and idealism. He decided to change the subject. But to what?

Before he could decide on a subject, she reverted to the old one. "I w
ready to tell Don that maybe we should talk. I mean, after a year and fo
months of going together, something should be happening. But it wasn
Before I could tell him how I felt, he said we should see less of each oth
saving me the trouble. But now he's feeling guilty and blaming himself for n
accident."

"Accident?" Rick blurted. Surely she didn't mean the accident he, hir
self, caused.

"Yeah," Jennifer said and laughed. "In case you haven't noticed, I have
arm in a cast, and my ribs are strapped."

"And I didn't even ask about it," Rick said, realizing he should have, as
he didn't know.

"Well, you're used to seeing people in worse shape than this, I'm su
Anyway, that's the first question everybody asks me, and I've told the story
million times."

Rick stood. "Here, let me clean up our supper dishes, and you can t your story again. First, we're going to need more blankets, and I don't know if I can stay awake much longer."

"You mean I'm that boring?"

I wish, Rick thought, but just laughed lightly and walked toward the kitchen with the paper plates.

They each took a candle into her mother's bedroom far down the hallway on the right side.

"You may sleep in here or the guest room, if you like," she told him.

"The couch will be fine," he said. "The way I feel, I could sleep on the floor."

Jennifer didn't want to go into a back bedroom and lie in the cold dark while Rick was piled up on the couch or in another room. After all, he'd risked his life for her. He was her hero. She could at least try and be there for him. "I'll just sleep in the chair," she said.

"You can take the couch, and I'll sleep in the chair," he said.

"I thought you'd decided on the floor," she quipped.

He gave her a disgusted look, then followed her into the bedroom.

"In the closet," she said, standing in front of a sliding door. Rick opened it and held his candle up until he saw several folded blankets on the top shelf. He set the candle on the dresser.

Jennifer set her candle on the bedside table. Rick reached up and got a blanket and turned to give it to her. "Under my arm," she said. "I think I can only handle one at a time."

He shook his head, angry with himself. She wouldn't be so good-natured if she knew he was the one who caused her predicament. "Why don't you just let me handle this," he said.

"Fine," she replied. "I can't hold a candle and a blanket at the same time anyway. Just get whatever you think we need. I'll be across the hall for a little bit."

Jennifer took her candle and went to the bathroom in her bedroom to brush her teeth and get ready for the night. When she was ready to leave, she picked the candle up more quickly than she intended and poof! Out it went. Everything turned black.

Maybe if her eyes adjusted or she got the door open, she'd see a ray of light from her mother's bedroom. She had to feel around for a surface to put her candle on, then felt around for the door. Finally, she found the knob. Slowly, she opened the door. Again, pitch black. She knew her own room. Surely she could find her way out. But with one hand, she couldn't take the candle with her. Of course she should come back for it later.

Cautiously, she felt for the side of the doorway. She scooted her tennis shoes the best she could on the carpet, felt her dresser, tried to make her way around it when her hand hit a picture on her dresser and it fell over with a thump. She shrieked, jerked her hand away, and hit it on part of the dresser. "Oh, good grief!" she wailed, reprimanding herself for being so clumsy and skittish.

"What's wrong?" she heard Rick call.

"My candle went out," she yelled.

"You just stand still, and I'll come and get you. Oh, no!"

"What?"

"I dropped my candle. Now we're both in the dark. Just hold out your hand in front of you, and I'll hold mine out and find you."

"It's pretty much a clear path over to me." She tried to steer him with her voice. "You walk my way, and I'll walk your way, and we'll meet. . .hmm-hm-hmm. . . innn the mid-dle," she sang, reminiscent of a country song.

She heard a deep chuckle in his throat as he neared, and she wished she could see if he were smiling. There was such a tenseness about him. She felt his hand touch hers, then both his hands enveloped it.

"You saved my life again," she exclaimed.

I ruined your life, he was thinking, but at least he was there to help her. He hated to think of her here alone having to do the everyday things a person took for granted. And would she ever have gotten the blankets off that top shelf? Yes, he knew she would have. . .some way. He had a sneaky suspicion she could have made it out of the bedroom, too. She was a fun girl. But he was the wrong person for her. He was not a fun kind of guy.

Once he had her safely back in the family room, she asked, "Why don't you just take the flashlight that's back there on the countertop and go after the blankets?"

His laugh this time was one of irony. "Now you tell me about a flashlight!"

She shrugged. "You didn't ask."

A little later, Rick returned with all the blankets.

"You want to play some board games or something?" Jennifer asked. "Monopoly? Scrabble? Checkers?"

"Thanks, but I'm a little tired for games," he said politely. "Why don't you sleep on the couch, and I'll take the chair."

"I prefer the chair, if you don't mind," she said.

"Whatever's comfortable for you," he said, and when she insisted that was the chair, he covered her with several of the blankets, then blew out the candles near her. Rick sat in one corner of the couch near the end table on which a lone candle glowed softly. He had that thoughtful, brooding look again. She wished he'd talk more about himself. She wanted to know him better.

"Okay," she said. "I told you about my love life, now what about yours?"

"Mine!" His laugh of irony was short. "No. No love life. No wife. No girlfriend." His head turned slightly, and he seemed to focus on the candle, as if he'd like to blow out the flame. Why was he so uncomfortable? Suddenly, he glanced at her again and smiled. She didn't think it reached his eyes. "No children, either."

She laughed lightly, knowing he was trying to cover whatever discomfort had come over him when she asked the question. Was he one of those married guys who denied it? She didn't want him to be. She liked Rick. She believed he was really concerned about her welfare.

She wasn't one just to let things pass, however. If she couldn't come in through a door, she was the kind who'd try a window. "You mentioned an uncle. Do you have any other family?"

"Parents in South Carolina," he said. He drew in a deep breath, then exhaled audibly. "My dad's a preacher."

His tone of voice and solemn expression suggested he wasn't too pleased about that. She waited, but he offered no other information.

"Ah," she said. "So that's why you can quote Scripture."

His laugh sounded almost genuine. "A few words of Scripture, if I remember correctly."

"Right, but it wasn't a common passage. Not exactly John 3:16."

"Not obscure if you've been raised in the church and had a dad like mine."

Seeing his frown, she questioned, "Was he overly strict?"

Rick shook his head. "If there is a perfect man, it's my dad," he replied, and she didn't think it was the cold that made his voice tremble. "Anyway," he continued, "I went to church every time the doors opened and sometimes opened them myself. At one time I even thought God. . ."

He cleared his throat as if something were stuck in it, then began again. "At one time I thought I was being called into special service of some kind." He shook his head. "No," he said. "No."

Jennifer spoke softly. "It looks to me like you are in a special service, Rick."

He snorted. "Not really. Not the way you mean it. I'm an EMT and volunteer fireman because I like helping people." He stared at the blanket over his chest. "Something happened several years ago, Jennifer. But I don't talk about it."

He quickly changed the subject. "You were going to tell me about the accident. What happened?" he asked, as if he didn't know.

"Somebody ran a stop sign and hit my car. Wham! Instant concussion, broken arm, cracked ribs. That's it."

That's it? "Do you know who did it?" he asked, knowing that question should follow, and obviously she didn't know or she would have said something about his being the culprit. She'd have every right to order him out where she'd wanted to throw that medicine bottle earlier.

"No, I heard it was a man in a truck."

"Don't you want to know?"

"I thought if the person wanted me to know, he'd contact me."

"And he didn't."

"Nope."

"That sounds heartless, don't you think?" he asked.

"Oh, not at all," she said. "I can't imagine that someone would deliberately run into me and risk his own life. I think he's probably afraid to face me, afraid I'll be angry with him."

"Aren't you?" he asked.

"No. It was an accident. I forgive him."

An accident! Forgiveness! Again, idealism. He wanted to force his mind away from it, but it was ever present. She made him think of things he hadn't had in his own life for many years—goodness, purity, innocence, kindness.

She doesn't even know I'm the one who ran into her. Yet she forgives me. That only adds to my guilt and misery. I want to tell her. But how do I go about doing that?

Rick took off his shoes, crawled under the blankets, and blew out his candle, plunging them into total darkness. He slipped farther down in the covers, his head on a pillow. Should he tell her he was responsible for her accident?

Was it too late for that? Wouldn't she fear him for keeping it from her?

She'd talked about forgiveness. Forgiveness! Did it bring anybody back? Make any difference?

His eyes closed, and he heard the terrible wind. Who knew when this storm might end? Or when the roof might blow off, or the windows and doors suddenly give way, or a tree fall through the roof? Who knew if this might be his last—only—chance to say he was sorry?

If they made it through the night, would it matter whether or not she knew?

"Are you asleep?" he asked quietly, half-hoping she couldn't hear him.

"No," she answered softly.

Maybe if he could let her understand him a little, she wouldn't be too upset or too frightened that he let her eat with him, smile at him, laugh with him, look at him as if she thought him a trusted friend. Perhaps she would not think him too great a hypocrite for pretending to be a good guy.

But he hadn't spoken of this in more than seven years. He felt like one of those trees being shaken by the wind until its limbs cracked and fell to the ground. Would he, too, fall apart with the telling?

"It's what happened to a former friend of mine," Rick began, knowing in a way that he wasn't lying. This "former friend" he referred to was entirely different from the man lying on the couch. "This man I knew turned away from God about seven years ago. He couldn't accept that a loving God allowed what happened to his sister, a young, beautiful girl who lived for God and was on her first real date. He can't think of it, and the boy who caused Francine's death, without anger and bitterness rising up inside him."

For a moment, Rick wondered if Jennifer had fallen asleep. If she had heard him. Then, her soft voice sounded across the darkness. "How long do you think your friend will stay mad at God?" she asked.

Rick drew a deep breath, then replied seriously, "Perhaps. . .forever."

"That's a shame," Jennifer said after awhile. "Your friend is only a breath away from forever. Simple belief, repentance, and acceptance of Jesus in his heart could mean forever in heaven. From what you said about his sister, I think she's in heaven saving her brother a place. It would be a shame for him to lose out on spending eternity with her. However," she continued, "if that boy and your friend are not Christians, then the two of them will spend eternity together in a different place. Isn't that ironic?"

Rick stared toward the dark ceiling without replying.

"So in a way," Jennifer added, "your friend is letting that boy determine his destiny. I think your friend needs counseling."

Rick felt like coming off the couch. "Counseling?"

"Yes," she said, "by a Christian counselor or a pastor."

Rick gave a short laugh. He'd already been counseled by a pastor. "At the moment, since I'm here on the couch, I have a strange feeling you're trying to be my psychiatrist."

"Are you your *friend*, Rick?" she asked softly.

Rick took in a deep breath, then exhaled. "I'm no friend of mine," he said.

❧

Jennifer got the point. Rick had been talking about himself. Francine was his sister. And now she knew what the sadness was inside him. Rick was his own worst enemy.

Rick's dad was a preacher. Rick knew about God. He just couldn't accept what God had allowed to happen. Well, she knew a little about the power of prayer. She didn't have words for Rick right now, but she could pray.

Jesus had calmed a storm on a raging sea before. He could quiet the storm outside her mountainside home. He would know how to say to Rick's troubled soul, "Peace. Be still."

Her tears felt hot on her cold face, then felt as if they were ice water making rivulets down her face. But she wouldn't chance any movement. She'd just pray.

Rick could say no more. He'd intended to lead up to telling Jennifer that three weeks ago had been the anniversary of Francine's death and then talk about his accident.

But Rick's throat seemed to have closed up. He could find no more words. He could only feel the grief and pain that never went away.

Rick's mind plunged into the past. He had told his parents he'd wait up for his seventeen-year-old sister to come home from the prom. She'd looked so grown up in her first prom dress, so pretty it could almost be a wedding dress. Rain threatened, and the last thing his mom had said to the young couple was, "Be careful."

His parents had gone on to bed. Francine was to have been home by midnight. Rick had stayed up to wait for his sister, and at 1:00 A.M. he was fuming, ready to go look for her, when the doorbell rang. What happened to her key? Or had this guy harmed her in some way and she was too nervous for a key?

With mixed emotions of anger and concern, Rick opened the door. There stood, not Francine and her date, but a policeman. At first it didn't register why a policeman was there. The next instant, he recognized the look in the policeman's eyes, the starkness on his face. He'd had to do it himself on occasion—tell someone that something terrible had happened.

Rick knew the policeman. He knew them all. He came in contact with them all the time. But at the moment, he couldn't think of his name. Francine was all he could think of.

"Rick," the officer said. "Are your parents home?"

"What happened?" Rick asked, grabbing the officer's arm.

"You know I have to tell all of you at once." He lowered his eyes to the floor.

Yes, Rick knew that. Suddenly, he felt the dampness of rain blowing through the door. What had that teenage kid done to his sister?

Rick strode to the bedroom of his parents. "Mom, Dad, wake up. Something's happened."

"Huh? What?" he heard and hurried back to the door where the officer still stood with the spring rain blowing around him. There had been times that Rick didn't feel the elements, either. This was one of those times. He felt numb when he asked, "What hospital is she in?" and the officer just looked down at the floor, holding his hat so tightly his knuckles turned white.

Rick didn't want to know any more.

His sister had died. She hadn't fastened her seat belt. Rick often chided her for that and always made her fasten it before he'd move the car an inch. This kid hadn't. Rick would have killed that boy if he'd been able to get to him. Later, he waited for the courts to do their job. But they let him go. Rick could have killed him then, and everybody in town knew it, but the boy's parents took him away. Rick didn't attend the memorial services at church and at the school for his sister. No, he would not sit there and pretend it was all right. That God was in His heaven and all was right with the world. His preacher-dad would speak at the service.

Francine should have lived. She was an ideal Christian girl. She made a difference, and she was the kind of person the world needed. Why had God let it happen? Why hadn't God taken him instead of a beautiful seventeen-year-old girl who'd just gone to her first prom?

Accident? Her date had been drinking. He'd claimed he didn't know the punch was spiked. He'd claimed his car skidded on the rain-slick road. Sure, he didn't know the punch was spiked! Then he was an imbecile! Rick had drunk spiked punch, and he knew it! The boy was a liar as well as a killer.

He could never have Francine back. His parents would never have their only daughter back. And, too, in a way, they'd never have Rick back, either. All that family togetherness was gone. Never to be returned.

What was the boy doing now? Was he happy-go-lucky? Still drinking and driving? Killing other girls?

The boy's name was Rory! He'd never forget it. Rory McPherson. A so-called nice boy. From a good family. A church-goer. Had it made a difference? Had that kept Francine alive? No! No, it had not! And why not? Why had God let it happen?

Nobody knew. Then why be concerned with God? If it. . .He. . .made no difference. . .then what did?

That boy—that Rory McPherson—continued to cause havoc from that one fateful night.

Seven years later, three weeks ago, had been the anniversary of Francine's death. Rick had passed the high school and seen young girls doing ordinary things like chewing gum, laughing, talking. Things his sister would never do again. It made him feel more acutely than ever that grief and pain that never went away. And the urge for revenge that never left him.

But was that a reason for me to run a stop sign? came Rick's uncomfortable thought. *I could say I'm sorry. Rory had said he was sorry. But it changed nothing.*

No, he mustn't burden Jennifer with this. Hopefully, exhaustion would overtake him, and he'd sleep.

Chapter 11

At around ten o'clock that Saturday night, several rescue workers brought in one other stranded couple. "I have a message for a Don Ramsey," said a worker.

"That's me," Don said, lifting his hand and hurrying toward the worker.

The worker looked at the small notepad he'd taken from a pocket. "The medication was taken to the people you have listed here. One of our volunteer firemen arrived late this afternoon at the home of Jennifer Collins."

"Arrived?" Don questioned "He didn't bring her here?"

"He apparently couldn't get through to let us know the situation. We've been swamped with calls and getting a lot of static on the radios, too. But he got there. That means she was fine and either he went home or he's staying with her until we can get up there and bring her down the mountain or somebody can get up there to take care of her."

"Take care of her?" Don questioned.

The worker shrugged. "That's what he said. I mean, didn't somebody here ask him to go up there?"

"Yeah, I did," Don said. "She has a broken arm and cracked ribs. Other than that, she's fine."

The worker snorted. "Well, you may not realize it, being down here with all the necessities, but up there on those mountains are people freezing to death. Even people with two good arms and legs. I don't mean to worry you, but she's lucky to have ol' Rick with her."

Ol' Rick? The one Don had asked to check on her hadn't looked very old to him. And come to think of it, he hadn't seemed very friendly, either. Don just nodded. "I appreciate it. Um, we had another couple up that way. The Mercers. Do you know about them?"

The worker flipped through some pages in the small notepad. He nodded. "Yep. A tree fell on their roof. They weren't hurt, though. It took a crew four hours to reach them, but they got 'em out. They're at a Red Cross shelter." He shook his head. "They're lucky. We can't even get up some of the mountains to check on all the people on our list. You guys just pray they find a way to keep from freezing to death inside their own homes."

"Yeah, we will."

"You probably won't see us any more tonight unless we find somebody stranded between here and the motel. We've got to get some shut-eye." The worker pocketed the notepad and glanced at the drink station. "Mind if I have another cup of that hot coffee before battling the elements?"

"Take all you want," Don said.

Don called for lights-out around ten-thirty. He lay in a sleeping bag near his youth workers in a corner section of the fellowship hall. He dozed off and on for awhile. He'd learned to spend long hours without sleep, be on call at all times, and never count on a weekend for rest. Working with youth was not an eight-hour job, but it reminded him of what the single mom's were always saying. They never got enough sleep and rarely made it through the night without having to get up for one child or another.

This night, everyone seemed to sleep soundly, except for himself. Fatigue should have overtaken him, but he could do nothing but lie there and think. And it seemed his thoughts continually turned in one direction.

God forgive me. I don't understand what's happening to me, Lord. I haven't seemed to make right decisions for over a month now. If I'm walking in Your will, Lord, then good will come from this.

But am I in your will, Lord?

What is good about being attracted to the best friend of the woman I've dated for over a year? What's good about Ashley being constantly on my mind? What's good about worrying that Tina is growing up without a father figure, and I'd like to be that for her? What's good about saying cool it to Jennifer when the relationship wasn't even hot? What's good about causing Jennifer to be distracted while driving, which she surely would be? What's good about sending a stranger, even though he's a rescue worker, up to check on a girl whose helplessness could incite the wrong kind of emotions from someone who didn't know the Lord?

Lord, I know You, I serve You, I love You, and yet look at all the poor judgment calls I've made. I don't even know if this rescue worker is one of Your followers. What kind of person did I send to see a helpless girl? What's wrong with me? When did I become so confused? How did these bad choices slip up on me like this? Or was it that I just didn't want to admit I was dating one girl while becoming increasingly drawn to another?

I tell the young people they should date, not go steady, but use dating as an experience of finding out about a person. That is not the time to become attached, but to learn about the character and personality of another. Go in groups. I've done that myself, Lord. And when I first met Jennifer, my heart leaped within me. She is perfect for me. She's a beautiful person, inside and out. She's a dedicated Christian. She's everything a man should want. And I've grown to appreciate and cherish her more and more over the months I've known her. I have a desire to influence and encourage young people. Her focus is on younger children. We're a perfect match, Lord. You know that. I know that.

Then why, why all this inner conflict? How many times I've thanked You for her. She is a perfect mate for me. And yet my eyes, my heart, my mind, all lean toward Ashley since Leo left her. Is this just my wishing she had a man in her life? Is this just compassion and caring for her? Is this just wishing Jennifer's friend could have a strong relationship with a man like Jen and I have. . .had? I'm ruining everything, Lord. I've pushed Jennifer away, caused her accident, sent a strange man to her, and have a roving eye.

Oh, God! How do I get back on track with You and with my relationships? God, I'm nearing thirty years old. I know my calling. I'm not a kid trying to discover who is compatible with me. No one is more compatible with me than Jennifer. I know that. I've thanked You for that. Was I just trying to make things work? What's wrong with me? Can I be an effective minister with this turmoil in my life? Can I lead young people when I can't follow my own common-sense advice and control my emotions?

Ashley wondered if Don, too, was unable to sleep. She quietly tiptoed around sleeping youth and stared at the back of Don's head. She wanted to apologize for her flare of temper. That had been no way to behave toward Don, who had only goodness in his heart for other people.

"Don?" she said quietly.

When he didn't answer, she knelt down and touched his shoulder. "Don?"

Still no reply. She rose to her feet and bit hard on her lip. Why did she keep coming back to torture herself like this? A glutton for punishment? She'd only meant to make amends. She wanted to console him, reassure him. Was that really what she wanted? Or did she want Don. . .for herself?

Dear Lord, has my loneliness brought me to this? That I would even consider hurting my friends? I'd rather die, Lord. I won't do it. And, too, the only way I can do it is to reveal my wayward feelings. For what purpose? Just to cause them distress? Just to cause myself embarrassment? To ruin the relationships of the two most faithful friends I've ever had? To keep my Tina from her favorite man and woman other than her grandparents? I see it all clearly, Lord. This must be the devil tempting me. I've got to get it under control.

"Forgive me," she said aloud to the back of his head. Tears spilled from her eyes, and she hurried from the dark corner of the room. She was saying it to Don, to Jennifer, to God, to anyone.

She returned to her cot, crawled under the cover, and put her arms around her sleeping little girl. *Thank You, God, for this most wonderful blessing*

in the world. Thank You for the assurance that You'll answer my prayer. You said,
"Ask, and you will receive." I'm doing that. I'm receiving Your forgiveness and Your
cleansing. Oh, please protect Jennifer. . .for Don.

The tears started again. Why did she have to add his name? Why. . .
always?

Little did she know that Don, too, had tears trickling from the corners
of his eyes.

✐

Irene had slept as well as one could in a strange place, in a strange bed, and
with the wind trying to blow the earth into another galaxy. Her mind had
eased some after the impromptu prayer meeting of the night before and then
Don's late call that a rescue worker had gone to check on Jennifer. She knew
she shouldn't worry. Jennifer wasn't an invalid like Sue, just inconvenienced.
But she couldn't turn off that protective motherly instinct of hers.

Something as ordinary as taking a shower made her realize how much
she took for granted every day. Thousands of people couldn't wake up to that
privilege this morning. Perhaps they hadn't even slept, being in houses without heat where the temperature kept plummeting all night long.

She'd been waiting for JoBetty's knock on the door. It came at 6:45.
"Here's your hairspray," the grateful desk clerk said. "I couldn't have shown
my head around here without it. Thanks a mil."

"Well, I think you'd look just fine even without hairspray." She smiled.
Knowing JoBetty was trying to look her best, she complimented her. "Your
clothes look nice, too."

"I thought I'd wear the blouse without the sweater. Gives the impression
of a different outfit." She held out her beads. "I doubled these over, too.
Maybe they won't look like the same ol' same ol'. I'd better get down there
and let my hubby go get some shut-eye. He's been at the desk all night." She
started to leave, then looked over her shoulder. "And don't you worry about
that girl of yours. The Lord takes care of His own." She grinned. "Even supplies you with hairspray when you need it." She laughed and left.

Irene kept smiling for quite awhile after JoBetty left. That woman knew
everybody's business by now and tried to encourage them all. Maybe she didn't
know how to run a kitchen, but she sure knew how to relate to people.

There would be breakfast and a morning workshop. She'd noticed the
considerable decrease in wind and had even seen a ray of sun shining on the
ice-plastered windows. Would there be any chance of going home today?

When she walked into the lobby and heard the twenty-four-hour continuous forecast, the answer to that question was confirmed. She'd known it
in her heart anyway.

"The sun is shining," the reporter was saying. "But don't be deceived. It's ore dangerous out today than it was yesterday. Over 250,000 are without ower. Water lines are freezing. Phone lines are down all over. The governor nd president have declared a state of emergency, but others can't get in to elp us. There are pileups on the interstate, and some of those are covered ith snowdrifts. Emergency vehicles are rescuing emergency workers. Trees nd limbs are down all over. Maybe today the National Guard helicopters will e able to try and rescue that group of hikers in the Pisgah National Forest ea."

The unfavorable reports continued. *No,* Irene knew, *there'd be no going ome this day.*

Chapter 12

Rick heard the sounds during the night. Howling winds shoving ove trees whose branches were weighed down with heavy snow and whos roots became loosened by the wet earth. He heard the cracking an the falling of trees and wondered when one might hit the house. Fortunately none had—yet.

If Jennifer heard the trees or was frightened by the possibilities of th destructive storm, she showed no sign. It wasn't until he got up and began t shovel the ashes out of the stove into an ash bucket that she spoke. "Oh, w have a little light in here without using candles. But I can see my breath. I must be freezing in here."

"You're right," he said, his own breath like puffs of smoke in the frigi room.

"Oh, but listen," she said optimistically. "The wind seems to have calme down to a roar."

Rick made a sound to acknowledge he heard the quip, but he didn't lool at her. He swallowed hard, trying to keep back the realization of how clos he'd come last night to bending her ear with his inner darkness. For the firs time in seven years he'd wanted to share, wanted someone to listen, to sym pathize. He thought she'd understand. Now, in the cold, dim morning light he shuddered at that thought. Why burden anyone else with it?

"Should be safe to have a fire now," Rick said, putting the lid on th bucket although the ashes were cold. "We might get some downdraft, bu that will be easier to handle than this cold." He set the bucket back agains the stones. "You have a carbon monoxide detector?"

"Fortunately," she said, and from the corner of his eye he could tell she' propped herself up. "One morning I emptied the hot ashes into the bucket an because the morning was unusually cold, I left the lid off to feel the warmth It was Sunday morning. I got a headache and was sick to my stomach. Mon got up and said she didn't feel well so we decided not to go to church. I lay o the couch and she stretched out in the recliner. Just as I started to doze off, th alarm went off."

"Oh, boy!" Rick exclaimed, knowing what had happened. He'd encoun tered carbon monoxide poisoning in his line of work. It was a silent killer.

"We knew immediately what it had to be," Jennifer said. "We jumped up, grabbed the ash bucket and set it out on the deck, and Mom began opening windows. I just didn't think about the hot ashes giving off carbon monoxide."

"That's why it's so important to have an alarm," Rick said, placing kindling on the paper he'd put into the stove. "Carbon monoxide is something a lot of people don't think about, but it can sure sneak up on you." He struck a match and immediately felt the warmth of flame burning the paper and catching the kindling. When the wood was burning well, he put on a bigger piece, then closed the door. "I'll wash up, then see about some breakfast," he said, rising.

Jennifer laughed. "I'll stay right here until my frozen nose thaws out."

When he came back to check the fire, she was sitting up, shivering in her blankets. "Chef Rick at your service, Ma'am," he said, "ready to take your breakfast order."

Jennifer smiled. "Now that we have a stove, we can eat anything you like. Heat water for oatmeal. Cook eggs in a frying pan." She shrugged and lifted her eyebrows.

Rick went over and touched his fingers to the stove. "It's starting to heat up," he said. "Oatmeal sounds great to me. I'll need something that sticks to the ribs before I go out and start working on that tree." He went into the kitchen and turned on the faucet he'd left dripping overnight so it wouldn't freeze. "Bingo!" he said. "We still have water."

❦

Jennifer decided she'd better wash up and get ready for the day, whatever it might bring. She shivered as she shed her blankets and looked toward the glass doors. She could tell the sun was shining against the drapes. That was an encouraging sight.

She stretched her one good arm, then turned to see Rick puttering around in the kitchen. That warmed her heart. She liked being cooped up here with Rick and his seeing after her. She just wanted a little more time with him, to talk personally, to get to know about his inner self that he guarded so secretively.

"I found the oatmeal," he said. "Now where's a pot?"

"Second door on the bottom, on your left," she said, then exited the room and went into the dark hallway. She backtracked. "Better take a candle," she said. "Still gloomy back there."

"I left the flashlight in the bathroom for you," Rick replied.

Their eyes met and held for a moment. "You like waiting on me hand and foot?" Jennifer asked.

"Well, hand anyway," Rick said and grinned. "I haven't gotten to the foot yet."

"Which reminds me," she quipped, "after I brush my teeth, you might
me the favor of tying the laces on my tennis shoes."

"Nag, nag, nag," he said. "Next you'll be ordering me to take out t
trash."

Jennifer liked the connotation of that. Reminded her of an old marri
couple. And to think, for the past few months, she'd had depressing feelin
when she thought of herself and Don possibly getting married. But that h
been something she had to entertain seriously. She and Rick were joking.

She went to the bathroom and washed up as best she could but decid
against changing clothes. It was just too difficult, and she certainly could
ask Rick to help. She managed to wash her face and brush her unruly cur
When she returned, Rick was putting another piece of wood in the stove a
had the pot of water heating on top. "Never brushed my teeth in ice wa
before," she quipped, causing him to glance up.

He laughed. "Never brushed mine with a washcloth before."

While the pot was heating, Jennifer had Rick help her wrap a blanket arou
her shoulders, then she went over and pulled the drapes aside. "Oh, Ri
Come here." Astonishment was in her voice. "You have to see this."

He walked over and stood beside her while she shivered and gazed
awe at the scenery. "How anybody can look at a scene so beautiful and i
believe in God is beyond me," she said, wonder filling her voice. "Look he
everything is completely white except a few tree trunks. And look how t
sun shines on the ice, making it sparkle and shine. Oh, this is so spectacula

"It is beautiful," Rick agreed, seeing how their breath was making
steamy fog on the doors. He wiped it off with his bare hand so she could co
tinue looking at the mighty handiwork of God.

Everything she did, everything she said, just served to emphasize the d
ferences between them. Their characters were opposite. They looked
things differently. He knew the picture before them was fantastic. Howev
that's not all he saw. He saw frozen trees with heavy snow and ice tl
weighed them down and knew their limbs were on the verge of breakin
their roots might not hold in the soft ground, and they could fall any minu
causing damage and destruction. He knew that beneath the whitened lan
scape were still the debris and quagmires into which one could step or fall a
lie hurt and freezing to death, becoming one with the elements.

*What does she see? The handiwork of God. His artistic, creative painting
the earth in yet another original landscape. She sees the ice crystals and calls th
sculptures. She lifts her eye to the uplifted arms of sparkling treetops and sees
small patch of blue sky and thinks of heaven. How different. How different we a*

My heart is frozen. Hers is warm. She's sunshine to a frozen heart.

The ice cannot cool the sun. But the sun can melt the ice. But what good would that do? Would he not end up with his life broken in even more pieces? Or falling flat on his face? Or standing in a puddle, exposed like the debris that lies out there under the snow? What would she see then? A man in his misery. How could he leave here—leave her—and ever be the same?

But she needs to know. Know who I am and what I am. Could he stand it if he told her that he crippled her? Could he stand it when she would look up into his face with her clear green eyes and say, "I forgive you. I'll pray for you."?

She looked at him then and caught him staring at her. Her eyes glinted with the early morning light. "What are you thinking?" she asked gently.

The words were in his heart, on his mind, but they didn't reach his tongue. She was waiting, anticipating, but all that rose in his throat was a hard, aching lump.

When he found his voice, his words came out gruff. "I need to take a look at the tree that's on my truck." He put on his outer clothes that he'd left by the door last night, angry because he couldn't bring himself to confess.

Jennifer watched Rick stomp through the snow on the deck, using a trash can to dump snow over the side of the deck, then shoveling, then sweeping. *What is he running from?* she wondered, as the pot began to boil on the stove.

❧

More than two hours later, Rick eventually made it to the truck and beat on the ice until he finally managed to open the frozen door. He sat in the driver's seat, suspended above a snowdrift with the back weighted down by the pine tree. When he finally made contact with the crew in the valley, they told him no more than he had reasoned. He'd seen winters that weren't nearly as treacherous as this one, and the crews couldn't make it up the mountains.

Rick wasn't overjoyed at having to say he was sitting several feet in the air with his truck hovering over a snowdrift and a pine tree on his truck bed. They'd rib him till kingdom come. But they needed to know why he wasn't in the valley helping them. He told them he'd stayed at the Collins house.

"I'm glad you and the girl are okay, Rick," his ops chief said. "You just stay put. There's no way we can get up any roads on the mountain. We can't even get the roads down here cleared. I've never seen anything like it. We're moving at a snail's pace. There's no place to put the snow. We don't know if the lumps are drifts or cars. A little bit of the interstate is cleared," he scoffed, "but none of the exits. People still can't get around."

"Maybe the end is in sight," Rick said.

"At least the snow has tapered off, and the wind's not too bad except for the gusts. But I'm sure you know there's going to be more trees and power lines down before this is over."

"Wish I could help, Charlie," Rick said.

"You'll get your share, Buddy," he said and laughed. "We'll leave enough trees around for you to cut."

"You do that," Rick said and laughed, thinking of the tree behind him. "Oh, can you get word to the church shelter that Miss Collins is fine? She can use her woodstove now."

"Great. I was wondering if we'd have to get a helicopter up that way. Don, at the church shelter, called us first thing this morning asking if we'd heard anything."

"Tell him she's fine." *Yep*, he kept thinking, even after the call ended, as he stared ahead at the top of the carport in front of him. *She's a mighty fine lady.*

❦

"You're going to freeze or work yourself to death," Jennifer chided while Rick ate a peanut butter sandwich for lunch and a can of spinach she'd warmed on the stove to give him energy. All the good food that her mom had left in the refrigerator was out on the deck, hard as a glacier. "Why don't you rest for awhile? After all, this is Sunday, the day of rest."

"Don't you know your Scripture, Jennifer? 'Who of you, if a sheep fell in a ditch on the Sabbath, wouldn't pull it out?' " His voice was playfully gruff. "That truck out there is my livelihood as much as a sheep was in Bible days."

"Okay," she relented. "But I feel so useless. . ."

"Useless?" he interrupted. "You've graciously shared your home with me, Jennifer. And you're keeping the coffee hot. That's far from useless."

"I wish I could do more," she said sincerely.

She watched as he took another big gulp of coffee before saying, "If I'm ever going to get out of there, I have to keep working on that tree. Thanks for lunch."

Jennifer sighed after he went outside again and started the chain saw. She put water on to boil for more coffee, then searched the cupboards for food. She spied a bag of marshmallows. Maybe tonight they could roast them together in front of the woodstove.

Then it occurred to her she could do something else for Rick. She'd heat water so he could take a nice, warm bath. He'd appreciate that after being out in the cold all day. Maybe she should take a bath while he was out there working.

With only one usable hand, she had to use a small pot. She smiled, taking the water to the bathtub and pouring it in. By the time she took the second pot into the bathroom, however, the first pot had grown cold.

She finally gave up on the idea that she could do anything for Rick other than ply him with coffee and open a can of beef stew for supper. She curled up with the romance novel she'd planned to read over the *quiet* weekend, only partially attentive to the words on paper. Her mind kept anticipating a marshmallow roast after supper.

Rick could hardly believe he was doing this. He couldn't recall ever being so fatigued, but he had finally gotten the tree off his truck. He'd planned to eat supper, stretch out on the couch, sleep through the night, and awaken early to see if he could get his truck started.

However, he was roasting marshmallows in the stove—burning them half the time, even catching the skewer on fire, catching one for her that was about ready to fall off into her lap, reaching over to wipe a smudge of black ash from the side of Jennifer's mouth, and laughing in a room whose only color was the orange candlelight aglow on her face, turning her hair to reddish gold.

How could something so simple, so basic, make his heart flutter as if he were just beginning to notice girls? Was it possible he'd only known her for about twenty-four hours? He felt like he'd known her always. Wanted to know her always. And that was all the more reason to get out of there as quickly as possible.

"Just a minute," he said. He went into the kitchen and wet a paper towel, then came back and gently wiped off a smudge of sticky ash on her left cheek.

"All this would have been frightening and dull without you, Rick. I'm so glad you're here." Her voice was soft, her steady gaze was warm, her lips trembly with a half smile as if she were uncertain about how much to say.

He lowered his gaze to her hand and wiped away the stickiness with the paper towel. "I appreciate your sharing your home with me, Jennifer." He paused, wondering if this were the time to tell her about himself.

Instead, he merely said, "I'm exhausted, Jennifer. I really need to get some rest."

Chapter 13

Jennifer had slept well Sunday night and awoke to a bright, sunshiny day. The temperature was slightly above freezing, and the icicles hanging under the eaves at the French doors began to look wet and form a small drop of ice water at their tips. Jennifer knew anything that melted during the day would freeze over again during the night. And ice could be even more hazardous in the morning. Perhaps Rick would have to stay another day.

But he'd been out all morning and afternoon for longer periods of time than yesterday since the wind had calmed to a stiff breeze, and the snow had ceased to fall. She kept the fire going for him to warm his hands and the coffee hot for him to drink. He'd turned his truck around so he'd be ready to go down the long road after it was cleared. He cleared a spot for a front-loader to come up and turn around. Rick was preparing to leave.

It was midafternoon when he came in and said he'd made contact with the crew down the mountain. "Everything still looks like a frozen marshmallow and is just as hard to get around in," Rick said. "But one of the crew is going to try and make it up here. They need every tree cutter they can find."

He'd be leaving soon. "I'll make sure you have everything you need before I go," he said and took off his Gore-Tex pants and jacket and laid them on the floor in front of the doors.

He brought up wood from the basement.

"That's enough to last me two weeks," she exclaimed, seeing that he not only stacked it high against the stone, but filled some cardboard boxes that had been in the basement.

"I want to make sure you have enough to burn all day and all night." Last night he had fastened a blanket over the open doorway separating the kitchen/family room from the rest of the house, so the heat from the stove would stay in the long room. He'd kept the fire going all night. She'd felt safe and protected.

Jennifer had stood near the stove, watching him. Finally, he came near. "Are you sure you don't want me to take you down to the church?"

She shook her head. "The worst part's over, Rick. I'll be fine." Her head turned toward the front window. She must have heard it, too. "That sounds like a front-loader," he said. He could visualize it scooping up the snow and ice, dumping it to the side of the road.

The worst part's over, Rick, she'd said. But not for him. There was still the matter of telling her the truth. Could he go away and never look back? Should he just blurt out the truth about himself and run away?

In the awkward moment, she said something he'd begun to realize was typical of her. "You were truly a lifesaver, Rick. I wish my arm were well so I could give you a big hug."

So, some good comes from everything! flashed through Rick's mind. He was glad Jennifer couldn't get any closer to him physically. She was going to be hard enough to forget. He did not need a memory of holding her close.

He turned and headed for the door. The front-loader was getting closer. He needed to put on his Gore-Tex.

"Wait," she said and went into the kitchen and picked up a small notebook and pen. She sat at the countertop and asked for his phone number. On the bottom half of the sheet she wrote her own, managed to tear it in half, and took it over to him. "I'd like for us to stay in touch, Rick."

At his hesitation, she pulled the paper back. "Am I being too forward?"

Rick didn't want to hurt her any more than he'd already done. But he couldn't let her think he wasn't interested in her. She interested him more than any woman he'd ever known. "Jennifer. If things were different, if I were different, you wouldn't have to ask that question. But I'm no good for you or anybody."

He knew he couldn't tell her now. He'd run out of time. The front-loader would be there any minute.

"If you were no good, you wouldn't be trying to protect me from yourself," she replied.

"I'm just being honest," he said. "You're on the rebound. Soon, you and Don will probably get back together. And. . .there's something else I need to say." However, hearing the front-loader right outside the house, he picked up his hat and gloves and shoved them into his pocket.

"Rick, what?" she encouraged. She looked out the glass doors where everything was still frozen solid. Even the sunshine wasn't enough to melt it. Just as she couldn't melt Rick's heart. But he had goodness in him. He'd shown that. His life showed it. His regard for her showed it. She turned back to face him as he shoved open the door. "You're a coward, Rick Jenkins."

He blinked. "A coward?" A laugh escaped his throat. "In what way?"

"You're afraid of me."

He stared at her, with the sun shining through the door onto her face, giving a soft glow to her smooth skin. Giving a golden glow to her green eyes. Making a halo of her curly hair. Outlining her soft, full lips. "You are so right," he said adamantly. His hands came up and grasped her arms. But before he could prove what a cad he was, from somewhere deep inside a stronger urge overtook him. He'd rather die than hurt her any more than he had already.

"I'll be back to cut up the tree," he said.

He let go of her arms, turned to shove the door open wider, and hastily exited.

❧

Jennifer looked out the window and watched Rick drive down the road behind the front-loader. He was gone. Had he been about to kiss her? Then why hadn't he? Or. . .had she thrown herself at him so many times that he felt he should pretend to like her?

Had she been wrong in thinking there was something special between them? She'd felt it. She'd known it. But was he right in saying she was on the rebound? Had God brought him her way to reinforce how close Don was to the Lord and that he was her intended mate?

Well, she'd just do as she planned before the storm hit. She didn't want to wait for anything to cook on the stove, so she made herself a sandwich and wished it would have been taped for the million-dollar funniest video. Of course it wasn't funny when she was trying to spread peanut butter on a piece of bread with one hand, but someday she'd look back and laugh about it— perhaps. If she had a working phone, she'd call Rick and tell him to come do this for her. That thought brought a smile to her face.

She lit a candle from the stove and set it on the end table and pulled up the chair Rick had set in front of the stove. Picking up her book, she turned to the page where she'd left off before the storm. After reading two paragraphs, she went back and tried again. No use. She couldn't concentrate. Her gaze moved to the far window where darkness had begun to press upon the pane.

Would he be thinking of her during this long, cold, lonely night?

She didn't want him to forget her.

❧

The following day, Irene felt a great sense of relief, being able to return to her house and her daughter. She inched her way up the mountain roads, grateful they had been plowed. But trees were down all along the way. A big pine lay on both sides of the driveway, but she was able to pull into the carport underneath the deck.

Another three days passed before the electricity was restored. Irene enjoyed the time with Jennifer, as if the two of them appreciated each other even more after the harrowing experience of a deadly storm. The entire house was freezing cold except for the family room and kitchen, where they spent much of their time huddled near the stove. At night, Irene slept on the couch and Jennifer in the recliner.

She was interested and grateful when Jennifer related the stories of how Rick had stayed with her and helped her. She was sympathetic when Jennifer told her about Rick's loss of his sister and hopeful that he would find peace in his soul.

"I'm looking forward to meeting this man who saved your life," Irene said, after her daughter's glowing description of all he'd done for her. She didn't miss the wistfulness in Jennifer's eyes, either, when she talked about Rick. "He's coming back to cut up the pine tree that fell on his truck," Jennifer said.

Finally, the electricity and phone were restored. They were back to the routine of daily living—only busier. Jennifer helped as much as she could with only one hand, but Irene faced the brunt of cleaning out the refrigerator, catching up on the laundry, and scraping candle wax off the floors and tables.

That evening, when she and Jennifer sat down to a cooked supper in a well-lit kitchen for the first time in days, she laid her hand on Jennifer's, saying, "Don't you think it's time you and Don got back to normal?"

Irene wasn't so confident about "normal" when Jennifer took a call from Rick and then, bubbling with enthusiasm, reported that he was coming on Saturday to cut the tree.

When Saturday came, Irene looked out to see him examining the missing deck railing. She was giving him the once-over when he turned and met her eyes. She walked out onto the deck. Jennifer, right behind her, greeted Rick warmly and introduced them.

"I came to finish cutting the pine tree that's beside your driveway," Rick said. "And I'll be glad to fix this railing for you," he offered.

"Oh, just cutting up that pine will be good enough." Irene smiled. "Jennifer said you met Don. He and the young people are doing repairs like this on damaged homes."

"Right," Jennifer said quickly. "So isn't it nice that Rick has volunteered to take some of the burden off them?"

Irene took a deep breath and cleared her throat. "Of course, Dear."

"Mrs. Collins," he said politely. "Do you want the pine for your stove, or would you like me to haul it away?"

"No, we don't burn pine," she said, knowing by his question that he was aware that pine collected in chimneys and could be a fire hazard if not cleaned frequently and properly.

Irene watched the kind young man as he pulled his tree-cutting equipment from the back of his truck. Jennifer had been right about his looks. He was tall, dark, and handsome, with dark, brooding eyes. But Irene had been astute enough to have seen a gleam of light leap into those dark eyes of his before he averted them from Jennifer, pretending disinterest.

Jennifer didn't pretend at all. She was as excited as a child about to open Christmas presents.

Ashley drove up around noon and parked behind Rick's truck, the bed full of pine logs. She heard a chain saw buzzing back in the trees. Last spring, Don and some of the youth had cut up fallen trees and stacked the pieces at the back of the carport. But that wasn't Don's truck. He was so busy at church, perhaps Irene and Jennifer had decided to hire someone to do the cutting.

"Who's out there?" Ashley asked, taking off her light jacket and running her fingers through her dark hair.

"Oh, that's Jennifer's storm hero," Irene said, shaking her head.

Ashley blinked. "The rescue guy? What's he doing back here?"

Jennifer shrugged. "Like Mom said, he's my hero. When we were stranded, he waited on me hand and foot. Oh, not foot," she said and laughed.

"What?" Ashley questioned.

Jen shook her head. "Never mind. It's a private joke."

Ashley looked at Irene for clarification but received only a slight shrug and a statement that it was lunchtime. "You staying, Ashley?"

"Sure," she said, then turned to Jennifer. "Tell me more about this hero."

Irene could hear the conversation from the kitchen. Jennifer told Ashley about the blankets, the darkness, the marshmallows. Irene failed to see the humor in all of it or the significance of it. Or maybe she simply didn't want to admit it.

"Jennifer talks about this Rick all the time," Irene said from the kitchen.

"Well, Mom," Jennifer rebutted. "Everybody I know is still talking about the blizzard. The papers are still reporting things about it. Every morning there's a special report about which schools are starting late because some back roads are still icy. And you're still getting calls from the conference women who are now your friends."

"Oh, I have to tell you about this, Ashley." Irene walked in to stand by the couch.

Ashley listened with great interest as Irene related the story of a special friend she'd made out of the whole ordeal. A friend named Phyllis Johnson, who also had a stranded daughter in the storm of the century. Irene described how her concern about Jennifer, who had a broken arm, compared with Phyllis, whose daughter, Sue, had spina bifida.

"Anyway," Irene said, continuing her story, "Phyllis and Sue have decided that Phyllis should sell her house. She's going to build a duplex so Sue can have her separate section of the house and be independent. Sue plans to take courses in literacy and illiterate persons can come to her house for lessons."

"So the conference was a big success," Ashley said.

"Oh yes. This will be a new life for Phyllis and Sue." She smiled appreciatively. "She calls me almost every day. She just can't thank me enough."

Jennifer got that impish look on her face. "You're her hero, huh, Mom?"

"She seems to think so," Irene replied, feeling she'd lost the battle with Jennifer over considering Rick a hero.

"There really were a lot of heroes during the storm," Ashley said and thought of her own knight in shining armor. She paused and quickly looked down at her hands. The first person who came to her mind was Don. It was he who ran around night and day helping people. It was he who organized things at church and made sure everyone's needs were met. He was a leader, called by God, and who could be a better hero than that? So she'd helped. But had her motives been right? She just wanted to be near him.

"Ashley, where'd you go?" Jennifer asked.

"Oh, sorry. My mind wandered."

"Jennifer," Irene called from the kitchen. "Why don't you introduce Rick and Ashley. After all, they're both single. You're always saying you wish there were more single men in your group."

"I saw him at church the night of the storm," Ashley said, picking up on Jennifer's reticence.

"Wasn't he gorgeous?"

"I didn't really notice that," Ashley said honestly.

Irene walked toward the entry, carrying a plate on which were two sandwiches, chips, and a pickle. "Well, then, come on. I'd like your opinion."

Ashley reluctantly followed her through the house, down the stairs, and out through the carport to where Rick was throwing pine logs into his truck. Irene called him over and made the introductions.

"We met at church," Ashley said, smiling.

Rick took off his gloves and extended his hand. "I remember," he said and then thanked Irene as he took the plate she held out for him.

Ashley tried to evaluate Rick. Yes, he was gorgeous. She could see that if one must be stranded, then Rick would be a good candidate with whom to be stranded.

However, she had been stranded with a hero, too. But her hero had another woman on his mind. Don had talked of Jennifer during the storm. He was head over heels for her. And now, here was another one. All the gorgeous men fell for Jennifer. And rightly so. Jennifer was a beautiful, wonderful person.

"Well?" Jennifer asked when the two women returned upstairs. "What do you think of him?"

"I think," Ashley could say honestly, "if you must be stranded with someone, he'd run a close second."

"Second?" Jennifer stopped on the stair. "Who's first?"

"Don, of course," Ashley replied. She studied her friend as Jennifer's thoughts seemed to drift elsewhere.

Ashley didn't say so, but maybe she and Irene had the right idea. Jennifer didn't seem to appreciate Don enough.

Chapter 14

Irene was glad Jennifer had returned to school full time on Monday morning. Just after she'd left, Rick came with all the materials for repairing the deck railing. Irene took him water a couple of times and a cup of coffee. She couldn't help but think how nice it would be to have a son-in-law to help with repairs that her husband used to take care of.

She had to admit Rick Jenkins was a fine-looking specimen of a man. Quite robust, like her husband had been. He'd been an outdoorsman, too. Loved to work outside. But he had also been a gentle man. Rugged but sweet. A wonderful combination for a man. One who stood tall among men and knelt low before God. Nothing was more appealing.

Wasn't Don like that? Well, yes, but in a different way. She began to see the appeal of Rick. But he had problems. He was older than Don but didn't have his life on track like Don. But he'd had a rough time. Jennifer said he'd been devastated by his teenage sister's tragic death.

Irene thought of her own loss. She missed her husband all the time. Sometimes she'd come to the table and expect to see him there. Crawl in bed and turn toward him. Walk into a room ready to speak to him. But he wasn't there. Except in memory. But she accepted that. There was appointed a time to die for everyone.

But suppose it had been Jennifer. Oh, just the thought was devastating. Losing a child was like having your own heart cut out, she was sure. Yes, it was worse when it was a young person just beginning life, rather than one who had lived a long, productive one. Rick Jenkins had experienced that loss of a sister whom he'd apparently loved dearly. No, it wouldn't be easy to accept.

After he finished the railing and put the stain on it, Irene was greatly pleased with his professionalism, but not so glad that he wouldn't accept compensation.

"I was stranded, too, Mrs. Collins," he said. "So Jennifer was more a hero to me than I was to her. This is the least I can do to try and repay the two of you for the use of your home." He smiled, and she detected the sadness in him.

Yes, she could identify with this young man. "Would you like to come in and have lunch with me?" she asked.

433

To her great surprise, he replied, "Yes, Ma'am. Thank you."

She invited him to wash up and realized he knew where the bathroom was located. He'd been here two days and two nights with her daughter. Apparently, he'd been a gentleman and a wonderful companion; otherwise Jennifer wouldn't think so highly of him.

Irene couldn't help but compare Rick and Don. Don's calling was special, yes. But that didn't make him any better or any more spiritual than other Christians. Rick had a good Christian background, according to Jennifer. Jennifer saw Rick's worth. She had a tender heart. And didn't all people rebel against God at some point, many times more than once, during their lifetimes? Hadn't the apostle Peter denied even knowing Jesus? And look what a great witness he'd become. Hadn't the disciple Thomas doubted Jesus? But he'd come to believe, affirming, "My Lord and my God."

Jennifer recognized Rick's need and potential. She was reaching out to one who had turned from the Lord, who had stopped his spiritual growth. She was reaching out to one she considered a lost soul. *The Lord Jesus requires such of us.*

✍

Rick wasn't sure if he should have accepted Mrs. Collins's invitation to lunch. But he knew she wanted to know more about him. He wanted to reassure her that he had no intention of pursuing her daughter. And he knew eventually they would all know he was the one who'd run into Jennifer. That would be the final break. He would no longer be anyone's hero once they knew. This would be the last time he'd come to this house, the last time he'd talk to Mrs. Collins, and perhaps Saturday was the last time he'd ever see Jennifer.

No, there'd have to be one more time. The time when he faced her with the facts of his having hurt her and not having said he was sorry.

"You're in a real life-saving job, aren't you, Rick?" Irene said after he came to the countertop and accepted the lunch she'd made for him.

He looked at her for a long moment. Was she being sarcastic? Comparing him with the youth pastor? He knew he was not the one she wanted for her daughter. She was a sensible woman. But now her smile reached her eyes, and he knew she was trying to be cordial, trying not to give a wrong impression.

"Yes, Ma'am," he said, "sometimes. And it might surprise you to know that cutting trees sometimes saves lives." He began the story of the tree breaking through the roof of the couple, trapping the woman in her bed, and how he'd cut the tree up around her until the crew could lift off the trunk.

She pulled up a stool and sat, listening, as if she were really interested. After his story, she told a few of her own from when her husband had been alive and the two of them had been stranded on the mountain. None of the storms had been as bad as the recent blizzard, however.

After he finished, he thanked her, extended his hand, and said in a tone that he hoped would reassure her that he probably wouldn't be seeing her again, "Good-bye, Mrs. Collins."

When Rick picked up his mail from his post office box on Tuesday, he stopped short. He had a letter from the clerk of courts. In it was the date and time he should appear in traffic court.

He couldn't put it off any longer. He had to tell Jennifer. He mustn't let her hear about it from anyone else. He might have let it pass if he hadn't been at her house during the storm, hadn't met Don, Ashley, and Mrs. Collins, all of whom knew his name.

He called on Tuesday evening. "I need to talk to you, Jennifer."

After a few words, they decided on the following evening. She had preschool choir practice on Wednesday night. They'd be finished at seven o'clock. She'd meet him in the parking lot.

"And Rick," she said. "My cast is off."

Hearing the excitement in her voice, Rick felt his spirits lift, remembering she'd said she wished the cast were off so she could give him a big hug. "I'm glad," he said.

Then he frowned. *There'll be no hug.* The time had come to tell her the truth. His court case was coming up soon. She'd be gone from his life—once and for all.

Rick felt something tighten in his chest when he pulled into the church parking lot where only a few cars were parked, including a little, blue one that he assumed was Jennifer's. The door had been repaired. His insurance had paid for it. Would he pay for it further by never deserving to have a wonderful woman like Jennifer in his life?

He parked in a space marked "guest" in white letters, close to the side of the building, then got out and walked along the dry, paved lot. Some snow still lay under the big bushes next to the church. The evening was chilly but felt like a heat wave compared to the temperatures during the blizzard the area had so recently experienced. After waiting five minutes, he saw Jennifer exiting through a side door.

She saw him and smiled broadly, her beautiful eyes dancing as if she were thrilled to see him. When he was away from her, he told himself she couldn't be as pretty or as perfect as he remembered. But each time he saw her, he realized she was not angelic, but she was real. A real woman with smooth, fair skin, green eyes the color of early spring leaves, light brown curls with a reddish cast in the sun or in the light, lips soft and inviting with a ready smile.

"Where's your truck?" she asked.

"I drove my car," he said and led her toward his maroon sports car. She smiled.

He leaned back against the car, and Jennifer stood in front of him. He figured she'd bolt as soon as he told her that he'd been deceptive in keeping from her the fact that it was he who ran into her car. Before he could get the words out, she held out her arms. "See. No cast," she said and turned daintily in a circle.

He smiled faintly. She was wearing a long-sleeved bulky sweater and slacks. The arm would be thin for awhile until the muscles grew strong again. He shuddered inwardly at the thought that he might have killed her. Just as easily as Rory had killed Francine.

He grimaced. "Before you say anything more, I have to tell you something that's going to make you hate me."

He saw the apprehension leap into her eyes, and she tried to hide it with a jest that she might well have thought held an element of truth. "You've found someone else to be hero to."

He frowned. "This is serious, Jennifer."

She waited.

He couldn't find the words. He just held out the letter from the court. He watched her curious expression turn to confusion. "What's this about?" she asked.

"I'm the one who ran into you, Jennifer. I'm the one who caused you to get hurt and to wear that cast all these months."

"You?" she rasped, visibly stunned.

He took the letter from her shaking hand, folded it, and shoved it into his pocket. "You call me a hero. I'm not that. I'm a villain. Or worse. I could have killed you, Jennifer. I'm so glad I didn't. I didn't tell you because I didn't want to face this. You see. . .I'm no better than that boy who killed my sister. I've spent seven years hating him, hating God, and now I've done the same thing."

Her face paled with surprise. Then she'd stared at him with her mouth slightly open like she couldn't believe what she was hearing. She looked down at the pavement.

"This probably won't make a difference," he said, believing she felt the same kind of disgust as he and was shocked by the sudden realization that tears were streaming down his face. "But I want you to know I'm sorry. I don't expect you to forgive me for not telling you. Whether or not you forgive me is your own private matter. I'm not asking for that. I've burdened you enough.

If there's anything you want to say to me, go ahead."

She lifted her head, and he saw that her face was as wet as his own. "Yes, Rick," she said adamantly. "Yes, I have something to say to you."

Rick looked beyond her in the distance, afraid to see what her eyes might reveal. He wanted her to unburden any misgivings she had of him. He wanted her to lash out at him. He wanted her to tell him how he could easily have killed her by his inattention to the road. How he had no excuse, no matter what reasons he might offer.

"I forgave you before I ever saw you, Rick. Now I want you to know that I forgive you for crashing into me and for not telling me."

She might forgive him, but it wouldn't change anything. It might make her feel better. It certainly hadn't made him feel any better harboring his bitterness against Rory.

I am the potter, You are the clay. The Scripture verse flashed through his mind. But he hadn't allowed the master potter to mold him. He was just a lump of hard, dried-up clay. And Jennifer's words weren't helping at all.

He wished she wouldn't forgive him. Her forgiveness disturbed him more than if she'd torn into him. "What if you'd been hurt worse?" he asked. "Just a little faster, or a few more inches, and. . ."

"Rick," she said. "I can't speak for what might have been. But I'm thankful to the Lord that it wasn't worse. And you know. . ." She smiled. "Since that first night when you told me about your sister, I've believed God brought you and me together for a reason."

Then she placed her right hand on his shoulder and raised up on her toes and lifted her face to his and placed her soft, sweet lips on his grim ones. The warmth of her lips threatened to melt his reserve.

He drew away. This was like being in the darkness for so long when suddenly a ray of light hits your eyes and the feeling almost blinds you. His rescue training reminded him that one must thaw out slowly from having been frozen, otherwise complications set in. He did not need any more complications.

Maybe her kiss was only a friendly one, like a hug. But if so, why had her lips lingered? Why had they stayed upon his long enough for him to taste the sweetness of her and feel her warm breath against his face? Why had she strained toward him? Why was he the one to move away? He didn't deserve someone like Jennifer.

"I'm no good for you," he said gruffly, stepping back.

"You've been wonderful for me," she rebutted. "And I would like to help you through this difficulty that weighs so heavily upon you, Rick."

His lips turned into a wry smile. "Everyone tried to help me, Jennifer. And I know all the answers. My dad is a preacher. I've heard the right words all my life. I can quote you Scripture on all the right ways to live and think. But unless I do this myself, it won't be done."

Jennifer was nodding. She knew that.

He stepped close again. "If I ever get myself straightened out, I'll come back. But don't wait for me. It's a journey I'm not sure I can make."

"I'll pray for you," she said.

He grinned, his eyes displaying a warmth she hadn't seen before. "I could have predicted you'd say that."

"Rick," she whispered, letting him see the longing in her eyes.

"Jennifer," he said and drew her to him instead of looking into her eyes that spoke of things he wasn't worthy of. He whispered against her ear hoarsely, "If I'd been different, Jennifer. . ."

She shook her head against his own. "If you'd been different, we'd never have met."

Chapter 15

Don stopped short. He could kick himself for staring. But he'd just exited the church building and begun walking toward his car, looking at the paved lot in front of his feet, deep in thought. Then he'd looked up when he was almost upon the couple embracing near the sports car. He recognized Jennifer immediately and stood transfixed until they moved apart.

A flood of emotions washed over him. Jennifer was not pining away because he'd broken up. She had a man in her life whom she obviously cared deeply about. Finally, he realized he mustn't stand and stare. He decided against walking up to them, lest they feel embarrassed.

He had a feeling Jennifer was doing just fine. She was moving on with her life. Perhaps it was time he did the same. Maybe he was in God's will after all.

Quickly, he turned and ducked back into the church, his heart lighter than it had been in a long time.

☙

"Isn't that Don?" Rick asked, seeing the retreating figure.

Jennifer looked. "I guess he saw us." She smiled, seeming to enjoy the fact that Don had seen them together.

"He seems so perfect for you," Rick said.

"I know," she said and looked lovingly into Rick's eyes.

He shook his head. "Maybe that accident rattled your brain."

"No," she said. "I was going to tell Don we should break off. He told me first. That accident did rattle my brain, Rick. And my heart. I think Don and I both hoped we were right for each other. I know I had an image of the ideal man, and Don fits that description. If marriage were a job and I were hiring someone, he'd get the job. But if he and I were meant for each other, the doubts wouldn't have come. If Don and I were meant for each other, then I would not have a roving eye, and I would not find another man. . .um, let's see, attractive, I guess is the word."

"You wouldn't be talking about anyone I know?" he jested.

"I'm talking about someone you've tried to forget."

"Don't tempt me, Jennifer. I know what I should do and say to be the kind of person you think I can be. But I'm not that person anymore. I'd better say good night." He started to get into the car. But something drew him. Once more. One more time. And the temptation was too strong. He wasn't accustomed to refraining from yielding to temptation. And this one was so much sweeter than any other—so much more. And his lips met hers this time in a long, demanding kiss and still she did not pull away.

Where he found his strength, he didn't know. But he managed. Maybe, for the first time in a long time he thought of someone other than himself.

He stepped back. "I'll remember that forever," he said. "And I don't know if I should thank you or reprimand you, because this will haunt me. But Jennifer, maybe there's still a decent spark in me. I won't see you again as long as I have all this garbage inside me. I don't even know if I will try and rid myself of it. It's like a bad habit I've had for a long time, and I think it might just be as addictive as drugs."

"I'll be waiting," she said.

"I'm not asking that."

"Just remember it," she said. "Let it work on your conscience."

"Are you trying to hurt me?" he asked.

"Yes. I don't want you to forget that I believe in you. That I think you're worth saving. That I know you have the strength of character to get through this. And I know God brought us together for a reason. I want you to find out what that reason is."

Rick felt a painful knot in his stomach at her remark. He knew, all too well, what the reasons might be. *But thawing out, Jennifer, after one has been frozen, is painful.*

⁂

After watching Rick get into his car and waving at him, Jennifer went back into the church to find Don. He apologized, saying he hadn't meant to intrude upon them. He didn't know they were out there.

"No harm done," Jennifer said. "I've tried to tell Rick that you and I are no longer dating. But he thinks you and I are suited for each other."

"You and I thought that, too, didn't we, Jennifer?"

She nodded. "We both made assumptions about our relationship that proved not to be true." She smiled suddenly. "Just like you have assumed responsibility for my accident. Our relationship was on my mind that day, but it was Rick who ran that stop sign and plowed into me."

"Come to think of it," Don said. "You didn't seem all that upset about my saying we needed to rethink our relationship."

"I was about to tell you the same thing, Don."

She smiled at him. They looked into each other's eyes for a long time, then rushed into each other's arms. Friends! The best of friends! She felt better in his arms as a friend than she ever had as a girlfriend. Maybe her reticence toward him hadn't been fear of temptation after all, but because something deep inside knew he was not her lifetime mate.

He released her. "You're a wonderful woman, Jennifer. But I think we've really broken up."

"I've come to the same conclusion. But I don't think 'breaking' is the right word. Maybe we're moving on with our lives. I'm doing that, Don. I want you to do the same."

He nodded, his eyes clouding over. "Thanks for a wonderful year and four months. I needed our relationship."

"So did I," she said, realizing she wouldn't have known the difference in kinds of love if she hadn't spent those wonderful months with Don. Now she was ready for whatever might develop with Rick.

She didn't know all the answers, but she believed God sent Rick her way for a reason.

❧

Two days later, Rick went to court. He remembered that Rory had stood before a judge, too. Rick had wanted the boy to be sent to jail or maybe even get the death penalty. Rory had gotten a strong reprimand, a lecture about youth and drinking, and a six-month suspended license. That's when Rick lost it. If he hadn't been held back by his parents and friends, then officers of the court, and if Rory's parents hadn't ushered the boy out of there in a hurry, Rick would have done his best to kill him.

Francine was gone. The boy got a license suspension and paid a fine.

Now, Rick listened with a hurting heart as the judge said what his own punishment would be for running the stop sign. For breaking Jennifer's arm. For cracking her ribs. For giving her a concussion. For crashing her car.

He would have to pay a small fine.

That's all!

No lecture. No license suspension. No penalty. Pay the small amount of the fine and go on your way.

It was over.

Except what gnawed at his heart and mind. How was it with Rory?

Rick bowed his head and stood for a long time looking at the floor. He could have killed Jennifer.

Rory had killed Francine. Rick could hear it plain as day. "It was an accident. I didn't mean to. I didn't mean to hurt her. I loved her." Those had been Rory's screams, Rory's defense. "It was an accident. Please. I'm sorry. I'm sorry."

Sorry didn't get it. Sorry hadn't brought Francine back. When Rory killed Francine, he'd killed something in Rick, too.

And Rick had spent seven years rebelling.

After he paid the fine, he drove along the curves toward his home. He tried to, but could not, block out the image of Jennifer. It wasn't good for either of them. He had too much baggage in his life—too many unresolved matters. He must push aside any thoughts of her.

How long would it be until he forgot? Maybe, with time, he'd forget the accident. But her kiss would haunt him until his last breath.

It did all through that night. He dozed. He had nightmares about Francine's accident, then Jennifer's. He could not rest. Before dawn he rose from his tumbled bed, dressed, put on his boots and jacket, went out into the darkness, and got into his truck. He had to get away, do something to keep the thoughts and nightmares from his mind.

There was a spot on top of the mountain where he and his uncle had often hiked and looked down into the valley. Maybe there his mind would clear. He told himself he was more miserable after meeting Jennifer than he was before.

But Rick knew the greater problem was not between him and Jennifer. It was not between him and his parents. It was not between him and Rory McPherson. What it came down to was between Rick Jenkins and God. Just the two of them. Almighty God and puny Rick.

Rick drove past his uncle's house, where the road ended and a narrow dirt trail began. Only it wasn't dirt now. Patches of ice still lay on some of the road, and he knew the trail would be icy. He drove as far as he could to where the trail narrowed and the truck could no longer drive through the thick trees. It was dark here, except for the white snow on the ground. He couldn't tell where the trail lay, but if he just kept moving up, he'd reach the top.

A stiff breeze came up, and he felt sharp icicles land on his head and hit his jacket. He stumbled over a tree limb blocking his path. Were the trees trying to warn him? Go back. . .back. . .back. . .

He looked back down toward the valley from where he'd come and saw only shadows that deepened into darkness. That's what lay in the valley for him. Darkness. Debris. After the snow had melted, what remained was a mess. At times, he'd felt his heart might melt. But wasn't what lay there just a mess?

He should go back.

It's better for one who has never put his hand to the plow than one who looks back.

"I looked back, Lord. I deliberately turned my back on You, God. You know that. What are the consequences I must pay?"

Jesus paid it all.

While looking toward the darkness, Rick put his hands over his ears. Why was his mind always filled with impressions of hymns, memorized Scripture, sermons, church life, and images of God that he could never completely block out no matter how hard he tried? They kept knocking on his heart's door.

Behold, I stand at the door and knock. If anyone hears my voice and opens the door, I will come in to him and sup with him, and he with me.

Rick wondered if he'd shut his door too hard, kept it shut too long.

He knew what it was like to wallow in the pigpen of life. He knew how the prodigal son felt when he'd hit bottom.

He lifted his arms to shield himself from a pile of snow and shards of icicles falling from a tree. He looked away from the darkness and up toward the top of the mountain. A faint light appeared along the ridge of the peaks as if someone had painted a jagged silver line along the horizon.

I lift up my eyes to the hills—
where does my help come from?
My help comes from the LORD,
the Maker of heaven and earth.

Morning was coming. The top of the mountain drew him like the burning bush had drawn Moses. Just as God had spoken through the fire in the bush, was He now speaking through the snow and the ice?

I am that I am.

Had Rick not lain in the pigpen of life long enough? What did the prodigal do? What did the prodigal say?

I will arise and go to my father.

"Will I arise and go to my Father?" Rick asked aloud. He focused on that thin line of light. In the back of his mind he could hear the words of an old hymn. "Where could I go? Oh, where could I go? Where could I go but to the Lord?"

Brighter rays of sunshine illuminated the tops of trees, turning the scene into a mountain of crystal trees. Every tiny twig sparkled with myriad colors as the early morning sun gently touched them.

The light beckoned him. The virgin snow, where no human foot had trod, was his pathway. Here was only pristine beauty. He began to tromp up the trail, ever focusing on an opening in the treetops where a small patch of blue began to appear.

He began to run. Away from the darkness. Away from the piercing cold.

Toward the sun. Toward the Son. "Father, the prodigal is coming home."

He stood in the opening and, like the frozen trees, lifted his arms toward heaven, seeking the melting warmth, seeking the Father, seeking the Son. He turned in a circle in this haven where only he and God were present. His gaze fell upon the ground, and he saw his footprints in the snow.

But were they his?

" 'When there was only one set of prints,' " he'd read somewhere, " 'that's when I carried you,' said the Lord."

He again lifted his face toward the sky, growing brighter by the second. *I turned, Lord. I deliberately turned my back on You, God. You know that. Will you. . . would you. . .accept me now?*

You see, I'm not like a sinner coming for the first time. I'm a sinner who knew the way and got angry with You and bitter with Rory and disgusted with life and wanted You to suffer. But I'm the one who suffered.

"My Son suffered and died for you before you ever sinned. Before you ever knew about Jesus. I made the way. Jesus is the way. Anyone who comes to me I will in no way cast out."

Rick fell on his knees and bowed his head.

If we confess our sins, he is faithful and just and will forgive us our sins and purify us from all unrighteousness.

Rick began to cry. His tears poured like rain as he gave his all to the Lord. There wasn't a sound, not a human voice, not an animal moving, not a bird calling, not an icicle falling, not a breeze blowing. All he heard was a still, small voice penetrating the darkness of his soul, saying, *I'll wash you and make you whiter than snow.*

Chapter 16

Jennifer didn't know what to make of Rick's silence. She could only hope and pray that he would renew his relationship with the Lord. But she could not force him. And God gave him a choice. Rick had to find his own time and place.

In the meantime, she would get on with her life, leading the preschool choir as they practiced for their Easter program and planning for her kindergarten graduation. She must trust the Lord to send into her life what she needed and what was best for her.

After the monthly singles' meeting, Don asked Ashley if he could talk with her a moment. He saw no need to put this off. "Ashley," he began. "You're Jennifer's best friend. I have to try and explain. . ."

"Don," she interrupted. "This is so hard to believe. I know things have looked strange between you ever since her accident. But I. . .everybody. . . thought you and Jennifer were perfect for each other."

"I think Jen and I did, too, Ashley. We had an ideal built up in our minds. She fit mine. She has said I fit hers. But. . .sometimes the heart doesn't listen to the mind."

He lifted his head and looked at her. He meant only to glance, but he saw something gleam in her dark eyes that seemed to reflect a joyful sadness. Could it be. . .?

He shook his head and looked away from her. His hand came up and brushed across his flattop. "I didn't know what to do. You remember how Leo left you and hurt you. I didn't want it to look like I was doing that to Jennifer."

"Don," she said softly. "I had told Leo that I wasn't ready for a serious relationship. It took a long time for me to get over my husband's death. And Leo wasn't that interested in children. I had to put Tina first. I could never consider a man who didn't fall in love with my little girl."

"How could anyone not love her?" Don asked. *Or you, Ashley? Or you?*

She bit her lip to keep away the tears. "Everyone doesn't feel that way. And I understand Leo. Before I had a child, I didn't know the kind of parental feelings that are awakened when you hold your own baby. I see all children differently since I've had Tina."

"I've never had a child, but. . ."

Ashley interrupted. "You have a special calling and a burden for children and young people, Don. I've seen that. I know it."

"Yes, I do," he admitted. "My heart goes out especially to the unchurched ones. And I treat them all according to their needs. But Ashley, I can't help having favorites."

Ashley was smiling. "And Tina is one of them," she said. He nodded in agreement.

"I know," she whispered. "I know." She touched his arm ever so gently before turning and quietly leaving the room.

∽

The following evening, Ashley went to see Jennifer. "Is it true that you and Don have really broken up? I mean, are you heartbroken? He says you prefer Rick to him. Can that be true?"

"Absolutely," Jennifer said, smiling. "I love Don, but I am in love with Rick. You know the difference, don't you?"

"Definitely. I was in love with my husband. I loved Leo, not expecting to be in love again, but. . ." Her voice trailed off.

"I've learned something, Ashley. It shouldn't be we who choose whom to love. We need to let God choose for us. Even if Rick and I can't get together, I know I'm not the one for Don, nor he for me."

"So it wouldn't bother you for Don to find someone else?" Ashley asked, biting on her lip, trying not to let the tears flow down her cheeks. She'd tried not to love Don. She'd prayed and fought it and thought of leaving town. Now Jennifer was saying. . . Oh, this was hard to believe.

"I hope he finds someone else, Ashley," Jennifer said sincerely, looking at her with what appeared to be a question in her eyes.

Irene came into the family room just then. "I couldn't help but overhear," she said.

"Well, no," Jennifer chided playfully. "When you stand back there in the hallway, that's not too difficult."

Ashley and Jennifer laughed as Irene pursed her lips together. Ashley feared what Irene might say. She knew how much the older woman had wanted Don and Jennifer to marry.

Irene sighed heavily. "I've been wrong," she said. "I've tried to push that relationship. But Jennifer is right about this. Sometimes we try and look for the perfect person for us. But there is no perfect person. We need, instead, to allow God to give us the person who is perfect for us."

"Thank you for saying that," Ashley said. God certainly did work in mysterious ways.

❧

Early Saturday morning, Ashley and Tina came to see Jennifer. "You have to be the first to know," Ashley said, holding out her left hand, which sported a diamond ring. "Don and I shopped for this last night. He asked me to marry him, Jen. As soon as possible."

Tina stood in front of Jennifer and gave a big sigh. "Mommy says she's going to marry Mr. Don. I thought you was going to marry him." She put her hands on her hips and tapped the floor with one extended foot. "I don't know who's doing what."

Jennifer drew Tina over to her. "Well, you see, I thought that I might marry Don. Then I realized that he was just a very good friend. I'm not really in love with him, although I love him as a friend. Your mommy and Don are in love. Do you understand that, Honey?"

"Um hm," she answered immediately. "I used to be in love with Jason. And then Billy till he moved away. And now I'm in love with um. . ." She touched her cheek with her index finger and looked toward the ceiling thoughtfully. Then she looked back and said very seriously. "I'm in love with either Todd or Wade." She shrugged. "So I understand."

Jennifer drew her lips in a tight line to keep from smiling. "Ooo-kay," she said. "Now let's talk about your being the flower girl."

"Oh, I'm getting married, too. Mommy said Don wants to marry me, too." She spread her hands and got that "oh, well," look. "He's in love with me. But not like Todd and Wade. Don's in love with me like a daddy."

"Yes," Jennifer said, nodding. She was smiling, although she felt a moment of loss over something good that had ended. She and Don had had a meaningful relationship. It was over. But she had no regrets. She could honestly say, "I'm sure Don will be a wonderful daddy to you."

❧

Rick drove down to Anderson, South Carolina, about a two-hour drive, and arrived at a service station around 6:30 P.M. He didn't know if the boy had ever returned to Anderson. He knew the parents had sent him up north to a college. He'd been told they were afraid Rick would kill him. That's exactly what Rick had been afraid of.

He looked in the phone book. A Rory McPherson was listed. Rick drove by the house a couple of times—a modest frame house bordered by neat bushes and colorful petunias. A woman was setting up a portable playpen on the front porch near a swing. He drove by, traveled a few blocks, and turned.

The second time he passed, the woman was sitting in the swing, holding a book, and a small girl sat beside her. A young child stood in the playpen, holding onto the side, facing the woman, waving a hand as if trying to reach the book.

Rick felt a gnawing in his insides. Although he hadn't eaten supper, he knew the feeling was not hunger, but nausea. Francine would be about the age of that woman. Was this Rory's wife? Rory's children? Was he living in a neat house with a mate, and children, and flowers, while Francine was cold in her grave? Wouldn't Francine have wanted to live for evenings like this? A pleasant spring evening? Was this Rory's family? And where was he? Did he appreciate what he had? Or was he still destroying people's lives?

Rick had slowed and seen the woman's head turn toward him. She stared when he slowed down, as if he were a criminal or something. But Rory was the criminal. Did she know it? Had Rory told her he'd killed a girl? What would happen to Rory's sweet little home life then? Rick felt it. Although he had forgiven God, and God had forgiven him, he feared how he would react seeing Rory face to face. He turned at the next corner, went around the block again, and approached the house for the third time.

This time he saw Rory on the porch staring straight at him. Rick pulled over next to the sidewalk. He sat for a long moment, then switched off the engine. After taking a deep breath, he got out of the car, walked around, and stood on the sidewalk. He was close enough to see Rory's eyes widen in surprise before his face lost all color.

"Rick," Rory breathed, and Rick knew that seven years hadn't clouded Rory's memory, either.

"I'd like to talk to you," Rick said from the sidewalk. Rick saw the fear in Rory's eyes. *He's not a boy anymore, but a man with a family.*

Rory nodded. He kept staring at Rick with fear in his eyes. *Does he think I've come to kill him? Is that what I've come for?* Rick asked himself. Then he recognized the truth. *I've come to end it, once and for all.*

Rick started walking up the front walk and heard Rory order, "Marla, why don't you take the children and go on to the park? I'll catch up with you there."

Rick wondered if she knew the situation. For a moment she looked as if she wasn't leaving. Then after Rory smiled reassuringly, she picked up the baby and took the little girl's hand. "Come on kids," she said. "Let's go to the park and swing."

The children sounded enthusiastic. Rory opened the screen door. "Come in," he said.

Rick stepped inside.

"You want to sit down?" Rory asked.

Rick shook his head. "I don't think so. Now that I'm here, I don't even know what I wanted to say. Well, yes, I do." He had trouble finding the words.

"Come in the kitchen," Rory offered. "Maybe have a cup of coffee or something."

Rick followed him. The house looked like kids lived in it. Toys all over the place. Pillows on the floor. Cartoons on TV. Rory switched it off.

They sat at the kitchen table. Neither mentioned coffee.

Rory didn't have trouble finding words. "You can't tell me anything that I haven't told myself. Not a day passes that I don't think of her in some way. Sometimes consciously, sometimes it's just there in the back of my mind. Even on my wedding day, I wondered if we would have married. I loved her. It was young love, but it was as much as I was able to love. I didn't want to hurt her."

His voice broke and his body shook as sobs filled his throat and tears clouded his eyes.

Rick had come to say. . .something to Rory. Perhaps to let him know he wouldn't kill him. But Rory was doing the talking. Pouring out his heart. Rick felt his misery.

"Would she and I have married? Would these be our children? This is not to take anything from my wife. I love her and I'm blessed. But I think of. . ."

Rick realized Rory couldn't say Francine's name, either. The man was hurting.

"I think of her and the loss. I know God has forgiven me and I have forgiven myself. But it's a part of me that never lets go. It's always in the back of my mind. I think of her. I have a daughter. . . . I see high school girls. Everything. . .everything reminds me of her. Anytime I hear of a drunk driver, or a young person, or a girl, or a boy, or a prom, or high school. The thought was in my mind when I married. She would never marry. When my first child was born and I held that little girl in my arms, I thought of Francine. She'd never have a baby.

"I tell myself she is in a better place, and I know it's true. But at the same time, I know we all want to live this life. She wanted to live. She wanted to make a positive difference, and she would have."

They both were crying. Rick was nodding. He thought of her, too. Never a day passed, maybe never a moment, when her presence was not with him in some form.

"I've hated you," Rick said.

Rory nodded. "I'm glad. That helped. I hated myself. I needed somebody else to hate me. How could I live with total forgiveness? I wasn't worthy of it. I should have died instead of her."

"It was all I could do to keep from killing you myself," Rick admitted.

"For a long time I hoped you would. I heard that you couldn't accept it, couldn't forgive me, and I thought about confronting you so you would kill me. But it dawned upon me that such an act would ruin your life, too. I'd done enough damage without adding your having to spend your life in prison. The law wouldn't see it as a justifiable act."

Rick sat for a long time, studying the floor tiles that wavered beneath his watery eyes. After a long moment he glanced up. "I've been in prison just the same. One of my own making, but a prison nevertheless. I've hated you, hated God. I hated my mom and dad for forgiving you. I've wanted revenge. I haven't even been able to think your name without getting sick to my stomach."

Rory was nodding, while tears ran unchecked down his face.

Rick had difficulty talking over the aching lump in his throat. "Maybe, Rory," he said. "Maybe it's time to. . .to let it go."

Rory leaned over the table, his forehead pushing against his fists, and he sobbed. Long, hard, heart-wrenching sobs. Rick got up and walked to the kitchen sink, where he stood and looked out the window. Finally he tore off a paper towel and mopped his face, then returned to the table with a paper towel for Rory.

When Rory felt the towel brush against his head, he looked up and took it. "Can we," he whispered painfully, "let it go?"

Rick pulled out the chair next to him and sat down. He talked about what his dad had preached as far back as he could remember. He said what Jennifer had said when his heart was as cold as the blizzard of the century. "Nothing is impossible with God."

Rory stared at Rick for a long time. The tears dried on his face. Rick knew Rory was having a hard time believing what he just heard.

"After Francine's funeral, your dad came over to me," Rory said. "He invited me to the church where he preaches. I've gone every Sunday that I could in all these years. During the service, I sit there, and when I don't cry openly, I cry inside. I want to pay, but there's no payment I can render."

"Yes, there is," Rick said.

Rory stared.

Rick took a deep breath. "We can be the kind of Christians that we believe Francine would have been."

"Yeah," Rory began slowly, "but that's impossible. . .for me."

"For me, too," Rick admitted. "All during my life I've heard that God will make us into new persons. I've never put Him to the test. But I don't want to live with this bitterness anymore."

Sunday morning, Rick stayed outside in the church parking lot until after he heard the music stop. Then he slipped into the building and sat in a chair in the vestibule, listening to his dad preach for the first time in seven years.

When the altar call was given, the choir sang softly about turning your eyes upon Jesus, looking full in His wonderful face, and about the things of earth growing strangely dim, in the light of His glory and grace.

Rick knew he had to do this publicly. The whole town had known of the tragedy. Church members would not have forgotten. They would have prayed for him over the years. And Jesus said that if anyone acknowledged Him on earth, He would acknowledge that person before the Father in heaven.

Rick wanted his parents and the other church members to know that his bitter reign of unforgiveness had ended. He wanted to acknowledge his Lord publicly. He strode to the doorway and walked down the aisle, his eyes on his dad, who stood at the front, looking for anyone who might make a move to come forward.

The prodigal son is coming home, Dad. When Rick neared the front, he saw his dad's eyes widen and heard a choked sound from his throat. Then he heard a woman's voice, in this considerably conservative church, sounding like an inadvertent shout of joy.

"Son," his dad said brokenly, and they fell into each other's arms.

"Forgive me, Dad," he said. "I've come home."

"Yes," came his dad's joyful cry. Then he felt his mother's arms embracing him and her tears against his neck.

"I need to get on my knees," Rick said, as he saw his dad embrace someone else. It was Rory. Rick and Rory embraced each other, then knelt at the altar. In the background, while hearing his dad pray, he could hear a few voices still singing praise to the Lord. He could hear prayers of thankfulness being said aloud and sniffing by those who cried with joy. Most of all, he heard the voice that he never again wanted to still. It was the voice of the Lord, reassuring him.

Nothing—neither death, nor life, nor angels, nor demons, nor fears, nor worries, nor the powers of hell, nor anything in all creation can separate you from the love of God that is revealed in Christ Jesus our Lord.

Chapter 17

A couple weeks passed before Jennifer received a card from Rick. "I'm getting on with my life, Jennifer. I knew you'd want to know. Best wishes, Rick," was all he wrote. Jennifer cried. The postmark was Anderson, South Carolina.

She couldn't be sure what he meant. Did he mean he wouldn't try and see her again? Or did he mean he'd returned to the Lord? She knew God would accept Rick the moment he sincerely turned to Him, but Rick had said he had a lot of baggage in his life to deal with. He hadn't related to his parents in seven years. Was he visiting them? Or had he moved back to his hometown?

"I'm praying for you. Love, Jennifer," she wrote back to his mountain address.

Two weeks later she got a beautiful card from him. "I could have predicted you'd say that. Smile, Rick," he replied.

Smile? Should she read between those lines? It was a far cry from "love," but coming from Rick, who had seemed to smile by accident, it was a start, wasn't it? She shared it with her mom and Ashley, who looked painfully skeptical.

"But look at the picture," Jennifer pointed out. "It's a mountain scene of springtime. I mean, we can look out these doors and see the little green leaves on the trees. The white dogwood sprinkled throughout the forest. The azaleas are budding. Look! No snow!"

They didn't seem to get the significance of that, either. "Well, Honey. All the shops would have springtime cards out now," her mother said and patted her shoulder as if consoling her.

"Oh, Jennifer," Ashley said guiltily, "I hope you're right. I don't think he would send a reply to your saying you'd pray for him if you weren't special to him."

"You're a good friend," Jennifer said with a big smile. "Now, let's get on with these wedding plans of yours."

For the next few weeks, Jennifer busied herself with finishing up the school year.

In early June, on a Friday morning, her kindergarten class had a special graduation service in the auditorium attended by family and friends. Each child had a speaking part, representing all the months of the year. Jennifer deliberately gave Tina the month of February, representing Valentine's Day.

At the end of the program, each child walked proudly to the front to receive a graduation diploma, and the audience applauded.

Tina was all grins and looked at Ashley and Don, sitting together looking at her and each other lovingly.

Jennifer knew that she was seeing a family unit brought together by the Lord, and it was good. Her only touch of regret was that perhaps Rick didn't think she was the woman for him. More than anything, however, she wanted him to find peace with God and himself.

Rick knew he had the greatest parents in the world. They went out of their way to "kill the fatted calf," so to speak. Rick was glad he didn't have an older brother to be jealous like the biblical story of the prodigal's return to his father. He became part of the family again. He told his mom and dad about Jennifer and how his accident could have ended the way Rory's did.

"Can we meet her?" his mom asked.

"I hope so," Rick replied, and his dad touched his arm encouragingly.

He renewed some past relationships and visited the high school where a memorial plaque was set inside a glass case in the front lobby for Francine. He visited her grave, cried, and told her that he knew she was happy with the Lord and that he'd be seeing her one of these days. He looked through old scrapbooks and remembered his sister as a vibrant, beautiful Christian girl and could thank God that, although her life had been short, it had been full and productive. She would never know sickness, pain, or disappointment.

After returning to the mountains, he and his uncle became even closer. No longer did Uncle Joe have to be careful to avoid mentioning Francine or God. Now they talked freely and discussed the Bible. After work, Rick went almost daily to the spot on top of the mountain where the Lord had spoken to his heart so vividly. He was aware of daily changes when bare limbs sprouted buds, small leaves, then lush green ones. The forest changed from black and white to fantastic color. White dogwood peeked out from every tree trunk. Wild azaleas produced little orange trumpets, heralding spring.

Leafy green ferns and waxy galax leaves carpeted the forest floor. Rabbits, squirrels, and chipmunks didn't seem to mind his presence. The bears and mountain lions kept their distance. Once, he saw a deer run through. He reminded himself that he didn't live in a spiritual desert anymore. He knew there would be rough spots in life, but he wasn't alone anymore. He had the Lord's Spirit to comfort him, to guide him.

He wanted desperately to share this with Jennifer. But he knew he couldn't return to the Lord and then go directly to Jennifer. He could not chance her being his reason for coming back to God. He knew too much about spiritual living to allow that. One couldn't fool God with his motives. But it wasn't easy, telling God he would serve Him for the rest of his life, whether or not he had a chance with Jennifer, whether or not he would ever have a wonderful woman as his mate.

Years ago, he had felt God wanted him in special service. He now realized that whatever occupation he had was special service when it was done for the glory of God and when he took advantage of the opportunities to witness about the power of God. If the Lord had something else in mind for him, then He would impress it upon his heart and mind.

And, too, Rick wanted to give Jennifer time to reconsider her relationship with Don. They were fine Christians who deserved each other. *Deserve?* came his thought. No, there was no way a person could ever deserve the wonderful blessings that came from the Lord, no matter how hard they worked, no matter how hard they tried. Salvation and God's Spirit were free gifts, undeserved.

Then in early June, Rick got an envelope that was unlike the usual business ones. He stared for a long time. This looked like a wedding invitation envelope.

With shaky hands, he opened it. A wedding invitation!

Had Jennifer come to her senses and realized Don was the one for her after all? He didn't want to read it. *Lord, are You punishing me? I know You forgive me. I know You love me. I have a long way to go before I can come close to deserving a woman like her. It's Your choice, Lord. You know best.*

King David was a man after Your own heart. You loved him Lord, and forgave him, but he had to pay the consequences for his sins. He didn't get to build the temple for You. He'd been too much of a warrior.

And Lord, I have to suffer the consequences of my sins, too. I'm not good enough for Jennifer. You've forgiven me, cleansed me. But. . .have I been too much of a sinner?

He took a deep breath and read the words. His eyes widened. Ashley Beaumont and Don Ramsey were to be married.

⬤

Rick's heart leaped within him when Jennifer, the maid of honor, slowly made her way down the aisle. Could he possibly be fortunate enough to have the heart of such a beautiful woman? He didn't deserve such. Only God could be so generous. She was a delight to look at in the flowing, light green dress, the color of her eyes. Her glowing face was surrounded by curly hair shining with reddish gold highlights.

While her former boyfriend exchanged vows with another woman, Jennifer smiled broadly as if she genuinely approved.

Rick couldn't take his eyes off her until the part in the ceremony when Don got on his knees to the little girl standing beside Ashley and promised to be a dad to her, the kind she deserved.

It was a long wait while photographers took pictures and then the guests greeted the bride, groom, their attendants, and the families. Rick stood back until after people were served and began to mill around. Several people introduced themselves, and when he said he was Rick Jenkins, many eyes opened wide and they expressed extreme pleasure at his presence. Apparently *someone* had been talking about him.

Then Irene spied him. She came up and gave him a hug. "I'm so glad you came today, Rick," she said, and he felt she really meant it for her eyes grew moist and her smile was welcoming.

Rick thought about how he didn't feel out of place in a church anymore. That's where he belonged. Christians were one big family. But he stood back in a corner, wanting to let his eyes feast upon Jennifer as she made the rounds of people in the fellowship hall. He knew the moment she saw him. Her face froze, her mouth flew open, and after staring for a stunned moment, she hurried toward him, even bumped into a person and apologized.

She came up to him. "You almost made me drop my punch."

"I did?" he questioned.

"You're here."

"Could I refuse an invitation from a beautiful woman like you?"

"I hoped not," she said sincerely.

He took a deep breath. "I have a lot to tell you."

"I think I already know a lot of it, Rick," Jennifer said. "After all, you're in a church. And. . ." She took a deep breath, looked toward the ceiling, then grinned. "You look fantastic in that suit. Wow!"

"Jennifer!" he chided.

"Well, truth is truth."

"Yes," he said. "And maybe it's my inner glow you're seeing."

"I think I am," she said. "But I see a man, too, who appeals to me. Oh, Rick."

"Let's get out of here," he said.

When they reached the parking lot, Rick laughed. "I was going to take you somewhere—maybe an overlook—and say what I need to say to you. But I don't know if I can wait."

"I've seen the overlooks and the mountains all my life, Rick," she replied. "I just want to look at you."

His warning look stopped her. "You need to know this, Jennifer. God has forgiven me. I have forgiven Rory. I'm starting over. But it's like so many things. You can't go back to innocence."

"Um, like, the tenth kiss can't be as sweet as the first one?" she asked teasingly.

Rick grinned. "Well, we'll have to test that."

He did. When he drew away, he took a deep breath. "No, that was nothing like a first kiss."

"I agree," she said, smiling. "And I think your relationship with God will be deeper and stronger, too. I know my love for Don was greater and deeper than my relationships in high school, which were deeper than my crushes in junior high, and they were deeper than my first crush when I was four years old. And Rick, my love for you is even greater and deeper than all of them. More mature."

"So you're saying my relationship to God can be even greater?"

She smiled. "He who has been forgiven more, loves more."

"Forgive me, Jennifer. Forgive me. Forgive me."

She laughed. "Oh, Rick. I love you so."

They embraced. "I don't want to give you the chance of finding someone else that you will love even more," Rick said against her hair.

"No," she said. "It stops with you."

He moved away just far enough to see her face. "Do you want to go down and meet my parents?"

"I do," Jennifer said.

Rick gazed at her lovingly. "You know, I answered when the preacher asked, 'Do you take this woman to be your lawfully wedded wife? Do you vow to love her and protect her?' On each question, I looked at you and in my heart I answered, 'I do.' "

Jennifer's arms came up and encircled his neck. "If you're not asking me to marry you," she said, "I'm asking you."

"I could have predicted you'd say that," he replied and then obliged her waiting lips.

A Letter to Our Readers

Dear Readers:

In order that we might better contribute to your reading enjoyment, we would appreciate you taking a few minutes to respond to the following questions. When completed, please return to the following: Fiction Editor, Barbour Publishing, Inc., P.O. Box 719, Uhrichsville, OH 44683.

1. Did you enjoy reading *Carolina?*
   □ Very much. I would like to see more books like this.
   □ Moderately—I would have enjoyed it more if _____
   _____
   _____

2. What influenced your decision to purchase this book?
   (Check those that apply.)
   □ Cover   □ Back cover copy   □ Title   □ Price
   □ Friends   □ Publicity   □ Other

3. Which story was your favorite?
   □ *Mountain Man*   □ *Call of the Mountain*
   □ *Smoky Mountain Sunrise*   □ *Whiter than Snow*

4. Please check your age range:
   □ Under 18   □ 18–24   □ 25–34
   □ 35–45   □ 46–55   □ Over 55

5. How many hours per week do you read? _____

Name _____

Occupation _____

Address _____

City _____ State _____ Zip _____

Grace Livingston Hill Collections

Readers of quality Christian fiction will
love these new novel collections from
Grace Livingston Hill, the leading
lady of inspirational romance. Each
collection features three titles from
Grace Livingston Hill and a bonus
novel from Isabella Alden, Grace
Livingston Hill's aunt and a widely
respected author herself.

Collection #7 includes the com-
plete Grace Livingston Hill books *Lo, Michael,*
The Patch of Blue, and *The Unknown God,* plus *Stephen Mitchell's*
Journey by Isabella Alden.

paperback, 464 pages, 5 ³⁄₁₆" x 8"

❤ ❤ ❤ ❤ ❤ ❤ ❤ ❤ ❤ ❤ ❤ ❤ ❤ ❤ ❤ ❤

❤ ❤ ❤ ❤ ❤ ❤ ❤ ❤ ❤ ❤ ❤ ❤ ❤ ❤ ❤ ❤

Grace Livingston Hill Collections

Readers of quality Christian fiction will love these new novel collections from Grace Livingston Hill, the leading lady of inspirational romance. Each collection features three titles from Grace Livingston Hill and a bonus novel from Isabella Alden, Grace Livingston Hill's aunt and a widely respected author herself.

Collection #8 includes the complete Grace Livingston Hill books *The Chance of a Lifetime, Under the Window* and *A Voice in the Wilderness,* plus *The Randolphs* by Isabella Alden.

paperback, 464 pages, 5 ³⁄₁₆" x 8"

❤ ❤ ❤ ❤ ❤ ❤ ❤ ❤ ❤ ❤ ❤ ❤ ❤ ❤ ❤ ❤ ❤

❤ ❤ ❤ ❤ ❤ ❤ ❤ ❤ ❤ ❤ ❤ ❤ ❤ ❤ ❤ ❤ ❤

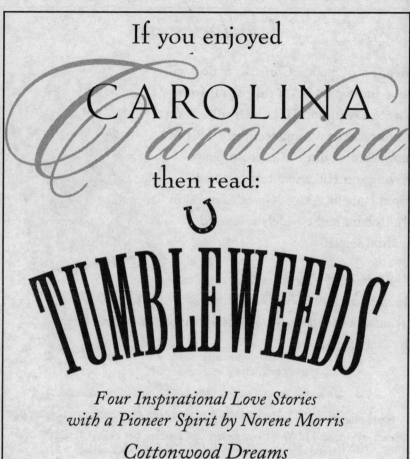

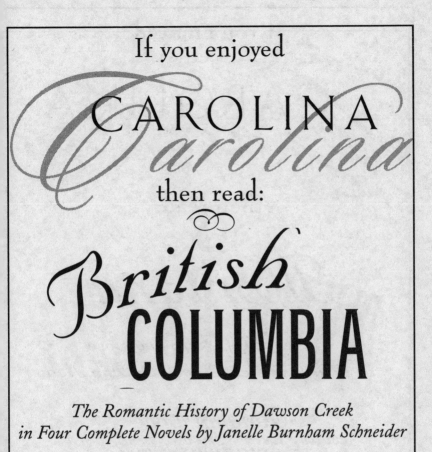

If you enjoyed

CAROLINA

then read:

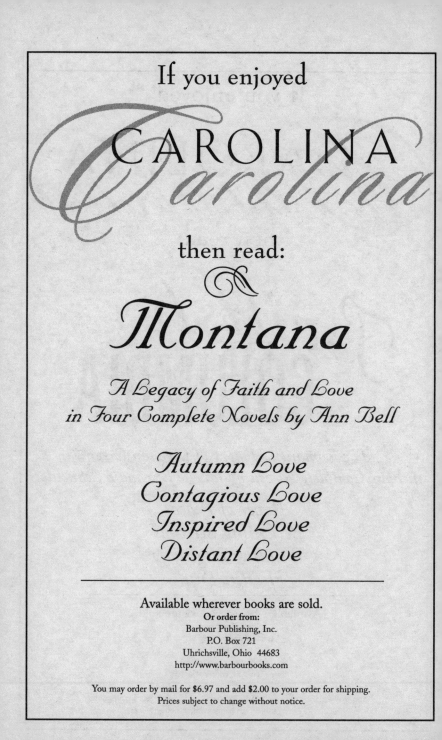

Montana

*A Legacy of Faith and Love
in Four Complete Novels by Ann Bell*

*Autumn Love
Contagious Love
Inspired Love
Distant Love*

$\mathcal{H}$EARTSONG ♥ PRESENTS

Love Stories
Are Rated G!

That's for godly, gratifying, and of course, great! If you love a thrilling love story, but don't appreciate the sordidness of some popular paperback romances, **Heartsong Presents** is for you. In fact, **Heartsong Presents** is the only inspirational romance book club, the only one featuring love stories where Christian faith is the primary ingredient in a marriage relationship.

Sign up today to receive your first set of four, never-before-published Christian romances. Send no money now; you will receive a bill with the first shipment. You may cancel at any time without obligation, and if you aren't completely satisfied with any selection, you may return the books for an immediate refund!

Imagine. . .four new romances every four weeks–two historical, two contemporary–with men and women like you who long to meet the one God has chosen as the love of their lives. . .all for the low price of $10.99 postpaid.

To join, simply complete the coupon below and mail to the address provided. **Heartsong Presents** romances are rated G for another reason: They'll arrive Godspeed!

YES! Sign me up for Hearts♥ng!

NEW MEMBERSHIPS WILL BE SHIPPED IMMEDIATELY!
Send no money now. We'll bill you only $10.99 postpaid with your first shipment of four books. Or for faster action, call toll free 1-800-847-8270.

NAME _____

ADDRESS _____

CITY _____ STATE_____ ZIP_____

MAIL TO: HEARTSONG PRESENTS, P.O. Box 719, Uhrichsville, Ohio 44683